PARADISE FALLS

Paradise Falls

DON ROBERTSON

VOLUME ONE

G. P. Putnam's Sons   New York

NOTE: There is no such place as Paradise Falls. With the exception of historical personages, those who populate this book are entirely the responsibility of the author.

Thanks are due to the following for their advice and encouragement: Max Gartenberg, Sally Gartenberg, Irving Gitlin, Peter Israel, W. S. Kuniczak, Walter Minton, Gerald M. Simons and William Targ.

For my wife, Shari, with love and gratitude

What does it profit a man? It profits a man the world, and the world is enough.

—TOBIAS G. FRYE

If God strikes down the last tree, it will be no outrage. But what if the dead hand of man is there before Him?

—GEORGE McC. PILLSBURY

Let every thing that hath breath praise the Lord.

—PSALM 150

PARADISE FALLS

1865 . . .

Here, then, to begin, is the Truth of this place:

Listen to the Truth. It abounds. Everyone has his own truth, and every truth is true in the eyes of its beholder, but all individual truths are simply fragments, and thus the only true Truth (the only true and *complete* and *unswerving* Truth) is the sum and total of all the right and proper—and incomplete—individual truths. Ah, this place. It is a saint. It is a whore. It is all.

Here is a sunrise in May. The war is finished, and today the men of the old Paradise Falls Blues are coming home. The sunrise is a green thief, green and moist. It has abducted the night. A red squirrel sits chattering high in a pin oak behind the Underwood place on Cumberland Street. Young Phil Underwood, darkly handsome, lying inertly, his bones unvexed by sleep, makes fists. The red squirrel is speaking for him. The red squirrel wants to fight. It is a brave and unpleasant red squirrel, and it is Phil Underwood's brother.

The thieving dawn brings a pale stuttering wind, and here and there, hugging the grass, are thin tracings of mist. The wind spins the mist, and the mist goes away. On Main Street the flags and banners hang limp. The wind is too weak to make them move. Leaves rub. Phil Underwood is eighteen. His parents never should have deprived him of this war. He cannot, however, hate them. It all would be so easy, if only he could hate them. He listens to the red squirrel, and the red squirrel's anger is dry and terrific. Phil Underwood closes his eyes. He hears drums and gunfire. He imagines himself brandishing a great silver sword.

They are coming, these survivors of the Paradise Falls Blues, in the steam cars of the Columbus, Paradise Valley & Marietta. The train is scheduled, God willing, to arrive at 11:38 this morning. Phil Underwood will be at the depot. He will stand off to one side. And he will mourn. And his parents, his loving parents, will understand not a thing.

The federal census of 1860 set our population at 2,991. We are served by one railroad, the CPV&M. Its tracks reached here in 1858. We have one bank, the Paradise Falls State Bank. Its president is Isaac (Ike) Underwood, father of Phil. Our newspaper is the Paradise Falls *Democrat*. Its publisher is Isaac (Ike) Underwood. It is a daily. It is the only daily in this part of the state. Its editor, a young hunchback named J. K. Bankson, is aggressive and thorough, and the paper makes more money for Ike Underwood than one would expect. Our largest industry, employing more than a hundred men, is the Paradise Falls Clay Products. Its president is Isaac (Ike) Underwood.

(Quiet, please. Permit, if you will, the dawn to come gently. Pinky, an aged tomcat owned by Oliver W. Purvis, county superintendent of public instruction, comes quickly awake in the cellar of the Purvis home. Pinky is called Pinky because he is utterly, irretrievably black. He yawns. His teeth are uneven. He pads across the cellar floor. Fut, fut, fut, fut, fut. Pinky is hungry. He climbs the cellar steps to the door that opens into the kitchen. Waow, says Pinky. Waow. Waow.)

Young Bill Light, fourteen and tumescent, is not yet awake. He is dreaming a silent smoky dream. The girl's name is Amelia Burkhart, and she is sixteen, and he seeks only to rest a cheek against her belly. Yes, yes, says Amelia Burkhart, her smile timid and soft against the golden sky and plump hazy clouds that sit lightly over the happy kingdom of his dreams, yes, yes, dear Bill, I love you. Do it. Fall down. Rest your cheek. I am warm. (Bill Light's humid adolescent bed is narrow, and in the next room his mother lies crouping and dying, and today everyone expects him to be proud of his father, who is a genuine Warrior if there ever was one. Outside his window, wrens tremble and scold. Oh indeed this will be a day for young Bill Light. It is more than four years since he has seen his father.)

To the east sit the foothills of the great Appalachians. The sun comes up in white tatters and smears. Its shadows dapple the flag that old Jake Phillips has just raised to the top of the pole in front of the Paradise County Court House. Old Jake, who has been the building's janitor for all fifteen years of its existence, has decided to hide himself in the courthouse cellar later this morning when the men come marching up Main Street. His son Jim marched away with those fellows, but Jim was killed last autumn at Petersburg, and he was all the family old Jake Phillips had. Grunting, old Jake raises the flag, grimaces off toward the hills and the raveled sunlight. Jim never was much to brag on, but he was better than nothing. Jim drank too much for his own damn good, and he never was able to hold a job for more than a month or so, and he was about as pretty as a cow pie in the parson's parlor, but *still* . . . great God, he'd never done anything *really* bad, and old Jake Phillips has no choice this day but to hide in the courthouse cellar. Old Jake Phillips is tall, bald, skinny and without teeth. Surely he is too old to grapple with the questions and anger that his son's death has brought him. But what choice does he have? He was a father. He loved his boy. And so he must ask the questions. He must permit the anger. The cellar is cool. The courthouse has a stone foundation. There is no cooler place in town. And the stone foundation is splendidly thick. He will not be able to hear the noise. The noise of those who this day will rejoice.

The sunlight trickles through the openings between the trees that line the foothills. It is now 6 A.M., and the town blinks, tongues saliva, bathes the roof of its mouth, digs gum from the corners of its eyes. Priscilla Purvis, daughter of Oliver W. Purvis, slips into a plain blue dress and goes downstairs to the kitchen. She sets out table scraps for Pinky, places the cat's dish in a corner by the stove. Then she fills another dish with water. She sets this dish next to the one containing the scraps. Then she opens the cellar door. Pinky is a very loving cat in the morning. He rubs himself against her skirt. She clucks at him, tells him to go about his business. Waow, says Pinky. Waow. Waow. A yawn from Pinky. Teeth. Ah, says Priscilla Purvis, dear Pinky. Pinky the fiend.

Dogs growl, yip, sniff, sprawl.

The river, the lovely Paradise, chucks and hisses, and the sound of the falls is white and unrelenting. One can, if one watches closely enough, observe fish flop over the falls. The mill there, Isaac (Ike) Underwood's old grist mill, is no longer used for that purpose. Now it serves as a storehouse for brick and tile manufactured by the Paradise Falls Clay Products. Its walls are damp, and mice debate within.

The flag, the dappled sunlight flag, the valiant Stars & Stripes . . . the month of mourning is past, and now the dear old flag is no longer flying at halfmast. The martyred President has been seen to his Illinois tomb; the assassin's treacherous bones have been hidden in an unknown grave; the affair is done; the Republic survives. God bless the Republic.

There are those who keep chickens. Now the chickens cluck and peck. And the cocks preen and prowl. And, now and again, a chicken shrieks; a cock crows; bellies palpitate. Feet. Feathers. Outrage. Thrust. Spasm. Triumph.

There is a statue atop the Paradise County Court House. This statue is ten feet high. It is a female figure, thick of bust and flank, chastely draped, arms spread widely apart, face expressionless. A man named Rossi carved that statue fifteen years ago. He was something of a sissy, or at least so it was generally believed. He called the statue Beauty. Its head is cocked in the direction of the sun. There are those who say: Poor old girl. Too bad she can't blink.

There are those who keep chickens, and there are those who grow corn and tomatoes—and not out in the country but right here within the corporate limits of the village. The thing of one's own earth, the home-grown thing . . . this is a thing to be savored and cherished. Now, with the mist gone, the stalks and clumps glisten in the new sunlight, and the word is Renewal, and it is a perfectly adequate word, an excellent word. These people . . . here and now, within this time and place . . . are, most of them, children of the earth, of farms, of homesteads, of the high sweet stink of horses, and they are, most of them, reluctant to inter their past. So some of them keep chickens. And others keep gardens. And others keep both chickens and gardens. And so the odors persist. And the nostalgia. And the feeling of continuance. (Destroy Arcadia? Never!) Berries. Grapes. Apples. The orchard and the arbor. The village treasures *all* its blessings, not simply its chickens and its gardens. The trees stand tall, and some of the trees bear fruit, and God is a good and loving God, and the village can be counted on to raise its collective voice loudly in its several churches. Chickens, gardens, fruit . . . ah, the poor old girl indeed. She has her head cocked in the wrong direction. Better she should be looking down. The bounty of the Almighty is so much closer down there. (Destroy Arcadia? For heaven's sake, *why?* It is such a large proclamation. Destruction would be sacrilege.)

So comes the morning. So comes this pretty day of homecoming.

Old Jake Phillips retreats into the courthouse cellar. Bill Light awakens. He is ashamed of himself, and he is ashamed of his dreams. In the next room, his mother coughs. Catherine Anne Light is just thirtytwo. She was only seventeen when she married Bill's father, the large and sturdy Warrior who is returning today. Bill was born the next year. He breathes deeply, pulls the sheet to his neck. His mother has not been well for years. He has never heard her complain, and he can barely remember her when she was well. The skin on her face is transparent. He is able to see the vessels in her temples. They jerk. They throb. She is dying. Of course she is dying. She has been dying for a very long time. He climbs from bed. His mouth is sour. He puts on his clothes. His erection is just about gone. He goes into his mother's room. She is awake. Of course she is awake. She does not believe she cares for any breakfast. Perhaps a cup of tea, she tells him. Do you think you could rustle up a nice hot cup of tea for your mother? Bill Light nods. He watches the vessels in her temples. He is fourteen years of age. He goes downstairs. As he heats the water, he thinks of Amelia Burkhart. He rubs his belly. He has to. He is fourteen years of age. He wonders if he will recognize his father. Out in the big house on Cumberland Street, Isaac (Ike) Underwood embraces his wife. He is sixtythree. His wife, the former Phoebe Bowers of New Haven, is fortysix. She is tiny and rigid, and she wants to laugh, but she resists the temptation. She does not want to be rude. Isaac (Ike) Underwood still is asleep. He presses his nose against the hollow place at the base of Phoebe's throat. She sees that there still are a few dispirited gray hairs sprouting from the top of his skull. They are mussed. She smooths them. She decides she is lying too rigidly. Sighing, she permits her muscles to relax. She pats her husband's substantial rump. She hears a red squirrel. It apparently is angry about something. Oh well, red squirrels always are. Across the hall, her son rises, walks to his bedroom window. He squints toward the trees but he cannot see the squirrel. Maybe, for all he knows, there is no squirrel out there. Maybe, for all he knows, the squirrel is in his belly. Our mayor's name is George McC. Pillsbury. He is taking breakfast with his wife. He is to give a speech today. It will be delivered from the courthouse steps. George McC. Pillsbury wears a pince nez, and it is doubtful that he weighs more than one hundred thirty pounds, and he has fathered seven sons. His wife, Irene, is vast and silent. She bore the first of George McC. Pillsbury's sons when she was nineteen. She bore the last when she was fortythree. Now she is sixtytwo, and most of the time she breathes with her mouth open. Three of the Pillsbury boys will be coming home today—the youngest three. Says George McC. Pillsbury to his wife: I've never met Ben Wade. This is quite a day for us. Quite a day. Says Irene Pillsbury: Yes. Her knees are pressed tightly together. The youngest boy's name is Lamar. He is not yet nineteen. He was wounded in the right arm last year when the Army of the Potomac met the rebels in a place called The Wilderness. He could have come home, but this he refused to do. He recuperated in a Washington hospital, and then he returned to duty. His parents visited him in that Washington hospital. He is a slight lad, and his eyes are not particularly good. He blinks a great deal. When his father asked him why he wanted to go back to duty, Lamar Pillsbury said: I like it. Irene Pillsbury cannot understand such talk, but of course she has offered no opinion. It is not her style to offer opinions. She has extremely fleshy lips, and they flap as she breathes. Says her husband, slicing a piece of ham: Ben Wade, by God. Now *there's* a genuine Tartar. Says Irene Pillsbury: Yes, dear. So I've been told. Ferdinand James Purvis, son of Oliver W. Purvis, is the last member of the Purvis household to come awake. Like Bill Light, he has been dreaming of the girl whose name is Amelia Burkhart. But Ferd Purvis' dream has been a happier one. He is seventeen, and he has been sparking Amelia Burkhart for more than a year, and he seeks to marry her, and the expectation is that he *will* marry her, and thus there is a warm and heavy optimism in his dreaming. When he awakens, he is not ashamed of his erection. Amelia is pale and blond. She lives on a farm, but you wouldn't know it from her complexion. She is no florid farm girl, not his Amelia. She stays inside the house, and her parents permit her to purchase salves and lotions for her complexion. She is the darling of their existence. In her father's words: Our love for her, young man, knows no bounds. And Ferd Purvis can understand the man's words. She is quiet, and when she goes outdoors she is never without a hat. She has told him: I freckle. It is a scandal how quick the spots just sort of pop out on my face. And, Ferd, it's not like I don't *want* to go outside; it's just that the sun makes me look so *tacky*. And I don't want to look tacky. Years from now, when I'm old and nothing matters, then all right, then I *can* look tacky. Won't matter a hill of beans. But right *now*, no. Ah, *listen* to me. Such blabber. My. Not like me. As he pulls on his britches, Ferd Purvis smiles. He loves her, and the sweet green May morning has done away with all defeats.

Today he will drive the buggy out to her place and call on his darling. He will take her back into town, and they will watch the splendid celebration that no doubt will attend the return of the Paradise Falls Blues. And they will *participate* in it. And today will be a great day. And later perhaps she will permit him to kiss her. He has kissed her a total of twentyfour times. This comes to twice a month, and it is an extravagant frequency, and he is properly delighted and humble. He hums. He goes to the washbasin. He washes his face and hands. He washes them very thoroughly. Outside his window is a sound of horses and voices, and now there is no mist, no mist at all, anywhere. Young J. K. Bankson, the alert little hunchback who edits the *Democrat*, has been engaged in a sight of figuring. As closely as he can determine, a total of 342 men marched off with the Paradise Falls Blues back in April of '61. Since then, according to his unofficial figures, a total of 1,115 men and boys enlisted or were conscripted. Not all served with the Paradise Falls Blues, of course. The Blues did most of their fighting in Virginia and Maryland. The later enlistees and conscripts, or at least a large percentage of them, were attached to various Ohio regiments that served in the west under Grant, Halleck, Grant again and finally Sherman. These men got to take part in the destruction of the Commonwealth of Georgia, and it must have been a splendid experience, and J. K. Bankson envies them. He was born and lived his first seventeen years in Savannah, and on his mother's side he had people who had more than four thousand acres of land and owned something like a thousand darkies. These people were named Depew, and they would have nothing to do with J. K. Bankson's father. They called him a drunkard. They said he had soullessly seduced J. K. Bankson's mother, staining her for all eternity. They said the fact that their son was born a hunchback was proof of Divine displeasure. J. K. Bankson's father finally shot himself. He stood on the gallery of the Depew place, and one of the Depew darkies, a gigantic coachman named Oscar, attempted to wrest the pistol from Paul Nelson Bankson, but Paul Nelson Bankson would have none of it; Paul Nelson Bankson inserted the barrel in his mouth, and the sound was not particularly loud (it was, said the darky, like the dull clap made by two shoes when they are struck together), and the poor darky was splattered with blood and brains, and yes, Paul Nelson Bankson was intoxicated; oh he surely was. His last words, hollered just before the barrel entered his mouth, were, according to the darky: *O you Depews, all of you! May all of this fall about your heads! May it crush you! God damn you all!* That was eighteen years ago, and J. K. Bankson was just eleven, and the fact that he and his mother were taken in by the Depews did nothing to strain away his agony, and it was not even enough for his mother to say: James, they thought they were behavin properly. The things they said, they thought they were the right things to say. Your father was an outlander, you see. They didn't know him. I had many beaux, and they knew all my beaux,

but then when I upped an married your daddy . . . well, they felt
slighted. An so they called him a seducer. An the hate came. An I've had
enough of hate. I hope to tell you. But his mother's words were inadequate,
and he just bet even *she* knew they were inadequate. His father had
harmed no one. At the beginning he had been by no means a drunkard.
But the Depews had made him a drunkard. Their contempt had trans-
formed him into a moist and belligerent rake and scamp. Paul Nelson
Bankson had come from a good Augusta family, but the Depews had not
known that good Augusta family, and those things they did not know they
did not recognize. Paul Nelson Bankson became a lawyer without clients
(he had read law with one of the most prominent judges in the Commonwealth, and the judge had told him he had a true feeling for the profession, and he came to Savannah with what had to be considered brilliant
prospects, but the damned Depews refused to recognize him, and in no
time at all his clients transferred their business elsewhere), and then,
after giving up the law, he took up carpentry, but by that time he was
drinking too much, and so his carpentry business failed, and it was then
that he shot himself, and one night when the young hunchbacked James
King Bankson was fifteen (his father dead and buried four years) his
mother took him out on that damned Depew gallery and they seated
themselves in a pair of wicker rockers (the wicker was uncomfortable
against his hump), and Carrie Bankson said: I want you to know some-
thin, son. And James King Bankson said: All right. And Carrie Bankson
said: Your daddy did not *have* to marry me. He did not seduce me. And
James King Bankson said: Please, Mama. Please don't talk about it. I
can't stand hearin about it. And Carrie Bankson said: He came here
with a friend, a boy named Colfax. I was sixteen, an there was a party.
My mama's birthday I believe it was. He an the Colfax boy shared a room
at the university. You've never been to Athens, have you? I surely must
take you there someday. A pretty little town. Prettiest little town I know.
Ah. Yes. Athens. It was a right an proper courtship I tell you. He didn't
even kiss me until a week before we were married. It was in Augusta,
you know. An no one from my family came. Your daddy was nervous
about it, an his mother an father didn't really know whether we should
go through with it, but your daddy had a mind of his own, an of course
that was why he insisted on comin here an settin himself up in the practice of law. I was eighteen years of age, an you were born a year later,
an I watched the way he fell apart. I watched the way my mama an
papa treated him. Wouldn't even nod to him on the street. Wouldn't even
hardly nod to *me* on the street. An so the drink came. An the thing that
happened happened. Right here on this gallery. Right over there by the
front door. Look at it. Yes. I want you to look at it. See those boards there?
There enough light for you to see them? Well, I can see them. You think
long an hard on those boards. You think long an hard on them. You know
what those boards tell *me*? They tell *me* PRIDE. They tell *me* PRIDE is

just about the worst thing there is. Ah, maybe you can't remember, but
I was a pretty woman. Everyone said so. White was my best color. White
with maybe a touch of deep dark red. But that's all gone now. My parents
got PRIDE, an your daddy had PRIDE, an is there anythin more awful on
this earth? *Pride goeth before a fall:* You mark me well. It will all fall
down. Your daddy called for it all to fall down, an he will be answered.
I know it. I swear by Almighty God I do. (Carrie Bankson died three years
later in an asylum. The last time her son visited her, she was unable to
control her saliva. She thought he was a horse. She thought he was Jack,
the old gelding she had ridden as a girl.) At seventeen, James King Bankson left his grandparents' home. You must understand, young man, said
old Samuel Depew, that we only tolerated you this long because of your
poor abused mother. And James King Bankson said: An just who was it
who did the abusin? And old Samuel Depew said: If it weren't for that
damned Affliction of yours, I would have you horsewhipped. And, grinning, James King Bankson said: Some day, old man, it will all fall down,
an oh how I shall rejoice. Wherever I am, I shall dance in the streets.
That I promise you. And then old Samuel Depew came at his hunchbacked
grandson with a cane. Sniggering, James King Bankson scuttled out of
the house before the old fool could catch him. There followed a time of
harsh wanderings. People called him Humpy, and drunkards were fond
of rubbing his Affliction for what they said was luck. It wasn't until 1860
that he came here to this village. It was at the invitation of Isaac (Ike)
Underwood. They had met in Columbus, where James King Bankson
was working as a reporter on the *Argus,* an afternoon newspaper of no
particular distinction. He had been working there three months, and he
was generally acknowledged (even by his colleagues) to be the best reporter on the staff, and never mind his Affliction. The harsh wanderings
had devoured six years of his life, and there was no indignity he had not
suffered, and thus there was nothing that frightened him. (Printer's devil
in Atlanta: One night, as he walked along the street, a fleshy whore came
up to him, embraced him, lifted him, turned him upside down, dropped
him on his head, relieved him of his purse. The street sang with all the
laughter that came from all the whores and ruffians who stood and
watched his disgrace. He said nothing. He did not weep. It was not too
difficult to learn the fleshy whore's identity. One night he climbed in her
window. He was, and still is, exceedingly agile. She was with a customer.
James King Bankson held a pistol at the fleshy whore's head. At the same
time, he held a razor about an inch from the private parts of the customer,
a small dark fellow who had a certain local reputation as a gambler. For
God's sake, said the small dark fellow, who are *you?* And James King Bankson said: Helen here knows who I am. And the fleshy whore said: All
right. All right. All right. I'll give you the money. I was drunk. And James
King Bankson said: It was six dollars an fourteen cents. Not countin
the price of my purse, which was thirtyfive cents. So I'll be thankin you

for six dollars an fortynine cents. The fleshy whore trembled in all her fleshy parts. She whimpered, but she had no words. James King Bankson pressed the pistol's muzzle against her forehead. Oh, said the fleshy whore, *cold*. The small dark fellow tried to seize James King Bankson's wrist. He was not successful. The wrist moved, and the razor slashed a shallow cut across the small dark fellow's knuckles. It scarcely bled, but the small dark fellow gave a great scream. He sucked his knuckles. The fleshy whore gave James King Bankson the money. He thanked her. He clambered out the window. His last view of the whore and the small dark fellow was of them embracing like terrified children in a stormtossed rowboat.) No, there was more to James King Bankson than the misshapen creature that met the superficial eye. (Telegraph messenger in Memphis: Boys and a dog. A residential street. The dog was tan, moist of eye and mouth, very old. There were eight of them, eight of those boys, and at least half of them were larger than James King Bankson, and they were beating the old dog with rocks. They held the dog's legs, and one of them had a knee on the dog's neck. It was screaming and slavering. An old woman came running from across the street. She had chinwhiskers, and she was perhaps eighty, perhaps older. She wielded a cane. James King Bankson picked up a rock. The old woman was screaming more loudly than the dog. James King Bankson went after the boy whose knee was on the dog's neck. He clubbed the boy about the shoulders and neck. Shrieking, the boy rolled to one side. The dog threshed. The old woman smacked two boys broadside with her cane. *Homer!* she screamed. *Homer! My poor Homer!* The boys whooped and kicked. James King Bankson burrowed into them. His rock moved in quick jabs. Two of the boys began to weep. They were clutching their bellies. The dog's legs were released. The boys fled. All of them. They flapped and staggered, and they did not look back. James King Bankson's teeth were exposed, but this is not to say he was grinning. The dog rubbed itself against the old woman's legs. She squatted beside the dog. Poor old Homer, she said. Poor old boy. Her voice was like pebbles on a marble floor. She insisted that James King Bankson come home with her. She said something about tea. She said he surely did deserve a cup. Her name, she said, was Letitia Burbank, *Miss* Letitia Burbank, and she told him that as a young woman she had been a bridesmaid at twentytwo weddings of her dearest friends, and now all twentytwo of those brides were dead, and then, chuckling, Miss Letitia Burbank said: Always a bridesmaid but never a corpse. And James King Bankson said: Yes ma'm. And Miss Letitia Burbank permitted herself an outright laugh. And so did James King Bankson. She was, she told him, eightyfour years of age. She said she'd once met George Washington. A quiet man, said Miss Letitia Burbank, with a peculiar mouth. And James King Bankson said: Yes. So his pictures show. Miss Letitia Burbank nodded. She had an acrid odor, yellowish and really quite strong. Homer nipped and sniffed at her skirts. Perhaps the acrid odor came from the

dog. James King Bankson wasn't quite able to tell. Perhaps he was being
unfair to Miss Burbank. He escorted her to her home, and she insisted that
he come inside. He told her he had a telegram to deliver. She told him oh
bosh, pish and tush. She said: You have nothin to fear. And James King
Bankson said: Yes ma'm. I know that. And he accompanied her inside
the house. And the front door needed oiling. And the dust made him
sneeze. And there were five pianos in the parlor. I gave music lessons
for almost fifty years, said Miss Burbank. This was the third house of
frame construction in all of Memphis. We came here in 1804, Daddy an
me, from Chittenden County, Virginia. Mama had died, an Papa could
not look at certain trees an fields an woods without burstin into tears.
We had money, an when we came here Papa started up one of the first
cotton brokerages, an he married again, an my halfbrother, Ratcliff Burbank, who has a large name in this city, operates the business to this very
day. But I haven't seen Ratcliff Burbank since 1847. Haven't so much as
laid eyes on him. He doesn't even want my money. Doesn't need it, so
he doesn't bother with me. Those boys who were out there devilin my
old Homer, those boys call me Crazy Lettie. Well, that's one thing, an
maybe they're right. But devilin Homer, that's *another*, an they had no
right . . . no sir, I remember real clear how Papa would go walkin with
me back there in Chittenden County, Virginia, an maybe it'd be a tree,
maybe a field, but he'd get to rubbin his eyes, an, well, it sure was a sight
an a caution. I took care of him until 1838 when he died, but don't think
it was *that* that kept me from marryin. I was thirty years of age, thirty
goin on thirtyone, when we came here from Chittenden County, Virginia,
and if I'd really wanted a husband, I would have found one by then. So
I expect I never had much use for the married state. Oh, I had beaux back
in Chittenden County; oh, I was just sparked an sparked until I wanted
to fall down in a heap, but whenever a beau got to talkin serious I just
sort of grinned at him an turned him back. Now you take old Homer. I
love old Homer. He loves me too. Now I call *that* love. Look at his eyes,
will you? You ever seen anythin so outright an forever *good*? Miss Letitia
Burbank's recitation was delivered in the kitchen of her home. It was
delivered as James King Bankson politely sipped at a cup of weak yellow
tea. Her sharp little voice was very clear. The table was slippery to the
touch, and James King Bankson didn't know whether it was grease or
what. He supposed the five pianos were not in tune. Homer scrabbled at
the feet of his mistress. She patted his head. He whined. He probably
had bruises. I surely do thank you, said Miss Letitia Burbank. He is buried
back in Chittenden County, Virginia. I bought the coffin. Ratcliff Burbank
never offered to pay a thing toward it. But, ah well, maybe it slipped his
mind. Come see the house. And Miss Burbank took James King Bankson
on a tour of the house: Must. Dust. Torn curtains. Dabs and slices of
the yellow Memphis sun. She chattered and sniggered, and the house was
enormous, and her father's likeness hung over the mantel (a small man,

he held a whip, and his eyes were wounded and smashed), and she insisted that James King Bankson write down his name and address on a scrap of paper, and the next day a cheque for five hundred dollars was delivered to his roominghouse. A note accompanied the cheque: *Please use this as you wish. I am most appreciative of your kindness. And please do not feel called upon to visit me and waste my time with remonstrations. Homer and I are most grateful, and we would consider it inexcusably poor manners if you refused this expression of our thanks.* James King Bankson honored the old woman's request. He converted the cheque to cash and left Memphis by nightfall. He was reasonably certain she would understand. Homer, too, as far as that went.) No. The history of James King Bankson does not in the slightest reveal him to be a milksop. Fleshy whores, bullying boys, rascals and miscreants of whatever stripe . . . none got the best of *him*. He has refused to yield to his deformity. And, in point of fact, it probably has helped him. He stands barely five feet two inches, and he walks in a rolling lurch, and his face is thick, gelatinous, with immense lips and ears. Had he been of normal shape and dimensions, he perhaps would not have survived. The suicide of his father, the madness of his mother, the unabashed contempt of the Depews: these things could very well have torn a normal man apart. But James King Bankson never has been a normal man, and thus he has never been weakened by a normal man's vulnerability. A normal man would not have gone after that whore with a pistol and a razor. A normal man surely would not have leaped to the defense of an aged dog, especially when his antagonists were eight in number and several of them larger than he. But James King Bankson has a large feeling for outrages, and his Affliction has provided him with a courage not shared by normal men. He has, as a result, a large feeling for personal honor, and he never has compromised it. (He could have paid another call on the old woman whose name was Letitia Burbank. Of course he could have. And probably, had he acted with intelligence, he could have moved in with her, as her servant or keeper or whatever. Which would have meant a great deal more money for him. Which would have been an outrage. No, the five hundred dollars had been honestly earned, and so he accepted it. Beyond that, however, he would not step. Another visit, another tour of the musty and tattered old rooms, another pilgrimage to the painting of the little man with the wounded and smashed eyes—no, no, no, morality demanded that the first tour also be the last. Propriety insisted that he convert the cheque to cash and quit Memphis as quickly as possible. What? How's that? You say five hundred dollars seems a large price to pay for the rescue of an old dog? No. Value is value only in the eyes of the beholder. What is trash to one man is a treasure to another. The old woman had valued the rescue at five hundred dollars. James King Bankson was too sensitive, too much of a gentleman, to question her judgment. No, he did the only proper thing. He honored her good sense. He took the money and he got out of

town. He has thought back on the incident many times, and occasionally
he has even managed a sort of smile. But it is not the smile of a cynic. It
is a smile of kindly sentiment. And he feels no guilt. He cannot. None
exists.) After Memphis, his wanderings took him to Frankfort, Louisville,
Evansville, Indianapolis, Toledo, Akron and finally Columbus, where he
was hired off the *Argus* by Isaac (Ike) Underwood, who was (and still
is) fat, who chewed (and still chews) tobacco, who cursed (and still
curses) with the virtuosity of a Brooklyn dockwalloper, who was (and
still is) a man of loud stabbing honesty, who said: Look you, I don't give
a damn if you're a hunchback. I want that known right away. All I seek
from you is a good day's work. Your employer happens to be a friend of
mine, and I trust his word, and he says you are the best fucking man for
the job. So how about it? You're making three dollars a week here. I'll
pay you twelve. Are you interested? And James King Bankson said: When
do I begin? And Isaac (Ike) Underwood said: Tomorrow. And James
King Bankson said: I'll be there. And it worked. And James King Bankson (now known as J. K. Bankson) has prospered. And, hump and all, he
even has a wife. Her maiden name was Frieda Alexander, and she is by no
exertion of rhetoric a beauty, but she is fecund, and her plain square face
fair glows with admiration and love for her gnomish lurching little husband, and she has given him two little girls, and J. K. Bankson is by no
means an unhappy man. He is twentynine and Frieda is thirtysix, and
they and their daughters live in a neat little house on Mineral Avenue.
Frieda, broad of hip and flaccid of bosom, with enormous brown eyes
that do not quite seem to focus, with large protuberant ears and a nose
that droops down on itself like the beak of an eagle that has hurled itself
fulltilt at the trunk of a tree; Frieda, who is almost six feet tall, whose
voice is fluted and fragile and preposterous coming from one of her size
and aspect; this Frieda Alexander Bankson, who had resigned herself to
a life of sandy aching maidenhood, who was rescued by her marriage
four years ago to this clever little hunchback with his soft Georgia words
and his large knowledge of outrages; this woman is grateful for her life,
and the days pass for her in a bright and happy rhythm that clearly cannot
help but go on forever. All is affection. All is white skies. She is a good
cook, and he has put on weight, and he has made her into a person of
some importance. She is the wife of that peculiar little bugger who edits
the newspaper, and his success has been hers, and there are few women
in this village who face their mornings with more delight. (Back in 1860,
when J. K. Bankson first came to Paradise Falls, there were those who
said they didn't trust him. And who was to blame them? After all, he was
deformed, and the deformed of this life are almost always seen as being
sinister. And then there was the matter of his Georgia accent. What had
possessed Ike Underwood to hire such a man? The Southrons would soon
be the Enemy, and *that* just about everyone knew, and now a Southron
was in their midst, editing their newspaper, and who knew what treachery

he would perpetrate? But J. K. Bankson is not a stupid man. He understood the suspicions, and so he dealt with them summarily. His editorials
were absolutely splendid; they seethed with anger at the South and the
recklessly destructive course it was pursuing; one would have thought they
were being written by that Garrison fellow, the Abolitionist zealot from
New England. And J. K. Bankson let out the story of how the Depews
had driven his father to suicide and his mother to the madhouse. He told
his acquaintances: You have to be born an reared down there before you
really can hate. Believe me, you people don't know what it *is* to hate. Look,
I *know* I'm suspect. I come up here an every time I open my mouth it's
like you're listenin to the shade of John C. Calhoun. Well, if you think
that means I'm a genuine Southron, you're as wrong as wrong can be. I'll
tell you the truth. I want a war. I want that war to burn the South to the
ground. All of it. My daddy called for it. Just before he died. He cursed
the South, an I curse it too. He called for its destruction, an I call for its
destruction too. This new President, this Lincoln, I pray to God he moves
against these insurgents an traitors. An with force. Proper an righteous
wrath. Fire an sword.) And of course the result of the late War of the
Rebellion has been a joy and an inspiration for J. K. Bankson. No one
greeted the news of Lee's surrender more jubilantly. Last month, on that
fine morning when the first Associated Press dispatch came on the *Democrat's* leased wire, when his telegrapher, Mace French, handed him the
scrap of paper that tolled the bell for the rebellious Confederacy, J. K.
Bankson became so wrought up he nearly choked on his own saliva. It
was a gray morning, and there had been rain. He did not bother with a
coat, however. He simply ran out into the middle of Main Street, splashing and sliding in the mud, and he literally *jumped up and down,* and
people came running from all directions, and his lips flapped and his
saliva flew. *It's done!* he hollered. *It's done, an the judgment has been
wrought! God bless the United States of America!* And then of course
came cheering and tears, and after a time churchbells were tolled, and
their tolling was loud and dark, and the gray sky shook itself, split and proclaimed the sun. Ah, those bells. Ah, that blessed morning. The bell had
tolled for the Confederacy, and another bell was tolling the joy attendant
on this supreme occasion, and the joyous bell was joined by other joyous
bells, and their heavy rhetoric made the citizens of the village whoop and
clap, and the muffled funereal bell, the bell that tolled for the despised
rebel nation, was overwhelmed by all the victorious bells, and especially
in the happy soul of J. K. Bankson, whose spirit stood atiptoe, announcing
its sweet vengeance. Oh those Depews! Oh now God surely would inun-
date them with rot and despair! J. K. Bankson jumped up and down, and
he splattered his shirt and britches with the Main Street mud, and the
new sun was soft and easy across the back of his neck, and later, when
the people of the village talked about his reaction to the glad news, there
was one general opinion, and it went like this: It takes a genuine

Southron to hate the South genuinely. A wise analysis, and the village knew this, and the village was rather proud of itself. But that was all more than a month ago, and since then J. K. Bankson has been very busy indeed. He is chairman of the committee that has been busy making the arrangements for a proper celebration to welcome home the Paradise Falls Blues. Mayor Pillsbury appointed him at the instigation of Ike Underwood. He really loved this war, said Ike Underwood, and so he's the perfect man for the job. Mayor Pillsbury did not disagree. He has never disagreed with Ike Underwood about anything. He knows better. If it weren't for Ike Underwood, he would not be mayor. And he would not be vice president of the Paradise Falls Clay Products. If Ike Underwood told George McC. Pillsbury to fly to the sun, there is every reason to believe that George Pillsbury would sprout wings and go flapping off, pince nez and all, the obedient Icarus of Paradise Falls. But his subservience to Ike Underwood does not embarrass him. He knows, and the village knows, that Ike Underwood is the largest human being hereabouts. Large in the sense of greatness. And so it is no disgrace to be subservient to him. Ike and his wife Phoebe and their son Philip constitute the First Family of Paradise Falls. Which is as it should be. First of all, Ike Underwood is the richest man in the county. Secondly, he is responsible for the village of Paradise Falls. He and a man named Morris, a storekeeper, actually laid out the streets. His bank, his newspaper, the Paradise Falls Clay Products, the various other commercial establishments and small manufactories he controls (a feed store, a chair factory, a shoe factory, a tanning works, a notions & sundries store) . . . these institutions enable the village to exist. Without them, it would die. Without Ike Underwood, it never would have been brought into being in the first place. And so he is honored. As well he might be. And so when he tells George McC. Pillsbury to do something, it is done. (But the instructions are benevolent. Ike Underwood is a hard man, and he always has been an ambitious man, but he never has been anything less than a Christian. There are those who says he lacks manners, but there are none who accuse him of gratuitous cruelty. He came here a long time ago, and he established—or had a hand in establishing—just about everything worth a damn in this entire part of the state, and of course his activities have created victims and enemies, but the creation of the victims and the enemies was unavoidable. He has always been governed by a design, and the fruits of that design have brought the greatest good to the greatest number, and his sleep is sound and firm and energetic.) And, as is usually the case, Ike Underwood's choice of J. K. Bankson to head the Paradise Falls Blues welcoming committee was a wise one. Rushing about the village with lurching hunchbacked fury, J. K. Bankson formed a subcommittee of church ladies who were charged with preparing a gigantic feast that would be served to the returning heroes and their families the day of their arrival. He obtained the use of the largest building in the village—St

Luke's Lutheran Church. The pastor, a dour fellow with the clamorous name of Horst G. Leppelmeier, wasn't too sure that the use of a religious edifice for such a secular affair was precisely proper. But J. K. Bankson had his way with the Rev Mr Leppelmeier. He said: Look, we only want the *basement*. What's the matter with you? You think people are goin to be eatin gooseliver off the altar? The little editor's words were delivered with such righteous outrage that the Rev Mr Leppelmeier's objections were sundered, splintered, crushed. All right, said the Rev Mr Leppelmeier, all right, all right, vhatever it iss you vant to do, do it, ant may the blessingks of Gott attendt you. And so the plans proceeded. A total of fortythree women was enlisted to prepare the meal under the supervision of Mrs Barbara Sturgeon, wife of J. Lloyd Sturgeon, county recorder of deeds and a candidate for reelection next year. J. K. Bankson next enlisted the services of a band, some sixteen members, sponsored by Paradise Lodge #171, Free & Accepted Masons. Then he sent a telegram to Senator Ben Wade. It had Ike Underwood's signature. (In this part of Ohio there is a morass of Democratic counties. The Copperhead movement was quite strong during the war, and dozens of peace sneaks held public office. But Paradise County was, and is, and probably always will be, a Republican bastion. And Ike Underwood has been, since the party's founding nine years ago, a loyal and generous financial contributor. He and Ben Wade are dear friends, and thus J. K. Bankson had every reason to believe that the Senator's reply to the telegram would be favorable. As indeed it was. The answer came the next morning: *Would be delighted to participate in ceremony. Am honored to have been invited.*) J. K. Bankson's next chore concerned itself with the matter of flags and banners. Thanks to the generosity of Ike Underwood, he was able to rent two hundred flags from a Columbus firm. Then he dragooned a number of women, expert seamstresses all, and pressganged them into creating four gigantic banners. Each of these banners is forty feet long and ten feet high. One has been hung at the CPV&M depot. It reads: Liberty Forever!! The other three have been hung across Main Street. It is assumed that the Paradise Falls Blues will march from the depot to the courthouse steps, there to be greeted by Mayor Pillsbury and Senator Wade. When they do so, they will pass under the three banners. The first reads: The Republic Indestructible!! The second reads: Victory!! The third reads: Let There Be Peace!! J. K. Bankson is very pleased with the seamstresses' work. In an editorial a few days ago, he wrote: *The energy and devotion of these fine women have been an inspiration and a blessing. To those who say that the late war has drained this nation of enthusiasm for its ideals and sacred institutions, we can only say: Nonsense. Examine, if you will, the hearts of these women of Paradise Falls. Honor them. Honor their zeal. Perhaps, in the large scheme of history, their contribution is insignificant—but is it really? What more noble estate is there than that of loyal womanhood? Ah yes. No question*

about it. This will be a happy and prideful day for J. K. Bankson. He
has done his work well. Main Street is gussied up to its very most victorious
eyeballs, and the women are already laboring over their pots and bowls
and kettles (some of the women have been up since 3 A.M.), and here
and there the soft morning is punctured by the wheeze and thump and
tootle of practicing bandsmen, and J. K. Bankson comes awake with a
damp grin. The first thought that crosses his mind is the figure 1,457. It
represents, according to his arithmetic, the number of Paradise County
men who served their blessed country in the late war. He reaches for his
wife Frieda, but she already is up and about her business of the day. He
hears her moving about downstairs in the kitchen. And he hears the
voices of their two daughters, Mary, who is three, and Ruth, just fourteen months. He grins. He is lying on his side. His hump prevents him
from lying on his back. He sits up in bed. He allows his mind to caress
the figure 1,457. He is proud of Paradise County, proud of Paradise
Falls, proud of the choice he has made, proud of his belief that he
will hate the South until his final breath. He climbs out of bed. He pads
across the room to the washstand. His feet are cold. He washes his hands
and face in cold water. Sometimes, in these Yankee mornings, there is
a scum of ice spread across his washwater. But not this morning. His
feet are cold, but the rest of him is as warm as warm can be. He grimaces
into the mirror: 1,457. Last week he talked with a man named Henry
Mohr, a farmer from up in the northern end of the county. Henry Mohr
had served in the Georgia campaign, and he had taken part in the
Christmas capture of Savannah. Henry Mohr was perhaps the two-
hundredth man J. K. Bankson had questioned about the Depews. And
he was the first who remembered encountering them. Depew? said Henry
Mohr. A man named Samuel Depew? Old fellow? And J. K. Bankson,
pulse slamming hotly, said: Yes, yes, that's the man. He's my grandfather.
And Henry Mohr said: Oh. Well. I'm *sorry*. And J. K. Bankson said:
Sorry about what? And Henry Mohr said: Well, I expect we went and
burned his place to the ground. Godalmighty, I didn't have no idea he
was your— And, breaking in, J. K. Bankson said: How'd it happen? And
Henry Mohr said: Uh, well, God damn, so he was your grandpa. And
J. K. Bankson said: *How'd it happen?* Henry Mohr stared at J. K.
Bankson. Then, after much hemming and throatclearing, he told a
story that made J. K. Bankson's soul leap up and whistle. It was cold, said
Henry Mohr, cold and gray and wetter than hell, and all we wanted was
to get in out of the rain. There was three companies of us, and we didn't
want to cause no trouble; all we wanted was to find someplace where it
was dry. Look, we'd burned and hacked our way clear across the Commonwealth of Georgia, and the truth was: we was tired. And I mean
tired. By that time, the meanness had been squeezed out of us. We was
mostly conscripts anyway. Look, Mr Bankson, let's face up to it. Mattie
and me got seven little ones, and the army it had to come and *get* me. It

wasn't until June of '63 that I went in, and by that time, well, the regiments was being filled by them as the government could get by hook or by crook. My regiment was from Iowa to begin with, but at the end there was more Ohio men than Iowans in it, and by a whole lot. And I'll tell you the truth—we wasn't exactly the cream of the cream, if you know what I mean. Conscripts, bounty men, even a few rebels who'd come over to our side . . . we was raggletaggle and meaner than a mouthful of glass. At least at the beginning. But that walk across Georgia took it out of us. The burning, the drinking, the stealing . . . well, even that gets to be wearisome, and so by the time we got to Savannah we was too whipped to be looking for trouble. But that old man, that Depew, he was bound and determined to give it to us. He should of had better sense. Well, anyhow, it was Christmas Eve, and we was marching along this here old mud road, and Major Everhart (who was commanding the three companies) was up forward somewheres looking for a place to bivouac. Then, allofasudden, we heard shots. Oh Lord God in Heaven, I said to myself, what'd we run into? Some platoon of dogeared militia? The officers yelled at us, and we moved forward at a trot. It was twilight, and I was so damn cold I had to blow on my fingers to get them to working proper. We formed a skirmish line on both sides of the road, and then we saw Major Everhart running toward us, running hellbent for election or however the saying goes. His horse was nowhere to be seen. He came running up to a couple of the captains, company commanders they were, and we seen him waving his arms and jumping up and down. Me, I thought he was about to have a stroke and drop dead on the spot. But he didn't. He got to hollering at us, and now we ran instead of trotted, and we came over a hill, and there they were, there the rebels were, and there couldn't have been more than thirty of them, and the major's horse lay dead in front of a barricade of treetrunks, and none of them rebels even wore a uniform, and two of them, old men and I could see them real clear, actually honest to God wore *high silk hats*, and the major hollered at us to charge, and I swear to you it was over just about before it'd begun. We killed nineteen of them in maybe two minutes, maybe three. The rest, all except one, throwed up their arms and gave up. They sort of hunched themselves into little balls when we came whooping and scrambling over their damn barricade; they hunched themselves into little balls and they threw down their rifles and that was that. All, like I said, except one of them, and that was the man named Depew, Samuel Depew, the man you say was your granddad. He'd gotten himself backed against one of them there old trees with that Spanish moss hanging from it, and he was sort of frail and small, you know, his white hair stringing off in the damp breeze, his chest heaving and jerking, and he had in both of his hands, aimed straight forward, the damnedest biggest old horse pistol I've ever seen in my whole entire life. And he was aiming it straight at Major Everhart. And then he got to yelling. *You swine!* he yelled. *How dare you come here!* And, what the hell, we didn't none of us need no telegram from the old boy to give us warning on what he was going to do. So we shot him. About fifteen, maybe twenty of us. We shot him from about thirty yards. We sure did shoot him good. The bullets slammed him back against that there tree, and his chest and his face got all red and smeary, if you know what I mean, and that was the end of him. He slid to the base of the tree, and it wasn't much of a thing to be seeing, no sir. Well, we found out his name from one of our prisoners, and we found out that his wife had died in I think it was '62 and his niggers had run off a week or so before, and Major Everhart he was madder than a whore with her tit caught in a wine press, and so he marched a company of us to the old man's house, and a big house it was, and we burned her to the ground. We burned her good. We burned her proper. Huh. Sure is funny, come to think of it. Those men, those fellers I mean who tried to stop us back there at that barricade, they was all of them old men, and it turned out they was all of them rich, with a whole lot more to lose from fighting than from giving up. Hell, if they'd of gave up, maybe they'd of been able to pick up some of the leavings . . . you know, land is land, with or without niggers. But this they did not choose to do. Instead they chose to fight. And we killed nineteen of them—twenty, counting old Depew. Boys, oh, the Southron mind, whoo. So that's it, Mr Bankson. I'm afraid we killed your granddad. But we couldn't help it. Swear God we couldn't. Huh. Peculiar, ain't it? I mean, that *me*, a Paradise County man, should of been in on it. What with *you* being a Paradise County man too. Small world. Yes *sir*. I surely am sorry though. If I'd of knowed he was your granddad, maybe I could have stopped it. *Maybe*. Doubt it, though. I mean, he was bound and determined to fire that old horse pistol. I'll go to my grave believing that. And here Henry Mohr concluded his recitation. He spread his hands in what J. K. Bankson supposed was a sort of apology. And so J. K. Bankson smiled, pulling taut his fat lips; J. K. Bankson smiled and patted Henry Mohr on a shoulder and said: You don't have to feel sorry. You've told me what I've wanted to hear. I thank you kindly for the good news. And then, with Henry Mohr frowning at him, J. K. Bankson took his leave of the fellow. He snapped and clucked at the horse as he drove his buggy back to Paradise Falls. He breathed deeply of the delicious Yankee air. He whistled. He slapped his knees. Yes *sir*, he said to no one. Oh my yes sir *indeed*. And so today, on this morning of triumphant homecoming, J. K. Bankson is encumbered by no defeats. He washes his hands and face. He puts on his best suit, his finest and most elaborate cravat, his most expensive studs and links. He examines his beard in the mirror. It is full. It is a Burnside beard. He combs it. Ah. Perfect. Splendid. Triumphal and grand, he lurches downstairs to his waiting wife and daughters. The streets abound with voices and laughter. The Paradise Falls Blues, first to leave to participate in the war and the last to return from it, will have sunshine in honor of their apotheosis, sunshine and oratory and flags and food and reverent joy. Ah, says J. K. Bankson to his wife and daughters, the day finally is here. Praise the Lord.

Flags. Chickens. Gardens. The village's collective fingers have wiped the collective gum from its collective eyes. Dogs yip. Children roll hoops. Young women, wives of men serving in the Paradise Falls Blues, primp and quiver, fight to control their breath. The streets begin to fill, and by 9 o'clock a goodly crowd already has gathered at the CPV&M depot. (The Paradise Falls Blues . . . ah, indeed a fine group of men. First to answer the call. Last to return. There is a rightness to this, a sort of justice, large and perhaps profound. These men marched away in April of '61, and for more than a year they did garrison duty in Kentucky and what is now West Virginia. But then, in late '62, they were transferred to the Army of the Potomac. They did not see action at Fredericksburg, but they did participate in poor old Muttonchop Burnside's infamous Mud March, and it was an excellent initiation for Chancellorsville, Gettysburg, The Wilderness, the siege of Petersburg. And they did well. The statistics attest to this. There were 342 of them the day they marched away. To-day, according to J. K. Bankson's figures, only 221 of them will return. And, of these 221, only 198 were among the first complement that marched away back on that April day more than four years ago. The rest of the original Paradise Falls Blues either died in battle, died of disease, vanished or were invalided out of the army because of wounds or disease. And so the rightness of today's celebration proclaims itself with irresistible eloquence. Of the original 342, some 144 were casualties of the hideous war just past. This represents a staggering percentage, and no doubt Ben Wade will mention it when he gives his speech on the courthouse steps.)

J. K. Bankson walks to his office. Passersby nod and smile at him. They congratulate him on the excellence of his preparations. He thanks them, strokes his lush Burnside beard.

Claude Dill and his son open their saloon. It immediately fills with customers. Going to be a great day, says young Ed Dill. Wouldn't be surprised, says Claude Dill, pouring whisky. Claude Dill's saloon, on Main Street just opposite the Acterhof House, is the largest and most elegant in Paradise Falls. Claude Dill has a cast in his left eye. He is tall and silent. He drinks at least a quart of whisky a day, and no one has ever seen him drunk. The same cannot be said, however, of his son Ed.

The hills would appear today to smile.

Ferd Purvis hitches up the family buggy and drives out to Lake Township to fetch his beloved, the pale Amelia Burkhart. He breathes odors of damp earth. He tastes odors of damp earth. He is seventeen years of age and he is immortal, and behind him, loving him and protecting him (or so he would believe), are the great smiling hills.

Trees. Listen to the trees. Hear the new leaves. Renewal. Green. God bless God.

Morning, and the people come from all over the county. Wagons. Carriages. Buggies. The horses trot, and the horses drop heroic steaming balls of shit, and women giggle, hold their noses, cling tightly to their bonnets.

Young Bill Light walks to the CPV&M depot. Will I recognize him? he asks himself. Will I recognize my father? He thinks of his mother. Old Mrs Pett is taking care of his mother this morning. Mama, Mama. Poor dying Mama. She knows her Warrior husband is to return today. She has made no comment, however. She has been too busy coughing. She has been too concerned with having a nice cup of tea. She has been too occupied with, if the truth were known, dying. Young Bill Light walks on the balls of his feet. He walks as though he expects to be set upon by assassins. His features are small, a bit pinched, but he is by no means homely. His complexion is light, and his hair just about turns white in the summer. He is fond of fishing. When he goes fishing, he never has company. Fishing for him means time to dream, mostly of girls and young women. His papa, his Warrior papa returning today, has his papa ever dreamed?

Banners. Banners and flags. The musicians are gathering at the depot. They tootle. They thump. They grin. They nudge one another, exchange ribald jests. They await the arrival of their leader, Prof Karl J. Baer, a skinny man with a gambler's moustache and a certain peculiarly successful way with maiden ladies who are beyond the first dear flush of girlhood. Many are the warm and airless parlors that have welcomed the learned Prof Baer; many are the crowsfooted spinsters who have been enchanted by the lilt and swoop of his rhetoric. Some day he no doubt will make a good match. One that includes a handsome dowry. There can be little doubt of this.

Mayor and Mrs Pillsbury call for Ike and Phoebe Underwood. They ride to the depot in Mayor Pillsbury's gleaming carriage. It is pulled by a team of matched grays. Mayor Pillsbury devotes all his Sunday afternoons —weather permitting—to the maintenance of his carriage. He especially enjoys polishing it.

In her bed, Catherine Anne Light smiles at a window. She tells herself: I do not hate my husband. How could I? He cannot help being what he is. Then Catherine Anne Light, thirtytwo and as good as dead, is seized by a massive fit of coughing. Mrs Pett runs into Catherine Anne Light's bedroom, but of course there is nothing Mrs Pett can do.

Riding in Mayor Pillsbury's resplendent carriage, Phoebe Underwood thinks of her son Philip. She is just fortysix, but no one would guess her age. She has the dimensions of a girl just past puberty, and they please her, and she knows they please her husband. She says to herself (putting aside for a moment the thoughts that have to do with her son): It is good for a woman to be tiny. It is also good for a woman to be strong. Then

(and she chides herself for permitting her mind to wander so shamefully)
she forces herself to consider her son. He has insisted on walking to the
depot. Last year, when he made so much trouble about joining the army
(of course Phoebe and Ike would not hear of it; they forbade it, and he
honored their orders), last year a change came over her son, and she
does not understand it. All she does understand is her love. She says to
herself: I expect I am an almost unspeakably uncomplicated person. I
only wish our Philip were also that way. Then, shaking her head, Phoebe
Underwood smiles at her husband. He winks at her. As all this is happening, Mrs Pillsbury is talking of her activities at sewing. She says: I
never could put a decent hem on a dress. And her husband nods. And
Phoebe Underwood nods. And Ike Underwood nods. Even *him*. And the
hills grin, and fear not, humanity, life is precious, and there still are
many places where the air is clean. (Assassinate Arcadia? Such rot.)

Prof Baer arrives at the depot. It is 9:45. He gathers the bandsmen
around him. He smiles his thin seducer's smile. The first selection, begun
at 9:51, is *Marching Through Georgia*. De de de de, de de de de, as we
go *ma*rching through Georgia; wumpa wumpa wump wump wump, &c,
&c, world without end, God spare us all.

And now come the members of the clergy, the Rev Mr Leppelmeier,
pastor of St Luke's Lutheran Church; the Rev Clovis T. Reader, per-
sonable young pastor of the First ME Church of Paradise Falls; the Rev
Edwin P. Rathbun, thin and diffident, rector of Grace Episcopal Church;
the Rev Fr Paul K. Messer, pastor of St Thomas Aquinas RC Church
(a good fellow this priest, red of face, jovial of manner, thick of belly, his
breath almost always clamoring with fruited proclamations of *spiritus fru-
menti*, surely an eloquent demonstration of the fellow's essential humanity), and the Rev Durward E. Lillis, pastor of St Mark's Presbyterian
Church (all grimness is this fellow, a true believer in the Elect and Pre-
destination, a blocky grayfaced fellow with an inappropriate squeak in
his voice that never fails to manifest itself when his sermons reach their
points of highest and most intense zeal, which sort of emasculates his
words, to say the least).

They emerge, the people of the village, from their dwellings of brick
and stone and clapboard; they climb into their buggies; they promenade;
children are gathered up; hoops and balls are left lying on lawns. Dogs
mourn, skulk, cover their faces with their forepaws. A child toots on a tin
whistle. Laughter. Several of the dogs look up. And tiny flags emerge. And
the fists of the children clutch these tiny flags. And the flags are waved.
And the Republic will never die. (The dogs crawl under porches.)

Young Phil Underwood sits at the base of an elm tree just across the
tracks from the CPV&M depot. He watches the crowd, the gathering
moiling happy throng, bright and undefeated in its bonnets and waist-
coats. He listens to the music. He smiles as he watches the excellent
flapping of the arms of the good Prof Baer. (This should have been young

Phil Underwood's war too. His parents made a mistake by keeping him
out of it. They have taught him honor but they have not permitted him to
exercise it. He cannot fathom their reasoning.) His smile goes away. He
is darkly handsome, and many girls are interested in him, and he wishes
there were someone he could hit. Grunting, he tears at the bark of a tree.
He splits a fingernail. He sucks on the finger. He sucks blood, spits it
out with a small fastidious patoo!

J. K. Bankson joins Mayor and Mrs Pillsbury and Ike and Phoebe
Underwood at the depot. They congratulate him on a job well done.
His grin is crooked and almost shy, but he does sort of puff up.

Carriages. Clatter. Music. Senator Ben Wade is due on the 10:27 from
Columbus. J. K. Bankson learns from Ed Sauer, the stationmaster, that
the train is on time. So is the train that is bringing the Paradise Falls
Blues up from Marietta. Ed Sauer smiles. Miracles never cease, he says
to J. K. Bankson.

Tootle. Thump. Flap. Jabber.

Above the depot entrance, the banner proclaims: LIBERTY FOREVER!!

Mrs Frederick L. Magill, wife of the commanding officer of the Paradise Falls Blues, chats briefly with Phoebe Underwood. Mrs Magill's husband has been quite ill with dysentery. He is a small man, wiry and dark,
and Mrs Magill is, to be frank about it, terribly worried about his condition. He has been in a Washington hospital for the past three weeks, but
he has insisted on returning to Paradise Falls with his men. In his last
letter to his wife, he wrote: *Madeleine my dear, my health cannot be
permitted to thwart my leading the men back home. Surely you can understand this. Remember, they elected me their captain by a unanimous vote.
I have an obligation. This has been a long & hideous war, but their loyalty
and devotion have never faltered. Thus, I owe it to them to bring them
home &, in a sense, balance the books on this adventure. Perhaps this
belief is an excess attributable to my lawyerish mind. If so, I apologize.
But, as you no doubt must understand, I cannot help being what I am.*

Ferd Purvis and his Amelia ride into town. He holds her hand. She
wears a white shirtwaist, and her chest is exquisite. They wave at acquaintances they see on the street. Amelia makes mewling sounds when
she sees the flags and banners on Main Street.

Frederick L. Magill has not permitted his wife to visit him in the Washington hospital. He has sought to spare her that much of his dying. He is
a brevet major now. He is proud of the promotion. Today, on this happy
morning, he reclines in a litter in the train that is bringing the Paradise
Falls Blues up from Marietta. The train has just stopped at the Athens
depot. Won't be long now, someone says. Murmurous sounds come in
reply. Major Magill's litter is surrounded by men. They are smiling at
him. He looks at his hands. He is fortyseven years of age, and his hands
should not be papery, but they are. Yes, he says, smiling a bit, won't be
long now at all.

Oliver P. Purvis, county superintendent of public instruction, walks to the depot with his two daughters, Priscilla and Editha. He is very proud of them (as he is proud of his son Ferd), and he has a right to be. Priscilla, who is twenty, is strong, alert, pretty and brave, and she has no time for foolishness. Editha, who is just nine, already shows signs of becoming a beauty of the purest ray serene. She walks in a skip, and she puts her father in mind of feathers and warm breath. She is, in that sense, very much like her late mother.

Phil Underwood sucks all the blood from his bleeding finger.

Madeleine Magill is forty. Her two small boys, John and Frederick Jr, stand silently next to her as she chats with Phoebe Underwood. John is eleven; Frederick is six. She is a tall woman, blunt of jaw, devoid of breasts. At first glance, she appears grim, rigid, sour. Nothing could be further from the truth. All her life Madeleine Magill has been a creature of deep and steaming passions. No one except her husband knows this, however. They were married back in '47, and on their wedding night she enveloped him like a python, and the next morning he smiled and told her: My darling, you are one of the great revelations of the age. And then he laughed. And so did she. And no one has ever known. Now, chatting with Phoebe Underwood, she struggles to control her breath. She is remembering certain feverish carnal episodes. She wishes she could feel ashamed of herself for permitting such memories, but she cannot. She stands tall, and she stands grim, and she is such a lie.

The Rev Fr Messer permits himself a priestly chuckle and says to Mayor Pillsbury: The kraut. I have prepared it myself.

Kraut? says the mayor.

Yes, says the priest. My brother Thomas. His last letter was all about kraut.

All about kraut? says the mayor, an obedient echo.

Yes. He wrote and told me he has not had kraut in four years. Thomas has always been an absolute lunatic about it. So last night I prepared it. Today we will share it. All it needs is to be warmed up. I would not let Mrs Gill touch it. She knows nothing about kraut.

Mrs Gill?

My housekeeper.

Ah. Yes.

It will be a fine feast. I love my brother very much. I pray he will get married soon.

Well, he certainly made a good record for himself. Lieutenant and all.

Yes, says the Rev Fr Messer, and I am proud of him.

You have every right to be, says the mayor.

And perhaps we shall share a drop or two.

Oh yes, says the mayor, a drop or two. Wouldn't blame you a bit.

Another priestly chuckle from the Rev Fr Messer. Fragrant.

Frederick Magill Jr cannot remember his father at all. His older brother

John has a sort of memory of the man, but it is indistinct. The boys are
very proud of their father, however. After all, he is the *commanding officer*. They know he is ill, but he will recover. It is not time for him to die.
Both boys are dark, small for their ages, but they have good nimble minds,
and their mother is more than a little proud of them. Chatting with
Phoebe Underwood, she says: Ah, these two. Such scholars they are. I
expect they can thank their father for that. They surely don't get such
abilities from *me*.

Now, says Phoebe Underwood, you deprecate yourself too much.

No. Not a bit. Last week there was a spelling bee for the fourth, fifth,
sixth, seventh and eighth grades, and did you hear who won?

No. I'm sorry. I didn't.

John here. Even though he's just eleven and only in the fifth grade.

Phoebe Underwood smiles at John Magill. Congratulations, young man,
she says.

John Magill looks off toward a stand of trees beyond the CPV&M
roundhouse. His face is warm.

John! says his mother.

Reluctantly John looks at Phoebe Underwood. Thank you ma'm, he
says.

That's better, says Madeleine Magill.

I can do sums, says little Frederick Magill Jr to Phoebe Underwood.
His voice is small, splintered, proud.

Now now, says little Frederick's mother, hush with that boasting.

And I can spell too, says little Frederick.

Hush! says his mother.

Twelve and seventeen is twentynine, says little Frederick. And horse
is h-o-r-s-e.

John speaks up. Luncheon is l-u-n-c-h-e-o-n, he says.

Phoebe Underwood laughs delightedly.

Prof Baer pumps with increased vigor, and the band plays more loudly.
Ferd Purvis and his fair Amelia arrive at the depot. They sit for a time
in the buggy and survey the crowd. Along come his father and two sisters. They smile and wave. Old Karl Hellmann's boxer dog Franz goes
sniffing at the base of a CPV&M Maintenance of Way Dept privy. Ike
Underwood and his old friend Harlowe Morris, the storekeeper, get to
talking about the political situation. Neither man has much use for the
new President, a Unionist Democrat named Johnson. Prof Baer smiles at
Miss Virginia Miller, a virgin of thirtysix whose late father allegedly left
her an estate valued in excess of forty thousand dollars. Miss Miller is
aware of a fugitive tingling in her loins. She tells herself: Oh *you*. Miss
Miller is plump and pink, and her reddish hair is thinning, and her voice
is burdened with a heavy salivary lisp. It makes her sound as though she
is speaking from the bottom of the river. She is standing with a cousin, a
Mrs Myrtle Hoerner. She turns to Mrs Hoerner and says: Myrtle, I

swear he is the mosht flirtasheoush man I've ever met. Mrs Hoerner, who knows more of the world than she expects her poor innocent cousin ever will, says: Yes. And you'd better stay away from him if you know what's good for you. And Virginia Miller says: Yesh. Of coursh. (He who would assassinate Arcadia perforce must be a monster among monsters. It is inconceivable that a *human being* would entertain such an ambition.) Alleys. Earth. The right hand of Ferd Purvis rests casually on Amelia Burkhart's left knee. She says nothing to him about it. Horses. Tootle-thump. Alleys and earth and secrecy are not always needed. Turmoil hides a great deal, including courageous hands resting on sweet innocent adored knees. (Buildings here sit flatly, and most of them are as plain as good Paradise County brick and mortar can make them. The Guglielmo Rossi statue of Beauty, standing openarmed atop the courthouse, is without question the village's most ambitious and flamboyant acknowledgment of esthetic considerations. The village, if it were called upon to comment on its apparent lack of appreciation for the artistic creations without which a civilization is said to be arid and desolate, no doubt would reply: What need have we for statuary and socalled pretty pictures? We have, surrounding us, the works of God. We have, breathing sweetly across the fields and down from the hills, the languorous bounty of Arcadia. We have sumac and bloodwort and pussytoes and cabbages and squirrels and owls and the dark abiding earth. We praise God, and He is the true Beauty, and God bless God; God save Him from Whom all lasting blessings flow in such happy abundance. Yes, this is Arcadia, and no doubt about it. Babylonians will never be welcome here.)

To the deafening cheers of one & all, the 10:27 arrives exactly on time from Columbus, and United States Senator Benjamin Franklin Wade, a Stalwart if there ever has been one, a seeker of Justice not to mention right & proper Vengeance, a man whose hatred of all things Southron has become a national legend, is the first person down the steps from the CPV&M daycoach, and he waves his hat, and he smiles, and he bows, and the band strikes up *Hail, Columbia.*

The engineer, a Democrat named Finnerty, digs at a nostril with a thumb. My God, he says to his fireman, listen to them idiots. (Bill Finnerty is a Columbus man, and there are niggers in Columbus, and he could tell these people a thing or two about these here Abolitionists and their damned niggers, oh he surely could.)

Ben Wade points with obvious enjoyment at the banner that proclaims: LIBERTY FOREVER!! The band rushes into *Yankee Doodle.* Ben Wade is engulfed by the crowd. He shakes hands with Ike Underwood, who claps him on the back. He shakes hands with Phoebe Underwood, who lets him have something that almost could be called a smile. Almost. He shakes hands with Mayor and Mrs Pillsbury. He shakes hands with J. K. Bankson. He has met J. K. Bankson before, and thus he is not thrown off by the editor's creamy rebel accent. He nudges J. K. Bankson and says (covering his mouth with a hand): You glad you picked the winning side? Then, opening wide his mouth and sending spittle flying in a great jubilant spray, Ben Wade guffaws, and J. K. Bankson guffaws right along with him. J. K. Bankson is not a stupid man.

(Finnerty, who lost a son at Shiloh Church back in April of '62, shakes his head.)

Young Bill Light spies Ferd Purvis patting the fair Amelia's knee. Young Bill gnaws on a fingernail. Across the tracks, Phil Underwood, his own fingernail in reasonably good condition, closes his eyes and listens to the clamor and sees blood and bones and the splendid gleam that is said to suffuse the eyes of heroes. The band essays *When Johnny Comes Marching Home*. Prof Baer keeps smiling at the salivary Virginia Miller, the prosperous—albeit balding and plump—virgin. Over on Main Street, Claude Dill's saloon is full of roisterers. Earl DeWitt, who was wounded in the left arm at Gettysburg while serving with the Paradise Falls Blues, becomes involved in a lurching and most ineffectual fistfight with a man named Borden. It seems this Borden was a conscript who was invalided out after fighting under Joe Hooker at Chattanooga in what came to be known as the Battle in the Clouds. After the battle, Borden was laid low with a fever, and he lost so much weight he was given a discharge and sent home. He has resented the Paradise Falls Blues for a long time. To hear people talk, a man would think the Paradise Falls Blues represent the sum and total of all the Paradise County men who participated in the war. Which is of course not a bit true. And so Borden loses his temper. And, after listening to Earl DeWitt brag on the Paradise Falls Blues for more than an hour, Borden goes after Earl DeWitt, and their fight is ludicrous and stupid. Borden still is weak from the fever; Earl DeWitt has a bum left arm. The two men thrash and gasp, and the other customers laugh, and the consensus is that there have been better fights between women of seventy. The guffawing Ben Wade drapes an arm around Ike Underwood's shoulders. Accompanied by the mayor and J. K. Bankson, they repair to the Depot Hotel, which adjoins the CPV&M station and was opened only last year. The owner and manager, Milt Youngblood, meets them at the door. Milt Youngblood is grinning, but then Milt Youngblood always is grinning. He is new to Paradise Falls, and thus it is required of him that he always grin. Ike Underwood has reserved a suite for the use of Senator Wade. It is the largest suite in the establishment, and the senator and his retinue are ushered there personally by Milt Youngblood. Whisky awaits. Good whisky. The gentlemen all smile.

Aboard the train that is bringing the Paradise Falls Blues home, Major Frederick Magill lies smiling in his litter, and strong hands grasp its sides to prevent the roll and sway of the car from pitching the poor fellow to the floor. He is able to see out the window. Sunlight freckles the gray and brown waters of the Paradise River. He sees the river quite clearly. It is a

miracle. He thinks of his wife and sons. Dear Madeleine and her embarrassment of passion. He chuckles. A man asks him whether he feels
all right. Oh, says the major, I feel fine.

Says Ben Wade, sniffing his whisky: This Johnson is a good man. Feels
the way we do. Drinks too much, but other than that little fault he's as
good a man as you'd want to meet. I don't give a damn if he *is* from Tennessee; he sees this rebellion for the filthy treason that it was. I have talked
with him personally, and he has assured me that we all . . . well, ah . . .
that we all shall, uh, benefit from his administration. That Lincoln . . .
well, I don't have to beat around the bush with you fellows do I? I detested him when he was alive, and I see no reason not to detest him just
because he's become a fucking martyr all of a sudden. But, ah, gentlemen,
that martyrdom . . . such a wondrous fine stroke of good fortune it has
been for us.

How so? says Ike Underwood.

Ben Wade downs his whisky. His tongue comes into contact with the
roof of his mouth, and the resultant popping sound is loud and brisk.
Ah, he says. Good. Then, grinning, he continues: There have been those
who have suggested leniency, and Lincoln was in the vanguard of that
particular group. So what happens? He is murdered most horribly, and
by a Southron zealot. He, the champion of *leniency*, is killed by an ex-
tremist. And so he has become a martyr. And the reaction has been swift.
And so the South will pay, my friends, and I for one will rejoice at its
every agony. Last year, when Zach Chandler and myself and the other
fellows issued our statement chastising Lincoln for his milksop attitudes
toward the rebels, well, there were those who said we were too harsh.
Now, though, that criticism has vanished. Ah, to be perfectly candid
about the situation, the assassination was not precisely an unalloyed
tragedy.

Does that mean you're glad Lincoln was killed? says Ike Underwood.

Now, Ike, you know me better than that.

Well, says Ike Underwood, it just so happens I had a great deal of respect for Lincoln.

Ben Wade smiles. He knows enough to smile. Ike Underwood is one of
the most powerful Republicans in this part of the state, and Ben Wade
would not antagonize him for the world. And so he says, looking Ike
Underwood straight in the eye: We *all* had respect for Lincoln. But
times change, and the peace will call for the abilities of other men, men
whose devotion to justice will not flag.

Justice?

Yes.

What sort of justice? You mean vengeance?

Yes, says Ben Wade, pouring himself another drink. He lifts his glass,
then: Gentlemen, to the whirlwind.

Ike Underwood looks at him.

Mayor Pillsbury and J. K. Bankson lift their glasses.

Lincoln had no devotion to justice? says Ike Underwood.

Ben Wade shakes his head. His voice permits itself a gentle and affectionate exasperation. Still holding high his glass, he says: Of *course* Lincoln had devotion to justice—but it was justice of a different *sort*. It was a gentler justice. Ours is a justice of fire. Nothing cleanses better than fire. We all know that. So, Ike, allow me to expand on my toast. I give you the whirlwind. I give you fire. I give you the ultimate humiliation of those Southron bastards. Their cleansing, if you will.

Well . . . says Ike Underwood, shaking his head. Then, shrugging, he lifts his glass.

The gentlemen drink.

Grass. Dooryards. Song. Old Jake Phillips falls asleep on a pile of sacks in the courthouse cellar. He dreams of his dead son. Bill Finnerty rings the bell, pulls the whistle cord. The crowd cheers. He shakes his head. He eases open the throttle. The drivewheels slip, then catch. The train moves away from the depot. It has thirtysix minutes to make a place called Earlham, where it will pull into a siding to allow the train coming up from Marietta to pass. The distance is only eleven miles, but all of it is uphill. Bill Finnerty's train clears the Paradise Falls yard limit, and he opens up the throttle. He is talking to himself, and he is repeating one word, and that one word is: Shit.

Madeleine Magill and Phoebe Underwood seat themselves on a bench inside the depot. Outside, the clamor and hooraw continue unabated. Madeleine's two boys have been permitted to go running into the crowd. She has warned them, however, to stay clear of the tracks. They have promised her they will. Sighing, she removes a handkerchief from her handbag. She dabs at her temples. My, she says, it surely is *warm*.

Phoebe Underwood, whose face is perfectly dry, nods.

I can't believe it, says Madeleine Magill.

Believe what?

That he's finally truly coming home, says Madeleine Magill. She returns the handkerchief to her handbag. Then, frowning: I look all right? My hair, I mean?

You look fine.

I do love him.

Of course you do.

Never a leave. Not once. Four years and a month. Phoebe, I *mean* it. I have *missed* him.

Surely.

Not a single leave. All those men. Tonight will surely be a night.

Yes, says Phoebe Underwood, I expect so.

I'm, uh, more of a, uh, warm person than I appear.

Phoebe Underwood says nothing.

Madeleine Magill continues: I always have been. I fool a lot of people. I know I do. To look at me, a person'd never know.

Well, perhaps not.

It was not a normal thing.

I beg your pardon?

Oh. Excuse me. I was just thinking out loud about the leave situation. Other regiments had leaves all the time. I have a cousin in Washington CH, and she was forever writing to tell me about her husband being home on another blessed leave, and that's the truth. Why, back in '63 he even got her *pregnant*. A nice little boy it was. She sent me a picture.

A woman named Dallas? Isn't that her name? Hilda Dallas?

Yes it is. Have I told you about her before?

Yes.

Oh. I'm *sorry*.

Don't be foolish. There's nothing to be sorry about. If I were you, I'd be saying the same words.

Madeleine Magill reaches for one of Phoebe Underwood's hands. She squeezes it.

Phoebe Underwood smiles.

Bill Finnerty's train labors up through the hills to Earlham, where it pulls into the siding to await the northbound from Marietta. Bill Finnerty climbs down from the cab and lights a cheroot. He is still mumbling to himself. Across the track is a field of white flowers, the names of which he does not know. They are delicate little flowers. He crosses the track. He bends down. The flowers have no odor. He straightens up. He feels foolish. He looks around, but evidently no one has seen him. He says to himself: Jesus Mary and Joseph I'm *bawling*. He digs at his eyes with the dirty thumbs of his engineer's gloves. His son Tim, the boy who was killed at Shiloh Church, was a delicate sort of lad, very fond of flowers. Bill Finnerty snuffles, kicks at the earth, spits out the cheroot. Aboard the northbound, Major Magill has a conversation with Captain Virgil T. Light, a large bald man with a large bald voice. Captain Light is second in command of the Paradise Falls Blues. Major Magill does not have much use for the man. Oh, Virge Light has been a good enough officer, but he has a habit of talking too much, and the war has done nothing to alleviate the affliction. Grinning, he stops at the major's litter and says: Well, Fred, we'll be pulling into Earlham in a minute or so. Then Paradise Falls. Ah. Praise God. It won't be long now. The parade and all. The band. I'm really looking forward to it. Says Major Magill: Yes, Virge. I know. Says Captain Light: One final formation. One final parade. Then we all scatter and . . . well, perhaps I am exhibiting a weakness, but I am moved. (A handsome blond private named Christian Soeder is among those who are supporting the major's litter so it will not fall. He turns his face to one side and covers his mouth.) Says Captain Light: This has been a splendid group of men. Smiling, Captain Light

raises his eyebrows and inclines his head, taking in the other men of the
Paradise Falls Blues who are sitting and standing and lounging here in
this swaying and clacking CPV&M daycoach. He repeats himself, this
time more loudly: A splendid group of men. Ah, we have gone through a
great deal together. We have memories, ah indeed we do. The men pay
no mind to Captain Light's words. Most of them are too busy looking
out the windows. Some of the windows have been wrenched open. A
man named Hendrickson leans out. *Ah Jesus Christ!* he shouts. *Paradise
County air!* The northbound slows for Earlham but does not stop. It
passes Bill Finnerty's southbound. Bill Finnerty has returned to his cab.
He is smoking another cheroot. His bawling is done. Eleven miles to go.
Eleven miles to home. The men cheer. Several of these men come from
around Earlham, and they probably could have prevailed on the train
captain to make an unscheduled stop there, but they have been asked by
Major Magill to participate in this one last formation and parade, and
they revere the man far too much to refuse him. And anyway, they all
know he is dying.

A man named Rossford enters the Paradise Falls depot and asks Ed Sauer
is the northbound still on time. Far as I know, says Ed Sauer. Rossford
thanks Ed Sauer. On his way out, Rossford smiles and nods at Madeleine
Magill and Phoebe Underwood. The two ladies are holding hands.
Phoebe Underwood is wearing a subtle lavender scent. Madeleine Magill asks her where she obtained it. It is perfectly *lovely*, says Madeleine
Magill.

The Masonbrinks arrive. They are led by their patriarch, old Ben
Masonbrink, who must be ninety if he is a day. More than a dozen of
them come riding up to the depot, and they all are riding mules, and they
all stink to the very utmost reaches of the Kingdom of God.

Phil Underwood walks across the tracks and joins the crowd. He says
nothing to anyone. In the Depot Hotel, his father is taken aside by Ben
Wade, who says: Listen, Ike, I didn't mean to offend you with my talk.
You know me. Sometimes I sound rougher than I really am. And Ike
Underwood says: No offense taken. It's just that I wonder what good it
will do to treat the Southrons like criminals. Says Ben Wade: Well, God
damn it, what else do you call traitors? Says Ike Underwood: All right,
Ben. All right.

Ferd Purvis and his Amelia, still sitting in the Purvis buggy, watch
the arrival of the Masonbrinks. Amelia moves closer to Ferd. His mind's
ear hears an announcement: *God bless the Masonbrinks.*

The band plays on, and never mind the Masonbrinks.

Major Magill looks up from his litter and says to Captain Light: My
idea about Ferris, have you given it consideration? Says Captain Light:
Yes, Fred, and I feel it is a good one. Says Major Magill: And will you and
Tom Messer go see his widow? I mean, I've talked to the men about sign-
ing the declaration, and you know they're all for it. Says Captain Light:

Don't fret yourself. Tom and I will take care of it. Says Major Magill:
Thank you. Says Captain Light: Now, Fred, I'm only too happy to do it.
After *all*, I know how much we owe the man. It is the least we can do. It is
only right and proper that we— Says Major Magill, interrupting the impromptu oration: Yes. Yes. Thank you.

The Masonbrinks are all descendants of the very first white family that
settled in what is now Paradise County. As a matter of fact, old Ben was
the first white child born in this part of the state. But the Masonbrinks
have been in decline for decades. And they know this. And the knowledge has made them angry. They squat in the hills in the southeastern
edge of the county, and they take to strangers about as happily as a hog
takes to those who have a weakness for ham. It is not clear what they are
doing in the village today. No Masonbrinks serve with the Paradise Falls
Blues. The crowd keeps its distance from the Masonbrinks, and the Masonbrinks keep their distance from the crowd. They dismount from their
mules and stand in a knot in the shade of a feeble little tulip tree next to a
freight shed. Two of the younger Masonbrinks support old Ben. He stares
toward the band and the urgent arms of Prof Baer. He is grinning and he
is drooling, and his head moves from side to side, not in time with the
music. Above the old man and his descendants, the sky is white and blank
and terrific.

Tootlethumpflapjabberbang. Oh the eyes of the village surely are this
day witnessing a glory. Clickscratchgabble. Oh the sounds, the victorious
sounds. The war has been so thoroughly won. Let now pass unvexed
the seasons of Arcadia. Again. As they were.

Now this day, this historic day of noise and teeth and exaltation, this
day of birds and sky and Arcadia atiptoe with its triumph, now this day,
punctuated by the urgent flappings of Prof Baer and the whump and
blast of the F&AM band, now this precious day accelerates, and 11:38 A.M.
approaches, and with 11:38 comes the northbound from Marietta, all
sparks and flanges, whuffling hollowly, and the men of the Paradise Falls
Blues lean from the daycoach windows and wave at the moiling throng,
and then come cheers, and cheers upon cheers, and the sky smiles, and
the hills smile, and tears come in hot happy surges, and screams, and a
woman named Sarah Cornwall takes one look at her son Horace and collapses like a punctured fish, flopping bonelessly at the feet of Phoebe
Underwood, who kneels next to her and applies smelling salts, and the
men come from the train in a whooping avalanche, and Horace Cornwall runs to his supine mother, and he is crying, and he is a grown man,
and at Spottsylvania he personally sent to glory at least eleven rebels by
his own count, and oh what the hell anyway: blubbering, he kisses his
mother and strokes her dear old gray head. United States Senator Benjamin Franklin Wade and his retinue have emerged from the Depot Hotel.
He grins at Ike Underwood and J. K. Bankson. Mayor Pillsbury is running toward the train. The three Pillsbury boys have come down off the

train. They are embracing their mother. Lamar, the youngest, the one
who was wounded in the arm at that place called The Wilderness, the
one who refused to be invalided out, has his arms around his mother's
generous waist and he is dancing a sort of jig with her and his mouth
is hollow and he is making sounds but they cannot be heard. As he
pushes through the crowd, Mayor Pillsbury is proud. His four oldest sons,
all of them farmers from up in the northern end of the county near a
settlement called Blood, have come here this day to welcome home the
three who are returning with the Paradise Falls Blues. At the war's outset,
they were jealous of their younger brothers. But now this all apparently
has passed. The three younger brothers are pummeled. They are embraced. Their hands are squeezed. Mayor Pillsbury's pride is like a large
white bird. Seven fine men, and his skinny loins have produced all of
them, and ah, ah, ah, such, such are the joys of love and family, and he
bursts into the happy family circle, and his pince nez are knocked from
his nose, and he doesn't care a jot about his pince nez. Hugs. Kisses. He
even kisses his wife. Irene Pillsbury is trembling, and he cannot blame
her a bit. Her fleshy face quakes, and it is entitled to quake, and the world
is huge and splendid, and the scope of its joys is without limit. Gleaming and grinning, Captain Virgil T. Light supervises the unloading of
the litter on which reclines Major Magill. Madeleine Magill scrambles
toward the litter. She has to claw like a cat. Her husband reaches for her.
She bends down, kisses him. He smiles. The boys come running. My God,
says Major Magill, just *look* at them will you? Then, to his wife: You have
warm lips. She barely can hear him, but she *can* hear him, and his words
create in her a sort of spasm that makes her pound her palms together
like a little girl who has just been given a pretty puppy for her birthday.
The Masonbrinks lean against the tulip tree, and old Ben wheezes. Young
Bill Light approaches his Warrior father. They shake hands. It is a fine
manly reunion. Virgil T. Light narrows his eyes and says: Ah, such a
day. Young Bill Light says nothing for a moment, then finally clears his
throat and permits the words to emerge: In case you're interested, Mama
isn't too good. Virgil T. Light frowns at his son, starts to say something,
thinks better of it. Instead he grins, and then he is saved by someone
who comes up to him and claps him on the back. Mrs Cornwall has
emerged from her swoon. She is helped away by her son. Phoebe Underwood looks around for her own son. Phil Underwood is nowhere to be
seen. Actually, he is hiding behind the CPV&M Maintenance of Way
privy. He is embracing old Karl Hellmann's boxer dog Franz. He is
shrieking, and no one hears him, and Franz is licking his nose. The Rev
Fr Messer embraces his younger brother, Lieutenant Tom Messer. The
two men speak to each other in German, and their voices are moist. They
speak of God, of good fortune, of the blessings of continued life. Prof
Baer flaps, winks at Virginia Miller, who makes a dry O with her tight
maidenly lips. Major Magill is helped from his litter and lifted into a car-

riage. Captain Light begins hollering at the men to get into formation. *One last parade, boys!* he hollers. *Remember your promise to the major!* The blond Christian Soeder is greeted by his older brother, Wilhelm Soeder, who owns what probably is the most prosperous farm in Lake Township, up in the northwestern corner of the county. Few words are exchanged between these men. The proper ones never have been found. Christian Soeder smiles, pats his blond hair, spies Amelia Burkhart sitting with Ferd Purvis. Mm, he says to no one in particular. Then he hears the shouts that are coming from Captain Light: *All right, boys! You promised him! It's the least you can do!* Lamar Pillsbury frowns. His father asks him is something the matter. He shakes his head no. He is thinking: Why couldn't the captain for once do a thing on his own without bringing up the major's name? What's the matter? Don't he think we'd obey? Well, maybe he's right. Maybe we wouldn't. Shrugging, Lamar Pillsbury excuses himself, joins the rest of the men, who are reluctantly forming ranks. Well, at least they don't have rifles to carry. Lamar Pillsbury thinks back on the Grand Review held in Washington a few days ago. He thinks back on the fireworks and the cheering and the heavy tramp tramp tramp and drum drum drum of the men of the Army of the Potomac who marched up Pennsylvania Avenue. He thinks back on the war and the killing and all and he says to himself: I don't ever want to see dead things any more. (The worst place for Lamar Pillsbury, and the worst place for all of them, was the place called The Wilderness. Old Grant gave a shit for no one, and old Grant said *I propose to fight it out on this line if it takes all summer,* and it was a time of roots and branches and mud and insects, of brambles that sliced a man's legs until they were nothing but scars and scabs and lumps, of remnants of dead men, damp souvenirs of the casualties of the Chancellorsville fight the year before, men who never had been buried after that awful battle that saw Fighting Joe Hooker lose his nerve and go scuttling back across the Rappahannock like a whipped dog, and the dead flesh was everywhere, the proclamation of that impotent antique adventure, and all right, dying in battle was one thing. But just to lie there, to lie there and greet one's returning vertical comrades, this was an obscenity beyond which there was no obscenity. The rebels had allies in that fight, and the allies were ghostly and frightful, and it was a miracle of God that anybody was able to survive the combination of rebels, ghosts and old Butcher Grant, him and his goddamn stubbornness. It was a summer of inches, of swamps, of rocks, of attrition, and at the end there was maybe a victory, but oh God, all the dead ones who fell because of that place, and that time, and those rebels and those ghosts and that general . . . oh God no, dead things are bad, and there is no room for dead things in Arcadia, and oh God the stink, oh God the foolish laughable pity of it. What are men but *men* and where is the sense of the things that happened?) The May sky has no memory, however, and so it smiles, and United States Senator Benjamin Franklin

Wade makes a clucking noise and says to Ike Underwood: Good fellows, all of them—the stuff of a nation. And Ike Underwood nods, escorts the senator to a waiting carriage. They are joined by J. K. Bankson and the Honorable Philetas E. Swallow, Judge of the Paradise County Court of Common Pleas and a former county Republican chairman. Judge Swallow is a florid fellow, heavy of belly and rather worried about his heart. He is convinced he is suffering from palpitations. So far, though, no doctor has believed him. He has an appointment later this week with a Columbus physician of distinguished reputation. This fellow will get to the bottom of the trouble. Of this, the judge is convinced. Captain Light hollers at the men. More of them fall into ranks. They are grinning, and most of them are clung to by women and children. Captain Light's son Bill stands next to his father. Bill does not know what to say. His father is just as he remembered him. His father is full of gas. His father is a fraud. His mother is dying, and his father doesn't care, and thus his father is also a monster. What Bill Light *really* wants to do is *hit* his father. Captain Light smiles, pats Bill on a shoulder. Bill flinches. *One last time!* shouts the captain. *Come on, fellows!* (Captain Light has a secret, and it comforts him beyond measure. He *understands* the amused contempt the men have for him. But he also understands the nature of men. Right now they are weary. They want to forget the war. They want to brush away the remembered killing. But their weariness eventually will vanish. And, after a few years, sentiment will rise up and take possession of what they like to think of as their good sense. He has discussed this with other men—none, however, from the Paradise Falls Blues. Several weeks ago he had a fine conversation with a colonel from a Wisconsin artillery regiment, and that colonel said: I give them five years at the most, and then by God they'll come to realize that this war has been the largest single event in their lives. They'll look back on it with a soft loving fondness, and they'll get together to talk about it, and you just wait . . . they'll form clubs and hold parades and sing all the old songs. It'll be an interesting situation, believe me, and it'll probably have repercussions we can't imagine. By that I mean power, political power. Think of the votes those men will represent, and mostly for the Republican party. The Democrats will be lucky to survive it. Ah, there's a new day coming, Captain. This country has just begun to feel its oats. The war has served to speed up the change. We are entering the age of the locomotive, the loom, the machine. And it will produce riches beyond measure. And those who control the politics will control the riches. And it is my contention that for the next twenty, thirty, maybe forty years the political power will lie with the men who are now going home from this war. So, take my advice—when the time comes for the clubs and the parades, *participate*. Place yourself in a position of leadership. You'll be glad you did, believe me. And Captain Light understood what the colonel was talking about. Thus contempt does not daunt him. His time will come. When it does, he will seize it firmly.) And

so the captain shouts, pleads, grins. And the men form a column of fours.
A few of them have vanished with their families, but (perhaps surpris-
ingly) most of them apparently are willing to participate in what they
consider to be a final gesture. The crowd cheers. The F&AM band is silent
for a moment while it moves to the front of the column. Smiling, Captain
Light calls the Paradise Falls Blues to attention. (Over by the tulip tree,
old Ben Masonbrink gulps and blinks. One of the younger Masonbrinks
wipes spittle from old Ben's chin.) Captain Light wheels, nods to Prof Baer.
The music resumes. *Forwaart haar!* shouts the captain. Preceded by the
band, the Paradise Falls Blues march away from the depot. Up ahead,
moving briskly, is the carriage containing the dying Major Magill. Then
comes the carriage containing Ben Wade, Ike Underwood, J. K. Bankson
and Judge Swallow. Then comes a buggy in which ride Mayor and Mrs
Pillsbury and Phoebe Underwood. Then a tallyho carrying the assembled
clergy. The procession moves up Mineral Avenue. The crowd trots alongside. A man walks past the Masonbrinks. He stares at them. Enos Masonbrink, one of old Ben's grandsons, rushes at the man and seizes him by
the lapels. The man quails. Enos Masonbrink shakes the man. You sonofabitch, he says, what you staring at? You think I'm going to kill you?
You sonofabitch, I don't even *know* you! We ain't here to do you no harm!
It's just the music, God damn it! Grandpa wants to hear the music! We
brought him here so he could listen to that there band! Enos Masonbrink
lifts the man off his feet. The man whimpers. Shit! hollers Enos Masonbrink. He hurls the man away. The man lands on his rear end. He
scrabbles off like a crippled cat. Enos Masonbrink shudders, then smiles
at his grandfather. *You like the music?* he hollers. *How's that?* hollers
Ben Masonbrink, slobbering. And Enos Masonbrink groans. He helps his
grandfather remount a mule. Then Enos and the other Masonbrinks remount their own mules. The mules guffaw. The Masonbrinks ride away
from the parade. Old Ben Masonbrink moves an arm in rhythm with whatever music it is he is hearing. The parade: horses, manure, the men of
the Paradise Falls Blues marching behind Captain Light, who is marching
past the manure, which is coming from the horses that pull the carriages and buggies and the tallyho. The bandsmen pant and sweat, but
the pumping arms of Prof Baer are indefatigable, and his eyes are quick
and alert, missing not a single female soul. Yessir! shouts Ben Wade over
the music, nudging Ike Underwood and bestowing on him a brave Republican grin. Yessir, my friend! These are the days of our dreams! Justice,
I say! Glory! And the hard earth streets tremble as the happy procession
passes dooryards and abandoned hoops, as dogs emerge from their hiding
places and slaver and howl at the heels of the marchers, as an abrupt
May wind causes the new moist leaves to clap and hiss, as the wives and
sisters and sweethearts trot beside the marchers and pluck at their sleeves
. . . ah, this day of joyful mouths, this day of clicking tongues and jubilant throats sore from their exertions. Old women, faces pink, dance and

skip. Children scream and flop, wave their flags. North, due north now, past Meridian Avenue and Second Street and First Street, then east on Grainger Street, then north on High Street, then east again, this time on Main Street, with a thump and a fanfare and a sound of tearful exultance, neath elms and oaks, sycamores and tulips, pounding up this precious thoroughfare, this Main Street, this most beloved street of streets, and now dear friends can be seen the famous J. K. Bankson banners: THE REPUBLIC INDESTRUCTIBLE!! Followed by: VICTORY!! And then: LET THERE BE PEACE!! And now begins the apotheosis of the day, and the men of the Paradise Falls Blues stand tall and straight, and the sound of their feet acquires a discipline, and Main Street is lined with people, and the drinkers come stumbling and blinking out of Claude Dill's saloon, and one of them, a tubercular wastrel named James Perry Blood, actually hawks and wheezes in rhythm with the music, and he grins as he coughs, grins and permits his mind to explore patterns that have to do with honor and valor (he knows honor; he does not know valor); he holds a glass of whisky; he lifts it high. *The Republic indestructible!* he shouts. Then, sniggering, he withdraws back inside Claude Dill's saloon. The marchers thump past the saloon. Ben Wade and Mayor Pillsbury and Ike Underwood and the other dignitaries have already alighted from their carriages and buggies. Major Magill is not present, however. His wife has taken him home. The depot celebration has tired him. Two neighbor men help Madeleine Magill carry her husband into their home. The two little Magill boys ask for permission to go see the festivities over on Main Street. All right, says Madeleine Magill, but just be sure you watch out for the horses. The boys nod. Then, whooping, they take off in a tumblejumping run. The neighbor men carry Major Magill to an upstairs bedroom. It smells of soap. They place him on the bed. The sheets crackle. He smiles, thanks them. Grinning, examining their knuckles and their feet, the two neighbor men tell Major Magill they're sure happy he's come home safe and sound. Major Magill nods. The neighbor men leave. Madeleine Magill covers her husband with the sheets and a blanket. He pats the back of her neck. He asks her to lie down beside him. You don't have to take off your clothes, he says. Just please lie down here with me. Madeleine Magill nods. She lies down next to her husband. They embrace. They listen to birds and the wind and the distant sounds of victory. Mayor Pillsbury speaks. Ben Wade speaks. Captain Light grins. Christian Soeder looks around for Amelia Burkhart. The men of the Paradise Falls Blues stand at parade rest, and Beauty holds wide her arms over the happy scene. Says Ben Wade: The rightness of our cause shall be unquestioned to the final generation! Says Lamar Pillsbury (to himself, as sweat dribbles in crooked streaks down from his forehead): When I told Mama and Papa I liked the war I was lying. What I should of said was: It's important for me to go back to duty so I can be there when it's over. Says Ben Wade: Believe me, my friends, our vengeance shall be most properly severe! The transgressions merit the

severity, do they not? Lenience would be an abject betrayal of those who
have shed their life's blood so that we can stand here today and participate in this joyous homecoming! Captain Light says to himself: Yes. The
Widow Ferris. Yes. We'll visit her. It is the least we can do. And, beyond
that, it will give me the opportunity to circulate among these men and
prepare them for the eventual organizing. I remember Ferris used to talk
about her good looks. Ah, dear Ferris. Ah, this dear war. Says Ben Wade,
raising his fists: May the judgment of Almighty God consign my soul
to hell if I in any way turn aside from my espousal of right! (Spectators
frown, nudge one another. How's that? says one. What'd he say? says another.) Ben Wade speaks for more than an hour, and his great triumphant
voice pounds and claps with rancor, non sequiturs, holy oaths. At the
conclusion of his oration, the applause is considerable, but the reasons for
this vigor are varying. Whistling and cheering, the crowd repairs to St
Luke's Lutheran Church, where the ladies are waiting with their great
feast. It is now nearly 2 o'clock in the afternoon, and many are the bellies
that rumble and hiss. Commotion. Kisses. Ben Wade and the mayor and
Ike Underwood and J. K. Bankson and Judge Swallow walk from the courthouse to the church. Such an oration, says the mayor, such a perfectly
splendid feeling for the uses of rhetoric. He smiles at Ben Wade, and Ben
Wade returns the smile, and then Ben Wade says: Well, I hope I got
through to those people. Says Ike Underwood: Ah, one thing is for sure—
you had an *effect* on them. No doubt about *that*. Ben Wade nods. He does
not quite know what to make of Ike Underwood's words, but he figures
he'd better not ask for clarification. In the church basement, the Rev Mr
Leppelmeier says the blessing. His grainy accent brings grins to the faces
of a number of those present. Clatter. Scrape. Crunch. Laughter. Ham.
Turkey. Beans. Potatoes. Slaw. Pies. Gravy. Bread. Milk. Coffee. Surreptitious snorts from small brown bottles. Teeth. Ears. Tongues. Outside,
the abiding hills smile and smile and smile. At 4:30 Captain Light goes
home to his dying wife. Children chatter of bullets and cavalry charges.
Phil Underwood stands at the door to the church basement, but he cannot bring himself to enter. His coat and britches have an odor of dog. He
spies his mother and father, and they are smiling, stuffing themselves.
Ferd Purvis and Amelia Burkhart eat quickly. (Christian Soeder watches
them.) Then Ferd and Amelia run outside and drive away in his buggy.
They drive to a grove down by the old mill. They seat themselves in the
shade of a pin oak. They kiss seven times. Now they have kissed a grand
total of thirtyone times. Ferd Purvis embraces his beloved, and he can
feel her bosoms flatten themselves against his chest. She breathes with
her mouth open. Ah, the sweet river, the lovely freckled Paradise: gently
it plashes past the old mill and over the falls. Ferd Purvis and Amelia
Burkhart breathe each other, and they say nothing, and nothing is needed
to be said. Thirtytwo. Thirtythree. Saliva. Tongues. J. K. Bankson eats
well. His flesh is cool. He thinks back on Ben Wade's words. They have

delighted him. He tells himself: It has all fallen down. Hallelujah. Christian Soeder questions his brother Wilhelm about the Burkhart girl. Ah, says Wilhelm, it doesn't take you long does it? Laughter from Christian Soeder. He slaps his brother on a knee, helps himself to more ham. (Christian Soeder has been the despair of his elder brother for a number of years. Before the war, the blond Christian had a considerable reputation as a seducer. Apparently he has in no way changed his attitudes.) No, says Christian, it doesn't take me long at all. She was a child when I went away. She is no longer a child. Correct? And Wilhelm Soeder says: Correct. At a neighboring table, Priscilla Purvis keeps glancing in the direction of Christian Soeder. She wonders what she has to do to make him look at her. Next to her, her father is saying something about the senator's oratory. I wouldn't want to have that fellow for an enemy, says Oliver Purvis. No indeed. The others at the table all nod in agreement. Now some of the taller trees are scratching at the sun. The name of this place is Paradise Falls. To begin with, it apprehends as many truths as there are hearts for the knowing of truth. Ah, the abiding hills. This is a place where an understanding of morality is not unknown. Bloodwort. Iris. Hemlocks. Tomatoes. Corn. The women have taken up the use of mason jars with enthusiasm. Rabbit. Polecat. Dog. Cat. Turds. Earth. Headstones commemorating the beloved and unforgotten dead. Licorice. Lamb. Jawbreakers. Taffy. Horses. The spit and puke of drunkards. Oil of cod. Banners. Flags. Oratory. Vengeance. Victory. Justice. The name of the place is Paradise Falls, and all its hymns are believed. The conscious malefactor is rejected here. Wheat. Barley. Timothy. Grass. Here the apple has managed to devour all worms. Here, to begin with, is a fine and felicitous Arcadia. The old girl's name is Beauty, and why should she *not* face sun and God? Her name is Beauty, her name is Beauty, her name is Beauty, and she is no ingrate, and her arms know whereof they stretch. Truth is the undefeated apple. Truth is the defeated worms. Truth is Arcadia. God bless Arcadia. God bless God. (There is a great bell that hangs in the Grace Episcopal Church. It was a gift of Ike and Phoebe Underwood. Engraved on that bell are the brave words of the final line of the Hundred and Fiftieth Psalm: LET EVERY THING THAT HATH BREATH PRAISE THE LORD. And why not? Especially now, what with blessed peace again reigning over the happy Arcadian landscape.)

To begin with, then, the Truth of this place is—more or less—a plump annihilating joy.

A Great Man:

EVEN THOUGH HIS REAR END was just about raw from the chafe and slap of the wooden daycoach seat, and even though the immense July sun cut through the dusty windows in cruel white slashes, making him squirm and perspire, Charley Wells (full name: Charles Palmer Wells) still managed to grin at this fellow, this train captain or conductor or whatever he called himself. Next to Charley, his plenteous bride Nancy also smiled.

Yessir? said the man. He glanced at Nancy.

How far now? said Charley Wells.

To Paradise Falls? That's where you and the lady are going ain't it? Yes.

The conductor glanced out the window. He was a skinny fellow with a white moustache that drooped at the ends. He rubbed the moustache. Well, he said, about fifteen miles. We ought to be there in about half an hour.

Ah, said Charley Wells. Good. Thank you kindly.

The man nodded, moved off down the aisle. His eyes were rather large.

Nancy, the former Widow Ferris and now Charley's plenteous albeit tarnished bride, made a deep shuddery sound. She was Charley's age (twentyseven), and back in Indiana her boobies had been legendary. She wore a white dress. Her flank rested against Charley's, and it made him think of her warmth last night aboard the packet that had brought them to Marietta. Leaning to Charley, moving her lips against his ear, she said: The old goat. I thought he'd never take his eyes off of them. I thought he was going to reach out and touch them.

Well, no blessing is unalloyed.

Very funny.

Charley chuckled. He licked the roof of his mouth. Sometimes he almost was ready to believe he still could taste the tar and the feathers. But of course this was ridiculous. The tar and the feathers had been applied more than three months ago, and those two women had done a fine job of removing them. (*Kill the Copperhead sonofabitch!* Ah, Indiana vengeance.)

No, there could not still be a taste of tar and feathers. Foolishness. Fool-

ishness. Charley ran his tongue over his lips. The remembered taste went
away. He glanced at Nancy. It surely was too bad about her weak chin.
Kept her from being a beauty. But then perhaps it made her more desirable.
As far as Charley was concerned, there was something to be said for such
a flaw. Perhaps perfect beauty would have been too intimidating. The
sunlight speckled her chestnut hair, gave it glints of gold. He sucked
saliva through the openings between his teeth and said to himself: God
damn.

Nancy wriggled her flank, moved closer to the window. Pretty hills, she
said.

Yes, said Charley.

They were really nice men.

Of course they were. Good loving Christians doing a poor widow lady a
good turn. A scroll and all, signed by all those men. *My.*

She glared at Charley. They *meant* what they said, she told him.

Of course they did. I know that. Why do you think we're going to this
town?

Nancy sighed.

Nancy?

Yes?

I am going to be a great man.

I know that.

There will be no dull moments for you.

Well. Good.

The grocery store will be just a beginning.

Nancy nodded.

Charley grimaced. He had several missing teeth. His body was thick,
blunt. He had great bushy eyebrows but wore no beard. He tried to keep
himself very clean at all times. He enjoyed soaps, pomades. The tarring
and the feathering had caused this enjoyment to increase. (*Destroy the
assassin!* Ah, his dear old home town.)

Charley?

Yes?

Whatever it is you want, I want it too.

Good.

I expect maybe I even love you.

Charley patted his bride's knee. Thank you, he said. And I expect I
love you too.

A lot surely has happened.

A lot more *will* happen. And better things.

I wouldn't be surprised.

Charley grinned. Then: Like the Professor said, if a man keeps his eye

on the *possible* and remembers that all things are mortal, if he doesn't go
chasing after concepts and ideals . . . you know, like our old friend George
Peters . . . well, the man who keeps his eye on what is real will turn out
to be a great man.

That Professor really meant a great deal to you didn't he?

He straightened out my thinking. I got to be grateful to him.

Nancy pinched the bridge of her nose. She looked out the window.
The river is below us, she said.

Charley nodded.

Look at the hills, said Nancy.

Charley nodded.

They surely are steep, said Nancy.

I'm told that west of the town, though, the land is flat, good for farming.

Mm, said Nancy. Her hair was drawn into a bun at the back of her
neck. She reached around and patted the bun. Her hands were not small.
Several fingernails were cracked. Well, her life as the Widow Ferris had
not been easy. But Charley would change all that. Now he understood
greatness, and he figured there was hardly anything he would not be able
to accomplish.

They had come a long way, both of them, and their adventures had not
been easy. Charley drew a deep breath. He thought of her first lover, his
friend George Peters, the late *hero* who had been so summarily ushered out
of this life more than two years ago at a place called Fredericksburg. The
thought made Charley smile. George Peters was so splendidly and heroically dead, and nothing had been proved, and there was the beauty of his
death: the nothing that had come from it. Charley remembered what the
fat and flatulent Professor had said to him one night last year in Washington: Honor nothing other than yourself. Nothing else can be trusted. This
is the thinking that will guide the future. Adhere to it, my friend, and the
riches of the earth shall accrue to you. What does it profit a man? It profits
a man the world, and the world is enough.

Charley licked his lips. He tasted no tar. He tasted no feathers. The
name of the place was Paradise Falls, and the name made him smile.
Christian generosity was bringing him and his Nancy, the former Widow
Ferris, to this village, and it would provide the beginnings of his greatness.
The tar and the feathers were gone, and so were the lingering thoughts he
had held on the subject of honor. They had vanished with the tar and the
feathers. It surely was remarkable the truths a man could extract from a
humiliation.

He shifted his weight, which provided some relief for his aching rear
end. He and Nancy had boarded the train this morning in Marietta after
four days aboard the steamboat that had brought them up the Ohio from

Evansville. There had been a stop in Cincinnati. He had taken her ashore there and had bought her a blue velvet gown. She had worn it at supper that evening, and all over the dining saloon men had twisted their necks to stare at her. He had grinned, had told her she was quite the rage of the evening. She had blinked at him, and her eyes had been just about moist. He had bought her a large diamond wedding ring. Her late husband, the martyred Ferris, had been unable to buy her a ring. He had been very poor, this Ferris, and now he also was a dead hero, and oh sometimes Charley just wanted to laugh and laugh . . . especially in view of the fact that it was Ferris' heroism that was bringing Charley and Nancy to Paradise Falls.

Nancy looked at Charley. Would you go over it with me one more time? She asked him. I don't want anything to slip out.

Surely, said Charley. Then, after a hesitation: First of all, we don't mention your family.

All right.

And we don't mention the tar and the feathers.

Yes.

And we don't mention the Democratic party.

Yes.

We have to make a good impression.

I understand.

It's all for the best.

Yes. I know.

Nancy, I had a thought last night.

Oh?

Yes. Uh, what would you say if I asked you to join the Church of England? I mean, are you so much of a Baptist that you can't change?

No. I can change.

I'd appreciate it.

Consider it done.

I'm going to join too. It's worthwhile to belong to the Church of England.

Yes.

It could help a man.

Yes.

Help a man make the proper impression.

Yes. I *understand*.

The world has rules.

Yes, Charley.

I didn't create the rules.

Yes.

Are these things too much to ask?

No.

This place doesn't know what it's in for.

I expect not.

Chuckling, Charley rubbed his palms together. He cracked his knuckles. Nancy frowned. He patted her hip. The daycoach bounced and clattered. Nancy looked out the window. Charley breathed deeply. He tasted smoke. The hills were beginning to level out. He looked around. Across the aisle, a woman was reading to a little boy from a book. Charley could not make out the woman's words. The little boy was staring at him. Charley smiled. The little boy looked away. Charley supposed the little boy was very innocent. He did not envy the little boy. He moistened the roof of his mouth. He tasted no tar, no feathers. All he could taste was greatness. He thought of the Christian charity that had been so generously displayed by those two men, Light and Messer, who had come calling on the poor Widow Ferris. He grinned. He had to. Ah, the uses of goodness.

1865 . . .

The village will endure forever. Its works are a miracle. Its horse population is in excess of five hundred, and it has sanitation difficulties, but it will prevail. Wonders abound. Blessings multiply. The village is in no way final. It embraces tranquillity, but it also embraces reasoned progress, and it rejects those who say it cannot have both.

Arcadia: the apple triumphant. God bless God. And so on.

There is little question that the village is by and large the creation of one man—Isaac (Ike) Underwood. Were it not for him, the county seat no doubt still would be upriver in the damp and undistinguished hamlet of Egypt. But Ike Underwood is a man of zeal and stubbornness, and he had his way, and his way was right and proper, and the village and the county and the valley all owe him an immense and clearly unpayable debt.

And, in a sense, his wife Phoebe must share the credit . . . if not for the creation of the village, at least for its grace. And there *is* grace here. Strangers are forever commenting on it. Which pleases Phoebe Underwood no end. Her fine Connecticut progenitors treasured grace, and she has felt a responsibility to bring their good taste out here to what is, after all, an area only a generation or so removed from wilderness.

Undoubtedly her largest accomplishment is the Paradise County Court

House, which was dedicated fifteen years ago. It was built to her specifications, including the massive statue of Beauty that stands atop the roof. Although principally constructed of good plain Paradise County brick, the building is decorated with ornate stone trim, and its inside courtrooms and offices are filigreed in dark heavy woods. But it is the statue of Beauty that is Phoebe Underwood's great joy and triumph. It was created by a man named Rossi, who was imported from New York City in 1849 at Phoebe's express urging. The county commissioners paid him a thousand dollars for the statue. A quiet little man with pale skin and famishingly moist and luminous eyes, Guglielmo Rossi worked for more than six months in a shed at the rear of Hapgood's Blacksmith Works. The statue was chiseled from marble that had been shipped by wagon, rail and canal boat all the way from Vermont (at an expense that caused a great deal of grumbling . . . none of it, however, public). Still, the matter of expense aside, the village was impressed by the fruit of Guglielmo Rossi's labors. The lady of Beauty is ten feet high, and she weighs several thousand pounds, and it was an engineering feat of no mean consequence the day a crew of more than thirty men rigged up the block and tackle contraption that enabled them to lift the statue to the courthouse roof. The veterans of that day still talk about it. Hands on hips, they often pause to stare up at the weighty lady. Ah, her name is Beauty, and bless her. The mind and heart are pleasured by the memorializing of those things that are larger than life.

Unfortunately, no one has been able to convince Ike Underwood of the truth of this sentiment. As far as he is concerned, the statue represents a lot of profligate foolishness. A hawker and spitter (outside of his home), a roarer of great Homeric oaths, a man who would as lief say be damned to you as shake your hand, he has long been at odds with his wife over matters of esthetics, especially when they have to do with the expenditure of money. When the question of the statue first came before the county commissioners back in '49, Ike Underwood minced no words. It's all damned nonsense, he told the commissioners. I don't know what's gotten into you people. All the things that need being done in this county, and so what do you propose to do? You propose to spend good money hiring some New York City sissy, and a foreigner to boot, to come here and play with a chisel. Well, if that isn't madness, I don't know what is.

And yet the county commissioners, though they respected Ike Underwood and even had reason to fear him, went ahead and authorized the expenditure. At first blink this might seem peculiar. But it isn't the slightest speck peculiar. The commissioners did what they did because there is one person in the village whose zeal and stubbornness are more profound than his. That person is Mrs Ike Underwood, the former Phoebe Bowers of New Haven, Connecticut, a frail and gentle little woman who is at the same time about as timid and inconspicuous as a pack of wolves. When Phoebe Underwood *wants* a thing, she gets it. One does not question her. One does not attempt to stand in her way. She went to the commissioners back in '49 and she said: Gentlemen, we do not want to be lacking in tone. We have an obligation to our children and all the future generations to provide them with a heritage of taste and, if I may, Beauty. The statue will mark a beginning. It is about time don't you think? *Tone,* gentlemen. *Values.* Our responsibility is clear.

The commissioners looked at one another. There was a deal of coughing.

Well? said Phoebe Underwood. A closed parasol lay on her lap. Her fingers drummed on its handle.

The money was voted.

Splendid, said Phoebe Underwood. She stood up. She smiled, and her teeth and lips were perfect, and the total effect was of a holy benediction.

Later, after she had left them (her skirts made genteel whispery sounds, and her tiny rump switched from side to side with quick ladylike authority), later, after the commissioners had had time to restore their composure, they all grinned, and then one of them said: Now that there is what I got to call a *woman.*

The others nodded. It was generally agreed that old Ike really had come up with something when he'd taken this Connecticut woman as his wife. Something mighty damned awesome.

And so the limpid Guglielmo Rossi came to Paradise Falls, and be damned to Ike Underwood. Be double damned to him, in fact, since Guglielmo Rossi actually took up residence in the Underwood home on Cumberland Street. At the invitation, naturally, of the indomitable Phoebe. Well, it turned out that Guglielmo Rossi was precisely the sort of fellow Ike Underwood had expected—a bower and scraper, a wearer of ruffled shirts, a damned sissy whom Ike even suspected of dabbing his ears with perfume.

I tell you, said Ike to Phoebe one evening, I can *smell* him.

Shush, said Phoebe, inclining her head toward the upstairs bedroom where their guest had retired for the night. He'll *hear* you.

Ike snorted.

Sh, said Phoebe. If he does wear perfume, it's no business of ours. Maybe that's his way. The poor man.

Shit, said Ike.

Isaac! said Phoebe.

Another snort from Ike Underwood. There are snorts and there are snorts, and this particular snort was a snort of surrender. He never had been able to argue with this woman. She always made him feel like a damned oaf. As far as that went, he never really had been able even to cope with her. She was seventeen years younger than he, but one never would have known it from their conversations. Especially their disputes. They always ended with her treating him as though he were a child of imperfect mentality. She never raised her voice. She never wept. She

simply sat there and spoke in that crisp little icy voice of hers and . . .
ah, hell, there was no defeating her and there never would be.

And there hasn't been. Ike Underwood has been guilty of no hyperbole.

Phoebe is New Haven, and Ike is Paradise Falls, and the difference is
vast and all in her favor. True, Ike's origins also are in Connecticut, but
he is of a different generation—and, beyond that, he has lived in the Paradise valley since the age of twelve. His widowed father, a bankrupt carpenter from Stamford, emigrated to Ohio in 1814, settling in the hamlet
called Egypt and opening a sawmill there the following year. Egypt is six
miles northwest of Paradise Falls. It always has been a precarious and ramshackle little settlement, but back in 1814 it was more than precarious
and ramshackle; it was just about intolerable. Ike Underwood kept a journal in those days, and it provides a splendid record of the conditions that
attended his youth. In that journal, under the date December 12, 1818, he
wrote:

> *Father kilt by the brain-fevor. Dyed hard. Dyed Screeming.*
> *Cursed Egypt. Made me promiss to go back to Connecticutt. I*
> *said yes, but I have no intention of doing so. So farr 9 here*
> *have perished of the brain-fevor. Only 7 remain. 6 pray to God.*
> *I work in sawmill. Made coffin. Presided at buriel. 4 indians*
> *attended buriel. Scurvy beggars. Drove them off with Gun at*
> *concluseon of prayers. Work is best Healor. I work. I shall en-*
> *dure. Later is time enough for Grief & Tears.*

Ike Underwood's fortunes, if not his spelling, improved steadily once
his hapless father was out of the way. The country was wild and incomplete, and he thrived in it. He was just sixteen when his father died, but
by the time he was twentyfive he was worth more than forty thousand
dollars. The sawmill prospered; he bought hundreds and then thousands
of acres of cheap land; he scored a remarkable coup in cornering all the
available hand tools and farm equipment in the area.

It was this last venture, the Tool Coup, that established him as a young
man no one could afford to ignore. It was all very simple, really, but no
one before him had thought of it. He journeyed to Columbus and Zanesville and visited all the hardware firms in those cities. Paying a ten percent
premium, he purchased large quantities of axes, hammers, shovels, hoes
and the like. In exchange for the premium, he extracted promises from the
hardware merchants that they would sell to no one else from the Paradise valley. Then, shepherding several wagonloads of tools, he returned
to Egypt and waited for the business to come to him. Which it did. It had
to. Thus did he become a rich man. The Paradise valley was filling with
settlers, and it soon became a question of either buying tools from him
or doing without. There were several hardware stores in the area. When

the proprietors of these stores discovered they could not replenish their stock, their screams echoed up and down the valley. But Ike Underwood did not give a damn; he was not the sort to concern himself with the pulings of those who were unable to look out for themselves. Within a year the other hardware merchants were out of business, and most of them had to flee the state in order to escape their creditors. One of them decided to take sterner action, however. The man's name was Jackson, and he was from a settlement called Blood. In the spring of 1827 he came after Ike Underwood with a pistol. The incident was recorded in the journal under the date April 8, 1827:

> Owe Harlowe Morris a favour. He came running in-to store today to tell me Jas. Jackson on way with pistol. Got pistol of my own. Met Jas. Jackson at front door. He called me swine, then fired shot but aime not good. Ball hit side of store 3 or 4 inchs from my head. I fired. Ball hit him in thygh. Crawled off weeping. Cool day for Aprel. Rain.

Jackson vanished from the Paradise valley that day and never was seen again. Still, for thirty years after the incident Ike Underwood never ventured outdoors without a pistol. Wise men profit from experience, and Ike Underwood never has been accused of stupidity.

The Tool Coup thus did more than make money for Ike Underwood. It also earned him respect, and after the incident few were so foolish as to attempt to thwart him. He went into the moneylending business, opened a second sawmill, built a grain mill on the Paradise River, secured the state contract for the digging of more than twenty miles of a branch of the Ohio Canal, founded the village of Paradise Falls, got himself elected its first mayor, constructed several kilns and established what later became the Paradise Falls Clay Products Co, opened the first gravel quarry in the county and obtained a charter for the county's first formal financial institution, the Paradise Falls State Bank. Then, over the years, he acquired control of the chair factory, the shoe factory, the tanning works, the notions & sundries store. Periodically have come attempts—by strangers, of course, sleek businessmen and financial manipulators from Columbus and Lancaster—to provide competition. Rival banks have been opened to great hoopla—and they all have failed. As have rival newspapers. As have two rival chair factories and a rival shoe factory. The world is larger than Ike Underwood, but Ike Underwood is larger than Paradise Falls, and this is as it should be. After all, he *founded* the place.

Paradise County was established as a political entity in 1831. The hamlet of Egypt was the first county seat. This place proved intolerable, and so Ike Underwood set himself to creating a new county seat. Which is how Paradise Falls came into being. The reason was expediency, and Ike Underwood never has said it was anything else. Certainly, in the larger meaning of the word, he cannot be considered to be a pioneer. He simply did what had to be done. And it was rather easy. He was no effete visionary, his head abounding with concepts that addressed themselves to posterity, concepts dedicated to the building of a richer and therefore superior life for subsequent generations. He founded the village of Paradise Falls simply because it was only right and logical that he do so. The 1830 federal census listed the population of Egypt as 197, which made it the largest settlement in the new county that was formed the following year. But life there was almost unbearable. Located in a shallow trough of the valley of the upper Paradise (a valley within a valley, so to speak), Egypt is extremely vulnerable to spring floods, and nearly every year there are drownings and considerable property damage. Ike Underwood had no idea who had established a settlement there in the first place. Whoever the man had been, he must have had a brain the size of a dried berry. Still, the land that surrounded Egypt was dark and rich, the best bottomland in the county. It still is the best bottomland in the county . . . whenever, that is, it is free of flood waters long enough for a crop to be brought in. But, back in '31, the first county commissioners could not be governed by considerations of floods. Egypt was the largest community in the county; therefore, it became the seat. But then came the terrible spring of 1832, and that year sixteen persons (seven of them children) drowned. The water rose to more than thirty feet in places, and it wasn't until eleven days after they had receded that the last rotting body was found. That did it. Within two months most of the survivors had moved away. Those who weren't farmers emigrated southeast to the relatively high ground that adjoined the falls. Ike Underwood's grain mill was there, and so was a general mercantile store owned by a man named Harlowe Morris. This was the fellow who had warned Ike Underwood about the irate Jackson. About a dozen homes were clustered near the store and the mill, and the place called itself Paradise Falls. Ike Underwood and Harlowe Morris owned a great deal of the land there. When they realized that most of the residents of Egypt had suffered through one flood too many and sought to live elsewhere, the two men sat down with pen and paper and laid out what they called *The Village of Paradise Falls, Ohio*. Under the date May 28, 1832, Ike Underwood wrote in his journal:

> *Have, with help of Harlowe Morris, devised Plan. Streats to lie north of River & east of my mill. Have estableashed streats in patern of gridds. Fair profit anticepated. Will begin talks tomorrow with families that are leeving Egypt. Will seek to sell land. Many of these families owe me money & cannot leave County under penalty of Law, whitch places me in good bargening position. Anticepate little Trouble. Splendid location for a settlment. High ground. My ground. Praise God.*

And it all worked out as Ike Underwood had expected. Most of the emigrants were more than happy to settle in Paradise Falls. It was only Egypt—not Paradise County—that they disliked. His high ground was indeed a splendid location for a settlement, and on January 1, 1833, Paradise Falls officially became the county seat. Papers of incorporation were filed in July, and in November Ike Underwood was elected mayor. He served for eight years, then saw to it that the job was passed on to Harlowe Morris, who held the office until 1858, when it was in turn passed on to the present incumbent, George McC. Pillsbury.

For more than a decade Paradise Falls clattered and clapped with the noise of things abuilding . . . homes, stores, mills, public edifices. In those days it was a place sweet and rich with odors of wood and shavings, loud with the thuck and slap of mortar, the squeal of saws, the hearty urgency of shovels and hammers. And Ike Underwood was overseer to all this activity. Overseer and participant—especially in the year 1841, which was the year he built his fine home on Cumberland Street and was joined in wedlock to the indomitable Phoebe. It was the latter event that provided him with his first defeat. He fought gallantly, however, and the defeat was no disgrace. Evidence of the ferocity of his resistance is found in this journal entry, dated July 7, 1840:

> *Frivulus nature of Man is his undoing more times than we like to think. The capacety of Man for serious thought is limited by this nature. The skrt & the pettycoat distract him, & so do the birds, the winds, the sounds of his Belly. I love her. I swoon. I am suffering. I acke. Would she had never come here. There is no nead for this. I protest. I must seak out the company of men. Resolve to imerse Self in sports &c. Hardyness needed. Cold water. No talk. No frivulus pursutes. Prefearence lies with quiet men. No lies from quiet men. No frivulus pursutes. As situation finds me now, I languesh too mutch. Strength needed. Resolve to ignore sky & warm winds & laughter.*

But all his resolve was for naught. Despite his better judgment, despite his selfreproach, he married her. And she has been his only defeat. He was thirtynine when he married Phoebe, and she was twentytwo, and he sought immortality from her: he wanted her to be the vessel and brood mare of his flesh. But he got more than he bargained for. Phoebe Bowers Underwood was not then, and is not now, the sort of woman to be content with simply a biological place in the scheme of her husband's life. Her mind and spirit were then, and are now, exclusively hers. And she was bound and determined to exercise them. And she did. And she still does. No roaring oaf of an Ike Underwood was about to suppress them. Frail she is, and pluperfectly gentle, but within her narrow bosom sit sinew and rocks and great slabs of iron. And Ike Underwood knows all this.

And knew it when he married her. But went ahead and married her anyway. He had been propelled into a ridiculous and degrading passion. He did, in fact, just about swoon. He was, in fact, too aware of sky and warm winds and laughter. The name of his Affliction was Love, and it rapped on his skull with small blunt hammers, cruel and relentless. And he came to understand that he would die unless he had her. Die. His skull would split, and his brains would leak out, and that would be the end of him.

Phoebe Bowers was a niece of Harlowe Morris, the storekeeper. Her mother was his sister. Her father was a prominent attorney in New Haven, and he was a bit distressed when Harlowe Morris' wife wrote a letter inviting Phoebe to Paradise Falls for the summer. The year was 1840, and travel was difficult, and Phoebe's father wondered if his little girl had the strength for the trip. He shouldn't have bothered himself.

Of *course* I have the strength for the trip, said Phoebe. Father, *please*, don't you know me well enough by now? And besides, it's not as though I'm going to the *ends* of the *earth*. It's only *Ohio*.

And so, a bit reluctantly but at the same time feeling rather proud of his gritty little daughter, Cyrus O. Bowers gave his permission. Phoebe arrived in Paradise Falls one afternoon in early June of 1840, alighting from the Columbus stage directly in front of the H. Morris Grocery & General Mercantile Store on Main Street. It so happened that Ike Underwood was conducting some obscure business there at the time. (So happened? Well, perhaps not *quite*. Harlowe and Ida Morris had a son but no daughter, and for years they had dreamed of some sort of union between themselves and Ike Underwood. Lacking the daughter, they set the focus of the dream on their niece Phoebe. They waited for her to grow up. They waited for her to complete her elegant schooling at the very chic Miss Watson's Academy in Falls Village, Connecticut. Then they acted. Ida Morris sat down and wrote the letter inviting Phoebe to Paradise Falls for the summer. A little later, after the letter of acceptance had been received from New Haven, Ida Morris and her husband let it be known—to Ike Underwood—that the most extraordinary female creature they knew was honoring them with a visit. Neither Harlowe nor Ida Morris had set eyes on Phoebe in about fifteen years, but this did not stay their hyperbole. She is such a lady, said Ida Morris to Ike Underwood, and her father incidentally is quite rich.) His curiosity thus piqued, Ike Underwood saw to it that he just so happened to be at the H. Morris Grocery & General Mercantile Store the afternoon the Columbus stage arrived bearing its fair burden.

She surely was a small one, this Phoebe Bowers of New Haven, Connecticut, and her face was perhaps a bit too heartshaped for Ike Underwood's taste. Still, her physical accouterments certainly were rounded enough, and she surely was quite a talker. In point of fact, she had a fine talent for carrying on conversations the likes of which were just about guaranteed to send even the most reasonable of men lurching off to the lunatic asylum . . . and gratefully, kissing the hand of his keeper.

Well, said Phoebe to her aunt and uncle as soon as she had alighted from the stage, who is this fellow with you? Is he the storied Mr Isaac Underwood? The one you wrote me about?

Harlowe Morris permitted himself a pained snort.

Well? said Phoebe. She placed her hands on her hips.

Ida Morris tried to smile. She pressed her hands against her stomach and she tried to smile and tried to smile and tried to smile.

Ike Underwood looked up toward the sky. It was altogether unremarkable.

Mr Underwood? said Phoebe.

He looked at her.

Aunt Ida has told me a great deal about you in her letters.

Rumm, said Ike Underwood, clearing his throat.

How's that? said Phoebe.

He looked away.

I'm *talking* to you, said Phoebe. Her voice was sweet as a summer morning. *You,* Mr Isaac Underwood. Please acknowledge my presence by at least *looking* at me.

He looked at her.

She was frowning. I seldom draw blood, she said.

Ike Underwood leaned forward a bit. Again he cleared his throat. Then, after placing his own hands on his own hips, he said: Is that so?

Yes. It is indeed so.

Would you take an oath on it?

I would.

I see, said Ike Underwood. He stroked his chin. Then, because he didn't know what else to do, he began to laugh. He laughed until his belly hurt. He laughed until all his breath was gone.

And his laughter was joined by laughter from Harlowe Morris, and finally there even was laughter from this small frowning girl, this Phoebe Bowers, this female nonpareil from New Haven, Connecticut. And then everyone got to talking at once, and damned if Ike Underwood didn't begin to feel as giddy as a maiden on the threshold of her first touch of male flesh. And damned also if he didn't feel like a damn fool.

That night he took supper at the Morris home, and nothing happened there to ease his feeling of foolishness. He and the Morrises and this Bowers girl did a fine job of work on the turtle soup and the chicken and the baked potatoes and the boiled beets and the steamed cabbage, and for dessert Ida Morris served cherry pie, and as was his usual habit Ike Underwood ate too much, and the girl talked of New Haven and her parents and her beaux and Miss Watson's Academy. Most of her remarks were directed to her aunt and uncle, and after a bit Ike Underwood got to squirming a little, what with his full belly and his suspicion that this damned girl was trying to take him down a few pegs. He was not used to this sort of treatment. Young ladies usually paid a great deal of attention to him. After all, he was *Ike Underwood,* and that was a large name, and there was not a mother in Paradise County who wouldn't have more than willingly bundled her daughter off to his marriage bed. Stout, vulgar, never one to pussyfoot or utter perfumed lies, Ike Underwood was nonetheless—for obvious materialistic reasons—very popular with these mothers. He understood the obvious materialistic reasons, but they did not vex him. He was a great man for his pussy, was this Ike Underwood, and if his money helped him attain it . . . well, such were the ways of the world. He wasn't about to change them, and so he lived with them, and quite gratefully. A fellow as stout and clumsy as he was *needed* money. Otherwise, his nights would be cold and barren. So, his appreciation of the power of his money was considerable. But this particular night, this Phoebe Bowers night, was different. Or was it? In a larger sense it probably wasn't a bit different. By not paying a bit of attention to him, by chattering with her aunt and uncle and behaving as though Ike Underwood didn't exist, she was by God *seducing* him, and he *knew* he was being seduced, and he knew *she* knew he knew. It was a sweet and rigid little game she was playing with him, and all he had to do was get up and walk out, and he might as well have tried to build a ladder to the sun. He sat stiffly, and gas rose warmly in his belly, and his crotch hurt, and his eyes followed the way her mouth moved, and she just chattered and chattered and chattered, and he had to admire her. None of the eligible Paradise County maidens had had the courage to do what she was doing. And of course there was a great risk involved. After all, no one had pressed a pistol to his head. Any time he wanted, he could simply rise and wish them all goodnight. But he didn't. He simply sat there and grappled with the gas in his belly, and the devil take his crotch. He had a curious premonition of what he supposed was doom, but then he was thirtyeight, and a man could postpone doom only so long. Only a simpleton refused to admit this, and Ike Underwood was by no manner or means lacking in awareness of such matters.

Later, he sat alone with Phoebe Bowers in the parlor. Her aunt and uncle had withdrawn to the kitchen. They certainly were eager to have this thing happen. Otherwise, they never would have left the girl unchaperoned. Harlowe and Ida Morris had always been a sight more prim that most people. So, when such as *they* chose to jettison the proprieties, it was clear that a serious and dangerous situation was developing (or at least so they hoped). As for Ike Underwood, about all *he* could do was trust in the Lord. He had not as much as touched this girl's hand, but already he had been most thoroughly devoured.

He lounged on a sofa. Phoebe Bowers was across the room. She perched on the lip of a straightbacked chair, and her knees were tight. Outside was a sound of insects and wind.

Ike examined his shoelaces.

Warm, said Phoebe.

He looked up. Yes, he said.

I expect you have unpleasant summers here.

They can be.

My aunt and uncle are foolish.

How's that?

They certainly can't believe it will happen.

I don't know. No telling *what* they believe.

But they want us to get *married*.

Yes.

They're so hideously *obvious* about it.

Yes.

Are you enjoying this?

No.

Phoebe Bowers smiled. Well, she said, I must give you credit for candor.

Thank you.

I am very candid too.

I wouldn't be a bit surprised.

Phoebe Bowers made a dry clucking noise. I feel ridiculous, she said.

So do I, said Ike.

Really?

Yes.

Do you feel stupid? Do you feel that you're being manipulated?

I do.

Me too, said Phoebe Bowers. But it's not proper of me to complain.

Why not?

Young maiden ladies are expected to *allow* themselves to be manipulated. At Miss Watson's we were told that our elders always know what's best for us.

Do you believe that?

No.

Do you allow yourself to be manipulated?

No.

Ike smiled. I didn't think so, he said. I got a feeling you are just about a girl and a half and then some.

Phoebe Bowers' hands came together and made a brief sound that was not quite a clap. She said: I thank you kindly for the compliment. I expect you mean it.

I do.

You know what would serve Aunt Ida and Uncle Harlowe right and proper?

What?

If I tore off all my clothes and hurled myself at you.

A fine idea, said Ike, grinning.

Are you funning me? Do you think I lack the courage?

I'm not funning you. And I don't think you lack the courage for anything.

Most men are shocked when I talk this way.

Do you talk this way with most men?

Yes, said Phoebe Bowers. She frowned. Her frown dared him to do anything about it.

Mm, said Ike.

My mother says it's my trouble. My mother is forever saying: Phoebe, I know you're just having your little joke, and *you* know you're just having your little joke, but *those poor young men* don't know it. *They* happen to *believe* the things you say. You scare them half to death. You'll never get a husband *that* way.

Maybe she's right.

I know, said Phoebe Bowers.

Don't you want to marry?

Of *course* I want to marry. But I want to marry the man *I* want to marry.

And you'll know him when you see him?

I'll know him.

I wonder if Harlowe and Ida are listening in on all this. If they are, I expect they've had a couple of catnip fits by now.

Well, said Phoebe Bowers, it'd serve them right for eavesdropping.

Mm, said Ike. Again he grinned. Then he said: I wouldn't of missed this for all the silks of Araby.

You're laughing at me.

Kind of.

You have your way with most girls, don't you?

Yes.

I like you, Mr Underwood.

Oh?

You give direct answers. Most men all they do is clear their throats and tell great bald lies.

The same can be said of most women, Miss Bowers. Only maybe they don't clear their throats so much.

That so?

Yes. But not you. What I mean is—I don't see you as being much of a liar.

Thank you.

I am enjoying this.

A little while ago you said you weren't.

Well, I've changed my mind.

Good. Tell me, do you derive satisfaction from having your way with girls?

Yes, Miss Bowers. I surely do.

Would you derive satisfaction from having your way with *me*?

I can't tell. A man never can until the thing's an accomplished fact.

That's not a very nice thing to say.

No, Miss Bowers. I expect it isn't.

Well, we'll let it pass. *Now* then, try to guess what it would be like with me. Try to imagine it.

I am. I have been.

And?

I don't know.

Phoebe Bowers shook her head. Then she almost smiled. But at the last instant she passed a hand over her mouth, and the hint of the smile went away. Finally she said: This is really all very remarkable.

Yes, said Ike. But we shouldn't comment on it.

Why not?

If we comment on it, we become too aware of it. Then it could go away.

A very perceptive observation, Mr Underwood.

Thank you.

I really do like you.

Thank you.

Even though you are far and away one of the least handsome men I've ever encountered, you have a certain blunt charm I find quite fetching. I expect it is one of the larger reasons for your successes with girls. But I must give you fair warning.

Fair warning?

You will have to work for it.

Work? Work for what?

Me.

And Ike Underwood did indeed work for the peppery little Phoebe. Both before and after their marriage. It was not an easy courtship. He never knew from one day to the next what her attitude toward him would be. He understood precisely what she was up to, but this in no way alleviated his discomfort. One day she would be all glitter and smiles; the next she would stare at him as though he had just emerged, all dripping and befouled, from the muck and offal of a humid and clamorously noxious bog. Within a week of her arrival in Paradise Falls, everyone in the village knew he had been smitten by her narrow snappish charms. There was a good deal of discreet sniggering, especially after people learned of the fine sweet highhanded way she was treating him. Serves the rascal right, said the ladies of Paradise Falls (especially those ladies whose daughters had been shabbily treated by him), and most of the ladies made tiny cackling noises behind their hands. Ike Underwood, the *great* Ike Underwood, mooning and staggering like a headless chicken in its final extremities! Ah, such a splendid turn of good fortune, and the ladies' eyes became small and wet and crinkly with delight. And of course Ike Underwood knew he was making himself appear ridiculous, but *knowing* his trouble and *doing something about it* were two entirely separate propositions. In his journal he gave himself the absolute devil, and a lot of good *that* did. He might as well have tried to crack a nut with a fistful of feathers. There was only one answer, and it was this: he would have to make his peace with his wretched condition; he would have to surrender; he would have to marry the girl. And eventually he did just that. On May 4, 1841 (Phoebe's twentysecond birthday, before a large and distinguished assemblage gathered in St Andrew's Episcopal Church, New Haven, Isaac Underwood and Phoebe Louisa Bowers were united in holy wedlock—or, as they later most candidly admitted to one another, mortal combat. The skirmishes were over; the war had begun. It has never ended. It is a great and noble war, bravely fought, abounding with mutual respect. It is a war predicated on Love, and this means it is a very enjoyable war, and from time to time Ike and Phoebe Underwood give voice to their enjoyment:

Isaac?

Yes?

Why do you love me?

I have no idea.

Now don't be *smart*. You love me because I stand up to you.

I suppose.

Would you have married me if I *hadn't* stood up to you?

No.

Ah, that is why I love you. Old and fat as you are, you still have the strength to be truthful.

Old and fat as I am. I am much obliged to you for that remark.

Sh.

She is my loving wife and she calls me old and fat. O God, how have I offended Thee?

Sh. Don't be impious.

And so his wife has been Ike Underwood's defeat. But all men suffer defeats, and he considers himself luckier than most. The Almighty has chosen to make *his* defeat an enduringly pleasant one. True, he and Phoebe are almost constantly at one another, but nonetheless their marriage is a genuine Love Match. They actually *enjoy* one another. They treasure the alertness that has evolved from their incessant squabbling. Their life together is a succession of ambushes, melees, surrenders and reconciliations, and from it they draw great nourishment, exaltation of the spirit. It is a perfect union of happy duelists, and they permit nothing to disturb it. There have been those who have predicted nothing but doom as the final destiny of such a marriage, but Ike and Phoebe know nothing of doom. They know a great lot, however, on the subject of Love.

Phoebe's father was one of the original doomsayers. During Ike's courtship of Phoebe, Cyrus O. Bowers became more than a little alarmed. His distress increased once he had met Ike. It increased by great leaps.

In the fall of 1840 Ike visited New Haven. It was his first trip east, and he had little use for what he saw. I must say, he told Cyrus O. Bowers, that most of the men I've met here are the sickliest looking crew of sissies it's ever been my poor fortune to run across. What's the matter with them? Don't they ever get out in the sunlight? They look like they'd be knocked over by the first hard breath came their way. Well, Cyrus O. Bowers, who'd never been noted for the frequency or zeal of his outdoor activities, took a bleak view of Ike Underwood and all the egregiously hearty talk. The man is an oaf, Cyrus O. Bowers told his daughter. You can't honestly tell me you're considering taking him as your *husband*? He is crude, has no rhetoric, curses outrageously, lacks even the most elementary awareness of manners, has no conception of how to wear clothes, and . . . uh, well, I hate to say this, but he certainly is more than a little, ah, corpulent. In ten years he will be absolutely *obese*. Ah, I don't mean to seem indelicate, but you must know that excessive weight can be a, well, a . . . a *hindrance* to the fulfillment of the proper purpose of a marriage. Uh, do you understand what I am trying to say? Phoebe nodded. She understood what her father was trying to say. She understood very well. And she didn't care. Folding her hands in her lap, moistening her lips, drawing a large shuddery breath, she said to her father: Yes. Yes. Perhaps Isaac *is* an oaf, but at least he is also a man. He is the first real man I have known. The others —Jimmy Hoover, Bob English, Wesley Nichols and all the rest of them, all my fine ardent young swains—are *boys*. They dress well, and they speak well, and surely they dance a fine waltz, but Papa there is no *flavor* to them. Please. Try to grasp what I am saying. I am serious about this. You can take my word for it.

And thus was her father routed. Phoebe's words came calmly, and they were invulnerable, and finally Cyrus O. Bowers gave his consent. Not that she really cared, though. Her father and the rest of the world could go jump off the highest parapet of the Leaning Tower of Pisa for all that any of their objections mattered to her. Ike Underwood was the man of her choice, and the word for what she felt was Love, and that was absolutely unequivocally all there was *to* it. She married Ike Underwood, and they have prospered, and their private war has given them delight and a mutual quickstepping agility of intellect, and they are convinced there is nothing they lack the strength to endure.

Isaac?

Yes?

I was just thinking of little Sarah. She would have been twenty this year. With blond hair, I expect.

Yes. I expect so.

I love you.

Yes, Phoebe. I know that.

There were two children, a daughter and then a son, but the daughter Sarah died of diphtheria when she was nine months old. This was difficult to *comprehend* let alone recover from, but Phoebe and Ike Underwood did recover. The birth of their son Philip was a great comfort to them, aided in the recovery. Now Philip is eighteen, and he is handsome and silent, and he will enter Harvard this fall, and their pride in him is immense. It is really of no importance that they deprived him of his war, and someday he no doubt will come to understand this. All arguments aside, Phoebe and Ike Underwood have a true and proper understanding of Love. It is larger than wars, death, diphtheria, obesity and terror. It is never final, and it cannot be destroyed.

The journal of Ike Underwood came to an abrupt end with the entry of May 3, 1841—the eve of the day he married Phoebe Bowers:

> *Marriage is to-morrow. Breast near bursts with anticepation. No more need for this Jrnl. No more need to keep in-most thoughts to Self. Praise God.*

Ferdinand James Purvis:

HE WROTE POETRY for his beloved Amelia, and their embraces were chaste. Later, after they got married, would be time enough for carnal explorations. He was skinny and undefeated, and his poems were full of swoonings and warm breath. He was seventeen and she was sixteen, and they took long walks; they picked flowers; they pleasured themselves with odors of earth and grasses and gentle animals. He could span her waist with his hands, and he did not have particularly large hands. Whenever she went outdoors she wore large hats. Freckles embarrassed her. Her eyes were gray, and her blond hair was of a texture so fine it seemed to be spun from motes and the breath of infants. She had told him she loved him.

It was a Saturday afternoon in early June. Ferd and Amelia sat at the crest of a hill overlooking Paradise Lake. They sat in the shade of a beech, which enabled Amelia to remove her hat. One of his hands rested against the back of her neck. Her hair was done up in a bun. Several strands had come loose. They tickled his fingers.

Ferd, she said, I want it to last forever.

It can't.

Why not?

If it lasted forever, it would be no good.

Her lips drew themselves into a tight line. She rubbed her eyes. She blinked toward the lake. Sunlight lay across the lake in golden smears. The lake plashed. The lake was very blue. She said: Why would it be no good?

Because then we wouldn't be human.

What?

Nothing that's human lasts forever.

Oh.

Does that sound too morbid?

Yes.

I'm sorry.

Ferd, I love you so much.

I love *you*.

I expect a lot of it sounds stupid.

A lot of what?

Our talk. The mooning and all. The words.

Well, it doesn't sound stupid to *us*.

No, said Amelia.

Does my poetry sound stupid?

No.

It's no good. I know that. But it comes from the heart.

Oh, Ferd! Ferd! It's *good* poetry!

Well, it *feels* good when I write it.

Amelia smiled. She twisted her neck and looked up at him. She kissed his chin.

Sixtysix, said Ferd.

What?

That's the sixtysixth time you've kissed me.

Ferd?

Yes?

You know what my lucky number is?

No. What is it?

Sixtyseven.

As far as Ferd Purvis was concerned, there could have been nothing beyond this. Nothing more clear. Nothing more golden and clean. He had told his father something of how he felt, and his father had said: Son, never feel ashamed. There are those who would deprive us of pleasure. Such people say pleasure is sin. Well, don't you believe it. A man's pleasure, as long as it does not inflict pain on others, is one of the large reasons he breathes air. Ah, Ferd Purvis loved his father above all men. His father encouraged Ferd's interest in poetry. As a small boy, Ferd had been read to by his father. Oliver P. Purvis, the Paradise County superintendent of public instruction, had a splendid voice. Reasonant. Profound. Like applause in a great empty room. It was an ideal voice for a superintendent of public instruction; it was an ideal voice for a father. Oliver P. Purvis was fond of discoursing on what he liked to call the Music & Rhythm of Rhetoric. Ferdinand, he said, there is almost a *physical* satisfaction to be gained from eloquence, whether it be your own or that of others. The magical process that permits the communication of ideas from one human being to another . . . ah, Ferdinand my boy, it *moves* one; it brings a catch to the breath, a euphoric tightening of the pectorals, a blessed joyful awareness of one's *heart* and one's *blood* and the very woof of one's *soul*.

Ferd Purvis enjoyed his father's hyperbole. He knew it was hyperbole (and so did his father), and the knowledge enlarged the enjoyment. The Music & Rhythm of Rhetoric: ah, such a father . . .

Granted, Ferd Purvis was too skinny. Granted, his eyes were set too closely together. Granted, his voice had a raspy catch that from time to time made him sound shrill and preposterous. But he didn't believe these things particularly mattered. He had his health, and he had a sweetheart, and he would be entering Oberlin in the fall, and he had his father available for advice and guidance, and he loved his sisters, Priscilla and little Editha, with fervor and devotion, and what else was there a young man required?

(He treasured what he thought of as the darling trivia of his days. He devoted much attention to the flavor of a slice of fresh warm bread. And cold water. On occasion he even sucked grass. He honored such diverse manifestations of the human spirit as the smile of brother for sister, of son for father, of lover for the beloved; he concerned himself with the breath of those he loved, with the sound of trees, with gaps between teeth, with old antimacassars, cracked plates, blankets, pillows, cicadas, the dimensions of a specific room, the odor of a dog. He remembered a day in June of 1863, which was the year his mother died. He was fifteen, and it was the day of his class picnic. She packed him a lunch. It included two hardboiled eggs. He remembered opening the lunch and unwrapping the eggs and wishing he had some salt to flavor them. But he didn't think there was any salt, and so he went ahead and ate the eggs. Then he found the salt. His mother had poured some into a scrap of old newspaper; then she'd very carefully folded the scrap of old newspaper so the salt would not leak out. When Ferd Purvis found the scrap of newspaper and discovered what was inside, he felt a sweet and terrible emotion that caused warm moisture to blur his vision. And so he did the only thing he could have done. He poured the salt directly into his mouth. He swallowed all of it. His dear mother had *remembered*. Her love for him had been so large that she'd even thought of such a trivial matter as salt for his hardboiled eggs. Sitting there on the soft warm grass of Bunker's Grove, surrounded by his laughing chattering classmates, Ferd Purvis had to hide his face in the crook of an arm so no one would see him. The salt was delicious. The flavor never left him. In October of that year, when his mother dropped dead most unexpectedly of a coronary seizure, there was nothing anyone could say to him . . . nothing . . . his loving God had wanted her all for Himself; this was the only explanation that made any sense at all, and Ferd Purvis arrived at it on his own. A packet of salt . . . a simple thing . . . sweet trivia . . . oh the mournful soul of Ferd Purvis clapped and roared, and life was very dear.)

It was another Saturday afternoon, this one in late July. Ferd and Amelia were driving up to Blood, a settlement in the hills northeast of Paradise Falls. They were on their way to a picnic at the Bethel ME Church there. Amelia had packed a lunch. Ferd clucked at old Henry, an ancient spotted gray who walked favoring his left rear leg. There was nothing wrong with the leg, but old Henry had been favoring it for years. It was a dry summer. The road was firm. The sky had no clouds, and the sun was hard and crisp. Old Henry loafed along, and Amelia was seated as close to Ferd as she could get without just plain up and draping herself on his lap. The lunchbasket lay on the seat next to her. He could smell fried chicken. She had prepared it herself. She was a good cook, her mother had told Ferd. (Joanna Burkhart was a great deal more friendly toward him than her husband Heinz was. Heinz Burkhart struck Ferd as being a very small man—in all possible ways.)

I sure do wish my folks liked you better, said Amelia.

So do I.

They haven't even ever asked you to take supper with us.

I know.

I want them to. I want to fix the meal myself.

I'd like that.

It bother you? That they haven't asked you, I mean.

Yes, said Ferd. He flapped the reins. Old Henry looked back over a shoulder. It was a reproachful look, and Ferd immediately was sorry he'd flapped the reins. There was no sense taking it out on old Henry.

It shouldn't bother you, said Amelia. I'm all they've got. If I'd of had brothers and sisters, then it'd be different.

I expect.

Ferd?

Yes?

You'll come back?

Come back?

From Oberlin I mean. You're such a *scholar* and all. Maybe I'm not smart enough for you.

You're smart. You love me.

Conceited!

Amelia, did you pack salt with the lunch?

Salt? Why, yes. Of course I did. What good's chicken without salt?

I love you. I could go off to China but I'd come back. You don't have to fret about Oberlin. I mean that. I love you. I love you.

Amelia didn't say anything. She kissed his ear. He felt as though someone had set a torch to his flesh. He blinked at the strong high sky. A week and a day later his father was murdered by Heinz Burkhart.

It was not a bullet, and it was not a knife. It was contempt. Oliver P. Purvis, Paradise County superintendent of public instruction, threshed away his life right smack in the middle of Heinz Burkhart's kitchen floor, and Heinz Burkhart stood with his hands on his hips and frowned ah such a very little bit, and the contempt came out of him like juice from a berry. Ferd Purvis was there. His father's eyeballs had rolled up. Ferd Purvis screamed. He dropped to his knees. He touched his father's face. He loosened his father's collar. His father coughed. Oliver P. Purvis, Paradise County superintendent of public instruction, coughed with such violence that his tongue shot out. He died with his tongue protruding. Ferd Purvis tried to stuff it back inside his father's dead mouth. Ferd Purvis tried and tried, but his father's tongue was too slippery. His fingers ran with his father's warm dead saliva, and finally he had to stagger out back by the pigpen and vomit.

People called it a wretched business.

It is best forgotten, they said.

They shook their heads. They frowned. They mused on the ways of the Lord. They told Ferd and his sisters how terribly sorry they were. They told Ferd and his sisters what a splendid man their father had been.

Attendance at the funeral was excellent. The undertaker, a man named Zimmerman, had managed to stuff the corpse's tongue back inside its mouth.

The murder of Oliver P. Purvis had its beginnings the day preceding his death. That day was a Saturday, and Ferd had arranged to take the lovely Amelia for a buggyride. A quiet buggyride. He had nothing special in mind. Perhaps they would go somewhere quiet and sit by a stream or the lake. Perhaps they would chat. Perhaps they would kiss. Perhaps they would speak to one another of love. Perhaps they would watch blackbirds. Perhaps they would drink cool water and listen to insects. Perhaps they would discuss the clouds. It didn't particularly matter what they did. They would be together, and this was enough. Surely they required no external music.

But they never went for the buggyride. When Ferd called at the Burkhart home, he was met at the kitchen door by Heinz Burkhart, and Heinz Burkhart was smiling. Which meant a calamity was imminent. It was the first time Heinz Burkhart ever had smiled at Ferd. It was not a good smile. The smile that comes over the face of a person who seldom smiles is hardly ever a good smile. It is pinched, narrow, really more of a grimace. As far as Ferd was concerned, Heinz Burkhart gave every indication of being the sort of man who smiled only when he saw a puppy with a broken leg.

Come in, said Heinz Burkhart. Please. We have to talk with you.

We? said Ferd.

Yes, said Heinz Burkhart, holding open the door. Please. Come in.

Ferd entered the kitchen. It was empty.

We are all in the parlor, said Heinz Burkhart.

Oh, said Ferd. Now he had no doubt but what something terrible had happened. He'd never been in the Burkhart parlor. Never. Not once in all the time he had been courting Amelia.

Heinz Burkhart led Ferd to the front of the house. Speaking softly, his words drifting back over a shoulder, he said: We have been waiting for you. It is a fine thing that you are so prompt.

Ferd did not reply.

He was a small man, this Heinz Burkhart. His eyes were like pellets that had sat in grease. He breathed with his mouth open, allowing his tongue to rest limply on his lower lip. This gave him something of a feebleminded aspect. Now, as he led Ferd toward the parlor, he was humming under his breath. Ferd's scalp itched. (Feebleminded? Well, perhaps Heinz Burkhart *appeared* that way, but in his case the appearance was a lie. He was one of the most prosperous farmers in the county, and his tongue was famous for its quickness. It was a stabbing and jabbing tongue; it inflicted lacerations without number. It was a small man's tongue, and it had been known to reduce far larger men to quaking impotent fools.)

Four persons were waiting in the parlor. It was dark. Ferd blinked. It took a second or two for his eyes to become accustomed to the darkness. There was a strong odor of dust, but the room was cool. The first thing his eyes were able to make out was a photograph of Heinz Burkhart. It hung over the mantel. Apparently it had been taken back in Germany. Heinz and Joanna Burkhart and their small daughter had emigrated to Paradise County from Saxony only fourteen years before. Evidently Burkhart had served in some sort of army back there. In the photograph he was wearing a resplendent uniform decorated with epaulets, enormous buttons and even a sash and sword. His right hand was curled over the handle of

the sword. He wore a magnificent plumed hat. His facial expression was
all tight eyebrows and narrow lips. Perhaps it was meant to be warlike. His
left hand was thrust inside his tunic. The photograph put Ferd in mind of
pictures he had seen of Napoleon and General McClellan. He almost
wanted to laugh, but of course this was no time for laughter. He now was
able to make out the faces of the four persons sitting in the parlor. One
was Amelia. She sat on the settee, and she had been crying. She wore a
white dress, and she was the virgin princess of the world, and a handkerchief lay damply in one of her hands. She was sniffling. Ferd looked at
Heinz Burkhart. Then he said: What's this all about?

It is good news, said a man who sat next to Amelia on the settee. The
man's name was Christian Soeder. He was large and blond, and there
were those who said he was handsome. He was the younger brother of a
rich farmer named Wilhelm Soeder.

Good news? said Ferd.

Yes, said Christian Soeder. He smiled. His teeth gleamed. He was
twentyfive, and he was just back from the war. He had come calling on
Ferd's sister Priscilla a number of times. Ferd did not like him. Christian
Soeder had a reputation. There were those who said Christian Soeder had
never had a thought that wasn't centered below his waist. His depreda-
tions against the county's maidens had become a matter of some public
concern before the war, and apparently he was taking up where he left
off.

I don't understand, said Ferd.

You will, said a voice.

Ferd looked around. The voice had come from Wilhelm Soeder, who sat
in a rocker near one of the front windows. Wilhelm Soeder was a thick
man. He had a plump wife and two small daughters. Ferd had always liked
Wilhelm Soeder. The man's reputation was quite the opposite of his
younger brother's. Wilhelm Soeder was an absolutist, a believer in straight
lines and direct discourse. He never bargained, cajoled or threatened; he
simply set out to do a thing and *did* it. He was as broad as he was tall, and
his ears had no lobes. His skin was grainy, tough, and perhaps it was his
skin that gave him such an appearance of thickness.

Terror danced and quivered in Ferd's throat.

A cluck.

Ferd flinched.

The cluck had come from the fourth person sitting there in the darkness.
It was Joanna Burkhart. I am so sorry, Ferdinand, she said. I truly am.

What? said Ferd.

Joanna Burkhart sat in a straightbacked chair by the door. She was
large, florid. She almost always smelled of flour and sweat and scouring

powders. She was not a talkative woman, and she seldom smiled, and here she had gone and *volunteered* something, and . . .

Amelia began to weep. The sound of it was not loud, but it *was* loud to Ferd Purvis, and perhaps it also was loud to the others.

Sh, said Christian Soeder. Grinning, he patted one of Amelia's shoulders.

What's going on? said Ferd Purvis.

Heinz Burkhart began to speak. He nodded as he spoke, and Wilhelm and Christian nodded with his words. He said: My Amelia and young Christian here have this day become betrothed. It has all been settled. An agreement has been reached. It will be a fine match.

Ferd Purvis tried to look at Amelia. He could not. She still wept.

A smile snipped at the corners of Heinz Burkhart's voice. He said: You are very young. You will recover.

Amelia began to wail. She covered her face with her handkerchief.

Her father glared at her. You be quiet, said Heinz Burkhart.

Don't talk to her that way, said Ferd.

You mind your own business, said Heinz Burkhart. He walked to where his daughter sat. He reached down and pulled her hands away from her face. The handkerchief fluttered.

Amelia stopped wailing. She swallowed, sniffled.

That is better, said Heinz Burkhart. He smiled at her, and then he smiled at Christian Soeder.

Ferd felt as though spikes were pressing on him. He was holding his breath. He trembled. He said to himself: God has come. God has tugged the bones out of me.

Heinz Burkhart turned away from his daughter. Smiling at Ferd, he said: It is settled. I am sorry it—

Sorry? said Ferd.

Yes.

She loves me. She does not love this fellow. How can she? She can't but hardly *know* him.

That is of no importance. She—

Ferd looked at Amelia. Tell your father what you feel, he said.

Amelia closed her eyes.

There is nothing to tell, said Heinz Burkhart. In this family, the word of the father is the word to be followed.

Christian Soeder patted one of Amelia's hands.

Ferd rocked on his toes. He started toward Amelia.

No, said Wilhelm Soeder, the grainy and stolid Wilhelm Soeder.

Ferd hesitated. He turned to face Wilhelm Soeder.

Wilhelm Soeder's face was flat. It has been arranged, he said, and arrangements are not things to be broken.

Is she *pregnant?* shrieked Ferd. Is *that* it?

Amelia opened her eyes and moaned. Joanna Burkhart made a growling noise. Christian Soeder started to get to his feet. Wilhelm Soeder held up a hand. No, said Wilhelm Soeder. Christian Soeder settled back. Heinz Burkhart came at Ferd and hit him across the neck. Ferd gagged, fell back, put up his arms. Heinz Burkhart's blows struck Ferd's forearms and elbows. Ferd backed into a table, knocking over and smashing a lamp.

Amelia stood up. *I am not pregnant!* she shrieked. *Ferd! Ferd! It has nothing to do with that! It's just that an arrangement has been made!*

Ferd pushed away Heinz Burkhart, held the little man at arm's length, blinked hotly at Amelia and yelled: *I love you! What do you expect me to do? Cock my hat and whistle a gay tune and walk out the door? My God, Amelia, I am a HUMAN BEING and I LOVE you!*

Amelia shuddered.

Ferd pushed Heinz Burkhart toward a wall. Wilhelm Soeder stood up and seized Heinz Burkhart by the arms, restraining him.

Love . . . said Amelia, shuddering. Love . . . please . . . I don't want to hear a lot of talk about something that doesn't . . .

Doesn't what? said Ferd. Why don't you finish what you're trying to say? How come you can't?

Christian Soeder stood up. I am going to thrash you good, he said to Ferd. I am going to thrash you good and proper and right.

You thrash nobody, Wilhelm Soeder said quietly. He pushed Heinz Burkhart into a chair and then he advanced on his younger brother. You sit down, said Wilhelm Soeder. You sit down and you be quiet. I have had enough of your trouble.

But—

Sit down.

Christian Soeder sat down.

Amelia looked at Christian Soeder.

You too, Wilhelm Soeder told her.

Amelia nodded. She seated herself next to Christian Soeder.

I am sorry, said Wilhelm Soeder to Ferd. You can believe me or not believe me, as you choose.

Believe you? What does that have to do with anything? I love her.

I have my family's interests to look after, said Wilhelm Soeder. My brother needs a wife. Without a wife, he will ruin himself. I will not tolerate that.

Well, find him *another* wife.

No. That I cannot do. This is the one he has chosen. If he marries a woman he does not want, he will continue to be a scamp and a seducer. So I am giving him what he wants. That way there will be no betrayals.

You filthy pig!

No. I am not a filthy pig. I can understand why you would say such a thing, but it is not true. I am simply seeing to it that the necessary is accomplished. There is no sense railing at me. Nothing will be changed. The young lady is marrying into our family, and I shall see to it that my brother is an exemplary husband to her.

Has she been *sold?* Is *that* it?

Wilhelm Soeder looked at Heinz Burkhart. He shrugged.

Is it?

Wilhelm Soeder spread his hands. His eyes were large. Yes, he said to Ferd. Yes indeed. Precisely.

Ferd? said Amelia.

Ferd looked at her.

It is done, she said. Never mind about it. An agreement has been made.

Christian Soeder spoke up. She is very pretty, he said. She will be a faithful and loving wife, and she understands what it means to live up to an agreement.

There are larger things than love, said Amelia.

Ferd jumped at Christian Soeder, pulled him off the settee and began beating him about the head and chest. Amelia moaned. So did her mother. Wilhelm Soeder came at Ferd from behind. Ferd's hands were around Christian Soeder's neck. Heinz Burkhart was shouting. Wilhelm Soeder knocked Ferd down. Ferd tasted the parlor carpet. The flavor was thick and dry. Bending over him, Wilhelm Soeder said: I do indeed regret all this. Ferd looked up. Christian Soeder had fallen back onto the settee. The eyes of Wilhelm Soeder were clouded with what Ferd supposed was regret. He helped Ferd to his feet. Ferd looked at all of them. Then he looked at the photograph over the mantel. He looked at that ridiculous little man in the resplendent uniform, hand tucked inside his tunic, eyes awash with cardboard bravery and zeal. Ferd began to laugh. It was a white soundless laugh. It took Ferd's breath away. It made him bend double. Wilhelm Soeder nodded. Yes, he said. Yes. Correct. This is the proper thing to do. He took Ferd by an elbow and steered him to the kitchen and out the back door. Heinz Burkhart followed. You are a fraud, said Heinz Burkhart to Ferd. You languish, and your eyes are full of feathers and moonbeams, and you never will amount to a pile of hog turds. Go away now. Go away and stay away.

Ferd was too warm. He was perspiring, and he was not the sort to perspire. Too skinny. His skin felt as though it was a paradeground for vermin with sticky feet. Wilhelm Soeder's hand released Ferd's elbow. Now all the laughter was out of Ferd. He stumbled down the back steps of the Burkhart place. Heinz Burkhart spat toward him. Ferd did not look back.

Moonbeams, said Heinz Burkhart. Moonbeams and nectar and sweet stupid words. You are an ass, young man. If you thought for one instant that I would allow you to marry my—

Heinz, said Wilhelm Soeder. Please. Not that tongue of yours. Not now. It is not necessary.

Ferd wrapped his arms around his belly. The sun was hot. The sun was too hot. The sun was like a rock.

Wilhelm Soeder and Heinz Burkhart disappeared back inside the house.

Ferd staggered across the barnyard. Old Henry was tethered to a tree near the barn. Old Henry nickered. Ferd pressed his forehead against old Henry's neck. Old Henry stamped his bad hoof, and Ferd heard flies. Ferd rubbed the flesh of his wrists. He wanted to soak them in cold well water. He unhitched the horse from the tree, then climbed up into the buggy. He clucked at old Henry, and slowly the buggy moved out of the Burkhart barnyard. Old Henry limped. A rain began that afternoon as Ferd drove home. The sun skittered off. The clouds were low, in gray smears. The rain came in a quiet clamor, tapping leaves, rooftops, bricks, the earth. When Ferd drove into Paradise Falls, he saw occasional children. They ran shrieking, rollicking and splashing in the rain. They kicked up sprays, and the earth smelled green. The rainwater drove against Ferd's face. It felt like spikes. It occurred to him that he was just seventeen years old. It occurred to him that he was taking it all too hard for someone of such slender days. It occurred to him that calendars sometimes were in error. It occurred to him that he had a right to take it all as hard as he pleased. The rain tapped and spat, and there was little wind.

After unhitching the buggy in the barn and leading old Henry to his stall, Ferd joined his father and sisters on the back porch of the Purvis home. Oliver P. Purvis was seated in a wicker rocker. He was reading a volume of Shakespearean sonnets. Priscilla sat in a straight chair next to her father. She watched the rain. Little Editha was perched on the back steps. She was just out of range of the rain. Now and then she leaned forward, turned her face toward the sky, opened her mouth, licked at raindrops. They taste gray, she said.

Ferd seated himself in another wicker rocker.

Oliver P. Purvis looked up from his book. Where's Amelia? he said.

Uh . . . oh . . . she doesn't feel so good.

Oh, said Oliver P. Purvis, that is too bad. I hope it is nothing serious.

Mm, said Ferd.

Smiling, Oliver P. Purvis returned to his sonnets.

Nice rain, said Priscilla.

Ferd nodded.

Might cool things off.

I wouldn't be surprised, said Ferd.

Little Editha licked at raindrops.

Do my tomatoes good, said Priscilla. They've been needing this.

Yes, said Ferd. It's been a very dry summer.

The rain makes everything slick, said little Editha. Look at the roof of the barn.

Yes, said Priscilla.

Courage, said Ferd to himself. She is not worth mourning. She accepted the *agreement* too readily. How can she be worth much if she would do such a thing?

Pinky got wet, said little Editha.

Oh? said Ferd.

Yes. He was out back somewhere, and the rain came too quick for him. He came running into the kitchen like a streak. Priss put him down cellar. He was all slick and mad. Howling. You know, howling like he does.

Yes, said Ferd. Howling. I know how he does.

He sure can howl, said Editha.

Ferd nodded. After supper, he told his father what had happened. Priscilla had fixed a particularly fine veal stew. Priscilla was an excellent cook. She would no doubt make some fellow very happy and very fat. The veal stew had been very well seasoned. It lay hotly in Ferd's belly. He had eaten too much. He was ashamed of himself. Skinny as he was, he had the appetite of a pride of lions, and apparently no tragedy was large enough to interfere with it. He had a schoolmate, a fellow named Jeremy Grainger, and this Jeremy Grainger didn't have half Ferd's appetite, yet at the age of fourteen Jeremy Grainger had weighed two hundred pounds. Now, at seventeen, Jeremy Grainger weighed two hundred forty if he weighed an ounce, and he hated Ferd with a large and unwavering devotion. It occurred to Ferd that the news of Amelia's defection would no doubt delight Jeremy Grainger.

When Ferd told his father, they were sitting on the back porch again. The rain still fell. Ferd and his father had been listening to peepers. His father was speaking of Priscilla's tomato plants. Ferd interrupted him. The words came in a burst. They came so quickly he could feel them scrape his heart and lungs and his bloated belly.

My Lord, said Oliver P. Purvis. He looked at his son.

Ferd was weeping. He tried to keep it quiet. The veal stew was doing battle with him, and finally he had to belch.

Oliver P. Purvis stood up. He went to Ferd and placed a hand on Ferd's shoulder. My Lord, he said. My Lord. My Lord. Those German pigs.

Ferd shuddered.

Priscilla came to the back door. I hear something? she said.

Never mind, said her father.

Something the matter?

No. No. Nothing's the matter.

Oh, said Priscilla. All right then. She retreated back into the kitchen.
Oliver P. Purvis pulled his chair next to his son's. He sat down. Oliver
P. Purvis was more than six feet tall, but he'd never weighed more than
about one hundred forty pounds or so. He was fiftyfour years of age, and
he had been married three times. His first two wives had died in childbirth. His third wife, Ferd's mother, had survived three births, but then
the coronary seizure had taken her at the age of fortyone, and who ever
heard of a *woman* dying of a coronary seizure at *that* age? There was no
question but what Oliver P. Purvis knew a thing or two about tragedies.
But he hadn't become hardened to them. Now, sitting next to his son, he
began taking tight outraged breaths through his nostrils, and finally he
said: God in Heaven, did they call it an *arrangement*? Is *that* the word they
used?

Yes, Papa. Arrangement. And they used agreement too. Arrangement.
Agreement. Those were the words.

But what do arrangements and agreements have to do with human
beings?

I don't know.

Of course you don't know. It was a rhetorical question.

Ferd choked off another belch. He wiped at his eyes, looked at his
father. There's nothing I can do, he said.

Yes there is.

Papa, I can't go back there and—

We'll go back there. First thing in the morning.

What?

This is an obscenity. It cannot be allowed to happen. We'll call on
this Burkhart.

He won't change his mind.

We'll just *see* about *that*.

I don't see where it'll do any—

Do you believe in love?

Yes.

Do you believe in honor?

Yes.

Is Amelia a slave?

No.

Then we're going there, said Oliver P. Purvis. It is only right that we
go there. She has been intimidated by her father. She is a human being,
and he is trying to take away her dignity.

I *know* that. And I *tried* to make her understand what was happening.
Well, son, sometimes two cooks can prepare a better broth than one.
Papa?
Yes?
I love you.
Thank you. Ah, look at the rain. Good for the rain. I must say, my preferences lie with the cooler weather.
Papa?
Yes?
Do we have to say anything to Priss and Editha about all this?
No. Of course not.
Thank you.

The next morning, Sunday morning, Ferd and his father were up early. They told Priscilla and little Editha they would not be going to church. There is a matter we have to attend to, said Oliver P. Purvis. Priscilla nodded. I expect the Lord will bear with us just this once, said Oliver P. Purvis. Again Priscilla nodded. She asked no questions. She was not the sort to ask questions. She fixed eggs and coffee for her father and brother, oatmeal for her sister, nothing for herself. She sat and watched them eat. Pinky lay in her lap. Waow, said Pinky, purring, licking his forelegs. Waow. Waow. It was a golden morning. Ferd hitched up the buggy. His father drove. Old Henry limped along the hard dirt road that wound toward the Lake Township farm of Heinz Burkhart. Nothing remained of yesterday's rain. The new sunlight baked the earth with such intensity that it actually was dryer than it had been before the rain. Oliver P. Purvis wore a derby and a crisp brown suit. His cravat was elaborate.
Papa?
Yes?
You should have been born rich.
Oh?
Yes. You would have been able to cope with it. You know how to dress well. You have a way about you.
Well. Ah. Thank you kindly.
Ferd sighed. Then, speaking in what was at most a whisper, he said: This will change nothing, Papa.
Do you resent me? Is that it?
For what?
Do you think I am interfering in your affairs?
Papa, if I thought it would do any *good*, I wouldn't care if you pulled a pistol from your coat and shot Heinz Burkhart dead. But nothing's going to do any good. With these people, an arrangement, or an agree-

ment, or whatever you want to call it, is holier than Jesus and all the saints.

I know that. I know how the German mind works. But we have to make our representations.

Why?

Because you are my son.

It's more than that.

Yes. I expect it is.

How is it more than that, Papa? All right, so she has jilted me. It's not the first time a girl has—

Oliver P. Purvis held up a hand, cutting off his son's words. He spoke calmly, and his voice was sweet and logical, magisterial, and he said: Ferdinand, there is such a thing as humanity. You love that girl. I know you do. And I have every reason to believe she loves you. I have seen the two of you together. I know the way you look at her, and I know the way she looks at you. When you two are together, you walk in the company of the elect. Do you think for one moment that I will permit such a thing to be destroyed? It is beautiful, and what sort of man would I be if I permitted an *arrangement* to destroy beauty? All my life I have valued beauty above all things. I am too old to adjust my beliefs. Far too old. And far too convinced that my beliefs are the only reasonable and proper beliefs a sane man, a *Christian* man, can hold. You share that view, don't you? Ah, but you must. Otherwise you would not be mourning your Amelia with such fervor. So please, do not demur. Between us, we will destroy this *arrangement*. Wilhelm Soeder will have to look elsewhere for a wife for that neerdowell brother of his. We shall prevail. Our hearts are pure.

Is that enough?

Yes.

Are you sure?

Yes.

He has a tongue. He lacerated me. He spoke to me of feathers and moonbeams, and I had no reply for him.

Leave the replies to me.

Papa, he'll hurt you.

No. He won't hurt me. And he won't hurt you. Our hearts are pure. Remember that.

Yes, Papa.

Feathers and moonbeams?

Yes.

And he belittled them?

Yes.

He is stupid.

Yes, Papa. If you say so.

Amelia came running from the Burkhart house as soon as the buggy turned into the barnyard. She wore a Sunday dress, and there were circles under her eyes. Heinz Burkhart came out of the barn. He was leading a horse. The Burkhart buggy stood outside the barn door. Amelia ran toward Ferd and his father. *No!* hollered Heinz Burkhart.

Amelia hesitated. She looked toward her father.

Go back inside the house! hollered Heinz Burkhart.

I want to speak with Ferd, she said.

No!

Yes, Papa, said Amelia Burkhart. She turned and walked back toward the house.

Ferd jumped down from the buggy. He began running after Amelia. Amelia ran inside the house, slamming the kitchen door behind her. Ferd stopped. He breathed dust. He rubbed his eyes.

Oliver P. Purvis came down off the buggy. He tethered old Henry to a fencepost near the barn. Still leading his own horse, Heinz Burkhart walked to the same post. He tethered the horse next to old Henry. Oliver P. Purvis said something to Heinz Burkhart, and Heinz Burkhart shook his head no. The two men walked across the barnyard. Ferd watched them. He followed them. They all climbed the back steps and entered the Burkhart kitchen. Heinz Burkhart was telling Ferd's father there was no sense arguing; done was done, and that was all there was *to* it. Amelia and her mother were standing in the kitchen. Heinz Burkhart told them to go upstairs. Amelia looked at Ferd. Her mother took her by an arm. They went out of the kitchen. In a moment, their footsteps could be heard as they climbed the stairs. They were heavy, slow. Ferd sniffed. He smelled pepper. The kitchen was very clean. Oliver P. Purvis spoke. Standing by the door, glaring directly at Heinz Burkhart, he said: Nothing is immutable, Burkhart. This cannot be allowed to happen. It is monstrous.

What is monstrous? said Heinz Burkhart.

This *arrangement* between you and the Soeders.

That is our business. It is not your business.

It *is* my business. It has to do with my son.

Kindly go away, said Heinz Burkhart. My wife and daughter and I were just about to leave for church.

You can forget church today. We have to settle something that is larger than church. My son loves your Amelia. What you propose to do is a crime against nature.

What?

You are denying them their humanity.

Are you crazy? Humanity? What is humanity? You are a madman. Next thing I know, you'll be speaking to me of feathers and moonbeams. Your son here has great love for feathers and moonbeams. He is a poet. Hah. A poet.

He loves your daughter.

Love, said Heinz Burkhart. You get out of here.

No.

I'll kill you.

You will not, said Oliver P. Purvis. You will do as I say.

Heinz Burkhart smiled at Ferd and said: You should have this lunatic put away.

You keep still with that kind of talk! shouted Ferd.

Oliver P. Purvis made a shushing noise and said: Ferdinand, don't bother yourself with anger. I'll take care of this.

You'll take care of nothing, said Heinz Burkhart. He inclined his head toward the door and said: Please go now. I don't want an argument.

Have you no decency?

What's decency got to do with this?

There is no decency in you! You would destroy my son! You would destroy your own daughter!

Get out of here! shouted Heinz Burkhart.

My God, can't you understand? If you do this thing, you are a murderer!

I know what is best for my daughter! This son of yours will never amount to a sack of dog shit! All the time sighing! All the time feathers and moonbeams! All the time composing his stupid poetry! All the time corrupting my Amelia with his perfumed talk!

You filthy hypocrite!

What?

How can you talk of corruption? You, a man who would sell his own daughter! Where is the corruption beyond that?

Gasping, Heinz Burkhart moved toward Oliver P. Purvis. An arm was drawn back, and the arm ended in a fist. *You sonofabitch!* he screamed.

Oliver P. Purvis' face was purple. He made a gagging sound. His tongue shot out.

Heinz Burkhart hesitated.

Oliver P. Purvis looked down at his tongue. Then he fell forward. He bumped into Heinz Burkhart. He tried to seize Heinz Burkhart's shoulders, but his hands did not have a proper grip. He fell to the floor. Ferd hollered something to Heinz Burkhart. The tongue of Oliver P. Purvis drew back inside his mouth. Ferd screamed. He dropped to his knees.

Heinz Burkhart was frowning ah such a very little bit. Ferd touched his father's face. He loosened his father's collar. His father coughed. He coughed with such violence that his tongue again shot out. His eyeballs had rolled up. He died with his tongue still protruding. He died in a spasm, quickly, kicking out, banging the heels of his shoes against Joanna Burkhart's fine clean floor. Lord God, said Heinz Burkhart, shuddering. Amelia and her mother came rushing into the kitchen. Amelia's mother shrieked. Amelia's face turned moist and tight. She made fists. She held them high, as though she were preparing to defend herself. It was then that Ferd began fussing with his father's tongue. Later, after he had vomited out by the pigpen, he ran into a field. He ran across the field. He ran until he came to a stand of beech trees. He embraced one of the trees. Its trunk was smooth and gray and hard. He slid to his knees. He gagged. He was drooling. He wiped his mouth. He sat down. Heinz Burkhart and Amelia came running after him. He watched them. When they came to where he sat, he looked up at them and said: Well, you surely have gone and done it.

No, said Heinz Burkhart, we have done nothing. It was your father did it to himself.

You killed him. Both of you.

No! screamed Amelia.

You are a murderess, said Ferd. And your father is a murderer.

Amelia started to say something, but her father interrupted. No, said Heinz Burkhart to his daughter, don't argue with him. It will do no good. Come. We have to go back to the house. I have to summon the sheriff.

Murderers, said Ferd.

Amelia whimpered. Her father pulled her away. She was pale against the fields and the golden sky.

Ferd's rear end hurt. He lay down. He closed his eyes. His fingers still were slippery from his father's saliva. He wiped them on his shirt. The vomit had made his throat raw. He breathed with his mouth open. He was able to smell his own breath, and it was rancid. He tried to think of sonnets and flowers and the gray flavor of rainwater. He even tried to think of feathers and moonbeams. He curled his fingers, scrabbled at the earth, shredded a number of fingernails. Several of his fingers began to bleed. He sucked on them. He told himself: Amelia couldn't help it. I shouldn't have called her a murderess. Her father is the one. Her father is the murderer. He killed my father with his contempt. Oh? Really? But why was Papa there? He was there because I could not grapple with it alone. I needed help. Then who is the murderer *really*? Had I been man enough, I would have refused his help. O God forgive me I am dead.

It was Priscilla who found him. Ferd? she said.

He opened his eyes.

She squatted beside him. Her own eyes were dry. Here, she said. Let me help you.

He allowed her to seize one of his hands and pull him to his feet. She led him back across the field and the barnyard. Zimmerman the undertaker had already loaded the body aboard a wagon. He and Priscilla spoke together quietly for a moment. Ferd could not make out what they were saying. He stood in the barnyard. He looked around for the Burkharts. He saw not a sign of them. He supposed they were hiding inside the house. Priscilla came to him and led him to the buggy. They rode home. She attended to all the arrangements. She even chose the Scriptural passages that were read by the Rev Mr Reader at the funeral. It was quite a successful funeral. There was not an unoccupied seat. Little Editha wept throughout. The Rev Mr Reader, a young fellow and rather a decent sort, spoke with authority, and his delivery was especially effective in the reading of this passage from Mark: *He that soweth the good seed is the Son of man; the field is the world; the good seed are the children of the kingdom; but the tares are the children of the wicked one; The enemy that sowed them is the devil; the harvest is the end of the world; and the reapers are the angels. As therefore the tares are gathered and burned in the fire; so shall it be in the end of this world. The Son of man shall send forth his angels, and they shall gather out of his kingdom all things that offend, and them which do iniquity; And shall cast them into a furnace of fire: there shall be wailing and gnashing of teeth. Then shall the righteous shine forth as the sun in the kingdom of their Father. Who hath ears to hear, let him hear.*

(There were that day O God squadrons of birds.)

1865 . . .

Seen on a map, Paradise County is a plump

7

with the village of Paradise Falls located almost smack in the center of the area formed at the junction of the horizontal and vertical legs of this incomplete triangle. It is just eleven miles due south of the settlement of Blood, which abuts the county's northern line. Actually, the county divides neatly into two parts—the flattened farmland west of Paradise Falls, and the hills and ravines east and south and north of the village. Most of the horizontal leg of the

7

is substantial, cleared of trees and wild vegetation, abounding in large farms whose owners (most of them Germans who came to the county in the decade after 1848) are thrifty, industrious, humorless and more than a little afraid of their rigid Lutheran (and, in some cases, Papist) God. Their names are Soeder and Brandt and Buehler and Stumpf and Rapp and Burkhart and Neumark and Osterhaus and Jurgens, and one could safely eat off the floor of any of their homes. These people are numerous, vertical, silent. They handle their wives roughly, but their wives never complain. They would sooner worship the Devil than yield to sloth. They make up their own minds—and, once made up, those minds will resist change no matter what the contrary argument. These people are not indigent. They raise corn, wheat, hay, barley, cattle; their chickens lay excellent alabaster eggs; their cows give forth thick warm milk that is sweeter than the smile of a virgin with her arms full of daisies. The heads of these families came to Paradise County because they did not choose to serve in the armies of their Prussian and Bavarian and Hessian and Saxon governments; these men are egalitarian; they believe in personal initiative; they neither borrow nor lend; their minds are clear as a slap; their tongues are icy; they are not confounded by the uses of rhetoric. Seldom do they yield to public passion. They are not reluctant to take of the heavy waters, but they do so among their own kind. They may covet their neighbors' wives, but most of the time they restrain themselves from overt pursuit. They neither snigger nor flatter, and they are not offended by the odor of sweat. They keep their privies and their fingernails spotless. Their children are silent. They eat heavily, and their cellars swarm with regiments of masonjars full of pickles, jellies, jams, tomatoes, peaches, corn, beans, peas. The labels on the masonjars are neatly lettered, and the masonjars with the earliest dates on the labels always are taken down first. There is no deviation from this practice. To these people the only proper life is the life methodical, and deviation is nothing less than naked immorality. To these people all hymns are loud. Being vertical and more than a little afraid of their rigid Lutheran (and, in some cases, Papist) God, they need to believe that He hears them. Unless He has chosen to render Himself deaf, the chances are He does. And it is good that they shout their gratitude. Surely, when the conditions that surround their lives are compared with the conditions governing the existences of those who live in the vertical leg of the

7,

these newcomers, these Germans, are very blessed indeed. Consider, for comparative purposes, what is known as Masonbrink Country. This area is located in southeastern Paradise County. It encompasses what is without question the poorest farmland in this part of the state, and yet it was the earliest to be settled. As far as can be determined, the first white family to take up residence in what is now Paradise County consisted of a

man named Masonbrink, his wife, his nine children and his younger
brother. They were squatters, and they came in either 1772 or '73. They
had no legal right to the land. A treaty signed by the Virginia colonial
government and the chiefs of the several tribes of the Mingo Indians had,
in exchange for territorial concessions to the east, reserved the area for
the Indians. As a result, one morning in the spring of 1774 Masonbrink,
his wife and nine children were slaughtered. The younger brother, who
was off chopping wood, managed to escape. A year later, however, he returned at the head of a party of twentytwo. A rough fort was built, and
then this new contingent of squatters began clearing land. This time
there was little trouble. The Mingoes had withdrawn westward after suffering a serious defeat in the Battle of Point Pleasant, fought October
10, 1774 near a settlement just south of the Ohio River in what is now
the new state of West Virginia. A small force of Virginia colonial troops
under General Andrew Lewis was attacked there by a much larger body
of Mingoes. Although the colonials suffered more casualties, they repulsed
the Mingoes, who then fled to the west. In the meantime, a regiment led
by Lord Dunmore, the Governor of Virginia, was pushing in from the east.
Together, the forces of Lewis and Dunmore secured the area—for the
time being, at least. But then came the War of the Revolution and the
collapse of British rule. The Indians began acting up again, and so it
wasn't until the late 1780's that southeastern Ohio was forever cleared
of them. The first permanent settlement, Marietta, was established on
April 7, 1788, at the confluence of the Ohio and Muskingum rivers.
It originally was called Adelphia, but the name later was changed in
honor of the then Queen of France, Marie Antoinette. The original Marietta settlers represented the vanguard of the immigrants who were then
brought to the area by the Ohio Company, which had purchased more
than a million acres of land from the federal government under terms set
forth in the Land Grant Act of 1787. Most of the immigrants were from
New York and New England, but not so most of those who came to what
is now Paradise County. They were Virginia people, most of them. The
unfortunate Masonbrink, for example, hailed from a mountain hamlet
near Lynchburg. His brother, young Tom Masonbrink, recruited his entire party of twentytwo from the same hamlet. These people later were
joined by several dozen veterans of the Lewis and Dunmore campaigns
against the Mingoes. By 1788, when the first Ohio Company officials arrived in what is now Paradise County and set up their land offices, there
already were some seventy persons living down there in Masonbrink
Country. These people had absolutely no legal title to their land, but
there was little the Ohio Company could do about the situation. So it was
tacitly agreed that the squatters owned the land they were working, and
the Ohio Company went about its business of filling the rest of the area
with settlers. By 1803, when Ohio was admitted to the company of the
several States, about seven hundred persons resided within a twentymile

radius of the original Masonbrink fort. There also were about a hundred
Mingo survivors living in the area. Oldtimers remember them as a skinny
starving lot who kept their indifferent bodies and souls together by a little
desultory hunting and fishing. The journal of Isaac (Ike) Underwood
calls these Mingoes *scurvy*, and the adjective is apparently a good one,
judging from the oldtimers' testimony. At any rate, by 1845 the last Mingo
family had died out, to the great relief of just about everyone. The damn
savages had been little more than public charges for decades. And so, with
the dispersal of the Mingoes and the assured safety that came from their
removal, the center of population moved northwest from the old Masonbrink fort. The land up there was much better for farming. The original
Masonbrinks had known this, but they'd been reluctant to settle there.
They had better sense. Rich as it was, that land also was flat and thus
more vulnerable to attack. So the Masonbrinks and their friends had made
do with the hilly country to the southeast. And hilly country it indeed
was. And still is. It is full of impecunious Masonbrinks, and there is even
a settlement *called* Masonbrink on the McArthur-Jackson road about three
miles north of the county line. One branch of the family operates a shabby
little store located within fifty yards of the original fort. There are at
least two hundred Masonbrinks in southeastern Paradise County, and
just about all of them live in brokendown little shacks back in the hills.
Their patriarch is old Ben Masonbrink, who reputedly was born in the
Masonbrink fort in 1775. He is the son of Tom Masonbrink, the young
fellow who brought the original twentytwo from the hamlet near Lynchburg. It is conceded by almost everyone that old Ben was the first white
person born in what is now Paradise County. As such, he is something
of a monument. Lamentably, he drools a good deal, and he never has been
what a person would call too allfired alert in the head. In point of fact,
mental agility never has been a Masonbrink hallmark. The subsequent
generations have been, if anything, even more dull in the head. And, to
complement their enervated intellectual achievements, they have developed a slovenliness that is an absolute scandal. In Paradise County, when
women gossip about the indigent, they never say the poor Soandsos live
like black niggers; instead they say the poor Soandsos live like absolute
dyedinthewool Masonbrinks. In Paradise County, this is the most devastat-
ing thing the human mind can comprehend—to be a Masonbrink, to live
like one. And of course this is all rather sad. The Masonbrinks *were*, after
all, the first people to come to the area, and there is little question but
what they were shabbily treated by their pioneering impulses. Had they
come to Paradise County later, they would have had access to the rich
farmland to the northwest. As matters turned out, it was those damn
Soeders and Brandts and Buehlers and Stumpfs and Rapps and Burkharts
and Neumarks and Osterhauses and Jurgenses who ended up with the
good land. For that time, in this place, the race went to the tardy. The
Masonbrinks' pioneering impulses had betrayed them. Back up there in

the hills of southeastern Paradise County, with the sky scratched and
blotted by oaks and poplars, the earth so scarred and precipitous, the poor
Masonbrinks have had to make do with what precious little their bleak and
impotent land has been willing to yield, and so yes, *of course* the Masonbrinks have become embittered and shiftless. The point is: they have
reason. Those damn Germans. Never discuss the Germans with a Masonbrink. Those who do should be able to defend themselves. This warning
also applies to those who would mention the name of Isaac (Ike)
Underwood within earshot of a Masonbrink. If the truth be known, the
Masonbrinks hate *him* more than they despise all the Germans combined.
As far as they are concerned, he is the blackest and most pestilential villain in all Creation. Their enmity dates back to the late 1840's and early
1850's. These were the years the Germans came to Paradise County. In
those days, Ike Underwood owned more than seven thousand acres of the
best land in the county—almost all of it up in the northwestern section.
He operated two extremely prosperous farms up there, but there still was
plenty of acreage he was willing to sell—provided the purchaser had sufficient wherewithal. He sold it to the Germans fast as they arrived. Most
of them had brought substantial sums of money over from the old country,
and thus they were able to make generous down payments—and, in some
cases, buy their land outright. True, these people were political refugees,
but this in no way meant they were insolvent. Far from it. And Ike Underwood knew his Germans. He knew they valued thrift above everything
save possibly breath. Which meant they were excellent risks. Which meant
they surely were better risks than the scrabbling impecunious Masonbrinks. And so he did business with the Germans. And, with each transaction, the Masonbrinks grew more furious. Several of them visited Ike
Underwood, but all he honestly could do was shrug. He reminded them
of a few basic facts of economics. I'm sorry, he said, but the whole damned
bunch of you couldn't scrape together fifty dollars if your lives, your
sacred honor and the fate of the Republic depended on it. So please don't
come sucking around me. The word, gentlemen, is wherewithal. Our
German friends have it. You don't. So, for that reason and that reason
only, believe me, I have to do business with them. When *you* come up with
the wherewithal, I'll do business with *you.* Until that time, good day.
(Granted, Ike Underwood's tact is not his most salient attribute. But a
tactless man is not necessarily a fool. Ike Underwood was speaking the
truth. And not as he saw it, but as it was. And still is. In the Masonbrink
Country, truth is harsh, and truth is hideous, and it does not change.)
When the Masonbrink delegation came stamping and cursing out of Ike
Underwood's office, they made a great lot of angry noise, and one of the
younger men even went so far as to kick over a cuspidor. But then of
course it was necessary that they make their noise and kick the cuspidor.
It was necessary for them to hide their pain. And so they hate. They
have no choice. The infliction of that sort of pain cannot be forgiven.

And thus the Masonbrinks, those descendants of true pioneers (who is more of a true pioneer than an original slaughtered squatter?), have remained on their little farms back there in the hills, and there is no reason to believe they will not remain on their little farms until the day of the final terrible Trump. They scrabble, and they curse, and they fight, and they breed, and they make the rest of the county purse its collective lips and shake its collective head, and the county's collective mouth, when discussing the Masonbrinks, usually utters weighty paragraphs having to do with Filth and Shiftlessness and Lack of Good Old Gumption. The Masonbrinks and their dreary Country provide the flaw that has stitched a scar across the sweet face of Arcadia, but then perhaps even the flaw has its place in the Divine Order. After all, without the Ugly how would one recognize the Beautiful? Yes, the Masonbrink Country enhances Arcadia, and ah, the wonders of the Mind of God. Ah, God bless God. But kindly do not bless God in the presence of a Masonbrink. He might take serious offense. In point of fact, it is wise to stay away from the Masonbrinks altogether. Let them rot down there in their Country. They are welcome to it. They can loaf there and curse there and fight there and hate there until the days fall down dead and dark, and it is just as well that they keep their corruption to themselves. Elsewhere in the county, especially in Paradise Falls and up in the northwest where the Soeders and the Brandts and the rest of the despised Germans have their fine fat farms, there exist (in florid abundance) hope, vigor, a sense that the best is yet to come, that the potentialities of sweet Arcadia have by no means been extended to their fullest. Down in the Masonbrink Country, though, it is clear that the best never was and never will be. Down there the scabrous Masonbrinks sit by the hour on the front stoops of their dispirited little shacks. Their corn comes up at a slant, and each rain washes the rest of their crops downhill, and what are they supposed to do? Laugh? Ride into Paradise Falls and fire shots at everyone in sight? No. The time for laughter is long past, and it is doubtful that the Masonbrinks have enough of the blessed wherewithal to purchase sufficient bullets to do any appreciable good. No, all they can do is sit. They hug their knees. Their awful companions, the hills and the rocks and the scruffy enervated vegetation, press in on the Masonbrinks, and at night there is a surreptitious sound of wind and small desperate beasts. Ah well, at least there are the small desperate beasts. Were it not for them, the Masonbrinks probably would have starved to death years ago. There is a belief held by the respectable and vertical of Paradise County. It goes like this: As long as the Masonbrinks have the strength to carry dead animals home from their traps, there will be Masonbrinks among us. (Ah, some country, some adjunct of Arcadia. Slanted corn. Crops sliding downhill. Rotten teeth. Sores. The old man's name is George Masonbrink. He is seventy, and he is the oldest surviving son of the ancient and still breathing Ben Masonbrink, and clearly it takes a great deal to kill a Masonbrink. Next

to shiftlessness, the tribe's outstanding characteristic is its witless and utterly pointless longevity. If a Masonbrink male dies before his seven-
tieth birthday, he is considered cut down in his prime, no matter how
scabrous and ramshackle he might appear to a stranger. Old George
Masonbrink grins, and his grin is a moist pink slash, all gums and spit
and green breath, devoid of even the memory of teeth, and his adamsapple moves in a bony spasm and he says: Far as I care, a man who
isn't a Masonbrink is a man who eats shit for breakfast. Yessir. This here
sure is some country. Good for wild hogs and Masonbrinks. Some country,
and so how come we got to love it? I be goddamn but it's like a woman
with tight drawers and a cold heart. The tighter her goddamn drawers
and the colder her goddamn heart, the heavier we get to breathing after
her. I be goddamn. Maybe it's a curse. Maybe we done something wrong.
Wild hogs and Masonbrinks. Heh. Yessir. Shit.) No, there is little to be
said for the Masonbrink Country, and there is even less to be said for the
Masonbrinks themselves. As far as anyone can tell, the existence of the
Masonbrinks serves just one function. It reminds the rest of Paradise
County's population of how very fortunate it is. This comparison even
applies to the people who live north and northeast of Paradise Falls, up
in Blood and Orland townships. This is also a hilly area, but it is not quite
as grim as the Masonbrink Country. Its farms are nowhere as plump or
large as those owned by the Germans to the west, but at least the people
who live up there are able to buy a cow now and again and wear clean
clothes to church. The histories of most of these families date back to
the 1790's and early 1800's. Lamentably, though, the oldest family is about
to die out. Its name is Blood, and its only survivor is the drunken and
tubercular bachelor wastrel, James Perry Blood. These days he spends most
of his time in Claude Dill's saloon, and he is very fond of gambling with
cards. His is surely a classic corruption, melodramatic and purplish, and
the word people use when they discuss him is Waste. His only living relative is a cousin, a clubfooted little lawyer named ElRoy Mauk, and ElRoy
Mauk's only explanation for James Perry Blood's dissolution is this: Jim
couldn't stand the responsibility. Last of the line, I mean. It's ripped and
torn at him for a long time, and in the face of it he did the only thing he
could do: he fell apart. All he wants is to die, and that's the truth. No
one disputes ElRoy Mauk's analysis of the situation. It is all very Tragic,
and many are the stony clucks that issue from the mouths of those who
take the bother to concern themselves with James Perry Blood's ruin. Ah,
it is all indeed a shame, and the stony clucks are fervent and mournful.
But please do not for a moment think that the north and northeast of
Paradise County are a hotbed of wastrels. This is absolutely not so. True,
there exists up there an abundance of hills and gullies and rocks, but this
is not a Masonbrink abundance, which means that a living *can* be wrested
from the coiled and reluctant earth. This country is not Arcadia undi-
luted, but it is an Arcadia of sorts, even if not of the highest rank. And,

in the spring, when trees and wildflowers explode in their proclamative greens and pinks and whites, when the cool hillcountry air claps and seethes with wind and birds and clicking insects, this country's beauty is of the highest order, and it becomes a favored spot for picnickers and lovers. But, for genuine yearround Arcadia, fullblown and triumphant, nothing surpasses that part of Paradise County that lies west and northwest of the village of Paradise Falls. This is the German country, the country of dark abiding earth, of masonjars and loud hymns and men whose bellies are thick with ropes of virtuous hardworking muscles. Geologically, the western and northwestern sections of Paradise County mark the last stand of the Great Plains, and a gallant last stand it is. These sections also mark the source of the Paradise River, which slices an increasingly deep valley from northwest to southeast as it makes its way toward the Ohio. This valley is not unlike those of the Hocking and the Muskingum, which also debouch into the Ohio. The source of the Paradise River is an elongated and rather narrow body of water called Paradise Lake. It is located in northwestern Paradise County, and it is fed by seven creeks that join it from the east and southeast. They are the Tuesday, the Henry, the Blood, the Orland, the Miller, the Yancy and the Cooper. The lake is shaped like a wurst, which is rather appropriate when one considers the recent influx of Germans into that part of the county. It is almost exactly eight miles long. Its widest measurement is a little less than three miles. It extends from west to east, and at places its northern shore is less than half a mile from the county line. The Paradise River leaves the lake at its western end, but then almost immediately describes a large arc and proceeds southeast, cutting its valley. The great bend in the river, almost one hundred eighty degrees, is the site of the best farmland in the county. This farmland is owned almost exclusively by Germans. The valley there is shallow, and thus the danger of floods is a recurrent worry, but the Germans do not complain too loudly. The land is too rich. The Germans do not want the Lord to think they are ingrates. From the great bend all the way some fourteen miles southeast to the village of Paradise Falls, the river sweeps through surpassingly lovely farm country, fragrant and misty country, golden and damp in the morning, a country of sunshine and blackbirds, Arcadia unfettered. It throws the lie into the faces of those who dispute the abiding goodness of the Almighty. The witness to this country comes away from it a better Christian, and that is an absolute fact. This fourteen miles of magnificence is interrupted by only one settlement—Egypt. Now, more than three decades after Ike Underwood and almost all the rest of the then residents of Egypt pulled out and reestablished the county seat in Paradise Falls, Egypt still is a place of floods and frets and floods and floods. Its population is less than a hundred. It supports a post office, a general merchandise store and a CPV&M telegraph station, and every March the inhabitants tote all their belongings up to their attics. The county has built and rebuilt a levee on both sides of the

river, but it has not been particularly successful. When the Paradise is of
a mind to overflow, nothing less than an act of God will turn back its
waters, and acts of God simply aren't very frequent in Egypt. To the rest
of Paradise County, the stubborn Egyptians are a peculiar bunch. Their
floods have become an annual joke, and no one understands why they
persist in living there. Not even the Egyptians themselves can explain it.
Amos Holiday, who owns the general merchandise store, puts it this way:
You can talk about them Masonbrinks all you want to, but when it comes
to Crazy your average Egyptian has got your average Masonbrink beat
eightynine ways come the second Sunday of next week. I expect maybe
it's a foolishness of the blood. Or maybe we're all descended from some
sort of creatures that's got webbed feet. One thing though for sure: If you
want to live in this here place you learn to *swim* before you learn to *crawl*,
let alone *walk*. Ah, poor old Amos Holiday. His throat works itself in a
rueful chuckle that is like sand on a tin plate. Yessir, he says, the human
race. God save the human race. Then, likely as not, Amos Holiday points
toward the levee, shrugs, permits the corners of his mouth to resolve themselves mournfully downward and finally says: Look at them goddamn
sandbags. Big lot of good they are. God save us all. Amos Holiday shakes
his head, and it is a valiantly lugubrious aspect he presents. But it is not
successful. The suppressed laughter within him has made his belly tremble. Crazy, he says. Crazy. Crazy. And no one disagrees with him. Ah,
those Egyptians . . . surely they are more mysterious than the night side
of the moon. Ah yes, talk about Crazy. Perhaps someday the collective
madness of Egypt will be explained. Yes. Someday. The day rocks fall up.
Meanwhile, the belly of Amos Holiday will continue to quake like the
leaves of the fair aspen. Let us, however, move on to the southeast, following the Paradise as it flows in a sweeping arc down to Paradise Falls,
where the high ground can be said fairly to begin. The name of the village has been of some interest to those hereabouts of literary persuasion.
They enjoy commenting on its curious Miltonian undertones, but they've
not found a very interested audience. The village has little use for those
who traffic in shallow irony. And the only Milton most of the village's
residents know is a fellow named Hosea Milton, who has a little farm up
in Orland Township. Nice man, Hosea Milton. Plays a strong fiddle at
dances. Fond of hard cider. No, the name of Paradise Falls is a very logical
name, and never mind the literary Milton. As to the falls itself, it is sixty-
eight feet two inches wide and twentyseven feet seven inches high, which
of course gives it comfortable rank among the lesser of the Republic's natural phenomena. Still, it is the only natural waterfall of any consequence
in eight counties, and so it is the object of a deal of pride. Paradise Falls
people enjoy showing it to visitors. The best view is from the south shore,
and there has been talk of establishing some sort of public park over there.
It is considered a choice spot for picnics, and lovers pay it numerous
nocturnal visits. The rushing of the water is said to have a decidedly aph-

rodisiacal effect. It is a sweet sound, fresh and Arcadian, and it brings to
mind love and smiles. To the southeast, as the water tumbles through the
Masonbrink Country, the sound deepens, and rocks are rubbed white,
and there is a hurried eroded menace to the river; it becomes a thing of
mud and vermin and beavers and dead treetrunks. But the Masonbrink
Country is not Paradise Falls, and thank the Lord for that. As a place, then,
Paradise County is not without its contrasts. The resident of one part can
live out his days without really knowing his neighbors in the other parts.
The German farmer, the Egyptian, the resident of Paradise Falls, the farmer
up in Blood Township, the hapless Masonbrink with his slanted corn—
all inhabit a territory of strangers. All abide in the light of a single Lord,
but geography determines how He is viewed. Says Wilhelm Soeder, the
most prosperous of the German farmers: God is the earth. God is Work.
Says Amos Holiday, the Egyptian storekeeper: God is that damn river
pushing over them damn sandbags. Says James Perry Blood: Hell with it.
Let's have another drink. Deal the cards. Says George Masonbrink: It's
like God keeps following us and hitting us with a stick. Says Isaac (Ike)
Underwood: God is whatever we make Him to be. And of course not a one
of these statements is false. There are, after all, so many truths, and this
blessed flawed Arcadia is large enough for all of them. The joy annihilates,
but the joy is not all, and so God bless God and the infinite variety of His
terrible creatures and their sweats and humours.

A Great Man:

OH DIDN'T THIS CHARLEY WELLS, this great man who had come to Paradise Falls with his high ambition and his opulent wife, oh didn't this
Charley Wells, this fine fellow, this believer in possibilities and mortality,
oh didn't he just grin at the world! Oh didn't he *ever!* Oh yes *sir,* he did,
he *did!*

And oh wasn't this place ripe for Charley Wells!

He would prevail! No doubt about it!

Paradise Falls . . . ah, such a name!

He tasted the air, and the air was sweet! *Delicious,* by God!

The name of the place was Paradise Falls, and it appeared to be more
prosperous than his Indiana home town ever had been. He grinned at the

village, this new Home Place for him; he grinned and he tipped his hat and he always had a polite howdydo for everyone, and *yes indeed,* ah *glory!*

But of course at first he moved quietly, cautiously. He insinuated himself on no one. He figured, what with his wife being the widow of a martyred local hero, the people of the village would come to him. Which they did. And he reacted well. And so did Nancy. She knew how to smile, and she was learning how to dress well. And she had her legendary breasts. He bought her parasols and billowy summer dresses. He taught her to say *would have* instead of *would of.* He taught her to modulate her voice. He taught her to giggle rather than shriek. Always, he told her, be sort of fluttery. Use your hands a lot. Seem helpless. Make men want to do things for you. We can profit from this place. I can feel it already. Grinning, Nancy assured Charley she would do everything he wanted. She told him he surely was a smart one. He told her well, he didn't think anyone was about to volunteer to be smart *for* him. He reminded her that the Lord helped those who helped themselves. She laughed, punched him lightly in the belly. I don't guess, she said, I'm going to need to fret an awful lot about dropping over weak and trembly from starvation. Charley also laughed. He told her good things surely would come. He told her he was not afraid of work, of deviousness, of whatever would be necessary to provide him with his undoubted greatness. It'll be a good journey, he told her. I'll see to it that things happen. It's going to be a life and then some, my girl. You just wait.

They took a suite of rooms in the village's new hotel, the Acterhof House. They could afford it, at least for the time being. Charley still had most of the money left to him by his parents, plus the proceeds from the sale of the grocery back in his Indiana home town, a little river settlement called Titusville. And Nancy had the money from the sale of her late husband's farm near Evansville. So she and Charley established themselves in the best suite the Acterhof House had to offer, and Charley began working toward his greatness.

Charley?

Yesm?

This here greatness you're always talking about, how's it going to happen?

When the luck comes along.

Luck? What luck?

I don't know. But, when it comes, I'll know what to do with it.

What if it don't come?

It'll come. And I'll grab it by the neck. Look, Nancy, I know what I'm talking about. Just believe me.

I believe you. The only thing is—how long do we wait?

Not long.

How do you know?

Because I got it coming to me. Because I'm twentyseven and it still hasn't happened. A man usually by the time he's twentyseven runs across it. But not me. All that's happened to me is that I've lost two elections and got myself tarred and feathered. Which means things got to change. And, when they do, I'll be ready. I'll take that old Lady Luck and I'll squeeze the juice out of her. All *you* got to do is have faith.

I do.

Good. That's my Nancy.

The grocery business would do just fine for a start. The village's principal grocer, a skinny old fellow named Harlowe Morris, was just about on his last legs, and the trade surely was there to be taken away from him. Within a month after he and Nancy arrived in Paradise Falls, Charley had opened a store directly across Main Street from the Morris place. Nancy helped Charley with the clerking, and—as he had figured—she brought in the customers. She was the widow of a man the village had judged a hero, and people came to the store out of curiosity if nothing else. Once in the store, however, they were assaulted by Charley's grin and his rhetoric (he never forgot a face; he never forgot a name), and few of them could resist him. The store prospered almost from the start, and the distress of old Harlowe Morris was really rather sad to behold. According to reports Charley received, the old fellow had become downright querulous, much given to delivering long and incoherent speeches on what he called the village's ingratitude. A widower and former mayor whose only son had gone off to New York or some such place to make a living playing the violoncello in a cheap theatrical orchestra, old Morris liked to tell people he supposed the world had passed him by. He was fond of reminiscing on the days when his store had handled yardgoods and hardware as well as groceries, when it had been a fullblown general mercantile store, and it was clear he was far too painfully aware that time was another word for rot. All in all, he was a dilapidated and preposterous old man, but this did not mean he did not have friends. And it wasn't long until Charley learned how large and influential at least one of the old man's friends was. The name of this friend was Isaac (Ike) Underwood.

In the meantime, however, Charley moved forward serenely, and people by and large took to him. When they asked him why he and Nancy had rented a suite in the Acterhof House, his reply was quick and easy: We are taking our time looking for a home. We don't want just any old place. We plan to live here the rest of our lives. We want to bring up children. We want for them to have a good home, a home where they can bring their little friends, an airy place full of sunshine and laughter and good cheer. Ah yes, good cheer. As perhaps you suspect, old Charley Wells is a great one for good cheer. Ah. Heh. Well, anyway, we're taking our time. One of these days we'll find something that's just right for our needs. I don't even know whether we'll build or buy. Depends on what we like.

The foregoing wasn't precisely a lie, but it wasn't precisely the truth either. Charley and Nancy really couldn't have bought a decent home if their lives had depended on it. He had spent nearly six thousand dollars equipping and stocking and paying the first year's rent on his store. The day the place opened, he and his wife had barely a thousand dollars between them. This was because of Isaac (Ike) Underwood, and it was the first manifestation of the man's hostile attitude toward them. His bank had refused Charley a loan on either the store or a home, and so Charley had had to use their own money to open the store.

(Oh indeed it was a lovely town, but it was a town like all towns. Lamps flickered, and the ladies of the prosperous swished expensively as they walked, and the sniggerings of young lovers came damp and fresh, and the preachers spoke fervently of honor and courage, and they all took care of their own. Old Harlowe Morris had been a friend of Ike Underwood for more than forty years, and no newcomer from Indiana, no grinning loud-mouthed oaf whose history was vague and perhaps disgraceful, was about to destroy one friend at the personal profit of the other. Charley understood all this, and he was wise enough not to bear Ike Underwood any particular grudge. Not even after Ike Underwood's later and more elaborate chicanery did Charley particularly hate the fellow. There really was nothing to be gained from hating Ike Underwood. Charley was in no position to destroy him—therefore, why hate him?)

Busy as they were with the store, Charley and Nancy still had time to assess Paradise Falls and most of the persons (or at least the persons of importance) who lived there. They divided these persons into two classes: Doers and Talkers.

We leave the Doers be, said Charley. We stay out of their way. The ones we got to get are the Talkers. That Isaac Underwood is a Doer. We stay out of his way. For now anyway. Maybe later, when we take on some strength, we can go up against him. But not right now. We give him a wide berth, him and that wife of his, that skinny little Phoebe. I tell you the truth, sometimes I honest to God think she's got more hardness and snap to her than he does. I mean, she's such a *lady* and all, but I wouldn't want to be caught with a hand in *her* cookiejar, no *ma'm*.

Nancy smiled. Yes, she said, I know what you mean.

Oh?

Yesterday she crossed the street to avoid me.

Really?

Yes.

Good.

What's good about it?

It's a start. Don't you see? By crossing the street, she *recognized* you. If you didn't matter, she wouldn't bother to cross the street.

Oh, said Nancy. Oh yes. I never thought on it that way.

I give you two or three more years and then thoughts like that'll be second nature. Your mind'll be like mine.

Nancy nodded. Yes, she said. I expect so.

Won't that be fine?

Yes, Charley. Very fine.

Aw hell, he *knew* she was being sarcastic, but a lot he cared that people sometimes were sarcastic with him. The first twentyseven years of his life had provided him with a leathery skin, and anyway, she was *his* wife wasn't she? His *friend* George Peters, the great *hero* who had seduced and abandoned her back in Titusville a decade ago, all right, so perhaps Charley had to live with the knowledge that Nancy had loved George more than she ever would love him, but at least Charley was *living* with the knowledge. George Peters was living with no knowledge. George Peters had been a *hero,* and a sniper's bullet had done in the great *hero* at Fredericksburg, and so George Peters was living with nothing, and so who *really* had won her? George Peters who was *dead* or good old Charley Wells who was *vertical* and taking nourishment just fine thank you very much? Ah, damn all heroes. Charley never had been a hero, never would be, hadn't even *wanted* to be for a long, long time. Greatness precluded heroism. And heroism had been the first thing he had shucked out of his boyhood and young manhood. Later he'd also shucked out honor, love, loyalty and belief, but the very first thing to go had been heroism, and he was happy to be shut of it. Swear to God he was.

It left him at age fourteen. It left him on a day the wind screamed high. It was a lunatic day, and a lunatic woman was responsible, and the rain laughed at him, spat in his face. And he was wretched. And he called himself a coward. But what did cowardice have to do with anything? Actually, he had taken his first stride toward greatness, as later he came to understand.

Charles Palmer Wells came all burly and bawling into his Indiana world, a world that was not unlike the world of this village Paradise Falls. His father, a good and loyal Democrat, was Titusville postmaster and operated a grocery. James C. Wells was a skinny man, but soft in the sickly wattled way skinny men sometimes can be soft. Charley was the only child of James C. and Caroline Wells. From the beginning he was the spark and devotion of his father's existence. His mother, a doughy woman with thin blood and a bad ear, was not as open in displaying her love, but it existed just as strongly, and Charley had few difficulties with his parents. He came and went as he pleased, walking in a jocose aimless stagger, pausing to kick at pebbles and sticks, to holler, to hop, to squawk. Titusville was on the Ohio River, and by the time he was five he had taught himself to swim. He was as wide as he was high; he had no loose flesh. He liked to stand with his legs far apart. He liked to glare into the ancient river sky. He felt as though he were challenging God. His blood slammed from all the courage that went squirting through him, and he had little doubt but what he would live forever.

The Wells place was high on a damp and fragrant hill. From its front steps a person could see for twenty miles, across the great coruscating river and beyond, to the Kentucky hills all blue and faded, softer than a kitten's neck.

On Sunday afternoons he sat on those front steps with his father, and the truth of the matter was that his father talked too much. Son, said James C. Wells, this is all very precious. We don't want anyone ever to take it away. People say there may someday be a war. God help us if what they say is right. Abolitionists, slavers, makes no difference. A plague on them both, I say. What this country needs is compromise, and only the Democratic party can provide it. Trust the Democratic party. It will see us through. We must all learn to live in peace. Understand that and you understand the secret of life.

The secret of life? Well, perhaps James C. Wells was exaggerating, but of course young Charley did not know this. Neither did he know that James C. Wells talked too much. He always listened carefully to his father. He did not see his father as a soft wattled bag of flatulence. He saw his father as knowing what the world was all about. He loved his father very much.

The year of Charley's birth was 1838, and it was an unfortunate year for the birth of a young man. When the War of the Rebellion broke out, he was twentythree, just the ripest age for a soldier. But he did not serve, and he went away from Titusville, and when he returned he was tarred and feathered and banished, and all he ever had done was try to tell people the truth, and so what good was truth? The hell with truth. Forever and ever. World without end.

But it was not truth that Charley first jettisoned. It was courage. Or perhaps the better word is heroism.

Looking back on it from the vantage of his twentyseven clanking years, perched now in this place Paradise Falls, he saw it all as being splendidly absurd, and he almost was able to laugh. Lying next to Nancy these warm nights in the best suite available in the Acterhof House, lying quite still and listening to the clatter of his particular truths, he sometimes felt his memories tug at the corners of his mouth. Ah, boyhood. Ah, the sweet and thank God dead days of Titusville.

Titusville, Indiana, a river town of no particular importance, a spot where gathered dust and giggles and hair and odors and heat, and Charley lurched through his green days, collected many friends, grinned on all of them, bestowed on all of them his loudmouthed affection, and those green days always were too brief.

Charley? said Nancy, sitting up in bed, tucking the pink Acterhof House coverlet under her chin.

Yes?

Remember the time you and those other boys stole Bill's britches?

Yes.

It was a Christmas wasn't it?

Yes.

And cold?

Very cold.

You shouldn't have done that to him, said Nancy. He was my brother, and it hurt him real bad.

I know. I'm sorry.

Really? *You?*

Yes.

He bawled about it. He wanted my papa to go beat on your papa, but of course my papa didn't do any such a thing.

He went to our house. Took Bill with him.

He did?

Yes. But when he got there he sort of backed off.

Sounds like him.

Charley remembered the incident very well. One Christmas Day he and two of his cronies came upon a skinny little boy named Bill Quimby. The little fellow was doing nothing special. He simply was sitting atop a pile of snow. He was sort of scooping at the snow with cupped hands. Little feller, said Charley, if you ain't the sorriest sight I ever seen, I don't know who is. Then Charley and his cronies jumped on Bill Quimby and rubbed snow against his forehead and lips until they bled. Then they rubbed his face back and forth against the earth. Bill Quimby was beyond screaming. He was beyond even wanting to scream. He simply whimpered and drooled. After Charley and his cronies tired of rubbing, they pulled off Bill Quimby's britches. He wore no underdrawers, and his little dingle was all shrunken like a dead worm. Charley and his cronies ran away and tossed the britches high in a tree. I hope he don't freeze that poor little thing! shouted Charley, and his two cronies just laughed like anything. Later that day, little Bill and his father showed up at the Wells home. Rufus Quimby was far and away Titusville's most notorious tosspot and neerdowell. In addition, he was a coward. His breath whistled through the gaps between his teeth. He was very thin. His bones looked to be made of old dry sticks. He had not much of a chin. Scuffling his feet, clearing his throat, he knocked timidly on the Wells front door. He was holding his skinny little son's hand. The afternoon had brought a thaw, and both Rufus Quimby and the boy had tracked mud on the porch. Charley, who had been sitting by a front window, had seen the Quimbys come up the walk. Charley's belly was sour. His father went to the front door and opened it. Charley hid behind a curtain and listened to the conversation between his father and Rufus Quimby.

What do you want, Rufus Quimby? said James C. Wells, his voice loud and annoyed.

A cough. A hesitation. Then, from the tired throat of Rufus Quimby: Well Mr Wells, my boy here, my boy Bill, he tells me your boy Charley gave him kind of a thrashing today . . .

James C. Wells closed the door in Rufus Quimby's face. He went into the parlor.

Charley ran to a front window and watched Rufus Quimby and the boy retreat back down the walk. Then Charley went into the parlor and seated himself on the sofa across the room from his father's chair. James C. Wells sat with his hands folded in his lap. He said nothing to Charley. The Christmastree was in the parlor. It abounded with candles and candycanes and plaster angels. It flickered, and Charley waited for his father to say something, and his father said nothing. A week or so later, Charley had pretty well forgotten the incident. But not altogether. And he never did. Not altogether.

Whenever he recalled that day, the sourness again flooded his belly. It was a special sourness, and it came only with his bad memories. It was perhaps a special *Titusville* sourness, and he had hoped his coming to Paradise Falls would do away with it. But no, the memories still scraped and gouged, and some of his Acterhof House nights were just about more than he could bear. (Paradise Falls. Paradise Falls. Paradise Falls. The clear thing to do was fill his mind with thoughts of this new place. There was a statue that stood atop the courthouse here, and the statue represented Beauty, and its arms were spread wide in womanly supplication, and the statue to him represented optimism, the glories that lay ahead for his greatness, and of course it invited him to erase his past, and of course this he could not do. He was the sum and total of his past, and it was unique, and therefore *he* was unique, and therefore he could not inter it.)

Of all Charley's multitudinous boyhood friends, the closest was a quiet and palely handsome lad named George Peters, an orphan whose parents and little sister Bess had died in a steamboat explosion on the Fourth of July, 1852, when both Charley and George were just fourteen. Altogether, sixtyfour persons were killed in the great disaster. The explosion blew George into the water, and he never talked about it, and Charley never asked him. George went to live with a childless couple named Harris. It was not exactly the worst thing that could have happened to him. Richard T. Harris was just about the richest man in town. He owned the Harris Tanning Co, which had been founded by his grandfather away back in 1808. The tannery employed more than three dozen men, and the Harrises' redbrick home was the finest in Titus County, even finer than the Wells place on the hill. George Peters was exactly eight days younger than Charley. They had run and played together as long as either could remember. George's father had been a magistrate, a man of great dignity and rectitude. People called him The Judge, and Charley's father and other Democratic officials had made several attempts to persuade him to run for higher office. But William Kimball Peters had refused. It just so happens, he told them, that I prefer Titus County to Indianapolis or Washington or any other place on the face of the earth. I thank you for your interest, but I must decline. Charley had often wished his own father were more like William Kimball Peters. For that matter, he had often wished *he himself* were more like *George*. It would be pleasant, he supposed, to be quiet and handsome. It surely would help get the girls, and at fourteen Charley already had a ravenous interest in them. He was especially intrigued by what he liked to call tiddies, most specifically the tiddies of a girl named Nancy Quimby. He decided he loved her. He decided he always would love her. He did not know what to do about this love. All that occurred to him was to snicker and nudge. She was a large girl, soft and pillowed in the bust and hindquarters. The rest of her was nice and girlishly skinny, however. She had high cheekbones, a wide mouth, not much of a chin. Apparently she had inherited the poor chin from her father, Rufus Quimby, the tosspot and neerdowell. Ah, it was some family, the Quimbys. Nancy's mother took in washing and sewing. There was a younger sister, Charlotte, and a younger brother, Bill, the nondescript little victim of Charley's shameful Christmas prank. Lord, Charley wished he could rub the memory of it from his mind. The incident had taken place when Charley had been just eight, but he didn't think that was much of an excuse. What if Nancy remembered it? If she did, surely she never would have anything to do with him. Charley and his parents were Methodist, and sometimes the Rev Mr Chorpening spoke of the Sinner being Re-

visited by his Transgressions, and yessir, the man surely knew whereof
he preached . . .

One day in the spring of 1852 (before George Peters' family was wiped
out in the steamboat explosion), Charley and George went swimming. It
was a warm day, and the boys swam until they had no breath. Then, lying
naked on the riverbank, they got to discussing one thing and another, and
Charley permitted himself all sorts of thick thoughts that concerned themselves with Nancy. But of course he gave them no words. Instead he said:
She don't wear no underwear. I'll wager you my daddy's house and lot
she don't wear a stitch under her dress. I'll tell you something. You know
what I pray for? I pray for a strong wind, that's what I pray for, a strong
wind to come along and whoosh, lift up her skirt so's I can see and get it
straight in my mind once and for all. I mean, if she ain't got nothing
down there, then she ain't going to have nothing over them tiddies neither.
I sure would like to find out.

George Peters nodded, grunted. His eyes were closed, and nothing was
revealed on his face.

Sort of a peculiar one, that George. Sometimes Charley wished he didn't
admire George so damn much. A person never really got any *help* from old
George. If he understood what you were talking about, why didn't he *say*
so? Why did he leave you like you were perched up in a tree? Didn't he
know that a thing wasn't nearly so bad when you knew somebody else
understood how you felt? Most of the time Charley did all the talking for
both of them, and God damn anyway, wasn't fair.

The river was slow and heavy, and the sun was like knives, and so
Charley baked, and no words came from his *friend* George Peters. Charley
grimaced. He listened to the river. He listened to the glassy sounds of
birds. He fell asleep. When he emerged from the sleep, George was gone.

Ah, that was good old George for you. Leave you somewhere naked to
die and a whole lot he cared. Sighing, Charley put on his clothes and
slowly walked home. He mused on Nancy Quimby's tiddies. He picked up a
long stick and trailed it on the earth. He held it loosely. It clicked over
rocks and pebbles. His *friend* George Peters. Some friend. It was like old
George was waiting for a Signal, a sound of trumpets perhaps. Once the
Signal came, George would no doubt move resolutely forward and perform deeds of immense heroism. Ahhh *shit*, there was no understanding
George Peters. Charley shrugged, threw the stick away. He told himself:
Think on Nancy's tiddies. He decided all he could do was lurch through
his days as well as he knew how, and the hell with George Peters. Maybe
some day something would come along to take George down a peg or
two. Until then, Charley had other friends, lots of them.

Friends: oh yes, Charley had had many friends. His youth had by no

means been lonely. People had liked him. It was perhaps the way he
grinned, the width and wet candor of his pale gray eyes, the way he
shrugged and scuffed and laughed at himself . . . surely these qualities
had been helpful to him, and now, here in this village called Paradise
Falls, they still had their uses, and he did not hesitate to employ them.
Most people saw him as a gentle oratorical oaf, and splendid. Hurrah
for appearances.

But of course now there was a difference. In his boyhood, the grinning
gentle oafishness had sprung from him in truth. Now, though, what with
his pursuit of greatness, what with his knowledge that heroism and honor
and love and belief were a lot of tinfoiled lies, the grinning gentle oafishness was about as genuine as a skinny woman with paper bosoms.

One evening in August of 1865, as he took supper with Nancy in the
diningroom of the Acterhof House, he looked up from his chicken purée
and said: Do you think back much on George Peters?

Nancy sighed. You're always asking me that, she said. She dabbed at her
mouth with her napkin, then: I wish you'd stop.

I was thinking back this afternoon on the explosion.

You mean the *Molly G. Edwards?*

Yes.

And it got you to thinking about George?

Yes.

Well, you shouldn't ought to think about him so much. He's dead. You're
not dead.

It's been thirteen years and a month and then some.

Mm, said Nancy.

I used to envy him. Do you know that?

Yes, said Nancy. I know that. But now maybe you don't have to envy
him.

No. I expect not.

It's all done. Dead is dead.

Dead and buried, said Charley.

Yes, said Nancy.

You being honest?

Yes, said Nancy, glaring at her soup, yes, yes, *yes.*

I'm going to be a great man.

I *know* that.

I'm going to win. I've learned a lot.

Yes.

You'll be proud of me.

Yes, Charley, *yes.*

People will remove their hats for me.

Mm, said Nancy, sipping soup.

He's dead, and your husband's dead, and I'm not.

Mm.

Well, don't you forget it.

Nancy looked up. I'm not about to, she said.

It's cost me a whole lot.

Mm.

When that boat blew up, it made George different didn't it?

Yes.

Like a martyr. Something special.

Sort of.

And then, when the storm came and I run off like I did, he was your big *hero* wasn't he?

Charley . . . Charley . . . why do you have to nip at it all the time?

Like a dog with an old bone, chewing and worrying the old bone?

Yes.

Well, that's my way. I don't forget.

It help keep you going?

Yes.

And there, in that particular question, Nancy had scraped against truth. Charley Wells was rigidly the sum and total of his past, and he believed he was much more so than most people. He could cite chapter and verse to illuminate the reasons why he lost his respect for heroism, honor, love, belief. And he figured the day that saw the beginning of it all, and per-haps the beginning of his understanding of greatness, was the day of the explosion, the Fourth of July in the year 1852, a loud and splendid day of band music and picnics and footraces, a day Titusville lay golden and clean in the light of the immense river sun, a day of tumblejumping children, of shrieks and candy and tongues and flags. It was afternoon, and Charley and his parents sat quietly on the front porch of their home on the hill. They watched the excursion boat, the *Molly G. Edwards,* go steaming downstream from the Titusville wharf. Charley had wanted to go on the excursion, and his father had bought tickets, but his mother wasn't feeling well, and at the last minute his father had turned in the tickets. Son, you won't mind staying home with your mother and me just this one day? James C. Wells had said. And Charley, amiable Charley, the gentle oaf, had shrugged. What else was he supposed to do? Tell his father to go to the devil? He could have done no such thing. The man was his *father,* and he loved his father, respected him even, and this despite an emerging awareness that James C. Wells perhaps talked too loudly and often to be really much of a man. Still, the love was there (and it included his mother), and so Charley stayed home and did not complain. They all three of them heard the explosion quite clearly. Charley had just fetched his mother a glass of cold well water. The explosion came just as he was handing the glass to her. He dropped the glass, but it did not break. His father stood up and squinted toward the river. The smoke came from a spot two or three miles downstream. It came from behind a line of trees at the riverbank. Charley ran out back and hitched up the buggy. He and his father rode off to see what had happened. The first thing Charley found at the riverbank was a headless rag doll. Then he found a foot. A woman's foot, judging from its size. Strands of muscle and tissue trailed away from the foot, and all of the foot was bloody, and all of it glistened. Charley's belly contracted, but he managed to keep from throwing up. People ran up and down the riverbank. They yelled and gesticulated. Charley looked out across the water. He saw only water, and the hazy blue of the Kentucky side. He didn't see even a single floating board. There had to be debris somewhere, but he didn't know where. Some of the survivors had made it to the riverbank. He supposed others were over on the Kentucky side. The survivors lay flat. They made few sounds. People squatted next to them. Several corpses lay at the edge of the river. Charley recognized them all. For some reason he picked up the headless rag doll. He hugged it to his chest. He walked to where the corpses lay. He stroked the headless rag doll. He wept. He inspected all the corpses: Sally Lewis, a thin redhaired little girl a grade or two behind him in school; Mrs Bertram W. Marshall, widow of a former Congressman from the district that included Titus County; Jim Wheeler, a carpenter; L. T. Smith, vice president of the Titusville Savings & Trust Bank; Miss Irene Ball, a narrowly constructed young woman of about twenty, pretty in an unfleshed way, daughter of Edward A. Ball, Titus County Clerk of Courts; Lloyd Redpath, operator of the stage line to Evansville and the betrothed of Miss Irene Ball; Mr and Mrs E. Y. Knapp, who had one of the most prosperous farms in the county; Mrs Naomi Redpath, widowed mother of Lloyd Redpath; Zebulon Harrington, hardware merchant; John F. Burt, barber; his wife, Eloise; their sons, Donald, about two, and David, about six months; G. P. Nance, attorney; Calvin H. Horsleigh, eightytwo, who had served under Andrew Jackson at New Orleans in 1814 and earlier this day had been grand marshal of the Titusville Fourth of July parade (he had walked erectly, and the applause for him had been loud and affectionate), and T. T. Riddle, about sixty, a bricklayer. Charley counted the bodies, and the total came to seventeen. He pressed his face against the headless rag doll's torn and muddy belly. Some of the bodies were not whole. Miss Irene Ball had no right foot. He supposed hers was the detached foot he had seen back there where he had picked up the headless rag doll. He had spoken with Miss Irene Ball only yesterday. They had passed the time of

day over on Kentucky Street. My, Miss Irene Ball had said, you are really
becoming quite a *young man*. No time at all and I expect you'll be spoiling all the girls for a faretheewell. And she had smiled, and Charley had
bestowed on her a properly oafish blush. And now she was dead. And
now one of her feet was missing. He coughed. His throat stung. Mrs
Knapp's right arm and leg were gone. Most of little Donald Burt's neck had
been torn away. Calvin H. Horsleigh was without a nose. Blinking, Charley looked around. He had lost track of his father. Papa? he said. Papa? He
found his father kneeling behind a tree. James C. Wells was reciting the
Lord's Prayer. James C. Wells' mouth held too much spit. A puddle of
bile was off to one side. Charley knelt next to his father, helped him with
the words. People still were yelling and gesticulating. Rising, Charley
threw the rag doll out into the river. He wondered how his friend George
Peters had fared. He knew George and the entire Peters family had gone
out on the *Molly G. Edwards*. There was no sign of George, and there was
no sign of George's family. Ah well, perhaps they all were on the Kentucky
side. Charley shuddered. He bumped into a man named Grover, a farmer
whose land adjoined the river here. He didn't have to ask Grover any questions. The words simply came from the man, and they came with warm
breath, and they were hurried, desperate, mad. My God, said Grover,
my God, my God, I mean it happened faster than I can tell it. She blowed
up and then what was left of her capsized neat as you please and it all
was done in less than a minute and the worst was the capsizing. The explosion was a loud sound and all that, but the *capsizing* . . . my God, my
God, my God in Heaven, it was like hogs sucking from a trough, only it
was like all the hogs in the world, and they was farting too, and the people
. . . my God, the poor *people* . . . there was so many of them who got
pulled in by the suction and taken right down to the bottom of the river. I
seen them. I seen the way their arms waved. My God. My God. As he
spoke, Grover seized Charley by the shirtfront, and finally Charley had to
wrench the man's hands loose and lurch away. Enough was enough.
Charley went to a tree. He sat down. He squinted toward the Kentucky
side. He smelled blood, and the blood smell was more than a blood smell:
something charred lay within it, something charred and splintered. Again
Charley shuddered. He hugged himself. His flesh was wintry. It turned
out George had been literally blown out of his shoes and over the side. He
was a good swimmer, though, and he made it to the Kentucky side. Charley did not see him until the next night. He had nothing to say, and
Charley did not press him. More than twenty bodies still were missing.
This total included George's father and mother and little sister Bess. George
insisted on working with the men who went out in small boats and sought
bodies. Charley worked right alongside George, but George said not a

word. (Later, a long time later, George told Charley it all was very dim. *You* were out there with me? said George. I swear I got no recollection of it. Swear to God.) Once, after seeing what he thought was a body, George jumped into the water. It was a body all right, but it was just part of a body. Hips. Hips and legs. No feet. Sex: male. It turned out to be all that was left of a man named Abraham Killpack, who had operated a small furniture store and undertaking establishment. It wasn't until three nights after the explosion that the bodies of George's father and mother and little sister Bess were washed ashore. They came up on the Indiana side of the river, and they had bloated. They had bloated to such a size that their clothing had split. Mrs Peters' face had been bitten by fish. Half her face was gone. She was purple, and her hair was tufted, revealing her scalp, and her mouth was a pinkpurple hole and she had no eyes. George insisted on looking at the bodies. Grover and several other men tried to talk him out of it, but he shook his head from side to side. No, he said (his voice was pale), I want to see them. Don't argue with me. I want to see them. Grover held the lantern for George, and George vomited, and then George wept, and it was the first time he'd wept, and later everyone said it was good he had been able to weep. It was a historic week for the undertakers in that part of the state. The late Abraham Killpack had been Titusville's only undertaker, and so all the undertakers in six neighboring counties (including the four established firms in Evansville) did handsomely by the tragedy. Charley had never seen so many frock coats. There were thirty-seven funerals the afternoon of Thursday, July 8. Coffins were shipped in from as far downriver as Paducah. One Titusville cabinetmaker, a man named Lemuel Summerfield, was so busy he managed only about six hours' sleep in four days. On that Thursday afternoon, July 8, the funeral traffic was so heavy that at one time the town's main street, Titus Avenue, clopped and echoed to the sound of fourteen separate processions. And of course the sound of the horses and the hearses was augmented by wails and lamentations. Charley never forgot that afternoon. It was warm and bright, and it was no day for funerals. He stood leaning against a store-front, and finally he had to weep: the noises of grief were too much for him. Some of the hearse drivers lost their tempers. They shouted foul oaths. Processions became entangled. Bereaved glared at bereaved. Crepe flapped. Coffins bounced and slid. Shuddering, Charley ran home. It was as though the world had come to an end, and he wanted no part of such horror. That night he walked down to the river. He watched a crow strut at the edge of the water. Off to his left, the lights of the town were weak; their re-flection barely brushed at the sky. The lights were orange and yellow, and they appeared to blink and sputter with the easy river wind. Charley seated himself on an old log. He was alone, and he did not like it. He'd never

liked being alone. A person was alone when he died, and that was enough
aloneness. He did not know what had made him come out here. He did
not know why he was sitting on this stupid log. He rubbed his hands together. He looked at his feet. They were bare. He rubbed his left leg with
the heel of his right foot. It made dry scraping sounds. He had wept that
afternoon. He had wept for all those dead people and all those processions. He had wept for the hearse drivers and their foul oaths. He had
wept for the entire wretched spectacle of all those entangled hearses and
buggies and wagons, all those frock coats, all those keening angry mourners. He grimaced. He'd always thought of himself as being hard, a sturdy
fellow who didn't waste time with sentiment. But this afternoon he had
wept, and many of his tears had been for people who'd been practically
strangers to him. He supposed he was nowhere near as hard as he had believed. Maybe this was why he detested being alone. He shrugged,
grunted, scratched the back of an arm. The mosquitoes really were out tonight, and they were magnificent mosquitoes, gorged, healthy, energetic.
Waving an arm, dispersing the mosquitoes at least for the moment, Charley
thought of his old *friend* George Peters. George's father and mother and
little sister had been planted today in the welcoming earth of Mount Zion
Cemetery. The coffins had been sealed. Charley wondered how George
had behaved himself. Had George wept again? Had he displayed an opening? Godalmighty, said Charley to himself, what a thing to be thinking.
Then, shaking his head, Charley tried to force away his thoughts. His forehead was tight. He relaxed it. He took several large breaths. He studied
the river. He listened to the river. All that water, night and day, and God
kept it coming, and who could not believe in Him? Charley shook his
head. No, he told himself, you stop that *thinking.* He looked up. The sky
was broken by stars. The sky still had a trace of gray from the remembered
mournful afternoon. Charley closed his eyes. He saw Nancy Quimby.
God save him but he did. Her and her tiddies. She was naked. Charley
groaned, bent forward a bit, opened his eyes. He listened to his blood. He
stood up, walked to the edge of the water. He squatted there and dampened his hands and wrists and neck. He returned to the log and again sat
down. He decided he might as well think. At least thinking kept his
mind from caressing visions of a naked Nancy, her and her tiddies and all.
Again he studied the river, but this time he did not think about God. He
told himself: Lord, if the fellers I run around with was to know the thinking I do. Well, why not? Ain't nothing wrong with it. Maybe, if I think
real hard *now,* I can use up all my thinking time for oh I don't know
three weeks or so. Then, for all that time, I won't have to bother none
with it. George, him so quiet and all, like he's waiting for a Sign. Well, I
expect he's had him his Sign. And me too. My mother she was sick, only

she wasn't too sick, but she *said* she was too sick, and so we didn't go on
no boatride, and maybe, what with what went and happened, that was *my*
Sign. God forgive me, but better old George than me. Can't help what I
feel. Can't. Can't. Here Charley shook his head. He felt as though a taut
wire had been drawn around his scalp. Again he stood up. Again he
walked to the edge of the water. Better old George than me, he said aloud.
He looked around. He saw nothing. He didn't believe anyone had heard
him. He looked up. The grayness was gone from the sky. Better anyone
than me, he said aloud. Better anyone, anywhere, ever. He trembled. His
face and eyes were hot. He took off his shirt. He dropped his britches,
stepped out of them. He waded into the river. The water was very cold.
He waded until the water became too deep for wading. He began to swim.
He swam slowly, lazily, and he swam for a long time. He swam in circles.
He treaded water. He floated. The river was loud in his ears. He could not
hear his arms and legs as they worked against the river. The wire was
loosened; the pain went out of his scalp. He wished Nancy were with
him. He wished that more than anything. He breathed in gulps, and each
gulp was a gift. Nancy . . . Nancy naked and playful and loving, tiddies
flopping in the water, Nancy splashing him, sniggering with him . . .
yes, he wished that more than anything, ever. (People said he was a big
lurching oaf, maybe even stupid. Lord God, people surely didn't know
much, and that was a fact.) When he came out of the water he didn't
bother with his shirt and britches. He flopped damply next to the log.
Water ran off him in dollops and rivulets. He breathed easily. Better thee,
George, he said aloud, than me. He closed his eyes, ran his hands over his
chest and belly. A breeze came up, and it was not a chilly breeze, and he
told himself it was Nancy's breath. It was a very inoffensive breeze, leafy,
timid. He rubbed his neck, the muscles of his upper arms. Better old
George. Better anyone. Better the world. Living was the largest thing there
was, and bereavement was the next worst thing to not living. Lord, spare
me, said Charley aloud. He grimaced, pinched the bridge of his nose. He
rubbed his closed eyes. They exploded in reds, greens, smears of white.
Naked and playful and loving, tiddies flopping, Nancy came dancing
through the explosions and said: I love you. Please let me kiss you. Charley moaned. He kicked his legs from side to side. Better *anyone*. Oh sweet
gentle Jesus. Charley grunted. He held his breath. He threshed. Nancy
ran and laughed, and the explosions cast lovely wild shadows across her
face, and the shadows made it so he didn't have to see her weak chin.
Better anyone *at all*. (George was an orphan now, and George never would
be the same again, and better George and the world, yes, forever.) Charley
bit his lips. He threshed. His head went from side to side, and his teeth
were exposed, and the back of his head gathered smears of the muddy

river earth. (It had been an advantage, George and his damn silence, his damn Sign. But now where was George's advantage? It was inside those three sealed coffins, which meant it did not exist, which meant the advantage now was Charley's, and praise the Lord. At fourteen, advantages were very important. Boys slid into manhood when they were fourteen. They required advantages. It was no longer enough to play games of toss and speculate on courage and tiddies and ambition.) Charley groaned. Charley shuddered. Charley sighed. The explosions went away. A silence. A bare clean flick of a silence. He opened his mouth. His tongue protruded. He held his breath. Then no more silence. Then no more naked Nancy. He listened to the river. He listened to his breath. He flung an arm across his forehead. Sweat trickled down his belly. He fell asleep. He dreamed of moisture and betrayals, but they did not matter. Better anyone, ever. Better any dreams.

Thus, for Charles Palmer Wells, ended the first part of the first lesson.

There would be a second part to this first lesson, and it would complete the destruction of all value he ever would attach to heroism. Which was, in retrospect, rather amusing. After all, what if not heroism had brought him to this village of Paradise Falls? Granted, it was the heroism of another man, but still, the situation did have its laughable aspects. Those two men, a captain named Light and a lieutenant named Messer, had come all the way to Indiana to tell Nancy how much they revered her late husband. All the way to Indiana. All. That. Distance. Hah! The human race!

In discussing Paradise Falls with Nancy, in dividing its residents into Doers and Talkers, Charley placed the man named Light in the forefront of the Talkers. The fellow's full name was Virgil T. Light, and he owned a furniture store, and he surely was a Talker of the purest ray serene. Charley was quite interested in the man. He figured he would be able to use Virgil T. Light very nicely. He hadn't yet precisely figured out *how*, but he knew he would when the time came. Virgil T. Light was a large bald man with a large bald voice, an invalid wife and a skinny son who was said to be something of a mooner. Virgil T. Light was in his middle thirties, and it was said he wanted among other things to be mayor of Paradise Falls. Now, home from the wars, Light was expanding his store. It was said his wife was dying of consumption, but he never was seen to brood over it. It also was said he was a very shrewd and ambitious businessman. Charley wasn't too sure about that. He detected too much flatulence in Virgil T. Light. Too much talk. Too much strut and preen. Behind his back, Virgil T. Light was called the Warrior, and the drinkers in Claude Dill's saloon sniggered whenever they discussed him. Especially the drinkers who had served with Virgil T. Light in the Paradise Falls

Blues. He'd been only a captain, but from the way he talked and carried on one would have thought he had sat at the right hand of George Gordon Meade. In the summer and fall of this year 1865, he busied himself in three activities: the store, the Republican party and the organization of all Paradise County veterans into a sort of club. Those of us who are veterans have to stick together, he told Charley one day. We were away for a long time, and it seems only fitting and proper that we band together for our mutual profit and benefit. There is, as I'm sure you know, a national movement afoot to bring into one huge group all the veterans of the late War of the Rebellion, and it seems to me most reasonable that we participate in it. Thus, if we are organized ahead of time, we perhaps can assume a position of leadership, at least in state affairs. Perhaps, ah heh, *national* ambitions are beyond our capabilities, but I see no reason why we cannot wield immense influence here in Ohio—*if we are organized, if we know what we are about.*

Naturally, Virgil T. Light wanted to know what Charley had done during the late war. Smiling, Charley tapped his chest and said something about an unfortunate coronary condition. I fear I spent most of the war in Washington, he told Virgil T. Light, where I served as secretary to a Congressman from the state of Illinois. Not a very heroic position, I must admit, but it represented the best I could do under the circumstances. A grave nod came from Virgil T. Light. Yes, he said, of course. And please don't for a moment think I bear you any ill will. And Charley said: Thank you, Mr Light. And Virgil T. Light said: Call me Virge.

Virgil T. Light and Charley became close friends, and many were the hours Charley suppressed yawns while Virgil T. Light delivered discursive monologues on the war and courage and duty and such. And Charley told Virgil T. Light oh yes, every word he said was the absolute gospel. He would not have disagreed with the man for all the whores in Babylon. (Virgil T. Light had a way of rolling his eyes heavenward as he spoke. It was as though he was hoping they would be heard by the Ear of Ears. Charley enjoyed watching the gyrations of Virgil T. Light's eyeballs. Peculiarities always had interested him, especially peculiarities that revealed weakness.)

Still, for all his talk, Virgil T. Light did have one thing to say that made good hard sense. If in every city and town and village veterans' groups are organized, he told Charley, they will be in effect militant arms of the Republican party. Militant and disciplined. Do you understand how this will affect politics? I wouldn't be a bit surprised if the Democratic party were destroyed as a result. Can you imagine! My God, what a blessing! Charley, who had been born a Democrat, whose father had been a Democratic postmaster, who had canvassed for office twice as a Democrat, who had been tarred and feathered and run out of his home town because of his allegiance to that party (*Kill the Copperhead traitor! Lynch the damned assassin!*), who was bound and determined that no one in Paradise Falls ever would learn of his unfortunate politics, smiled, smiled widely, smiled and told Virgil T. Light oh yes indeed, the Democrats surely would have trouble surviving. He was not surprised or ashamed that the smile came so easily. He knew it *had* to come easily. Otherwise, he was not a great man. At one time he had espoused the Democracy with loud and furious zeal. He had been tarred and feathered for speaking his mind. All right then, he would no longer speak his mind. The hell with telling people what he thought. He knew he would have to proclaim himself as a devoted Republican in order to achieve his greatness here in this place that called itself Paradise Falls. This he would do. He'd had enough of tar and feathers; martyrs frightened him; he would not join their lunatic company.

Light will help us, he told Nancy one night in their Acterhof House bed.

Good for him, said Nancy. Let there be Light, I always say.

Charley smiled.

He was in the store today, said Nancy.

Oh?

Yes. It was while you were down at the depot seeing about the canned meat.

Mm. What'd he want?

Coffee. He bought a pound. He couldn't keep his eyes off my bosoms.

Good.

How's that?

Now. Please. I didn't mean anything by it. Anything about you.

You'd *better* not, said Nancy. Grunting, she shifted her weight, leaning on a thigh so that she faced her husband. Then she said: If you think you're going to use me to get *at* him some way . . .

No. No. Farthest thing from my mind.

Then why did you say good?

Because it proves he's no Doer.

Oh?

Yes. There's not a Doer in the world who looks at bosoms when he's buying coffee. He buys the coffee and goes on about his business. He doesn't clutter his mind with thoughts that won't do him any good.

How do you know they won't do him any good?

I know *you*.

Oh.

Yes, said Charley, I know you good. Right?

Right.

Anyway. About Virge Light. He's got to be a Talker. He clutters his mind with thoughts on bosoms.

Well, I like *that*.

What?

My bosoms a clutter to *your* mind?

Charley grinned. I don't need to work them in my mind, he said. Why should I *think* when I can *do*?

Scamp.

Yes ma'm. I expect so.

Charley?

Yes?

You ever get tired?

Not these days.

Sometimes I get tired, Charley. Sometimes I wish I was somewheres picking flowers and bathing my feet in cold water.

Mm.

Somewhere sweet.

Fine. Good for you. Go to sleep.

Little yellow flowers in my hair. Yes. I would like little yellow flowers in my hair, and I wouldn't care if the dew was still on them. Flowers and birds, a sun that smelled like milk and babies—

Sh.

Pretty things, you know?

Yes.

I have pink dresses, but there are prettier things than pink dresses.

Mm.

When I was married to Henry Ferris, we used to talk about quiet things.

Mm.

There's gentle things in life too.

Surely.

Old woman came in the store today. She told me she could remember when Indians lived all around here. Mingoes. She told me she could remember from before there even was a village called Paradise Falls. Just the Morris store was here in those days. A couple of houses and Ike Underwood's grist mill. Nothing else. She told me Harlowe Morris' prices were dear even in those days. She remembers him as being something of a handsome man, full of talk, the way you are now.

Charley opened his eyes. Handsome? he said.

No, said Nancy, chuckling. I meant full of talk.

Charley closed his eyes. Oh, he said. He punched his pillow.

A nice gentle old woman, said Nancy.

Good for her.

Her name is Tayloe. Husband drove the Lancaster stage before the CPV&M came in. You've waited on her. She says she likes you. She says you surely do remind her of the way Harlowe Morris was years ago. Her husband's name was Reeve Tayloe. She gave him eleven children. Eight are dead now. Two live up in Fairfield County, near some town called Basil. The other one, a son, ran off in I think she said 1834. She's never heard from him. She's got a real gray face. She uses a cane. She says she liked to dance. Says she never could hear enough music. Nice gentle old woman. She just about bawled when she talked to me today. I don't know why. Or maybe I do know why. Gentle people. The world steps on them.

Mm.

She remembers when Ike Underwood ran a sawmill up by Egypt, a sawmill and then a hardware store, and he drove all the other hardware store people out of business. She says he's never let a thing stay in his way for long. Says she had a daughter who would have married him at the drop of a hat. Says the daughter was a pretty girl. Susan Tayloe was the girl's name, and she died in '28 of the diphtheria. She was seventeen. A nice old woman. Got hardly a soul now, only the son and the daughter living up by that Basil. She says she doesn't see them from one year to the next. I expect we talked for half an hour. Old people got a lot to say. She dips snuff. Pink hands. Nice old woman.

Mm.

She's known love.

Mm.

Maybe some day we can too.

Mm.

Nancy sighed. Her lips made a gentle sound, loose and moist. She lay back flat. *Good* love, she said. *Honest* love.

Charley did not reply. He could not. Maybe, if he was lucky, she would believe him to be asleep.

Nancy waited.

No words from Charley.

Oh dear God, said Nancy, and it was quite a long time before the heaviness of her breathing announced that she had fallen asleep.

No words from Charley. He barely breathed.

Good love! *Honest* love! What was the matter with her? Why did she have to be so stupid? Why did she refuse to accept the conditions of his greatness? Didn't she understand that all the socalled *good* love had been sucked out of him a long time back? Oh at one time he'd surely known it, this *good* love, but his personal history had cruelly assassinated it, hurling it into the same grave with the heroism he had betrayed. If indeed he'd ever experienced a *good* love, its object had been this Nancy. But then

along had come the day the wind had screamed high, the day the pale
rain had laughed at him, the day a lunatic woman had made him a coward.
It was the day that saw born his greatness, but of course he had no way
of knowing that at the time. It was a day in April of 1853, a day just two
weeks before his fifteenth birthday, and after that day he would hate his
friend George Peters with a ferocity that only Nancy ever would learn.
And there of course was the great unblinking beauty of the hate. Out-
wardly Charley remained the lurching oaf. But within his tattered soul
there was born a delicious little poison tree, and its fruit was juicy, unparalleled, full of sweet vermin. It was a day of grays and greens, damp and
heavy, and from the west came occasional thunderclaps and brief white
sticks of heatlightning. Charley and George walked to school together that
morning. They walked silently. Ever since the day George had lost his
family Charley had tried to find the proper words, but none had been
forthcoming, and George had volunteered none. Most people found it
almost impossible to talk to George. When they did, they just about whispered. It was as though they were fearful of interrupting his concentration on his grief. After stating their business, they moved thinly away.
There were many other Titusville families that were equally bereft, but
for some reason George's bereavement appeared to be more profound.
Perhaps this was because his father had been such an important man, a
magistrate and all. Or perhaps it was because George, being so quiet and
such an apparent lover of secrets and Signals, therefore seemed so much
Deeper than anyone else. When people spoke with George, they not only
just about whispered; they rubbed their hands together; their arms made
vague flapping movements; their pity and their awe sat on their faces in
lumps, like a cluster of warts. That particular April morning, as Charley
and George walked together, the only sounds they made were caused by
their breath. It had been nine months since the sinking of the *Molly G.
Edwards,* but time had created no words—or at least none Charley could
find. (He had found out all there was to know about the funeral of
George's parents and little sister Bess. He now knew, for instance, that
George had wet his pants at the cemetery. And he now knew that George
had, for some peculiar reason, *embraced* none other than *Mr Pearsall,* a
drunken old man who dug graves at Mount Zion Cemetery. *Mr Pearsall,* of all people! An utter stranger and—next to Nancy's father, Rufus
Quimby—the most thoroughgoing noaccount in all Titus County. It made
no sense. It baffled. It vexed. Why a stranger? And why especially *that*
stranger? Good God, craziness. Grief. Yes, yes, yes, better George than
Charley. Better anyone.) Charley glanced from time to time at his *friend,*
but nothing was revealed. The two boys walked slowly. They had no
reason to be in a hurry to get to school. Their teacher, a Mrs Weatherly,

was a mean old rip. Thirty years before, her husband had run off with a barge captain's daughter. As a result of this betrayal, Mrs Weatherly had weaned for herself a new life of outrage and sour distrust, questioning everything, relying on no one, living alone and timeless like a monument in a small clapboard house filled with gewgaws and cats and cutglass and rancor, a small clapboard house where no one was welcome (no *human being*, that is; *cats* were always welcome; she called them her *babies*; she liked to kiss them; there were those who said she also liked to witness their desperate furry couplings). In short, Mrs Weatherly was seen as a true eccentric, but of course her personal habits did not keep her from teaching school. There was just one school in Titusville, and it had just three classrooms, and only eight grades of education were provided, and thus it was not particularly necessary for a teacher to be of a particularly high caliber. If the teacher kept discipline, that was just about enough. And Mrs Weatherly surely did keep discipline. For thirty years she had kept superb discipline. People said she should have been a man. They said she would have been a truly splendid muleskinner or jailer or army sergeant. She was small and gray, all knots and sinews. When she was angry, her glare was enough to grind away rocks and brick. That April morning she was in excellent form. Perhaps it was the sky. Perhaps it was the heatlightning. At any rate, whatever had caused it, her voice was particularly shrill that morning, and she went through the lessons with a sort of gray frenzy (a thing of blinkings, of an urgent handkerchief constantly rubbing her mouth) that made a number of the children draw back and look at her with narrow apprehension. Then, at about 10 o'clock, after giving the class a quantity of sums to do, Mrs Weatherly scuttled out of the room, presumably to go outdoors to the privy. As soon as she was gone, the mischief began. Charley sat directly behind Nancy. Laughing, he went to work on her hair, tugging it, pulling back her head. He blew into one of her ears. He was the oaf. It was expected of him. He blew into one of her ears, and she shrieked, and so did just about everyone else—not including George, of course, who simply stared out a window. Nancy shrieked, and then she giggled. She had no temper, absolutely none at all. Tugging, Charley leaned forward. He could smell her hair. What he really wanted to do was kiss it. What he really wanted to do was stroke it with soft and gentlemanly hands. But he was the oaf, and an oaf had to be consistent, and so he began making allusions to her underwear (or lack of underwear). Tugging, he said: Come on. Tell me. Nancy's head was on Charley's desk and she still was laughing. Tell you what? she wanted to know. Charley lowered his face over hers. He could smell her breath. It was like grass and flesh. You know what, he said, whispering, but whispering loudly enough so everyone could hear.

And, not angrily, Nancy said: You ought to stop asking me that. Now you let me go. And Charley said: I'll stop asking it. And Nancy said: You will? And Charley said: Sure. When you give me the answer. And Nancy said: *You.* And Charley said: I got to know. And Nancy said: It's a nasty thing to ask. And Charley said: You don't seem so het up. And Nancy said: *Charley Wells!* And Charley said: Just say yes or no, that's all. Nancy never had a chance to answer. Mrs Weatherly reentered the room just at that moment. Quickly Charley released Nancy's hair. She giggled. Mrs Weatherly glared at her. Charley looked out a window. He hoped his face was properly innocent. He supposed the old rip was about to give him the devil. But Mrs Weatherly surprised him. She did nothing. She frowned, shook her head vaguely, said nothing. Charley saw that the sky was turning purple. Sure was a peculiar color. He couldn't remember ever having seen it quite that color before. He looked at Mrs Weatherly. She kept glancing out the window. She called for recitation of the sums. She had Charley do 27 and 14 and 32 and 12 and 9. Charley stood up. Ninetyfour, he said. Mrs Weatherly nodded. Charley sat down. He always had been good at arithmetic. Nancy glanced back at him and winked. He made a small dry sound with his tongue against his teeth. Now the purple sky was streaked with yellows and pinks. Mrs Weatherly sat down. She called on several more pupils to do sums, and then she seemed to lose interest. She simply sat there. She said nothing. She sat very straight, and she did not seem to be breathing, and the gray in her face was like the ashes from an old fire. Charley was cold. A wind was rising. It rattled the windows. He looked back toward his old *friend* George Peters. Dampness lay across George's forehead. Now some of the children were whispering. Mrs Weatherly paid them no mind. She sat rigidly. Her teeth were exposed. Her lips were curled back. She put Charley in mind of a dog, an angry old dog with a shredded coat, an angry old dog that had flopped too long in the dust and the hot sun. Some of the children stood up and stared out the window. Charley's belly felt warm, and his breath came in grunts. A girl began to cry. Mrs Weatherly stood up. She went to the window. She leaned forward, stared out. Her hands were clasped behind her back. They twitched. They rubbed. She tugged at her narrow gold weddingband. Charley watched her. Everyone watched her. Even George Peters watched her. Another girl began to cry. The children were whispering. The whispers and the weepings blended into a sort of keen. Mrs Weatherly turned away from the window. There's going to be a storm, she said, not loudly. I think it will be a bad one. You're dismissed. I want all of you to go straight home. Straight home. Right. Away. Now. Her voice seemed squeezed. Now the wind whooped. Leaves and twigs and branches slapped

against the side of the schoolhouse. A branch broke one of the windows,
scattering glass. Rain came in. Screaming, the children made for the door.
The peculiar purple light had darkened their faces. Some light. A light
that darkened. The rain came horizontally. Papers swirled. Slates fell,
crashed, splintered. The children shoved. A girl was stepped on. She
shrieked. Mrs Weatherly made her way to her desk. Her hands still were
clasped behind her back. Her eyes were wet, and she was whispering to
herself. Everyone was shouting. Everyone except Mrs Weatherly and
maybe George Peters. Even Charley was shouting, but he was not shouting words. He simply was shouting. His chest was full, but he was not
afraid. And by damn if he didn't have a stiff pecker. All this terror, all
this shouting and shoving, and by damn it was stiff as a railroad spike.
He just about wanted to laugh. He looked around. Where was Nancy?
He wanted Nancy. Ah Lord didn't he *ever*. Another girl was stepped on.
She roared. Now the children were one enormous screaming squirm.
Charley pushed, and he hoped his pecker didn't stab anyone to death.
A small tree came through a side of the building. Mrs Weatherly was
showered with glass. She fell down. Some of the children had forced their
way out of the building. There was no sign of Charley's old *friend*
George. Charley laughed. He was drenched, and he smelled of earth and
leaves, and then he saw Nancy crouched behind a desk. He pulled back
from the mob at the door. He went to Nancy, bent over her, held out
a hand. Her hair had fallen over her face. She pushed back her hair.
The wind caught at her hair, sucked it horizontally, drawing it back
from her ears. Her ears were quite pink. He wanted to lick them. She
blinked at him. He pulled her to her feet. He put an arm around her,
braced her against the wind. By this time most of the children had forced
their way through the doorway. One of the fallen girls still lay on the
floor. Her name was Janie Kelso, and she had no tiddies at all. None whatever. She rolled on the floor. Her face was plastered with wet leaves. She
got to her hands and knees and crawled out the door. Charley pulled
Nancy toward the door. She was grimacing. The schoolhouse groaned.
Mrs Weatherly still lay on the floor. Charley did not bother with her.
He pulled Nancy out the door. The air was white and horizontal. Nancy
wrenched free of Charley's arm. She began to run. She skidded and
sloshed across mud and grass. She flailed. She vaulted fallen branches.
Charley took after her. He shouted. He laughed. He fell. His
pecker throbbed. He shook his head. The odor was so damp he had to
sneeze. He felt himself, and by damn he could have pounded a nail with
it. He laughed more loudly. The wind made wrenching splintered sounds.
He got to his feet and resumed the pursuit of his Nancy. He had a gift
for her. Yes. He tasted his breath. It was sweet with a flavor of earth. He

ran. He ran and ran. His arms churned, and his fingers curled around slices of the lunatic wind. Nancy was not far in front of him. She bounced as she ran. She bounced and she flopped. Charley laughed until he cried. His face was peppered by flying sticks and hunks of earth. He did not concern himself with them. He kept his eyes on Nancy's skirt. It was thoroughly soaked, and he was able to see every movement of her rump. He laughed, and by damn the thing was so stiff it could have dug a hole to China. A tree came up out of the earth. It flew over Charley's head. It was a large tree. It was a very large tree. Its leaves whispered and spat. When Charley caught Nancy he began shouting to her about her under-wear. The wind knocked both of them down. They rolled in mud in the middle of a road. Nancy giggled and shrieked. Charley tugged at her skirt. He thrashed. So did Nancy. He kicked. So did Nancy. Then Nancy's skirt began to rip. And, still giggling, she began to shout: Ou ou ou ou now *stop* ou ou for heaven's sake! But Charley wasn't about to stop. Not *now*. Stiff as he was, he couldn't have, not even if the sheriff had come along with a pistol. And besides, the world was coming to an end. What difference did anything make? He figured he just had to know about her underwear. At least that way he would die happy. A dog ran past. It was old Bill Rossiter's collie, Tyrus. Bill Rossiter had a farm at the north edge of town, and on that farm was perhaps the finest peach orchard in all Titus County. Charley moistened his lips. Damn but what he was tasting peaches. Tyrus ran in a sideways lurch. Tyrus was howling. The sight of Tyrus made Charley laugh and laugh and laugh. Nancy also laughed. Tyrus skidded smackdab into a deep pool of mud. He sank. Only his snout could be seen. Yipping, Tyrus emerged from the pool of mud. He had been a brown and white dog. Now he was a black dog. He ran off. Charley laughed. Nancy laughed. Charley kissed Nancy's eyes. He licked them. His hands dug at her magnificent tiddies. She clucked, shrieked. Her breath came hotly. He pressed himself against her. She fell back. He moved on top of her, and his big old ramrod was pressed against one of her thighs. Her eyes enlarged. Then someone kicked Charley across the neck. He whooped. So did Nancy. He rolled himself off her and sat up. Nancy also sat up. The rain came straight into their faces. Mrs Weatherly kicked Charley's chest. Hollering, he fell back. Mrs Weatherly's dress was dark blue from the rain. She kicked Nancy's chest. Hugging her breasts, Nancy also fell back. The wind did not bend Mrs Weatherly. Her mouth had no lips. Apparently she was concentrating on something. Apparently she was trying to remember some-thing. Then, abruptly, she relaxed. She bent a little. She clucked. She kicked Charley and Nancy several more times. *Did you think I was stupid?* she shouted. The shout was louder than the storm. Nancy and Charley embraced. *Did you?* shouted Mrs Weatherly. She pointed toward the sky, toward the trees that were bent from the wind. *This is my doing!* she shouted. *My doing! Nobody will survive this!* She leaned closer to Charley and Nancy. My dear, she said to Nancy (her voice softer, but still loud enough to carry over the sound of the storm), I know you are not to blame. A woman never is. And anyway, what with your father being a barge captain I expect you haven't been too intelligently reared. I am sorry for you. Then Mrs Weatherly turned to Charley. She kicked him in the stomach. He mewled. Nelson, said Mrs Weatherly, you are an animal. I have been a good wife to you. There is no excuse for this, and if you think for one minute that I'm not going to punish you, and punish everyone else for that matter, then you are very much and very sadly in error. There's no sense staring at me like that. I have planned this. No, I am not mad. You must think I am mad, but I am not. I have known all about this. I saw It. Yes. It. It was like a Hand. I saw It in the sky. I had been waiting for It. Then I went outside and there It was. You shouldn't have done this. I am not perfect, but then who is? I always say that the punishment should fit the crime. Nelson. Nelson. Nelson. You don't love her. You only think you do. I've always had to keep an eye on you haven't I? You have a penchant for error. Mrs Weatherly suddenly kicked Charley again. He didn't understand what was happening. He didn't understand it one bit. He cringed. He wrapped his arms around his head. Mrs Weatherly seized him by the neck and pulled him to his feet. Her hand was all tight bones. The wind sucked Charley's hair. His britches flapped. He was no longer stiff. His arms still were wrapped around his head. He was bent forward. He faced the wind. Mrs Weatherly propped him against it. His ears pounded. He was no longer stiff at all. It had curled back, drawing into itself like a wary turtle. Leaves and twigs slapped at him. Everything roared. Again Mrs Weatherly spoke to Nancy, and again Mrs Weatherly's voice carried over the sound of the storm. My dear, said Mrs Weatherly, I don't hold you responsible. I really don't. I know my man too well to hold you responsible. I know the effect he has on young girls. Then Mrs Weatherly grabbed one of Charley's elbows. His arms came away from his head. She pushed him. He stared whitely, blinking. His britches were torn. He used his free hand to wipe water from his face. He wiped and he wiped and a lot of good it did. Again Mrs Weatherly pushed him. He looked at Nancy and he tried to smile. Nancy frowned, spread her hands. Now Nancy was sitting up, and all Charley had to do was tear himself loose from this insane old woman. Yes. Yes indeed. It was all he had to do, and he might as well have tried to walk on the waters of the great Atlantic Ocean. He was twice Mrs Weatherly's size, and a lot of good *that* did too. He felt as though something was sucking the bones out of his ears. He knew nothing of madness. He leaned into the great white rainswept wind. He might as well have been a board. Mrs Weatherly pushed him. She dragged him. She clucked. Her eyes were large, whiter than the rain. Charley's knees and elbows were loose. They rattled, clicked. Mrs Weatherly was pulling and pushing him back toward the school. Her home was half a mile or so the other side of the school. He supposed she was escorting him to her home. *Charley!* shouted Nancy, her voice stringy and weak in the wind. He did not look back. Neither did Mrs Weatherly. Usually Mrs Weatherly kept her hair in a bun. But the storm had caused it to come undone. It flapped and streamed. Charley groaned. His teeth hurt. He pushed at Mrs Weatherly. She staggered back. He let out a wail. He turned and ran back toward Nancy. He glanced over a shoulder, and Mrs Weatherly was simply standing there, arms outstretched, shouting something gray and soundless, making no attempt to pursue him, but still he ran. Nancy was standing. She was bent forward and she was trembling and her hands were cupped over her crotch. Her skirt had blown away. By damn by damn by damn if it hadn't. He ran straight toward Nancy. Arms churning, he lowered his head. His face stung. He ran splashing and skidding, kicking up immense spatters of mud and water. He ran squarely down the middle of the road. He did not look at Nancy. He looked in no direction except down. By damn by damn by damn her skirt had blown away, and he had seen her hands pale across her crotch. He ran toward her. He ran right on past her. She had to step aside in order to keep from being knocked down. He ran. The oaf ran. Charley Wells ran. Charles Palmer Wells ran. He ran. He ran. He ran. He ran groaning. By damn by damn by damn trees swayed and ripped, the sky spat and pounded, and by damn by damn by damn the oaf, this Charley Wells, this Charles Palmer Wells, was a coward. By damn by damn by damn he was a pig, helpless in the face of madness. He deserved nothing. He never would deserve anything. Nancy's sweat was too good for him, the dirt off her feet. He ran squarely down the middle of the road. He ran. He ran. He ran. By damn by damn by damn how he did run. The storm rapped and tore and blasted and wrenched, and on ran this great enormous shambling oaf, on and on ran this clamorous stinking pile of human sheep dip. And of course it was his *friend* George Peters who found Nancy later that day. And of course Nancy still was without a skirt. And of course she became George Peters' sweetheart. Which meant that George Peters had been a great fucking *hero*.

Thus, for Charles Palmer Wells, ended the second and final part of the first lesson.

In the face of that madness, it had been better anyone, even Nancy.

And so, at fourteen, Charles Palmer Wells buried heroism. In rock.
Forever.

Why, he asked himself, try to be something that is beyond me?

So he buried it. Scrape. Thud. Thump. RIP.

Hell with it.

He had loved Nancy, but his terror had devoured his love. (Better anyone. Better the world. Better anything other than Charles Palmer Wells.)

But ah what an amusing place the world was! George Peters the *hero*
now was dead. And Nancy's first husband, a man named Ferris, also
a *hero,* also was dead. And it was because of the heroism of this Ferris
that Charley had been brought to the proper arena (this village called
Paradise Falls) for the flowering of his greatness. He and Nancy had come
to Paradise Falls by *invitation*. Because of Christian gratitude. A tribute
to a hero. (The veterans of the Paradise Falls Blues even had, to a man,
signed a goddamn *scroll* testifying to the heroism of the splendid Ferris.
The scroll had been presented to Nancy by Light and Messer. They had
traveled all the way to her Indiana farm to deliver it. Charley had been
lying in bed in the back room. Charley who had been at that time by no
manner or means her husband. Oh gentle Jesus, a *scroll!*)

When Charley and Nancy came to Paradise Falls, they did not make a
point of looking up either Virgil T. Light or the other fellow, the younger
one, the one whose name was Messer. There was no reason to seek out
those men. Paradise Falls was only a village. The news would get around.
Either Light or Messer would see Nancy on the street. As soon as that
happened, Charley would proceed. He did not have to wait long. He and
Nancy encountered Virgil T. Light on Main Street the morning after
their arrival on the CPV&M steam cars. They were taking a leisurely
promenade in the direction of the courthouse. Charley was admiring the
Guglielmo Rossi representation of Beauty. Mighty fancy for a little town,
he said. Sort of ambitious, too. As though maybe this town has got aspirations. Well, good for aspirations, I say. I tell you, Nancy, I'm just the
sort of man to fit in real good in a place that thinks a lot of itself. It's
something I can work on, yes ma'm. We're going to do just fine. No doubt
about it. (Nancy smiled at him. She wore a billowy pink dress. It crackled.
She carried a parasol. She walked erectly. Her bosoms were a glory.)
They encountered Virgil T. Light in front of the courthouse. He came
running up to Nancy, and he was grinning, and his eyes reached for
her glorious bosoms, and he said: Uh, my Lord, it's Mrs Henry Ferris
isn't it?

Nancy squeezed Charley's elbow. She matched Virgil T. Light's grin
and then she said: Yes. Or at least I was. Now I'm Mrs Charles P. Wells,
and this gentleman here is my husband.

Hands were seized.

Virgil T. Light's face was red. It was a warm morning, but it was not that warm a morning. Pumping Charley's hand, he allowed as how this all surely was a surprise. He insisted Charley and Nancy accompany him into the courthouse. He wanted them to meet a friend, a man named Lester W. Bowles, the Paradise County sheriff and a signator of the fabled Ferris scroll. Old Les was wounded at Gettysburg, said Virgil T. Light. Got it in the leg. He was invalided out, came home, ran for sheriff last year, got himself elected. A fine fellow. He'll be very pleased to meet the widow of Henry Ferris—and, uh, you too, Mr Bell.

Wells, said Charley, smiling.

Virgil T. Light apologized. Charley told him no apology was necessary. Virgil T. Light escorted Charley and Nancy into the courthouse. Again he apologized. Charley wanted to tell him he apologized too much, but the devil with it. And anyway, a man who apologized too much was a man who could be manipulated. Charley and Nancy were introduced to Sheriff Lester W. Bowles and several other leaders of Paradise County's allpowerful Republican Party. The men clacked and fussed over Nancy, and she grinned at them and swung her bosoms to and fro, hither and yon, &c, &c, and Charley quietly stood off to one side, and he figured Nancy would be a very large help to him indeed.

The following evening Charley and Nancy took supper with Virgil T. Light and Mrs Light and their son Bill. The Virgil T. Light residence was a splendid place, with high ceilings, cool hallways, dark and heavy furniture. Virgil T. Light's wife, who must have been a beauty in her day, apparently was dying of what appeared to be consumption. The meal was prepared by the Lights' housekeeper, an elderly woman named Pett. Young Bill Light had very large eyes. They were drawn again and again to Nancy's chest. Charley very much wanted to laugh, but of course this was neither the time nor the place. What needed to be accomplished this night was the mendacity. He had to begin to spread the lies about himself, his background, his politics, his marriage . . .

You see, said Charley, smiling toward his plenteous bride, Nancy here and I are in need of new beginnings, so to speak.

New beginnings, Mr Wells? said Catherine Anne Light. She cleared her throat, coughed into a handkerchief. I beg your pardon, she said. I have not been well.

Charley jabbed at his roast beef. Ah, he said, I am sorry.

Thank you, said Catherine Anne Light. Please continue.

Charley nodded. Thank *you*, he said. Wellnow, about those new beginnings. Nancy and I both hail from a little Indiana town called Titusville. It's about thirty miles or so up the Ohio River from Evansville. We

of course have a love of our little town, but we cannot honestly say that
Titusville is the sort of place to provide much of a future. I fear it has
grown as much as it ever will grow. It is a stop for riverboats, and it is the
site of a rather substantial tannery, but it has little else to offer. And I'll
tell you the truth—not to be indelicate about it, but the odor of hides
always has turned my stomach. I fear I do not have the, uh, olfactory
stamina for the work.

Catherine Anne Light smiled. Did you say olfactory stamina? She
wanted to know.

Yes, said Charley.

Ah, a fine turn of phrase. You apparently have a way with words.
Thank you.

You're quite welcome, I'm sure.

Charley smiled. He hoped this damn woman wouldn't be long in dying.
He smiled. He smiled gently. He nodded to Catherine Anne Light. Then
he continued: Well, at any rate, I felt that my future did not lie in Titusville. But a man just does not simply pack up and go wandering off. He
needs *prospects*, some *goal*. And of course this is where Paradise Falls enters
the picture. Nancy was invited here by your husband, ma'm, and Mr
Messer. Or, if not precisely *invited*, she was told that this village always
would welcome her.

That's right, Catherine Anne, said Light to his wife. That's what we
told her.

Catherine Anne Light nodded.

Charley pushed on: A few months ago I journeyed from Titusville to
see Nancy on her farm near Evansville. I have loved Nancy for a great
many years. I courted her some time ago, but I lost out to Mr Ferris . . .
a blow from which, incidentally, I was a long time recovering. But then
Mr Ferris (a man for whom by the way I had the most profound respect
and admiration) was killed in the late war. So this past spring I called
on Nancy. I was, to be frank, determined to resume my campaign. I have
always been something of a stubborn one. Eh, Nancy? Isn't that so?

Oh yes, said Nancy, spearing a number of peas.

Good old Charley Wells may not amount to much, but he does not
easily shut himself of love. Isn't that right, my dear?

Oh yes.

Charley grinned at Virgil T. Light. He chewed, swallowed, then: Mr
Light, you and Mr Messer called on Nancy after my arrival in Evansville.
The night after your visit she showed me the scroll. She told me the
things you and Mr Messer had said. She was—and I do not believe it is
anything she need be ashamed of—near tears. As I say, and as I am sure
you know better than I ever could, her late husband Henry Ferris was a

fine man. She was touched by your scroll and the splendid gesture that lay behind it. She was deeply and genuinely *moved*. We read the names on that scroll and I said to her: Nancy, how often in this life is such generous sentiment encountered? I said to her: Nancy my darling, it would be good to live among such people. There is nothing to keep us here. Not any more. From what you've told me of your two visitors, they are decent and honorable men. I said to her: Marry me, Nancy. Let us together discover new beginnings.

Yes, said Nancy, that's what he said.

Charley chuckled. He blinked at Virgil T. Light. He said: And she did me the greatest honor a man could hope for. She consented to marry me. And here we are. And we are here quite honestly in a spirit of *love*. We are young. We face the future with confidence. Henry Ferris, a stranger from Indiana, had—by indirection—a great respect for this place. His letters reveal that. Nancy has shown me some of them. They reveal the love he felt for his comrades, the men of the Paradise Falls Blues. He was a good judge of people, sir.

Yes, said Nancy. He was a fine man.

Charley worked his face into what he hoped was an expression of humble sincerity. It consisted mostly of a narrowing of his eyes and a firming of his lips. Speaking to Virgil T. Light, he said: We seek no charity, sir. We ask no special consideration. All we desire is to become members of your fine community—one that, from the superficial look we have had in the past two days, apparently has a large destiny.

Oh? said Catherine Anne Light. Is that so?

Yes. Timber, agriculture, clay products, the manufacture of shoes and chairs—we have noted all these activities, and it seems to me that a young man of at least moderate abilities should be able to do very well here. I have had experience in storekeeping (my father was a grocer back in Titusville), and between us Nancy and I have adequate funds for at least a beginning, and so, well, what else is there to say? God willing, we shall remain here the rest of our lives.

Mm, said Catherine Anne Light, and then she began to cough.

The table was silent.

After a time Catherine Anne Light worked her way out of her coughing. I *am* sorry, she finally said, wiping her mouth.

The boy's eyes had not strayed from Nancy's chest. Inadvertently he made a popping noise with his lips.

Everyone looked at him.

He blushed.

Charley covered his mouth and gently coughed.

Nancy was quite pale.

Charley understood everything that was happening, and that was a fact, and he felt no resentment. At least not because of the *boy*. This woman was quite another matter. Perhaps, if he was lucky, she wouldn't last much longer. He smiled at her. She returned the smile.

Later that night, back in their suite in the Acterhof House, Nancy got to sniggering. She was easing herself out of her corset. Her body was pale and soft. She sniggered and sniggered, and then she gasped.

What's the matter? said Charley.

Noth . . . nothing . . .

Then why the laughing?

Ah Charley Charley . . . what a one for *talk* you are . . .

Guilty as charged.

That Light took in every word you said. Just like it was Gospel. And so did his son.

But not his wife, said Charley.

She doesn't matter.

Oh?

She's dying. And anyway, she'd never be enough of a person, sick *or* healthy, to get in *your* way.

Well, thank you. I'm taking that as a compliment.

I figured you would.

Charley visited Light's Furniture Store the next morning. He took along the scroll. He carried it very carefully. It was wrapped in muslin. He wanted the world to know how dearly he valued it. Virgil T. Light greeted him with a large bald smile. The boy Bill was there too, but he could not quite negotiate a smile. Charley asked Virgil T. Light if there were someone available to make a frame for the scroll. This is just about our most cherished possession, said Charley, and we want to ensure its proper preservation. Light nodded. Do it myself, he said. Be pleased to— and at no cost. Charley thanked the man. Ahh, said Light, think nothing of it. We try to be friendly here in this little village of ours. Said Charley: Yes. I can see that. Said Light: I'm not a bad cabinetmaker, you know. Said Charley: That so? Said Light: Yes indeed. I've been one just about all my life, and so was my daddy before me. Look around the store. Some of the merchandise has been Shipped In, of course, but not all of it. Before the war I did a lot of hand work. Look here at this drop table. It's my work. Made it in '58 if my memory serves me correctly. Note the finish. I'm quite proud of this drop table. It doesn't bother me a speck that no one's bought it yet. As long as no one buys it, I get to look at it every day. This may sound foolish, but I thought about this table a great deal while I was away in the army. I believe it was good that I did. A man requires sentiment, isn't that so? This table is a creature of my hands and skill, and I was touched whenever I thought about it. The price was fifty dollars the day I completed working on it, and the price still is fifty dollars, and that's too dear for most of the people in Paradise Falls, but I don't care too much. It is my humble effort to create beauty, and I do not believe it should be sold cheaply. Do you follow my reasoning? Yes? Good. When I finally do sell this table, I figure it'll be to someone who appreciates good things and doesn't mind paying something extra for the beauty. Said Charley: Yes. I understand. Said Light: The Shipped In merchandise is cheaper. Of course it is cheaper. But where's the workmanship I ask you? Where's the pride? Said Charley: You have a point. Then, scratching his chin, Charley examined the drop table more closely. He rapped it with his knuckles. He said: Fifty dollars? Said Light: Yes. Said Charley: Well, I just happen to have fifty dollars. Suppose I buy it. You can keep it here until Nancy and I find a proper home for ourselves—and it. Does that strike you as being a fair offer? Said Light (grinning): It surely *does*. Said Charley: Good. Said Light: I have a feeling you and I are going to get along very well. Said Charley: So do I.

Light delivered the framed scroll the next day. He and Charley repaired to the Acterhof House tap room. Charley bought the drinks. It was then that Light asked Charley what he had done during the war. Charley's answer was not completely a lie. He *had* been employed as secretary to an Illinois Congressman. He did not, however, suffer from any sort of coronary condition. He said he was a Republican (a lie). He said he was Episcopalian (a lie; he had been born and reared a Methodist). He exchanged mildly ribald jests with Light. They laughed. They nudged. They spluttered. They became rather tipsy. Charley finally had to escort Light to his home. The elderly Mrs Pett met them at the front door. The boy Bill came running from somewhere in the rear of the house. Mrs Pett and the boy helped Charley steer Light into the parlor. He flopped on the sofa. He was murmuring brave old songs of war. Mrs Pett told Charley Mrs Light was asleep upstairs. Mrs Pett thanked Charley for bringing Light home. Light looked up from the sofa. He moistened his lips. Then he spoke, and he spoke very deliberately, and he said: You're a good man, Charley Wells. A good old fellow with a big heart. A fine fellow to be coming here to live . . .

All the way back to the Acterhof House Charley whistled and snapped his fingers.

The next few days, Charley and Nancy were visited by a number of the village's most prominent citizens. They told Charley he surely was held in the highest regard by old Virge Light. Charley smiled. I am flattered, he said. He had Nancy serve drinks to his distinguished visitors. She wore billowy dresses that had radical décolletage. The visitors con-

ducted an impromptu competition in hyperbole. Their compliments were
florid and heroic, and from time to time she managed to blush. Most of
the visitors, even the older men, perspired. Some paid a great deal of
attention to clearing their throats. Their eyes, however, seldom strayed
for long from her décolletage. The visitors included Sheriff Bowles; Mayor
Pillsbury; the Honorable Philetas K. Swallow, judge of the Court of Common Pleas; D. Ferguson Strawn, feed & grain merchant; J. K. Bankson,
editor of the Paradise Falls *Democrat,* and even the Rev Edwin P. Rathbun, rector of Grace Episcopal Church. This man had heard from Virgil
T. Light that Charley (and Nancy too, presumably) embraced the Episcopal faith. Speaking softly, shyly, the Rev Mr Rathbun assured Charley
and Nancy that he would do everything he could to make them welcome
at Grace Church. Nancy smiled at the Rev Mr Rathbun, told him this
Paradise Falls surely was a *hospitable* place, goodness yes.

Most of the time, when she was alone with Charley, Nancy had the
good sense to laugh at their new friends' behavior. But not all of the time.
Sometimes she became quite solemn. She said to him: Charley, it doesn't
seem fair.

What doesn't seem fair?

The way we've been lying to them.

Ah, Nancy, it's not wise to try to interfere with the way of the world.

The way of *what* world? *This* world?

If by *this* world you mean Paradise Falls, yes. Don't be fooled by it.

No. I don't believe you. This is a sweet place. I wish I went for more
walks. The trees. The shade. People smile at me. They compliment me.

The Underwoods don't smile at you. They don't compliment you.

Well, that's because we're threatening their friend. After all, Harlowe
Morris *is* her uncle.

Nancy, I want to tell you something.

Go ahead.

I want you to understand the nature of lies. I want you to understand
that people *expect* lies. Suppose everyone told the truth, and nothing
but the truth, all the time. We'd all turn into lunatics. The truth, Nancy,
can be very ugly.

That's a terrible way to think.

No. It's the only proper way to think.

Nancy shrugged. All right, she said. All right. Let's don't fuss about it.

That's a good idea, said Charley, grinning. Why don't you take off
your dress? *I* don't feel like fussing at *all.*

Fresh.

Mm.

Charley's unsuccessful application for the loan from Isaac (Ike) Underwood's Paradise Falls State Bank came as no particular surprise. Ike Underwood was just about the only Paradise Falls dignitary who did not call on Charley and Nancy at the Acterhof House. Still, it was good that Charley had confronted the man. Now he knew that Ike Underwood was a person to be avoided whenever possible. When he called on Ike Underwood, he was prepared for the worst. And the worst was precisely what he experienced. Ike Underwood was a fat man, but mean fat, not soft fat. He chewed tobacco. When Charley entered Ike Underwood's office, the old bastard neither stood up nor offered to shake hands. Charley was smiling, and he continued to smile, but he knew damn well his smile was useless. He seated himself on the edge of a hard chair, and Ike Underwood didn't waste much time telling him no.

A large blot of tobacco sat fatly in Ike Underwood's right cheek. A spittoon was on the floor at a corner of his rolltop desk. The legs and sides of the desk were streaked in brown. All four legs. Three of the four sides. Apparently Ike Underwood had tried a number of different locations for the spittoon, and obviously none of the experiments had been particularly successful. Shuffling papers on his desk (it was littered with a wild crackling profusion of ledgers, pencils, pens, penwipers, paperweights, boxes, memoranda and immense tottering stacks of documents), Ike Underwood finally came up with what Charley supposed was the loan application. He glanced at it for a moment, then wadded it into a ball and tossed it in the general direction of the spittoon. It missed the spittoon. It rolled, stopped, gradually came unfolded, spreading, crinkled and final, on the not particularly clean gray carpeting of Ike Underwood's not particularly clean little office. He looked at Charley. Leaning toward the spittoon, he spat. The juice splattered against a leg of the desk. Shit, he said.

Charley kept his voice polite. I expect, sir, he said, you're not approving my application for a loan.

You expect right, said Ike Underwood.

Would you mind telling me why?

Wouldn't mind a bit, said Ike Underwood. He chewed for a moment. He bathed his teeth in juice. Then (after sending another unsuccessful spray of juice in the general direction of the spittoon) he said: It's got two parts. Listen close. Part One: I don't know you from a sack of turnips. I've heard about you, though, and I kind of think maybe there's a few things you got to hide. This Ferris, or whatever his name was, was greatly beloved by the men of the Paradise Falls Blues. Or so I am told. So now who should come to town but Ferris' widow, and she's got herself a new husband, and this new husband is quite a talker, and he wants to go into the grocery business. Sure, I know that Virge Light and the Messer boy went to see her in Indiana and told her she was welcome to come here if she wanted. And I don't mind that a bit. After all, those fellows feel they owe Ferris something. Fine. Let them support his widow if they want to. But what happens? She comes here with a *new husband,* and this new husband proposes to open a grocery. Well, maybe I'm doing you a wrong, but I got to figure something peculiar's going on.

No sir. That's an incorrect assumption. I have no intention of—

Be quiet. Let me finish.

Yes sir.

All right. *Now.* Like I was saying, I expect you're here looking for some advantage. Well, all right. Look away. As long as you don't try to interfere in *my* affairs, you can look until your eyeballs fall out. You can use your mouth and your wife and her dead husband and her big tits, and if Virgil Light and those other damned fools can't see through you, well, that's no concern of mine. That's Part One, Mr Wells. I just plain and simple don't trust you.

And Part Two?

Part Two is Harlowe Morris. He's my wife's uncle. And, beyond that, he's been a friend of mine for forty years. He once saved my life. Warned me a man was coming after me with a gun. A man named Jackson. Well, I had a gun of my own, and Jackson was the one got shot. But, if it hadn't been for Harlowe Morris, I wouldn't of been ready. So, you see, I'm not about to finance someone whose aim is to run old Harlowe Morris out of business. I'm sixtythree. Harlowe's damn near eighty. We're too old for betrayals. So good day to you. Find some other source. I expect you will. Now get the hell out of here.

Charley still smiled. Yes sir, he said. Yes *sir.*

Ike Underwood frowned.

Charley rose and left Ike Underwood's office. Once out of the bank, he breathed deeply and jubilantly. He smiled at everyone on Main Street. He squinted at dear Beauty atop the courthouse. He lighted a cheroot. He puffed. He had been acknowledged. Ike Underwood had put on an impressive performance. One did not put on such a performance every day. One only did so for the benefit of persons of importance. Therefore, Charley was a person of importance. Therefore, Ike Underwood (willingly or not) had acknowledged the greatness. Charley lifted a hand toward the sun. The hand blotted the sun. The hand was larger than the sun. It was *his* hand. He puffed. He was all lips and teeth and jaw. He was great. He would indeed prevail.

But it would not be easy. He knew this. He also knew he did not want it to be easy. He used his own and Nancy's money to get the grocery business started, and immediately the pressures began. He of course did not know for sure, but he had to guess that Ike Underwood was responsible. The first pressures came from the Columbus wholesale firms that supplied canned goods. Shipments began arriving a week late, ten days late. Columbus was barely fifty miles northwest of Paradise Falls, and the CPV&M passenger trains made the trip in less than two hours, and so apparently his canned goods were being routed by way of Milwaukee, Rochester, St Louis, Boston and perhaps, for all he knew, the Cape of Good Hope. As a result, his shelves never were properly stocked, and some of his customers became miffed and returned to Harlowe Morris' place. The second pressure came when old Harlowe's prices abruptly began to plummet. Obviously Ike Underwood was underwriting the competition's losses. Well, Charley also could play *that* game . . . at least for a time. He kept his prices one notch below old Harlowe's. After a month of this, old Harlowe gave up (or perhaps Ike Underwood, weary of underwriting the losses, was the one who gave up), and prices returned to their normal levels. The housewives of Paradise Falls had become somewhat spoiled by this dandy little contest. Many of them became peevish when it was over. Some even accused Charley of having made an arrangement with old Harlowe. The accusation made Charley laugh like the devil. Considering the circumstances, he figured he had a right to laugh like the devil. In late September, when the undercutting finally ended, Charley had precisely $217.43 to his name. Ike Underwood and Harlowe Morris had driven him *that* close to the edge. But of course they didn't know that. Had they continued their undercutting perhaps ten more days, that would have been the end of Charley. But, praise God, they *hadn't known*. Ah. Whoo. Yes. Praise God. But then came a third pressure, and it was by far the most subtle and dangerous. It pushed Charley within a hair of ruin. He received a shipment of spoiled canned goods—fish, to be specific. A boy of six, one Harold Swallow, son of no less a personage than the Honorable Philetas K. Swallow, judge of the Paradise County Court of Common Pleas, became wretchedly ill after stealing a tin of sardines from his mother's pantry and gobbling down every fish in the can. He became convulsed with vomiting. A physician was summoned. According to the physician, the sardines had most definitely gone off. The boy recovered, but J. K. Bankson wrote a lengthy account of the incident for the *Democrat*. The account mentioned the fact that the sardines had been purchased by Mrs Swallow in Charley's store. The next day, Charley's business was just about zero. Nancy asked him what on earth was he going to *do*. He told her he didn't have the slightest idea. And he didn't. Not then. That night, however, while lying in bed and twisting and tossing and trying to sleep, he had an inspiration. He sat up.

Glory! he hollered. Nancy groaned. She had been asleep. She opened her eyes. *I have it!* shouted Charley. *I have it! I have it!* As soon as he opened the store the next day he ate a twofoot length of raw sausage. Then he ate three large ripe onions. Nancy stood with her hands on her hips. She asked him if he had gone out of his mind. Belching gently, he said: Hardly. Just you wait. Then he ate a dozen large chocolate cookies. He rummaged under the counter. He came up with a quart bottle of a purplish preparation called Mother Burwell's Pectate Elixir. It foamed. He drank it down. All of it. It tasted like rat piss. Not that Charley ever had *tasted* rat piss, but he just bet he could guess what it tasted like, and he just bet it tasted like Mother Burwell's Pectate Elixir. A salesman had left the stuff several weeks before. The salesman had smelled dreadful. And now, apparently, so did Charley. Nancy went to him and made a face. You stink, she said. Charley nodded, belched. He wanted to throw up, but of course the time had not yet arrived. He took down a bottle of alcohol from the shelf where the soaps were. My Lord! shouted Nancy. He waved her back. He washed out his mouth with alcohol. He ran into the back alley and spat out the alcohol. It burned. It surely did. Godalmighty! he said, gasping. His eyes were soaked with tears, and Jesus how he wanted to throw up. His belly grumbled. He farted. Jesus. Jesus. Jesus. He wiped his eyes. He reentered the store. Nancy's hands again were on her hips. Maybe I ought to call the sheriff, she said. Charley grinned. Or maybe a doctor, said Nancy. Charley shook his head. He cleared his raw throat, ate halfadozen sugared lemon drops. Come here, he said to Nancy. She came to him. He breathed in her face. Smell better? he wanted to know. She nodded. Good, said Charley. He went to the shelf where the sardine tins were. He took down a tin. He put the tin in a pocket. He belched. He covered his mouth, excused himself. I'll be back after a bit, he said. Now don't you fret. Smiling, he walked out of the store. Nancy stared after him. He walked very erectly. He breathed shallowly. He smiled at everyone he encountered on the street. He received few smiles in return. He was, after all, Charles Palmer Wells, the Evil Poisoner of Children, the Fiend Incarnate. Naturally, few were so depraved as to smile at such a person. He understood all this. People were people, and he understood. It was a fine warm morning, and the sun slapped and rang. His belly twitched. He patted it. He brought a hand to his mouth and permitted himself a moist and fruity belch. Steady on, he told himself. Ten minutes more and you can let her rip. Be brave. Show the stuff you're made of. Yes. Heh. *Well.* You just do that. Just show it all. Just whoop and gag to beat all. Ah, you goddamn devil you. Now Charley was perspiring. He itched. He wiped his forehead. He was in front of the courthouse. He stared up at the massive lady of Beauty. Sunlight dazzled her head. He

blinked, grinned, entered the courthouse. He went to the office of the
Honorable Philetas K. Swallow. The judge was not particularly glad to
see him. Smiling, Charley asked after the health of poor little Harold. He'll
be all right, said the judge, his voice short, but no thanks to *you*. Charley
nodded humbly. Yes, he said, I know. And that is why I'm here. I feel
we should get to the bottom of this. The judge stared at him. He asked
Charley what he meant. Said Charley: Sir, I had no idea those sardines
had gone off. I paid the highest wholesale price for them. If they are indeed spoiled, then I very much desire to take legal action against the wholesale firm that sold them to me. Perhaps you know the firm, the Ralph F.
Wood Food Co of Columbus? So I want you, sir, to bear witness to a little
experiment I propose to conduct. Then . . . before the Honorable Philetas
K. Swallow could say ah, yes or no . . . Charley produced the tin of
sardines. You will note, sir, said Charley, that this tin has not been
tampered with. Charley held up the tin. The judge, his face numb,
nodded. Quickly Charley opened the tin. Then he produced a spoon from
a coat pocket. He had taken the spoon from the Acterhof House diningroom that morning. Spooning away, he ate the contents of the tin. Then
he drank down the oil. His belly felt green. He told himself: My God, I
may swoon. The judge stared at him. The office stank of sardines. Sam
Garson, an old fellow who was the judge's bailiff, stuck his head in the
door. You smell something peculiar? he asked the judge. The judge pointed
toward Charley, who still held the spoon and the empty tin. A smile
worked at the corners of Charley's mouth. Then it went away. He vomited. It came out horizontally, and it was yellow and green, and it
drenched poor Sam Garson from head to waist. Then Charley bent double.
He vomited all over the judge's floor. Hawking and gagging, he staggered
toward the judge's desk. Jesus God! shouted the judge, drawing back. A
plaster bust of John Marshall was on the judge's desk. Charley inundated
both bust and desk. Then, groaning, he sagged to the floor in a fine
faint. He took care not to faint in such a way that he fell onto his vomitus.
The legal proceedings against the Ralph F. Wood Food Co were begun two
hours later, and the next afternoon the firm's president paid a personal
call on Charley. The man's name was William D. Stone, and he was the
soninlaw of the company founder. He was corpulent. His flesh was
purple. Apparently he had some sort of trouble with his sinuses. His
voice sounded as though it were being fried in hog fat. He told Charley
he had received a telegram from A Friend. According to the Friend, Mr
Wells had begun legal action. Perhaps Mr Wells was acting with
an excess of haste. Perhaps something could be arranged. Surely Mr
Wells was not an intractable sort of person. Said Charley: No. Of
course not. I can be talked to. Said William D. Stone: Perhaps a settle-

ment can be arranged? Said Charley: Perhaps so. Perhaps five thousand
dollars will do a great deal to relieve me of my discomfort. Said William
D. Stone: Please do not consider me rude, but my thinking was more in
the neighborhood of one thousand. Said Charley: Four five. Said William
D. Stone: One five. Said Charley: Four. Said William D. Stone, grinning: Two. Said Charley, also grinning: Three—and I'll go no lower. I
propose to sue you, Mr Stone, for two hundred thousand dollars. I have
the tins, and I have the bills of lading. They will make splendid evidence.
When you were put up to selling me the spoiled tins, apparently you didn't
think of the evidence. If I were you, I would complain to Ike Underwood,
or Harlowe Morris, or whoever was associated with you in this lamentable
adventure. So why not be shut of the matter? Three thousand is better
than two hundred thousand. Said William D. Stone: Yes. You surely have
a point. And, I must say, your tactics have been splendid. Throwing up in
the judge's office. A brilliant maneuver. Said Charley: It served its
purpose. Now the judge figures I have to be innocent. He figures no guilty
man would subject himself to such an ordeal. He sees me as having been
terribly wronged—which of course I have been. So how about it? Will it
be three thousand or two hundred thousand? Said William D. Stone: Do
I have a choice? Said Charley: I don't believe you do. Said William D.
Stone: All right then. Three thousand it is. Said Charley: Splendid. Said
William D. Stone: My goodness, you must think I am a dreadful person.
Said Charley: Well, I don't exactly think you're a saint. Said William D.
Stone: Ah, neither, in point of fact, do I. Said Charley: I hope you take it
out of Ike Underwood's hide. Said William D. Stone: Ike who? Then
William D. Stone permitted himself a large purple laugh. Charley also
laughed. He had to. Rascality always had pleasured him.

1865 . . .

Queenie, a threadbare old spitz bitch owned by the Rev and Mrs Edwin
P. Rathbun (he is the rector of Grace Episcopal Church), becomes
hungry one September afternoon and eats all of Nahum, Habakkuk,
Zephaniah, Haggai, Zechariah and Malachi from the family Bible in the
Rathbun parlor. Mrs Rathbun is appalled. Bad dog, she says. My. My.
Bad Queenie. Mrs Rathbun embraces Queenie, shakes a finger in the old
dog's face. The Rathbuns have no children.

Amelia Burkhart is married to Christian Soeder. His brother Wilhelm
has given him fifty acres of good bottomland near Paradise Lake. Christian

Soeder builds a house on this land. The marriage takes place in late August, and perhaps two weeks later Amelia becomes pregnant. An astounding thing has happened to Christian Soeder. He has fallen in love with his pale little wife. For the first time in his rakish life he has been made aware of leaves and clouds. He says to Amelia: It will be more than an arrangement. Our life, I mean. I will make you proud of me. Amelia nods. She bakes excellent pies, keeps their new home spotless. She has never mentioned Ferd Purvis to him. Not once. (Her mother and father are delighted beyond words. Of course they regret the fact that Oliver P. Purvis gasped away his life on their kitchen floor, but this unfortunate incident has in no way mitigated against their joy in the marriage. They know Christian Soeder is a good boy. They know he will now settle down. They figure it is good that he has gotten all the wild oats out of his system. They also are delighted that their blood has been joined with the Soeders'. They admire Wilhelm Soeder with fervor and devotion. And they admire his money.) Amelia takes silent walks. She shades her fair face from the sun. She walks in leaves, and the leaves are dry and crisp and brown, and there is a burnt odor in the air. Sometimes she is accompanied by her husband. She tells herself he surely is handsome. She tells herself she no doubt is the envy of most of the girls in the county. She tells herself: He wants to be a good husband. I must let him. But what about the poetry? Where will the poetry come from? Oh Ferd, the poetry . . .

The Honorable George McC. Pillsbury, mayor of Paradise Falls, is re-elected without opposition.

Priscilla Purvis insists that her brother Ferd go ahead and enter Oberlin College. It was what their late father had wanted. Ferd protests, but she will have none of his arguing. She tells him he needs to get away. She and little Editha escort him to the train. Little Editha weeps. Ferd says not much of anything. Priscilla takes a position as clerk in old Harlowe Morris' grocery. From time to time Christian and Amelia Soeder stop there to buy coffee. Priscilla never waits on them. Her face is like a rock, and her soul screams. She has loved Christian Soeder as long as she can remember. Each time she sees him she wants to kiss the soft blond hairs that trail across his forehead. She tells herself she is obscene. She tells herself she should be ashamed. Her face is like a rock, and she dare not look at him. Ferd seldom writes home from Oberlin. When he does, his letters are perfunctory, dispirited.

It is a splendid golden autumn. Sumac slashes the hills.

Young Bill Light has become wretchedly enamored of Mrs Charles P. Wells. A slatted and aimless boy at best, he has now fallen into the habit of taking long and feverish naps. Mrs Wells prances and grins across the field of his dreams. He supposes he is becoming a degenerate.

The ladies of St Luke's Lutheran Church hold a bake sale. It realizes $41.17.

A second Paradise Falls youth leaves for college this autumn. It is the

silent and darkly handsome Philip Isaac Underwood, only child of Ike
and Phoebe Underwood. The last hour before his departure, he sits in
his room and leafs through the scrapbook he kept of the war. It is an
elaborate scrapbook, crammed with cuttings from more than a dozen
newspapers and magazines. His parents were kind enough to take out the
subscriptions for him. There is nothing they will not do for him. He cannot hate them. True, they would not permit him to participate in the war,
but this is no reason to hate them. They have picked out a fine college
for him—Harvard. He has no reason to believe he will not do well there.
He grimaces. He is neat. He gleams. He despises dust. He flings the scrapbook into a closet. He clears his throat. He goes downstairs and braces
his parents. He smiles. He carries his luggage to the carriage. His parents
drive him to the depot. His mother smells fine. His smile does not relent.
The trip to Cambridge takes the better part of two days, and a number
of girls—several of them not unpretty—engage him in conversation.

The countryside is elegaic. The countryside murmurs. Hear the leaves.
Smell the dry smell. Prayers are offered. Scripture is read. The warm brown
air is heaven's breath.

The village sits soft and humble, a thing of homes and sheds and privies
and steeples and a lady of Beauty. Hear now a locomotive laboring uphill toward Earlham. Smell now straw and manure. See now the pin oaks,
the slits of sunshine that dart and slash over roofs and lawns and streets.

Frederick L. Magill, commander of the old Paradise Falls Blues, dies in
late September. Prof Baer leads the funeral band. With Virgil T. Light
marching at their head, the men of the Blues parade behind the hearse
on its trip from St Mark's Presbyterian Church to Oak Hill Cemetery.
Virgil T. Light marches erectly, and from time to time he almost appears
to be smiling. It is a glorious day, awash with sunshine, and Virgil T.
Light draws deep breath upon deep breath. Poor Fred Magill. Sure is too
bad. Ah, the deep breaths abound, and poor Fred Magill. The gravesite
is crowded. Madeleine Magill, widow of the deceased, never has heard
muffled drums before. She stands pale. She holds the hands of her two
small sons. General debility brought on by the dysentery was the cause
of death, the attending physician told her. But Madeleine Magill knows
better. Her husband told her the real reason. He told her many times.
He said: This war. This damn war. I was a man to be reckoned with. I
had ambition. I was a good lawyer. I've tried not to behave like a coward.
Fred Magill spoke often in his last days. He was yellow in the cheeks,
and his wristbones protruded in gray lumps. He said: Do what you can
for the boys, Madeleine. Always remember the boys. Try to make them
understand virtue. I still cherish virtue. I do. I do. If I didn't, this wouldn't
be so painful, this leaving, I mean. Her dead husband's words pound and
slap in Madeleine Magill's ears. The earth is heavy and dark. The coffin
has brass handles. The men of the Paradise Falls Blues stand at attention.
Madeleine Magill's sons weep for the father they barely knew. She

squeezes their hands. Virgil T. Light holds high his large bald head. The golden day is a splash, a proclamation. Wind. Heaven's breath. Arcadia. Sweet love. Madeleine Magill shrieks, writhes. She is led away. Her sons cling to her.

A Great Man:

THE SARDINE INCIDENT ended the harassment of Charles Palmer Wells' grocery business. In one loud and volatile and triumphantly accurate spew and spatter of sausage and onions and chocolate and Mother Burwell's Pectate Elixir and alcohol and lemon drops and sardines not to mention the oil from the sardines, Charley sent his adversaries skittering away, and from that moment his store prospered.

I don't expect I'll ever know, he said to Nancy.

Know what?

Whether it was deliberate.

You mean the sardines?

Yes. For that matter, I'm not even sure they'd gone off. After all, maybe the little Swallow boy just has a delicate stomach. I mean, the only reason I threw up was because of the sausage and the onions and all.

Don't forget Mother Burwell's Pectate Elixir.

I'm not about to.

Stone didn't admit a thing did he?

No.

But he did pay you the three thousand dollars.

Yes, said Charley, but maybe he was just avoiding trouble.

Three thousand dollars is a lot of money.

But I could have given him a lot of trouble.

Charley?

Yes?

You're sure it all has to be this way?

Yes. The way of the world, remember?

Some world.

Well, I didn't make it.

No mistake about it. The sardine incident represented Charley's first

clear victory in Paradise Falls. But it was small cheese indeed compared to
the one he achieved a month or so later. In point of fact, this second
victory was more than a victory; it became nothing less than the instrument that brought him to his greatness.

It was a poker game.

In this poker game, Charley destroyed a man.

The man was James Perry Blood.

James Perry Blood was the wastrel—and wasting—bachelor scion of a
family that had once been perhaps the most prideful in the valley, a family
that at one time had owned most of the northeastern quadrant of what
later became Paradise County, a family that had come to the valley in
1799, had labored, had wielded ax and spade and hoe and flail, had built,
had razed, had sown, had caused the hand of man to spread itself across a
succession of stony pessimistic hills aswarm with oaks and birches and
evergreens and tulip trees and bloodwort and squirrel corn and miterwort
and wood geraniums, a family that had hopped across tiny creeks chirping
with white water, a family that had beat its urgent way through brambles,
bilberries, wild strawberries and buckeyes, a race of workers and doers
that had been undaunted by lizards and toads and blacksnakes and
narrow blasted weedstrangled gullies, a crew of optimists that had thrived
there among pike and perch and the bitter mud cat, grappling with deer
and bear and puma and squirrel and coon and wolf, a clan of zealots that
eventually wrenched from God's reluctant grip a kind of brutal bounty,
a small and most thoroughly *earned* domain. The first of the race to come
to the valley was a man named Joseph Mauk Blood, who arrived from
Maryland in 1799. By 1811 a settlement had been named after the family,
and in 1845 the settlement officially became a village. But the area thrived
more than the Blood family did. The Blood women had a frailty in them.
They gave birth to too many dead infants. The family went into a decline.
Not enough babies were born. And now, in 1865, the only surviving direct
descendant of old Joseph Mauk Blood was this wastrel James Perry Blood,
who was rumored to be dying of consumption, who hawked and spat continually, who apparently was bound and determined to preside over the
full and final destruction of the achievements that had been wreaked by
his valiant progenitors. There were certain girls and women who saw
James Perry Blood as being handsome in a bony and tottering way. These
women and girls were either stupid or doomed, and sometimes they were
both. They were the sort of women and girls who wrote impassioned notes
drenched in perfume, who sang sad songs while accompanying themselves
on the piano and rolling pale eyes heavenward, who read fervent poetry
that addressed itself to Tragic Lost Loves. They sighed and gushed over
James Perry Blood, and as a result he was never at a loss for a mistress.

There were at least a dozen women and girls in Paradise County who had had rancorous arguments with their families over this man. Three of them had been evicted from their homes. After James Perry Blood was finished with them, all three went to Columbus and took up lives of prostitution. One, a dark little girl named Sara Quayle, whose widowed father was postmaster until his death in 1859, drank herself into a premature grave in 1861. It was said that she had held herself responsible for her father's death. There probably was some truth to this. Prior to his daughter's descent into whoring, Sam Quayle had been a robust and cheerful man. But, once he learned what had become of her, he went into a rapid decline; he spent ten hours a day in Claude Dill's saloon; a cerebral hemorrhage took him in an instant, and he rode to glory directly from the sawdust and the cigar butts there on the floor of the place. James Perry Blood was as shocked as anyone by the death of Sam Quayle. Why, he and good old Sam drank together in Claude Dill's place almost every day, and sometimes half the night. Sam Quayle really had had nothing against James Perry Blood. Neither had the families of the other women and girls who had gone running after this wasted inheritor of the Blood bloodline. James Perry Blood had a simple explanation for this curious phenomenon. Look, he told his drinking cronies in Claude Dill's place, it's not that difficult to understand. I am, and those people know it, *nothing*. I have never pursued a woman in my life. I am no seducer. I have no prospects. I simply drink. But there are those females who seek to degrade themselves. And there is the important point. *I* do not degrade them. They degrade *themselves*. If they choose to thrash and gasp with a ruin, all right, I'll not refuse them. But I never have *sought* them. And their people know this. So, when it happens, they never come after me with murder in their hearts. I am not *worth* murdering. Instead, they try to reason with the afflicted young ladies. But corruption is too large for reason, and so there you are: I, James Perry Blood, from time to time find myself in bed with a young woman who has been destroyed by what for want of a better word I shall call poetry. How can I be blamed? That would be foolish. My God, just *look* at me. My ancestors. All that work. And just look. Such a fine serving of lunacy it all is. The sick Blood blood. The blood of Blood has thinned to water. The weak bloody Blood bloodline. Ah, my friends, such a jest. And most of the county agreed with James Perry Blood's estimate. And most of the county agreed that he would not die until everything was gone. Which wouldn't be long. Of all the land that had been owned by the Bloods, just two hundred acres remained. Its market value was about five dollars an acre, by the most generous estimate. His grandfather's house was on those two hundred acres. It sat on a hill overlooking the village of Blood. The view from this place was conceded to be just about the best in the county.

On a clear day it extended almost all the way to Paradise Falls, a distance of eleven miles. James Perry Blood lived there alone, and it was said the place had become literally a mare's nest. A few of his women and girls had described the house, and their words had touched on dust, cobwebs, rats, splintered floorboards, grimy dishes, broken candles, shattered glass, a litter of old newspapers, immense stacks of wormeaten books, piles of tumbled gray bedclothing, cockroaches in the pantry, spiders in the beds, brown scum lying thickly over ruined ancestral portraits. All their words were believed, and all their words were true. All one had to do was look at the man. One look and the truth was believed. James Perry Blood was thirty, but his voice was shrill as a boy's, a thing of uneven teeth and gross breath and raging obscenities. His skin was the color of dirty feet. Yellowish grime usually was caked in the corners of his eyes. Crinkly brown hairs straggled from his nose and ears. He was very tall. He always wore a spotted morning coat, stovepipe hat and striped brown trousers. His appearance was that of an unfrocked undertaker, one who perhaps had been discovered taking his pleasure on the corpse of a freshly deceased lovely young woman. His knees wobbled as he walked. When strolling along Main Street, he had a habit of baring his teeth and spitting on the shoes of unwary passersby. There were many theories on the reasons for James Perry Blood's decay—and his wholehearted dedication to hurrying it along—but perhaps the best one was held by a man named ElRoy E. Mauk, a clubfooted little lawyer who was first cousin to the man. Said ElRoy Mauk: Jim Blood was the only one of nine children who lived past the age of four. The only one. It was truly terrible for his folks. I remember that his father and mother buried two boys and a girl in one span of I think it was just eight months. The family cemetery is right behind the house. It is something to see. I've never seen so many tombstones packed so close together this side of a stonecutter's shed. Well, anyway, getting back to the family—Jim's father's name was Perry Joseph Blood, and all the dying caused what I'd have to call an unfortunate thing to happen to Perry Blood. He turned on the boy Jim as though the boy was the Hope of the World. Fifteen years or so ago Loretta and I used to visit Perry and Jane Blood oh maybe once or twice a month. Now then, Jim was only about fifteen at the time, and just a boy the way most boys are boys—you know, what with the fishing and the looking after girls and the swimming and all that sort of thing. But, to listen to his father talk, you'd have thought this boy was going to grow up to be Napoleon and Shakespeare and George Washington and Socrates and I don't know who all. He was just a boy, but he was the last of his line, and so old Perry Blood tried to make him something, uh, larger than human, if you can understand what I mean. Oh, I tell you, there was nothing Perry and Jane wouldn't do for that boy. I remember how one time they sent away for a pony. A *farm horse* wasn't good enough for *their Jim*. He had to have a *pony*. It was brought here in a canal boat as I recollect, and it was a pretty animal, white mostly, with a great black smear spread across its forehead and its neck and its withers. Well, anyway, that pony got itself tripped up in a squirrel hole, and Perry Blood had to go shoot it. This happened *just two days* after Perry gave it to the boy. Well, the boy bawled and carried on something terrible (I was there that day, happened to be visiting, had some legal business to attend to), and who could blame him? But his father didn't want him to bawl and carry on. No *sir*. Perry Blood walked to the boy and clapped him hard on a shoulder and said: By God now you just *stop* that! You are a *man!* You will behave in a manly fashion! You are a Blood! You *stop* that! And surely the boy did stop. The bawling, the carrying on—all of it was swallowed, and the boy went off somewhere and sat on the side of a hill. Well, maybe that should give you an idea of the way things went. He had violin lessons, by the Lord Harry. *Violin* lessons. His dad made him practice three hours a day. And, when Jim Blood was seventeen, he was packed off to Kenyon College. Well, he got fired from there before the first year was out. Went to Cleveland, worked as a clerk in some hotel, and it's my understanding he gave some girl a real fine dose of the clap. Girl from a good family, too. Methodist preacher's daughter, if my memory is accurate. Well, at any rate, when he was twenty he came home for good. That would be ten years ago: 1855. I don't think he's been out of the county since then. Perry and Jane both of them died in '59, and within no more than two weeks of each other. For Perry it was the heart. For Jane it was a stroke. Perry didn't want to die at all. I know that because I talked with him and Jane shortly before they both passed away so suddenly. Perry wanted to get his boy straightened out. He still hadn't given up. The day I talked with him and Jane, damn if old Perry didn't cry. But then he went and died, and Jane hurried along after him, and I expect Jane was just as happy about it. Eight little dead ones were waiting for her, and the one live one was headed straight for hell in a bushelbasket, and what was there *for* her? So she went and died, and she was laid away next to her husband back there behind the house where all the tombstones are, and yessir, it's been quite a situation. That talk I had with Perry and Jane gave me I think a glimpse at the truth. Or at least the truth the way Perry and Jane saw it. Clear and plain, there had been just too much put on Jim's shoulders. And he wasn't near strong enough. So he collapsed. And came to hate his family. And so now he's conducting the funeral of all the dreams of all the people who were there before him. He keeps selling property and throwing away the money, and it's the same thing as throwing shit on his father's grave, and it's all tragic and terrible, but where else is the answer?

Charley had heard this story (and its attendant theory) from ElRoy Mauk, and he supposed Mauk's estimate was reasonably accurate. Not that it mattered. If James Perry Blood chose to do away with his bloody Blood bloodline, that was his right. And maybe Charley would be able to scoop up some of the leavings. One simply never could tell.

And this was precisely what happened. Only the leavings were of a value undreamed of. And they catapulted Charley to his greatness. They came to him in the poker game, and of course the poker game immediately assumed the proportions of a dark and thrilling legend. The date was October 11, 1865. The game was played in Charley's suite in the Acterhof House. It lasted all night. Throughout the playing of it, Nancy sat on the sofa and worked on a piece of embroidery—a doily for the back of a chair. As the game wore on, James Perry Blood's drinking became increasingly more heavy, but Nancy seldom looked up from her work. From time to time she hummed. There were five players in the game: Charley Wells; James Perry Blood; Virgil T. Light; ElRoy Mauk, the clubfooted lawyer, and John K. Reeser, a plump young physician who wore ruffled shirts and had something of a reputation as a dandy. Charley had been playing poker with these men for several weeks. The stakes had been relatively low. As far as he could tell, the most that had been won by any one man was about a hundred dollars. And, as closely as he could estimate, the most that had been lost by any one man was about two hundred. The games usually were held in Virgil T. Light's home, but that particular week the walls of all its downstairs rooms were being papered. So Charley offered his suite in the Acterhof House. It's about time I hosted something, he told the others. So please do me the courtesy of accepting my invitation. There were no objections, and Charley outdid himself in providing food and libation. He hired a bartender from the hotel tap room. The bartender, a young fellow, was named Johnston. Charley provided Johnston with a case of assorted whiskies, plus two bottles of gin (James Perry Blood was fond of gin). The hotel sent up an ice chest, a keg of beer, several pots of coffee, three boxes of cigars and an immense tray of sandwiches. The cost of all this was almost a hundred dollars, but Charley figured it was a wise investment. He didn't think it would be good for him to be thought of as anything less than generous. In some way, such a reputation just might put obstacles in the way of his greatness.

Johnston set up his bar on a table next to the sofa where Nancy sat. She paid no attention to him. She declined all offers of food and drink. He was a sandyhaired young man, and he had a fine moustache, and from time to time he smiled at Nancy. She did not notice the smiles. Or, if she did, she did not let on.

For some reason the game got out of hand. Charley never could quite understand why. Perhaps it had something to do with the new surroundings. Or perhaps it had something to do with Nancy's presence. Or perhaps it simply was the phase of the moon. At any rate, the game fed on itself, derived much nourishment from itself and thereby enlarged itself into something that finally was a great deal more significant and beautiful than a mere game of cards.

It probably all began with James Perry Blood's drunkenness. James Perry Blood always drank heavily during the games, but that night his drinking was something to draw back from in wonder and admiration. He had done away with an entire bottle of gin before the game was two hours gone, but in no way did he become incoherent. Instead he simply smiled, said little, played good poker. Which, for him, was quite an achievement. None of Charley's new friends played the game particularly well, and usually James Perry Blood was the worst of the lot. He bluffed two hands out of three as a general rule, and he deceived no one. He might as well have fired off rockets to announce what he was up to. Actually, Charley had in previous games played easy with the man. He sought to antagonize no one, not even this ruined and tubercular rake of a James Perry Blood. In previous games Charley always had managed to win a little, lose a little, antagonizing no one, never revealing his clearly superior abilities at the game. (His Washington days during the late war had provided him with the experience that had made him an excellent player. Ah, his good old Washington days . . .)

But on this particular night something came to suck away the informality and provide the dark and thrilling legend. Ah, but perhaps that was to be expected. Poker can be approached informally only so long. Then it becomes larger than passion and honor. It seizes a man's viscera and gives his soul a profound and heady wrench. It is an experience no genuine pokerplayer can avoid, something he will carry with him to his last terrible night.

In the past, the table limit had been ten dollars. This particular game started out that way. An hour later, at James Perry Blood's suggestion, the limit was raised to fifty dollars. By midnight, one could open for fifty dollars, then wager a sum equal to the total amount in the pot. At that time Charley was more than a thousand dollars ahead. He watched the other players. None of them appeared to be angry. Not even James Perry Blood, drunk as he undoubtedly was, appeared to be angry. None of the men had brought sufficient funds for such a rich game, and so now it was understood that cheques would be exchanged at the conclusion. The smallest chip now was worth fifty dollars. From time to time Charley glanced over at Nancy, but she did not look up from her embroidery. Johnston, the young bartender, had pulled up a chair behind Virgil T. Light's shoulder. Johnston had undone his cravat. He was sweating. He fidgeted. Charley smiled at him. Johnston gave Charley a narrow look. Charley bit his tongue, then decided oh what the hell, he had held back long enough; there was real money to be made here tonight, and he'd be the worst sort of fool if he didn't plunge in and have at it. The money from William D. Stone had made him solvent again, and so what the hell indeed—why not?

The game was stud. Fivecard stud. No other game was permitted. Charley was a cautious player, and therefore he was a very good player. He did not bluff. He did not succumb to wishful thinking. When he had the cards, he bet them to their eyeballs. When he didn't, he dropped out. He never stayed beyond the deal unless he had either a pair or a face card (the face card could be either up or down; it made no difference). And he never stayed unless he had the board beaten. He venerated stud. A good player could make a great deal of money and risk comparatively little. Ah, he *had* to venerate this game. Any game that permitted him to see four of his opponents' five cards surely was a game to be cherished. Such information, weighed in the mind of a player who knew what he was doing, was priceless. (In the earlier sessions, the ones held in Virgil T. Light's home, Charley had deliberately thrown money away on poor cards. This had of course been necessary in order that he not make enemies, but it had offended his respect for the pure and lovely delights of the game. This night, however, he could let it all rip. Which he did.)

Shortly after midnight, with the plump Dr Reeser dealing, Charley received the jack of clubs and the jack of hearts backtoback.

James Perry Blood had the ace of hearts showing. He bet fifty dollars. Next came Virgil T. Light. Deuce of clubs showing. He folded. Then Charley, who called with the jack of clubs showing.

Next came ElRoy Mauk. Nine of clubs showing. He called.

Then the dealer, Dr Reeser. Nine of diamonds up. He also called. Then he dealt the new round.

Ace of spades to James Perry Blood.

A pair, said the doctor. Two big ones.

Six of hearts to Charley.

Nothing, said the doctor.

Three of diamonds to ElRoy Mauk.

Nine-three-nothing, said the doctor.

Shit, said ElRoy Mauk. He glanced toward Nancy, covered his mouth. She did not look up.

Dr Reeser dealt himself a card. It was the nine of spades. Ah, he said, the fat dealer has a pair.

Two hundred on the aces, said James Perry Blood.

Out, said Charley.

Out, said ElRoy Mauk.

Dealer calls, said Dr Reeser.

James Perry Blood was dealt the seven of clubs.

Dr Reeser dealt himself a third nine.

Mm, said Virgil T. Light.

Dealer bets his three nines, said Dr Reeser. Dealer bets five hundred.

How much? said James Perry Blood.

Five hundred.

I've got you beat.

I don't believe it, said the doctor.

Five hundred, said James Perry Blood. And five hundred better.

Don't bluff, Jim. You can't afford to.

I'm not bluffing. I've got you beat.

Dr Reeser cleared his throat.

Well? said James Perry Blood.

Call, said the doctor.

James Perry Blood's hole card was the ace of diamonds.

Charley turned down the corners of his mouth. James Perry Blood grinned. Dr Reeser loosened his collar. Nancy hummed over her embroidery. Johnston the bartender made a whistling sound. Well, said Virgil T. Light, look there. ElRoy Mauk said nothing. James Perry Blood had Johnston fetch him a refill of gin and a cheese sandwich. The game continued. It occurred to Charley that perhaps James Perry Blood didn't seek to destroy himself after all. In the previous sessions, the man had bluffed two times out of three, and a man who bluffed so often surely was a man who sought to commit suicide. But tonight James Perry Blood was not bluffing. When he bet, he had the horses. Tonight he was a good player, a worthy opponent. Charley lighted a cigar, grinned at everyone. Dr Reeser won several quick pots. James Perry Blood played calmly, cautiously. So did Charley. Virgil Light and ElRoy Mauk, who had been staying about even, began to lose consistently. James Perry Blood watched Charley. James Perry Blood's shirt was gray, and there were grimy lines in his forehead. He used his fingernails to dig dirt from his palms. He grinned, hummed, drank gin, ate his cheese sandwich, studied his cards. Something large had happened to him. Charley was wise enough not to try to guess what it had been. James Perry Blood hawked, cleared his throat, coughed and spat into his smeared and filthy handkerchief. Nancy looked up. James Perry Blood blinked at her. He smiled, excused himself.

She told him there was nothing to excuse. He thanked her. The game moved on. There seemed little question of it—James Perry Blood was taking up arms against his ruin. The players spoke softly. Usually the sessions broke up at about 3 in the morning. This one did not. Nothing was said about the lateness of the hour. James Perry Blood was the only player whose breathing could be heard. Charley smoked so many cigars his tongue stung. From time to time Nancy withdrew down the hall to the toilet, but she gave no indication of wanting to retire. It didn't matter to Charley. And, anyway, he couldn't spare the time to worry about her. James Perry Blood was giving him too much trouble. At about 4 A.M., Charley lost fourteen hundred dollars when his three kings fell to James Perry Blood's nines over sevens full. Half an hour later, James Perry Blood won more than two thousand dollars from ElRoy Mauk and Virgil T. Light on a flush over two straights. He kept glancing at Nancy. Johnston the bartender stretched out on the floor and fell asleep. By 6 A.M., Charley was twenty dollars ahead. James Perry Blood was about seven thousand dollars ahead. The other three men had been hit about equally. Charley's eyes smarted. James Perry Blood hawked and spat. Nancy fell asleep over her embroidery. Charley paid her no mind. At 7 A.M., Virgil T. Light dropped out of the game. He had lost twentyseven hundred dollars. At 8:30 A.M., after losing thirtyone hundred dollars, Dr Reeser dropped out. But ElRoy Mauk, who'd lost more than four thousand, refused to surrender. The game moved on. By 9 A.M., Charley was ahead by about two thousand dollars. James Perry Blood had won about eightyfive hundred dollars. Now James Perry Blood was drinking whisky. The second bottle of gin had been emptied hours earlier. Johnston came awake. So did Nancy. James Perry Blood sent Johnston out for more gin. Virgil T. Light and Dr Reeser still were there. This is really what you'd have to call an epic contest, said Virgil T. Light. No one said anything in reply. Charley's eyes were so hot he felt they were about to melt. His shoulders hurt. His back hurt. He nibbled at the corners of his fingernails. From time to time he spat out tiny gray slivers of nail. ElRoy Mauk was leaning so far forward his chin just about rested on the table. At 9:15, Charley won four thousand dollars on a pair of tens over ElRoy Mauk's pair of eights and James Perry Blood's pair of sixes. Shit! said ElRoy Mauk, and he dropped out of the game. Nancy looked at him. He waved a hand in her direction. I'm sorry, he said, croaking. I apologize. Nancy smiled, yawned, shrugged. James Perry Blood hawked, blinked, rubbed his eyes. Charley covered his mouth, suppressed a yawn. He looked at James Perry Blood and told himself: He was a damn fool for staying with that pair of sixes. Maybe his concentration and judgment are going. Praise God.

Now, with only the two of them left in the game, Charley and James

Perry Blood played almost without words. James Perry Blood asked Nancy to draw the shades. The sunlight, he said, is just a little too much for me. Nancy smiled, drew the shades. James Perry Blood thanked her. Johnston the bartender took over the duties of dealer. Charley's underdrawers were clammy in the crotch. He kept having to rub the muscles in the back of his neck. By 10 A.M., he was four thousand dollars ahead to James Perry Blood's more than six thousand dollars in winnings. Charley stood up. He stretched. He grinned. Well, he said, I expect this is to the death, isn't it. He did not speak the words as a question. James Perry Blood coughed, excused himself, then said: Yes. To the death.

Virgil T. Light took over the deal. Charley tore off larger slivers of nail. The third hand dealt by Virgil T. Light was the one that destroyed James Perry Blood.

Including Nancy, there were seven persons in the room. Seven witnesses to what she later called a murder. Five witnesses, really. One could not include the murderer or his victim. The hand was inexorable. Charley saw it coming. He saw the beauty of its development. He had been waiting for it. He knew James Perry Blood was weakening. Otherwise, the fellow never would have stayed with that pair of sixes. To Charley, the final hand almost was funny. To the others, however, it was a thing of horror. He could not understand this. He had tried to prevent James Perry Blood from betting so heavily. He *had*. He *had*. He'd done everything but seize the man by the throat. What else *could* he have done? It all began innocuously enough . . .

Sucking spit, Virgil T. Light dealt the down and up cards.

Charley's up card was the jack of diamonds.

James Perry Blood's was the four of spades.

Charley bet fifty dollars.

James Perry Blood called him and raised him fifty.

Charley frowned at James Perry Blood's four of spades. He shrugged, called the raise, raised back a hundred.

James Perry Blood called.

Out came the second round of up cards.

Charley's was the jack of hearts.

A pair, said Virgil T. Light.

James Perry Blood's was the ten of spades.

Two spades showing for Mr Blood, said Virgil T. Light.

Pair bets two hundred, said Charley.

Two hundred better, said James Perry Blood.

Call, said Charley, and five hundred more.

Call, said James Perry Blood.

Now everyone was leaning forward. Even Nancy, who wasn't bothering with her embroidery now.

Out came the third round of up cards.

Deuce of spades to Charley.

Jack-jack-nothing, said Virgil T. Light.

Ten of clubs to James Perry Blood.

Ten-ten-nothing, said Virgil T. Light. Jacks bet.

Jacks bet a thousand, said Charley.

A thousand more, said James Perry Blood.

Call, said Charley. He glanced at his hole card. He could see what was coming. He sure as hell God damn could.

Out came the fourth and last round of up cards.

Jack of clubs to Charley.

Gasps.

Godalmighty, said Virgil T. Light, the man has jack-jack-jack-nothing.

Ten of hearts to James Perry Blood.

Louder gasps.

Ten-ten-ten-nothing, said Virgil T. Light. The three jacks bet.

Charley looked at James Perry Blood. I have, said Charley, about a thousand dollars in winnings here. To that, I'm adding four thousand. I bet five thousand.

Lord, said Dr Reeser.

ElRoy Mauk began twisting a ring on the little finger of his right hand.

I'll call that, said James Perry Blood. His voice was dry. And I'll raise you five thousand.

Charley smiled. Mr Blood, he said, do you have that kind of money? I mean, I know you can call. You have won enough to do that. But the raise, sir, do you have funds to cover the raise?

I do.

My three jacks have you beaten.

This game includes a hole card.

I am aware of that. And I still have you beaten.

I am raising you five thousand dollars, Mr Wells. Are you calling or not?

ElRoy Mauk breathed with his tongue resting on his lower lip. He looked at James Perry Blood and said: Jim, you don't have that sort of money.

I have my land, said James Perry Blood. It is worth five thousand dollars with the house thrown in.

I have you beaten, said Charley. I really do.

Will you or will you not accept my land and home as the equivalent of five thousand dollars?

Mr Blood, if I call your raise, I'll have to put up my store.

Splendid. Your store against my land and home.

Charley shook his head. I *mean* it, he said. I *know* I have you beat. There are no two ways about it.

Then call me.

Charley looked at Nancy.

Her face had no expression.

He looked at James Perry Blood. He sighed. All right, he said, I hate to do this, and I'm sorry about it, but I call.

Good, said James Perry Blood. He flipped over his hole card. It was the fourth ten.

That's what I figured, said Charley. He turned over his own hole card. It was the fourth jack.

James Perry Blood moistened his teeth.

No sounds.

Nancy covered her mouth.

Charley looked at all of them. Well, he said, I expect that's that.

It didn't matter what I had did it? said James Perry Blood.

I beg your pardon?

Your four jacks *had* to be boss didn't they?

Yes.

Shuddering, Nancy rose and left the room.

James Perry Blood was seized with a fit of hawking and spitting. It was loud. Everyone was silent, waiting for it to finish. He coughed into his filthy handkerchief, wadded the handkerchief, stuffed it in a pocket. His eyes were pink and moist. He smiled at Charley.

Charley's breath came hotly into his raw throat.

I can't complain can I? said James Perry Blood.

I don't see how, said Charley.

You warned me.

Yes.

I hope you do well by the land.

Now, now, I'm sure we can work out some sort of arrangement whereby—

No arrangements. The land is yours. You won it. You warned me, but I went ahead anyway. I have a few possessions in the house, a few small personal things of no value. I'll fetch them this afternoon. ElRoy here is my lawyer. As soon as he has me sign the papers, I'll see that the deed is delivered. So don't speak to me of arrangements, you fucking swine.

Jim, said ElRoy Mauk, there's no sense calling him names.

Be quiet.

Jim, for God's—

Be quiet.

ElRoy Mauk grunted, subsided.

James Perry Blood leaned forward until his elbows were resting on the table. He dug at a nostril with a thumb, sniffled, then said: Mr Wells, you have indeed done it.

Done what?

Murdered me.

What's the matter with you? What was I supposed to do? Drop out of the game? Throw away all my money? Let you have a pot I knew I'd won?

I'd have done the same for you.

What?

I repeat: I'd have done the same for you, you sonofabitch.

I don't believe that.

James Perry Blood stood up. He began fumbling at the front of his trousers.

Here! Here! said Virgil T. Light.

Get me a razor, said James Perry Blood. I want to give Mr Wells here his due.

Virgil T. Light and Dr Reeser went to James Perry Blood and seized his arms. James Perry Blood wheezed. He hawked. He spat on the rug. Virgil T. Light and Dr Reeser dragged him from the room. The door was slammed behind them.

Charley sat numbly.

Outside in the hallway, James Perry Blood sniggered and mewled.

ElRoy Mauk stood up.

He can keep the land and the house, said Charley. I don't give a damn. If he sends me the deed, I won't accept it.

Yes you will, said ElRoy Mauk.

What?

You *have* to accept it. If you don't, you'll be pissing all over his honor. He has just two things remaining to him—his property and his honor. He'll sacrifice one in order to preserve the other.

I thought you said he wanted to destroy himself. How come, if that's the case, he's taking it all so hard?

A man has a right to change his mind. Dying is hard.

Well, I'll accept *that*.

All right then.

He said he would have let me win if the situation had been the other way around.

Yes, said ElRoy Mauk. And I believe him.

What does that make him? It makes him a damn fool doesn't it?

No. It makes him a hero.

A hero?

Yes.

Well, fuck him.

I beg your pardon?

Fuck him, said Charley. When the deed comes, I'm *taking* it. He can die. He can rot. I got no use for heroes.

Oh? That so? said ElRoy Mauk.

Yes. That's so. That's exactly so.

I don't think I want to know why you feel that way.

I don't believe you would.

You don't even feel sorry for him do you?

Would that change anything?

You're not what you seem to be, said ElRoy Mauk.

Hardly anyone is.

A lot of people are.

Oh?

Yes. And they suffer for it. Transparency is no advantage in anything.

I agree, said Charley.

Surely has been some night, said young Johnston.

ElRoy Mauk and Charley glanced sharply at him. Charley had forgotten he still was in the room, and he supposed so had ElRoy Mauk.

Johnston was packing empty bottles in a box. Grinning, he said: I surely got something to tell my grandchildren.

Are you married? said ElRoy Mauk. I didn't know that.

No, said Johnston, not yet. But someday I *will* be. And I'll live to see my grandchildren. I got a reason now. I want to talk to them about this night. I want to talk to them about the human race.

The human race? said Charley.

Yes, said Johnston. I figure this night has taught me a lot.

How so?

Johnston shrugged.

How so?

Johnston looked squarely at Charley. He kneaded the knuckles of his right hand with the palm of his left. Then, speaking slowly, he said: Mr Wells, if I'd of been holding the cards you was holding, I'd of done just what you done.

Good.

But I wouldn't of liked it, said Johnston. He spread his hands. He scraped at the rug with the toe of a shoe. Then: I'm sorry. Maybe I shouldn't of spoke up.

You're saying I liked it?

Yes sir.

What does that make me?

I don't know.

Charley stood up. He placed his hands on his hips. He looked at ElRoy Mauk and said: Do *you* know?

I wish I did. Whatever it is you have, I could use some.

Charley went to a window and opened it. He breathed deeply. It occurred to him that today was Columbus Day. He grinned. He decided oh what the hell anyway. He passed on the Columbus Day information to ElRoy Mauk and young Johnston. They both grinned. The air was gray and crisp. He decided he needed a bath. Again he breathed deeply. He gave young Johnston a twentydollar tip. Young Johnston thanked him. Now, said young Johnston, this here game has got *two* winners. Charley nodded. ElRoy Mauk chuckled. A few minutes later he left. Young Johnston followed along. Alone, Charley rubbed his eyes. Damn smoke. He decided he was too tired to take a bath. He went into the bedroom. He decided he even was too tired to take off his clothes. He lay down next to Nancy. She was chewing on her lips. He said nothing to her. He closed his eyes. Nancy was breathing through her nose. He supposed she was mourning what had happened to James Perry Blood.

Charley?

What?

Do you like being Episcopalian?

What?

I mean, it's such a lie.

What do you mean? It's a good church. Teaches virtue and all that.

I don't mean *that*. I mean *us belonging* to the church. Us lying that we were Episcopalians back home.

I've explained all that.

I don't like it that we got to lie so much. And I don't like it that we got to hurt people.

You mean Blood?

Yes. Of course I mean him.

He *wanted* to be hurt.

No.

You want me to feel sorry for him?

Yes. That such a terrible thing?

All right, said Charley, sighing. I feel sorry for him.

Mm, said Nancy.

. . . and, drawing his hands into taut fists, Charley slept. The sleep came abruptly, and it was heavy, and it was warm, and it made his mouth brown and scummy, and it brought a memory, and that memory was of heroism, his own heroism, a heroism forever lost, and dear God why was

he breathing again the sweet muddy riversmell of his home town, that
hateful old Titusville? Why again did he have to return to that day of
the storm and the mad Mrs Weatherly and his betrayal of Nancy? But
return he did, and the year was 1853, and he was skittering and slithering,
the terror chewing his throat, and by damn by damn by damn he surely
did run. He ran. He ran. He ran. Sobbing, he flailed and flopped across
the pocked and littered streets and fields, and the shame came from him
like a certain warm and moist variety of green shit that he'd sometimes
seen issue from frightened cattle. He was fourteen going on fifteen, and
he was a worm; he was vermin; he was not worth a single golden dollop
of her sweet sweat. He ran. He ran. He ran. He ran all the way home.
Nancy was behind him, skirtless and abandoned standing there in the
mud, her hands pale across her honeyed and now forever unattainable
crotch; she had stood there and he'd damn near knocked her down, and
this was the sort of hero he was, this was the sort of hero he would forever
be. He kept looking back over a shoulder. Mrs Weatherly was nowhere
to be seen. But still he ran. He just ran and ran and ran and ran, and then
he was home, and he scrambled upstairs to his room, and he collapsed all
muddy and torn across the clean bedspread, and after a time the great
storm died away, and so, trembling, coughing, he went back outside and
again he ran, but this time he ran toward the river. He ran down the
long green hill from his home to the river. He ran to the edge of the river.
His legs gave way. He knelt in the mud. He looked up, and he spoke to
Almighty God, and he said: Mrs Weatherly thought I was her husband. Why did You make her think such a thing? I was doing fine. I
didn't mean nobody no harm. So I wanted to grab at Nancy's tiddies a
little. Is that so bad? How come, if it's so bad, You had to go and make
them so big and sort of squishy and all? I love her. *I love her!* I wouldn't
hurt her. *I wouldn't! I wouldn't!* So how come You had to go and make
it so I'm not even big enough to kiss the hem of her dress? Then Charley
fell on his stomach. He kissed mud. He lay there a long time. He lay there
until all of the storm's cold whistling gray afterlight was gone. Finally
he had to piss. He stood up, pissed in the river and went on home. The
tornado had cut through Titusville in the shape of a ragged S. Damage
was estimated in the thousands of dollars. Dozens of homes and business
establishments and farm buildings were shredded like pulp. One large
oak tree was uprooted from the courthouse lawn and carried almost four
miles. All its fresh spring leaves were torn off. It came to rest inside the
barn of a farmer named Wooley. Damn thing just dropped through the
roof, said Wooley. Came out of the sky and fell straight down. Damnedest thing I ever seen or hope to see. One minute there was just the big
wind. Next minute down comes the tree. I was standing in the yard. I

seen the whole thing. Mabel and the little ones was in the cellar, but I couldn't bear to stay down there. I had to *see*. Oh yes *sir*. Old John Wooley can't abide not knowing what's going on. So, anyhow, she came down just after I'd come outside into the barnyard. I was wet to the skin. Damn rain was *white*, and that's the truth of it. I was standing there, and I was leaning into the wind so's I wouldn't fly off, and then crash splinter thump down comes the tree. The courthouse elm. God damn. I recognized it right away. Down it came, and it ripped my barn roof all to hell, and you know what I done? Oh I was real smart. I ran inside the barn and I stood there and I cussed out that tree. *God damn you, tree!* I hollered. *What's the damn idea doing a thing like this?* And then I done an even smarter thing. I went to the tree and I *kicked* it. Kicked it good. Kicked it *so* good I damn near kicked off the big toe of my right foot. It was quite a dance I put on. I expect some people would of paid good money to of seen it. I mean, when it comes to me and brains, we don't hardly nod on the street. You might say.

But, despite all the property damage, the great storm killed just two persons. One was Old Man Pearsall the drunken gravedigger at Mount Zion Cemetery, the man Charley's *friend* George Peters had inexplicably *embraced* the day George's parents and sister had been buried. Old Man Pearsall apparently had been majestically drunk. His body was found in an open grave. It had filled with water, and he'd somehow fallen into it and drowned.

The other victim was the mad Mrs Weatherly. A neighbor watched her die. She was standing on the lawn in front of her home. She was standing erectly and she was staring at the sky. A tree fell on her. It just about cut her in half. Said the neighbor: It sure was strange. I mean, she should of gone inside. Can't figure out why she'd want to stand out there and stare at the sky like that. Didn't she know where she would of been safe?

Charley didn't know what to make of Mrs Weatherly's death, and all he could do was shudder. But then he didn't suppose he knew what to make of much of anything. Maybe crazy people were the only ones who truly understood the world. Ah, some life. Like cockroaches in Cousin Tillie's rice pudding.

Oh it surely was some storm. And it did more than destroy and kill. Or at least for George Peters it did. Good old George Peters, blond and tragic George Peters, the orphaned George Peters, Charley's *friend*. Ah, too bad about George Peters. This storm, this destroyer and killer, actually made George a gift, and the gift was Nancy, and Charley's hatred for George never would end. It was an immense and conclusive hatred, and Charley never showed it, and it clamored him to the beat of cym-

bals and drums, and not even George's crimson faceless death at Fredericksburg did away with it.

Of course George had to be the one to find the skirtless Nancy the
day of the storm. He gave her the shirt off his back, and she tied it around
her waist, and they ran to an old barn. George told Charley all about it.
After all, they were *friends* weren't they? Silent George, whose tragedy
had made it so he had talked to no one about anything, just talked and
talked and *talked* about his adventure with Nancy, and the words made
Charley want to stuff George's tongue and teeth down his treacherous
throat. Silent George, whose grief had removed him from the howdydos
and handshakes of normal society, suddenly began proclaiming himself
and even sort of strutting. She was in love with George. No doubt about
it. And George was Charley's *friend*. And George told Charley all about
it, even to the size of the tiddies and the honeyed fragrance of her flesh,
and Charley's teeth felt as though they had been dipped in vinegar.

They spoke, the oafish Charley and the handsome George, these two
who had not truly spoken since the day the *Molly G. Edwards* blew
up, they spoke at some length the morning after the storm. Charley said
nothing about the incident involving Mrs Weatherly, but George (a grinning new George, all minted and gleaming) told Charley he had heard
all about it from Nancy.

The boys met that morning on Titus Avenue in front of Thompson's
Dry Goods Store. There was no school. The schoolhouse had been too
severely damaged. There would be no school for two weeks. George was
grinning to beat anything. His feet were bare, and the legs of his britches
were rolled up. This was the first time Charley ever had seen him with
the legs of his britches rolled up. Oh this surely was a different George,
and maybe *he* was crazy too, like Mrs Weatherly and who knew how
many other people. He came up to Charley, and his grin did not diminish,
and he said: It surely was some day.

Charley was more than a little startled. He had to be. These were the
first words George had *volunteered* since the day of the explosion. Charley
nodded, grunted, said something about the storm having been a true
wonder.

Don't look at me like that, said George.

What?

I'm all right.

You're all right?

People don't have to draw back from me. I'm just what I always was.

Oh, said Charley. He shifted his weight from one leg to the other. The
street was so muddy that horses' hoofs made loud sucking sounds. The
horses moved carefully. Their legs were delicate, tentative, fastidious.

Drivers were easy with reins and whips. They didn't want to frighten the poor horses.

She doesn't wear any underwear, said George.

What?

Nancy. I saw her yesterday. She doesn't wear a stitch of underwear. I know that for a fact. Thought it might interest you.

It sure *does* interest me, said Charley, making his voice oafish and hearty. He showed George his teeth.

We went to a barn, said George.

Oh?

Yes. And she told me about you and Mrs Weatherly. Sure was something about what happened to Mrs Weatherly. She must have been crazier than a loon.

Charley nodded. He retained his display of teeth. She sure was, he said. I'll swear to that any day. Now then, what's all this about a barn? You took old Nancy to a barn?

Yes. We sort of fussed and wrestled.

And she told you about me and Mrs Weatherly?

She did.

She told you I was ascared?

No. All she said was Mrs Weatherly dragged you off. She said Mrs Weatherly looked like Death.

Oh. Hunkydory.

Forget it, said George.

What?

It doesn't matter.

You think I was ascared.

Forget it, said George. What difference does it make?

You think I was ascared.

Well, if you were ascared, I don't blame you.

Charley sighed. He was good old Charley. He was Charley the oaf, and George was his *friend*. He grinned. He said: Well, maybe I *was* ascared.

Well, said George, don't you fuss about it.

Charley grinned. He was Charley the oaf. He was Charley the oaf. He was Charley the oaf. Mud lay all around him, and the air was rich with the green and brown stink of uprooted trees and splintered boards and the heavy gelatinous earth. Charley grinned and grinned. He was Charley the oaf. He grinned and grinned and grinned, and then he said: You, uh, you fuck her?

George frowned.

Well?

No, said George.

No?

No. She'd lost her skirt. *You* know that. I gave her my shirt to wear. She was standing right there where you'd left her. We went to the barn, and that's where we fussed and wrestled. And that's all we did. I wouldn't have minded fucking her, but I didn't. I'll tell you the truth . . . I was kind of ascared myself. I swear nothing happened. You think I'd tell you I hadn't when I *had?* Maybe I'd tell you I *had* when I *hadn't,* but I wouldn't lie about it the other way around now would I? I mean, if a fellow is going to fib about a thing like that, there's only one way he does it. Right?

Right, said Charley, nodding.

George grinned.

The mud's sweet stink made Charley's eyes water.

So there it was: the hate. It flourished. But of course Charley did not let on. Charley was a fine boy. Charley was the oaf, the oaf, the oaf. He said and did not a thing, not even after Nancy began trailing George and sniffing at him like a bitch hound. Everyone laughed about it. Even Charley laughed about it. His heart was being clawed by immense rusty hooks, but he just laughed and laughed and laughed. Nancy would stand behind the handsome George and sigh, giggle softly, place one hand over her mouth and use the other to point at him, her eyes narrow and crinkly, her shoulders shaking with her warm secret mirth. And always she had other girls with her. And always *they* placed *their* hands over *their* mouths too, and their laughter was just as silent, just as warm, just as carnal. George professed not the slightest knowledge of what to do. Which was sheep dip, and Charley knew it was sheep dip, and how could George expect him to believe it? There was only one way for Charley to deal with all this. Whenever he was with George he never failed to urge his *friend* to take her somewhere private and spread her legs and pound it into her as far as it would go. I'm told it ain't the most complicated thing in the world, he said to George. You get her to lay down for you and the rest just sort of takes care of itself. It's real natural, I'm told. Like the rain falling from the sky. Yessir, the *rain.* Charley's words were hearty; they leaked oafish good fellowship. They were very necessary words. If they'd not been uttered, he would have revealed himself. He would have shown that he gave a damn, and of course Charley Wells the oaf gave a damn about not a thing. George smiled at Charley's urgings, smiled and allowed as how it wasn't all that easy. This brought guffaws from Charley. *Hog mess!* he roared. My Lord, just look at them tiddies will you? You're telling me you don't *want* to? If you was to tell me you didn't want to breathe, I'd be more likely to believe you! Go on, god damn it!

Do it! Fuck her! Fuck her good! Fuck her until she sings *Hail Columbia!*
Give her what she wants! What's the matter with you? Don't you know a
gentleman should give a lady what she wants? (In the schoolyard Nancy
had the habit of rubbing herself against George, quite *accidentally* of
course, acting as though she had lost her balance. Charley witnessed a
number of these *accidents*. They made him go off somewhere and slam his
fists against fenceposts and walls and treetrunks.) In the spring of 1854,
when all three of them—Nancy, George and good old Charley—were sixteen, George went ahead and did it. He took Nancy to that same damn
barn and he spread her legs and he gave it to her good. He said nothing to
Charley about it, and he didn't have to. It all was proclaimed in the
narrow grin that appeared the next day on his pale pretty face.

Eleven years later, shortly before Nancy and Charley were married,
she told Charley all about it. It was a Saturday night, she said. I was
just leaving the house. I was carrying a basket of wash to Mrs Ashbaugh.
You remember Mrs Ashbaugh don't you? Well, anyway, along came
George and he took the basket from me and he put it on the ground.
I recollect all of it real clear. He put the basket on the ground, and we
walked away. Just left it there. He took me by the hand, and we walked
clear across town to that old barn, and I don't believe he said a word.
Straight down Titus Avenue we walked, and the whole town saw us. He
was big where he was supposed to be big, you know? And he was strong.
And he didn't hurt me. But now he's dead, Charley. *Dead.* And *you're*
not dead. What is it you want me to do? Eat dirt?

Although George said not a word to Charley about the seduction (if
it could be called a seduction, what with Nancy's pursuit, her giggles,
the little *accidents*), he made no denials either. When Charley brought
up the subject, George smiled, and the smile was all that was necessary;
it permitted Charley's imagination to gallop to the moon. And of course
Charley professed an oafish admiration for George's accomplishment. It
flapped like a flag. He figured George didn't suspect a thing. (Oh yes,
those were the days. Charley Wells, at sixteen the cowardly oaf who had
betrayed his beloved, was no longer anything resembling a boy. Oh days
of leaves and the first gray winds of a dying year. Charley Wells, oaf and
clown, walking the quiet streets of the town of Titusville—1850 population: 1,101. Charley Wells scruffling. Charley Wells kicking the hard contracting autumn earth. Charley Wells hating. Charley Wells grinning at
his damp Indiana world, and Charley Wells hating. Charley Wells, his
lesson on heroism (its lack) most thoroughly learned, saying to himself:
His people are dead. *He* is an orphan. Better him than me. Better
anyone. Charley Wells closing his eyes and seeing the disreputable flesh
of his beloved. Charley Wells virginal as a nun. Charley Wells stiff and

stoppered and mute. Charley Wells saying to himself: Someday something'll happen. Maybe I'll have a part in it and maybe I won't, but
it'll happen good, and he'll pay, and I'll be there to laugh. Swear I
will. Charley Wells puffing his cheeks. Charley Wells watching his *friend*
parade with the adoring Nancy. Charley Wells observing with agony the
way her pillowy tiddies press against his *friend's* elbow. Ah, but Charley
Wells showing not a thing. Charley Wells chortling. Charley Wells red
in the face. Charley Wells always and forever the oaf, the clown, wouldn't
hurt a bug, not good old Charley Wells, not *him*. Charley Wells, all
teeth and arms and chest, hands on hips, feet wide apart, a lively fellow,
this Charley Wells, oh indeed, especially at night when, wrapped in his
blankets, he trembles and threshes, his ears echoing with the terrible silence of the hard Indiana nights. Ah, gray winds. Snow. His belly
abounds with cruel pink coals.)

But all he ever displayed was envy, goodnatured and comradely. Yessir
boy, he told George one day, do you have any *idea* what you got there?
I mean, them tiddies. Ohhh Heavenly Father what a pair! God save my
poor black Catholic heart but what I don't never get them out of my
mind for long. I mean, all I got to do is *look* at her, and *stiff*? My God,
I like to be bent over double. Whoo.

Catholic? said George. Did you say Catholic?

That I did.

You're a Methodist.

Maybe I'm going to get myself converted.

Oh? How come?

Change my luck. Maybe, if I was to turn Catholic, I'd grow six ten
twelve fifteen inches on my dingle and give you a run for your money.

Ahhh, you and your jokes.

Yessir, said Charley. Me and my jokes.

George laughed. Charley smote George on the back and also laughed,
very loudly and oafishly, throwing back his head and opening wide his
mouth and permitting the laughter to come in spasms and roars. He was
good old Charley. He surely was. Him and his jokes.

So passed the wretched unheroic days. Charley floundered. His greatness was a secret to him, and probably—if it hadn't been for a man
known as the Professor—it always would have been. But the Professor
had words for him, and those words showed him truth, and he would always revere the Professor above all men. This was quite a fellow, an
orator, a fraud, an oracle, a man of urgent flabby carnality, a wise man, a
prophet, a fool. He called himself Tobias G. Frye, and he had come to
Titusville like a fat orating wraith one summer day in 1845 after the
captain of the *Y. N. Bates* had thrown him ashore for cheating at cards in

a friendly poker game in the firstclass saloon of that pride of the fair Ohio
River, taking an estimated seven hundred dollars by the simple and
efficient means of marking the cards, but drinking too much and bragging
on the feat (certainly a poor and unintelligent thing for a cheater at cards
to do, but Tobias G. Frye was the first to admit that his tongue became
inordinately loosened by the heavy waters) and thus, because of the drinking and the subsequent loosening of the tongue, finding himself relieved
of the seven hundred dollars and abruptly propelled ashore, bag and baggage, such as it was, onto the Titusville wharf, to the guffawing merri-
ment of the loafers who clustered there those golden riverdamp summer
days. But Tobias G. Frye was not the sort ever to call retreat. He recon-
noitered, and he liked what he saw, and two weeks later, after a great deal
of blather and jaw and scurry, he announced the fall opening of the
Southern Indiana Eclectic Institute, Prof Tobias G. Frye, PhD (Harvard),
principal, A College for Young Men and Women Dedicated to the Basic
Intellectual Concepts of Christian Society, and if the Southern Indiana
Eclectic Institute didn't exactly coin money for Prof Frye, PhD (Harvard),
it did enable him eventually to repay those who had loaned him the funds
for the establishment of his temple to the intellect, and it also enabled him
to achieve a certain Superiority of Mind to most of the oafs and ruffians, as
he called them, who inhabited Titusville and its environs, its green fat environs where it was said he occasionally took female students off for private
field trips dedicated to the study of botany and perhaps other less eso-
teric of the physical sciences. With certain of his favored male students
and other friends of less intellectual bent Prof Frye grinned and admitted
that he had indeed occasionally strayed from the thorny path of virtue,
but he was among friends, and he was a good fellow, not the sort to lord
it over a person because of any real or fancied erudition, and so when
these friends did spread the word of his strayings, they did so with high
good humor, and their telling of tales brought Prof Frye nothing but
smiles. After all, what did any reasonable person expect from one of
those professorial types? But there also was a harsh sense of the real
within this man, and it was he, this Prof Tobias G. Frye, who conducted
the Southern Indiana Eclectic Institute in a secondfloor room over Thompson's Dry Goods Store, a tiny room full of hot air and oratory and a
vague emanation of bedpussies that came from God knew where, since
there were no beds at all in the building; it was he, this Prof Tobias
G. Frye, whose doomed and halfsmothered student enrollment seldom
exceeded half a dozen, due no doubt to what can most kindly be called
his informal teaching methods; it was he, this Prof Tobias G. Frye, this
cheater at cards *manqué*, who taught Charley the terrible severity of truth,
and Charley (despite all laughter, despite all awareness of the fellow's

fraudulence) always would look back on him with fondness, always would cherish his memory. Already shut of heroic aspirations, Charley learned from Prof Frye how to sidestep love, honor, belief. The lesson came after Charley had lost his parents. He sought out the Professor, and the Professor had the proper words for him, and from that moment he had no doubt whatever of his eventual greatness.

After completing his eight years in the Titusville school Charley went to work in his father's grocery store and post office. He did not protest. He could have gone on to the Southern Indiana Eclectic Institute, but he didn't particularly want to. I don't see what would be gained by sending you to that Frye fellow's humbug institution, said Charley's father, and Charley had to agree. We might as well get you some experience in the business eh boy? said James C. Wells, nudging Charley, grinning, adjusting the flaccid wattled lines that squirmed across his face. Sure, Papa, said Charley, why not?

But of course Charley's *friend* George Peters attended the Southern Indiana Eclectic Institute. George and the Professor became close friends. Sometimes Charley saw them sitting alone on the riverbank. They spoke in low voices, and Charley was unable to hear their words. A couple of real talkers, oh yes. He supposed they were comparing carnal adventures. He supposed George was telling the Professor about Nancy. All about her. Nancy. Ah, sweet Jesus: Nancy.

Charley was a good grocery clerk. His lurching oafish amiability served him well. He always jested with the ladies, never failed to compliment them on their clothing, their complexion, their hair, their general sparkle and feminine desirability: Why, Mrs Spooner, you ought to be ashamed of yourself! How come you don't let the other ladies in on your little secret? Here they are, every day getting older and older, but not *you*, oh no, *you* never change, and that's a fact! Your daughter Annie, she's got to be at the very least eighteen years of age, and what's a tiny breath of a girl like you doing with a daughter that old? Now I ask you, is that fair to the other ladies of this here town? You ought to go back to the woodshed and hang your head! My! My! *Shame* on *you!* Of course the ladies smiled at Charley's eager hyperbole. Some even gasped and blushed. Many of them told James C. Wells his son surely would Go Far. Yes ma'm, said James C. Wells, measuring out coffee or sugar or dried beans or whatever, I wouldn't be at all surprised. He's taken hold real good. He was made for this business, no two ways about it. Gives me a good feeling, I tell *you*. What I mean is—I know that when Caroline and I are Gone, the place'll be in good hands. Now then, was it one pound or two? In the late spring of 1856, less than a week after Charley's eighteenth birthday, his father fell ill of a chest congestion. James C. Wells took to his bed, but he did not be-

lieve the ailment to be very serious. Neither did his wife. Neither did
Charley. Caroline Wells treated her husband with poultices and several
varieties of liniment, wrapped his chest in muslin, chided him for being a
lazy old slugabed. James C. Wells grinned his wattled grin, kissed her
hands, told her he was much obliged for her kind attentions. She stayed
home with him. Charley took care of both the store and the post office all
by himself. He did not mind. As people said, he had plenty of the old snap
and ginger. He worked like a pack mule, and his customers (especially the
ladies) were agreed that he surely was something. (It had been more than
three years since the incident of the storm and the mad Mrs Weatherly,
but Nancy still was trailing Charley's *friend* George like a bitch hound.
George had an ambition now. He sought to enter West Point and embark
on some sort of splendid military career. He had taken to walking very
erectly. And—tiddies heaving, mouth moist and anxious—Nancy scuttled
after him, and every time Charley saw her his heart curled into a gray
knot. But he showed nothing. He was the oaf. He was the clownish
Charley Wells, a good one for footraces and the drinking of beer, a good
one for talk and music and gritty ribaldries an excellent flatterer, adroit
of tongue and tonsil, a good fellow all round, and he surely would Go very,
very Far indeed. Definitely. The world loved a good fellow.) Four days
after James C. Wells became ill, his wife Caroline fell victim to the same
chest congestion. Charley clucked and orated over his parents. He closed
the store and left the post office in the care of an old fellow named Stock-
still. He stayed at home and fed his parents broth and jelly. He rubbed his
father's chest with various of his mother's preparations. She would not,
however, permit him to rub *her* chest. My bosoms, she said, smiling palely,
coughing, clearing her throat, are not for you to be looking at. Charley
nodded, grinned, told his mother sh, she didn't have to talk; he understood. He decided it might make her feel better if he blushed. So he did
blush, and his mother's smile became larger. His father lay in the bedroom. His mother lay in the guest bedroom. Charley ran back and forth
between the rooms. Within a week his mother and father were coughing
and wheezing in concert. Charley summoned Dr Horsleigh, who was a
son of old Calvin H. Horsleigh, the elderly fellow who had been killed in
the explosion of the *Molly G. Edwards*. Dr Horsleigh did not care for what
he saw. He shook his head and murmured soft defeated words that concerned themselves with fevers and influenza and the damp spring weather
and such. Early in the morning of Sunday, June 8, James C. Wells began
to vomit phlegm. The sound of his gagging brought Charley at a run. Charley wiped his father's mouth with a muslin rag. In the guest bedroom,
Caroline Wells was coughing dryly. It had a sandy sound. James C. Wells
waved his arms and wheezed and tried to say something. His face was

crimson. The phlegm came out horizontally, with great force. It spattered Charley's forehead and cheeks. Charley wadded the muslin rag, wiped his father's face, wiped his own face. Now the rag was too damp, too slippery. Charley tossed it into a clothes basket in a corner of the room. Then he ran into the hall and fetched another rag from the linen hamper. In the guest bedroom, his mother persisted with her sandy sounds. James C. Wells' vomitus had slowed to a dribble. Charley wiped the corners of his father's mouth. The room stank. James C. Wells smiled. His wattles appeared a good deal more pendulous. They were like old gray meat. He closed his eyes. The corners of his mouth relaxed. The sandy sounds no longer came from the guest bedroom. Charley stripped the spread off his father's bed. The spread was decorated in a checkerboard pattern, yellow and brown. It had been made by Charley's mother. Now it was streaked with vomitus. Charley carried it to the clothes basket, folded it, tucked it under the rest of the soiled linen. He brought another bedspread from a closet. This was a plain white bedspread. He tucked it in at his father's feet. James C. Wells lay flat. He breathed with his mouth open. Dr Horsleigh had said something about a Crisis. Perhaps this was the Crisis. Charley didn't know. He wished Dr Horsleigh were here, but he knew he didn't dare leave the house long enough to fetch the man. He wondered what his father had been trying to tell him. He clucked, shook his head, wiped his father's forehead. Now the new muslin rag was wetter and dirtier than the old one had been. Charley tossed it into the clothes basket. Nancy's mother was supposed to come tomorrow to do a washing. It wouldn't be a bit too soon. Charley crossed the hall to the guest bedroom. This room was on the east side of the house, and Charley was aware of dawn. It was gray and blue, and it had dampened the windows. The moisture clung to the panes in strings and clots. He touched his mother's forehead. It was warm. Perhaps she also was going through a Crisis. It was just his luck to have the two Crises take place simultaneously. He seated himself on a straight-backed chair next to his mother's bed. The chair had knobs, and it was the most uncomfortable chair in the house, but his mother always had loved it. She did all her sewing in that chair. I can get my work done in this chair, she'd told Charley. In a comfortable chair I might just take me a little nap. Charley smiled. He wondered if his mother were asleep. Mama? he said, very softly, the sound barely emerging. She did not open her eyes. Her doughy face was almost yellowish. Veins and vessels were caught by the reluctant morning light. Mama? said Charley. No reply. He listened for the sound of her breath, the sandy sound. He heard nothing. He leaned forward, placed an ear against her chest. He heard nothing. He placed the ear in front of her mouth. He heard nothing. He lifted her right hand, released it. Down it came, straight and true, thumping against the bedspread. The sound was flat and stupid. This also was a homemade checkerboard spread, but its colors were blue and white. Charley stood up. He glanced out a window. Lord God, she was dead. Dead. She was good and dead, and she would be dead forever, and what was he supposed to do? He looked at his hands. Then he gave a great shout: *Papa!* Another: *Papa!* Another: *She's dead!* Then, groaning, Charley ran across the hall to the room where his father lay. James C. Wells' mouth was open. James C. Wells' tongue lay curled deep in his throat. James C. Wells' lips were streaked with spittle. *She's dead!* shouted Charley, lurching across the room to his father's bedside. James C. Wells' hands were in fists. James C. Wells' eyes were open. James C. Wells was not breathing. Charley leaned forward and listened. There were no sounds. His father was good and dead, and he would be dead forever. Charley stared into his father's eyes. They were yellow and green, laced with pink. Charley screamed. He ran out of the room. He stumbled down the stairs. He ran outside. He ran and he ran, and it all was like the day with Mrs Weatherly, only this time there was no storm; there was only dew, grass, the silent gray and blue sky. He ran and he ran. He ran all the way to the river. The river was misty, grayer than the sky and at the same time more blue. A person didn't often see the river that blue. He ran up and down the riverbank. He made no sounds. The scream had been his last sound. He was barefoot. He didn't know it. He ran back and forth, and then he ran up an embankment; he ran until his breath was gone. He sat down on a large rock. He shuddered. A hateful thought came to him; it made his belly jerk. The hateful thought was: *Better them than me.* He pressed his hands against his face. His feet were cold. His poor feet. He wrenched his hands away from his face. He looked around. He did not know quite where he was. Now then, he told himself, you get hold. *Right now.* He grimaced. He frowned. Now he knew where he was. The Evansville road was just beyond a line of sycamores a few yards in front of him. He stood up. He walked toward the sycamores. He heard a lark. The sound came from beyond the sycamores. It was a pretty sound. It trailed high and clear. It trailed into nothing. He walked through the line of sycamores. He walked to the road. His teeth were clicking. He flopped down at the edge of the ditch. He wept for a time. His tears were hot. Then he sat up crosslegged like a tailor. He did not move. A squirrel ran past. It did not stop to look at Charley. It ran in a flash of brown fur. Charley rested his elbows on his knees, cupped his chin in his hands. He exhaled. The lark came back. More sounds. They quavered. Charley dug fists into his eyes. He asked himself: What's going to happen to me? Behind him, the river plashed and murmured. He told himself: This ain't really happened. None of it. I'll wake up, and the wind it'll be cold, and I'll be feeling the need to pass water, and I'll be stiff as a plank. It happened to George. That's enough. It don't have to happen to *me* too. Enough is enough. Charley shook his head. He snorted, snuffled, opened his eyes. He decided to try not to move. I am a rock, he told himself. Nothing fusses at me. I don't have to think.

The lark still sang.

But then along came another sound, a sound of whistling, and it intimidated the sound of the lark. The Professor came walking around a bend in the road. He was such a very fat fellow, this Professor, and several of the buttons at the front of his britches were undone. He wore a high silk hat. It was crooked. He wore a white scarf. It was gray. He wore a long topcoat. It was spotted. He wore high black shoes. They were white and brown, streaked and splotched from earth and dust and perhaps a suspicion of dog mess. The Professor walked slowly, and the music of his whistling came through the openings between his teeth. His lips worked with each note. They were purplish lips, liverish and cracked. They lay deep within a thick uncombed beard. Only God knew what Prof Tobias G. Frye, PhD (Harvard), was doing out here in the country at this hour. He looked at Charley, the silent rock. He frowned. He stopped. He placed his hands on his hips. The whistling was cut off in midphrase. Charley had not recognized the tune.

Well, said the Professor, it appears to be young Mr Wells.

Charley said nothing. Charley was a rock. Charley did not move. Charley listened to the river. He waited for the sound of the lark to return.

Mr Wells?

Charley said not a word.

The Professor bent forward and said: Do you hear me?

Not a word.

Boy? Do you hear me? What is the trouble?

Charley paid close attention to the sound of the river. His nostrils itched, and his skin was hot, but he did not move.

The Professor's voice was flatulent. His breath came yellow and rancid. Now then, he said, I've never known the cat to make off with *your* tongue . . .

Charley began to weep. He embraced the Professor's waist.

Great day in the morning, said the Professor.

They're . . . dead . . .

What? How's that, boy? Who's dead?

My papa . . . and my mama . . . both . . .

Both?

At . . . the same . . . time . . .

How?

I don't . . . know. It's just that . . . at the same time all at once just
. . . just like *that* . . . they were *Gone* . . .

An accident? Was it an accident?

No . . . no accident . . . they just up and . . . went . . .

Lord, said the Professor. One of his hands touched the top of Charley's
head.

Charley squeezed his face against the Professor's vast belly.

Yes, said the Professor. All right. Dead. He stroked the top of Charley's
head. There, said the Professor. Yes. Quite proper.

Charley screamed into the Professor's belly.

A little later the Professor escorted Charley into town. They went to
the home of a man named Weatherwax, an undertaker. The fellow's full
name was Clive F. Weatherwax, and he looked like an undertaker. Charley
and the Professor roused Clive F. Weatherwax from his bachelor bed.
Clive F. Weatherwax wore a magenta nightshirt. His hands were small
and pale, and his adamsapple stuck out like a prune. He had come to
Titusville in 1852, shortly after the *Molly G. Edwards* disaster had killed
the town's only previous undertaker, Abraham Killpack. No one knew
where Clive F. Weatherwax had come from, and no one particularly cared.
His prices were reasonable, and this was all that mattered. After receiving
the distressing news from the Professor, Clive F. Weatherwax assumed a
properly stricken expression. It included a certain shy and mournful
sequence of spasms by his epic adamsapple. Charley had difficulty keeping
himself from staring at this adamsapple. It was good though, he supposed,
to be concentrating on something. At least the tears were out of him. He
was feeling not much of anything. It was as though he had been stuffed
with cotton. He and the Professor sat in the kitchen and drank coffee
while Clive F. Weatherwax changed into an appropriate mourning livery.
Now the sun had emerged, and church bells rang, and the streets had a
sound of carriages, voices, the wind, debating birds. The Professor said
nothing, but he did smile at Charley from time to time. They rode to
Charley's home in the splendid hearse of Clive F. Weatherwax. It was
plumed, heavily draped. It appeared to be quite expensive. People stared at
it. Charley heard some of them wonder aloud who had died. The Professor
helped Clive F. Weatherwax carry the bodies out of the house. Clive F.
Weatherwax told Charley not to concern himself with a single solitary
thing. You are Methodist, is that not so? said Clive F. Weatherwax. Yes,
said Charley. He was standing at the front door. He had just shaken one
of Clive F. Weatherwax's tiny hands. Clive F. Weatherwax's palm had
been dry and cool. The Professor stood behind Charley. The Professor was
breathing heavily from the exertion of helping Clive F. Weatherwax
carry the bodies. Well, said Clive F. Weatherwax, I shall notify Mr Chorp-

ening. We'll work out the time of the funerals. I'll stop by this afternoon and let you know. And again, Mr Wells, my most profound condolences. Charley nodded. Thank you kindly, he said. Smiling, Clive F. Weatherwax tipped his hat. He walked to his great elaborate hearse and drove away. The hearse moved slowly, with ponderous dignity, its plumes barely swaying. Charley closed the front door. He was thinking about names— Weatherly, Weatherwax. He frowned. Then he shrugged.

Yes? said the Professor. What is it?

Charley gave an involuntary little jerk. He'd forgotten the Professor still was here. Nothing, he said. He walked into the parlor.

The Professor followed him.

Charley seated himself on an ottoman. He looked at his knees, and then he said: You should of gone back to town with our friend.

No. I believe I'll sit here with you for a time. I expect you need someone to sit with you.

Charley shrugged.

The Professor looked around the room. He moistened his lips. Uh, wellnow, he said, perhaps we could have . . .

Charley frowned at him.

The Professor smiled. I was making reference to, uh, spirits, he said.

Whisky?

Yes.

There's a bottle over there on the sideboard. And some glasses. Help yourself.

The Professor made for the sideboard. He poured himself a drink, then turned to Charley and said: You'll join me? I find solitary drinking most unrewarding.

All right.

Good, said the Professor. He brought Charley a substantial drink. Charley was not unfamiliar with the taste of whisky. Occasionally his father had allowed him a drink. He preferred beer, though. The Professor handed him his glass. Then the Professor lifted his own glass and said: To your parents.

Charley nodded. He lifted his glass. He drank. He coughed. Some of the whisky got into his nose, but the sensation was not altogether unpleasant.

The Professor drank. Then he seated himself in a chair next to the ottoman. It was a thick chair, a very comfortable chair, all heavy leather, grainy and soft, and it had been Charley's father's chair.

Thank you, said Charley.

Ah, thank *you*, said the Professor.

I don't mean the whisky.

Oh.

You're right. I do need somebody to sit with me.

Splendid, said the Professor. I'll just sit here with you as long as you like. Sighing, the Professor settled back and studied his glass. A terrible affair, he said.

Charley nodded, drank some more of his whisky. This time it did not get into his nose.

The Professor breathed in a sort of rasp, but he said nothing.

He was trying to tell me something, said Charley.

Your father?

Yes. But he never got it out.

A shame. A tragedy within a tragedy.

Yes.

There are no explanations for such matters.

Both of them at once. Just like that. He was puking and she was coughing, and then she was dead and so was he, and it happened faster than it takes me to tell it.

A tragedy, said the Professor, rolling whisky on his tongue.

Charley drank. Yes, he said, I expect so.

Call it Fate. Call it Nature. Call it God. Call it whatever it pleases you to call it. We have to have agents for the things that happen. We cannot permit ourselves to believe that there is no pattern.

I got something I can call it.

And what might that be?

I call it shit.

Charley and the Professor became quite thoroughly drunk. And the words came from Charley. He lurched to the front window, pulled open the drapes. Sunshine came. It came in a cascade, scattering motes. Holy and most merciful Sabbath sunshine. Charley opened the window. He told the Professor the view extended twenty miles. He told the Professor about the day of the explosion of the *Molly G. Edwards*. We was sitting on the porch, said Charley, and I'd just brought Mama a glass of fresh cold well water. The sound made me drop the glass, but the glass didn't break. It sure was some strong glass. Hey, I'm eighteen years of age . . . you realize that? You think I'm old enough to have what's happened to me today happen? Grinning, Charley staggered to the sideboard and refilled his glass. He returned to the ottoman. He flopped down. The motes had gathered themselves around the Professor's head in a corrupted drunken halo. Charley spoke of the dead tufted scalp of his *friend* George's mother. He spoke of George's insistence on looking at the bodies. He spoke of George's good looks. He spoke of how long he and George had been *friends*. He spoke of swimming expeditions and games of toss. He spoke of rain and breath and laughter. He spoke of poor mad Mrs Weatherly. He spoke of love, of cowardice, of Nancy and her hair and her tiddies and her dear weak chin. He spoke of the new erect George who had taken Nancy to that old barn and had seduced her, this aloof George who now owned Nancy as completely as any of those Southron planters owned black niggers, this ambitious George who sought to enter West Point as the first step toward the seeking of splendor. Oh Charley talked and talked; he rocked from side to side; he beat his palms together; he talked and he drank, and after a time he told the Professor of his unworthiness even to kiss the hem of Nancy's dress; he told the Professor it was good to be a clown and an oaf; it made people cotton up to a person; he talked and talked, did this bereaved and flabbergasted Charley Wells; he talked and he drank; he talked and the Professor listened; he talked through spit and the hot sting of the whisky; he talked until the whisky came back on him; he talked until he swooned.

The Professor carried him upstairs to bed. He slept until nightfall, and when he awoke he heard voices. The house was full of mourners. The Professor was gone. People tiptoed in and out of Charley's room. They offered him their most sincere condolences. He lay gray and sick. An old lady brought him some lukewarm soup. He sipped at it. It was a beef and noodle broth, and it did not taste half bad. Later he went downstairs. More people were in the parlor. Slowly he moved among them. He had washed his face. He had combed his hair. He had rinsed out his mouth with salt. He wore a clean suit, and he had polished his shoes. The mourners shuffled timidly amidst the velvet and the cutglass and the mahogany and the ormolu of the parlor. Charley's face was solemn and drawn and unutterably brave. The mourners spoke to him of God's will. Oh yes, said Charley, I understand. His head hurt, and the salt had failed to rid his mouth of the remembered sourness of the whisky. Much later, after the last mourner had gone home, Charley again attacked the whisky, and this time he passed out on the floor in the hallway at the bottom of the stairs.

A week or so after his parents' burial, Charley walked into a riverfront establishment called Bagwell's Saloon. It was across the road from the Titusville wharf, and its general aspect consisted of equal parts heat, airlessness, rancor and the fume of drunkards. It was frequented by bargemen and the like. It did a good business. Bargemen liked to drink. Old Pete Bagwell, the irascible owner of the place, was rumored to be worth in excess of fifty thousand dollars, and Charley could believe the rumor. Pete Bagwell was stertorous and disputatious in the extreme, and no one understood why he had made such a success of the place, but a success it was, and the river people gathered there like worms on a dead goat. Charley sort of liked the place. When he was in Bagwell's Saloon, he could say and do as he damn well pleased. Elsewhere, he'd always had to think a bit on his talk and his actions. But none of the patrons did business in the Wells grocery; none carried tales; none gave much of a whoop about much of anything. Old Pete Bagwell's beer came in kegs from Louisville; he always kept it very cold. Charley had been drinking beer for more than a year now. It made him piss a great deal, but otherwise he detected no particularly adverse effects. Beer made him feel very strong and large. It made his oafish laughter even louder. He drank the beer from immense mugs, and the feel of the foam was cool and prickly against his nose, and sometimes it produced great delighted sneezes. He really did prefer beer to whisky. He could handle beer with a great deal more skill. It only made him piss; it had never made him swoon. The Professor was very taken with whisky, however. The Professor was a regular patron of Bagwell's Saloon. His favorite whisky was the Irish. When he had put away enough of it, he recited poetry and spoke at great length of stunning and heroic sexual adventures. Charley and the Professor had been nodding acquaintances before the death of Charley's mother and father. Now, though, they were closer, and never mind the fact that Charley hadn't seen the man since that wretched day. Charley had embraced the man's belly. Thus they had to be closer. And the Professor had heard Charley's confession, just like that Catholic priest from over by Boonville. Charley wished the Professor had attended the funeral. Just about everyone else in town—including George Peters—had been there. The day was gray and crisp, and a nice cooling breeze came from the northwest, and the Rev Mr Chorpening's vestments flapped and whipped and snapped as he read the graveside prayers, and at one point in the proceedings the breeze sent Clive F. Weatherwax's immaculately funereal high silk hat whirling into the branches of a nearby tree. A small boy shinnied up the tree and retrieved the hat, which was a bit dusty but otherwise none the worse for the adventure. Clive F. Weatherwax gravely gave the boy a dime. The double funeral was generally conceded to have been a splendid one. It was later that day, after the prayers and the lowering of the coffins and the solemn handshakes and kisses of the assembled mourners, after Charley had returned to the house and had sat alone in the parlor, after he had stared mutely for a number of dry racking hours at the smash and clutter of cutglass and ormolu with which his late mother had furnished that sad and forsaken room, after he had fingered antimacassars and pressed a cheek against the soft leather of his father's chair; it was then that Charley decided he had to seek out the Professor. In the first place, he was in the Professor's debt. The Professor had permitted him to talk, to expose and dissect his soul. A big fat bag of gas the Professor surely was, but who else ever had permitted Charley to do such a thing? Charley was the oaf, the clown; who gave a damn about such a person? Not even Charley's parents ever had permitted him confession. There had been times when he'd wanted to lay open some private agonies for them, but they hadn't ever given him the opportunity. He never had seen within them a willingness to listen. And he figured that, had it been there, he would have seen it. (A smile perhaps? A warm hand? He had waited for a sign, and none had been forthcoming. Oh they had smiled, and sometimes their hands had been very warm, but the willingness really to listen had not been there, and so he'd kept his own counsel. The oaf had never withdrawn.) And there was a second reason Charley wanted to see the Professor. Perhaps there was something the Professor could tell him. The Professor was a man of experience and perhaps a certain flatulent wisdom. Charley sought to listen to him. About what, he did not know. He simply sought to listen. And so, a few days after the funeral, Charley walked down to the river, to Bagwell's Saloon. He walked through a hazy purple twilight, and his belly was hot with alarms and tumults; he walked to that scabrous saloon and bought drinks for everyone and waited for the Professor. And did not wait in vain. Grunting, snuffling, bellying through the swinging doors, the Professor entered the place, waved at all his assembled cronies, waved at Pete Bagwell, grinned, chortled, bellowed obscene insults, was answered with hoots and laughter. Then he saw Charley, who was sitting alone at a table in the rear of the place. A man came away from the bar. He inclined his head toward Charley, whispered something in the Professor's ear. The Professor nodded, tugged at his beard, walked to Charley's table.

Jim Patterson tell you I bought drinks for the house? said Charley.

Indeed he did, said the Professor. Which makes me rue my tardiness tonight.

You shouldn't. Sit down. I'll buy you a drink.

I am honored, said the Professor, seating himself.

Charley hollered for Irish for the Professor, more beer for himself. Old Pete Bagwell himself in the flesh brought the beer and the whisky.

On second thought, said Charley, grinning at old Pete, bring the bottle for my friend here.

*Well*now, said Prof Frye, smiling.

You crazy? said Pete Bagwell.

No, said Charley. Do like I say.

Pete Bagwell shrugged. All right, he said, moving back toward the bar, all right, it's your money.

Charley lifted his beer mug. I owe you a debt, he said to the Professor.

You owe me nothing, said the Professor. He lifted his glass.

They touched glasses, drank. Old Pete returned with the bottle of Irish. He made a sour face at the Professor. This really ought to be a caution, he said. He placed the bottle in front of the Professor. Then, speaking to Charley, old Pete said: I hope to hell you know what you're doing.

I know what I'm doing, said Charley.

He talks a lot and raises the old Ned.

I know that.

All *right,* said old Pete, and his reluctance came in a whine.

The Professor winked at old Pete.

Jesus, said old Pete. He went away. He went behind the bar and mumbled.

The Professor sniggered.

Drink up, said Charley.

Our beloved publican does not lie, said the Professor, emptying his glass and pouring himself another drink of the Irish. He suppressed his sniggering, peered solemnly at Charley and said: Really, you owe me nothing. I did what anyone would have done.

No. That's not true. You *listened.*

I beg your pardon?

You listened to *me.* To what *I* had to say.

Oh. Well. The whisky was free.

That's not all of it.

Mm, said the Professor. He drank. He pursed his lips.

You had the decency to—

Don't use that word. Please.

All right. But I'm beholden to you. Believe that.

I believe it, said the Professor.

Charley sipped beer. How come you weren't at the burials?

The burials? Your parents?

Yes. I looked for you.

If I told you why, my dear young sir, you might just laugh in my face.

Take the chance.

All right, said the Professor. All *right.* If you *must* know, I was fucking your preacher's maiden sister.

Pamela Chorpening? *Her?*

None other than.

My God.

The intelligent Rake does not waste opportunities. With her brother presiding at the burials, Pamela and I were able to use his house. She is a splendid woman. I am quite successful with the kin of clerics, if I do say so myself.

Charley shook his head. He wondered if he dared believe what the Professor had told him. Miss Pamela Chorpening was about thirty, dark and slender, silent, almost beautiful. Again Charley shook his head. Then he said: I want to believe you. You know that? I want to believe you because then maybe you can tell me some things that are worth hearing.

I fear I don't follow you at all.

Godalmighty, Professor, what's it all about?

How's that?

Living. *Living.* Remember what you said at my house the morning my folks died? About Fate and Nature and all that? And remember how I called it all shit?

Yes. Vaguely.

Isn't there anything more to it than that?

Oh yes. A great lot.

Then *tell* me.

The Professor smiled. He finished his drink, poured another. He gulped it down, then said: Would you like for me to declaim?

What?

Declaim. It means to speak at great length, to harangue.

All right. I want to know if there's something *you* know that maybe I can use. I been thinking on a whole lot of things.

But I declaim too much. This whisky is excellent, but it never fails to loosen my tongue. I shouldn't have told you about Miss Chorpening.

I won't tell. I don't give that much of a damn.

Mrs Weeks, too.

What?

I have been fucking Mrs Weeks for the past three years.

Charley didn't know what to say. Mrs Sara Weeks was the *wife* of the *Presbyterian* minister, the Rev Abner D. Weeks. She was thin and blond, and she painted china. Again Charley shook his head, and finally he said: Now *there* I find it real hard to believe you.

Nonetheless, said the Professor, it is true. Our friend Mr Weeks calls her his Beloved Sister. He hasn't let her have any since their wedding night. I ask you—what is any reasonably healthy woman to do?

My Lord, how do you do it?

Kindness.

What?

Its uses are delicious. Sweet words. Gentle deceits. I may talk too much, but I am no brute. And anyway, the kindly approach is invariably more successful.

Tell me.

I beg your pardon?

Tell me about kindness. Tell me about the things you know.

It may take a long time.

Well, there is plenty of whisky.

The Professor smiled. Why me? he said. Why come to me as though I were some sort of authority?

I don't know. Maybe because you heard me out.

Like a priest?

Yes.

And now you seek wisdom from the priest?

Yes.

A priest who boasts too indiscreetly on his carnal conquests?

Well, it just means you're a human priest.

The Professor chuckled. Eh, he said, yes indeed.

So go ahead.

The Professor nodded. All right, he said. He squinted at the bottle of Irish. He shook his head. Remarkable, he said. Truly remarkable. Potatoes. Great God. *Potatoes*. Such unalloyed transport from such a homely source. Ah, the Irish. Fine people. Heh. Well. Be that as it may, as I understand it, you are urging me to overwhelm you with the rococo splendors of my rhetoric. You seek wisdom from me. Well, all right, I shall attempt to oblige you. Here the Professor hesitated. He drank until his glass was empty. He grinned, belched, patted his belly, refilled his glass. He resumed: The other morning, the morning of your parents' death, you spoke to me, young man, of many things. You may rest assured, incidentally, that I never shall divulge them to another human being. At any rate, I should say that the substantial preponderance of your words had to do with Miss Nancy Quimby, who is surely by any standard a marvelous female creature. Luminous. A young lady to make the blood simmer. Ah, no doubt about it. I tell you . . . if I thought there was the barest chance for me to—ah, but I stray from the point. Forgive me. To return to your particular difficulty, it is quite clear to me that you judge yourself to be in love with Miss Quimby, despite your knowledge that your friend, or perhaps I should say *erstwhile* friend, George Peters has been having sexual congress with her for some time now. You feel, because of some real or imagined cowardice, that you are not fit to, as you put it, kiss the hem of her dress. Is that a fair assessment?

Yes.

And you hate George Peters, don't you?

Well, I don't know as it's gone that—

Please. Please. Please. I implore you. Do not waste my time with denials of the hatred. I understand full well that you do not wish it to be known, but I am your *priest*, remember?

All right. All right. I hate him. Then, grinning, Charley said: I confess.

The Professor nodded. I believe I understand your anguish, he said.

And—in my own corrupted way—perhaps I share some of it. As you shall see later in the course of this harangue of mine. Provided, that is, I remember to bring it up.

What?

When one's habits incline toward the hortatory, one occasionally loses sight of one's point. But then I believe you have been thoroughly warned. You have *asked* for this, and so perforce I proceed.

All right.

You have spoken warmly of your love. Correct?

Correct.

And this even though you fully realize how thoroughly George Peters has smashed and shredded what no doubt was an excellent fine maidenhead. Correct?

Correct.

And now your parents are dead, and you don't know what to do about *that* either. Correct?

Correct.

Splendid. Now at least we have sketched the nature of your troubles. We can proceed. I believe I have a solution for you—although I must warn you that you will have to adhere to its principles with a great deal more devotion than *I* have been able to summon lately. In other words, do as I say, not as I do. Do you follow me?

Yes.

Good. Now then, the solution to your difficulties is centered on one word. That one word is Love. The intelligent manipulation of it. After all, no man is immune to its sweet conceits, but why should not an intelligent man use it to further his own ends? After all, fire can burn flesh, but it also can keep a house warm. Its qualities are dependent on the uses to which it is put. The same can be said for Love. A wise man should be able to reach an accord with it. This is only possible, however, if he understands its *mortality*. Human beings are mortal, and so is Love. You loved your parents, but now they are dead. Yes, yes, I know; it is all very tragic, but you haven't jumped into the river have you? No. Of course not. In point of fact, you have done just the opposite. Instead of doing away with yourself, you have come to your corrupted priest and asked him to tell you how to come to terms with existence. This means that, whether or not you understand it, you are aware of mortality. The end of your parents has not been the end of the human race. Clearly, what you have to do now is find other objects for your Love. There are, I am certain, many candidates, provided you take the time to seek them out. You say you love Nancy Quimby but she does not love you because you are unworthy. Well, kindly forgive me for speaking so rudely, but that is all a great heap of

frog shit. You have permitted yourself to become entangled in an empty
concept of heroism, and God spare us from heroes. And anyway, there is
such a thing as patience. I happen to be privy to some of the specifics of
the Quimby-Peters matter, and believe me, it will come to nothing. George
Peters is perhaps the most intelligent of those threadbare yokels who
attend my Southern Indiana Eclectic Institute, and he certainly has a
pleasing aspect, but he is a person of immense ambition, and for him
Nancy Quimby is just so much baggage . . . pleasant enough for now,
but certainly not the sort of young woman to be married, not by *him*, what
with his *ambition*. As you perhaps know, he is interested in a military
career. He sees himself as some sort of nascent hero, and Nancy Quimby
is inadequate as far as his lofty view of himself is concerned. God knows
who would be adequate. Perhaps an Arabian princess. As you perhaps
can deduce, I do not particularly like young Mr Peters, but at the same
time I would not care to attempt to thwart him. And neither should you.
And anyway, all you have to do is wait. Eventually the road will be clear.
He will abandon your beloved, and you can resume your pursuit. And
please don't aggravate yourself feeling ashamed because of that mad day
you think you were demolished by poor Mrs Weatherly. There is no cop-
ing with insanity. You behaved in a manner most sane. You ran. You got
out of there. I would have done precisely what you did. Any sane man
would have. Are you following the convulsions of all this?

I think so, said Charley, nodding.

Good, said the Professor. He poured himself another drink, wiped his
forehead, tugged at his beard, scratched his chin. Now then, he said, to
continue. It seems to me that human existence can only be dealt with in
terms of the *possible*. A reasonable man must avoid cosmic designs. He
must simply accept his life as it happens. We are all of us, after all, simply
human, and cosmic designs are beyond us, and so why should we waste
our time in such barren pursuits? Do you know Goethe? Do you know the
Young Werther and his fabled Sorrows?

Who?

Werther.

No.

Good. Goethe and his foolish hero have destroyed too many otherwise
worthwhile young men. Damn all Romantics, and damn all works of
Romance. They see existence in terms of Ideals that Dazzle. And that is
shit, sir. Absolute hogwash. Existence is the *possible,* I say. The man who
understands the *possible* is the man whose days will contain at least a
modicum of serenity, and of course a modicum is all any of us can expect.
This belief surely applies to Love. Exercise your Love in those places where

it will have the opportunity to draw breath. Do not expend yourself on the unattainable. If a certain Love eludes you, strike it. Bury it. Tamp down the grave with heavy boots.

How's that done?

The Professor smiled. It's done, he said, by *willing* it done. It's done by accepting the way things *are* and *not* the way one *wishes* they were. And, don't forget, there are certain, uh, fleshly immutables.

How's that?

Fleshly immutables, said the Professor, chuckling. Hear me out. As you perhaps know, I am a man whose interests have been confined to the pursuit of food, spirits and fucking. I call these conditions the fleshly immutables. They have nothing to do with Love, and they have nothing to do with Christian piety; they are neither good nor bad; they simply exist, and their existence gives pleasure. I have cast my lot in the pursuit of them. *However,* and I want to emphasize this, I do not believe myself to be an evil person. I have a certain personal code of belief. I call it my Fucking Principle. It's a simple code, and it is not hampered by the *mortality* of Love. Its principal ingredients—and please do not laugh—are kindness and consideration. When I pursue a woman, I of course prevaricate, but never with sinister intent. What is so dreadful about telling a woman the things she wants to hear? I understand the uses of rhetoric and hyperbole. I have never yet fucked a woman who didn't *want* to be fucked. God forbid that you should think of me as a rapist or seducer. Far from it. My lies are creations of beauty, and I honestly believe myself to be sweet and gentle. Liars almost always are. Think it over. Aren't most lies simply instruments for the avoidance of pain? I have fucked women in New York, Massachusetts, Vermont, Rhode Island, Ohio, Mississippi (a nigger, and I could talk to you about *her* for hours and perhaps days), Maryland, Tennessee, Kentucky, Pennsylvania, and of course Indiana (I have kept a list; it comforts me from time to time), and not once, *not one time,* have I been anything less than considerate, warm, devoted. Fuck them all, I say, only never be cruel. Display to them your special *mortal* Love. This is the nub of my Principle—awareness of the *mortality.* Have I lost you?

No. Not at all. This is real good. Just what I wanted. Don't stop.

The fleshly immutables, my boy. Remember them. And remember my Principle.

I will.

The Professor nodded. He drank, wiped his mouth, then said: Splendid. But be warned—one must be vigilant. I fear I have not been so vigilant. Lately I have had trouble keeping Love's *mortality* uppermost in my mind.

Oh? That so?

Yes. It is so. I have been having curious thoughts about Mrs Weeks. Not Miss Chorpening, who is a fine woman and all that but really rather dry and uninspired in carnal endeavors. I aim soon to break off with her. No, it is Mrs Weeks who vexes me, ravels my sleep. I am reluctant to admit such a thing, but lately I've almost come to disbelieve in Love's *mortality.* My feelings for Mrs Weeks almost make me want to grapple with the damn cosmos, and the devil take my Principle, my fleshly immutables. I sometimes am almost ready to believe I am experiencing a larger Love. I don't like it. I don't like it one damn bit.

How do you explain it?

I can't.

Does it mean that all the things you think are shit?

No. It simply means that sometimes I yield to weakness. *My beliefs have not changed.* The only sane life must be centered on an awareness of the *possible* and the *mortal.* This is my implacable belief. Freeze it, if you will. Stuff it in a pocket. And please do not think that such an attitude implies cynicism and defeat. On the contrary. Awareness of the *possible* and the *mortal* can transmogrify a man into a giant. Especially *now,* at *this* time, in *this* nation. I expect there will be a war soon, and it will be won by the side that has the keener understanding of reality, and of course that side will be the North, and the understanding of reality will do away with the need for heroes, and it will thus be a war like no other war. In one convulsion, the hero will be rendered extinct. The businessman, the inventor, the moneylender—all will combine to unhorse him, and the peal of innocent bugles will be only a memory of fools. . . .

Yes. Go on.

The Professor shrugged. This no doubt will come as a great shock to you, he said, grinning, but I have nothing further to say.

Charley laughed. He sipped his beer. The conversation drifted away from the Professor's attitudes, but this did not matter. Charley saw. Yes, he surely did. He smiled at the Professor, and the hortatory engines of the Professor's rhetoric churned at full throttle for several hours, and Charley understood quite clearly, and he even understood that from time to time he would suffer relapses and make mistakes (as indeed later he did, with his espousal of Copperheadism and his subsequent expulsion from Titusville), but he even would make the mistakes work for him (as indeed later he did, when Nancy out of loneliness married him, and because of her late husband's heroism she and Charley went to live in a wondrously Arcadian village called Paradise Falls), and he even understood that the relapses and mistakes were *mortal* and thus proof that the philosophy was viable, and so he smiled at the Professor that night, that ancient

doomed river night there in Bagwell's Saloon in dear old accursed Titusville, smiled and sipped, listened carefully to all the oratory, listened until
the Professor became too drunk for speech. Then, still smiling, Charley
helped the Professor out the door and supervised the Professor's noisy and
splendrous vomiting, an immense ejaculation of bile that carried off the
end of the Titusville wharf and far, far out into the silvery moonlit river,
and of course he always would revere this man, this Prof Tobias G. Frye,
PhD (Harvard), above all men (the words were *possible* and *mortal,* and
they had clamped themselves in Charley's brain with a high singing ferocity), and he thanked Fate or Nature or God or whatever for the existence of
this beloved friend and priest and teacher, and oh yes, now he knew *truth,*
and he always *would* know it, and everything was so terribly clear, and his
understanding never would be erased, *never,* come God or battalions of
angels, come horror or pain or shame, and now he knew he had the
capacity to face whatever sat waiting for him, no matter what (such a
knowledge! such a revelation! such a clear stinging slap of truth!), through
all the fine free clench and butt and fart and clank of all the days of all
the years of his life, a life that *now* surely would carry him to greatness . . .

Back to it, yes. A man was the total of his history. Charley Wells, the
Acterhof House sheets drawn tightly under his chin, his sleep warm and
gummy, traveled—in his accurate dreams—back to his boyhood as he snored
away that Columbus Day in the year 1865, and the accuracy of his
dreams was hideous, and thus his sleep was not much of a sleep, even
though it *was* heavy, even though Nancy, the precious pussy long withheld, *was* lying there next to him. He had gone, in his uncomfortable
sleep, back to the beginnings of his rakishness, to the fleshly immutables
and the Fucking Principle, and when he awoke he understood that it did
not matter that he had destroyed the wasted James Perry Blood. All that
mattered was the greatness. The time for feeling sorry for people had
passed a long time ago, and there was no returning, and he didn't even
want to return, and that was a fact.

After the poker game broke up, Charley and Nancy slept ten hours.
Charley had supper sent up to their suite. It included two bottles of champagne. Nancy smiled. She drank a great deal of the champagne. She
told him he was quite the fellow. He grinned, pinched her buttocks. She
slapped at his hand. She giggled. Oh *you,* she said. He watched her very
closely. He did not want her to hate him. Later he mounted her. She
threshed and groaned with proper abandon. She even spoke words of love.
He told her she was a fine girl.

I'm just where I ought to be, she said. People surely get their due.

What are you talking about?

Don't act so innocent.

Nancy, I love you.

I won't give you any trouble. I deserve being your wife.

Sh.

Sure is something.

What?

Being Episcopalian. All that kneeling and all. My.

The next afternoon a messenger came with the deed to James Perry Blood's land and home. The messenger brought it to Charley's store. It was a Friday (a Friday the thirteenth, in point of fact), and business was extraordinary. Word of the fabled poker game had reached everyone in Paradise Falls save the blind, the deaf and the incompetent. Charley personally waited on just about half the population of the village. He grinned at one & all, and the ladies were engulfed by mighty torrents of his rhetoric. The messenger's name was Arthur Sturgeon. He was a skinny towheaded boy of twenty, and he had been reading law with ElRoy Mauk for more than a year. He smiled when he handed Charley the envelope containing the deed. He said: Mr Wells, if you ever need a good lawyer, I'd be obliged if you tried me out. I got a feeling I could get along with you like a bug with his sweetie and the two of them laying in warm fur. Charley laughed. I just might do that, he said. I like a fellow who speaks out, even if he is trying to steal business from his employer. Art Sturgeon's smile remained. Ah, wellsir, he said, a young fellow he's got to look out for himself, isn't that so? And Charley said: Yes indeed. He smote the boy's chest, gave him a dollar. I thank you very much, said Art Sturgeon. He winked, and only the good Lord knew what the wink was supposed to mean, but Charley went ahead and laughed again anyway. Arthur Sturgeon walked out of the place in a sort of strut. Charley studied the deed. Everything seemed in order. A note from ElRoy Mauk was enclosed. Charley's signature would need witnessing, and then the deed would have to be filed with the county recorder. In the note, ElRoy Mauk volunteered to attend to all the legal arrangements. Charley visited ElRoy Mauk later that day. He told ElRoy Mauk to go right ahead. He signed the deed, and ElRoy Mauk shook his hand, and not a word was said about the destruction of James Perry Blood. Then or ever. Not even after the coal was discovered. Not even after Charley made all those millions of dollars.

1866 . . .

Ike Underwood decides to go out of the chair business. It never was much of a business, and he never should have bought it from old Frank Beeman's estate four years ago. But Frank Beeman was a close friend, and so was—and is—Frank's widow Edith. So Ike Underwood purchased the damn establishment for ten thousand dollars, which was more than enough money to set up Edith for the rest of her life. Frank Beeman had had eight men on his payroll, and Ike had retained them all, even though not a one of them had been worth a whole lot. But four years has been enough charity, and so on July 1 of this year Ike closes down the Beeman Chair Co works. He does, however, arrange new employment for all eight of the workers. His loss in the four years has been about fifteen thousand dollars—plus of course the ten thousand he paid the Beeman estate. He is chided by his wife Phoebe. You fraud, she says. You aren't nearly the bear you want people to think you are. Ah, such a reprobate. Shame on you.

Amelia Burkhart Soeder dies in childbirth in early May. The infant, a boy, lives for just eight days. Amelia dies with her bedroom windows open. She has asked that they be open. She has asked that she be able to feel sunshine. Her husband, the blond Christian, attends her at her death. She does not make much noise. She holds the noise within her, squeezing it. She smells the May air. It occurs to her that this sort of air needs the services of a poet. But the only poet she knows is off at a place called Oberlin. Her mother and father wail and lament. They embrace. They croon. Amelia Burkhart dies pale and moist, loins straining, teeth bared. Her mouth is open, and she is able to taste the fragrances of air and earth and sun.

O God of apples, we Thy humble servants do give thanks to Thee for seeing to it that our apples devour our worms. Protect us, however, dear Lord, from serpents. O magisterial God of Arcadia, love us, protect us from fiends and rascals and interlopers and Masonbrinks. Look Thee to our steeples, our hymns, attend to our baked beans, our rag rugs, the kindnesses we shower upon our dogs. We praise Thee, dear God. Blow us Thy loving clouds and winds and gentle green rains. Caress our fruit. Buttress our faith. Be all things. There is so little we know. In the name of the Father, and of the Son, and of the Holy Ghost, we do most heartily and resolutely thank Thee. Amen.

The new President, this Johnson, surely has turned out to be a disappointment. He apparently intends to treat those damned Southron traitors with softness. It is becoming more and more apparent that something must be done about this foolish drunken Tennessee Democrat weakling. Says Virgil T. Light: Perhaps a horsewhipping will bring him into line. When I think of all the lives that were lost in the late war, it makes my bile come to my throat each time that damn jackass speaks of his weak-kneed policies of what he calls reconciliation and what I call outright bare-faced *treason*.

The Grand Army of the Republic is organized nationally, and Virgil T. Light immediately obtains a charter for a Paradise Falls post. By the end of the year, the post has more than two hundred members, and of course Virgil T. Light has been chosen commander.

Christian Soeder vanishes from the county. No one knows where he has gone. Not even his brother. Amelia Burkhart Soeder's grave lies in the side of a hill behind the house her husband built just last year. The grave faces the morning sun. Christian Soeder dug the grave. He also dug the grave for his infant son. The two graves are set close together. The morning sun is splendid out there in the country. It is golden today, blue tomorrow. Christian Soeder dug the graves neatly. An excellent job.

But enough, dear God, of anguish. We love Thee. We do. We do.

A Great Man:

THERE WERE NO MORE poker sessions. Charley's cash winnings from that one dark and thrilling game had come to about fifteen thousand dollars, and it did not surprise him that there were no more sessions. His adversaries had not been that rich, and one of them—James Perry Blood—had not been rich at all. So the sessions were tacitly discontinued. Charley did not complain. He did not have to. He had made his. And anyway, the old well was dry. But he didn't believe it hurt anything for him to laugh —at least privately. He was especially amused by James Perry Blood's bloody honor. I knew the deed would be delivered, he told Nancy. Like ElRoy Mauk said, Blood is a man of honor.

And that makes you laugh? said Nancy.

Yes.

Why?

Ahhh Nancy, think a little on it. Ponder. Wrinkle your forehead. Ask yourself how come we're here. Don't you see? It's not enough that they *invite* us; they even go so far as to just about *give* us their money—and, in the case of this fellow Blood, their land as well. Believe me, I have encountered bad poker players and I have encountered bad poker players, but *these* people, God have mercy on their poor innocent pocketbooks.

I still don't think it's right that you should laugh.

I can't help it . . .

They didn't invite *us*. They invited *me*.

Well, said Charley, we're married.

Mr Blood didn't play so badly.

He did when it mattered.

He's as good as dead. Better than dead.

I can't help that. I warned him.

Charley?

Yes?

I want a glass of water.

All right.

My mouth tastes like mud.

All *right*.

Doesn't *your* mouth ever taste like mud?

Ah well, he couldn't really expect her to understand. He'd not yet made her that aware of *possibilities* and *mortality,* and she didn't really understand the greatness that was bearing down on him. But there were others in this village who did. Which pleased him a great deal. Which made him grin his large oafish grin. The poets spoke of victory, of empire. They were speaking to Charley. The orators preached greatness. They were describing Charley's future. The village trooped into his store after the fabled poker game, and there were those who looked at Charley with a sort of horror, and there were those who grinned and turned away their faces, and there were those who came right out and *said* how profoundly they envied him, and from all sides, from carpenters and housewives and politicians and small grainyvoiced boys, came a hot surge of admiration, and Charley detected it as an old hound detected the odor of a small wounded wild thing. It was a time of pilgrims, and the pilgrims came to honor Charley and praise him and look upon his countenance; they came in reverence; they came in order that they experience the oafish murderous flesh and heart and gristle of him, and the feet of the pilgrims slapped and scruffed, and all Charley needed was a sound of fifes and cymbals. He spoke; he blessed them all. Thank you, Mrs Evans. A pleasure to do business with you. No, Mrs Abernathy, I do not have the slightest idea what I'll do with the land. I truly regret the entire affair. In a very real way, I wish none of it had happened. But, now that it *has* happened, I have no choice but to accept the land. Otherwise I would be dishonoring Mr Blood's . . . ah, his *word.* Yes, Mrs Rathbun, it *was* a tiring night. Nuts

did you say? Walnuts? Yes, we have splendid walnuts. Well, Mrs Limbach,
I only hope I am not too deeply resented. After all, Mr Blood comes from
an old family. I expect there are those who feel he should not have been
permitted to gamble so heavily. Believe me, I regret all this as much as anyone does. But what am I to do? Please, if you can, place yourself in my
position. Look, Sheriff, I know as well as you do that it probably will kill
him. And, god damn it, I *tried* to give him back the deed. But he would
have none of it. You don't have to believe *me*. Jesus, go ask ElRoy Mauk.
Liverwurst, Mrs Tayloe? Yes ma'm. We have bratwurst as well, if ever it
should strike your fancy.

James Perry Blood took up residence with his cousin, ElRoy Mauk. From
time to time he was seen sitting on the front porch of the Mauk home on
South High Street, but he seldom ventured off that porch, and Claude
Dill's saloon saw no more of him. He had a small room at the rear of the
house. The room was full of books, and most of the books were histories,
great sweeping works that addressed themselves to empires and dynasties
and ruined ambition. It was said he had read all of Gibbon. Shakespeare
also was a favorite, according to what ElRoy Mauk told Charley, with
Richard III a most favored favorite. James Perry Blood never visited his old
home place. He ate little, coughed and spat less, took more baths, seldom
spoke. He even from time to time smiled.

Charley rented the old Blood place to a farmer named Wainscott. It
was this Wainscott who discovered the coal. His full name was Winfield
C. Wainscott, and he and his skinny wife had eleven children, the oldest
not yet twenty. He talked Charley into having the old Blood place painted
a bright yellow. He was a very fastidious sort of person. I have to be, he
told Charley. Otherwise, the children would take the place apart board
by board. Naomi and I are very careful with them. There is Scripture
every night, and we never permit them to raise their voices.

Winfield C. Wainscott was about fortyfive. He did not look like a
farmer. He wore spectacles, and his face was thin, clerkish. His hands
were red and thick, though, and his walk was heavyfooted, farmerish.
Still, one did not get the impression of a farmer. Perhaps this was because he talked so damn much. And yet he was a good farmer. He had
forced his oratorical and clerkish disposition into a pattern for which it
had not really been suited, and the forcing had been successful. (The
old Blood farm made money for him—not much, but some. He never was
arrears in the rent.) As far as Charley was concerned, this Wainscott
was something of a substantial human being, or at least a remarkable one.
Otherwise, he never would have made such a good farmer. He and his
family were from down in Meigs County by the Ohio River. His father's
farm had failed a decade and a half before, and since then Wainscott had

worked—and with large success—a number of farms in several southeastern
Ohio counties. His success hadn't been very fruitful, however. As he put
it: I come to a county and I rent a place, and nobody thinks it's worth
much of a damn. So I work it for a year or two, and the crops come good,
and the place begins to make money, and so what happens? The owners
throw me off and give the place to some relative, usually a son or a soninlaw. I tell you, I'm getting to believe it's not too smart to be too good at
your work. It gives people notions, and the next thing you know you're out
on the road and it's like your work didn't matter a speck except so some
boy could take what *you've* done and live off the fat of it. I call it a hell of
a state of affairs.

To Charley, Wainscott's complaining was something of a bore, but he
put up with it cheerfully enough. After all, the fellow was prompt with
the rent, and this was what mattered. As for the coal . . . well, Charley
had known nothing about it. As far as he was concerned, the Blood acreage
he had won in the storied poker game was of no overwhelming value. If
he could derive from it the rent money and perhaps a little extra from
timber, he was satisfied. It was hilly acreage, and the timber was of a low
grade, and he saw no riches in it. But then one day in the spring of 1866
he was visited by Winfield C. Wainscott, who told him: I do believe
there's a lot of coal on that land. I can see it in the sides of the hills. It
sets in streaks, and I can just about scoop it up with my bare hands.
Maybe I shouldn't be telling you about it. Maybe you'll decide to dig a
mine, in which case I expect you'll throw me off. But I got to be honest.
I mean, better you finding out from *me* than from somebody else. If you
was to find out from somebody else, maybe you'd figure I was hiding it
from you. I think maybe you ought to come out this Sunday and take a
look for yourself. Charley agreed. He wasn't quite ready to accept Wainscott's views on honesty, but he certainly was willing to pay close mind to
the possibility of coal deposits. And so the following Sunday he and Nancy
rode out to the old Blood place and went for a little walk with Wainscott,
who chattered all the way. Wainscott took along a scythe. He used it to
clear a path up the side of a hill. Nancy, who was wearing a new blue
dress, tore her skirt. Charley asked her if she wanted to turn back. She
shook her head no. She told him it was too good to be out here where the
air was clean. Charley nodded. Wainscott was up ahead. He scrambled
up the side of a hill. He swung the scythe, clearing a path through high
grass. This way! he hollered, pointing toward a cluster of large flat rocks.
Charley and Nancy picked their way through grass and weeds and high
spiky bramble bushes. The earth was damp, scummy; it sucked at their
shoes. Charley had hold of Nancy's elbow. He steered her toward the
cluster of rocks. He was grunting. So was she. He supposed they had been

spending too much time in the hotel. His breath was heavy, and sweat came off his forehead in great fat smears. Some of it trickled from the point of his chin. He grinned at Nancy. She was wheezing now. She opened her mouth, moistened her lips, said nothing. When Charley and Nancy arrived at the cluster of rocks, Wainscott dropped to his hands and knees and began scraping at the side of a ledge. He broke several fingernails, but after a time he came up holding several small chunks of soft black rock. Sure does look like coal to *me*, he said. Sure does *feel* like it too. And there's plenty of it all around. It just about jumps up and slaps a person.

Let's see it, said Charley.

Wainscott handed Charley the chunks. Surely does feel like it, said Charley.

Nancy took the chunks from Charley. She wiped her face with the back of a hand. Yes, she said, it surely does.

Charley grinned. Well, he said, we appear to be in agreement. Then Charley turned to Wainscott and said: You suppose you could run down to the house and fetch me a shovel?

Glad to, said Wainscott. He made a happy humming noise, and then he said: This may just be quite a day.

Perhaps so, said Charley.

Wainscott scrambled back down the hill toward the house. Charley and Nancy seated themselves on the rocks. He spread his coat for her to sit on. She thanked him.

He's right, you know, said Charley.

About this maybe being quite a day?

Yes.

I wouldn't be surprised. I remember how once you said something to me about luck, about how you were going to grab it and squeeze the life out of it.

I meant that.

I know you did, said Nancy. She made a small mouth, stared at the sun. Charley grinned.

Sure is a lot of dogwood around here, said Nancy. I've always liked dogwood.

We could be rich.

Mm. Sumac, too. The color of it in the fall. Mm. Takes the breath away.

Charley grinned.

Wainscott returned with the shovel. Charley dug up several larger chunks of whatever it was. He filled his pockets with the chunks. Later that day he placed the chunks in a grip. He locked the grip, deposited it in the Acterhof House safe. The next morning he left Nancy in charge of the store. He told her to say nothing about the coal or whatever it was. He claimed the grip from the Acterhof House safe, then caught the 10 A.M. train for Columbus. He held the grip on his lap. He hummed and whistled. An old woman said shush. He paid her no mind. She glared at him. He grinned. He arrived in Columbus shortly after noon. He had a fried steak dinner in the depot restaurant, then called at the freight sales offices of the Columbus, Paradise Valley & Marietta Railroad. He spoke with a fellow named Downing, a florid middleaged man with a splendid set of Burnside whiskers. Downing was cordial. He shook hands with Charley, offered him a seat. Charley introduced himself as Chester Fargo, a businessman speculating in coal. Downing smiled. Your name is not Fargo is it? he said.

No, said Charley.

Why won't you tell me your real one?

Charley grinned. I may have to buy some leases, he said. If I told you my real name and where I was from, you people just might try to beat me to those leases.

Well now, we don't do business that way, said Downing, still smiling.

Hah, said Charley.

Downing chuckled. Ah, he said, wellsir, you are a one, aren't you?

I hope so.

All right, *Mr Fargo*. No more fencing. What is it we can do for you? No hard feelings?

Of course not.

Good, said Charley. Now then, can you people recommend a good firm of mining engineers and geologists or assayers or whatever they're called?

We can. But why?

Charley nodded toward the grip. He held it on his lap. I need some expert help, he said.

You have samples? Coal samples?

How on earth did you ever guess? said Charley.

Downing laughed. By God, sir! he said, chuckling, his voice large and jovial. You are *indeed* a one!

By God, sir, said Charley, so are you.

Downing recommended a firm called Mellow & Leathers. He told Charley its offices were over on West Broad Street. It's without question the best in this part of the country, said Downing. Charley thanked Downing. He said: I expect I'll be seeing you again. Good day for now. He shook hands with Downing, walked out onto High Street, hailed a cab, had the driver take him to the offices of his old adversary, William D. Stone, the food wholesaler. Stone was glad to see him, and they talked for a time of poisoned sardines and the like. Then Charley got down to the business at hand. I need to find a good firm of mining engineers and assayers, he said. I understand the best is an outfit called Mellow & Leathers. Can you find for me the name of its largest competitor?

William D. Stone looked puzzled. Why not just go to Mellow & Leathers? he wanted to know. I don't know much about the mining business, but it seems to me that outfit has a good reputation.

Can't do that, said Charley. I got a suspicion Mellow & Leathers is sleeping with the CPV&M. It was the CPV&M recommended those people. I don't want whatever they do going right back to the railroad. That's why I asked the railroad to make a recommendation. The way I see it, Mellow & Leathers is the last outfit I want to deal with.

It all sounds terribly devious.

It *is*. Look, I don't know shit from hardboiled eggs about the mining business. But I *do* know that the railroads are using every resource at their disposal in trying to find good mining property. It's good business. First of all, they're converting their locomotives from wood to coal. Secondly, mines create towns, and towns mean money, and the railroads can take some of the money out of the towns. Third, if a railroad owns enough mines, it can just about support itself by doing business *with* itself.

Well, that all makes sense.

Of course it does. Now then, look at my position. It so happens I own some property where there may or may not be—ah, now, I have said too much.

What?

You and your friend Ike Underwood. I have a faulty memory. The sardines. My Lord, I have told you far too much.

Ike Underwood? Who is Ike Underwood?

Charley laughed.

No. Really. You have mentioned that name to me before. Who *is* he?

You know damn well who he is. Don't act so innocent. He put you up to the business with the sardines.

Ah, the sardines. The damned sardines. Would you believe me if I told you it all was plainly and simply an accident?

No.

Well, it *was*.

Of course, said Charley, grinning.

William D. Stone laughed. He shook his head. Ah me, he said, I expect I just do not have a trustworthy face.

Laughter from Charley. He and William D. Stone clapped one another on the back, and then William D. Stone told him: All right. I can understand. I like you. If you don't care to, you don't have to reveal anything

more. I have a friend. I suspect he will be able to help you. He usually is in
the Neil House tap room at this hour of the day. Come on. Let's take a
stroll over there. Grinning, William D. Stone escorted Charley over to
the Neil House. Sure enough, William D. Stone's friend was standing at
the bar in the tap room. He was a tall bearded man, and his name was
Donald F. Platt. He had brilliant teeth. They were like polished tombstones. He was a representative of the Ohio Coal Mine Owners' Associa-
tion. That means lobbyist, he said, smiling, and please, in the interest of
good fellowship, call me Don. Charley also smiled. So did William D.
Stone. They took a table in a quiet corner of the place, and Charley
bought the first round of drinks. He asked Don Platt to recommend a good
mining engineering firm other than Mellow & Leathers. Said Don Platt:
You got something against Mellow & Leathers? Said Charley: No—except
that the people there are too close to the CPV&M. I don't want everything
they find out getting back to the CPV&M. When I want the CPV&M
to know what I'm up to, I'll tell them myself. Said Don Platt: Well,
that makes sense. Said Charley: Can you help me? Said Don Platt: I'll tell
you the truth. There isn't another really good firm in this town. Said Charley: That makes no difference. I'll go elsewhere. Said Don Platt: Well, in
that case, there's Barlett, Roberts, McGettrick & Adams up in Cleveland.
Believe me, there's no love lost between those people and Mellow & Leathers. It's a sassy and alert company, young men mostly, and I expect it
would do a job of work for you . . . whatever it is you want done. Charley
grinned. Uh, he said, with no disrespect to you, that's for me to know
and you to find out. Don Platt laughed, and so did William D. Stone.
Charley bought another round of drinks, then excused himself. He sent
Nancy a telegram: *Leaving for Cleveland tonight. Should be home Friday
afternoon.* In Cleveland the next day, he visited the offices of Barlett,
Roberts, McGettrick & Adams. He talked with a bald young fellow named
Fritz Voss, an Alsatian who had been in the United States only about six
months. Voss did not waste time with superfluous words. When Charley
handed him the chunks of coal or whatever it was, Voss nodded, excused
himself, went out of the office. Twenty minutes later he returned. He
explained to Charley that the analysis was only preliminary. However, the
chunks appeared to be of an extremely highgrade bituminous. The volatility and the sulphur content apparently are very low indeed, said Voss.
Charley grinned at Voss and said: That mean it's good coal? Said Voss:
It means it is excellent coal. *Most* excellent. Especially for a bituminous.
Most bituminous is not of a low volatility. It is what you call in this country *soft* coal, and most soft coal is highly volatile, which means it burns
quickly. Hence, it is not as valuable as the socalled *hard* coal, the anthracite, which is of a lower volatility. Naturally, a pound of anthracite, being

longer burning, is more valuable than a pound of bituminous. That should be apparent. However, in the case of the samples you gave me, the quality of the bituminous is splendid. And of course the low sulphur content also contributes to the, uh, *longevity* of the burning. Said Charley: I own the property where this coal came from. Or at least I own *some* of it. There's a possibility the deposit extends for I don't know how many miles. Can you come down and determine for me exactly how extensive the deposit is? Said Voss: Of course—if my employers give me permission. Charley nodded. I understand that, he said. He had Voss take him into another office, where he conferred with a stout redfaced man named Barlett. The arrangements were made. Voss' services would cost Charley thirty dollars a day plus expenses. He gave Barlett a cheque for one hundred fifty dollars as a retainer. Barlett smiled, told Charley it was a pleasure doing business with him.

Voss and Charley left for Paradise Falls the next morning. Voss' test boring gear rode in the baggagecar. He had little to say. They rode the Big Four to Columbus, then the CPV&M to Paradise Falls. Voss supervised the transfer of the gear from one baggagecar to the other. They arrived in Paradise Falls late in the evening. The gear was checked at the depot. They walked to the Acterhof House. Voss registered himself as a salesman from Columbus. Upstairs in his suite, Charley kissed Nancy and told her to keep her fingers crossed. She asked him what had kept him. Your telegram said you were coming back this afternoon, she said. Well, said Charley, it took a little longer than I thought. The next morning Charley and Nancy had breakfast with Voss. It was a Saturday morning, and the Acterhof House diningroom was not crowded. Charley hired a carriage. He and Voss dropped off Nancy at the store, then drove to the CPV&M depot and picked up Voss' gear. They rode out to the old Blood place, and Voss went to work. He clambered over rocks and treetrunks, across streams, up and down hills. He hacked at earth and rocks with his exotic equipment. He worked for eight days, and each night he locked himself in his room and analyzed the samples he had gathered. He carried his search across a number of hills and eventually beyond the limits of Charley's property, but Charley said nothing to him about it. In the eight days Voss found nine major seams of coal. The largest was fifteen feet thick and about two and a half miles long. Charley asked Voss how much that particular seam was worth.

Just about any sum you care to name, said Voss.

What?

I mean millions.

On *my* property?

Yes—or at least on the property you have represented as being yours.

Jesus Christ.

Mm, said Voss.

Could you keep what you know quiet?

I have to make a report to my employers.

You do?

Yes, but do not fear. Your secret will be kept. My employers are men of integrity and discretion. I would not have consented to work for them had they not been. I am not, sir, a common immigrant. I came to this country at the *express request* of Barlett, Roberts, McGettrick & Adams. I had many offers. The one from Barlett, Roberts, McGettrick & Adams was the most attractive. In the sense, that is, of probity and not money. Probity is valued highly by me. Do you understand that?

Yes, said Charley. How much would it cost me to get you to keep your knowledge to yourself?

A share.

How much?

Ten percent of the profits—plus a position as general superintendent at a salary to be arranged.

Done.

Are you serious?

I am very serious.

The two men shook hands. Charley grinned. Voss did not. The next day Voss returned to Cleveland and resigned his position at that temple of integrity, Barlett, Roberts, McGettrick & Adams. In the meantime, Charley obtained a plat map of Blood Township and the Village of Blood. Using a red crayon, he marked the boundaries of his property. Then, using a blue crayon, he marked the paths of the seams. In addition to his own property, a total of fourteen parcels was crossed by the seams. Eleven of the parcels were owned by none other than his old friend Isaac (Ike) Underwood. To be more exact, they were owned by the Paradise Falls Clay Products Co, of which Ike Underwood was founder and president. Until about five years before, these parcels had contained excellent deposits of clay. Now, however, most of the usable clay had been scooped out, and the land no longer was of any real value to Underwood. He had taken out some of the lowgrade timber on the land for use by the chair company he had owned, but now there was no more chair company, and it seemed to Charley that Underwood just might be inveigled out of the land— provided the inveigling were done cleverly enough. After all, the land was too wild and rocky for successful farming, and the timber wasn't much good, so why would Ike Underwood want to keep it? No, it seemed to Charley that some intelligent maneuvering just might snooker Underwood out of the property. All he had to do was hit upon a method. As for the other three parcels, Charley anticipated little trouble. They were owned by an impoverished farmer and his two sons. The farmer's name was John Ellsworth, and it was said he drank too much. His two sons, Peter and Ben, also were rumored to be strong addicts of the heavy waters. Charley's evaluation of the Ellsworths was correct: he received little trouble from them. Ike Underwood, on the other hand, was a much more difficult barrel of cheese. If he got wind that Charley was after his property, he no doubt would raise the price beyond reason—or, perhaps more likely, not sell at *any* price. Ike Underwood was in no way stupid. With Charley interested in obtaining those eleven apparently worthless parcels, the old fart no doubt would examine them with a powerful glass. And, if he did, he unquestionably would find out about the coal. Or, rather, the *extent* of the coal. After making a few discreet inquiries, Charley had learned that the existence of coal up there in Blood Township had been known for some time. The only thing was—no one had the slightest idea it was worth anything. The consensus was that it was too poor for mining. How this consensus had come about, Charley did not know. He was grateful for it, though. Very grateful indeed.

Now then, how to accomplish the snookering of Ike Underwood? William D. Stone had accused Charley of being devious, and ah that William D. Stone didn't know the half of it, but this time Charley would have to outdo even himself. He worked the problem in his mind, worked it and worked it, and finally he came up with an answer, and it was a splendidly convoluted answer, and he saw it as having a fine chance of success. It made him grin. It made him grin very widely. It was as devious as a rat in a swamp, and thus it pleasured him. Ah, dear old rascality.

As soon as Voss returned from Cleveland, he called on Charley at the Acterhof House. They held a lengthy discussion of the situation, and Voss agreed that Charley would have to have someone buy Ike Underwood's parcels *for* him.

Ah, I am available, said Voss.

Charley grinned. He punched Voss lightly in the belly. Voss winced.

You find the suggestion inadequate? Voss wanted to know.

Yessir, said Charley. Yes *sir,* I do indeed.

And why is that?

I can see it all. I give you the money, and you buy the property, and that's the last I see of it. You open a mine, and first thing out of the barrel you pay me back, and that's the end of *that.*

It was Voss' turn to grin. Ah, he said, it surely takes one to know one does it not?

Charley laughed. He whooped. He whacked Voss on a knee. You rascal you! he shouted.

Nancy, who had been in the bedroom, came out to see what the matter was. She wore a pink wrapper and not much else. Voss ran a hand over his bald head. He stood up, bowed. She hugged the wrapper to her bosom. She did not like Voss. She had told Charley she saw something *dirty* in Voss. She looked at Charley and asked him was he drunk. He grinned, told her he was perfectly all right, it was just that his friend Fritz here had made an extremely amusing remark. Oh, said Nancy. She shrugged, turned, went back into the bedroom. As soon as she had closed the door, Voss sat down. He smiled at Charley and said: You are an extremely fortunate man, Mr Wells. Your wife is very handsome. I have always been partial to large fullbosomed women.

Charley nodded. Yes, he said, she is a good old girl. Now then. About that land. Let me explain my thinking to you. My plan may take six months or so, but I do believe it'll work . . .

Voss listened carefully. From time to time he nodded. He rubbed his head, clucked, smiled. When Charley had finished outlining the specifics of the plan, Voss made a dry cackling sound and said: Excellent.

You really think so?

I do.

Good.

But what in the meantime am *I* to do?

No one here knows what you do for a living. Would it be beneath your dignity to clerk at my store for six months? I can say you're a cousin of a friend. I can say you're just off the boat. I can say you're really quite an intelligent fellow, obviously too intelligent to spend the rest of your life storeclerking, but that you're doing the clerking in order to sort of, uh, get your feet wet. Now then, does it all sound that much beneath your dignity?

Yes. It does.

Oh. Ah. That's too bad.

But I'll do it.

Fine!

The more I consider this scheme of yours, the more I feel it will succeed. We need that land. I can think of no more expeditious way of obtaining it.

That's the way to talk. Good for you. Wonderful.

The following afternoon Charley called on his friend Virgil T. Light. He told Virgil T. Light he had an idea that had been working itself in his mind for some time. Virge, he said, are you as prosperous as you want to be? Grinning, Virgil T. Light said: No. Who is? And Charley said: Good. Then hear me out. I have a proposition, and perhaps it has merit. For obvious reasons, we shall have to be discreet. For the time being, at any rate. I'm sure you'll see why. It has to do with something you know a lot about—furniture. Yessir, chairs, tables, beds, the whole shooting match. It seems to me you can do better than deal in an inventory that's mostly Shipped In. Look, aren't most of the materials available right here in Paradise County? By that of course I mean lumber. Have you ever given any thought to manufacturing your own furniture? Now I don't mean *make* furniture. I mean *manufacture* furniture—cheap furniture, and lots of it. Ah. Ah. Ah. Don't interrupt. Let me get it all out. Now then, as I was saying, *furniture*. I expect you're thinking about Ike Underwood's chair factory, the Beeman company. You're saying to yourself: If Ike Underwood couldn't make a go of it, how can I? Well, there's a difference between what he was trying to do and what you should do. You got to remember that all that place made was chairs. And he kept on the cabinet-makers from when Beeman had the company. Wellsir, the day of the cabinetmaker is past. People are no longer willing to pay for workmanship. Nowadays when a person buys a chair he doesn't give a damn how carefully it was put together. All he's interested in is the price, how *cheap* it is. My Lord, *you* know *that*. Remember when I first came to Paradise Falls a year ago this summer? Remember that drop table you sold me? How long had it been sitting around the store? Seven years? Now, that is a hell of a beautiful drop table, but it *cost,* and people weren't willing to spend the money. The merchandise they buy is that tacky Shipped In truck, correct? Straight from Philadelphia or Chicago or wherever, made in factories by ignorant Irishmen, cheap and shoddy goods— *that's* the sort of furniture the people want. You know it and I know it. Where Ike Underwood made his mistakes was, one, he used cabinetmakers instead of buying the machinery that would have increased production, and, two, by only making chairs instead of branching into other items . . . tables, beds, sofas and whatever. The more items a company produces, the lower the cost per item. Correct? All right then, let's not bother our-selves with fretting over the fact that Ike Underwood didn't make a go of it. His chair company wasn't a comparable proposition. Let's go on to some other points. For instance, labor costs here would be low. And Lord knows there's plenty of cheap timber right here in Paradise County. Another thing, we could corner the business in this part of the state. A man in Zanesville, for instance, would be more than happy to trim his shipping costs by buying from us instead of from some manufacturer away up in Chicago or some such place. Stands to reason, doesn't it? I tell *you,* the more I think about all this the more intrigued I become. Now, about the timber. I can give us a good start on that. There's a good deal of it on that land I won from Jim Blood in the poker game. And what about all the prop-erty Ike Underwood owns up there? He's got about two thousand acres that aren't doing him a damn bit of good now that all the clay's gone and he's gone out of the chair business. All he's doing is paying taxes on two thousand acres that aren't bringing in a bit of return. I expect for twenty thousand dollars we could have the whole kit and kaboodle. It doesn't matter that the timber's not much good. What do we care? Our furniture wouldn't be designed for the grand ballroom at Buckingham Palace. We'd make it cheap, and we'd sell it cheap, and the more we'd make the more we'd sell and the more money we'd make. Do you follow all this? Does it make sense? Virgil T. Light frowned at Charley. Finally he nodded. Yes, he said, I guess so. Said Charley: Good. But of course you understand there are obstacles. Said Virgil T. Light, grinning a little: I do. Said Charley: Well, I believe we can overcome them, but we'll have to be a shade devious, if you get what I mean. Said Virgil T. Light: Yes. Said Charley: Ike Underwood doesn't like me. I'm a stranger to him, and I'm in competition with his friend Harlowe Morris. It means, if you go along with my plan, that *you'll* have to do the negotiating. Said Virgil T. Light: Yes. *If* I go along with your plan. Said Charley: Of course. Now then, I'll put up ten thousand dollars—what I figure will be half the money. Are you in good enough financial condition to put up the other ten thousand? Said Virgil T. Light: Yes. I could do it if I had to. Said Charley: Well? Said Virgil T. Light: Let me think on it. Said Charley: Fine. You do that.

The next morning Virgil T. Light dropped in at Charley's store. Charley introduced him to Fritz Voss, the new clerk. Virgil T. Light and Fritz Voss shook hands. Then, turning to Charley, Virgil T. Light said: Can we go into the back room? Virgil T. Light's face was tight, and he kept rubbing his hands against his thighs.

Grinning, Charley ushered Virgil T. Light into the storeroom.

I won't hem and haw, said Virgil T. Light.

Good, said Charley.

If I got one full hour's worth of sleep last night, I was lucky.

That mean you're in with me?

Yes. When do we get started?

Not right away. You'll have to give me oh about six weeks.

How come?

All my money's in Ike Underwood's bank. I got to get it out gradually. If I just up and withdraw ten thousand dollars and you go to him with your offer to buy the land, he'll figure I'm in on it with you. If that happens, we can forget about the land. So just be patient for a little bit. I'll let you know when I have the money.

Virgil T. Light smiled. You don't miss a trick do you? he said.

Can't afford to, said Charley. Mistakes cost too much.

I didn't tell my wife about all this.

Well, said Charley, I didn't tell mine either.

Catherine Anne would disapprove. She almost always disapproves of the things I do.

Well, she's been sick. Sick people can be contrary. She's a fine woman. I want to surprise her with it.

I expect you will, said Charley.

A few days later Charley withdrew five hundred dollars from his account at Ike Underwood's bank. He said something to the cashier about new showcases for the store. A week later he withdrew a thousand dollars. This time he spoke of some repairs to the roof and the floors. He mixed withdrawals with his regular deposits, but the withdrawals always were a bit larger. It took him five weeks and three days to extract the ten thousand. He gave the money to Virgil T. Light. All right, he said to Virgil T. Light, it's up to you now. Go to the old pirate. See what you can do. Virgil T. Light grinned, said he would do his best. And for God's sake, said Charley, don't mention *my* name. Said Virgil T. Light: Don't worry.

Virgil T. Light's first offer was fifteen thousand dollars. Ike Underwood refused it. They haggled for several days before settling on twentytwo thousand. Ike Underwood's original asking price had been thirty thousand, and so they had in effect just about split the difference. Charley came up with the additional thousand dollars of his share, and several days later the transfer was certified by the county recorder. Virgil T. Light then promptly like a good fellow went to ElRoy Mauk and had him draw up papers that gave joint ownership of the land to Charley. This was in late August, just three days after the funeral of James Perry Blood. The consumption finally had done him in. Charley and Nancy attended the funeral. Nancy wept rather loudly. That night before retiring she had three large drinks of Kentucky whisky, then made love to Charley with a sweaty and frenzied desperation that drove him to say: My God, you got you an *itch* down there? Maybe you ought to see about getting yourself some sort of salve. Nancy grunted, covered her face with her pillow, muttered words the sense of which he could not make out. My God, he said, and presently he was asleep.

Charley had to stop at ElRoy Mauk's office to sign the joint ownership papers. The little clubfooted lawyer grinned at him and said: I suppose it's the coal isn't it?

Charley raised his eyebrows. How's that? he said.

The coal. What'd you do? Sneak out there and find some?

I don't know what you're talking about.

There's coal out there . . . only no one, Ike Underwood included, thinks it's worth mining. Tell me, you got reason to believe differently?

I tell you, I don't know what you're talking about.

Virge Light tells me you two want the land because of the timber. Well, maybe *Virge Light* believes that, but not *me*.

Does it matter what you believe? The truth is that Virge Light and I have had to be a bit devious—seeing as how Ike Underwood doesn't care for me a great deal. My name had to be left out of the transaction, otherwise it probably never would have gone through. But none of this has anything to do with coal.

Jim thought there was good coal on his land.

What?

He did, said ElRoy Mauk. He told me about it. He told me he was about to send for some geologists to examine the land when he up and lost it to you. He was lying on his deathbed and he told me all about it. He said to me: I expect some day Wells will find out about it. He said to me: Wells will rip up everything. He said to me: Wells is a bastard.

A bastard?

Yes.

Well, imagine that.

Nothing much makes you angry does it? said ElRoy Mauk.

If you mean am I going to get violent because a dead man called me a bastard, the answer is no. What do you propose I do? Go to the graveyard and dig up his coffin and piss on it?

Suppose *I* were to call you a bastard.

Go ahead.

No. If you're a bastard, then so am I. It just so happens I believe most of the same things you do.

Well. Fine.

ElRoy Mauk rubbed his hands together. Jim Blood never would have mined that land, he said.

Oh?

No. Toward the end he loved it too much.

Him?

Yes. He honest to God didn't want to die. At the end he bawled. Like a baby. He hacked and he wheezed and he bawled.

How come he changed his mind?

I don't know. All I do know is that he told me he hoped you never found out about the coal. He didn't want to think of the land being wounded and chopped.

I'll be damned. And you were the one who kept telling me all he wanted to do was destroy himself and all the work his people had put into the land.

I know, said ElRoy Mauk. He blinked at Charley, cleared his throat, then said: You don't give a damn about the land do you?

Why should I?

You admit you plan to mine it?

I admit nothing.

Virge Light doesn't know about the coal does he?

What coal?

ElRoy Mauk chortled, wiped his forehead. His laughter was shrill, pinched.

Charley grinned at him.

Oh *ho!* You are truly *something!* First you get Virge to lead Ike Underwood down the garden path, and now, unless I miss my guess, you're about to take old Virge by the hand and lead him past those exact selfsame flowerbeds!

I really have to admire your imagination.

How are you going to do it?

Do what?

Snooker Virge Light.

You don't give up do you?

No, said ElRoy Mauk. Do *you?*

I suppose this all is leading to something.

Yes. I want in.

In?

Yes. You heard me. In.

Otherwise?

Otherwise I tell Virge Light.

Tell him what?

You know what. And he'll believe me. I'll get geologists if I have to.

Charley sighed. I give up, he said. I give up. I give *up.* How much will it take to keep you quiet?

That depends.

Let's stop this goddamn skirmishing. Depends on what?

Will it be a large operation?

Yes.

You'll need counsel.

Wouldn't be surprised.

I'm your man.

Somehow I thought you'd say that.

I'll draw up an agreement, said ElRoy Mauk, sniggering. And it'll be binding, believe me.

I believe you.

I'm betraying my cousin. In a way, that is.

That's your worry.

How are you going to snooker Virge Light?

You'll see.

I expect it won't be simple.

Well, just you be patient, said Charley.

A few nights later Charley and Nancy took supper with the Lights. It was at this supper that Virgil T. Light broke the news of the land purchase to his wife and son. Catherine Anne Light was aghast, and she made rather a nasty scene. You're idiots, she said, both of you. Isaac Underwood has swindled you. Said Virgil T. Light: Now, now, darling, I wouldn't go so far as to say *that*. Said Catherine Anne Light: Just how do you propose to finance this furniture factory of yours? Virgil T. Light started to answer, but Charley interrupted him. Uh, Mrs Light, said Charley, your husband is a respected businessman. Next week he and I will obtain a loan. Said Catherine Anne Light: Where will you obtain that loan? Certainly not from Isaac Underwood. Said Charley: There are other banks, Mrs Light. Many other banks. Said Catherine Anne Light: It is madness. I've never heard of such stupidity. There are already more than enough furniture factories in this country. Said Virgil T. Light: Now, Catherine Anne, don't be such a pessimist. This is a growing country. You say there are more than enough furniture factories. Not so. Growth creates shortages. We shall do all right, Charley and I. Just you wait. Said Catherine Anne Light: Eleven thousand dollars? You put *eleven thousand dollars* into this ridiculous scheme? Said Virgil T. Light: Yes. Said Catherine Anne Light: I ought to have you committed to a lunatic asylum. With those words, she stood up and left the table. She climbed the stairs to her room. She coughed and wheezed, and Charley was put in mind of the late James Perry Blood. Virgil T. Light was perspiring. He wiped his forehead, smiled at Charley and Nancy. I'm sorry, he said. She . . . well, her health, you know. Sometimes it creates in her a certain, uh, *depression*. Said Charley: Of course. I understand. Don't let it bother you. Nancy smiled at Virgil T. Light. Your wife is a nice woman, she said. And anyway, Charley and I don't believe in grudges. Charley glanced sharply at Nancy, but he said nothing. The boy, Bill Light, said not a word. His eyes caressed Nancy's bosom. Mrs Pett came in from the kitchen with the dessert—apple pie in warm cream. Her face was red, and Charley would have wagered a thousand dollars she had been listening at the pantry door. Quickly she served the dessert, then withdrew back into the kitchen. The pie was really quite delicious, and Charley commented on it. Virgil T. Light thanked him. The boy's eyes worked on Nancy's belly. Charley wanted very much to grin. He was reminded of his own attitudes back in that ruined and extinct Titusville time when he'd been a virgin. He had lost his innocence to a widow woman named Bumpus, and his eyes had behaved in precisely the same manner the Light boy's eyes were behaving now. Ah Lord, *that* had been a long time ago, and sometimes he almost was ready to believe he heard the flapping of great wings, the wings of immense birds that had the word TIME written on their bellies . . .

The Widow Bumpus. A fine woman. There was no question but what he owed her more than he ever would be able to repay. After the Professor, she was the most important person to cross his field of vision in the years immediately following the death of his parents. She was a good woman, and she understood the *mortality* of Love, and she gave Charley such transports as he'd never known existed. She believed in the Now of things, and she took his innocence gently, and she never made a nuisance of herself, and there were those who said she was a whore, and the hell with those who said she was a whore. And anyway, what was wrong with whores? As far as Charley was concerned, whores did not have to lie. An arrangement with a good whore was an honest arrangement, and later, looking back on all of it, Charley regretted not a thing.

The conversation with the Professor that historic night in Bagwell's Saloon went a great long way toward bringing Charley out of his confusion. He aligned his thinking into a neat and logical pattern centered on *mortality* and *possibility*. The year was 1856, and he was just eighteen and such a very ingratiatingly loud and oafish fellow, and he would be all right. The Professor, his revered priest, had seen to it. He now knew he would be all right no matter *what* happened. *Mortality* and *possibility* . . . ah, such golden words. He told himself: Now I will be able to look at Nancy. Now I will be able to look at anyone. The Professor has shown me the way. God bless the Professor.

The grocery was closed for a week after the death of his parents. At the end of that week, however, Charley's grief had abated to the extent that he was able to reopen the place. And, after receiving a temporary appointment arranged by his father's good Democratic friends, he took over operation of the Titusville post office. The following year, shortly after Buchanan was inaugurated President, Charley received a permanent appointment. It cost him two hundred dollars in payments divided between a minor postal official and two state committeemen, but he did not complain. It was worth it. And he did very well indeed in his operation of the store. People complimented him on how well he had taken hold. His flattery served him excellently: Mrs Gentry, I swear one of these nights I'm going to carry you off in a canoe! Now you look here, Mrs Bumpus, if you bat them eyelashes at me one more time, I can't be responsible for what I do! Mrs Dodd, you ain't going to stand there and tell me you been married twentyfive years! I know better! Ain't *no* woman gets married at the age of *three!* Mrs Piggott, you know what the color of your eyes reminds me of? The breath of angels! No, I don't know that the breath of angels has got a color—*but*, if it *does*, it's *got* to be the color of your eyes, so help me! Lord strike me dry and lifeless if I'm funning you! Ah! Ah! Ah! *See!* I'm still here, ain't I? Ain't no thunderbolt come down, so I expect I must be telling the truth!

As far as the details of his life were concerned, he decided to remain in the house on the hill. He hired Nancy's mother to come there twice a week and pick up the place. At the same time, he put himself on a schedule of regular visits to Bagwell's Saloon down by the river. He was very generous when it came to buying drinks, and he shared many a bowl with his revered friend the Professor. They spent a great deal of their time discussing Nancy, but they spent even more of it discussing Charley's *friend* George Peters. A West Point appointment had been arranged for George by his guardian, Richard T. Harris, the owner of the tannery. It so happened that a black Republican was the Congressman from the district that included Titusville, and it also so happened that Richard T. Harris was a generous financial contributor to that bastard hybrid gang of Abolitionist niggerlovers. So there was no difficulty about the appointment. From time to time, late in that summer of 1856, George and Charley had long talks, and George did most of the talking, and his words had to do with Destiny and God and West Point and War and Ambition and such. These were very serious unsmiling talks, the awkward discourse of friends who were no longer particularly fond of one another, even though of course they would not admit it, and this created a mendacity that was brighter than a bonfire at high noon. One Sunday afternoon the two of them went rowing. George did the rowing. The expedition had been his idea. The day was overcast, and the wind caused the water to make small lapping and plashing sounds. The river, the great river, the mighty Ohio, and George had lost his people in this river, but now he clearly was over all that, and he rowed placidly, easily, not even working up a sweat. Charley was uncomfortable. He figured there were better things he could have been doing. But George had insisted, and it did little good to argue with him when he had his mind set on a thing. He rowed for a long time before he said anything. He rowed until they were in the middle of the river, until they had been caught by the current and were beginning to drift. Then he said: I know I'm different.

How's that? said Charley.

You and everybody else, you can abide Titusville.

What's so bad about Titusville?

Titusville's not the world.

I expect I know that.

It's small.

I expect I know *that* too.

George leaned on the oars. His eyes focused themselves on the point of Charley's chin. They were blue eyes. They complemented his blond hair and his freckles. Girls surely were mad about him and his blue eyes and his blond hair and his freckles, and there was one girl who also was mad about his cock, and the name of that girl was Nancy Quimby, and by God it was all Charley could do to keep himself from smiting George with an oar and throwing him over the side, and that was an absolute fact. George stared at Charley's chin, stared at it, stared at it. Then, shrugging a little, he finally said: I have a feeling a large thing will happen to me.

What sort of large thing?

I don't know. Perhaps it will have something to do with the war.

You think there's a war coming? You mean with the South over the niggers?

Yes.

Well, I don't.

You're a Democrat.

What's wrong with being a Democrat?

Nothing, only the Democrats and old Doughface Buchanan won't face up to facts. Mr Harris thinks Buchanan will whip Frémont, but he says it won't make a bit of difference. Buchanan or no Buchanan, there's going to be a war. And I'll be in it. As a West Point man, I'll *have* to be in it. And something will come along. I think of it as a Deed.

Mm, said Charley.

I *feel* it.

That so?

Charley, you're my friend aren't you?

Surely.

I've talked with the Professor about you. He seems to think you're all right.

Fine.

People grow apart. That's why I wanted to row out here with you. I just wanted to let you know I won't forget you.

Thank you kindly, said Charley. He coughed. He spat over the side of the boat. Now the boat was drifting sideways. It was about a mile or so below town. Charley glanced at the Kentucky hills. They were smoky. He'd always had a large sight of affection for those Kentucky hills.

All my life, said George, it's like I've been waiting for a Deed. When it comes, then I'll *mean* something. You understand that? Nancy doesn't. All she wants is to get married. It's all she talks about. Her and her damn whining.

Fuck her, said Charley.

George smiled.

Charley again spat over the side of the boat.

Grunting, George pulled on the oars and brought the boat around until it was facing into the current. He began to row. Ah, he said, it will all be so grand . . .

Sure, said Charley. Grand.

The world is so large . . .

Mm.

There is so much more than Titusville . . .

Mm.

I'm sorry Nancy doesn't understand, but there's not much I can do about it . . .

Mm.

So much to explore, a Deed waiting somewhere . . .

Charley again spat over the side of the boat, and this time the wind caught his spittle and blew it back in his face. He grinned, wiped his face with the back of a hand, wiped the hand on his britches.

Plash went the river. Plash and lap. George rowed. Grunting, he said: I . . . oh hell, I wish Nancy could open up her mind and . . . try . . . to . . . ah well, you know what I mean . . .

That's right, said Charley.

Ah, good old Charley . . .

That's me, said Charley.

George rowed. Plash went the river. Plash and lap.

And so he left Titusville, this George Peters, this blond and handsome *hero* and seeker of a Deed. He went off to West Point, and he was undefeated, and it all made Charley want to throw up. *Heroes!* Ahhh *horse mess*, heroes and their convulsions! Perhaps the Lord intended to end the world by flooding it with heroes and their precious Deeds. This wasn't the sort of flood most people saw as being indicated in Scripture, but then Charley was no Baptist. He didn't particularly hold with those who believed the Word to be literal truth. As far as he was concerned, a flood meant anything, even heroes. The thought amused and delighted him, made his nights less cold. Then, in the spring of 1857, word came that George had been fired from West Point and wasn't coming home. Oh *my*, said Charley to himself, it sure does look like the Lord is making it hard for him to find his Deed. Ah hah ho hah, such a joke. How's it feel to fall on your face George old hero? Hah, sure is too bad old *friend*.

But Charley continued to hate George. The hate was apparently one thing in his life that was without *mortality*. He was grateful. And he also was rather grateful that he was able to see Nancy again, take her to dances and socials and theatricals and whatnot. But he was unable to bed her. As a matter of fact, it wasn't until that year of 1857 that he was able to bed anyone. His innocence was taken from him—or, to be more exact, he most enthusiastically thrust it out for the taking—by a Mrs Harriet Bumpus, a widow, aged thirtyseven, mother of three, a person of pleasing and rounded aspect and straitened circumstances. Her late husband had operated a barber shop, but he had been rather a poor barber. And, beyond that, there already were two tonsorial establishments in Titusville when Lloyd Bumpus opened his. So he quickly went out of business, and within a year he had drunk himself into a merciful grave, and his widow was left as the sole support of their three cunning little daughters. Mrs Bumpus was a passably fair seamstress, and under normal circumstances she no doubt would have been able to make at least a bare living for herself and the three little girls. But Lloyd Bumpus had left her with a number of sizable debts, and so she had to seek ways to augment her sewing earnings. She was plump, was this Mrs Harriet Bumpus, the former Harriet Clarendon of Xenia, Ohio, but she was not so plump as to be obese or in any way repulsive. She had large breasts and heavy black nipples, but the flesh of her belly still was firm, and her dark interior landscape still was rich and hospitable, wise and used but not exhausted, full of heat and moisture and lovely girlish zeal. She took Charley to her bed because he was an ideal person to take to her bed. He had money. He lived alone. She would not be threatened by outraged relatives. And, perhaps most importantly, he had a certain amount of stature in Titusville. He was, after all, the *postmaster*. The way she viewed the situation, he would protect her from any and all defenders of morality. So she quite honestly (to herself, that is, telling herself no lies) set out to take in the young oafish Charley Wells as her lover. Whenever she visited his store, she was most thoroughly aware of how closely he watched her. His eyes were like bright insects crawling happily across her breasts and crotch, savoring every blessed fleshly moment of it. The feel of his eyes was not unpleasant. He was sturdy, and he surely did have a great deal of energy, and Mrs Harriet Bumpus told herself: Ah, you could be doing worse, yes indeed. She waited for it all to begin, and she did not have to wait very long. Gently, easily, by cheek and hip and flank, moving softly, using her wise flesh with shy carnal skill, she insinuated herself into his dreams, and whenever she encountered him she made sure she greeted him with a soft and private smile that she felt sure he knew was an invitation like no invitation he'd ever received. She realized she wasn't being very ladylike, but a lot she cared about *that*. One morning, after giving him her secret smile, she decided she would go ahead and take the step that was necessary. In her mind she called it the Potato Step. His hyperbole that morning was magnificent: Why, Mrs Bumpus! What

a vision you are this morning! What a delight to these poor humble boyish
eyes of mine! He spoke very loudly, and his face held too much color,
and she knew she had him, oh she knew indeed. Clutching hotly, his
eyes scampered across her bosom and crotch, scampered back, skipped,
hopped, strutted. On and on went the flattery, and Mrs Bumpus' smile
was shy as the eyes of a kitten. Finally she spoke. Oh Mr Wells, she said
softly, you surely do have a sweet way with your words. If I wasn't such
an old woman and didn't know better, my head would have been turned
long ago. Charley smiled. No, Mrs Bumpus, he said, no indeed, you are
not an old woman, and you *know* it. You are pretty and your, uh, *aspect*
is more pleasing than I could ever hope really to tell you, and I just hope
your husband knew what a lucky man he was. The Widow Bumpus
summoned a fine blush. Oh *now*, she said, there you go *again* with your
talk. She bought a pound of coffee. Then, taking the Potato Step and
feeling rather delighted with herself for her nerve, she bought a twenty-
pound sack of potatoes. Charley rose to it like a good fellow. She had
felt certain he would. After taking her money, he said: Mrs Bumpus,
I don't want you carrying that big sack. It's too much for you. Mrs Bumpus
smiled. I was raised on a farm, she said. This sort of thing is no bother.
But Charley shook his head no. Leave them here, he said. I'll bring them
around to your place tonight soon's I close. Mrs Bumpus frowned. Well
. . . she said, letting the word trail off in a helpless feminine sigh. And
Charley said: Now, now, do like I say. I know best. A smile from Mrs
Bumpus, a very grateful smile, warm and moist. She had good teeth and
gums. All right then, she said. And I thank you. Soon's you close. You
know where I live? Charley nodded. Yes *ma'm*, he said, I do. Still smiling,
Mrs Bumpus again thanked Charley. Ah, said Charley, we aim to please.
Will seven o'clock be all right? Mrs Bumpus allowed as how 7 o'clock
would be just fine. She went home and prepared herself for the evening.
She dug around in her dresser and found some lavender bath salts an
aunt had given her as a wedding present. She opened the bottle. The
odor was faint, but this was just fine. She didn't want to be too obvious.
At the store, Charley spent the rest of the day trying to calm the action
of his heart. He took great deep breaths, and they did some good, but
not much. He knew what was happening, but he hardly dared believe it.
Mrs Bumpus? A respectable *widow lady?* A *mother of three?* Great God,
would tonight at last be the night he crossed that vast and coveted con-
cupiscent bar? Grinning, clucking, sweating like a pig in a swamp, he
passed through the rest of the day in feverish alternations of hope, suspicion, despair and wild anticipation, and finally—at about 5 o'clock or
so—he closed the store and post office and went on home. He could bear
himself no longer. The odor of his sweat was enough to make goats go

jump in the river. He took a very hot bath. He paid close attention to his
armpits and his parts. He hunted up some of his mother's old talcum and
sprinkled it all over his body. He sprinkled so much of it that he began
to cough. He laughed as he coughed, and finally tears squirted from his
eyes. He pomaded his hair. He put on his finest undershirt, underdrawers,
shirt, stockings, suit, cravat and shoes. It was almost 6:30 when he left the
house. He returned to the store and fetched the sack of potatoes. Grunting a little, he hefted the sack up onto his right shoulder and set off for
the home of the Widow Bumpus. It was a very small house. It was located
at the edge of town on a street that trailed off and became a narrow
path that wandered down toward the river. The house really was more
of a cabin, but its yard was neat, and a splendid trumpet creeper fussed
its way along the side of the house just to the right of the front door.
The dooryard itself abounded with small clusters of blue and yellow flowers, the names of which Charley did not know. He was breathing a bit
heavily when he knocked on the front door. Perhaps this was because
of the sack of potatoes, and then again perhaps it was not. Mrs Bumpus
was smiling when she opened the door for him. Come in, she said. He
thanked her, entered the house. The three little girls sat on the settee.
They gleamed. Charley followed Mrs Bumpus into the kitchen. She had
him set the sack of potatoes in a corner next to the stove. Yes ma'm, said
Charley. He set the sack in the corner. When he turned and faced her,
she still was smiling. I was just about to have a glass of cold tea, she
said. Would you like one too? Charley nodded, told Mrs Bumpus he was
much obliged. Some tea'd taste real good along about now, he said. I
mean, it was sort of a piece of work carrying that there sack. Mrs Bumpus
crinkled the corners of her eyes. She told him she surely appreciated his
bringing out the sack. She was wearing a blue dress. Her hair was
dark, and it glistened, and a row of fresh curls marched neatly across
her forehead. He was able to smell a faint odor of lavender. She told him
to go back into the front room. Say hello to the girls, she said. I'll be
with you soon's I pour the tea. Charley nodded, returned to the front room.
His belly hurt a little. He was breathing mostly through his nose. The
little girls still were on the settee. Charley seated himself in a large
rocker. A sampler hung over the mantel. The sampler said: GOD BLESS
THE REPUBLIC. The little girls all had brown eyes and their mother's dark
hair. They were delicate little girls, smallboned and pretty. They all
smiled at Charley, but their smiles engaged only the corners of their
mouths. The one on the left, obviously the oldest, said: I'm Victoria.
I'm eleven. The middle one said: I'm Hope. I'm almost nine. The one
on the right said: I'm Ruth. I'm seven. And Charley said: I'm Charley
Wells. I'm nineteen. It is an honor to make your acquaintance. Ruth,

the little one on the right, covered her mouth and giggled. The other two continued to smile their polite and reluctant smiles. Our mama says you're a nice man, said Victoria. Oh. Well. I must thank your mama, said Charley. Hope, the middle one, spoke up. Our mama took a bath today, she said. And she dressed us in our best dresses. Charley smiled. Mm, he said, and very nice dresses they are. Said Victoria: We haven't worn these dresses since the day Daddy was buried. That was last year, and Mama let them all out this afternoon. Said Charley: Mm. Well. Mrs Bumpus came into the room. The two glasses of cold tea were on a tray. Charley stood up. The little girls clambered down from the settee. Smiling, Charley took a glass of tea. Mrs Bumpus looked at her daughters. Time for bed, she said. Time for prayers. Time for dreams. The little girls all nodded. They smiled at their mother, and this time their smiles engaged all of their mouths. They went to their mother. She kissed them. They hugged her about the hips and waist. She patted their heads. They backed away. They turned to Charley and curtsied. He bowed. Great day, it was like he was attending a reception in a king's palace, and that was a fact. The girls trooped into a side room, closing the door behind them. Mrs Bumpus seated herself on the settee. Charley dropped back down into the rocker. I believe in sending them to bed early, said Mrs Bumpus. They're up with the chickens, and by this time of day they're very tired, even if they won't own up to it. I, uh, I could hear them from the kitchen. Victoria told you about the dresses, didn't she? Charley nodded, sipping at his tea. It was very cold, but it had a bit too much sugar for his taste. He moistened his lips with his tongue. Good tea, he said. Thank you, said Mrs Bumpus. I expect you need it. Couldn't have been much pleasure carrying that big old sack all the way out here. Charley made a deprecating movement with a hand. My pleasure, he said. Mrs Bumpus smiled. Well, she said, I'm very grateful. A woman gets tired, you know? She sipped at her own glass of cold tea. Her tongue rubbed a corner of her mouth. Charley decided to go ahead and permit his eyes to walk across her breasts and crotch. There were a few lines at the corners of her eyes. He wanted to kiss them. One of the girls made a giggling noise in the side room. The closed door muffled most of it. They go to sleep real fast, said Mrs Bumpus. Mm, said Charley. No time at all, said Mrs Bumpus. That's fine, said Charley. Sort of close tonight isn't it? said Mrs Bumpus. Yes, said Charley. He drank the last of his tea. He set his glass on a table. He stood up. Mrs Bumpus smiled up at him. How long a time is no time? he asked her. Mrs Bumpus blushed. Half an hour, she said. Would you care for another glass of cold tea? Charley shook his head no. He sat down again. Are you eighteen? said Mrs Bumpus. I'm nineteen, said Charley. I'm twice your age less

one year, said Mrs Bumpus. Don't mean a thing, said Charley. Mrs
Bumpus nodded. All right, she said, I'm not going to fuss with you about
it. You are a fine young man. It wouldn't do for me to fuss with you.
I mean, after all, we both know the way things *are,* don't we? I've never
done this before, and I surely don't want to start out with a *fuss.* No
indeed. Is it all right with you if we don't go chasing all around the
mulberry bush about this? I feel very peculiar. I don't think I have the
strength for that sort of thing. And anyway, I think I want to save my
strength. You are very sweet. You talk so well. You say such nice things.
Come sit here with me and *talk.* Mrs Bumpus cut off her words. She
slid over on the settee, patted the vacant place next to her. Another muffled
giggling noise came from the side room. Charley paid it no mind. He
stood up and went to the settee. His skin felt tight. He supposed she
could see what had happened to him. He sat down next to her. First
he smelled the lavender. Then he smelled flesh, juices, homemade soap.
He looked away from her. He looked at the sampler that said: GOD BLESS
THE REPUBLIC. He cleared his throat. His eyes remained focused on the
sampler. A sequence of squealing sounds came from high in his nose.
Then, reddening, he said: I, uh . . . well, maybe now you're not going
to believe this, but . . . uh, I ain't never . . . uh, what I *mean* is: I ain't
never *ever* . . . uh, never ever *you* know. Then, after again clearing his
throat, he rubbed his mouth with the back of a hand. He shrugged,
summoned spit, worried it with his tongue. He swallowed. God strike me
dead if I'm lying, he said. Curl me into ashes, and I *mean* that. Mrs
Bumpus laughed softly. Quickly he looked at her. She did away with
her laugh. Now, now, she said, don't make a long face. I'm pleasured,
that's all. Very much pleasured. And then Mrs Bumpus reached for
Charley and kissed him. Ah Lord God, he had been kissed before, but
never like *this.* It was a kiss that made all other kisses obsolete; it was
lips and tongue and teeth, and she sucked on his mouth, sucked wetly,
and her fingers tugged and tickled his ears, and it was as though she had
breathed sparks and hot oil into his belly and balls. And then, pulling
her mouth away from his and lazily nibbling at his neck, she whispered:
I am *real* pleasured. Yes. Kind of . . . kind of flattered too. So . . . kindly
don't . . . vex yourself. Everything will be . . . fine. Just . . . fine. Leaning forward, Charley said: Yes. He reached around Mrs Bumpus and
unfastened the buttons at the back of her dress. She sighed, smiled. He
kissed Mrs Bumpus, sucked on *her* lips. He pulled the dress away from
her shoulders. They were vast shoulders, warm and white shoulders. Yes,
she said. Yes. Yes. Everything will be . . . just fine. You are my lover.
My . . . darling . . . sweetheart. She groaned, helped Charley undo her
corset. Ah, she said. Yes. He pulled open her corset, and her belly was

warmer than her shoulders. It was a soft belly. She pressed down his head. He kissed her belly. It has been a . . . long . . . time, she said. Lloyd . . . wasn't much . . . good to me toward the . . . end. I expect I'm the sort of woman who needs a man to be . . . ah, yes darling, do that, *do that* . . . needs a man to be . . . good to her. Mrs Bumpus' hands went inside Charley's jacket, and then they went inside his shirt and undershirt, and presently they went inside his britches, and finally they went inside his underdrawers. Charley mewled. Charley grimaced. She led him into the bedroom. Her dress hung at her waist. Her nipples were dark and enormous. The bed was wide. The ticking in the mattress made dry crackling sounds. Like old leaves. Charley rode her easily, and she was ready for him, and she smiled and sniggered and gnawed her lips, and her breasts flopped and slapped against his face, and up came her knees, folding themselves tightly across the small of his back, and off galloped Charley, once, twice, three times, finally a fourth, and the room was damp with the pale proud odors of concupiscence, and Mrs Bumpus bucked and reared and nibbled and gasped, and once she even farted, and by God *finally* Charley had crossed that coveted bar, ah had he *ever*. Later she said: I hope we didn't make too much noise. I hope the girls didn't hear. Charley nodded. He told her they probably had slept through the whole thing. Then he told her he loved her. She smiled, kissed him. Yes, she said, of course you do. Naked now, naked and moist, gleaming pale yellow in the light of a weak new moon, a light that had insinuated itself around the crisp white curtains of this bedroom, naked and spent, Charley and Mrs Bumpus held one another and burrowed under the covers and grabbed and pinched and snickered like children in a sandbank. I love you, said Charley. Of course you do, said Mrs Bumpus. He told her about the talcum. She told him about the lavender bath salts. They laughed quietly. She asked him to rub her nipples. He did, and away they went, and later, recapitulating the night, Charley said to himself: Six times in maybe three hours at the most. God in Heaven. Mrs Bumpus did Charley the courtesy of waiting for him to bring up the matter of arrangements. She knew he would. She knew, despite his talk of love, he had an understanding of realities. And he did bring up the matter of arrangements. The sum he mentioned was ten dollars a week, and she told him he was very generous. Ah, he said, but I love you. Said Mrs Bumpus: Yes. Of course you do. Come here, my dearest. I have wisdom for you. And she smiled. And he came to her. And they wrung one another. And the ticking scratched. Ah, such a time, and what was ten dollars a week? It was nothing, not in exchange for the gift he received, the fine *mortal* Now she was giving him. He took two or three meals a week with Mrs Bumpus and her daughters. Victoria and Hope were the talkers. Ruth seldom said a word. Victoria wanted to be a singer of grand opera when she grew up. Now and then she sang for Charley, and her voice filled his ears with glass and icicles, but always he managed to smile. Hope wanted to be a preacher's wife. Mrs Bumpus and the girls attended the Methodist church, but of course they never sat with Charley. He hoped the girls didn't understand why. Hope loved the church. I like the music and the smell, she told Charley. I mean, if I was married to a preacher then I could go to church on a *Tuesday* if I was of a mind to. I could sit there and smell the smell and there wouldn't be nobody who could tell me: No. You go away. This is Tuesday. You aren't allowed to sit in church on a Tuesday and smell the smell. I'd say to anyone who fussed at me: *You're* the one should go away. *I* happen to be the *wife* of the *preacher*. I can sit here on a Tuesday or a Wednesday or a Friday or any day I *want* to sit here. Hope spoke the words belligerently, and Charley was wise enough not to smile. Mrs Bumpus was very proud of her daughters, and Charley wouldn't have laughed at them for the world. One night, after Charley and Mrs Bumpus had had at one another, she said to him: I think I am a good mother to my girls. Said Charley: I think you are too. Said Mrs Bumpus: They don't know what we do. Said Charley: Good. Said Mrs Bumpus: They eat better now. That's very important. Said Charley: That's fine. Said Mrs Bumpus: Lloyd had so many debts. I have a duty to pay them. Said Charley: It's to your credit that you feel that way. Said Mrs Bumpus: He was a good man, but he wasn't very strong. He had a fine tenor voice. Did I ever tell you that? It was a pure and sweet voice. He used to serenade me back in Xenia when we were courting. He stood outside my window at night, and he had a banjo, and he sang all sorts of lovely songs. I tried to make him understand about the barber shop. I tried to make him understand it didn't matter. But the corn whisky got him. Once or twice he even hit me. And one night he hit Victoria. He cried about that. All the next day. He just cried and cried. Ahhh, *shoot*. I talk too much. Said Charley: That's all right. Said Mrs Bumpus: Well, thank you for listening. Said Charley: My pleasure. Said Mrs Bumpus: He cried and cried, and for a day or two he slunk around the house like a whipped cur, and then he went out to Bagwell's or someplace and I didn't see him for I think it was a week. A whole week. (That night, for the only time in two years Charley was lover to Mrs Bumpus, she wept. She did not, however, weep loudly. She did not want to awaken the girls.) It ended in the summer of 1859, but there was no rancor. A widowed farmer named Fred Carson had begun courting Mrs Bumpus, and so Charley acknowledged the mortality of the situation by withdrawing. Mrs Bumpus was quite grateful. Mr Carson knows about you, she told Charley, but I guess it doesn't make any difference. He keeps saying he wants to marry me. I expect I'll say yes. I'm thirtynine now, and I don't believe I'll be getting any other offers. I mean, last time I looked outside I didn't exactly see a big crowd of men beating and shoving at one another trying to break down the door, if you know what I mean. And, well, Mr Carson is a good man. His wife never gave him children, and I swear he treats my girls just like they were his own. This'll be a good thing for all of us. You understand that don't you? Smiling, Charley nodded, told her he did indeed understand. The last time in her bed was quiet and slow, and it consisted mostly of kisses. Two years at ten dollars a week came to a little more than a thousand dollars, and it would have been a bargain at ten times the price. That last night he tried to tell her how good it all had been. It was the best thing ever happened to me, he said. Far as I know, there hasn't been a single lie. Smiling, Mrs Bumpus thanked him for the kind words. We aim to please, said Charley, and then he laughed, and so did Mrs Bumpus, and that was that; the mortality of the thing had declared itself. That last night, walking away from her little house with its trumpet creeper and its anonymous dooryard flowers, Charley did not look back, and the sentimental things that sweetly imprinted themselves on his heart were so delicious he just about had to gasp for breath. He was large. He strutted. Birds sang for him. It was, he supposed, a profound moment. He hitched up his britches, grimaced, gave the sky an eyeful of his teeth.

. . . and so how could he have been angry with this Light boy just because the poor tormented young fellow was making calf's eyes at Nancy? His grand renunciation scene with Mrs Bumpus had taken place just seven years earlier, and he was not so insensitive that he had forgotten the things he had felt on first encountering that remarkable woman. Things the Light boy no doubt was now feeling. Things all boys felt. Charley smiled. Mrs Pett had just finished pouring the wine. He lifted his glass. To success, he said. To the attainment of dreams. To cheap furniture. To cheap furniture and the manufacture of it and the realization of great fortunes. He touched his glass to Virgil T. Light's glass. Nancy lifted her glass, touched it to the boy's. The boy cleared his throat. Everyone smiled, even Nancy, even the boy. Everyone drank. The boy coughed, blushed. Charley smiled at the boy and said: Bill, you're going to be very rich.

The boy nodded. Yessir, he said.

Your mother's a little angry now, but she'll get over it. She'll come to be very proud of all of us.

Yessir.

But we can't say anything about any of this just yet. Your father and

I have to arrange the financing. It costs a lot of money to open a factory. We don't want anyone getting wind of it just yet—and especially Ike Underwood. If he finds out how well your father and I turned his pockets insideout, he might make it difficult for us to obtain a loan. You understand that?

Yessir, said the boy.

We're going to Columbus to see the bankers there. Your father will be very helpful, seeing as how his GAR work has put him in touch with so many people from all over the state, including bankers. A fine organization, the GAR. It's about time our veterans had a voice in the way the government is run. Right, Bill?

Yessir.

Ah, you're a fine young man.

I won't say a word about any of this, sir.

Good. That's the boy.

He's a good boy, said Virgil T. Light, smiling at his son.

You don't have to tell *me*, said Charley.

The boy squirmed.

Nancy patted one of his hands.

He looked at her sharply.

We all like you very much, she said.

Yes ma'm, said the boy.

On the walk back to the hotel, Nancy held Charley's arm fiercely. She was trembling. He asked her what the matter was. She told him nothing important was the matter, perhaps a slight chill, certainly nothing serious, nothing to cause him alarm, nothing to cause him to divert his attention from his precious scheme, whatever it was. Charley grinned, told her she surely was quite the one for ragging a fellow. She said: They don't know *anything* about the coal, do they? Said Charley, his words quick: No. And they're *not* to know anything. I mean that. I've told you before and I'll tell you again—you're not even to give them a hint. Said Nancy: Yes, Lord and Master. Yes. Yes. A grunt from Charley. Nancy continued to tremble. Perhaps she'd had too much wine after the supper. In their Acterhof House suite he told her he'd been thinking about Mrs Bumpus. Did she remember Mrs Bumpus? Oh yes, said Nancy, I remember her. Charley grinned. He went to Nancy and pulled off her clothes. He told her he knew what she needed to lift herself out of her mood. Mrs Bumpus, said Nancy. Yes, it follows that you would want to do this after thinking about Mrs Bumpus. Poor Harriet. I always sort of liked her. She never looked down on me because of my papa. Sighing, Nancy lay down. Charley kissed her breasts, and her nipples hardened, and she said: Oh yes. Ah, Charley. I. Yes. Yes. Just what I need. Now.

Now, Charley. *Now*. There's something better you can put there than a finger. Yes. Yes. Dear Charley. Charley the schemer. Ah. Ah. They think it is timber, father and son both. The mother wonders, but she is too sick to do anything. *Timber*. Ah God, where were they when You passed out the brains? Ah, Charley. Charley. *Charley*. How can someone so *bad* feel so *good*?

The next morning Charley wrote a long letter to a man named Wendell Archer Doggett, owner and proprietor of the Hotel Nonpareil, Washington, DC. Charley had lived at this hotel from January of '63 until April of '65 while serving as secretary to the Congressman from Illinois. The reply came eight days later. It said, among other things: *The man's name is Percy T. Disney. He is a virtuoso in his chosen field. Given a week's notice, he can be in Paradise Falls. (Such a splendid name for a village! It exalts my soul!) He has authorized me to inform you his fee is one thousand dollars, payable in advance. I can vouch for his efficiency. I have friends who have had occasion to call upon his services. They have had nothing but praise for his work. Tell me, when are you coming here for a visit? The girls all remember you with fondness, Dorcas Pfaff especially, our dear murderous Dorcas.*

The answer delighted Charley. He showed the letter to Fritz Voss, who said: Who is this Doggett? Some sort of whoremaster? Said Charley: Precisely. But he can be trusted in matters of this nature. Said Fritz Voss: Well, it's all gone according to plan so far. I only hope you know what you're doing. Said Charley: Don't fret. Just be a nice little grocery clerk for a month or so longer. Maybe two months. Then you won't have to bother with it any more. Then I'll have the land and the coal, and we can get to work digging the coal. Said Fritz Voss: Where will we get the money? Said Charley: Don't concern yourself about it. The money will come, believe me.

A few days after receiving the reply from Wendell Archer Doggett, Charley accompanied Virgil T. Light to Columbus. They conferred with officers of all the leading banks. None of these men had much enthusiasm for the proposed furniture factory. As Charley had figured they would, they all pointed out that the nation already had more than enough furniture factories. And, beyond that, did either Mr Wells or Mr Light have experience running *any* sort of factory, let alone one of such size as they proposed? The answer of course was no. The bankers were very polite, and some of them even were regretful, but not a one was willing to lend Charley and Virgil T. Light the money. (Had any of them *been* willing, Charley probably would have toppled over dead. An acceptance would have destroyed his scheme faster than a bullet from a pistol.) Charley and Virgil T. Light spent three days and two nights in Columbus, and Virgil T. Light became gloomier and gloomier. My God, he said to Charley the first night, what are we going to do? Maybe Ike Underwood'll have the last laugh after all. Charley grinned, clapped Virgil T. Light on the back. Cheer up, he said, things are bound to get better. After all, how can they get any worse? Their second night in Columbus they stopped in the Neil House tap room and ran into Don Platt, the coal lobbyist. Quickly, before Don Platt could say anything, Charley introduced him to Virgil T. Light as Don Platt, manufacturer of work shoes. Don Platt frowned. Charley winked at him. Don Platt smiled a little, then shrugged. Don Platt ordered a bottle of champagne. The shoe business has been good lately, he said, chuckling. When the bottle was empty, Charley ordered one. Presently it was Virgil T. Light's turn to buy a bottle. By this time, Virgil T. Light had begun talking about the GAR and his wartime experiences in the Army of the Potomac. He said to Don Platt: You know, I got my boys organized before there *was* such a thing *as* the GAR. So, when it came time to form a Paradise Falls post, naturally I was elected commander. Charley here can vouch for all of it. I'm real proud, I tell you. *Real* proud. The state commander complimented me. Told me I'd shown real foresight. I got a letter from him. And I tell you something—the men like it. Every other Saturday afternoon we drill over to a place called Bunker's Grove, and most of the men show up without fail. You can say what you want to about wars; you can decry all the killing and all that, but the fact remains that most men look back on war as the biggest thing ever happened to them. By God, when we drill together it's just like the old days, and there's something about the old days most of us miss. Call it comradeship. Call it whatever you will. Whatever it is, it is large, and it cannot be killed, and it grips a man's guts. All right, so perhaps some of the men are putting on weight, but that doesn't stop them from drilling, and I call commands just like in the old days, and we march in all the parades, and by God sir we march *in step*. It's a fine thing, this GAR, and don't ever let anyone tell you anything to the contrary. Ah. Whoo. This is what I call *good* champagne. I always have liked champagne. Drank some one night with a whore named Pauline. Never did find out what her last name was. It was in Virginia. She'd been brought to Falmouth by none other than General Fighting Joe Hooker. Her and about twenty other whores. I think he brought them from Baltimore. Or maybe Washington. Well, no matter. The thing was—what this Pauline didn't know about the act of copulation could have been scratched on the head of a pin with room to spare. She scowled when she was doing it. Scowled and drew back her lips. Now then sir, Charley here can tell you I'm a happily married man, but I'd been away from home a long time, and it's never

been in me to live like a monk for too long a time. Oh she gave it to me
good, that Pauline. Red hair. Big lips. Firstclass pussy, *I'll* tell the world.
Hooker was quite a man for his whores. Brought at least twenty of them
down there for the pleasure of his staff officers. Now then, I wouldn't
want you to get the wrong impression. I wasn't a staff officer, but I had
a friend who was, and this friend was a man of boundless Christian
generosity. Oh yes. He let me have the whole night with Pauline. And
the champagne . . . whoo, I mean, there was champagne and there was
champagne and there was *champagne*. General Hooker gave a party
earlier that night, and Pauline and I carried off at least six bottles to my
tent, and I *mean* . . . ah, excuse me for grinning, but a memory such as
that one has to be acknowledged, you understand? Don Platt smiled. So
did Charley. I understand perfectly, said Don Platt. Virgil T. Light gulped
down more champagne. Then, winking, he said to Don Platt: This talk
has got me into a sort of state, you know? Said Don Platt: Yes. I expect I
know. Said Charley: Are we all willing? Said Virgil T. Light: I vote aye!
Don Platt nodded. Two votes, he said. Unanimous, said Charley. Don
Platt took Charley and Virgil T. Light to a fancy whorehouse on East Gay
Street. It had crimson carpeting and drapes, and it was operated by a
young woman named Irene Hollingshead. She was the widow of a former
state senator who had been a brevet brigadier in the Army of the Potomac.
Charley grinned when he saw this Irene Hollingshead. He had known
her in Washington. Her name in those days had been Irene Weaver. The
world surely is getting smaller, he told her. She grinned, went to him and
hugged him. Don Platt and Virgil T. Light stared at them. Virgil T. Light
was swaying. He had spilled cigar ashes on his vest and trousers. Irene
Hollingshead made a happy chirping noise, told Don Platt and Virgil T.
Light that tonight they were to be the guests of the house. Mr Wells here
is a dear old friend, she said. Don Platt and Virgil T. Light grinned. You
rascally soandso! said Virgil T. Light, belching. Irene Hollingshead
blushed, took Charley's arm, steered him into a drawingroom. Don Platt
and Virgil T. Light followed along. The room was full of whores. Most
of them were young. Most of them wore their hair in braids. Men seem to
prefer girls who appear innocent, said Irene Hollingshead. At least *I've*
found that to be true. Charley nodded. I expect you have a point, he said.
He smiled at Irene Hollingshead. She was tiny, and she was quite blond,
and he knew for a fact that her tits were the smallest he'd ever encountered, and yet there was a quiet corruption within her, a sweet unblinking fragrant depravity, a thing of contortions and wild lips, that
made her infinitely more desirable than most women, that had made her
—back in those wartime days at the Hotel Nonpareil—one of the great
legendary whores of that great whoring city, a whore of whores, so to

speak, a miracle of the flesh. Well, she said now, turning to Don Platt and Virgil T. Light, take your pick, gentlemen. She clapped her hands. The girls all looked at her. Anything these gentlemen want, said Irene Hollingshead. Anything at all. The girls nodded. Some of them stood up and smiled. Virgil T. Light breathed through wet nostrils. He hiccoughed. He blushed. The girls could have been pupils in a boarding school. They all wore primly dark dresses, and their faces were without paint. Virgil T. Light wiped the ashes from his vest and trousers, then advanced on a small blonde who bore something of a resemblance to Irene Hollingshead. See? she whispered, nudging Charley. See what I mean? That Rosemary, I just hope and pray she doesn't wear out. I don't know, perhaps it is indecent of me to say such a thing, but do you think she is so popular because she reminds so many of them of their daughters? Charley grinned at Irene Hollingshead, told her she was beyond hope. Virgil T. Light leaned over the demure Rosemary and whispered something into her ear. She nodded. She said: Yes sir. Anything you want. She went out of the room with him. Meanwhile, Don Platt advanced on a tall brunette whose hair was in braids. She had great brown eyes. Her arms were folded at her waist, and she was rubbing her elbows. Don Platt took her by an arm and asked her where the drinks were. This way sir, said the girl, and she led Don Platt through a curtained door. Irene Hollingshead squeezed one of Charley's hands. Will I be all right? she asked him. He nodded. You will be fine, he said. I am honored. They climbed a wide staircase. She was very good. She was every bit as good as he had remembered her. When it was done, he told her so.

Thank you, said Irene Hollingshead. I mean that. It's been a year for me, and I wasn't sure how I'd do.

How's that?

You're the first man since my husband.

Charley, who was sitting up in bed, looked down at the splendid little Irene. He really was quite fond of her tiny body, its hardness and all, the things she knew to do with it. He said: And you're the first woman since my marriage.

Irene Hollingshead smiled. You're married now? she said.

Yes. Last year. An Indiana girl. Now we live in a place called Paradise Falls. It's about fifty miles from here. Perhaps you've heard of it.

Yes. I have. Do you know a man named Mauk, a little clubfooted man? He visits here quite often. He's one of Rosemary's steady gentlemen. *ElRoy Mauk?*

Yes.

Charley whooped. *ElRoy Mauk!* he hollered. Why, the old bastard! Rosemary tells me he's got enough of it in him to swamp a canoe.

Charley lay back, clutched his belly and laughed. Finally he said: Well, you just never can tell.

No. That's true. Well, Charley, what are you doing around here? Like I said, we live in Paradise Falls.

But why?

Would you believe me if I told you I was tarred and feathered and run out of my home town back in Indiana? It was right after the President was shot, and those damn people thought I'd had something to do with it.

Did you?

Now, Irene, that's not very funny.

Well, I just thought I'd ask.

Charley smiled. Sure, he said. That's my Irene. He hesitated, then: It's a long story. Let's just say that I came to Paradise Falls more or less by invitation—or at least my wife did, and I went along with her. I'm doing fine, though. And I'm *going* to do *better*. Now then, what about you? How come you call yourself Hollingshead? And where'd you get the money for this place?

Irene Hollingshead made a vague gesture with her hands. She pulled the covers over her body and Charley's. She smiled. It was part defeat, part astonishment, part rueful amusement. It was large in her eyes. She spoke softly of the late brevet brigadier. She spoke with sentiment. Her voice was girlish. Alf was fiftysix years of age, she said, and he and some other officers came to the Nonpareil about a week or so after that friend of yours, Wilkes Booth, shot the President. You did know Booth didn't you?

I knew him to talk to. But that doesn't mean I was in on the plot. I mean, who *didn't* know Booth? A person couldn't walk into a saloon without encountering him. You know that.

All right, Charley. All right. I believe you.

So go ahead about your husband.

Irene Hollingshead nodded. Well, she said, his name was Alf Hollingshead, and he looked very grand in his uniform, very grand indeed. The other men were drunk, but not him. He was almost shy. I mean that. He had the saddest eyes I've ever seen, the poor man, and he treated me with a gentleness I couldn't hardly believe. He told me I reminded him of his dead wife. He told me her name had been Margaret, and she had been the daughter of a preacher in the Methodist Episcopal church. Well, anyway, he and his wife hadn't ever had any children, and she'd died in '58 of I think he said it was an abscess following a quinsy, and then the war'd come along, and it had taken most of the starch out of him. You know where Massillon is? Well, it's upstate, not too far from Cleveland. He owned a drygoods store up in this Massillon. Anyhow, he visited the Nonpareil twelve nights running, and he told me all about his dead wife, and I

don't know, at the end of those twelve nights I married him. Mr Doggett
was awfully good about it. He gave me a little cameo pin as a wedding
present. Alf was mustered out a few days later, and we went off to
Massillon to live. And, you know, I got along pretty well with the people
there. I was there almost a year, and they were decent to me. I mean that.
Then one night this spring . . . well, Alf and I were in bed, and it was
going good, and then for no reason that I could see he upped and made a
sound like a horse makes when it works its lips in sort of a loose flap, you
know? He, uh, sighed, yes, and then he rolled off me, and then he was
passing water on the sheets, and that was the end of him. Three weeks
later I left Massillon, and I had an inheritance of more than sixty thousand dollars . . . me, little Irene Weaver . . . Irene Weaver *Hollingshead*
. . . with *sixty thousand dollars*. It had all been marked out for me in his
will. He had two brothers and a sister, and they didn't give me a bit of
trouble. Not a bit. They were nice people. Ah, but what was I supposed to
do with all that money? Well, I did the only thing I could have done. I
came here and opened this house. I mean, it's all I know anything about.
That's been four months ago, and the place is doing just fine. These are
good girls. I got the right people taking money from me, and this is the
capital of the state, which means it's full of politicians, which means it's a
good town for a whorehouse. I like it here. I really do.

But there have been no men for you?

Not until tonight.

Why?

I don't know. Not exactly. All I can figure is that maybe I loved old Alf.

Mm, said Charley. Love.

What's the matter, Charley? You got no use for it?

I don't know. And that's a fact. I expect maybe *sometimes* I got use for
love. But not all the time. It can't be trusted. I mean, it's like everything
else: it goes and dies on a person.

Oh.

If a man doesn't watch himself, it can ruin him.

Same with women.

I wouldn't be surprised.

Irene Hollingshead smiled. She punched Charley's belly. Listen to us go
on, she said.

Yes ma'm, said Charley. Surely is a caution.

The next evening, riding in the CPV&M steam cars back to Paradise
Falls, both Charley and Virgil T. Light looked like something the cat had
scraped out of the bottom of a cesspool. The night with little Rosemary had
lifted Virgil T. Light's spirits a bit at the time, but now the time was

gone, and he was gloomier than ever—and guilty on top of it. This is the first time since the war, he said.

First time for what? said Charley.

First time I stepped out on my wife.

Well, what the hell. You're only human.

No. Don't say that. It wasn't right. Catherine Anne is a good woman. How am I going to look at her?

Charley sighed, stared out the window, said nothing.

She's always been good to me, said Virgil T. Light. Maybe you wouldn't know it from looking at her now, what with her being so sickly and all, but before the war she was a true beauty. And she's always loved me. I don't think she's ever approved of me, but that doesn't mean the love hasn't been there. And so what do I do to show her my gratitude? I run off to Columbus and behave like a pig.

Jesus, said Charley.

And what about *you*? You're practically a newlywed.

Look. All we did was go to a whorehouse. We didn't piss on the flag. We didn't blow up a church. We didn't rape a baby.

I don't know . . .

Forget it. It's over. Done with. You couldn't change it if you wanted to.

Charley? Godalmighty, Charley?

Yes?

Where in the *hell* are we going to get the *money*?

We'll get it.

The eleven thousand damn near cleaned me out. If we don't get the money, I don't know what I'll—

It'll be all right.

I've had expenses. Store expansion. The place needed a lot done to it when I came back from the war last year. Sam Reddy, the man I had run the place while I was gone, you know old Sam Reddy don't you?

Yes.

Well, it wasn't his *own* place, and he didn't exactly coin money for me, and the inventory was all depleted, and I had to spend so damn much cash just to get everything in order again, and it's been no—

There are other cities. There are other banks. Columbus isn't the world. My Lord, I should *hope* not.

What city do we try next?

Let me think on it.

I should have been satisfied with what I had.

Now, Virge, that sort of talk doesn't sound like you at all. Tomorrow's another day. God smiles on the optimistic. I mean that. You'll see.

In the succeeding ten days, Charley and Virgil T. Light visited banks in Zanesville, Newark, Cleveland and Pittsburgh. They received no encouragement. In point of fact, they were turned down flat. The officials of these banks echoed what the Columbus men had said—the world did not number among its most urgent needs the establishment of another furniture factory, especially one that would be operated by men who, no matter how wellmeaning, were totally without experience. Sorry, said the bankers, and they were as cordial as whores on payday, but they were adamant, and of course each rejection made Virgil T. Light that much more frantic. It all was working out perfectly for Charley. He sat down and wrote another letter to his friend Doggett in Washington. Doggett's reply was prompt. Charley showed Doggett's letter to Fritz Voss, who said: So far, so good, eh? And Charley said: Yes *sir*. He spent part of each day with the disconsolate Virgil T. Light, and Virgil T. Light told him: I've said nothing to Catherine Anne about the delay. She hasn't asked me yet. Why do you suppose she hasn't? Said Charley: I expect she has faith in you. Same as I do. Same as I have faith in what we're doing. It'll come out all right. Did I tell you I have been in correspondence with banks in Detroit, Dayton and Cincinnati? I should receive a reply any day. *I* haven't given up, and I see no reason why you should. Said Virgil T. Light: You see no reason? My God, how many times do we have to be turned down? Said Charley: It'll work out. Trust me.

Percy T. Disney arrived in Paradise Falls one morning in early October on the 11:38 from Marietta. He was a short bearded man, and he was chewing on a cigar. He put Charley in mind of photographs he had seen of old U. S. Grant, who would be the next President of the United States as surely as God made the grass green and the little pigs go oink. Disney was carrying two large suitcases. Doggett's second letter had contained an excellent physical description of the man, and Charley had no trouble recognizing him. He handed Charley one of the suitcases. It was very heavy. Charley supposed it contained Disney's equipment. He had no idea what sort of equipment it was. Oh well, it was better that way. The less he knew of Disney's techniques, the better off he probably would be. The man would be in and out of town very quickly, and this was all that mattered. Charley escorted Disney to the Depot Hotel. Disney registered as Perry T. Dewhurst of Annapolis, Maryland. Charley accompanied him upstairs to his room. As soon as the door was closed and locked, Disney flopped on the bed. Goddamn trains, he said. I wish someone'd think up some way to put beds in them. Man who did that would make himself a fortune.

Charley nodded, sat down on a straightbacked chair.

If anyone asks you who I am, said Disney, just say I'm a salesman come here to try to get you to buy oh I don't know, showcases or some such thing.

Again Charley nodded.

I expect in a town this size there was someone saw us together down there on the platform.

Charley shrugged. I expect so, he said.

Don't shrug at me. I know what I'm doing. Doggett told me you had a head on your shoulders. Use it.

I use it. I'd already thought of a pretext for meeting you, in case anybody saw us. I was going to say you were an old friend from Indiana.

Fuck that. If you say I'm an old friend, then people'll maybe ask too many questions. I'm a salesman, and you don't give a damn about me, and that way the questions won't be asked. All right?

All right . . . and, uh, you're absolutely correct.

You got the money?

Yes.

Give it to me.

Charley stood up. He went to the bed. He dug out his billfold, opened it, extracted ten hundred dollar bills, handed them to Disney.

And a hundred dollars for expenses. Didn't Doggett tell you about that?

No. He didn't.

Well, it's part of the deal.

You're holding me up.

Disney shrugged. He leaned forward on an elbow and held the ten bills out to Charley. Here, he said, take them back. I'll be on the next train out of here.

Charley sighed. He handed Disney another hundred dollar bill.

Disney nodded. He lay back.

Charley returned to his chair and sat down.

Disney closed his eyes. His mouth made moist sounds with the cigar. He still held the money. He held it in a tight fist. Any time you're ready, he said.

The address is 16 West Main Street, said Charley. Light's Furniture Store.

A furniture store?

Yes.

Good.

Is that your, uh, *paraphernalia* in the suitcases?

It ain't Bibles.

Mm, said Charley.

You don't think I'm going to buy that stuff *here* do you? said Disney.

No. I suppose not.

Kerosene. That's all I'd have to do—me, a stranger, go sashaying into a hardware store to buy *kerosene*.

I see what you mean.

Disney opened his eyes. He stuffed the money into a pocket of his britches. He scratched the back of a hand. He inspected his fingernails, then said: It's frame ain't it?

Yes.

Good. Goddamn brick can be an aggravation.

I wouldn't be surprised.

Now, how about the winds?

You mean where do they come from?

I do.

They come from the west.

I figured so, said Disney.

Do the winds make that much difference?

Disney gave Charley a sharp look. Mister, he said, when I work on a place, it *goes*. Day after tomorrow there ain't going to be so much as a *board foot* of that store that ain't felt the warm touch of Percy T. Disney.

Well . . . uh, good enough.

Tell you something. This here is the one thing in the world I can do good.

Mm.

Women, gambling, things like that . . . they get the best of me, you know?

Charley nodded.

But, said Disney, this here thing I'm better at than anybody. You'll see. Your thousand dollars has earned you that right.

My eleven hundred dollars.

Disney sucked at the cigar. Have it your own way, he said.

Charley grinned.

You won't be disappointed, said Disney. I ain't disappointed nobody yet.

That's fine.

Doggett says you'll get the man drunk. That right?

Yes.

Good enough. Just keep him away from the place. I'll do her at midnight tomorrow night. I'll catch a train the next morning out of here. You don't have to come here no more. Uh, 16 West Main, right?

Right.

Now you can get out. I want to catch up on my sleep.

Charley stood up. All right, he said. He started for the door.

Disney removed the cigar from his mouth. He flipped the cigar on the rug. He shaded his eyes, rolled over.

Charley walked to the place where the cigar lay.

A snigger from the bed.

Charley looked at Disney.

Don't worry none, said Disney, his eyes closed.

What?

It ain't lit. Wouldn't do for me to throw a lit cigar on the rug. Be a hell of a fire hazard.

You sonofabitch, said Charley, laughing.

He laughed all the way back to the store. That afternoon he invited Virgil T. Light to take supper with him and Nancy the following evening in the Acterhof House. And bring along that boy of yours, said Charley. He and Nancy hit it off real good. We'll all have a little something to drink. Take our mind off our troubles. Virgil T. Light nodded gloomily. He told Charley he wished they had something to celebrate. Ah well, said Charley, it won't hurt anything to have a few drinks. Said Virgil T. Light: Sure. We'll be there. The supper was successful. Many drinks were put away by Virgil T. Light, and eventually he proposed toasts to (1) Nancy, (2) the Army of the Potomac, (3) the Paradise Falls Blues, (4) the late Henry E. Ferris, (5) the GAR, (6) the Republican party, (7) poor sickly Catherine Anne, whose condition of course prevented her from attending this gay gathering, (8) good old Charley Wells, (9) friendship, (10) loyalty, (11) the furniture business, (12) forgiveness for carnal transgressions, (13) luck, (14) the abiding and eternal damnation of all bankers, their families and their friends. It was 11 o'clock when the supper finally ended. Grimacing, young Bill Light told Charley he had had a grand time. Mumbling and humming, Virgil T. Light leaned against his son. Bill Light smiled at Nancy. She returned the smile. He reddened. Virgil T. Light's mumblings produced several audible words. Among them were *flag* and *war* and *death*. Charley asked young Bill if he needed help in shepherding his father home. No thank you sir, said young Bill, I'll manage. He shook hands with Charley, then dragged his stumbling father through the Acterhof House lobby and out onto Main Street. Charley smiled. He took Nancy by an elbow and escorted her upstairs to bed. She asked him why he had given Virgil T. Light so much to drink. To take his mind off his troubles, said Charley. They're *your* troubles too, said Nancy. Yes, but I'm not taking them so hard, said Charley. Is there a reason for that? Nancy wanted to know. What's *that* supposed to mean? said Charley. Oh never *mind*, said Nancy. She took off her clothes and went to bed. He sighed. He undressed and stretched out beside her. She kissed him. Her lips were hard and dry. Her breath was sour. She fell asleep almost immediately. Charley did not fall asleep. He waited. At 12:30, he was doing sums in his head. Next to him, Nancy was snoring. When he heard the firebell, he grinned. He could smell the smoke, and presently he could hear shouts, and God love Percy T. Disney. The next morning Virgil T. Light stood numbly amid the ruins of his furniture store. There wasn't a single board foot of the building that hadn't been destroyed. The place stank. The fire apparently had started in a back room. Several cans of varnish had been stored there. Spontaneous combustion they tell me, said Virgil T. Light. Spontaneous combustion. Sweet Jesus, I don't even know what spontaneous combustion *means*. They tell me it means the place *set itself* on fire. That make any sense to you? Charley spread his hands. I don't know what to say, he told Virgil T. Light. He wondered whether Percy T. Disney had anticipated the varnish. He supposed the rascal had. He didn't think Percy T. Disney was the sort to miss a thing. Solemnly he patted Virgil T. Light on the back. Ah Lord, he said, such a terrible tragedy.

Virgil T. Light rubbed his hands together, then ran one of the hands over his great bald head. He coughed briefly, and then he said: This . . . uh, well, Charley, you want to know something? This . . . uh, this does me in.

What?

It's . . . it's all gone. I got nothing . . .

A vigorous negative nod from Charley, who said: What are you talking about? You'll come back better than ever. You can take the insurance money and you can—

What insurance money?

You mean to say this place isn't insured?

I had to drop the insurance. I mean, it was all I could do to raise the money for that goddamn fucking sonofabitching *land*.

Oh Jesus God, said Charley, arranging his features into a properly stricken expression. He shook his head. He pursed his lips. He had a quick vision of Percy T. Disney's cigar butt. His chest and stomach began to give him pain. He rubbed his mouth. Then he put an arm around Virgil T. Light's shoulders. You'll be all right, he said.

Virgil T. Light kicked at a charred and splintered board. He pulled himself away from Charley's comforting arm. Shrugging, he said: I'm a dead man. Remember when Jim Blood said *he* was a dead man? Well, I know how he felt.

Shit. Stop feeling sorry for yourself.

What?

Something'll happen. You're not just anybody. You're Virge Light, and the people in this town respect you, and just you wait. *You'll* see. Something'll make it so you can rebuild this place, and it'll be bigger than ever, and then you'll laugh about what happened last night.

I slept through it all. You know that?

Mm.

I was so drunk. Bill tried to get me out of bed, but he couldn't. He and Catherine Anne both. They shook me and shook me, and they might as well have tried to shake a stone.

Well, you did have a lot to drink last night . . .

Fine time to get drunk.

Ah, well, who was to know?

Virgil T. Light's eyes moistened.

Now, *now*, said Charley.

What . . . what am I going to *do*?

You got no assets at all?

Virgil T. Light wiped at his eyes. He coughed. He wet his lips. Mm, he said. Pardon me. Now. About my assets. Maybe, if I was to sell my house, I could pick up five or six thousand dollars, and maybe that five or six thousand dollars could buy me an inventory, but what about this building? Ike Underwood's probably laughing to beat hell. He never has liked me a whole lot. He told me once I talked too much. Well, that doesn't matter. The thing that *does* matter is: Ike Underwood isn't about to lend me any money for a new store. Not even if I was to press a pistol to his head. And where else can I go?

There are other banks.

Other banks? My God, you and I have just gone traipsing all over the goddamn *state*, and what good's it done us? If the bankers won't lend *us* the money for a *factory*, what makes you think they'd lend *me* the money for a *store*?

Well . . .

Especially after they find out I let the insurance go. A man who lets his insurance go . . . well, the bankers don't exactly throw their hats in the air because of such a man.

Lord, Virge, I didn't know you had so little in reserve.

Well, now you know.

Our factory, suppose we get the money to build it. You'd have had to put up more cash to get the operation started. Your share, I mean. Where would it have come from?

I'd have sold off part of my half. It could have been worked out.

Charley shrugged. Yes, he said. I suppose so.

But never mind *that*. What about my store?

Charley made a clucking sound. There has to be a way, he said. You'll think of something.

Can *you?*

Not offhand. But give me time. And give yourself time. A good man can't be kept down, and that's a *fact* for the God's sake, and you *know* it.

Virgil T. Light sucked breath, spread his hands, kicked at another charred board, ran a hand over the blistered surface of a ruined chiffonier, made petulant sounds with his saliva.

You were brave through a war, said Charley, and you can be brave through something like this.

Thank you.

Nothing to thank me *for.* I'm just speaking the truth.

You're a good friend, Charley. I swear to God you are.

Ahhh, said Charley, lowering his eyes in affectionate modesty, *shit.*

Now all that remained was for Virgil T. Light to come up with the idea Charley hoped and prayed he would come up with. And Virgil T. Light did. It took him eleven days. He called on Charley at the grocery store, and they conferred in the back room. They seated themselves on a couple of crates. Virgil T. Light leaned forward. He rested his forearms on his legs. Charley, he said, I been thinking on something.

And what's that?

That land we bought.

Oh?

I don't think anything's ever going to come of our plan.

Mm.

I wondered if maybe I could—

Charley held up a hand. He smiled. Virge, he said, it's occurred to me too. But I don't think I can manage it.

But you haven't heard me out.

I don't have to. You want to sell me your half, correct?

Yes . . .

Well, I just don't see how I can do it.

Why not?

We each invested eleven thousand dollars. I, uh, well, the only fair thing would be for me to pay you eleven thousand for your share, and I just don't *have* eleven thousand. Remember the other day when you said you would have to sell off part of your share in the factory so you could come up with your half of the working capital? Well, that's what *I* would have had to do too. And, besides all that, if there's no furniture factory, what would I *do* with the land? The timber's not worth that much, and, well . . .

How about if I asked for just five thousand?

Charley forced down the corners of his mouth. It was working. It really was. He folded his arms across his belly. He was able to hear his pulse.

Well, Charley?

I couldn't do that. It'd mean you'd be out six thousand.

No, no, don't think of it that way! It'd mean a chance for me!

How's that?

Virgil T. Light folded his hands in his lap. He studied them. I beg your pardon, he said. I didn't mean to shout. It's just that I've thought it all through, and I figure I got a solution. I'm selling my house. Dr Reeser's buying it for eight thousand. That's about two or three more than I expected. I saw Ike Underwood yesterday. He told me he'd lend me ten thousand if I had ten thousand in hand. So all I need from you is five. That'd give me the ten thousand plus three for emergencies. It'd bring me back.

You mean to tell me it's going to cost you twenty thousand dollars to get your business going again?

Yes. Counting the inventory.

And you'll take a loss of six thousand dollars just so you can have five?

Yes.

Well, it surely would pinch me . . .

Charley, Jesus, do this thing for me.

Charley smiled. Well, he said, I guess I can.

You mean that?

Yes. But there's one thing I want you to understand real clear.

What's that?

Maybe someday that land will increase in value. You could be awfully put out with me.

Don't let the thought cross your mind. It's the chance I've got to take, Charley. And anyway, how could I be put out? You're saving my life. Believe me, on my word of honor, I'd never hold a thing against you.

You mean that, don't you?

Yes. I give you my oath.

All right. I'll do it.

Ah, Charley, Charley . . . God love you . . .

ElRoy Mauk arranged the sale. Charley and Virgil T. Light signed the papers in his office. Virgil T. Light pumped Charley's hand with great vigor. He even embraced Charley. ElRoy Mauk sat with a hand over his mouth. After Virgil T. Light had left, ElRoy Mauk was taken with a fit of giggling. He giggled with such ferocity that he had to remove his dentures. He held them in the palm of a hand. They dripped. Wheezing, he blinked at Charley and finally said: Thapor folish sumish.

How's that? said Charley.

Cackling, ElRoy Mauk replaced his dentures and said: The poor foolish sonofabitch.

Yes, said Charley, grinning. That's very true.

Grimacing, ElRoy Mauk tapped his jaw and cheeks with the heel of a hand. Back in '39, he said, when Loretta and I were married, we took a wedding trip to Alexandria, Virginia. She has relatives there. Well, at any rate, one day we borrowed a buggy and drove over to Mount Vernon. George Washington's dentures are on display there. Damnedest things I've ever seen. The poor fellow must have been in constant agony. It's no wonder he seems so sort of . . . oh I don't know, *constipated* . . . *prissy* . . . in the paintings that were done of him.

I've always had good teeth myself, said Charley. I've lost some—accidentally—but the ones I have left are fine.

A blessing, believe me. I envy you. I hate to think of how much money I've spent on dentures. The ones I'm wearing now are no damn good, and I'm the first to admit it, but at least they don't give me pain. At my age, one is grateful to be free of pain. At least in one's mouth. I refuse to discuss my other regions.

According to what I hear from Irene Hollingshead, you got one region that isn't giving you any pain.

You know Irene Hollingshead?

I surely do.

And she mentioned my name?

Yes.

She told you about my little Rosemary?

She did. And she said Rosemary had told her you had enough of it in you to swamp a canoe.

Ah, that Rosemary. I must lecture her on the evils of talebearing.

Shit. At your age, you probably wish she'd put a notice in the newspapers.

You know me too well.

I know *people* too well.

I believe you do.

Well, I didn't come here to talk about my wisdom. I came here to sign some papers. They've been signed. I expect I'll be going now.

Just a minute.

Yes?

How did you manage it? To burn down the store, I mean.

To burn down the store? You must be crazy. You know me better than that. I'm outraged. I didn't burn down any store. I was in bed when the firebell rang. I got witnesses.

You hired somebody, didn't you?

I don't know what you're talking about.

ElRoy Mauk chuckled. You're outraged, he said. I surely do have to give you credit. Like the night . . . when was it? Three months ago? The night you bought me all those drinks in Claude Dill's saloon.

I don't know what you're talking about.

I told you about Virge Light letting his insurance lapse.

You did?

Yes. And I remember how you sort of smiled when I told you.

That so?

And to think he trusted me with his personal affairs.

He is a very trusting fellow.

What are you going to do now?

Get the financing for the mines.

You think you'll have any trouble?

Charley smiled. No, he said. Not a bit.

Poor Virge Light.

Well, if you say so . . .

I'm still to be counsel?

Yes. I gave you my word.

Your word. Well.

It means something.

Of course it does.

Don't ridicule me, ElRoy.

Me ridicule *you?* It'll never happen.

Good.

I got better sense, said ElRoy Mauk.

Charley grinned.

1867 . . .

Mayor George McC. Pillsbury is reelected without opposition. Ferd Purvis is fired from Oberlin College because of chronic drunkenness. The particular offense that caused his expulsion came on a Sunday morning when he pissed on the steps of a Methodist church in full view of several dozen members of the congregation. He was heard to say he had waited up all night until a proper audience was on hand. He leaves Oberlin but does not return to Paradise Falls. His sister Priscilla hears from him now and again. At last report he is working in the Zanesville depot as

a baggage smasher or freight clerk or some such thing. Or perhaps it is
the Coshocton depot. Ah well, makes no difference. Priscilla still is clerking in old Harlowe Morris' grocery. He is relying on her more and more.
Back in 1817, long before there was such a place as Paradise Falls, he
planted twentytwo peach trees in his back yard. The trees still thrive. This
is the best peach orchard in the county, no question about it. Now that
his wife is dead, he tends the trees by himself. He spends more time with
the trees than he does in the store. The GAR boys are, most of them,
mighty upset with Andy Johnson. He is far too quick in declaring am-
nesty for the rebel traitors. Ben Wade and Secretary Stanton and Thad
Stevens have the right idea. When Johnson callously gets rid of Secretary Stanton, Virgil T. Light says: That goddamn fool should be forced
from office at the point of a bayonet. Joanna Burkhart, mother of the late
Amelia Burkhart Soeder dies of a malignancy on her right breast. Several
weeks later, fourteen of Heinz Burkhart's fattest and most productive
Guernseys are drowned in a sudden flood. When Harlowe Morris planted
his peach trees, there wasn't another home within three miles. Now, of
course, the village has grown up around his home and his trees. His home
now faces what is called Market Street. He has refused all offers to sell the
land where the orchard is. Ida was a young girl when they planted that
orchard together. She was so very shy, and she had a taste to her that was
like water from a spring. The orchard contains more of her than her grave
ever could. He likes to sit out there. He especially likes to sit out there
when the peaches are in season. He likes to suck on the peaches. He likes
to rub them against his face. He has often discussed the orchard with his
friend Ike Underwood. He has asked Ike Underwood: Do you understand how important it is? And Ike Underwood's reply always has been
the same: Yes. I expect I do. Harlowe Morris wishes his son Edwin would
come home. Edwin plays the violoncello for a living. He has not seen
Edwin since 1849. He has never approved of Edwin's line of work. He
wants to see Edwin just once before the end. He doubts that he will.
Edwin seldom answers his letters. He has never understood Edwin, him
and his damn violoncello. The C. P. Wells Coal Co is incorporated. Says
Ike Underwood to his wife: Do you suppose I've been snookered? Says
Phoebe Underwood: Yes, dear. I do. That man is many things, but he
is not stupid. Old Ben Masonbrink finally breathes his last. He literally
chokes to death on his own sputum. His coffin is homemade, and he is
buried in the Masonbrink cemetery near the site of the old fort. No mention of the event is made in the *Democrat*. J. K. Bankson wants to print
a short article, but it is vetoed by Ike Underwood, who tells him: We
can't. They hate me too much. If we print something, they'll think I'm
being a hypocrite. I won't allow that. Virgil T. Light builds a new store.
The opening ceremonies include a door prize—a sofa Virgil T. Light says
is worth thirty dollars. It is won by Mrs Phoebe Underwood. She does not
refuse it. She has for some time needed a sofa for her sitting room. Ah, says

Ike, them as has gets. Says Phoebe: For once in your life, you have a point. Virgil T. Light is seduced by Mrs Charles P. Wells, the plenteous Nancy. She tells him: It is the least I can do. He asks her: How can I face Charley? Says Nancy Wells: You'll manage. Now come here. I want to lick your feet. Mrs Jasper O. Lloyd, wife of the foreman at the Underwood Shoe Co, finds a dollar bill and thirtytwo cents in change on the walk in front of St Luke's Lutheran Church. She hurries over to Main Street and buys a new hat at Steinfelder's.

Philip Isaac Underwood:

THERE WAS NO DARKNESS at the beginning. There was not even a hint of it. He was a handsome little fellow, and he collected butterflies, and his mother spoke to him often of love and respect and honor. He loved his mother. He loved his father too, for that matter. And he respected them. And he honored them. He was frail, though, and his father, the loud tobaccochewing Isaac (Ike) Underwood, didn't quite know how to talk to him. Ike took the boy fishing, and always the dampness made little Phil shiver. He hugged his father, and his teeth clicked, his eyes moistened, and usually he came down with the sniffles. Ike took the boy hunting, and always the sight of the dead animals made little Phil weep. He preferred to gather up leaves and pebbles. He kept them in a box in his room. He liked to smell them. He liked to press the leaves against his palms. He never pressed them too tightly. He did not want to bruise them. He liked to rub the pebbles together and make them snap. Wintertimes he often amused himself by drawing pictures in the frost on the windows. Sometimes, when the sunshine struck treetrunks just right, he tried to lick the sunshine off the treetrunks. He never did this, though, when anyone was looking. He had long talks with his father, and he told his father: I'll try not to cry when I see the dead things. I promise. And he did try. He tried until his face ached from the trying. But always the tears came, and after a time his father no longer took him fishing and hunting.

Phil was born in 1847. There had been a girl, Sarah, born four years earlier, but a diphtheria outbreak had killed her when she was nine months old. There were no children after Phil. By the time he was eight, he had read everything ever written by James Fenimore Cooper and Sir Walter Scott. His mother had seen to it. Phoebe and Ike had reached an agreement about the boy. Isaac, she said, I believe it would be advisable if we approached this matter with intelligence. Just because Philip does not care for fishing or hunting, it would not be right for us to dismiss him as being a sissy. He is a manly little fellow, but his manliness is not of the conventional sort. I understand your exasperation with him, but it is not as serious as you believe it to be. Let him be my responsibility. I swear to you: I shall not turn him into a mama's boy. That I promise. Are you willing to accept my word?

Ike was willing, and so Phoebe began her campaign, and the first thing she did was send away for the Cooper and the Scott. And she spoke to Phil of courage. She told him courage did not always have to be loud. She told him the largest courage was the courage to be one's self. She encouraged his butterfly collection. It is what interests *you*, she said. Never be ashamed of it, no matter what anyone says. By the time he was ten, he had the most elaborate butterfly collection in Paradise Falls. At the same time, his mother had started him on a program of exercises. He carried out the program in the back yard, out of sight of the neighbors. He ran short sprints. He climbed trees. He taught himself somersaults, cartwheels, handstands. His mother sometimes, but only sometimes, watched him exercise. I won't stand over you, she told him. That would not be right. Either you do the exercises or you don't, but it's going to be up to you. Remember, you are not going to be a mama's boy. I made your father a promise, and I have every intention of keeping it.

When Phil was eleven a boy named Henry Oliver pushed him—facedown and flailing—into a pile of horse apples on Cumberland Street. It was a warm day, and the horse apples were fresh, which meant they gave off steam. Phil's mouth was open when he fell in the horse apples. The flavor caked his lips. Henry Oliver guffawed. He was Phil's age, but he was a good deal taller. He stood over Phil, and his hands were on his hips, and his voice was grand and inexorable, and he said: Ah, look at him! Look at the sissy! The sissy and his butterflies! Go home, sissy! Go home and play with your butterflies!

Grunting, Phil got to his feet. The front of him was smeared with squashed horse apples. Steam came off his chest. He wiped his fouled mouth with the back of a hand. Henry Oliver had been ragging him for more than a year. Henry Oliver's father was a teamster, and people said the man seldom was sober. A few years earlier, he had attempted to assault Ike Underwood right out on Main Street in full view of the world. Drunk, he had accused Ike Underwood of thinking he had clear title to Creation. Ike Underwood had tried to avoid a fight, but Oswald Oliver had insisted on one. Ike Underwood had tried to walk away from the fellow, but the attack had come anyway. From the rear. Roaring, Oswald Oliver had jumped at Ike Underwood, had caught him at the small of the back, had knocked him down. Oswald Oliver jumped on top of Ike Underwood and began pummeling him about the head. Grunting, Ike Underwood rolled over, seized Oswald Oliver by the throat and flung him back. Oswald Oliver gagged. Ike Underwood stood up. So did Oswald Oliver. Heads down, they had at one another. Ike Underwood broke six of Oswald Oliver's ribs. He broke Oswald Oliver's right wrist. He broke a small bone in the forefinger of Oswald Oliver's right hand. By that time Oswald Oliver was wailing like an old woman. He was carried off to jail. He served six months for aggravated assault. Phil knew this story, which meant he knew why Henry Oliver called him a sissy. He was sorry. He truly was. It occurred to him that his father probably could have killed Henry Oliver's father. In those days Ike Underwood had carried a pistol. Phil blinked at Henry Oliver. He wanted to tell him: My papa could have killed your papa. Phil shook his head. No, there was no sense saying such a thing. It would do no good. Sighing, Phil advanced on Henry Oliver.

Henry Oliver grinned. He was a skinny boy, knobbed and underfed. Oh now lookit here, he said, the butterfly boy wants to scrap.

Yes, said Phil.

A crowd of children gathered. It was an afternoon in late May. School had just let out for the day. The children were silent. They cheered for neither contestant. As the son of the richest man in town (and a collector of butterflies, to boot), Phil had no particular friends. And Henry Oliver always was too loud and angry, hadn't ever *wanted* friends. Phil hit him low, squarely in the belly. The air went out of Henry Oliver. He bent forward. Phil hit him across the side of the neck. Henry Oliver moaned, tried to straighten up. Phil smiled. He felt enormous. Henry Oliver finally managed to straighten up. He tried to hit Phil. A fist grazed Phil's nose. It wasn't much of a fist. Phil danced back. Grimacing, Phil embraced Henry Oliver around the belly. He pushed Henry Oliver to the ground. He jumped on top of Henry Oliver. His heart was like a bladder in his throat. He remembered his father's time with Oswald Oliver. He remembered how his father had been attacked from the rear. And now today Phil had been attacked from the rear. Like father, said Phil, smiting Henry Oliver's chest and belly, like son. Henry Oliver began to weep. He whimpered words that had to do with a pain he was feeling in his chest. You should have thought of that, said Phil, before you hit me from behind. A number of the spectators spoke up. Serves you right, Henry! shouted one. About time! yelled another. Phil slapped Henry Oliver's face. Henry Oliver wailed. Phil stood up, backed away. Sobbing, Henry Oliver pulled himself to his feet. Hugging his chest, he staggered away. A number of boys clapped Phil on the back. He'd had no idea it would be so easy. Indomitable and stinking, he walked home. I am, he told himself, unconquerable. My wrath is terrific.

When he told his mother what had happened, she was delighted. As for Ike Underwood, *he* just about burst his britches. Phil had a place of honor at the table that night, and his parents spoke to him lovingly.

It is good to be able to cope, said Phoebe.

Yessir, said Ike, always remember to give it to them good.

The next day was a Saturday, and Phil captured two particularly glorious monarchs (*Danaüs archippus*). A year or so later, Henry Oliver died of what people said was the consumption. His family moved away. Briefly something stabbed and gnawed at Phil, but his parents said nothing to him about the death of Henry Oliver, and the pain went away rather quickly. There was, after all, so much to *do*. And, great day, how could he have *known*?

Phil grew. His voice deepened. He kept up his exercises, and they enlarged his chest. His mother bought him fine clothes. There is no reason why you should not be a gentleman, she told him. Appearance and manners should never be a source of chagrin. Your father's generation has built. It will be up to your generation to consolidate, to create tradition and standards. It is a high calling.

As a small boy, Phil had been dark and frail. Now he was dark and slender, and girls were very aware of him. He made them whisper. The years of exercise, plus the years of chasing after butterflies, had destroyed any hint of fat. He moved easily and quietly. He never staggered. He never bumped into things. His mother taught him how to dance. He was a splendid pupil. She told him she envied him his natural grace. He did well in school, too. He was particularly interested in history and literature and the natural sciences.

He was just fourteen when the War of the Rebellion broke out. He loved the war so intensely it made his chest hurt. He kept elaborate maps. He persuaded his father to subscribe to all the Columbus newspapers, plus *Harper's Weekly*. He was soon acknowledged to be the village's foremost expert on the subject. In 1864, two days after his seventeenth birthday, he attempted to enlist. A lieutenant and sergeant of recruiters had set up headquarters in an office in the courthouse. But Ed Maxwell, a county commissioner, saw Phil enter the office. Ed Maxwell ran across the street to Ike Underwood's bank and told Ike what he had seen. Ike went to the courthouse. He walked in on Phil while Phil was talking with the recruiters. He knew the recruiters. One of them, the lieutenant, a

man named Savage, had people in Paradise County. Ike smiled at the
recruiters, told them he needed to have a few words with his son. Phil
looked at his father. Ike took Phil by an arm and escorted him across the
street to Claude Dill's saloon. They took a table in the rear. Ike bought
his son a glass of beer, and then he said: You can't do this.

Papa, I have to.

No, said Ike Underwood. I understand why you have to, but no.

Why?

Ike Underwood spoke quietly. He had bought himself a shot of whisky.
He drank it neat, directly from the shotglass. He said: Your mother. Suppose you got killed. It'd kill *her* too.

It wouldn't.

Ike Underwood sighed. You don't know, he said.

Would it kill *you* too?

I don't know. Maybe. No. That's wrong. I *do* know. It *would*. I mean
that.

Why? said Phil. He frowned at his beer glass, pushed it away. He said:
Why would it kill you? Why would it kill her?

You're our son. *That's* why. You shouldn't have to ask the question.

It's my war, said Phil. If I'm made to do without it, there has to be a
good reason.

Your war?

Yes. Young men require their wars. They have to find out things
about themselves.

But, my Lord, the danger—

No. No. Please. That sort of talk won't do. You can speak to me of
danger until the stars fall down and it won't do you any good. The
point is, Papa: I'm like everybody else. Just because I'm *your* son doesn't
make me different. At home, all my maps and cuttings: I could have all
the maps and cuttings in the world and they wouldn't be enough. Look,
if you *order* me to go home, I will. I would have to. Otherwise, I wouldn't
be showing the proper respect for you and Mama. She has taught me
about respect, and I believe the things she says.

All right then. I order you.

Are you sure?

Yes.

Papa, I love you. And I love Mama.

I know that.

You really want me that much?

Yes, said Ike Underwood.

All right.

I don't want you scraped up off some damn field in Virginia and sent home in a box. Is that so hard to understand?

Not a bit, said Phil.

Your beer. Claude Dill serves good beer. Drink up.

No thank you.

Oh?

The taste. I'm sorry, Papa, but it is too bitter.

At supper that night, Ike Underwood told his wife their son had attempted to enlist. He told her in front of Phil. He was no sneak. He never had been. Phil loved him, and that was the absolute truth. Phil also loved his mother, and so was *that*. Phoebe Underwood looked up from her soup. Her eyes were tight. She wiped her mouth. She listened carefully. Then, after her husband had finished, she looked at Phil and said: We understand. Truly we do. I know I speak for your father when I say that. But, Philip, you have to give us time to prepare ourselves. Perhaps, in a year or so, if you still insist on doing this thing, perhaps then we will be ready. Later that night, alone in his bed, Phil made fists. It was a warm and humid night, and tree frogs clicked. He was covered only by a sheet. His sweat was sour. He thought of duty. Which was the largest duty? The duty toward his mother and father? Or the duty toward his necessary war? Great bloody wounded Jesus, what of manhood? It was a time of heroes and terrors and awful excursions, of bugles and swords and brave beards. Where else lay true manhood? He told himself: I hope they know what they've done. I love them. I only hope they know what they've done. I only hope. He closed his eyes. He saw *Harper's Weekly*. He saw the neat engravings. He saw those Vermont men who had enfiladed the rebels on the third day at Gettysburg and in so doing had repulsed the grand attack there by that stone wall. He said to himself: I trace fastidious lines on my maps. I can speak for hours on this war. Grunting, Phil rubbed his eyes with his fists. He saw the face of Frederick Magill, the man who had been elected captain of the Paradise Falls Blues; he saw this Frederick Magill marching at the head of the men as they paraded to the depot; he saw himself running dark and silent alongside the men; the year had been 1861, and the month had been April, and the CPV&M locomotive had whooped and snorted; he saw himself holding a tiny flag; he saw himself waving the tiny flag; he heard himself shout *Hurrah!*, and at fourteen his voice had been like tin against glass; he saw the men of the Paradise Falls Blues lean out the windows of the steam cars and wave and yell; he saw how crimson their faces were; he understood why their voices were so loud and desperate; he recalled all the specifics of that great martial day, and then, pulling his fists away from his eyes, opening his hands and pressing them flat against the sheet, he forced himself to fall asleep, and of course he had visions of splendid carnage, frozen visions pilfered from the *Harper's Weekly* engravings. His heart thumped in cadence with drums and artillery, and his heavy dreaming tongue tasted the enemy's blood. At breakfast the next morning he told his mother and father he loved them. Within a year the war had ended, and he was packed off to Harvard. He majored in literature, and Harvard was a fine place, and he took to wearing elaborate vests. In the fall of his junior year, when he was twenty, a drunken professor named Lipscomb came up to him at a party and attempted to seize him by the genitals. Phil broke Lipscomb's jaw and one of his arms. The damage to the room was considerable, but the host, a classmate named Paul Starling, refused Phil's offer to pay. No, said Paul Starling, it's about time that damn sissy got what was coming to him. Weeping and screaming, Lipscomb was carried off to a hospital. Phil blew on his knuckles. They bled. The other guests congratulated him. Phil thought of splendid carnage. He smiled. He straightened his fastidious vest. He wiped his knuckles. He seated himself on a horsehair settee and kept his legs crossed so his erection wouldn't show. The edges of the darkness were upon him.

1868 . . .

What is the sense of fighting and winning a war if, at its conclusion, the enemy is not made to repent? Ben Wade and Thad Stevens and former Secretary Stanton have the right idea, and here in Paradise Falls it is most heartily endorsed. There is much gloom when Andy Johnson is saved from impeachment by one piddling vote. Crimes and misdemeanors, says Virgil T. Light to his GAR cronies. You're damn right the man committed crimes and misdemeanors. He has betrayed us. He has betrayed all those who forfeited their lives in order that the South be brought to its knees. As far as I am concerned, the troops can be kept down there until the final generation.

(In January, Mrs Charles P. Wells discovers she is pregnant. When she tells her husband, he says: Glory be to God. When she tells Virgil T. Light, *he* says: Oh Lord. He tells her he will have to stop visiting her. She says: I hear a click. Says Virgil T. Light: How's that? Says Mrs Charles P. Wells: The click of the lock on the barn door now that the horse has been stolen.)

During the impeachment trial, J. K. Bankson writes a number of editorials endorsing the work of the President's enemies. But Ike Underwood will not allow him to publish them in the *Democrat*. When J. K. Bankson asks him why, he says: Those people have gone too far. It is one thing to disagree with a man. It is quite another to try to silence him because of the disagreement. I don't like Andy Johnson any more than you do, but I don't think that's enough reason to have him impeached. If it happens, a lot will go out of this goddamn democracy we're always talking about. A whole lot. Maybe too much.

(Mrs Margaret Jellicoe, wife of George A. Jellicoe, a teller in the Paradise Falls State Bank, gives birth to a baby boy that has no feet. She is thirtysix, and this is her first baby. The annual spring floods do an estimated one hundred thousand dollars' damage to the hamlet of Egypt and the farms that adjoin it. The county commissioners authorize more money for sandbags. Says Amos Holiday, who operates the general store in Egypt: One of these days I'm going to pull out. One of these days. On the morning of June 5, little John Howdyshell, who is just four, manages to keep his hoop rolling for a distance of two squares. It didn't tip over once! he tells his mother. Not once! Please believe me! The Rev Edwin P. Rathbun, rector of Grace Episcopal Church, purchases a new Bible for his parlor. His wife delights in telling people of her dog Queenie and the day dear old Queenie feasted on Nahum, Habakkuk, Zephaniah, Haggai, Zechariah and Malachi. I mean to tell you, says Mrs Rathbun, it's been three years now, and that dog has been getting holier and holier.)

O dear God, protect our alleys and our sheds and our children and our shade trees and our cats. Guard well, O most blessed Lord, the sigh and whisper of leaves and the river and our beloved falls. Our streets are one day dust and the next day mud, but they are *our* streets and we love them as we love Thee, and teach us to understand that aggravation accomplishes nothing. Teach us to accept the dust and the mud. Teach us to place them in the context of elms and laughter and prayers and sweet corn. When the last tree falls, dear God, when the final morning comes, make the end Your act. Hear the babies. Apprehend love. Teach us not to back away from sentiment. It is all so very precious, O God, and we most humbly thank Thee. In the name of the Father, and of the Son, and of the Holy Ghost. Amen.

(Says the Rev Edwin P. Rathbun to his wife: I do wish you'd stop telling that ridiculous story about Queenie. It verges on blasphemy, and it surely is in rather bad taste coming from *you*, considering what *I* do for a living.)

Grant is the nominee, and Grant is the winner, and long live Grant. Virgil T. Light and his GAR people hold a gigantic torchlight parade election night. A large crowd gathers in front of the *Democrat* offices. Grant takes an early narrow lead, slowly pulls away from the Democratic candidate, Horatio Seymour. Long live Grant. Long live the Republican party. Everyone knows about Seymour. He was a Peace Sneak during the war, a damnable Copperhead. Why, when he was governor of New York he even encouraged the draft rioters in New York City! Why, *everyone* knows *that!* The Democrats of course dispute this story, but who can believe what *they* say? The Democratic party is the party of treason. Virgil T. Light has reminded one and all of the Democrats' perfidy and Seymour's Copperheadism, and throughout the canvass the windows of his store are blanketed with placards and banners that proclaim LET THERE BE PEACE! and GRANT FOR PRESIDENT! and SECURE THE VICTORY! In October he is elected chairman of the county Republican organization, replacing County Commissioner Edward B. Maxwell, who retires because of a bloodpressure condition. The choice receives the imprimatur of Ike Underwood, who says: It'll serve to bring the party and the GAR into one tent. We need the GAR, and so I'll not stand in his way, even though I never have given a damn about him. Ike Underwood delivers this confidence to his wife Phoebe, and her only reply is: Well, I just hope you know what you're doing. Grant carries the county, 1,129 to 322. He carries the village of Paradise Falls, 699 to 107.

A Great Man:

GOD ALMIGHTY, *of course* Charley knew that stupid ass of a Virgil T. Light had been smitten by Nancy, but what difference did it make? Charley understood his Nancy. She wasn't about to get herself entangled with that sort of clot. And anyway, what could they do? In a village of that size, they didn't dare meet privately. Where would they go? There was no such thing as privacy in Paradise Falls, and so of course Charley had to grin. Poor Virgil T. Light. The poor besmitten clot.

Charley said nothing to Nancy about the situation, but he did discuss it once with his colleague, Fritz Voss. It was in the winter of 1867–68, and they were riding the steam cars to Columbus to meet with officials of the CPV&M. Fritz Voss had long since given up his job clerking in the store. Now he was officially general manager for the C. P. Wells Coal Co. The story he and Charley had given out was that he just *happened* to have an engineering degree. They let it be known, however, that he knew little about mining. Fritz and I are getting started together, said Charley to his cronies, and I suppose we'll make some mistakes, but then that's to be expected. The important thing is that we profit from them, and I believe we're both smart enough to understand that. He didn't know whether the village accepted these stories, but he didn't particularly care.

He was acquiring something of a reputation as a rascal, and he found he enjoyed it. And he also enjoyed the fact that Virgil T. Light had given him no trouble, even after it became amply clear that the coal deposits up there at Blood were apparently of great value. He had retained Virgil T. Light as a friend, and Virgil T. Light never wearied of telling Charley how grateful he was for the financial assistance good old Charley had given after that unfortunate fire . . .

Outside was snow. Charley wiped steam off the window. The coach clattered and swayed. Next to Charley, Fritz Voss was staring stolidly toward the door that opened onto the front platform. Fritz? said Charley.

Yes?

Night like this, a man ought to be home with his wife.

Yes. You are fortunate to have such a splendid wife.

Thank you.

Someday I shall have a splendid wife like yours.

You like her don't you?

Yes.

Well, said Charley, can't say as I blame you. She surely has her . . . ah, attributes.

Yes. And she is of a sweet disposition.

I'm glad I see so much of you.

I beg your pardon?

Well, I was just thinking about Virge Light. He thinks the sun rises and sets on her. But he's a goddamn fool. *You're* no fool, though. I don't think I'd want to leave you alone with her for too long.

Thank you, said Fritz Voss. I take that as a compliment.

That's the way it was meant.

It is strange about Light . . .

You mean because he hasn't made a fuss about the land?

Yes.

It's not that strange. He has strong feelings about Nancy. They make him ashamed of himself. I mean, he's no better than that son of his. Oh that boy, such a mooner the world has never known.

You give Light credit for being very moral.

I'm sure he is. I remember one time I took him to Irene Hollingshead's place. He liked it all fine at the time. But the next day you'd of thought the world had come to an end. All he talked about was his wife, how he'd betrayed her and all that. And he was only with a *whore*. That's what whores are *for*, for the God's sake. For husbands who get an itch now and again.

Mm. You probably have a point.

Probably, my foot. Believe me, Fritz, old Charley knows whereof he speaks. If I've told you once, I've told you a thousand times, I am on my way to being a great man.

Oh yes, said Fritz Voss. Pardon me. I have such a dreadful memory.

Charley grinned.

A great man—if, in the years 1867 and 1868, Charley's pursuit of his greatness had been any more successful it would have entered beyond human belief. With the assistance of Fritz Voss and ElRoy Mauk and even the clerkish Winfield Wainscott, he built his greatness, built it slowly, built it easily, always aware of proper goals and *possibilities*. He did not rush. He concentrated on details. He laid down certain important lies and deceptions. He memorized the lies and deceptions. He never was caught up in them. In early 1867, when the C. P. Wells Coal Co was incorporated, he took steps to dilute any wrath or envy that might have been felt by the hornswoggled Virgil T. Light. He told Virgil T. Light his entire good fortune had come as a result of a visit to the Blood property by geologists in the employ of the CPV&M. I didn't have the slightest notion how valuable the land was, he said. But then along came those geologists, and you should of heard them! If what they say is true, I'm . . . well, let's just say there's a chance I'm going to make a good piece of money. As I expect you know, the CPV&M isn't exactly the most prosperous railroad in the world, and so it's had to sort of scuffle around looking for business. Well, some high mucketymuck in Columbus got the idea that maybe the road should go out and look for things to carry in its trains. Which is why it hired the geologists. There's a good sight of coal up in Hocking and Athens and Perry counties, and so the geologists came nosing around here. I didn't know a thing about it, not until a man named Downing came to me and said the CPV&M wanted to buy leases from me. Well, that's when I began looking into the situation for myself, and it wasn't long until I figured out how big those thieving bastards were out to swindle me. So I told them no thank you; I expect I'll go into the mining business for myself. Then they got smart. They said all right, we'll help you get a bank loan. And they did. The bank's up in Columbus. The CPV&M aims to build a branch from here to Blood, and it'll at least have the shipping business, even if it won't own the mines. The way I put it to them was like this: Half a loaf, gentlemen. Half a loaf. And they went along with my thinking. Not that they, eh, had much choice . . .

That was Charley's explanation to Virgil T. Light, and almost all of it was a lie, but apparently Virgil T. Light believed it. Nodding, smiling, shrugging his large shoulders, he said: Don't let it bother you, Charley. Those things happen. I bear you no grudge. Luck is a peculiar thing. And anyway, where would I be without your help after the fire?

Charley came away from the conversation just about convinced Virgil T. Light would give him no trouble. *Just about.* He decided he would permit Virgil T. Light no *opportunity* to give him trouble. Alertness was a prime characteristic of wisdom, or at least it was a prime characteristic of the sort of wisdom practiced by Charles Palmer Wells. Maybe, for the first time in his anxious lurch and stagger of a life, he had encountered a man who was precisely what he seemed. Maybe good old Virgil T. Light *was* as stupid as he gave every indication of being. Ah yes, and maybe the moon *was* made of chocolate; maybe fire *did* taste like grass. Ah, now, now. Who could tell? Perhaps Virgil T. Light *was* the last enfeebled survivor of the world's innocents. Lord, what a thought. Huh, Virgil T. Light and his GAR fuss and spit and oratory. Virgil T. Light and his closeorder drill exercises. Virgil T. Light shouting commands to young veterans already running to fat from love and potatoes and wives and whisky. Virgil T. Light and the strut and preen of him as he marched in the annual Fourth of July parades. Virgil T. Light and the *conscience* that was buffeting him because of his clear infatuation with Nancy, *and* because of the time with the little whore in Irene Hollingshead's place, *and* because of what he considered to be a betrayal of his dying wife. Ah, Virgil T. Light. Such a man. Such an ass.

It was in the eyes and mouth of Virgil T. Light, this passion he had developed for Nancy. Whenever his eyes beheld her, it was as though warm water had been thrown into them. And, at the same time, he pulled in his lips. The expression on his face took on a quality of constipated pain, and he forever rubbed his pate, patted it, made large bald raling noises deep in his throat. It was the sort of devotion one normally associated with dogs. And children of imperfect mentality.

One night in the summer of 1867, not long after Charley had told Virgil T. Light about the coal and the CPV&M, the two men sat drinking in the Acterhof House tap room. Virgil T. Light had an arm draped around Charley's shoulders. He said: Believe me, Charley, if it all works out I'll be the happiest man in the county.

Less one, said Charley, grinning.

Very *good.*

Virge, be honest with me about something.

Yes? said Virgil T. Light, and his voice cracked a little. He took a deep swallow of whisky, shuddered, then grinned. He cleared his throat. Go ahead, he said.

You really don't bear me any grudge?

No. No. Not at all. I mean that.

That's hard to believe.

Maybe so. But it happens to be the truth. I got myself in some trouble.

You helped me out of it. Now the land is worth a great deal of money. What should I do? What *can* I do? All my life I've tried to face facts. This is a fact. Life goes on.

That's really a remarkable attitude. Nancy thinks so too.

Na . . . Nancy?

Yes.

You've talked to her about it?

Many times.

And . . . and she . . . *admires* me for it?

Yes. She does indeed.

Virgil T. Light exhaled. The warm water had come to his eyes. He sucked his lips, smiled at the corners of his mouth, then said: She is a remarkable woman.

Yes. You really do like her a great deal don't you Virge?

I do. Yes . . .

Well, she likes you too.

Ahhh . . . yes . . . well . . .

She admires the way you've brought back your business. Why, only this afternoon she said to me: Charley, it takes a fine and courageous man to do such a thing. Charley, she said, I just hope his wife realizes how lucky she is.

Well . . . ahhh . . . said Virgil T. Light. Grunting, he wiped his forehead.

Charley's heart clapped and whooped.

Mm, said Virgil T. Light. Ah.

A great man—the obtaining of the bank loan had not been particularly difficult. Charley hadn't expected it to be difficult. In early 1867 Charley and Fritz Voss went to Columbus and called on Downing, the florid middleaged fellow who worked in the freight sales office of the CPV&M. Ah, said Downing, smiling, I remember you. The mysterious Mr Fargo.

Charley also smiled. My name is Charles P. Wells, he said. This gentleman is Mr Voss. I believe we have some business with you.

As I recall, said Downing, I believe you told me you speculate in coal.

Yes, said Charley. And now I'm in a position to seek assistance from you people.

Down went the corners of Downing's mouth. He fingered his Burnside whiskers. Then, abruptly, he sniggered. Ah! he said. Ah, *yes!* Fargo! Wells! *Now* I see!

Charley grinned. So did Fritz Voss.

A few moments later, after his sniggering had subsided, Downing asked Charley and Fritz Voss what he could do for them.

I need two hundred thousand dollars, said Charley.

Well, splendid, said Downing.

You and your railroad are going to see that I get it.

Oh? That so?

Yes, said Charley. He turned to Fritz Voss. A small bag was on Fritz's lap. Open the bag, said Charley.

Fritz Voss opened the bag.

Give Mr Downing the little present we've brought for him, said Charley.

My pleasure, said Fritz Voss. He withdrew a chunk of coal from the bag and placed it on the desk in front of Downing.

Downing looked at it. He did not touch it. He simply looked at it.

I would suggest, said Charley, you have this sample assayed. I feel certain you will be pleasantly surprised. I own twentytwo hundred acres of Paradise County land that is just about bursting with this sort of coal. I want to go about mining it, and I need your help for a bank loan. That's really all I have to say at this time. Mr Voss and I are staying at the Buckeye House. Perhaps, after you have the sample assayed, you will want to get in touch with us.

Downing looked at the chunk of coal. He did not touch it. He simply looked at it.

At 10 o'clock the next morning, a message was delivered to Charley at the hotel: Would Mr Wells and Mr Voss kindly stop in at the offices of the CPV&MRR at their earliest convenience? Charley rapped Fritz Voss across the shoulders, told him the gears and the wheels had begun to move. That afternoon they conferred with Downing and two other men—Chester W. Leathers, president of the engineering firm of Mellow & Leathers, and Harry E. Smallsreed, general superintendent, CPV&MRR. They questioned Fritz Voss as to the thickness and extent of the seams. After he had finished describing the deposit to them, Leathers sighed and said: If what you tell us is true, you have deposits worth—and I mean this very seriously—a great lot of money.

I know that sir, said Fritz. And you do not have to take our word for their extent. Come see for yourself. Bring your own men.

That's right, said Charley. Bring an army for all we care.

Leathers frowned at Fritz and said: How come you know so much about all this? Have you studied up?

Ah, said Fritz, yes.

But I thought a little earlier Mr Wells said you're a clerk in his store.

I am. But I have an education.

Well. Ah. Imagine that, said Leathers. He removed his spectacles, polished them with a sleeve of his coat. He was a small man with a pinched salivary way of talking. Returning his spectacles to his nose, he said: Remarkable.

Smallsreed, the railroad man, looked at Charley. Mr Wells, he said, if the deposits are all you and your colleague say they are, I feel sure we would be very happy to assist you with the financing. In point of fact, I am certain we would be interested in obtaining a share of—

No, said Charley. No shares. The holdings are mine, and I have worked diligently to obtain them. You have no idea.

Yes, but it may be difficult for us to agree to—

No. Please. None of that. Allow me to be frank. It is more than the financing that has brought us here today. Look, let's own up to the situation. With coal of such value, I'll have no trouble obtaining the financing no matter where I go. But I've come to the CPV&M first. Why? Because, as should be obvious, I must have transportation. I need for you people to build a branch from Paradise Falls the eleven miles to Blood. I think you will build that branch.

Oh? said Smallsreed.

Yes. If you refuse, I'll simply pay a call on those people who are building the new railroad from Lancaster to Athens down the Hocking Valley. I expect they might see their way clear to drop a branch down from Logan to Blood. True, the distance is considerably more than the eleven miles, but I understand those people are quite aggressive. As it is, their road will serve New Straitsville, Orbiston, Gore, Murray City . . . well, I don't believe I have to name for you *all* the mining towns this new road will reach. I'm sure you have them committed to memory.

Yes, I do, said Smallsreed. He made a rueful clucking noise with his tongue.

Charley smiled. I see from the expression on your face that you understand me, he said.

Smallsreed nodded.

You people chose the wrong route from Lancaster to Athens, and you know it. If you'd gone by way of Logan instead of Paradise Falls, you'd have been able to serve all those mining towns. But you didn't. And, as a result, the financial health of the CPV&M is not particularly good.

What?

Please, Mr Smallsreed. No demurrers. I have made a study of the CPV&M. It needs me just as much as I need it. Actually, it needs me *more,* since I can always go to those Hocking Valley people. Isn't that what they plan to call their road? The Hocking Valley?

Now, Mr Wells, you—

Mr Smallsreed, the CPV&M main line runs from Columbus to Lancaster to Paradise Falls to Athens to Marietta. Its primary freight business comes from agricultural products and manufactured goods. You know as well as I do that *that* isn't enough business to keep the road out of receivership more than two or three more years. For the fiscal year ending June 30, 1866, the CPV&M returned a *net profit* to its shareholders of just one thousand two hundred nineteen dollars thirtyfour cents. I have the figure committed to memory—*one thousand two hundred nineteen dollars thirtyfour cents*. There is only one answer to your dilemma, sir. It is coal. I offer you coal to ship. *If* I can raise the capital to open the mines. *If* you people help me raise that capital. But don't waste my time speaking to me of sharing in the operation. These will be *my* mines or they will be no one's. I will not compromise. So get me the money. Grease a bank for me. Go to your bondholders. Tell them what the prospects are. Arrangements can be made. We both know that. All I'm offering to do is save your goddamn railroad. Well?

Smallsreed fussed with a penwiper on his desk. He folded the penwiper, smoothed it flat, folded it, squeezed it into a ball. You'll hear from us, he said.

Good, said Charley. And soon, I hope. Thank you very much.

The CPV&M did indeed come through, and quickly. The loan was arranged through a Columbus bank, one of the banks that had declined to participate in Charley's spurious furniture scheme with poor stupid Virgil T. Light. The bank and the CPV&M had sent geologists and a platoon of mining experts swarming over the hills and rocks of Charley's land, and these fellows had been unanimous in their belief that the seams were worth who knew how many millions. Low volatility bituminous. Low sulphur content, less than seven percent. The combination was, as Fritz Voss had said all along, irresistible. This was precious coal, lovely coal, abundant coal, and the geologists and mining engineers were loud and ardent in their enthusiasm. And so in the late summer of 1867 the CPV&M began construction of the eleven miles of branch line from Paradise Falls to Blood. In the meantime, Charley spent five thousand dollars securing mineral leases from John Ellsworth, the farmer whose land Fritz Voss had included in his survey of the coal deposits. At the time of the transaction, John Ellsworth was so delighted he just about swooned. He signed the papers in ElRoy Mauk's office, and ElRoy Mauk paid him in cash, and he promptly spent almost a thousand dollars in an epic fourday miracle of tosspotism performed mainly in Claude Dill's saloon. Later, when John Ellsworth found out how thoroughly Charley had snookered him, his delight vanished, but what could he do about it? He was a huge man, thick of cheek and jowl, a person of heavy flesh and an immense voice that rumbled from behind a profuse and terrible black beard, and he did the only thing he could have done—he sought out Charley and tried to kill him. It happened on Main Street on a morning in November of 1867. It was witnessed by perhaps a hundred persons. Charley was on his way to ElRoy Mauk's office. He had taken to carrying a cane. He twirled the cane. People smiled at him. He returned their smiles. The sun was high and white. Leaves skidded. His jowls felt warm, and there was a smell to him of pomade. Then up came John Ellsworth, and John Ellsworth stank, and he was shouting words the sense of which Charley could not make out. But then John Ellsworth jumped at Charley and seized him about the neck, and oh yes, Charley suddenly understood it all. He was reminded of the night he had been tarred and feathered back in Titusville. The expression on John Ellsworth's face was the same as the collective expression that had been etched across the faces of all those who had applied the feathers and the brush. *Ahhh!* he squealed, clawing at John Ellsworth's hands. *You bastard!* hollered John Ellsworth. *You cheating pig!* Charley wriggled and threshed. He tried to hit John Ellsworth with the cane. *I'm going to kill you!* hollered John Ellsworth, squeezing Charley's neck. Charley felt his adamsapple being squashed, not to mention the bones in his neck, and what a Godawful hell of a way for a great man to die *this* was, and John Ellsworth's breath was sour as an oldmaid's armpit, and then Charley was knocked down, and then John Ellsworth was sitting on his chest, and then people were grabbing at John Ellsworth, and Charley moaned, gasped, gagged, said to himself: I'm just a country boy trying to make my way in the world. I don't know why I have to take so much abuse. Damn if I do. John Ellsworth snorted. Charley reared. Hands tugged at John Ellsworth. Reluctantly, with all the sweet sorrow of parting lovers, John Ellsworth's hands were disengaged from Charley's neck. Sheriff Lester W. Bowles came running up, bad Gettysburg leg and all. *See here!* he shouted. A deputy was with him. Aided by seven men, the deputy pulled John Ellsworth to his feet and ushered him off to jail. John Ellsworth still was yelling. *I'll even up with you, God damn it!* he hollered. *You ain't seen the last of John Ellsworth, you thieving sonofabitch!* John Ellsworth's legs shot out in spasms. His captors took care to keep out of their range. He clenched and unclenched his fists, worked his elbows against the ribs of those who were dragging him away, brayed and spat and cursed. *See here!* shouted the sheriff to John Ellsworth. *You stop that kind of talk!* John Ellsworth cleared his throat, hawked a great gray glob in the general direction of the sheriff. The sheriff shuddered, shook his head. He bent over Charley, helped him to his feet. Charley rubbed his neck. Ark, he said. He rubbed his adamsapple. He cleared his throat, and then he spoke: You know, nobody is without his enemies. Even the Lord has His enemies. But I ask you, how come I always seem to draw such *strong* enemies? All my life it's been like this, you know? Every time

I get involved in a dispute somebody takes it in his head to beat on me like I was an old rug. Huh, sure is a caution. And I'm not such a bad sort, for the God's sake. That I swear to you. On my mother's grave. A month later, John Ellsworth was tried and found guilty of aggravated assault and battery. He was given a year in the county jail. When Charley testified at the trial, John Ellsworth jumped to his feet and loudly reiterated his promise of revenge. He was not silenced until a deputy gave him a good one across the head with the butt of a pistol. Blood got into John Ellsworth's eyes, and he snorted and spat, and Charley drew back a little and tucked in his neck like a turtle. The judge thumped away with his gavel, and Charley felt like asking him for the loan of it, just in case John Ellsworth came toward him. But John Ellsworth finally was subdued, and he went off to jail for a year, and Charley resumed the pursuit of his undoubted greatness.

A great man—in January of 1868 Nancy told him she was pregnant. She told him at breakfast, and he just about choked on his coffee. They were in the Acterhof House diningroom. The morning was bright and crisp. It cast silvery reflections on the glassware and the chandelier. She looked up from her eggs and she said: Well, I did it.

How's that?

Nancy shrugged a little. She smiled. I'm pregnant, she said. I am in the family way. I finally did it.

It was here that Charley just about choked on his coffee.

Nancy continued to smile. It was a very calm smile. He supposed it was a motherly smile.

Finally he was able to speak: My . . . my *God* . . .

I finally did it.

We finally did it.

Oh, said Nancy. Yes. We. The smile went away. Now her face had no particular expression. She studied a point somewhere beyond Charley's left shoulder. She worked her tongue over her upper teeth. Perhaps she was trying to dislodge a sliver of food.

You're sure? he asked her.

Yes, said Nancy. She scraped at her eggs. Oh yes, she said, I'm just as sure as sure can be.

Well, don't just sit there like your pet cat died.

What do you want? You want me to dance a jig?

Charley reached across the table, patted her hand. Don't get aggravated with old Charley, he said. He doesn't mean you any harm.

Surely.

Would you like some champagne?

Champagne? For breakfast?

Yes. I thought maybe you'd like to celebrate.

No, said Nancy. No. Thank you kindly, but no.

Well, it was just a thought.

I appreciate it.

I mean, what I'd like to do is stand up and make an announcement.

That's nice.

You, uh, you feel all right?

My stomach's felt a little peculiar. But that's to be expected. First few months anyway.

I'm proud of you.

Yes, Charley. You're a fine fellow. A prince.

What?

Don't mind me. Maybe the way I talk has something to do with my condition. I'm sorry. Uh, Charley?

Yes?

Every so often I expect I'll throw up.

Charley grinned. That's all right, he said. You do that. You throw up. You throw up any time you want to. I won't say a word.

Will you clean it up?

What?

I asked you will you clean it up.

What sort of a question is that?

Never mind what sort it is. Just answer it.

Shrugging, Charley said: All right. If you want me to clean it up, I'll clean it up. But . . . ah now Nancy . . . come out of it, girl. This is a grand morning, and I've received grand news, and who wants to talk about throwing up?

Nancy nodded. Don't mind me, she said. She swallowed a mouthful of eggs.

Yes. Good. You eat.

Mm, said Nancy. She chewed. A grand morning, she said, and she opened her mouth as she spoke, and her mouth was yellow, and one of these days he would have to speak to her about talking with her mouth full of eggs.

A great man—ah, it made no difference that she appeared a bit sour. He could understand. Pregnancies worked at women's minds. He would bear with her. He was not a cruel person. He would cherish her, comfort her, protect her from dark winds. That morning, as he and Nancy walked up Main Street to the store, he felt a crisp full surge in his blood. He stopped people. He stopped people and pushed Nancy forward and loudly announced the news. He waited for their smiles. He devoured their smiles. He grinned, and he figured he now knew how roosters and stallions felt.

Nancy managed to smile and blush at all the kind congratulatory words
from all the people Charley stopped that morning. Even the normally
taciturn Fritz Voss seemed pleased by the news. He coolly kissed Nancy
on the forehead, shook hands with Charley, told them he was delighted.
Later that morning Charley walked over to the CPV&M depot to super-
vise the unloading of some desks and office furniture he had ordered for
the C. P. Wells Coal Co, desks and office furniture that would soon grace
the C. P. Wells Coal Co headquarters in a secondfloor suite of the Underwood Building, directly over old Ike Underwood's bank, and as he strolled,
grinning, stopping to chat, to blabber the splendid news, as he strolled
through this small gray winter village all frosty and quick, this fine and
inspiring place of one firebrick & tile manufactory, one planing mill, one
flouring mill, one shoe factory, a gas works, one bank, one public school,
one steam fire engine, six churches, five saloons, two boot & shine parlors,
four millinery & drygoods stores, one musical instrument store, one furniture store, one undertaking establishment, nine attorneys, seven physicians, two dentists, six clergymen, three restaurants, two hotels, one
photograph gallery, one tannery, three barber shops, one carriage works,
one wagon works, one jobprinting shop, two insurance agencies, one
news & book stand, one express office, one public cemetery, one Papist
cemetery, five grocery stores, three butcher shops, two bakeries, one monument works, one telegraph office and two drug & sundry stores, as he
made his quickstepping and jubilant way toward the depot, he said to
himself: Charley you old scoundrel you, you have come a long way, and
by God the greatness is no longer a *probability*; it is a *fact*. The Professor
would be proud of you. You have been an alert student. You have kept
your eye on *possibilities* and *mortality*; you have played the game as the
business of living has dictated it be played. And that is a fact. Later, as he
watched workmen unload the office furniture from a boxcar into a wagon,
Charley grinned to himself. He thought of Ike Underwood. He knew
full well how deeply Ike Underwood despised him, and yet the old fart
had rented him the office space. Well, why not? Business was business,
wasn't it? An enemy's money was just as good as a friend's. Charley was
rather sorry Ike Underwood despised him. Under other circumstances,
they probably could have been close friends. Ah well, who ever heard of a
great man who had no enemies? Even Jesus had had enemies. Ah. Yes indeed.

A great man—such a year, good God, such a year of scurry and crash it
was. In February Charley sold the grocery for thirty thousand dollars to a
man named Keller, an immigrant who paid him in good solid unadorned
pristine *cash*. Perhaps there were indigent immigrants elsewhere in the
nation, but not in Paradise County, at least as far as those Germans were

concerned. They were the most affluent people he'd ever encountered, and
close! Whoo. He'd heard talk that *Scotsmen* were close. Well, maybe so,
but he didn't see how they could be any more reluctant with a dollar than
these damn Germans. For all Charley knew, the Germans all had printing presses down in their cellars along with the pickle jars and the canned
watermelon rind. Maybe those damn people stayed up all night. He could
see them, and that was a fact. Testing the ink. Examining the paper.
Hanging the new bills to dry. God damn. Chortling. Smiling. Rubbing
their hands together. No sir, there was nothing like a German when it
came to money. After the Keller transaction, Charley decided he could do
a whole lot worse than hire one of them to handle the books of the C. P.
Wells Coal Co. With that in mind, he went to Columbus and engaged the
services of a young man named Erich Kahler, a plump and guttural fellow
who barely could speak the English language but nonetheless knew fiduciary arithmetic backward, insideout and upsidedown, in Greek, Latin,
Sanskrit, Hottentot, Chickasaw, Mandarin Chinee and you name it.
Erich Kahler was a second cousin of Fritz Voss, and he was practically
just off the boat, and Charley plucked him off the payroll of a Columbus
firm that manufactured brass and iron fittings for coffins. He was very
grateful to Charley, especially after it was explained to him how much
money the new coal operation stood to make. He moved into a roominghouse and joined the Lutheran church and sang bass in the choir and
began making calf's eyes at certain young ladies of the congregation, and
he was quite taken with Nancy, gravid and ungainly as she was, and he
hurled himself into his new duties with immense portly zeal. And, with
spring, there began the sweet blessed birthing season of the C. P. Wells
Coal Co. Construction of the CPV&M branch line to Blood had been de-
layed first by unseasonably cold autumn and winter weather, plus certain
legal entanglements involving farmers whose land blocked the rightofway,
but finally in March the work was finished, and the trains began to run.
And with the trains came the birthing. The C. P. Wells Coal Co opened an
office in the barn of the old Blood place. Charley and Erich and Fritz
were there every morning at 6, even though this meant rising at 4:30 in
order to start from Paradise Falls at 5 for the elevenmile trip to Blood.
The road was narrow and precipitous, but Charley, by dint of industrious
application of the whip to the shanks of a young gelding he had purchased from a Lancaster horse dealer, was able to negotiate the trip in a
little less than an hour. Sitting next to him in the buggy, his two associates
hung onto their hats and held their breath and no doubt uttered most
fervent silent prayers directed to their grim Lutheran God, and Charley derived great enjoyment from these mad sunrise gallops. They rid the circulation of any fugitive sluggishness, by God; they put a spark in the eye;

they made the heart shout. Hah. Yes *sir*. Ah, the birthing season. He, this Charles Palmer Wells, was not yet thirty, and it was a splendid season for being young and full of piss and steam. And the first manifestation of this glorious time was the clearing of the land. The loggers came, and the trees fell, and the underbrush was hacked and slashed and carried away. The trees. The trees fell. The tall trees fell. The small trees fell. The axes severed, and the trees fell. The loggers yelled, and the trees fell, and the earth was turned. Tulip trees. Cucumber trees. A few oaks. A few elms. A few sycamores. A few wild cherry trees. The wild cherry trees were especially lovely that spring. They were so tall, and the tips of their leaves were white, gently frail in the blue winds of that gentle season of strip and pound and smash and level and scar and scrape. The loggers pulled down the trees and shredded them and dragged them away. Then workmen came and pulled down houses and barns and sheds and dragged *them* away. The largest of the structures to be razed was of course the old Blood place. Wainscott and his wife and his multitudinous get had removed themselves to Paradise Falls, but Wainscott was not angry with Charley, not a bit. Charley had appointed him assistant general superintendent. Wainscott's gratitude shone like a star in the night, and he became an excellent assistant general superintendent, a fact even Fritz Voss had to admit. Well, said Charley to Fritz Voss, it stands to reason he would be. All his life he's wanted to get out of farming, and this has been the big opportunity for him. He's smart enough to know he can't waste it. Winfield Wainscott was put in charge of the tent city that was laid out on the old Blood place. In the meantime, Fritz Voss went scouting for men in Pennsylvania, visiting towns where the mines allegedly were beginning to play out. It was Charley's wish that the men who worked his mines not be local people. When Fritz Voss asked him why, he said: Look, let's be honest about it. Mining isn't exactly the sort of work a man would choose if he wanted above all things to uplift his immortal soul. I know. Back during the war, when I was secretary to that Congressman from Illinois, I visited his district with him when he was canvassing for reelection. There are a number of mining towns in that district. Compared with the people in those towns, your ordinary barnyard sow leads the life of an Arabian queen. I don't see how the living's going to be any different for the people *we* hire. A mining town is a mining town. It's not the Hanging Gardens of Wherever They Are. All right, so who's going to get blamed when it turns out our mining town isn't so much to look at? The President? The Tsar of Russia? Hell, Fritz, I'*m* going to get blamed for it. And no matter what I do. I could fix up the place so it looked like Commodore Vanderbilt's summer estate, but in a month or so it'd be filthy again. That's the nature of the coal business. It breeds dirt. So all right.

So should I hire *local* people and make myself into the blackest villain this side of poor old Andy Johnson? No sir. *That* I will not do. I expect a man who owns a mine isn't very popular no matter *what* he does, but I'm damned if I'm going to *ask* for trouble. I'm not going to get the whole damn county in an uproar about poor Cousin Billy and the way that awful Wells fellow makes him live. Instead, we're going to recruit strangers. Foreigners mostly, if we can come up with them. In the first place, they'll probably work cheaper. Second, nobody around here will give much of a damn how miserable life is for a gang of foreigners. After all, the strangers and the foreigners will have voluntarily *come* here, right? By God, we'll give the good folks of Paradise County some people they can look down on. We'll be doing them a service. Everybody likes to have somebody to look down on, right? Sure, you believe old Charley. He knows whereof he speaks. And Charley's argument made sense to Fritz Voss. Off he went to Pennsylvania. He leased daycoaches from the Pennsylvania Railroad, and these daycoaches brought people named O'Brien and Lewis and Llewellyn and Monahan roistering into the village of Blood and the tent city Winfield Wainscott had laid out for them. And the birthing season heated up, and then the birthing season was summer, and the oldtime residents of the village of Blood gathered in small fretful knots and spoke darkly of ruin and destruction (they were wise words, wise and accurate), and the O'Briens and the Lewises and the Llewellyns and the Monahans— accompanied of course by their skinny grayfaced wives and their sinewy dogpacks of halfstarved children, yellowish and splintered little creatures who scrabbled in the dirt and didn't know any better, who were odoriferously unaware of soap, who knew nothing of meat, whose teeth fell out in clicking green clusters—spread across the bare and corrupted land, and some of them were put to work digging the shaft of the first C. P. Wells Coal Co mine, and some were put to work building the houses that the C. P. Wells Coal Co was providing for its workers (at a nominal rental), and others were put to work building the commissary that this selfsame C. P. Wells Coal Co was providing for those selfsame workers, and of course by midsummer the first of the oldtime residents of Blood had moved away, and Charley bought their homes from them, and of course he was delighted. It all was working out precisely as he had anticipated. Erich Kahler kept a tight fat paw on expenses. Winfield Wainscott kept a tight thin paw on the work of the men, making certain that none of them malingered. Under the supervision of Fritz Voss and a team of Mellow & Leathers engineers (present at the insistence of the Columbus bank that was financing the operation), the first shaft was dug into the side of a hill behind the old Blood place. The CPV&M laid several spur tracks across what until so recently had been the dooryard and foundation. A privy was placed at the exact spot where the front door had been. By the autumn of 1868, the population of the village of Blood had been quadrupled, and the place had seen its first murder. The victim was a drunkard named Henahan. He was killed by another drunkard named O'Malley in a dispute over a bottle of whisky. By this time, the oldtime residents were holding weekly protest meetings in the Bethel ME Church, and delegations paid periodic calls on Charley. He told the delegations he was sorry if the operations had inconvenienced them. He reminded them, however, that he was doing nothing illegal. It is my property, he said, and I shall do with it as I see fit. The delegations of course could do nothing, and by early fall more than half of the village's original residents had moved away. The first mine was opened on Monday, August 3, 1868. It was called the Nancy, and by year's end it was earning damn near a thousand dollars a day, and of course this was only the beginning . . .

A great man—the baby came exactly a week after the opening of the mine. It was a girl, and Nancy had great trouble expelling it. It weighed ten pounds seven ounces. Nancy's labor began the previous night at about 9. She screamed almost all night. The baby finally came at 11:30 the next morning. Charley helped Dr Reeser pull it out of Nancy. The confinement took place in the Acterhof House suite. Several transient guests complained to the owner, a burly fellow named George Acterhof. He told them to go to hell. He told them he would be happy to arrange other accommodations for them—in the Depot Hotel perhaps? None of them took him up on his offer. He and Charley and Fritz Voss sat up all night in the tap room. George Acterhof was more than six feet tall. He weighed more than two hundred thirty pounds, and it was all bone and muscle and inexorable Teutonic belligerence. He discussed the complaining transients with Charley and Fritz. He punctuated his words with brave threatening bursts of phlegm and saliva. Charley listened to him with half an ear. Upstairs, Dr Reeser and the midwife, a Mrs Eunice Loeffler, were working on Nancy. George Acterhof broke out a bottle of Scotch whisky. He and Charley and Fritz nipped from it all night long. At about midnight Dr Reeser came downstairs to report to Charley on the progress of the confinement. She'll be all right, said Dr Reeser. The only thing is—we have to give it time.

Charley nodded. His face was flat. He rubbed the back of a hand on his whisky glass. Then he sipped at the whisky. All right, he said, all right. Now why don't you go back up there?

Quickly Dr Reeser nodded. I just thought you'd like to *know*, he said, pouting a little, rubbing his fancy shirt cuffs. The midwife is up there. If something serious happens, she'll call me.

Thank you, said Charley. Now go on back up there.

The doctor scuttled out.

Jesus, said Charley.

Upstairs, Nancy whooped.

Fritz Voss looked at George Acterhof, and George Acterhof looked at Charley.

She better not die, said Charley.

She won't, said Fritz Voss. She is a very healthy and very strong woman.

Another whoop from Nancy.

Charley winced. What's that child trying to do? he said. Kill her?

Childbirth carries with it pain, said Fritz Voss. It is to be expected.

Be quiet, said Charley.

Fritz Voss nodded, poured himself a drink.

George Acterhof breathed slowly. He removed a gold toothpick from his vest. He scraped at something in the back of his mouth.

Charley closed his eyes. He tried to bring Nancy's face into focus. He could not. He saw her eyes, her nose, her cheeks, her mouth, her weak chin, but he could not see them *together*. He said to himself: We have been married just three years. I should be able to do better than this. He opened his eyes. He moistened his lips. He cocked his head toward the ceiling. He heard nothing. He wished he knew how he felt. He thought of the mine, the glorious Nancy mine, the first fruit of his greatness. He shook his head. He told himself: The precious pussy long withheld—has she ever been anything else? Ah, Lord, Romance. No. Spare me that. Remember the Professor's words. No love. Ever. Only *possibilities*. Only *mortality*. She may die tonight. Prepare yourself. Rid yourself of all concepts. Be Charley Wells. Be hard. Never give a damn.

Upstairs, Nancy whooped.

Shit, said Charley.

George Acterhof poured him more of the Scotch whisky.

Thank you kindly, said Charley. He downed the whisky. It burned. He coughed, cleared his throat. He looked at Fritz Voss. He decided he never would be able to trust Fritz Voss. He hoped none of his enemies ever offered Fritz Voss thirty pieces of silver. Still, for all that, he did have to admit Fritz knew about the mining business. This was no small admission. After all, the sonofabitch *had* wormed and coerced his way into ten percent of the profits (at Fritz's insistence, all properly put into writing, the wording attended to by the fine legal hand of ElRoy Mauk), and—ah, what a thing to be thinking! Charley grimaced. For all he knew, Nancy was dying, and here his mind was nibbling at Fritz Voss.

Fritz chewed on a fingernail. Very little of his hair remained, and he was only just twentysix. His face was too bony, and his lips had no dimension, which made them like the lips of a fish. Charley knew nothing at all

about Fritz's life away from work. The chances were he had none. He lived
silently and frugally in a roominghouse operated by a widow named Ruple,
and he had none of the licentious flap and stagger that was characteristic
of most young fellows his age. Whenever he and Charley went to Columbus on business, Fritz never accepted Charley's invitations to come along
to Irene Hollingshead's girlish boarding school of a whorehouse. It surely
was strange. Perhaps, for all Charley knew, Fritz was a sissy.

Charley rubbed his cheeks. He slumped forward a little. He didn't care
much for sitting silently like this. It made him realize how tired he was.
And had been, all this year. The getting up at 4:30 in the morning, the
mad gallops out to Blood, the arguments with the angry delegations of oldtime residents of that doomed village, the finagling and the drinking and
the chopping down of trees and the digging of shafts . . . such a year it
had been, such a time for greatness—and such a time for a weariness of the
bones. God damn it, one of these days he would have to look at his wife
full and square. Busy as he had been, he had become increasingly aware
that she had begun to create mysteries for him. Her pregnancy had been a
silent time, and he'd not been able to get her to volunteer a thing about
how she really felt. It was as though her silence were increasing in direct
proportion to the growth of his greatness. And, the few times she *did* have
something to say, she didn't make very good sense. Take, as an example,
the subject of Fritz Voss. Charley remembered how at one time she had
told him she saw something *dirty* in Fritz. But lately she'd come around
just about full circle. She'd gone out of her way to tell Charley how wrong
she'd been about Fritz. Only a week or so ago she'd said: Charley, I don't
know what got into me. Fritz can't help it that he's quiet. It's just his way.
I was too quick to find fault with him. I expect I'm not very smart that
way. Pay no mind to what I said. He's a nice man. I got nothing against
him at all. She chattered on and on about Fritz Voss. The conversation took
place in bed, and her belly was a great white mound, and on and on went
her damned words, world without end, and the moonlight rubbed her
teeth, and she rubbed herself below her belly, and it all just about made
Charley wonder whether she and Fritz had been . . . ah, *shit!* The idea
was ridiculous. Not Fritz. Not *that* thinblooded little fart.

Charley rubbed his eyes. He was letting his thoughts run away from
him, no doubt about it. He asked George Acterhof for another drink.

Sure enough, said George Acterhof, pouring the drink.

Charley drank it down in one gulp. Ah, he said, thank you.

Upstairs, Nancy whooped.

Charley looked at Fritz Voss. Speaking slowly and deliberately, he told
Fritz a story about an old maid and her dog. Fritz did not laugh. George
Acterhof did laugh. Then George Acterhof told a story about a nigger

whore and an old man who had only one ball. Charley laughed until he cried. Upstairs, Nancy shrieked and groaned. George Acterhof kept Charley's glass filled. Charley felt nothing. He heard every one of the sounds that came from upstairs. At about 3 in the morning, George Acterhof went into the kitchen and fixed a pile of ham sandwiches. Charley ate five of them. Fritz Voss ate nothing. Charley looked narrowly at Fritz. George Acterhof went to bed at 7 in the morning. Fritz stayed with Charley. They drank coffee. At 8 o'clock, Charley went upstairs and seated himself on a straightbacked chair in the sitting room of his suite. Inside the bedroom, Nancy screamed and puled. Fritz Voss sprawled on the sofa. He looked at the ceiling. He blinked. He yawned. Charley got to thinking about chloroform. He wondered why Dr Reeser wasn't using any. Dr Reeser was supposed to be the best physician in Paradise Falls. A damn poor pokerplayer but a hell of a doctor: yes indeed. Charley looked at Fritz Voss and said: You've taken hold very well.

I beg your pardon? said Fritz.

Oh. I don't know. I was just thinking. About you. You know what's remarkable about you?

No sir. You tell me.

The way you speak English. A person wouldn't take you for a foreigner. Fritz smiled.

No, said Charley, I'm serious. When I first met you, you were practically just off the boat. But you spoke the language like you'd lived in this country all your life. Why was that?

Fritz shrugged. A small talent, he said.

For taking hold fast?

Yes. Precisely.

I don't believe I trust you.

I know that.

It doesn't bother you?

No. It does not. You see, *I* don't trust *you* either.

Charley chuckled. He leaned forward, rested his elbows on his knees. It is probably better that way, he said.

Yes, said Fritz.

If I were to trust you, you might cheat me.

The reverse is also true, said Fritz.

Mm, said Charley, nodding.

Nancy screamed. She screamed words. They came heavily through the closed door. *My sins!* she screamed. *My sins are all remembered! I—O dear God!*

Charley stood up. That's just about enough of that, he said.

Fritz looked at him.

Charley went into the bedroom. He could taste the ham sandwiches. Nancy lay naked and crimson, spraddled. The baby was emerging. Fritz came into the room behind Charley. Fritz mewled. Dr Reeser was tugging on the baby. *Ahhh!* whooped Nancy. *Ahhh!* Her tongue protruded. All her teeth were visible. They were yellow and wet. Dr Reeser tugged with one hand, wiped his brow with the other. Mrs Loeffler, a plump woman whose husband had been killed at Chancellorsville, wiped Nancy's face with a damp cloth. Mrs Loeffler clucked and crooned. Her body moved from side to side, and her breasts bounced. The baby kept coming. It was slippery. Dr Reeser used both hands, but they had trouble obtaining adequate purchase. Charley turned to Fritz Voss and told him to get out. Fritz nodded. He went out. *The baybee!* whooped Nancy. *The poor baybee! Don't let the baybee die!*

Charley advanced on Dr Reeser. *Where's your goddamn chloroform?* he yelled.

Dr Reeser did not look up from his tugging.

Godalmighty! shouted Charley. He went to the bed.

Nancy squealed, threshed.

I'll take one arm! shouted Charley to the doctor. *You take the other!*

The doctor nodded.

The betrayer! screamed Nancy.

Charley looked at her.

Nancy drooled. *The betrayer betrayed!* she shouted. She coughed. *Ah hah! Turnabout is fair play ah hah ah hah O God!*

Be quiet! hollered Charley.

Dear God save the baby! Save the baby! Dear God!

Charley bent over the emerging baby. Together, grunting in unison, he and Dr Reeser tugged. Dr Reeser's fine cuffs were wet and crimson. Nancy shrieked. Nancy shrieked. Nancy shrieked. Charley tasted sweat. Nancy stank. He tugged. Dr Reeser tugged. Nancy shrieked. Nancy shrieked. The baby was so goddamn slippery. Nancy shrieked. Nancy farted. Mrs Loeffler moaned plumply. The baby came out. The baby came out in a burst. Charley's face was splattered. He licked his lips. The taste was gummy and bland. He swallowed. He gagged. He staggered back from the bed. Nancy keened, whooped.

Dr Reeser was gasping. A . . . a girl, he said. A fine big girl. He cut the cord. He slapped the baby on its rear end. It hollered.

Charley looked at Nancy.

She was unconscious. Mrs Loeffler went to her and began fussing over her.

Charley looked at Dr Reeser. Jesus holy God, he said, where was your goddamn chloroform?

Dr Reeser did not answer. He held the baby cradled in his arms. He turned to Mrs Loeffler. Here, he said, take the child.

Mrs Loeffler came away from the bed. She took the baby. She cooed. She jiggled the baby. My, she said, such a *big* one . . .

Nancy breathed through her nose. The sound was wet. Her teeth still were exposed.

Mrs Loeffler brought the baby to Charley. It had a great deal of dark hair.

Charley turned away from Mrs Loeffler and the baby.

Dr Reeser looked at him.

Where was your chloroform? said Charley.

Dr Reeser sighed. We couldn't use it, he said.

What?

We needed your wife's help. If she'd been unconscious, how would she have been able to help?

Charley shuddered.

Mrs Loeffler placed the baby in a crib beside the bed. She washed the baby. Then, gently rolling Nancy first to one side of the bed and the other, she changed the sheets. Then she bathed Nancy. She used soap and talcum and toilet water. Dr Reeser congratulated Charley. He rubbed his hands on his britches; then he shook hands with Charley. His hand was slippery. So was Charley's. Dr Reeser smiled. I'm going home to take a bath and change my clothes, he said. I'll be back in about an hour.

She'll be all right? said Charley.

She'll be fine.

She's not going to *die* or anything?

Yes.

What?

The doctor smiled. Charley, he said, we're *all* going to die. Sometime.

What's that supposed to be? A joke?

Well . . .

Fuck you and your jokes! Jesus, I ought to kill you!

Mrs Loeffler gasped.

The doctor's smile went away. I, uh, I . . . meant no . . . offense, he said, clearing his throat, spreading his bloody hands.

That's *my wife* you got all over you and all you can think of to do is *joke!*

I'm . . . ah, I'm genuinely sorry . . .

Charley turned his back on the doctor.

The doctor went out.

Charley went to Nancy, bent over her and kissed her on the mouth. Her lips were sour. The odor of talcum and toilet water was dense.

Everything will be just fine, said Mrs Loeffler.

Charley nodded. He said nothing. He straightened. He rubbed his eyes with his bloody fists. He returned to the sitting room. Virgil T. Light and his young son Bill stood there with Fritz Voss. Their mouths fell open. Charley supposed it was because of the blood on him.

She all right? said young Bill, squeaking.

Charley nodded.

Young Bill exhaled. He flopped down on the sofa.

Splendid, said Virgil T. Light. He went to Charley and shook hands with him. His grip was large. His eyes were pale, and they were having difficulty looking at Charley head on. Charley had seen such eyes on frightened dogs.

And the sex? said Fritz Voss.

The sex? said Charley.

Of the baby.

Oh. Ah, it's a girl.

Excellent, said Fritz. Let us hope it has its mother's beauty.

Charley looked at Fritz.

Virgil T. Light nodded. Yes, he said, if that's the case she'll be a very lucky little girl.

Charley looked at Virgil T. Light.

On the sofa, young Bill Light studied his fingers. He linked them. His knuckles popped.

Later, after his visitors had left, Charley took a bath and changed clothes. When he reentered the bedroom, Nancy was nursing the baby. Mrs Loeffler sat in a chair by the bed. Charley told her to go out into the sitting room and get some rest. The sofa is very comfortable, he said. Mrs Loeffler thanked him. She went out. Charley seated himself in the chair that had been vacated by Mrs Loeffler. It was warm. He smiled at Nancy. She returned the smile. He said nothing, and neither did she. He sat with his hands folded in his lap. The baby sucked loudly. Dr Reeser returned. He was clean and crisp. He examined Nancy and the baby. He asked Nancy how she felt. I hurt, she said. Dr Reeser smiled. You will for a few days, he said, but otherwise I can find nothing the matter with you. Nancy nodded. Dr Reeser shook hands with Charley, went into the sitting room and spoke briefly with Mrs Loeffler. Then he left. Then, for the first time, Nancy spoke to her husband. She said: I've always liked the name Nell.

You want to name her Nell?

Yes.

All right, said Charley.

Thank you, said Nancy. Her voice was like warm cotton.

The baby still sucked.

Nancy smiled down on the baby. She grimaced. Hurts, she said. She adjusted her breast.

Charley said nothing.

I made an awful fuss didn't I?

Don't bother yourself about it.

I'm sorry. I didn't mean to. But it took so long, and I hurt so much.

Charley nodded.

Hairy little thing isn't she?

Yes.

Your hair.

I hope so.

That's not much of a joke.

Nancy, you remember what you hollered?

Hollered?

Yes. Something about betraying the betrayer.

Really?

Yes. What did you mean by it?

Nancy shrugged. I don't know, she said. I expect I was out of my head.

There anything you want to tell me?

No.

There anything you *ought* to tell me?

No.

I got to believe you.

Good.

1869 ...

Against the advice of her friends, Mrs Madeleine Magill is married to the resplendent Prof Karl J. Baer. That night, after the consummation, she asks him if he is shocked. He smiles. No, he says, I am delightedt. He puffs on a cheroot. He wears a crimson robe. He is sitting on the edge of the bed. You are, he tells his bride, a magnificent woman, ant I shall always cherish you. Your friendts are wrongk my dear. They are very wrongk indeedt.

Accompanied by his son William, Paradise County Republican Chairman Virgil T. Light attends the Grant inauguration. Due to her delicate health, Mrs Light is unable to take the trip with her husband and son.

The boy, who now is eighteen and beginning to fill out, is seduced by
the wife of a Michigan Congressman. The event takes place in the Congressman's bed. He is off attending some GAR function. The woman is
fortyfour and childless, with a thin clutching body and sour sweat. She
tells young Bill Light: We are obscene. Come, my darling, come do it
again. Young Bill Light, distended and enthusiastic, obliges. She asks him:
Am I your first woman? He tells her yes. It is a lie.

It is a good year for roses, corn, oats, apples, onions. The huge increase
in the population of the village of Blood has had its effect on Paradise
Falls retail business, which at the end of the year is up an estimated ten
percent. The storekeepers—and the saloonkeepers—are properly grateful to
C. P. Wells. Fritz Voss brings in more miners from Pennsylvania, and
two more mines are opened: the Orland and the Nell. By December, only
about a dozen of the original Blood residents still are there. The others
have sold out to C. P. Wells, and at just about any price he has cared
to name. The talk is that the Bethel ME Church soon will be abandoned.
Ike Underwood closes down his shoe factory. It has sixteen workers. He
finds them all jobs elsewhere. He does not want to close down the shoe
factory, but it is a losing proposition, and there is no sense throwing good
money after bad. The shoe factory closing is closely followed by the closing of a small tannery owned by a man named Peter O. Rothermel. This
tannery had supplied most of the leather used by the shoe factory. Ike
Underwood loans Peter O. Rothermel enough money to set himself up in
the retail shoe business. It is a success, and Ike Underwood is grateful
for *that*. He likes Peter O. Rothermel, always has. He truly regrets closing
the shoe factory, but truly he has no choice. He tells his wife: That railroad is not altogether an unmixed blessing. Says Phoebe: What do you
mean? Says Ike: It's all very simple. I've had to close down the factory because it's not competitive any longer. The railroad has enabled the big
manufacturers to ship in their shoes too damn cheaply. Go down to Sidlo's
tomorrow. You'll see. The price of a pair of Massachusetts shoes is oh fifty,
seventyfive cents cheaper. That's a lot of money. So, if you want to blame
somebody, blame the CPV&M. Blame its low rates. I opened that factory
when was it? '47? Well, nobody's sorrier to see it go than I am, but I'm
not about to lose money over it. That'd be lunacy. Pete Rothermel or no
Pete Rothermel, I got to do what *I* think is right. Says Phoebe: Yes, dear.
I understand.

Virgil T. Light and the Michigan Congressman have been friends
since the war. The Michigan Congressman was brevet colonel commanding an artillery brigade, and the 33rd Ohio helped cover its retreat after
the debacle at Chancellorsville. Virgil T. Light and young Bill were the
Congressman's house guests for the three days and four nights they were
in Washington for the inauguration. On the journey home, Virgil T.
Light asks his son what he thought of good old Vern Cobb.

Father and son are aboard a train of the Baltimore & Ohio Railroad. It is laboring through the crisp March mountains somewhere west of Harpers Ferry. Young Bill sits next to the window. His groin still has a vestigial ache from the ministrations of the fervent Mrs Cobb. Staring out the window (he does not of course dare look at his father), young Bill says: Oh, he was all right. Sure did talk a lot though.

Well, that's his way. Politics, you know. A man *has* to talk a lot.

I expect, says young Bill.

He's a good fellow. A Stalwart. Loves the party. And that's important.

Yes, Papa.

What'd you think of Georgia?

Georgia?

Mrs Cobb.

Oh. *Georgia*. Heh. I thought you meant the *state*.

Virgil T. Light chuckles. Well, that's not far from the truth, he says. I . . . uh, I wouldn't want you to repeat this, but last night she, uh, well, the plain truth is she was *in* a state last night. It was after you'd gone to bed. She and Vern and I stayed up until past midnight, and they both put away a good deal of wine, and then he excused himself and went off to bed, and a little later, *well*, it almost became, ah, *troublous*, if you know, ah, what I mean . . .

Oh?

Yes. Yes indeed. Quite a girl that Georgia, for such a skinny little thing.

Girl?

Well. Ah. A figure of speech. When you get to be *my* age, son, just about all the women in the world are girls.

Young Bill Light smiles. He decides it is the least he can do. He knows all there is to know about his father. He even knows his father's guilt. Mrs Wells has told him. He cannot think of Mrs Wells as Nancy. He wishes he could. It might make it all easier. A great deal has happened in the past four years, and he cannot be expected to understand all of it, but he understands enough of it so that he cannot hate his father. If only he *could* hate his father, though. If only.

J. K. Bankson devotes five columns to a detailed account of the completion of the transcontinental railroad. Two of old Harlowe Morris' peach trees die. Ferd Purvis is killed in a saloon fight in Zanesville. A friend escorts his body home. C. P. Wells learns, through a Columbus friend, of the Jay Gould gold plot. He buys $30,000 worth, gets out for $47,000. Mr and Mrs Frank J. Hill and their two children perish in a fire that levels their Mineral Avenue home two days before Christmas. It is a poor year for walnuts, beets, cabbage, barley, squash. A cool summer. First frost on October 3. Henry Perkins, aged three, cuts a finger on a page from the Paradise Falls *Democrat*. My, says Henry's mother, kissing the finger, such a sharp edge. Henry tells his mother he will stop weeping if she gets a pussycat for him. Margaret Perkins laughs, tells little Henry he is the absolute limit. The throat of John K. Busse, schoolmaster, is seriously torn by a chicken bone. He spits blood for almost an hour. Mayor George McC. Pillsbury is reelected without opposition.

Arthur Carmichael:

HE CAME TO AMERICA from his father's sweet tiny Ulster farm in the year 1862. The Union Army recruiters offered him free passage, and no Carmichael had ever rejected things that were free. God never left their table, and Arthur Carmichael saw Him as an Almighty Grimness, viewed as He was through dark lenses provided by the Presbyterian Church, and he was a great deal more interested in gentler pursuits—such as, for an example, the rendering of young women happily horizontal. He was a handsome young man, blond and glittery, and it pleasured him to know that most of the young women enjoyed the rendering. At any rate, he could not be called an unhappy young man, even though he was something of a despair to his father. His conduct did not adhere closely enough to the view of existence that his father held, and thus his father was quite pleased indeed when the recruiting men came to the village. He talked to his coltish son very seriously about the recruiting men, and finally Arthur grinned and said: Papa, it is all right. I *want* to go. That is the truth. I want to see America. And Patrick Carmichael said: Such an opportunity, and the passage is free. Ah, think of it. And Arthur Carmichael said: Yes, Papa. *Yes.*

The family gave a party for him the night before he left for America. A large sight of stout and ale and whisky was consumed, and one of the recruiting men (an honored guest) became so intoxicated he attempted to drag Arthur's elderly grandmother off to the barn. She would have accompanied him too, but then he had to go and make the tactical error of telling her he was of the Papist faith. Naturally enough, she clawed and shrieked and spat, and that was the end of *that.* Still, this one unfortunate incident notwithstanding, Arthur Carmichael's leavetaking was lubricous and splendid, and the memory of it stayed with him through many hard times.

The steamer that brought Arthur Carmichael and some two hundred other immigrants to America was slow and in poor repair, and two days out of Belfast it almost foundered in a storm off Clonakilty Bay. Also, life was not made any easier by the fistfights that continually broke out among the Irish and the Ulstermen. And, to boot, the captain apparently was a hopeless inebriate. Most of them became quite resolutely seasick and remained that way for the duration of the voyage. Arthur Carmichael was spared seasickness. Instead, he was flattened by a cruel attack of dysentery. Every other day the passengers received meat for supper, and most of them were willing to take their oath it was horsemeat. Arthur Carmichael, however, held out for dog. Whatever it was, he was convinced it was responsible for his dysentery. Whatever it was, it became inedible after about the sixth day at sea. But, after the eighth day or so, Arthur Carmichael and the others were too hungry to care. The ninth night out, he took to his bunk with cramps and running bowels. He spent the remainder of the journey groaning, breaking wind and searching out slop buckets. The day the boat steamed into New York harbor was the first day he'd been on deck in more than a week.

He could not really believe it. He leaned against the rail. Next to him was a little redhaired fellow named Patrick, a very taciturn sort, a former shoemaker from a place called Omagh. My Lord, said Arthur Carmichael, grinning at Patrick, such a city. Arthur Carmichael extended an arm, and there it was, there the city was, the great fingering city of gray buildings and squadrons of argumentative gulls. It had an odor of fish and coaloil and hot bricks. The month was July; the day was cloudy and humid; the immense stink came in sheets. Arthur Carmichael still grinned. His belly had begun to give him distress, but he fought it, and he managed not to vomit.

I expect this must be a place of unequaled Sin and Wickedness, said the taciturn little Patrick.

Ah yes, said Arthur Carmichael, a grand thought.

Patrick glared at him.

Arthur Carmichael covered his mouth.

The army people were waiting at the dock. They were representatives of the New York division that had sent the recruiters to Ulster. Arthur Carmichael and several dozen other young men, including the disapproving Patrick, were immediately sworn into the service of the United States. They rode a ferryboat across the Hudson River to New Jersey, and from there they were shipped in the steam cars to Washington, where they joined their regiment. They had no opportunity at all to sample the Sin

and Wickedness of New York. Arthur Carmichael and two other men
(not including Patrick, who ended up in the quartermasters) were assigned
to a company comprised entirely of men from an upstate New York town
called Schenectady. It took them several days—and they were ragged all
the while—just to learn how to pronounce the name of the place. This
company was part of a brandnew regiment that had been raised only six
weeks earlier. The men had as yet seen no action, which meant that
Arthur Carmichael and his two companions were at least on even terms
with these Schenectady fellows: *nobody* knew what this war was like;
they *all* were virgins; they *all* would participate in the fighting with the
same initial clumsiness and terror. For Arthur Carmichael, this knowledge
made the ragging bearable . . . and anyway, he gave as good as he got,
greenhorn or no. Their division was part of a force called the Army of
Virginia, which was commanded by a handsome and dashing major general named John Pope. It had been reported that this John Pope was a real
fighter, and he allegedly had told a newspaper correspondent he was
such a fierce and willing sort of fellow that his headquarters always
were in the saddle. Almost immediately, word circulated that John Pope
had his headquarters where perhaps his hindquarters should have been,
and the suspicion arose that perhaps he talked far too much and too
loudly. Late in August, the suspicion was eloquently borne out, and the
Army of Virginia was soundly defeated by a Confederate army commanded by people named R. E. Lee and T. J. Jackson. The battle, which
came to be known as the Second Battle of Bull Run, or Manassas,
marked the beginning and the end of Arthur Carmichael's military
career.

It was the twentyninth day of August in the year 1862, and the brandnew regiment came marching across a stone bridge that passed over a
little stream called Bull Run, and then it wheeled to the right, and Arthur
Carmichael's mouth was without moisture and his eyes had forgotten
how to blink, and he held his rifle at port arms, and his rifle was heavier
than doom, and other regiments were ahead and behind and to the left
and the right, and the regimental guidon whipped and flapped, and the
day was brilliant, and no one was saying much, and it was understood
that the Confederates under no less a person than *T. J. Jackson* were
waiting in front of a low ridge called Sudley Mountain, and officers rode
back and forth, and these officers were brandishing their swords, and
Arthur Carmichael told himself he was a pluperfect *ass* to be here participating in a strangers' war he was nowhere near to understanding, walking
alongside men the name of whose home town he had the utmost difficulty
pronouncing, men who spoke in peculiar harsh accents that gave large

testimony to the brutality of their raw new nation, and the fields became
ravines, and the ravines abounded with rocks, and the rocks made footing
difficult, and insects swarmed and hummed, and dust rose in immense
ochre pillars and smears, and Arthur Carmichael coughed, and the dust
lay in grains against his tongue, and he spat, and his saliva came out
mud, and he itched, and he grunted, and he bared his teeth, and his
shoulders hurt from carrying his rifle at port arms, and the officers continued to brandish their damnable swords, and Arthur Carmichael
devoutly hoped John Pope understood the great favor he (Arthur Carmichael) was doing him (John Pope) by participating in all this
hot and clamorous nonsense, and then the shooting began, and Arthur
Carmichael uttered a sound he'd never before known he even was *capable*
of uttering (it was somewhere between a sob and a shriek, embodying
the louder qualities of both), and the damn earth began to vibrate, and
something hot and whirring flew past his left ear, and the Confederates, or
rebels, or Secessionists, or whatever they were called, clearly were firing
at *him*, Arthur Carmichael, attempting to do away with *his,* Arthur Carmichael's, breath and lusts and dreams, and of course never in the history
of the human race had there been such an outrage, and so he did the
only thing he could have done: he roared a curse, and the curse was
without words, and he began running forward, and now his mouth was
moist, and now his eyes had remembered how to blink, and the rebels
were massed in a line of trees, and he could make out the shapes of
the individual rebels at those times when the protective dust briefly swirled
away, and he dropped to one knee and fired in their general direction,
and somewhere some idiot was blowing on a bugle, and Arthur Carmichael ran forward, again dropped to one knee, reloaded, again fired
(only six weeks ago he'd had no idea how to load and fire a rifle, but
six weeks ago was not today, and times changed sometimes even quicker
than that, and the killing and the hate and the firing of a rifle came
easily, too easily, almost joyously, and the horror built by the joy was
enough by God to make oceans run dry), and all around Arthur Carmichael the men of this brandnew regiment still were moving, and never
mind the rebel fire (and he was proud of these Schenectady men, and
never mind their harsh voices), and to the left of him a man named
Jenkins was split vertically by what apparently was grapeshot, and half
of Jenkins sailed off to the right, half to the left, and the half that sailed
off to the right just missed knocking Arthur Carmichael flat, but as it
was Arthur Carmichael was drenched by the blood of poor Jenkins, ah
the luckless devil, a fellow whose Christian name Arthur Carmichael
never had learned and never would, and the blood of Jenkins leaked into

Arthur Carmichael's mouth, and Arthur Carmichael spat, and for some
reason he said to himself

Skah

neck

ta

dee

by

Jesus

I

can

do

it

if

I

put

my

mind

to

it

and at first he thought the whimpering noises were coming from his own
throat, but they weren't; they came from an anonymous weeping redhaired boy who now was running next to him, and this anonymous weeping redhaired boy was without rifle or cap or knapsack, and Arthur Carmichael seized him by an arm, turned him around, told him for God's
sake to fall back and find himself a rifle, and obediently the anonymous
weeping redhaired boy ran back toward the rear, and Arthur Carmichael
figured that was the last he ever would see of *him* (the guess was a correct
one), and Arthur Carmichael just about laughed, and now up ahead
several men of the regiment were grappling with the shadowy Confederates, and Arthur Carmichael ran forward, and his outrage sang and
hooted, and forward he ran, forward, forward, over rocks and twigs and
holes and caps and britches and bloody flesh and splintered bones, forward he ran, forward, forward, grimacing and happy, saying to himself

Skah

neck

ta

dee

and sniggering all the while (submerging for the Here & the Now of this
thing his wretched awareness of the damage his enjoyment was inflicting
on his almighty soul), and he saw a Confederate, and this Confederate
would be *his* Confederate, and this Confederate was a middleaged man
who reminded Arthur Carmichael of a farmer he'd known back home

(a sot and rake named Purcell), and this middleaged Confederate was snarling, and he advanced on Arthur Carmichael with his rifle held in the manner of a flail, and Arthur Carmichael shot the middleaged Confederate squarely in the center of his face, and the middleaged Confederate then had no face, and soundlessly he flew backward, flapping, the impact of the bullet sending him sailing like an acrobat, a lunatic bird, and everywhere were shouts and cracklings and explosions and the massive pound and thud of cannon, and Arthur Carmichael staggered and gagged, looked around for someone else to assassinate, and it apparently was chain shot that hit him.

At any rate, whatever it was came whirling along the ground, digging a furrow. He never really saw it. He only caught a glimpse of it at the last moment, when there was no time to jump out of the way. Whatever it was, it struck his right foot. He shrieked. Part of his shoe was knocked away. So were three of his toes. His foot spouted blood. He dropped his rifle. Again he shrieked. He hopped on his good foot. His hopping did not take him anywhere. He simply hopped straight up and down, like an indecisive stork. He almost laughed. Damn him for a liar if he didn't. But he didn't laugh. Instead, he fell to the ground. He saw a sweet gray cloud, cool and moist. He saw his mother, and he saw pastures, and he saw cattle, and he supposed he was dead. It was a darling death; he loved it. The war for him was over.

Later, much later, he was aware of hands. He heard grunts. He felt himself being dragged. People lifted him. There was no feeling in the foot that had lost the toes. He said something. He could not make it out. He listened closely, said it again. This time he was able to make out what he was saying. It was just one word, and of course the word was Schenectady. He repeated it: Schenectady. He spelled it: S-c-h-e-n-e-c-t-a-d-y. He repeated it, lingering over each clicking syllable: Schenectady. Schenectady. Schenectady. The doctor had blood on his cheeks, his forehead, the front of his shirt. His hands were warm against Arthur Carmichael's poor mangled foot. The train lurched. Arthur Carmichael listened to the moans that came from the other men. The train seethed with an immense stench. Hospital. A man with a beard. Something about candy. Would soldier like some chocolate? Yes, thank you kindly, soldier would. Mm, fine chocolate this. Then, abruptly, came vomit. Soldier's chocolate had made soldier gag. The man with the beard retreated. Soldier slept. The doctor looked down at soldier and said: Poor fellow. I expect he must feel miserable. The fever is bad enough, but the damn dysentery. I had dysentery once, and all I sought was to be permitted to expire as expeditiously as possible. Well, keep watch on him, Hazlitt. I expect he'll come out of it. Change his linen now and again, will you? The cleanliness may be something of a comfort to him. And then the doctor's voice was removed from soldier's field of vision, and soldier groaned, and soldier's poor mangled foot was warm and full of pins, and soldier's belly hurt, and soldier passed his hands across his belly and pressed down, and the pressure provided some relief, and soldier was able to smell himself, and the odor was not a bit pleasant (sour it was, sour and gray), and it was damn near a month before soldier really knew what was happening.

Arthur Carmichael had lost nearly thirty pounds (the hospital scales registered his weight as a fleshless 111), and to walk across the ward was just about enough to make him swoon. The hospital was in Washington, and autumn was pushing in on the hot and corrupted city, and one morning a doctor came to Arthur Carmichael's bedside and said: Well, young man, the war is over for you.

How's . . . how's that, sir?

The doctor smiled. We'll be letting you out of here in a few days, he said. What do you think of that?

I . . . I just don't know what to think . . .

I understand you are recently arrived from Ulster.

Yes sir . . .

My name is Haverstraw. I have people in Belfast. On my mother's side. I expect this is a foolish question, but I'll ask it anyway—do you know the Whitechapels of Belfast?

Arthur Carmichael frowned. This doctor seemed like a decent sort, and he wished for the doctor's sake he did know the Whitechapels of Belfast. But he didn't, and he wasn't going to lie about it. He smiled at the doctor. The sheet was very clean, and it was tucked snugly under his chin. He smiled and then he shook his head no. I'm very sorry, sir, he said, but I've never heard of them. But then of course you got to understand I'm not *from* Belfast. My home was near Armagh. Have you heard of Armagh?

The doctor shrugged. Ah, he said, no matter. As I told you, it was a foolish question.

A week or so later, Arthur Carmichael was invalided out of the army. The hospital people gave him a suit of clothes, and he had twentythree dollars in pay. He took a room in a house on G Street and went looking for a job. He was hired to wait table in a Connecticut Avenue restaurant frequented by actors, gamblers, prostitutes, politicians and shadowy men whose activities were conducted with an impenetrable secretiveness that proclaimed to the world how industriously they were up to no good whatever. Arthur Carmichael was immensely amused by the persons who came to this restaurant. After working one night in the place, he was reminded of the dour Patrick's sour talk about the Sin and Wickedness of *New York*

City. Ah, New York City be damned! Next to *this* city, New York probably was about as Sinful and Wicked as a gaggle of virgins reciting the Twenty-third Psalm. Naturally, he was delighted. Happily he flung himself into the shriek and mischief of this altogether remarkable city. His foot still gave him pain, but he was able to walk on it. And he had a quite attractive limp. The absence of those three toes gave him a sort of roll to his walk, and he didn't really think of it *as* a limp. And neither did the young ladies whose acquaintance he made. It announced to them that he had been wounded in the war and thus had gained certification as a genuine hero, but he was in no way a cripple. And so, in a manner of speaking, he had the best of two worlds—the world of the selfless hero tragically maimed *and* the world of the civilian scamp for whom the war had become an exhilarating time to prey upon the hearts and quivering bodies of lonely women and girls. He remained in Washington a year, and his nights were sweeter than honey in a warm pan. And he even managed to push aside the occasional assaults of conscience that came nipping at him. He in no way saw himself as an evil person. He drank and fornicated with the strength of ten, but his heart still was pure. It was as though, in a sense, those wartime Washington days—and nights—did not truly exist. They did not, he believed, truly represent what he was. It was as though this time were separate from what his life had been before and would be again. The war had taken perfectly respectable men away from their farms and their banks and wherever and had made them the most wretched scoundrels imaginable. But were they *really* wretched scoundrels? Arthur Carmichael thought not, and thus he was able to absolve himself, and thus he was comforted. He told himself: Don't let it aggravate you. The war will end one day, and you'll go back to being what you were, whatever *that* was. An interesting thought, to be sure. Back in Ulster, Arthur Carmichael had by no means been a stranger to drunkenness and carnal debauchery, but at the same time he'd not gone *out of his way* in search of fleshly corruption. In Washington, however, he did go out of his way. But it was Washington, and no one cared. How could anyone have cared? How could the venal cast aspersions on the drunken? How could the drunken preach to the promiscuous? How could the promiscuous criticize the venal? Were whores outraged by swindlers? Were thieves rendered aghast by the sight of tosspots? No, in Washington there were few who were in a position to cast the first stone, and wisely those few kept their mouths shut. And the pious kept their cluckings at a minimum. Who would have heard? Or, more importantly, who would have *listened*? Ah, Washington: a wonder and a revelation. For Arthur Carmichael, the great miracle of the city was that it did not float away. He went for weeks without drawing what honestly could have been termed a sober breath. His mouth almost always held a flavor of brown. And he was invariably half tiddly even when attending to his tablewaiting duties in the Connecticut Avenue restaurant. But he had an advantage over the other waiters—his bad foot. He quickly discovered that he could use it to hide a great deal of inebriated staggering. He was not precisely the finest waiter ever to walk the face of the earth, and this he was perfectly willing to admit, but he also was perfectly willing to admit he didn't give a damn. As an indirect and somewhat surprising result, he rather intimidated the owner of the place. The man's name was Gifford, and he had a son serving in the Confederate Army. This Gifford mistook Arthur Carmichael's not giving a damn as a sign of patriotic hostility. On a number of occasions he took Arthur Carmichael aside and tried to apologize. One night he took Arthur Carmichael into a back room and said (all the while wringing his hands): Look, Art, I know you got it against me because Lloyd is fighting on the other side. I mean, you being a wounded veteran and all. But you got to remember that Lloyd's mother, Lord rest her soul, was born and raised in Alabama, and he's only doing what he thinks is right. Oh, I tell you, I get it all the time from so damn many people, and it doesn't do this place a bit of good . . . people can be so damn cruel; they come in here and they call my son a traitor and they dare me to do anything about it, and my God, Art, *look* at me. All I weigh is one twenty, and I got a bad heart; it'd *kill* me if I got in a fight. Is that what they want? Is that what those people want? To kill me? Jesus, don't hold it against *me*, Art. I see the way you look at me. Some nights it scares me; it really does; it's like you're wanting to hit me on the head with a board. Look, I tried to talk him *out* of it. Believe me I did. I'm as patriotic as the next fellow. Swear God.

Mr Gifford?

Yes, Art?

Don't. Just. Please. Be. Quiet.

What?

It's all right. Pay no mind to me, Mr Gifford. It's just, I expect, this city.

Washington?

Yes. I've never lived in a place like this. There was nothing like it back home, believe me.

Yes. Well. Things have been loose since the start of the war.

Mr Gifford?

Yes.

I got nothing against you.

Really? Honest to God, Art?

Yes, said Arthur Carmichael. He exhaled heavily. He moistened his lips, wiped them with the back of a hand. Then he continued: I . . . ah, this isn't the first time you've talked to me about your son. I . . . well, I should of stopped you the first time. You've got nothing to apologize for. I been taking advantage of you.

What?

God damn it, Mr Gifford, I'm *drunk.*

What?

I been drunk for four days. It's my limp. Makes me able to hide it. You—

Mr Gifford, I quit.

That night, walking away from the restaurant, Arthur Carmichael felt as though needles had been pulled out of his chest. He smiled at the clamorous Washington night. The time of delusions was done. A man could blame the war only so often and only so long. Good was good, and right was right, and the time of war changed nothing; the lunacy of this city was no excuse. He would no longer submit to the delusion. Arthur Carmichael grimaced. He snapped his fingers. The next morning he was shut of Washington. He drifted north, working first as a baggage smasher in the Harrisburg depot, then as a carpenter's helper in a little town called Stroudsburg. The carpenter was a testy old fellow named Hollreiser. The war had killed Hollreiser's two sons, one at Malvern Hill, one at Antietam. Horst Hollreiser and his wife took the limping Arthur Carmichael into their home. Almost immediately, Hollreiser began treating him as a son. He taught him a great deal about carpentry, told him he had a true gift for it. Arthur Carmichael worked hard, enjoyed it, especially when it took him outdoors. He'd never known how good odors could be. Especially the odors of fresh wood. And he'd never known how satisfying it could be simply to drive a nail straight and true or saw a board at the proper measured angle. But after six months he had to leave Stroudsburg and the Hollreisers. They were too zealously trying to make him into something he could not be—namely, a new son. Horst Hollreiser offered him a share of the business, but he declined. He told the Hollreisers he was very sorry. He said: I wish I could stay, but a man has only one life, and he has to make it his own. I need yet to see more of the world. I truly regret all this. Please be so good as to believe me. The day he left Stroudsburg, the Hollreisers drove him to the depot. They talked all the way. Arthur Carmichael smiled politely. He shook his head no. Mrs Hollreiser had packed him a splendid lunch of cold fried chicken. As soon as the train was safely away from the depot, Arthur Carmichael gave the lunch to a woman and her small daughter. He told them riding in the steam cars took away his appetite. The woman smilingly thanked him, and she and the little girl ate the cold fried chicken with enthusiasm and much smacking of lips.

Arthur Carmichael's next stop was Philadelphia, where he worked first in a brickyard, then a planing mill, then a factory that manufactured percussion caps for rifles. In early 1865 he again moved on, this time to Pittsburgh, where he again found a job as a carpenter's helper. His new employer's name was Newsom. This Newsom was quite fat and he had immense ears and he drank a good deal and he was letting the business go to hell. He was a widower. He lived alone with his daughter, who was seventeen and whose name was Ann. Her hair was long and blond, and she was a large girl, heavy of bust and thigh. She and her father took in Arthur Carmichael as a roomer. She visited Arthur Carmichael's bed the first night. The very first. She perspired a great deal, but he did not find the odor offensive. She took many baths. She was extremely interested in his mangled foot. Her father's almost continual semistuporous condition enabled her to visit Arthur Carmichael's bed almost every night. They could hear the old fellow's rich and moist snores very clearly. Poor Papa, said Ann Newsom. Please, darling, don't think he's always been this way. He was a good man until Mama ran off with Mr Rees the clock and watch salesman. That was five years ago. I seen Mr Rees once. He had a red moustache. I remember that red moustache real good. Well, it was two years ago when we got word she was dead. A train wreck it was, just outside Lima, Ohio. A terrible thing. Took both her *and* Mr Rees. When Papa heard about it . . . well, poor Papa. Then, sniggering, Ann Newsom kissed Arthur Carmichael and chided herself for being unduly morbid. She grabbed at him, and he sighed, and his bed rocked and groaned. And always, listening with half an ear, he made sure he could hear old Newsom's snores. Whenever the snores ceased, he sent Ann skittering from his room like a frightened buffalo. She ran flatfooted. She made the floor tremble. Her manner of running never failed to make Arthur Carmichael grin. But then one night Arthur Carmichael was not aware that the snores had ceased. Blinking, holding high a spitting coaloil lantern, Abner Newsom came into the room at a very inopportune time. The first thing he did was roar like a gored ox. Ann Newsom wriggled out from under the urgent and tumescent Arthur Carmichael, who immediately was seized with a severe attack of stomach cramps. At the same time, however, he drew himself into what he fervently hoped was an inconspicuous ball. He hugged his belly, prayed for the best. But Abner Newsom pulled him from the bed and began hitting him with the lantern. He broke the lantern over Arthur Carmichael's head, soaking Arthur Carmichael's hair with coaloil and setting it afire. Bleating, Arthur Carmichael rubbed his flaming head against the first object available. This object happened to be a bedsheet, and so within a few seconds the bed had caught fire. Ann Newsom tried to run out of the room. Her father seized her around the waist. She screamed and kicked. *My God!* shouted Abner Newsom to his naked flailing daughter. *How come I can't never find a helper without you got to jump into bed with him? Damn it all, helpers is hard to find, and how come you can't lay up with some BAKER or SCHOOLTEACHER or YARD-GOODS SALESMAN?* As Abner Newsom shouted, his daughter puled and wriggled. Arthur Carmichael managed to extinguish the fire in his scalp, but the bed was burning with great briskness. Quickly, while father and daughter struggled, he slipped into his clothes. He did not bother with his suitcase. All his money was in his britches anyway. He would obtain new clothes somewhere else. Right now the object was to *get* somewhere else. He staggered past father and daughter and out of the room. The smell of the burning bed was heavy. He coughed. He lurched downstairs and out into the street. His belly felt as though it had taken in a load of hot coals. He ran down the street. He did not look back. That was the last he ever saw of Ann Newsom and her father. He never did learn whether their house burned down.

Arthur Carmichael journeyed west, first to Youngstown, then Cleveland, then south to Wooster, then Zanesville. He took whatever jobs as were available to him. In Youngstown, he smashed baggage. In Cleveland, he worked as a printer's devil. In Wooster, he again was a carpenter's helper. In Zanesville, he again smashed baggage, and it was there that he met a thin and gloomy young fellow whose name was Ferdinand James Purvis.

It was the spring of 1869, and this Ferdinand James Purvis was from a town called Paradise Falls. He was just twentyone years of age, but he appeared to be about thirtyfive. He was unable to get through the day without pouring down at least a pint of whisky. He worked as a freight clerk for the railroad, the Columbus, Newark, Zanesville & Eastern, and the remarkable thing was that he was a *good* freight clerk, whisky or no whisky. Ah, but then he was by no means a stupid person. He had attended a college, and he knew a great deal of poetry, especially poetry that addressed itself to lost loves and broken romances. He told Arthur Carmichael a lost love had been the cause of the drinking. He talked a great lot about his lost love; he talked about it perhaps too much. And still, for all that, Arthur Carmichael was fond of the poor fellow. They drank together in a railroad saloon owned by a man named Stillinger. They invariably began their drinking sessions by toasting the good old CNZ&E, which provided the money for the whisky. God bless gainful employment, said Ferd Purvis. God bless the pain money can destroy.

No, amend that. God *damn* the *pain*. God *bless* the *money*. And then, this ritual attended to, the whisky flowed, and so did the words of Ferd Purvis. Her name had been Amelia, and she had married another man, and now this Amelia was dead, and one night Ferd Purvis frowned at Arthur Carmichael and said: You blond fellows, damn you all. And Arthur Carmichael said: How's that? And Ferd Purvis said: The man she married, Christian Soeder, *he* was a blond fellow. Looked something like you. He's gone off now, left town right after she died. Nobody quite knows *where* he is. I wish *I* did. Maybe I'd go find him and do something. Art, you see, that was my trouble—I didn't *do* anything. That's why my father's dead. Maybe someday I'll be able to make my peace with the way I lost Amelia, *but what about my father?* I just *stood there.* I let him fight *my* battle. He fell dead right there on the floor of Heinz Burkhart's kitchen, and he had no business being there in the first place. No business. I should have been able to attend to the matter alone. Why didn't I have enough manhood? Ah, now perhaps you can understand why I drink so much. Or perhaps you cannot. Perhaps you believe I have been too easily destroyed. Well, Art my friend, you boon companion of my drinking days you, you probably are correct no matter *what* you think. If, that is, you bother to think anything at all. I . . . ah, don't you see? I should have *taken* Amelia. And summarily. I should have dragged her away. Or, failing that, I should have been the one to die. But no. I did nothing. My father took the action *I* should have taken, and in so doing he ended both our worlds. My sister Priss writes to me. She tells me I am foolish. Ah, but what does she know? Women are so damn realistic, such excellent scavengers. Calamities seldom destroy them. They pick up the leavings; they go on from there; they make do. But *I* cannot make do, old friend. I cannot forget. I cannot cope. So I drink. I do not wash my clothing often enough. I am able to smell my breath, and it is foul. I neglect my fingernails. My sleep is vexed by peculiar conversations, and the gist of these conversations is gibberish. And, I ask you, what difference does any of it make? Does anyone require that I stay alive? Priss? Little Editha? Don't be ridiculous. They will be all right. I need not worry about them. *They* can cope. Ah . . . you do not . . . I see by the expression on your face that you, ah, have not ever before encountered such a one as myself. You are probably asking yourself what right I have striking such a tragic attitude at the frail age of twentyone. Well, let me tell you something about my age. I despise it. Consider me to be elderly and feeble. *There* exists truth. My calendar age is a lie. God damn you, Art, I am *not* mad. It is just that Amelia and my father were all things to me, and look what happened to them . . . just you God damn it *look* . . . I could have been a man . . .

but all I did was stand there, and my father fell dead at my feet . . . man-hood, Art . . . God damn you, *manhood* . . .

The friendship of Arthur Carmichael and Ferdinand James Purvis lasted about four months. It ended with Ferd's death. Arthur Carmichael saw Ferd die. It was a quick death. Ferd tried to be brave, and perhaps he was, but he also was very nearly decapitated. His blood was thick and warm, and a great deal of it flew in all directions. It was almost a heroic death, but only almost. In the final analysis, lamentably for Ferd Purvis, it was more of a stupid death. It did, however, get Arthur Carmichael a wife.

Ferd died in Stillinger's saloon. He died because he chose to stand up against what he considered to be an outrage. He was in enormous pain when he died. The outrage was of a commonplace nature, and it probably was not even an outrage at all, and it certainly was not worth the dying. Even the man who killed him admitted this. When the sheriff's men came and took Sam Stillinger away, he was weeping. He blinked at Arthur Carmichael and he said: Godalmighty, it wasn't none of his business. You know it wasn't. Arthur Carmichael nodded. Arthur Carmichael had been very drunk, but now of course he was no longer drunk. He nodded at Sam Stillinger and he said: Yes sir. That's the truth, Sam. But then of course you never really knew Ferd Purvis. If you had, you'd have known he was waiting for something like this. Sam Stillinger wiped at his eyes. He frowned (his wife, skinny little Olivia, was embracing him, and her grief came in thin white gulps and spasms), and then, patting Olivia, he said: I don't understand. And Arthur Carmichael said: I'm sorry, but you never will. I couldn't ever hope to explain it. Sam Stillinger shrugged. The sheriff's men pulled him away from Olivia and escorted him out the front door. Arthur Carmichael and Olivia Stillinger were alone in that saloon for several hours. They drank Irish whisky. They stood at the bar. Ferd's body lay behind the bar. It had a frayed quality. An undertaker came and took away the body. Arthur Carmichael and Olivia Stillinger watched Ferd's blood dry and cake. Olivia had stringy brown hair. Now, what with her sweat, it was ropy. Sam hits me all the time, she said. I don't mind. Wouldn't be Sam if he didn't hit me. He's not a bad sort. He's worked hard all his life, saved his money, set himself up in business with this here saloon, and what's going to happen to it now? What's going to happen to *him*? What's going to happen to *me*? Arthur Carmichael shrugged, turned down the corners of his mouth. He said nothing. He leaned on the bar. He drank. He allowed his mind to grapple with the death of his friend . . .

It had been no special night. It had simply been a night for drinking.

Sam Stillinger's saloon was just up Muskingum Street from the CNZ&E depot. Arthur Carmichael and Ferd Purvis had a favorite table at the rear of the place. It was not a particularly clean establishment, but the whisky was good, and the price was just a nickel a shot. It was a favorite drinking spot of railroaders, gamblers, sports and the like. It was visited by few women. This was not a good town for female companionship. Except for an occasional visit to a whorehouse down by the river, Arthur Carmichael had had not a single carnal adventure in this town. He had just about decided to pull out, and this was a topic he wanted to discuss with Ferd Purvis. But he never got around to it. Instead, he became drunk, and it slipped his mind, and then Ferd became involved in the dispute with Sam Stillinger. And then Ferd went and died.

Sam Stillinger was about forty, bony, tall, with heavy fists. Olivia was about thirtyfive, and at one time she probably had been at least reasonably pretty. The bones in her face still showed a certain delicacy. She had given Sam four dead babies, and now the skin lay in flaps and folds across her forehead and neck, and her teats were flabby, inconsequential. She and her husband ran the saloon alone. The incident began when she dropped a schooner of beer. She dropped it on the floor behind the bar. It broke, and evidently some of the beer splattered Sam Stillinger's trousers. He glared at her. She trembled. Goddamn clumsy bitch, he said. Arthur Carmichael and Ferd Purvis looked up from their whisky. God's sake, said Sam Stillinger. He seized a towel, bent over and brushed at his trousers.

He shouldn't talk that way to her, said Ferd.

Arthur Carmichael shrugged. None of our business, he said. She's *his* wife.

She's a *human being.*

All right, Ferd. All right. Drink up.

Olivia scuttled off and fetched a broom. She swept up the broken glass. Her husband finished brushing himself. He straightened, slapped her on the rump with the towel. She squealed. She continued sweeping. Sam Stillinger sighed, grinned at several men who were sitting at the bar. Well, he said loudly, I expect we all got crosses. Now Olivia was bent over. She was picking up glass. He pinched her rump. She shrieked. Sam laughed, and so did the men at the bar.

Ferd Purvis closed his eyes.

Arthur Carmichael called for two more drinks.

A grunt from Ferd. He opened his eyes.

Olivia came with the drinks. She pushed her hair off her forehead, collected the ten cents, returned to the bar. She rubbed her rump. More laughter from the men at the bar.

You can tell by looking at her, said Ferd.

Tell what? Arthur Carmichael wanted to know.

That at one time she was a handsome woman.

Probably so.

It's a damn shame, the way he treats her.

I'm told some women *like* to be treated that way. Treat them any other way, they just might drop over from the shock.

She's a *human being*, said Ferd. He drank. He wiped his mouth. He glared in the direction of Sam Stillinger. I call it, he said, a damn shame.

Well, there's nothing we can do about it.

There *ought* to be.

A little later it was Sam who did the spilling. He was carrying a tray of shotglasses full of whisky. He was on his way to a table at the far side of the room. He bumped into Olivia as he came around the end of the bar. He bowled right into her. He did not see her. It was his fault. Her back had been turned, and he should have watched where he was going. Arthur Carmichael saw how it happened, and so did Ferd. The shotglasses went flying. Sam's feet came out from under him. He sat down. Olivia let out another shriek. Sam roared. Most of the shotglasses were smashed when they hit the floor, and the floor ran with whisky. An old gray tomcat came sprinting out of the back room and began lapping up the whisky. A number of men guffawed. Again Olivia was trembling. She tried to help her husband up from the floor. He hit her. He used one of his heavy fists. It struck her squarely in the belly. The breath all went out of her. She grunted, staggered back against a wall. The cat yowled, ran across the room and hid behind an old piano.

Ferd Purvis stood up. By God, not *this* time, he said.

What? said Arthur Carmichael, looking up at him.

No, said Ferd, not *this* time. He was gasping. He swayed a bit. His face was gray. He moved toward Sam Stillinger, who had just stood up.

Olivia's fingers were laced over her belly. Her eyes were closed. Her breath came in strings and tatters.

Sam Stillinger shook his head. He looked down at all the broken glass and he said (speaking to no one and everyone, to God, to the heavens, to the Devil, to the dead, to the unborn, to the air and the sky and the grasses in the fields): Now there's no excuse for this. I go to church just about every week. I don't deserve this.

Laughter.

Olivia opened her eyes. They were moist.

Ferd Purvis ran across the room, straight toward Sam Stillinger. *You swine!* yelled Ferd.

Sam Stillinger gaped at him. So did everyone else, including Arthur Carmichael and Olivia.

Ferd Purvis came around the bar and struck Sam Stillinger across the face. Sam staggered back. Olivia came away from the wall and jumped on Ferd's back. She held his arms. Grimacing, Sam came forward and hit Ferd in the chest. Both Ferd and Olivia were knocked backward. Olivia lost her footing. She fell, taking Ferd down with her. They landed in the whisky and the broken glass. Olivia's skirt and petticoats were all hiked up. There was a large scab on her right knee. She still clung to Ferd's arms. Ferd was in a sitting position. He sat astride Olivia's belly. He tried to get up. Olivia would not let go. Sam Stillinger laughed. So did everyone else. Even Arthur Carmichael, who now was standing in order to get a better view. The whisky was sweet and warm in Arthur Carmichael's belly. Sam Stillinger's laughter was so enthusiastic it made him throw back his head. He had excellent teeth and a fine blue tongue. Olivia wrapped her legs around Ferd's middle. Ferd bellowed. Arthur Carmichael's laughter ended. Again Ferd bellowed. Arthur Carmichael brushed tears from his eyes. His breath had begun to hurt. Ferd pried Olivia's legs apart. Sam Stillinger and the others still laughed. Ferd rolled free of Olivia. He grabbed a large sliver of glass. He got to his feet. The laughter stopped. Sam Stillinger drew back. Ferd went after him. Ferd held the sliver at arm's length. You swine, he said to Sam Stillinger. Arthur Carmichael came running. He went around behind the bar. *No!* screamed Ferd. He waved the sliver toward Arthur Carmichael, who stopped dead. Olivia grabbed Ferd by the ankles. He kicked her away. He leaped at Sam Stillinger. The sliver just missed slicing off the tip of Sam's nose. *Now damn it all!* shouted Sam. He seized the wrist that held the sliver. Olivia clawed at Ferd's back. Ferd would not let go the sliver. Arthur Carmichael stood there. Arthur Carmichael plainly and simply just stood right where he was. Arthur Carmichael had killed a man in the war, and Arthur Carmichael had been very brave, and all Arthur Carmichael did was stand there. The space behind the bar was not large. Grappling silently, Ferd and Sam bounced from bar to wall to bar again. Sam bent Ferd's arm toward his neck. *Let go that damn thing!* shouted Sam. *Never!* screamed Ferd. Sam twisted Ferd's arm. He twisted it quickly, across and up. Obviously he was trying to twist Ferd's arm to such an extent that Ferd would drop the sliver. But Ferd refused to drop the sliver. As a result, its jagged edge dug across his neck. The skin and tissue were laid back in folds clear to the bone. Ferd looked at Sam. Ferd's eyes and mouth filled with blood, and more blood came from his neck, squirting. Sam stepped back. So did Olivia. Ferd fell dead like a bag of fat.

It all happened with Arthur Carmichael standing perhaps five feet away.
He looked around. One man, a tall bearded fellow, was biting his fingernails. Another man, shorter, beardless, had forgotten to do away with the
smile on his face. Olivia stood in a crouch. She stared whitely at the corpse,
and it was as though she were about to pounce on it and eat it. Men leaned
over the bar and looked down on the corpse. Arthur Carmichael remembered a story Ferd had told him. It had been about the death of Ferd's
father. Ferd had had the devil's own time stuffing the dead man's tongue
inside the mouth. Arthur Carmichael knelt next to Ferd and looked at his
mouth. It was all red, but he was able to make out the shape of the tongue.
Part of it protruded. Working carefully, Arthur Carmichael stuffed Ferd's
tongue back inside his mouth. Olivia's breath had a sound of pebbles. Sam
rubbed his elbows. Someone ran out to fetch the sheriff. Arthur Carmichael
straightened up. He didn't know what he was supposed to do, and so he
poured himself a drink of whisky. The Stillingers said nothing. Arthur
Carmichael drank. The other customers reached across the bar and poured
drinks for themselves. Arthur Carmichael leaned against the bar. The
blood had ceased coming out of Ferd. Arthur looked down at the corpse
and thought: Well, Ferd my friend, you did it. This time you stood up.
This time you took action. Jesus God Lord & Saviour from Whom All
Mercies Originate yes. Arthur Carmichael shook his head. Blood had come
from the corpse's ears. It was like curls.

The next morning Arthur Carmichael dispatched a wire to Ferd's sister
Priscilla in this town called Paradise Falls. Her reply was prompt: *Thank
you for your kindness in notifying us. Could you attend to shipping
arrangements? I would reimburse you. Please advise.* Arthur wired back
that he would be only too glad to attend to the arrangements. Late that
afternoon he learned that the county coroner had ruled the killing justifi-
able selfdefense. The undertaker sewed Ferd's neck back together, then
embalmed him. The stitches were crude, and the undertaker apologized.
It was a very difficult piece of work, said the undertaker. Cost of the coffin,
plus the undertaker's services, was $22, which was just $3.75 less than all
the money Arthur Carmichael had in the world. He arranged for the body
to be shipped COD to Paradise Falls. He accompanied it. His train fare
was $1.15, which left him with $2.60. The reason he accompanied the
body was obvious—he wanted his $22 back. The trip was via the CNZ&E
to Columbus and the CPV&M to Paradise Falls. He sat on the coffin in
the baggagecars during both legs of the journey. He took along two small
suitcases. One contained his own gear. The other contained Ferd's. Sam
and Olivia Stillinger had seen him off. Tell his sister I'm real sorry, said
Sam. Tell her we're *both* real sorry, said Olivia. Arthur Carmichael

nodded, told the Stillingers he would indeed do that. Olivia smiled. She had bathed. She smelled good. She had combed her hair. It appeared that some of the lines and flaps had been pulled out of her face. She held her husband's arm very tightly, and her voice was firm and clear. The interior of the CNZ&E baggagecar was cool. The interior of the CPV&M baggagecar was downright *cold*. And the month was August. Lord God. From time to time (and despite the acknowledged morbidity of it) Arthur Carmichael sniffed. He smelled nothing untoward, but after *all*, the month *was* August. He sat on the foot of the coffin. He did not want to sit directly over his late friend's face. He understood proprieties, by God. The sisters Purvis, Priscilla and Editha, were at the Paradise Falls depot to meet the train. Neither was weeping. They both curtsied when Arthur Carmichael clambered down from the baggagecar. They wore black. They shook hands with Arthur Carmichael. Priscilla told him how grateful they were. He made a deprecating sound, told them it was the least he could have done. He judged Priscilla to be about twentyfive (she was twentyfour) and Editha about fifteen (she was thirteen). He was especially impressed with Priscilla. Her handshake had in no way been frail. She was a large girl, and her black dress did little to hide her solid bosoms. Arthur Carmichael always had been partial to girls with large bosoms. Priscilla looked him up and down, and a sort of flush came into her cheeks. Arthur Carmichael smiled. Then the undertaker came up to them. The undertaker's name was Zimmerman. He wore a frock coat and a derby. He supervised the unloading of the coffin. He and another man carried it to a wagon, slid it into the wagon and drove off. Arthur Carmichael and the sisters Purvis seated themselves on an iron bench. Priscilla had dark hair. Her hat was small, and Arthur Carmichael was able to see a great lot of her hair. Her eyes were spaced widely apart. They were brown and dry; they seldom blinked. Her pink skin was set off by her hair and her eyes. Her mouth was wide, but its lips were too tight. Ah well, it was no doubt the grief. Arthur Carmichael supposed this girl was no beauty, but she surely was *impressive* in her bigboned way, and there was a good solid femaleness to her that he felt certain, given the proper opportunity, he could enjoy a great deal. He seated himself between the sisters Purvis. He was hungry. His $2.60 was inviolate, which meant he hadn't eaten for almost a day. He was very aware of the liquids in his belly; they plashed. His thigh touched little Editha's. It was soft and warm. Little Editha was very pretty for her age. Her features were gentler than her sister's, and perhaps someday *she* would indeed be a beauty. Her hair was darker than Priscilla's, and so were her eyes, and she breathed in reedy girlish gasps. But she was still no more than a child, and so Arthur Carmichael leveled his attention on Priscilla. The first thing Priscilla said was—as he didn't need much time to discover—typical. Not showing a thing, she said: I see you walk with a limp.

Arthur Carmichael started to grin, but then he thought better of it. He coughed into a fist, then said: It, uh, it was the war. Chain shot. Took off three of my toes. Or at least I *think* it was chain shot. It came real fast.

Does it hurt? Editha wanted to know.

Not now, said Arthur Carmichael. It did at the time, but that's been seven years ago. Seven years ago. My Lord.

Were you decorated? said Editha.

No. It was my first fight and my last. I didn't have time to get decorated.

Priscilla frowned at her sister and said: That'll be enough of that, miss.

You started it, said Editha, pouting.

Priscilla snorted. It was because I was seeking information, she said. I was *not* trying to be *morbid*. I spoke to Mr Carmichael about his limp because, in a sense, I sought to clear the air. It may have sounded rude, but in the long run it was a wise thing to do. We have spoken of the limp. Now we can go on from there. Now we do not have to pussyfoot. It would do you a great deal of good, Editha, if you applied yourself to an understanding of what I mean.

Arthur Carmichael smiled at Priscilla. Oh that's all right, he said. I don't mind. We can talk about it as much as she wants.

Mr Carmichael, said Priscilla coldly, she is my sister. If you don't *mind*, there is a certain amount of family discipline that must be enforced, and I'd be grateful to you if you attended to your own affairs.

Arthur Carmichael reddened. Yes, he said. Surely. I beg your pardon.

Priscilla moved a hand in a short chop, dismissing the subject.

Editha clucked, said nothing.

Uh, said Priscilla to Arthur Carmichael, there is a matter of money to be attended to. How much do we owe you?

Twentytwo dollars, said Arthur Carmichael.

Priscilla held a small brown handbag on her lap. She opened it, counted out the money, handed the money to Arthur Carmichael.

Thank you, he said.

Priscilla snapped shut the bag. It was very kind of you to come here, she said.

Well, I did have to get my money.

That is not amusing.

No ma'm.

I could have wired you the money.

Yes ma'm. I'm sorry. I spoke without thinking.

Editha giggled.

Arthur Carmichael looked at her. So did Priscilla.

That sister of mine, said Editha. She'd scare away rainstorms. Mean to tell you.

Editha! said Priscilla. *You are in mourning!*

Editha's giggling subsided. She covered her mouth.

The two suitcases were at Arthur Carmichael's feet. He decided the best thing he could do would be to change the subject. He used his good foot to nudge the suitcase on the left. That's your brother's grip, he told Priscilla.

Yes. I recognize it.

There's not an awful lot in it. I cleaned out his room. Some shirts and socks. Pair of britches or two. Pair of shoes. Couple of books. Man named Wordsworth. Englishman. Wrote very flowery poetry.

Yes. I *know* Wordsworth.

Well, good for you.

A glare from Priscilla. She stood up.

Arthur Carmichael quickly got to his feet. Well, damn it, she had it coming. Damned snippy—

Priscilla shook her head. She blinked. I apologize, she said. I didn't mean to be rude. Please forgive me. Sometimes I can be too abrupt.

Arthur Carmichael nodded. No matter, he said, smiling.

Priscilla was blushing. Damn if she wasn't. She held her handbag close to her belly. Ah, she said, and she smiled weakly, ah . . . we have hired a cabriolet for the funeral period. It would . . . ah, pleasure us if you consented to stay with us until after the funeral. *If,* that is, you *are* staying for the funeral.

Yes ma'm. I am. But, uh, I don't believe it would be proper would it for me to stay with two unmarried young ladies.

Mr Carmichael, *really.* We will be well chaperoned, have no fear. Our Aunt Patricia and Uncle Raymond are in from Junction City. They arrived this morning. I sent for them. Our mother's sister and her husband. They will watch over us. They will protect you.

Arthur Carmichael smiled. Oh, he said, in that case I thank you kindly.

The sisters Purvis led Arthur Carmichael to the cabriolet. He limped with the suitcases. He exaggerated the limp a bit. The three of them barely were able to squeeze aboard. Priscilla insisted on driving. She handled the reins with vigor. Her voice had authority. Cha, she said to the horse, and it moved off at a right smart clip. It was an old mare, and it moved with a sight more spirit than one would have expected from

such an aged steed. It was a smart old horse. It knew enough not to ma-
linger. Arthur Carmichael rubbed his mouth. That way, neither of the
Purvis sisters saw his grin. Priscilla's thigh touched his this time. There
was no room for it not to touch his. It was firm. It also was warm. Arthur
Carmichael breathed shallowly, looked around at the sights of the village.
Next to him on his other flank, Editha breathed through her nostrils. He
decided he would like Editha. He decided she just might someday be a fine
ally. After the funeral, he stayed on in Paradise Falls. He went to work as
helper to a carpenter named Osterhaus. He took a room with a family
named Ruple. He courted Priscilla Purvis, and she led him a solemn
chase, and nothing was easy, and he truly did earn her, and he never
regretted a thing.

1870 . . .

Mrs W. W. Phipps, wife of the owner and proprietor of the W. W. Phipps
Hardware, Saddle & Harness Store, braids a rug that measures twenty by
fourteen feet. Her friends all acknowledge it to be a genuine miracle. When
the weather is suitable, Prof Karl J. Baer never fails to walk over to a vacant
lot off South High Street and pick wildflowers for his bride. He gets
along with her sons better than anyone would have expected. John Magill
is sixteen now, and his younger brother Frederick Jr is eleven. John hopes
to go to college. He is conceded by everyone, and especially his teachers,
to be smart as a slap. He and his little brother were shocked when their
mother married Prof Baer. To the boys, the man had the manner and
appearance of a common swindler. But the boys have begun to change
their minds. Prof Baer speaks with them often, and he tells them: Chen-
tlemen, I shall not attempt to pass myself off as a father to you. Your father
vas a goodt ant brave man. I vouldt be foolish to attempt such a thingk.
Insteadt, I shall try to be your friendt. All I ask is thadt you give me the
opportunity. The boys move cautiously. They show little. At the same
time, however, they feel themselves being drawn to this fellow, this Prof
Baer, him and his wildflowers, his cheroots, his thin and villainous moustache. R. E. Lee is dead. It came about ten years too late, damn it all,
says Virgil T. Light to his GAR cronies. They laugh, but there is no joy
in their laughter. Virgil T. Light's wife, Catherine Anne, now weighs
less than a hundred pounds. She seldom leaves her bed, and no one—least
of all her physician, Dr Reeser—can understand what keeps her alive.
Virgil T. Light has a theory, however. He believes it is her contempt for
him. You always have been soft, she tells him. Always. As long as I have

known you. You still can't really believe that Wells person swindled you, can you? You think he simply was lucky. Hah, people such as *that* one create their own luck. If you believe otherwise, Virgil, you are an imbecile. How many millions of dollars is that land worth now? Oh God save you, Virgil. God save you from your vacant head. Of course Catherine Anne Light has no knowledge of her husband's involvement with Mrs Wells. Even if she did, she probably wouldn't believe it. Virgil T. Light himself sometimes doesn't believe it. Sometimes he feels as though he has been bound up in great straps. He knows his wife is right. He knows he should hate C. P. Wells. But how can a man be hated and betrayed simultaneously? (Ah, Nancy . . . sweet Nancy . . . all that flesh and urgency. There is nothing she will not do for him. It is said that secrets cannot be kept in a village. Not so. If a thing is incomprehensible, it is kept a secret forever. There is not a soul in Paradise Falls who can feature Virgil T. Light as Nancy Wells' lover. Therefore, the secret is inviolate. He is a constant visitor to her Acterhof House suite whenever her husband is off on a business trip. People see him come and go. They think nothing of it. Not *him*. Not *Virgil T. Light*. The very thought is absurd.) A debate of sorts has begun. There has been formed a school of thought that believes C. P. Wells has become the village's most influential citizen. This school is led by Virgil T. Light. He says: Ike Underwood me no Ike Underwoods. How come, if Ike Underwood is so grand and powerful, he's closed down the chair factory and the shoe factory? No sir, Paradise Falls has got a new leader, and he's Charley Wells. Those mines of his, damn it all, are bringing a prosperity we've never known. There's not a businessman in Paradise Falls who isn't making more money. But is he appreciated? No sir, not nearly enough. I keep hearing talk about how *terrible* it is the things that have happened to the village of Blood. I ask you—what's been so terrible? All right, he's dug some holes. All right, he's chopped down some trees. Are those things that important? Life is life, and sometimes holes have to be dug, trees have to be chopped down. You think Paradise Falls was built in the middle of a meadow? Hell, no. Ike Underwood and the rest of them, they *chopped down trees*. That's the way of the world, the way of people, the way of life. Progress is progress, by God, and nothing stays the same. I don't blame Ike Underwood for chopping down trees, and I don't blame Charley Wells either. This country's expanding. The way of the world is the way of the world, and we got to face up to truth as it exists, not as maybe it was when *he* was a boy, Ike Underwood I mean. I believe in *Charley Wells,* and I don't care who knows it. The year is a good one for tomatoes, beans, radishes, corn, coal. The C. P. Wells Coal Co opens its fourth mine, the Nancy #2. Two more of old Harlowe Morris' peach trees die.

A Great Man:

THE BEGINNING HAD BEEN FULFILLED, and the damp and the coalgas rose from the dark and corrupted land in direct proportion to the prosperity of Charley Wells and his associates, and the muzzle velocity of his greatness tore away everything in its path, and what did it matter that she had screamed something about the betrayal of the betrayer? She had been out of her head. She had said so. Her manner of saying so had been very convincing. He had to believe her. And anyway, now there was his daughter, his Nell, and he doted on the little girl with fervor and warmth. There was nothing he would not buy for her. She had dolls by the dozen; she had little wooden ducks on wheels; she had houses for her dolls; she had five stuffed dogs, a stuffed kitten, two stuffed rabbits. She was a dark and silent child, and she seldom spoke as she played with her dolls and all. He often held her. He often bounced her on his knee. He said to her: You are my girl, darling. My girl. I love you. I could eat you. Ah, you sweet thing. He dandled her and he stroked her, and Nancy warned him he would spoil her out of her wits. He told Nancy ahh, the dear little creature is barely two years of age. Later is time enough to worry about spoiling her. And Nancy said: All right, Charley. You're in charge. And of course Nancy was correct—Charley *was* in charge, and of a great many more things and persons than his daughter. The muzzle velocity was irresistible. He was just thirtytwo years old, but his greatness was no longer a matter for conjecture. It was *fact*; it could be proved in the books of the C. P. Wells Coal Co, the books the devoted Erich Kahler kept so assiduously. Charley's personal fortune increased by nearly one hundred thousand dollars that year, and the loan from the Columbus bank had almost been paid off. According to Erich Kahler's computations, the final payment would be made at the end of June, 1876, a *full five years* before it was due. It is all very remarkable, said Erich Kahler, and Charley didn't disagree with him. Not for a moment. It was a splendid life, and he kept it aswarm with activity, and by the end of the year he had learned a new thing about his greatness. This new thing frightened him, but it also exhilarated him, and the exhilaration was larger than the fright, much larger. In point of fact, there was little comparison. The new thing had to do with the muzzle velocity—unlike a bullet, the velocity of Charles Palmer Wells

did not expend itself. Instead, it increased. Five years ago, when he and
Nancy had come to Paradise Falls, Charley's ambitions had been vague,
and a certain charity had moved parallel to the vagueness. He recognized
old Ike Underwood as his chief competition, but he did not recognize Ike
Underwood as an adversary. Not even the sardine incident changed Charley's feelings on the matter. But that had been five years ago, and now
Charley knew that greatness could only derive nourishment from feeding upon itself. Now it was no longer enough to be rich. Now it was
necessary that he, this loud and gallumphing Charles Palmer Wells, this
oaf of oafs, achieve power. But the power was in the hands of Ike Underwood. All right then, Charley would have to wrest it away from the old
bastard. He would have to, if he could, destroy Ike Underwood. And here
lay the fright . . . and the larger exhilaration. The greatness of Charles
Palmer Wells would never be satisfied. Never. All his days he would seek
new worlds for it. Ah, Lord, this was some thought. Some thought indeed.
Within the bounds of his understanding of *possibilities* and *mortality*
(those two blessed tenets of his revered teacher, the late Prof Frye), Charley would forever hunger for larger prizes. He swam through his days,
this Charles Palmer Wells; he whooped and guffawed and found many
backs to clap; he felt worms gnaw his belly; the beginning had been
fulfilled, but there was no relief from greatness, and so now he no longer
considered Ike Underwood to be a competitor; now Ike Underwood was an
enemy, and now the fat old tobaccochewing sonofabitch would have to
be subjugated: the worm demanded this, and Charley was not the sort to
ignore the demands of worms. In June of 1870 the Paradise Valley Farmers' & Merchants' Bank was founded. Charley was chairman of the board;
Erich Kahler was president. Its initial capitalization was seventyfive thousand dollars, money that came directly from Charley's pocket. The new
bank opened its office directly across Main Street from Ike Underwood's
Paradise Falls State Bank. This situation was not without its amusing
aspects, seeing as how the C. P. Wells Coal Co still was renting office
space above old Ike's bank. It was not long before Charley learned that
the new bank was giving old Ike numerous attacks of the snorts and mads.
Well, the old rip hadn't seen anything yet. In August of that year, Charley
hired a man named David I. Millerspaugh to come to Paradise Falls and
establish a new daily newspaper, the Paradise Falls *Journal*. The new
paper's first issue had Charley's name listed on the masthead as publisher.
Millerspaugh was a compact man with a large voice and great shocks of
reddish hair. He had worked on newspapers in New York, Cincinnati,
Toledo and Cleveland. Charley paid him fifty dollars a week to chuck
his Cleveland job and come to Paradise Falls. I understand you're
something of a drinker, said Charley to Millerspaugh. Well, I don't give a

damn about that, as long as you get out a paper that makes trouble for the *Democrat*. You can drink until the cows come home. You can sprout wings and go flapping off to the planet Neptune. I don't give a whoop. All I care about is that you put out a paper that makes life miserable for Underwood and that little hunchbacked fellow Bankson. Said Millerspaugh: You mean dirty? Said Charley: If dirty gets the job done. Said Millerspaugh: We'll give her a try. The sixth issue of the Paradise Falls *Journal* contained a lengthy, and substantially erroneous, account of alleged misappropriations committed by Mayor George McC. Pillsbury. The article accused the mayor of purchasing a buggy for his personal use out of funds earmarked for civil vehicles, principally those used by the volunteer fire department. The story was true to the extent that the mayor *had* bought a buggy—*and* from the firm that supplied the fire department vehicles—*and* at a substantial discount, a discount usually reserved for city purchases. But the money had come from his own pocket, a fact that was quickly pointed out by J. K. Bankson in the *Democrat*. But the damage had been done. The mayor's admission that he had indeed bought the buggy at the city discount gave enough respectability to the Millerspaugh story and left the impression that there was something vaguely illegal about the entire affair. People began wondering what other kinds of mischief old George Pillsbury had been up to. The *Journal's* circulation jumped from two to six hundred, and a number of merchants (until then afraid to act for fear of antagonizing Ike Underwood) took out small advertisements in the *Journal*. Charley was delighted. He gave Millerspaugh a bonus of one hundred dollars. The next week the *Journal* published an article describing the mayor's activities as vice president of the Paradise Falls Clay Products. A bond issue had been passed the previous year for the construction of a village hall. The contract for the brick to be used in the building was awarded to the Paradise Falls Clay Products. Millerspaugh's article (this time a very accurate one) concluded with this question: *Has morality fallen to such a tragic state of desuetude that this sort of rank collusion can be countenanced?* Upon reading this article, Charley laughed so hard he just about fell out of his chair. As far as he was concerned, this man Millerspaugh was a genius of the purest sort. The screams of the wounded were heard for days. The *Democrat* quoted the mayor as saying he refused to dignify the slanderous charges with a reply. This reaction naturally made the entire village think that even worse misdeeds were being committed by the mayor and perhaps Ike Underwood as well. After all, a man didn't progress as far as Ike Underwood had progressed without cheating at least a *little*. The city hall was built, and the contract for the Paradise Falls Clay Products brick was not broken, but—again—the damage had been done. Charley couldn't have been more de-

lighted had he found a million dollars in his mattress. Next year the mayor
would be up for reelection. For years he had run without opposition. This
time, though, perhaps the story would be different. A strong candidate just
might defeat him. If that happened, Ike Underwood's loss of prestige
would be enormous. It certainly was something to keep in mind. Ah,
politics. Charley didn't suppose his interest in that ridiculous pursuit ever
would diminish. It went all the way back to his Titusville beginnings, to
his late father's ardent espousal of the Democratic party, and especially
to those two times he, this selfsame Charles Palmer Wells, now a black
Republican darker than the midnight sky, had canvassed for the Indiana
legislature as a candidate of the dear old Democracy. Those canvasses had
been very valuable to him. They—and his subsequent humiliation with the
tar and the feathers—had cleared his soul for once and for all of dedication to any concept or belief larger than the inevitable greatness of Charles
Palmer Wells. . . .

It went back a little more than a decade, and it had begun shortly after
the end of his relationship with the dear Widow Bumpus. The year was
1859, and all anyone in Titusville wanted to talk about was war, war and
abolition, war and the slavers, war and John Brown and those other lunatics at Harpers Ferry. Charley remembered that year 1859 with a special
vividness. Looking back on it, he saw that it had marked a start of his
greatness. A start in the sense that he began making decisions on his own.
Already, thanks to the teachings of the Professor, he had done away with
his feelings for heroism and love, but what was he to do with his new
wisdom? His first attempt lay in politics, in the zealous espousal of political
beliefs deeply held. This was of course a mistake, but at least it was a
beginning. It got him out among people; it gave him knowledge of their
behavior. Later, after he understood his mistake, he abandoned beliefs;
he tailored his opinions to fit those of the majority, and by the time he came
to Paradise Falls he fully understood how little it profited a man to utter
what he held to be the truth. And so he became a Republican, a Stalwart,
a hater of the late Confederacy and all its works. But this was not the case
in 1859. He was twentyone, a man in body and spirit, but his manhood
did not include acceptance of what was happening—the war fever or
whatever one wanted to call it. He had definite opinions, and he was
not shy about revealing them. To people who came into the store to pass the
time of day, to his cronies at Bagwell's Saloon down by the river, to anyone who cared to listen, he had this to say: What'll a war do except kill a
lot of people? Suppose the Southrons secede, or whatever they call it
down there. All right. So we go to war with the Southrons. And we whip
them. And we do like the abolitionists want us to do: we free the niggers.
Just what the hell is *that* going to solve? I mean, them Southrons got a

right to conduct their affairs any way they want to. How can we shove abolition down their throats? You call that democracy? I call it *tyranny,* by God. They got their own way of doing things down there, and I say we got no right to tear it up by the roots. Now that don't mean I hold with slavery. I ain't for slavery and I ain't against it. I'm for the people, North and South, deciding what *they* want. These here goddamn black Republicans, they want to make everybody live one way. Well, that ain't proper. It just ain't the way things are done in this here Republic. And besides, you got to remember: you can lead a horse down to the river but you sure as *hell* can't make him drink unless he's of a mind to. Them Southrons, we go down there and we fight a war and we free their niggers, but how much of it'll really change? You think that's going to make them *accept* the darkies? *Shit.* I'll tell you something, and you mark my words good. Maybe a nigger slave he don't live like the King of England, but what'll a *free* nigger live like? He'll be worse off than when he was a slave, a whole lot worse off. He won't have nobody to take care of him. He'll have to get by on his own. He'll have to pay taxes, bear arms, take out a mortgage at the bank. Now then God damn it, right across the river here is the state of Kentucky, and in that state of Kentucky there's free niggers and there's slave niggers, and the slave nigger is about a thousand times better off. Ask anybody who's been there. Anybody. The slave nigger is taken care of. He don't have to worry about a thing. No sir, a war would be the worst thing that could happen—to the North, to the South, to the niggers, to *everybody.* War ain't never settled nothing, and it ain't about to settle *this.* If the Southrons want to go, I say let them go, and good luck to them. Better secession than a war. Better *anything,* by God. I don't know about *you,* but *I* sure as hell don't want to die.

Charley was not alone in his opinions. In Titusville there was a substantial minority that felt as he did. Some of these people were former Southrons. Others were descendants of Southrons. The Indiana river counties had a great many of both. And, needless to say, few of those people had any use for niggers. Suppose there *was* a war. The North surely would win, and the niggers probably would be freed. What was to prevent those niggers from invading Indiana and competing for jobs? Being niggers, they would be satisfied with lower wages. A nigger was able to live on less than a dog; everyone knew that. White men would lose their jobs. It was a Godawful prospect, and so there were a lot of people who told Charley: Yessir, you sure God speak the truth. And Charley was delighted. He had to admit he enjoyed the attention. It was good to have people listen when you spoke. It was good to be able to make them nod their heads. He began thinking seriously about politics, and the possibility of someday declaring himself as a candidate for public office. For the

time being, though, there were enough other convulsions in his life, and
the largest still was Nancy Quimby, she of the epic tiddies, she who had
been corrupted by his handsome *friend* George Peters. He still was getting
nowhere with her. Mrs Bumpus had made him a man, but a lot of help
that had been. As far as Nancy gave a whoop, he was still good old loud-
mouthed oafish Charley, the poor wretch who had been so thoroughly
routed that mad day of Mrs Weatherly and the storm. This girl, this marred
girl who had been so excellently despoiled by his *friend* George Peters,
this girl who had whined and sucked around George for more years than
Charley's belly could bear remembering, oh this *fine* and *upstanding*
young lady would grant no favors to Charley; he escorted her to dances
and picnics and church affairs, but that was as far as matters went; he
was forever grabbing at her superb tiddies; she was forever clucking and
laughing and shoving away his hands, and on more than one occasion he
damn near knocked her to the ground and raped her. But he never went
through with it. Instead he persisted. He would be kind. He would follow
the teachings of the revered Prof Tobias G. Frye, PhD (Harvard). The
possibility of Nancy still existed. He would do nothing to jeopardize that
possibility. No sir & bob. (She had known, incidentally, of his arrangement with Mrs Bumpus. But she'd not criticized. It's your life, she told
him, and besides, I'm not the one to be throwing a stone, if you know what
I mean.) He still mused a great deal on the subject of George Peters. He
wondered if George had abandoned the idea of a Deed. According to
word from Mr Harris, the tannery man, George had somehow secured a
position as an actor with a Shakespearean repertory company that
traveled all over the country. Charley wondered what had caused George's
expulsion from West Point. Incompetence? A breach of the rules? Hah,
such a splendid development. Nothing warmed Charley more deeply than
the thought of a deflated hero. One night, while drinking with Charley
in Bagwell's Saloon, the Professor delivered a comment that Charley felt
was particularly apt. Smiling gently, the Professor said: Ah well, now
perhaps our young Mr Peters understands something of his mortality.
After all, he has become of all things an *actor,* and I cannot conceive of a
more mortal occupation than *that.* Acting is akin to the writing of fiction;
the initial presumption is one of mendacity, and what is more mortal
than mendacity? Laughing, Charley slammed a fist on the table and said:
Yessir! *Mortality!* Ah hah! *Mendacity!* Yes *sir!*

The days slid, and the seasons succeeded each other, and each day was a
day nearer the inevitable war, and Charley wondered how many dead
and maimed heroes would be required. The newspapers proclaimed nothing but ultimatums and anger and confusion, and nothing came from
President Buchanan save feeble pleas for reason and calm, and where was

the sense to any of it? Charley saw none, and so he spoke up more. The days slid into 1860, and Charley read the newspapers, shook his head, rubbed his chin, walked by the dark murmurous river, thought of drownings and tiddies and his late wattled father, his late doughy mother, the heavy nipples of Harriet Bumpus (now Mrs Fred Carson and living with her new husband and her three daughters on a farm about a dozen miles northwest of Titusville), thought of love and spit, of cowardice, of the foolishness of those who sought Deeds; he walked loose and spraddled, did this Charley Wells, and he was shepherded by clouds and the wind, and spindly birds swooped down gently upon him, worrying about his head but meaning him no offense, and willows sat graceful and green, and the fine old river earth lay in smears and chunks; he walked grinning, did this Charley Wells (he was *Charley Wells,* and he was the most amiable fellow a person could hope to meet); he walked and he listened to the hiss of trees; he walked and he told himself: There will some day be a greatness. I'll be ready for it, by God. Ready and willing. Yes.

He drank well; the grocery store prospered; his fancy talk was beloved by the ladies (they knew of the Harriet Bumpus business, and he figured they did not approve, and in truth they did not, but neither did they make their displeasure known; apparently they did not seek to deprive themselves of the flattery); he was *Charley Wells,* and his name had some importance, and he mourned what the inevitable war would do to this little town; he truly did mourn, and he gave not the tiniest solitary damn what the rest of the world felt.

His political career began in the spring of 1860. He was summoned to the office of one Morton C. Hightower, Titus County chairman of the Democratic party. This Morton C. Hightower was a lawyer and former Congressman. He was past seventy. He wore spectacles that were attached to his vest with a loose black string. He suffered from some sort of ague that affected his hands and arms. Talking with him was like conducting a conversation while riding in a wagon along a pitted and bumpy road.

Morton C. Hightower quickly got to the point, and of course the point was politics. Your father would have been very proud of you, he said. From what I am told, you make no bones about your opinions. And I understand they are opinions also held by the party. Is that so?

Yes sir.

Morton C. Hightower glared at his trembling hands and arms. God damn these things, he said. He hesitated, made fists. The trembling subsided a little. Then he said: Would you run against Frank Sturdevant for the legislature?

Sir?

You heard me. Two years ago, as you know, we had no candidate. We can't permit such a thing to happen again. You won't win, of course, but it will be a start for you.

A start?

Yes. This will be a bad year for us. Our party is being wracked by this issue of war or peace. We shall be fortunate if we emerge from this election still functioning as a meaningful part of the body politic. I very much fear that our largest objective this year can only be bare survival. Ah, I am making it very attractive, am I not?

No sir, said Charley. You are not.

Morton C. Hightower wheezed. Perhaps it was some sort of chuckle. Again he glared at his hands and arms, and then he said: This was Whig country for years. Now it is Republican country. But a Democrat is not necessarily doomed. I was elected to two terms in the Congress, and a really popular Democrat can make inroads. In a normal year, that is. This will be no normal year. I won't delude you. You have no chance whatever of winning. But of course that is not important. The important consideration is to get your name on the ballot. In 1862, I expect matters will have improved. If there is a war, it will be a Republican war. People tire of wars very quickly, which should leave us in a splendid position. So? What do you think? Yes or no?

Uh, wellsir . . .

Yes?

All right, sir. All right. I'll do it.

In order to devote all his time to the canvass for votes, Charley hired a middleaged couple named Thornton to take care of the store and the post office. Wesley and Verda Thornton were very thin, and they had damp eyes, and they looked more like brother and sister than husband and wife. They were very grateful, and they worked hard and well. Wesley Thornton had owned a hardware business in Evansville. It had thrived, and he'd had a splendid reputation in the business community there. He and Verda and their two sons had lived in a large and sunny home, and he had been a deacon in the Methodist church and very active in Masonic affairs. But then the two boys died, and they took a great deal of time in their dying. Henry was fourteen, and a congestion of the lungs did away with him. Wesley Jr was twelve, and he was dispatched by a kidney disorder. They had been quiet boys, undemonstrative and studious, and their room had been full of books. The medical bills came to several thousands of dollars. Wesley Thornton had to extend himself a bit to meet those bills. Still, there was enough money left over. His hardware business was in no danger. But it soon came *into* danger. Wesley Thornton became afflicted with a curious absentmindedness. He misplaced things. Stock vanished. He began

losing his temper for no apparent reason. He began bursting into tears
for no apparent reason. Occasionally he loudly declaimed on Fate and
God. He resigned his church position, dropped out of the Masons. Then,
in the summer of 1859, he took after his wife with an ax. She ran screaming from the house. He came after her, and his face was very red, but a
number of neighbor men managed to knock him to the ground and wrest
the ax from his grasp. That night he wept. He plucked at his nightshirt.
His wife wiped his face with a damp rag. He spoke of Fate and God. She
nodded. A month later, his hardware business went bankrupt. Verda
Thornton brought her demolished husband to Titusville. It was the only
place they could go. Verda Thornton's maiden name had been Killpack,
and she had been born and reared in Titusville. She had a sister still living
there. (A brother, Abraham Killpack, was the undertaker who had been
killed in the explosion of the *Molly G. Edwards* back in '52.) The sister's
name was Miss Marie Killpack, and she was immensely fat, and she gave
lessons in the piano, harp, organ and violin. There was no one in Titusville who did not like Miss Marie Killpack. She always had room in her
existence for laughter. Along with food and the piano, harp, organ and
violin, laughter was in point of fact the largest thing that ever had crossed
her corpulent field of vision. Naturally she welcomed Wesley and Verda
Thornton into her home. She told them not to concern themselves with a
thing. She told them she understood they needed time to make their
peace with their disaster. She also told them they had no reason to feel
beholden. She told them she was, after all, *family*. Her face was mostly
cheeks and great round blue eyes. Her mouth was tiny. She had blond
hair. She was fortysix, and her blond hair was all ringlets and combs. She
gave her music lessons in her home. When her pupils came, Wesley Thornton invariably went outside and sat on a large rock in the back yard.
There were two cherry trees in that yard. He enjoyed the smell of the
blossoms. He sat very quietly. He did not think. His wife and sisterinlaw
were wise enough to leave him be. He'll be all right, said Miss Marie to
Verda Thornton, if we just give him the time. A man needs sons. He had
two of them, and now he has none, and he's got to make his peace with
it. All we can do is sort of lay back and wait for him to, uh, well, come
home from wherever it is he's gone to. Verda Thornton agreed. And the
sisters waited. And in the spring of 1860 Wesley Thornton began to
emerge. One day he went to his wife and said: Just now, out back, I
picked up a little old stick. That's all. Just a little old stick. I pinched it. It
scratched. I *felt* it. A little old stick. Verda, I'm just fiftyone years of age.
If you was to cut me with a knife, I expect I'd bleed all over the place.
If you was to take away all the air, I'd die. Verda, I'm just like everybody
else. What do you think of that, huh? Ain't that something? That night

Wesley Thornton stuffed away three helpings of chicken, and the next morning he went out looking for work. Within a week he and Verda had been hired by Charley Wells at a salary of one hundred dollars per month, plus free groceries (within reason, of course). There were those in Titusville who viewed the hiring with more than a little dismay. Some of them asked Charley if he knew what this fellow Wesley Thornton had tried to do to Mrs Thornton back in Evansville. Grinning, Charley said of course he knew. And you're *still* hiring the man? said the astounded doubters. I sure am, said Charley. To the Professor, he explained his reasons: Those two'll do a good job of work for me—better than if it hadn't of happened. Said the Professor: How so? Said Charley: A thing happened to make Wesley Thornton fall apart. It would of made just about anybody fall apart. But now he's come out of it, and so has his wife. And now they're stronger. They have to be. Said the Professor: Oh? Said Charley: Yes, damn you. And they're grateful to me for giving them a chance. They'll do just fine . . . better than if it hadn't of happened. Adversity strengthens people. Don't you believe that? Said the Professor, smiling a little: Yes. Of course I do. But just don't let them become too grateful. Said Charley: Why not? Said the Professor, his smile gone: Because then they'll come to hate you. A human being who owes more than he possibly can repay of necessity comes to hate his benefactor. Said Charley: I don't believe you. That's a lot of shit. Said the Professor: All right. Just wait. Charley laughed, bought the Professor a drink, told him his view of humanity sometimes was just too bleak for belief. The Professor shrugged. As you wish, he said. (Five years later, after the Professor had been proved most abundantly right, Charley was tarred and feathered and run out of Titusville, and of course the Thorntons were right there among the ringleaders. Grinning. Spitting. Slapping on the hot tar with great zeal.)

Charley's 1860 canvass was hopeless from the start, as Morton C. Hightower had said. But nonetheless Charley hurled himself into it with all his considerable energy and loudmouthed blabber. The Titus County population that year was about four thousand. Subtracting women and children and the dim of wit, the total was reduced to about fifteen hundred ablebodied and soundminded adult males. In the 1858 election, running with no opposition, the black Republican incumbent—Frank T. Sturdevant, a farmer and cattle breeder—polled 872 votes. This left more than six hundred voters unaccounted for. They clearly hadn't been Frank Sturdevant's two years ago, so why couldn't they be Charley's now? Not that their votes would enable him to win, but at least they would enable him to make a respectable showing. In this year of almost certain defeat, that was the truly important consideration—to get as many, or more, votes than anyone on the Democratic ticket. He began his canvass with a brief

journey to Evansville, where he called on a signpainter named Folsom.
He paid Folsom fifteen dollars to paint three immense signs. Each of these
signs measured fifteen feet wide by four feet high. One said: VOTE THE
DEMOCRACY! Another said: HENDRICKS FOR GOVERNOR! The third said:
WELLS FOR LEGISLATURE! Folsom worked on the signs through the night.
The next morning Charley loaded them aboard a wagon and took them
home. He nailed them above the door to the grocery store. People came
from all over town to watch. Even the trembling Morton C. Hightower
ventured outdoors to see what was happening. Wesley Thornton helped
Charley lift the signs into place, and a number of boys climbed on ladders
and held the signs while Charley did the nailing. The spectators laughed
and hollered at Charley, and he laughed and hollered right back. I set out
to do a thing, I *do* her! he yelled. Everyone laughed. Won't nobody be in
the dark what side *you're* on! shouted a man named McGruder. No *sir!*
yelled Charley. That evening he put the second stage of his canvass into
operation. He went down to Bagwell's Saloon and purchased a keg of
beer. He loaded the keg aboard his wagon and drove to the store. After
unloading the keg, he crossed the street and purchased forty cheap mugs
from old Bill Nimmo, who operated Nimmo's General Mercantile Store.
Bill Nimmo helped Charley carry the mugs back across the street. The
keg was on the stoop in front of the store. Charley and old Bill lined the
mugs next to the keg in military formation. A man came along. Help
yourself, brother, said Charley, nodding toward the keg. Wet your whistle.
It's good and cold. The man grinned, took one of the mugs and filled it.
Your name is Keeling isn't it? said Charley. That's right, said the man,
and I'm the blackest abolitionist Republican you ever seen. Charley smiled.
Well, he said, that's your right. Keeling nodded, lifted his mug. Damn
right, he said, but, be that as it may, I thank you kindly. Charley jumped
up on the keg. You're welcome, he said. And help yourself to more. He
winked down at old Bill Nimmo. You too, Bill, he said. Bill Nimmo
nodded, grinned, drew himself a mug. Charley looked Keeling directly in
the eye. I'm going to make a speech, Mr Keeling. You're my audience.
You and old Bill here. So listen close. Keeling chuckled. Yessir, he said,
least I can do. Nodding, Charley looked out over the street. No one was in
sight. It was past 7 o'clock, and most of the sun was gone. Keeling and old
Bill looked up at him. Charley cleared his throat. He spoke of the threat of
war. He spoke of the menace of Republicanism. Two more men came
along. They frowned at Charley. He told them to help themselves to beer.
They did, told him they were much obliged. Charley resumed his oration.
Several small boys ran up. He motioned them back from the keg. They
flapped their arms, stuck out their tongues. Charley looked at Keeling.
I'm making you my deputy, he said. What? said Keeling. I'm deputizing

you to keep them there boys back from the keg, said Charley. Wouldn't
want any of this good brew wasted now would we? A nod from Keeling.
Sure hell wouldn't, he said. He shooed the boys across the street. Two
girls of about twelve or thirteen came along. They giggled and pointed. A
man came along in an open wagon. He clambered down from the wagon,
helped himself to a mug and some beer. Again Charley resumed his oration. Within half an hour perhaps thirty persons stood listening to him.
Most were men, and most were partaking of the free beer. From time to
time some of them even applauded. The Democracy! shouted Charley.
Up the Democracy! I say to you, and I say in all seriousness: *The Democracy is our only salvation!* Only ruin and despair will come to this lovely and
gentle nation of ours if it yields to the poisonous oratory of the abolitionists and coercionists and other charlatans who in verminous profusion
populate the ranks of the Republican party! We must do the South the
courtesy of permitting it to conduct its affairs as it pleases! We have no
legal or moral right to force it into patterns of conduct that are questionable at the very least! There are those among you who have roots in the
South! Scrutinize your minds and hearts closely, my friends! Do you truly
seek a war? I doubt it! I doubt it very much! Thus you must cast your ballot
for the party that is committed to the use of reason, not arms! You must,
my friends, *vote Democratic!* There must be *discussion!* There must be
negotiation! There must *not* be *war!* Ah, I know, I know, there are
those who say we Democrats are cowards. They say we do not have the
heart for a fight. Some even go so far as to slander us with the hideous
word Traitor. Well, let me put a question to you. Is it Traitorous to
love one's nation above war? Is it Traitorous to advocate calm in the face
of discord? I say no. And I say the people of this nation will not be taken in
by such wretchedly contemptible misrepresentations. Vote the Democracy,
my friends! Show the world that Titus County has faith in the sweet uses
of reason! These are uneasy days, and the electoral decision we make this
year will redound to the benefit—or the anguish—of generations without number! We must be wise! *We must not permit those generations to
be born into a nation vexed by narrow and hateful factionalism!* Please
think, my friends. Please do not destroy this nation. Please. Please. I implore you . . . Here Charley hesitated. His auditors all were leaning forward. There were no sounds. He grinned, pushed his hair back from his
forehead and eyes, resumed his oration. He spoke for about an hour, and
the audience gave him a good deal of its attention, even those out there
he knew were against him down to the blackest dregs of their foul Republican niggerloving souls. Along toward the end of his talk he had to step
down from the keg. The level of the beer had dropped below the level
of the bunghole, and it was necessary that the keg be tipped in order to

release the last of the brew. Several members of the audience were staggering a bit, and two or three men had dropped and smashed their mugs,
punctuating his words with impromptu tinkling noises. But no matter.
Most of his auditors had given him almost all their attention, and he figured he was off to a damn good start as a canvasser. He concluded his remarks at almost the exact instant the last of the beer was drained from the
keg. By that time about sixty persons had gathered—including Charley's
old friend Prof Tobias G. Frye, PhD (Harvard), advocate of the *possible*, exponent of *mortality*. He had helped himself to several mugs of
beer, and at the end his applause was among the loudest. He actually
whistled and hollered and waved his hat, and then he came to Charley
and shook his hand, and so did several other men. Their breath was
warm and brown with beer. Charley grinned until his cheeks hurt. He
assured one & all he had spoken from the heart. A little later, he and the
Professor took a walk by the river. Well, said the Professor, it was a fair
beginning. Charley looked at him. The speech had made him sweat heavily. He wiped at his face. His armpits were sticky. Fair? he said. Yes,
said the Professor. Now then, would you care for me to explain? Charley
nodded. All right, said the Professor. He led Charley to a log. They
seated themselves on the log. The Professor grunted, adjusted his buttocks,
and then he said: You must remember that the beer had a great deal to do
with your success tonight. Agreed? Charley sighed. I suppose so, he said.
The Professor grinned. You *know* so, he said. That's why you *provided* it.
A clever tactic. Most of those men would have listened to the Devil himself
as long as the beer kept flowing. It was an eminently successful device,
and you should retain it. You were very wise to conclude your speech with
the last of the beer. Had you gone on, they would have begun to drift
away. Believe me, there are few things in this life more appalling than the
sight of an orator whose audience has begun to disperse before he has
concluded his remarks. It is akin to the witnessing of an infant expir-
ing while still struggling to free itself from its mother's womb. But, having complimented you for having the foresight to provide the libation, I
must now list for you some strictures I feel. They have to do principally
with your mode of delivering a speech. I am not speaking now of your
reasoning. No one expects a political candidate to be, uh, *reasonable* in
his reasoning. And, as far as that goes, your words did after all make a
sort of sense. A war *will* be a national calamity. But it will *not*, as you
apparently believe, *destroy* the nation. This is too large a nation, too
energetic. Regardless of wars and alarms and rancor, the Republic will
survive. And remember, calamities quite often accelerate maturity, or at
least worldliness, and God knows we surely could employ some of *that*.
But no matter. Your opinions are your own, and I believe they are sin-

cerely held. But, my boy, O Lord, your *delivery*. Why so orotund? Informality, my boy. *Informality*. If you seek to do well in this canvass, *that* is what you must develop. It is not enough simply to grin and provide free beer. You must make those men believe you are one of them.

Charley interrupted. They know I'm one of them, he said. I've known most of them all my life.

Sadly the Professor shook his head no.

What's that supposed to mean? said Charley.

Your language was too hightoned, said the Professor.

Hightoned? Me?

Yes. I fear I have influenced your manner of speaking—or at least your manner of platform speaking.

Charley's face was warm. He rubbed his cheeks.

The Professor grunted. Let me make some suggestions, he said. First, curse a bit. Pepper your discourse with an occasional *by damn*. Second, show some sort of homely characteristic. Perhaps somewhere on your person a button should be left unbuttoned. After all, most of *them* seldom are properly buttoned, and the successful politician is the one who appears to be the mirrored reflection of his constituents. Third, speak plainly, even when you are equivocating. Appear to be straight, unhypocritical. These are plain people. They will love you if you display plainness. It is of course so much shit (there is no such thing as a plain and unhypocritical human being), but nonetheless you should let them see what they want to see. Ever since the beginnings of this Republic a foolish and hideous canard has been foisted on the body politic. It addresses itself to the socalled plain wisdom of the socalled plain people. It is, as I said, so much shit, but the people happen to *believe* it. So give them what they believe. If you do, if you manage to submerge your distaste, the riches of the world will be yours, and the plain people, with their insufferable snobbery born of ignorance, will be none the wiser. Ah. Now then, this is not to say that you cannot *occasionally* indulge yourself in dithyrambs of highblown rhetoric. By all means do so. These socalled plain people like to believe that, even though good old Charley Wells is one of them, he nonetheless possesses high intelligence. And nothing indicates high intelligence to them more eloquently than great nonsensical polysyllabic ejaculations that defeat their knowledge of the language. But exercise the rhetoric in moderation. *Always remember that success lies in making them believe that you are, in the final analysis, one of them.* If you can accomplish this, adulatory books will be written about you, and you will elbow your way into the company of the mighty. Even with these beginnings. Even with this insistence you apparently have to espouse an unpopular cause.

But I believe the things I say.

Of course you do. And when you emerge from the experience, you will be enriched. So go home now. Sleep well. Success awaits you. I predict it.

You old bastard, said Charley, grinning.

Yes indeed, said the Professor. Absolutely. Then, grunting again, the Professor stood up. He clapped Charley on a shoulder. He bowed. The *possible,* he said. The *possible* and the *mortal.*

Charley looked at him.

The Professor turned and walked away. He began whistling, and there were no other sounds, and the grayness from the river swirled around him in fat gusts and spurts. Witless. Preposterous. Profound.

Charley grinned again. He stood up, kicked at the log. He went on home. He slept very well, and he did not even dream of Nancy. At 8 o'clock the next morning he was awakened by a great pounding at the front door. Wesley Thornton was there, and Wesley Thornton was sweating. He insisted Charley come to the store right away. I just want you to know I had nothing to do with it, said Wesley Thornton. He would not tell Charley what the *it* was. Shrugging, Charley got dressed and accompanied Wesley Thornton to the store. A crowd stood in the street. Everyone in the crowd was at the very least smiling. Charley immediately understood why. He was, after all, not blind. He grinned at the signs he had placed over the entrance to the store. The signs said:

WELLS FOR LEGISLATURE!
HENDRICKS FOR GOVERNOR!
VOTE THE DEMOCRACY

Well, *by damn,* said Charley, and he burst out laughing. He left the signs that way. A good joke, he said to the crowd, and whoever played it was doing me a good turn. I wouldn't want folks getting *used* to them signs. Everybody and his brother has got signs that are right side up, and after awhile folks walk right on by *them* signs. But an *upsidedown* sign, by God *that's* a sign. Makes a man stop and crink his neck and *think* a little. By damn. And so, grinning, he invited the crowd into the store, where he had the Thorntons break out free candy for the women and children, free plug tobacco for the men. And the summer passed. And it passed in a spasm. And of course Charley lost the election. He'd not really expected anything else. But he also lost Nancy, and this loss was abrupt, and he'd not expected it at all. She married a man named Ferris, a farmer from over by Evansville. The fellow was old enough to be her goddamn *father,* and that was a fact. It all began at the Masonic picnic on the Fourth of July, and Charley was unable to do a thing about it. He had

brought Nancy to the picnic, but then he had become very drunk, and
Nancy had gone off with Ferris, whom she'd never seen before that day,
and a few weeks later she was Mrs Henry Ferris, and she was very sorry
if she'd hurt Charley, but ah, such was the way of the world: sometimes
the hurting could not be avoided. Looking back on the loss of Nancy,
Charley blamed it on the fool *canvass*. He was supposed to have debated
Frank Sturdevant that day, and damn it all he was *afraid* of Frank Sturdevant, and so when Nancy's neerdowell and tosspot father Rufus Quimby
offered Charley a swallow from a jug of cider that was harder than the
stone in a grist mill, Charley went ahead and had a good one, and Godalmighty such cider. Whoo. Ah.

It was a warm day, a day of silvered clouds, a day redolent with fiddles
and laughter and the whisk and quaver of willows, and Nancy was leaning on Charley's arm when they arrived at Garmaker's Grove for the gala
picnic. A bandstand had been set up. The great Sturdevant-Wells debate
would be held on that bandstand. It was decorated with bunting, and it
was six feet off the ground, and a great crowd no doubt would gather to
hear the debaters, and by damn Charley needed a drink real bad. Frank
Sturdevant made Charley's hair itch. Frank Sturdevant always smiled at
Charley. Frank Sturdevant always addressed Charley as Son. Frank
Sturdevant was tall and bearded, and his voice was like a knot of old rope.
When he spoke, it was like God speaking, and who was Charley Wells to
be canvassing for votes against *God*? Until that day, Charley had managed
to avoid any public confrontation of Frank Sturdevant, but this time he
could not avoid it. The Fourth of July political debate was a cherished
tradition in Titusville, and there was no graceful way he could get out of
participating. And Lord God, how he had dreaded it. He had seen Frank
Sturdevant debate other men. No wonder the Democrats hadn't bothered to put up a candidate two years ago. Frank Sturdevant never truly
debated with his opponents. He simply smiled on them, and it was as
though God were smiling on them, and no one defeated God, not in
Titus County, not anywhere . . . except perhaps on those infrequent
days out beyond the clouds when perhaps He was off His feed a little.
So, when Rufus Quimby offered Charley the swallow from the cider
jug, Charley didn't hesitate. It burned going down. Whoo. He bent double
and began to cough. Serves you right, Mr Smart, said Nancy. Charley
shook his head, paid no attention to her. He took another swallow, and
this time he didn't cough. Nancy shook her head. She disengaged her hand
from Charley's arm. You go ahead, she said. *I'm* taking me a little *stroll*.
And away she walked. Charley grinned at her. He watched her rump.
It was a glory. She wore a pink dress. It was cheap, but on her it was a
revelation the likes of which the eyes of man never had beheld. She

switched her tail. Charley sniggered. That's some daughter you got there, he said to Rufus Quimby. Thank you kindly, said Rufus Quimby. His eyes were the eyes of a thin starving bird. Charley looked at him. Charley was reminded of the Christmas his father had shut the door in Rufus Quimby's face. He thanked the Lord he was not Rufus Quimby. He thought briefly on the Quimby family. The boy, Bill, had run away from home in the spring of 1859. He reportedly was working on a farm somewhere down in Virginia. There was another Quimby daughter. Her name was Charlotte, and she was two years younger than Nancy. She was a large girl, dark and fullbreasted, and in 1857, shortly after her seventeenth birthday, she had married a retired farmer named Oliver I. Grimes. He died shortly after the marriage. He left her some money, and she used some of it to build a home for her parents. Otherwise, they would have moved in with her, and *that* she would not tolerate. Now she was the extremely youthful Widow Grimes, had many gentlemen callers, apparently enjoyed herself a great deal. The town was not overly disturbed by this. The consensus was that she had earned the enjoyment. Oliver I. Grimes had been one of the most scabrous old rips ever to have breathed good Titus County air, and everyone acknowledged this. (He had beaten her quite often, and he had been fond of tweaking her teats. A total of six persons showed up for his funeral. As far as most people were concerned, this was about six persons too many.) Still, even though the town begrudged her nothing, Charlotte Quimby Grimes was seen as being somewhat loose, and the feeling was that sooner or later she would be the central figure in some sort of scandal. She was, after all, a Quimby, and that name never had been pronounced in tones of reverential awe. Hardly. One son run off God knew where, one daughter a widow with tweaked teats, the other daughter most thoroughly despoiled by a now tarnished *hero* . . . no, the Quimby future did not precisely dazzle, and the Quimby past had known nothing but drunkenness and poverty, and ah, this was some family, and from time to time Charley wondered what illogic had placed the Quimbys on earth in the first place. Excepting, of course, Nancy. Always excepting Nancy. He still was having no luck with her, this opulent creature that had threshed and gasped so willingly for his *friend* George Peters, but this did not mean he was discouraged. She still was *possible,* and thus he would not give up. But, for right now, he could not concern himself with her. He had to find the courage to participate in this confounded debate. And so, after taking several more substantial swallows from Rufus Quimby's jug, Charley sat down in the shade of a tree with the foolish old scoundrel, and they got to talking about all manner and sorts of things. They passed the jug back and forth, and the talk kept Charley's mind off his fear, and hurrah for the talk. Children shrieked and yipped, and the silvered clouds were low and plump, speckled with dots and glints of gold, and somewhere was a mighty stink of sausage, and on the bandstand an impromptu orchestra was sawing its way through various reels and round dances and square dances and even an occasional enervated waltz, and Charley and old Quimby grinned and chatted, grinned and chatted, and back and forth went the jug, O blessed vessel. The tree was near the river. Quimby pointed across the river and said: They's more Quimbys over there in Kentuck than they's leaves on the trees. And Charley said: If you say so. And Quimby said: I *do* say so. And over there it ain't a bad name, the name of Quimby. But here on this side of the river, it's like I'm a nigger. And Charley said: How's that? And Quimby said: They think I'm *worse* than a nigger. And Charley said: Well, *I* don't. And Quimby said: That's on account of you want to fuck my daughter. And Charley said: That's no way to talk. You ought to be ashamed of yourself. And, belching, Quimby said: George Peters hit me oncet, you know that? And Charley said: How's that? And Quimby said: He was grabbing at Nancy. They was in his buggy over in Yarborough's woods other side of town. I came along, and I said something, so George Peters came down offn that buggy and hit me. Hit me right smart. Knocked me down. Tell me something. *You* going to hit me? And Charley said: No. I don't hold with hitting people. And Quimby said: I hope you get her. You want to marry her? And Charley said: I don't know. Maybe I do. Maybe I don't. I don't know. And Quimby said: Ain't much to be said for a man when people treat him like he was a nigger. Charley did not reply. He took the jug from Quimby, helped himself to a deep swallow. Then along came a man named Carleton and a man named Stringfellow. They were the captain and mate, respectively, of a small sidewheeler called the *Myra B. Carleton*. It had been built by Carleton's father. It was named after his mother. It carried passengers and general freight between Cincinnati and Cairo. It wasn't much of a boat, and Carleton wasn't much of a human being, and for that matter neither was Stringfellow. Whenever the *Myra B. Carleton* was in Titusville, Carleton and Stringfellow spent most of their time in Bagwell's Saloon. Carleton was stumpy and bald. He was about thirty, appeared to be about fifty. Stringfellow was perhaps in his late twenties. He was walleyed, very thin, with white hair and eyebrows. He had very thick lips, and he put people in mind of what a nigger would look like after being dropped into a drum of white paint. His nickname was Nig. He grinned when he saw Charley and old Quimby. So did Carleton. They had a cider jug with them. Ah, said Quimby, I got me an idea this here is going to be some afternoon. Grinning at Carleton and Stringfellow, he said: You boys giving out any samples?

Chuckling, Stringfellow handed Quimby the fresh jug. Quimby drank. *Ah,* he said, yes *sir.* He wiped his mouth, handed his own jug to Stringfellow. He passed Stringfellow's jug to Charley. Then Carleton had a turn at both jugs. Then Stringfellow had a turn. Then grins were exchanged all around. Later they all were joined by a couple of farmers named Ford and Griswold, and of course Ford and Griswold had a jug of *their* own, and it was like a convention. God damn and fuck a dog, said Quimby, his voice moist with delight. Everyone laughed. Nehemiah Ford and John Griswold laughed the loudest. Ford and Griswold had fat arms and bellies, and they weren't particularly good farmers. Still, their cider was tasty, and they were a very jolly pair of men, even though they were both black Republicans. Worthlesssss, said Charley, sighing. We're all of us worthlesssss. Passsss the fucking cider. Oh am I going to give it to old God good. Said Stringfellow: Old who? Said Charley: Old God. Otherwise known as Frank Sturven. Grinning, Charley drank deeply of the cider. Things he's God, thasssss wha he things, him an his why hair. Charley and his companions drank until the cider was gone, and then they sang a number of ribald songs, and the clouds skipped, and the sun came as a slap, and Charley tasted his breath and his belly, and after a time he fainted, and of course there was no debate. Carleton and Nig Stringfellow carried Charley home. They helped themselves to a great deal of whisky. They dropped Charley on the sofa, concentrated on the whisky, paid him no mind. When he came out of his slumber, Carleton and Nig Stringfellow both lay snoring on the floor. Groaning, Charley stood up and went into the diningroom. He took inventory of the silver. He nodded, moistened his lips. He went upstairs to bed. His dreams produced Frank Sturdevant, otherwise known as God. Frank Sturdevant patted Charley on the head. Son, said Frank Sturdevant, I forgive you. Charley looked around. He and Frank Sturdevant were standing on the platform at Garmaker's Grove. A large crowd was in attendance. Charley's feet became entangled in bunting and flags. He kicked at them. The more he kicked, the more entangled he became. The audience laughed. *Up the Democracy!* he shouted, and the audience laughed more loudly. He awakened late the next morning. Carleton and Nig Stringfellow were gone. Again he took inventory of the silver. None was missing. As far as he could determine, Carleton and Nig Stringfellow had made off with not a thing. Charley went into the kitchen. He scraped his tongue with his teeth. He opened a window, leaned out and spat. *Yach!* he said, and again he spat. Then, wiping his mouth, he brewed a pot of coffee and tried to figure out a lie that would explain his failure to appear at the debate. He wondered how many persons had seen him drunk. If not too many had observed his condition,

then perhaps he could plead sudden illness. And perhaps he could even
—brilliant stroke!—lay gentle hints that perhaps his food had been tampered with. He scratched his chin, shrugged, decided why npt. That afternoon he went into town. He walked into the store. Well, said Wesley
Thornton, I see you're up and about. Charley nodded, sucked spit, waited
for Wesley Thornton to continue. Surely must have been a bad piece
of meat or something, said Wesley Thornton. Mm? said Charley, picking
up an apple and taking a bite. Maybe it was the same bad piece of meat
that laid Frank Sturdevant low, said Wesley Thornton. What? said
Charley. Too bad you didn't see him, said Wesley Thornton. Throwing
up all over the place like he did. Terrible thing. Charley swallowed,
coughed, covered his mouth. Mm, he said. Mm.

A week or so later, Nancy told Charley she was in love with the man
named Henry Ferris. I'll marry him if he'll have me, she said.

She and Charley were standing on River Street near the wharf. Nancy
was barefoot. She had just delivered some washing for her mother. Charley
had spent the afternoon in Bagwell's Saloon. He had bought several
rounds of drinks, all in the name of the canvass of course, and hurrah
for the canvass. He shook his head. He'd just asked Nancy a simple question. He'd just asked her to go for a walk with him. It had been such
a very harmless oafish Charley Wells sort of question, and what right did
she have telling him *this* at *this* time? But he *was,* after all, Charley Wells,
and so he grinned. Henry *who?* he said.

Henry *Ferris,* said Nancy. The man I met at the picnic. When you
were off getting drunk . . . or sick, or whatever you want to call it.

Charley took Nancy by an arm. He looked around. Come on, he said.
He steered her toward the wharf. They went out on the wharf and sat
down. Their legs dangled over the edge. Charley breathed deeply. He
smelled mud. He tasted the green odor of the water. You mean Sherman
and Idarose Gentry's nephew? he said. You touched with the heat maybe?
He's about *fifty years old.*

He's *thirtyeight.*

You say you *love* him?

Yes.

But you just *met* him.

Don't matter.

Charley nodded.

I'm sorry, said Nancy. I'm real sorry. But I don't think you're going
to die. You don't love me or anything like that. With you, it's the wanting.
I don't say you're a bad sort of man. All I say is, with you it's the wanting.

Nancy . . .

I said I'm sorry. I expect that's all I know how to say.

All right.

Nancy stood up. I won't cross the street to get out of your way, she said. I don't want *you* crossing the street to get out of *my* way.

Charley nodded. All right, he said. Uh, you going to Evansville to live with him?

If he asks me. That's where *he* lives ain't it? Where *he* lives, *I* want to live.

Mm, said Charley. Makes sense.

Thank you, said Nancy. She walked away. Her bare heels made hard echoing sounds on the planks of the wharf.

Charley pressed his tongue against a loose tooth. He worried the tooth until blood came. He spat. The taste was like brass.

Ferris did ask Nancy to marry him, and she did accept, and they did go to live on his farm near Evansville. According to what Charley heard, it wasn't much of a farm. The ground was too low. There were floods just about every year, and earth was carried off, and crops were ruined, and Charley almost felt sorry for the man. But Ferris had Nancy, and feeling sorry for him made about as much sense as feeling sorry for a man who had a million dollars. (It was almost five years before Charley saw Nancy again. Ferris was dead. George Peters was dead. Her sister Charlotte was dead. Her brother Bill was dead. And, as for Charley, well, he had been tarred and feathered and run out of town, and he was damn *near* dead, and that was a fact.)

Charley lost the election, but his canvass surely had been a success. The official count was Sturdevant 714, Wells 506, and Charley did better than any Democrat on the ballot. The Democratic gubernatorial candidate, Tom Hendricks, lost the county to a man named Lane by 799 to 481, and the officially endorsed Presidential candidate, Stephen A. Douglas, received just 244 votes to Abraham Lincoln's 817. There were two other Presidential candidates, both of them nominally Democrats. They were John C. Breckinridge, who had 113 votes, and John Bell, who had 83. John Bell ran on something called the Constitutional Union ticket, but he was a Democrat same as the others, and damn the Democratic party anyway. Of all the times for it to split into three factions! Taken together nationally, the votes received by these three men were more than enough to defeat that wretched baboon of a Lincoln. Taken separately, of course, they were not. Douglas, the Little Giant of Illinois, had been the nominee of the regular convention, but the Southrons hadn't found him acceptable, and so they'd bolted the convention, meeting later to nominate Breckinridge. In the meantime, the socalled Constitutional Unionists were nominating Bell. Ah, it was a fine year not to be a Democrat, and that was a fact. But Charley did not particularly mourn. He had done well. He had done all that had been *possible*. Next time perhaps the outcome would be different. The Friday after the election, he encountered Frank Sturdevant on Titus Avenue. He walked up to Frank Sturdevant and grinned and shook Frank Sturdevant's hand big as you please, right out in front of the world. Frank Sturdevant, otherwise known as God, smiled and said: Thank you, Son. Thank you very much. And Charley said: It was a good canvass. I have no regrets. And Frank Sturdevant said: As well you should not. You received a fine substantial vote. The handshaking and politeness continued for another moment or two, and then the two adversaries parted, and Charley grinned, and deep in his throat sat the words: Just you wait, you old bastard. Just you wait until next time. Charley grinned all the way home, and yes, by damn, there surely would be a next time. Politics was for him. He had enjoyed the canvass immensely. It occurred to him that he had chosen a good year to get into the game, a good exciting year. In neighboring counties there had been a good sight of violence; passions had run mighty high; newspaper editors had been dragged from their homes and beaten; night riders had burned and smashed; there was an awful suspense hanging over the land, and from the suspense came frustration, and from the frustration came the violence, and Charley didn't have to be hit across the face with a bag of stones to understand that most people sought *any* sort of resolution, even a war. Well, at least in Titus County there had been no violence. And he was grateful for this. Had there been violence, he had no idea what he would have done. He just couldn't *see* violence. Damn if he could. Ah well, the hell with the violence. The pleasures of the canvass had been considerably larger than any threat of pain and dark deeds. He decided he would make politics his life's pursuit. Old Morton C. Hightower was very encouraging. You did far better than I expected, he told Charley. You apparently have a way with you. I have even noticed that business with the buttons. You are not stupid. Charley laughed, told Morton C. Hightower he (Morton C. Hightower) had good eyes for one of his age. Morton C. Hightower cackled dryly. Ah, he said, you *rascal*. And the winter of '60–'61 passed, and a war was coming as surely as grief and blood, and (if the Republicans made a botch of it, as almost surely they would) better days were in store for the Democracy. *And*, since Charley had led the Titus County ticket, there was little reason to believe he wouldn't do even better in '62, and perhaps even *win*, depending on the depth of the disaffection with the Republicans and their clownish Lincoln. So Charley returned to the store (but kept on Wesley and Verda Thornton: they were good workers; they were honest, kept honest books; they had brought in new customers—and, beyond all that, if he discharged them he might have lost some future votes), and once again Charley's loud and oafish good cheer reverberated there among the pickle barrels and the potato sacks and the brimming coffee bins, and once again his hyperbolic effusions delighted the ladies, and from time to time Wesley and Verda Thornton made small gray noises that he supposed indicated disapproval, but ah hell, they meant no harm, and so he ignored their noises, and the talk flowed from him like a mighty river, white and urgent, and it divided itself into two streams. One was of course the hyperbolic effusions, aimed at the women. The other was politics, aimed at the men. Right up until April of '61 he continued to talk against the war. He said a war would solve nothing at all. He deplored the fact that so many compromises had been rejected by the new Republican government. He spoke bitterly of the abolitionists and that brainless booby, Abraham Lincoln. He spoke just as bitterly of those hotheaded Southrons who apparently were bound and determined to destroy the Union because of their refusal to compromise. What's this country headed for? he wanted to know. Are we all lunatics? One day he had a long discussion of the situation with a farmer named Lew Bixby, a tall muscular man with a red face and enormous hands, a deacon of the Methodist church, a slowspeaking fellow with a growly voice. When Lew Bixby put a thing to a person, the person listened. People said there was a large quiet wisdom within him. At one time he'd been mayor of Titusville. Now he owned a farm out in the county, and it was a very successful farm, and it was a very successful farm because Lew Bixby had put his mind to *making* it a very successful farm, and yes indeed, he was the sort of fellow who could not help but command respect. Charley, he said, look, I'll tell you the truth: I was a Whig oncet, and I'm a Republican now, but damn if I didn't vote for you last year anyway. I don't want no war no more than anybody else does. But how long are we supposed to put up with all the fuss and talk? The people are just plain impatient for something to *happen,* something that'll be a start toward *settling* this here trouble. If it has to be a war, then it has to be a war. We can't go on like *this* much longer. Charley nodded. Yes, he said, I know what you mean. People have lost their patience. But, Lew, they got to hang on. A war is no answer, no *right* answer. Lew Bixby shrugged. Maybe, he said, a thing that's necessary isn't always right. For thirty forty years there's been nothing but talk talk talk, and you say we should sit still for *more* talk. No sir. No more talk. No more backing away from the situation. If it takes a war, then it takes a war. If the Southrons start something, there'll be no standing off. Again Charley nodded. Well, he said, it surely does seem a shame. Said Lew Bixby: Ain't nobody arguing with you about *that.*

When the war began, when those contemptible South Carolinians finally went ahead and set their artillery to bombarding Fort Sumter, when the ordeal of secession conventions and Congressional blather finally was over, when it irrevocably was determined *for* the federal government what it would have to do about the situation, when the time for negotiations and compromises was forever dead and gone, when finally the headlines read THE REBELLION BEGINS! and the newsboys ran screaming jubilantly in the streets of every city and town and village in what was left of the federal union, when finally the headlines read THE WAR BEGINS! and the newsboys ran screaming jubilantly in the streets of every city and town and village in that great hot groaning land that had chosen to disaffiliate itself from the federal union, when *finally* and *for once* and *for all* and *for good* the two sides began taking direct action to settle the dispute, the news was accepted—no, it was more than accepted; it was *welcomed*—with a witless flapping joy. In Titusville, even most of the *Democrats* were seduced by the excitement, and why shouldn't they have been? All over the nation, Democrats were urging support of the war. Even Stephen A. Douglas had been caught up. The Little Giant visited Indianapolis shortly after the beginning of the war, and he spoke from the balcony of the Bates House, and thousands stood in a rainstorm to hear him, and he delivered a lengthy oration on what he called the Sanctity of the Union. Charley read every word of the Douglas speech in the columns of an Indianapolis newspaper, and it surely didn't sound like the Little Giant who had led the northern Democracy only six months earlier; it sounded like the speech of a War Republican, and that was a fact. Well, what could anyone have expected? Douglas had met in the White House with Old Baboon Lincoln, and evidently they'd reached some sort of agreement, and God damn it, wasn't *anyone* left who understood this madness and was man enough to raise his voice against it? In Titusville, old Richard T. Harris, the tannery man and erstwhile guardian of the golden George Peters, spent (it was said) *thirtyfive thousand dollars* recruiting and outfitting a regiment of volunteers with himself at its head with the rank of colonel. The commission came from the new Republican governor, a man named Oliver P. Morton, who was outdoing himself in raising troops. Lincoln had called for seventyfive thousand volunteers nationally, and Morton had wasted no time oversubscribing Indiana's quota. The terrible corruption galloped; its first bloom created *drummers,* by God, and men who played the cornet and fife, and the maidens of Titusville sewed little flags for their sweethearts to carry away with them, and Dick Harris' recruiting campaign proceeded with urgency and dispatch. The talk was that none other than George Peters had been given the rank of major and would be regimental adjutant. Apparently good old George's Shakespearean acting troupe had been in Indianapolis when Dick Harris had gone there to obtain the commission from Gov Morton. The rumor was that Dick Harris had visited George, had talked him into joining up, had put him in charge of the regiment's training, which would be conducted in a camp somewhere near Terre Haute. Great God, the fellow had spent less than a year at West Point and now he was a bloody *major!* Heaven protect the Republic! What with all this yawp and clamor, Charley found himself losing his oafish amiability, and finally one day he could stand the situation no longer. He walked across the street to the front stoop of Thompson's Store. The recruiters had set up a table there. Charley said nothing to the recruiters. He simply walked to their table and jumped up on it. A crowd of men was gathered around the table, and none other than Dick Harris himself was standing out in the street and speaking with several young men who apparently were somewhat reluctant to join up. *Men!* shouted Charley, and then he glared down at the recruiters, who still were seated around the table. They looked up at him, but none of them made a move to try to force him down from the table. Dick Harris smiled at Charley and moved his head slowly from side to side. Charley paid no attention to Dick Harris, him and his goddamn smile. *Men!* shouted Charley. Do you know what earth you're standing on? I'll tell you what earth you're standing on! You're standing on American earth, that's what you're standing on, and now the government is trying to tell you that America's no damn good, that we got to go out and kill Southerners and destroy that Union that was paid for by the blood of our forefathers! Do you believe we have to do that? Do you believe we have to go out and die? I don't believe it! I ask you—why do we have to go out and participate in the murder of the American Republic? On and on rolled Charley's words, and several men moved toward him, and he didn't need to be slapped in the face with a wet chicken to know these men were about to attack him physically, but today he simply did not give a whoop. Maybe this would be the last time he would say these words, and maybe never again would he be so close to truth in a public utterance, but for once he *would* say them, even if his head were split open. But, after a few anxious and fretful seconds (seconds full of heat, mugginess, sweat, the glare and thump of a gray sun, small vexed eyes, fists like hams, the flap and crack of the recruiters' banners and pennons; seconds that for Charley were frozen), seconds that pounded and rang with Charley's uncorked rhetoric, seconds of white anger and the rigid silence of the patriotically outraged, Dick Harris gave Charley some assistance. Dick Harris quietly moved through the crowd. He whispered to the men. He nudged them, shrugged. He grinned at Charley, grinned and nodded and as much as said: Go on. Tilt at your windmills. Spit it all out. Get it over with. It was a kindly grin (Dick Harris was a kindly man; after all, hadn't he and his wife taken in the orphaned George Peters?), but it made Charley want to hit Dick Harris in the face and mash his goddamn condescending grin, shove it down his throat along with his teeth and his tongue and whatever else got in the way. Even though he despised violence, this was what Charley wanted to do, and he had to make fists in order to keep himself from jumping down off that table and going after Dick Harris. But those seconds eventually dragged past, and then Charley again had control of himself. He turned his rhetoric on Dick Harris; he pointed to Dick Harris and hollered: Them who wants to kill people can go ahead and join up and be damned to you! The rest of us, we'll stay home and we'll obey the Rule that says Thou Shalt Not Kill and we'll be the real patriots! Now damn it all you just better believe me! You just better! You fellers, you look at me! You got any idea the crossroads this country's at? You got any idea the terrible things that's going to happen if us, us people, us plain people, don't stand up to Lincoln and them others in Washington and tell them No Mr Lincoln we ain't going to fight no war against our brothers? You got any idea? Well, if you don't, then you just better start thinking! Then Charley spread his arms. *Think!* he yelled. Don't do this terrible thing! Think! Think! *Think!* He allowed his arms to fall. He jumped down from the table. He was gasping. He rubbed his eyes. A few of the men applauded. Then there were shouts, curses. The applauders stopped clapping. Charley crossed the street. Silence now. Somewhere a horse nickered. Wesley Thornton stood at the front door to Charley's store. Charley's eyes were damp, and God damn, God damn, God damn. He was just about to elbow past Wesley Thornton and enter the store when someone came up on him from behind, seized him by an arm and spun him around. It was a boy named Ezra Ordway. He was just seventeen, and he was enormous. You sonofabitch! shouted Ezra Ordway. You traitor bastard sonofabitch! He hit Charley across the adamsapple and then he hit Charley across the nose. Squealing, Charley fell down. Wesley Thornton stepped back. Traitor! shouted Ezra Ordway. He bent over, grabbed Charley, pulled him upright. He hit Charley in the belly. Coward! he hollered. Won't even fight like a man! Now, with Dick Harris in the lead, a number of men came running. Charley was gagging. He would not fight back. Ezra Ordway beat him across the shoulders and arms. Charley put up his arms, protected his head. Give it to him good, Ezry! someone hollered. Then Dick Harris was tugging at Ezra Ordway, and so were several other men, and finally they managed to pull him away. Charley reeled inside the store. Wesley and Verda Thornton stared at him. Their faces were gray and taut. They made no effort to assist him. Charley staggered into the back room and collapsed on the floor next to a case of tinned codfish. Later he learned that two or three men had turned away from the recruiters after hearing his speech. But he knew it all had been a failure; he knew—*now* he knew—that no single voice, no matter how loud, could turn men away from the seduction of alarms and the brilliant prospect of Deeds and all *that* sort of pig shit. He lay on that back room floor for several hours. Neither Wesley nor Verda Thornton came to see how he was. When he finally managed to get to his feet and leave the place, he went out the back door. Still staggering a little, he made for his home. He kept to vacant lots, back streets. An hour after he arrived home, he had a visitor. It was Morton C. Hightower, and the rage of Morton C. Hightower was majestic and irresistible. You damn fool, said Morton C. Hightower, you damn and doubledamn *simpleton*. If you want to deliver speeches against this war, I suggest you go find a cornfield somewhere and harangue the crows and the rabbits and the earthworms. Don't you understand? This is *not the time* for that sort of talk. *Not the time.* These are days of excitement and great expectations, and no one will listen to you. No one. And, if you persist in these public declarations of heresy, you surely will destroy yourself. Do you seek destruction? Is that your one large ambition? If so, you are performing splendidly. If not, then for God's sake keep your mouth shut. With those words, Morton C. Hightower turned and walked away. Charley had not uttered so much as a syllable. The entire onesided conversation had taken place on his front porch, the porch with the magnificent view of the river, the porch where he had brought his mother the glass of cold well water the day of the explosion of the *Molly G. Edwards*. Charley leaned against a pillar and watched Morton C. Hightower walk away. The twilight cast purplish streaks and smears across the old man's back. Charley frowned. There had been something different about Morton C. Hightower. Charley rubbed his chin. Then it came to him. Morton C. Hightower *had not been trembling*. Shuddering, Charley went inside the house and seated himself on the settee in the parlor. He stared at all the ormolu and cutglass. It was dusty. Nancy's mother, who kept house for him, was very slovenly. Ah, what difference did it make? Charley wasn't about to be entertaining the Queen of England. He frowned. He rubbed an arm of the settee. The old man *had not been trembling*. God save the world, he had been *that* angry. Now then, *that* just about had to be the angriest Charley ever had seen *anyone*. Whoo. Charley shook his head. He wished his revered teacher, Prof Tobias G. Frye, PhD (Harvard), were available. He needed advice, by God. Good advice. Advice that made sense. But Prof Frye was not available. Prof Frye had vanished. A terrible and grotesque thing had happened to Prof Frye, and Charley didn't suppose he ever would see the poor fellow again. Sighing, Charley lay back on the settee and thought of the Professor, of the suicide and murder and mad melodrama that had enveloped the Professor. He didn't suppose he ever would know the full truth of it. He didn't suppose anyone would. Which was a shame. Charley enjoyed melodrama, and that was a fact.

It had been the most delicious scandal ever to have spread itself across the Titusville consciousness. It had involved, in addition to the Professor, his surprising inamorata, Mrs Weeks; her husband, the skinny Rev Abner D. Weeks; and Nancy's younger sister, the girlish Widow Grimes, who now was a madwoman beyond hope or solace. It had been a thing of shrieks and terror, and—

Charley opened his eyes. He shook his head. Enough of *that*. There was enough melodrama in his own life. He had no need to dwell on the melodrama in the lives of others. He sat up. He cleared his throat, rubbed his head. It still hurt from the blows delivered by the righteous Ezra Ordway. Wincing, Charley thought back on his conversations with the Professor, especially that one profound conversation they had held that drunken night shortly after the death of Charley's parents, that oratorical and revealing night in Bagwell's Saloon. Gradually it came to Charley that he had lost sight of at least a part of his revered teacher's wisdom. Gradually it came to him that his beliefs had caused him to lapse into unrealistic attitudes. He had lost sight, by Christ, of *possibility*, of *mortality*. He had suffered a genuine relapse. Honor and courage and heroism had fled him, and also—or so he had thought—had belief. But this wasn't so. At least judging from the foolishness he had permitted himself today. Charley rubbed his elbows. You *are* a damn and doubledamn simpleton, he told himself. Mr Hightower is right. You stand up and you say what you think. Oh you are the biggest damn and doubledamn simpleton in the county. It's all right to say what you think as long as most *other* people think it. But to say what you think when you know you're as much as pissing on the flag . . . how can anything be *possible* for a man who doesn't know when to keep quiet? You are as ridiculous as George Peters, and that is a fact. *He* seeks a Deed; *you* seek to say what you feel, no matter the consequences. The both of you are equally brave. The both of you are equally stupid. Oh wouldn't the Professor have had a snake fit if he'd seen you today. You and your damn and doubledamn *beliefs*, he would have said. My Lord, my boy, don't you understand the *mortality* of beliefs? They are like love and a stiff pecker and everything else: they wear out. Be a true man. Understand the world as it *is*. Shut your mouth. Keep your eye on the possible. There always will be windmills, but why not leave them to *other* fools?

Charley stood up. He felt as though he had jumped into a lake full of ice. He grimaced. His belly hurt. His face hurt. His adamsapple hurt. He went to the sideboard and poured himself a substantial drink. It stung his adamsapple, but the sting was not unpleasant. He sneezed from some dust neglected by Nancy's mother. He shook his head. He went to bed.

Charley withdrew from public forensics for almost a year. He kept his political opinions to himself. He spent most of his time in Bagwell's Saloon. He no longer was postmaster, and he seldom visited the store. The postmastership had been turned over to a deserving Republican named Leander Dutton, who operated a small smithy and forge. Charley stayed at home the day Leander Dutton went to the store to claim the stamps and documents and other accouterments of the postmastership. Wesley Thornton represented Charley. Good old Wesley Thornton. The new post office was directly across the street from Charley's store, but he never visited the place. When he needed to purchase stamps or post a letter or pick up his mail, he had Wesley Thornton run the errand for him. As for the store itself, well, it was better that Charley stay away. Wesley Thornton had managed to keep the business reasonably close to the break-even point. I don't talk politics, said Wesley Thornton. I just sell groceries. People seem to like it that way. Charley nodded, told Wesley Thornton he understood what he was trying to say. The hell with the store. Charley's days passed in Bagwell's Saloon, and yes sir, the very utmost hell with the store. Those were not good days for Bagwell's Saloon. A great many of Pete Bagwell's best patrons had gone off to fight in the damned war, and the ones who remained didn't amount to much. They were older men, most of them, and they had too many stupid arguments. But Charley was wise. Charley had learned. Charley stayed out of the arguments. And anyway, the diffuse discourse of drunkards held no appeal for him. He sat alone. He drank beer. He smiled when he had to, but he seldom was loud, seldom was oafish. He subscribed to several Indianapolis newspapers, and each morning he had Wesley Thornton fetch them from Leander Dutton's black Republican post office. He took the newspapers with him to Bagwell's Saloon, and from time to time he tore out certain articles and stuffed them in his pockets. He had begun to keep a table of statistics at home. It mostly had to do with casualty totals. The blessed war was not going at all the way most of the people of Titusville had thought it would, and by God at the proper time he would see to it that they were reminded of all the butchery. At the *proper* time, the time when the *possibility* of gain would be the greatest. He smiled when he read of the ferocity of the Southrons' resistance. He smiled one of his ancient oafish smiles. He smiled the way he had smiled as a boy. He read of an Ohio Congressman, an apparently indomitable fellow named C. L. Vallandigham, a person whose opposition to the war had made him a national figure, a man who apparently was not afraid to stand alone. This Vallandigham had been a pacifist before the war. Now, of course, he could no longer preach outright pacifism (there were, after all, limits to indomitability). Instead, Vallandigham said the Democrats should do their duty as patriotic citizens —but only as long as the war's sole aim was preservation of the Union and defense of the Constitution. If and when that aim became subverted by abolition, Vallandigham would have no part of it. In the meantime, however, there was a serious issue the Democrats could take up in earnest. In the Midwest, many Democrats—including judges and even public prosecutors—were being summarily arrested by federal authorities, principally the military. Vallandigham's protests were loud. Again and again his public discourse made reference to the rights *guaranteed* by the Constitution the federal forces were supposed to be fighting to *preserve*. The arrests had been triggered by that damn ass, Edwin M. Stanton, Secretary of War. The way Stanton saw it, anyone who spoke against the black Republican government was in effect preaching sedition, and so the jails began to abound with incarcerated Democrats—especially in the Midwest. Ah, what a lovely issue the arrests would provide for the '62 canvass, and Charley and all other rightthinking advocates of the Democracy were immensely delighted. In the spring of '62, Charley met several times with Morton C. Hightower. They agreed that the Democratic party stood a large chance of doing well in the fall—provided it did not preach outright pacifism, provided it struck hard at the issue of unconstitutional arrests, provided it remained inflexible in its opposition to abolition, provided the federal forces gained no significant successes on the field of battle. This was a large sight of provisos, but there was nothing to make Charley believe they would not be fulfilled. Early in the year, the Union army did capture New Orleans and two strong Tennessee forts called Donelson and Henry, and for a few weeks there was jubilant talk that the war soon would be won. But the talk faded. In the spring, a huge Union army landed on a muddy Virginia peninsula east of Richmond and slowly made its way toward the rebel capital, but it was worn down in a series of Confederate rearguard actions and finally gave up trying to take the city by that route. And, in the Shenandoah valley of Virginia, a rebel general named T. J. Jackson just about drove the federal commanders mad in a series of brilliantly conceived and executed small battles. He won all of them except one, and the talk was that he surely was a genius. Farther to the west, at a place called Shiloh Church in southern Tennessee, the federal and rebel armies met in force, but the result was a stalemate and came within a whisker of being a calamitous Union defeat. All in all, it was a discouraging spring and summer for the Republicans, and Charley carefully collected and saved his casualty totals and other drear statistics. Late in the spring, he cut down on his visits to Bagwell's Saloon. One morning, brisk and grinning, he showed up at the store. Wesley and

Verda Thornton frowned at him. He paid them no mind. He rubbed his hands together. He breathed deeply of the splendid May air. He loved the fragrance of it, a fragrance that actually was enhanced by all the anonymous grocery smells, the fine conglomerate stink of sawdust and coffeebeans and licorice and earth and potatoes and brine. That day he once again revealed his teeth for the world to see, and up, up, up came his hyperbole, flapping like the fabled phoenix, and of course the women who came to the store that day were, despite themselves, despite their knowledge that Charley Wells probably was nothing more than an oily peace sneak, delighted. Said one of them that night to her husband: Clovis, I expect Charley Wells is fixing to stand for the legislature again. He showed up at his store today, and you should of *seen* him. He started talking about my brooch. Said it set off the *alabaster delicacy of my skin.* No, don't look at me like that. I mean it. That's what he said. Now, now, *he* was the one said it, not *me.* When Charley's candidacy was announced a few weeks later, few were surprised. His first beer keg speech was attended by a large crowd of men, most of them middleaged fellows. Some were wearing the uniform of a ragtag militia called the Indiana Legion, which was charged with protecting southern Indiana in case a rebel raiding party somehow came up through Kentucky and sneaked across the river. Grinning, clutching his lapels, inspecting his vest to make sure a button was unfastened, Charley climbed atop the beer keg and said: I know what you're thinking. You're thinking ah, here's old Charley Wells again, coming back for more punishment. Poor old Charley Wells is going to get his butt whipped again by Frank Sturdevant. Ah, but that's where you're all of you wrong. *This* time poor old Charley Wells is going to *win.* He's going to win for one reason. He's going to win because he speaks for the *Democracy,* and now the people are beginning to understand how much they *need* the Democracy. This war, my friends, has become a disaster. I know it. You know it. The world knows it. I see some of you fellers are wearing the uniform of the Indiana Legion. All I got to say to you is: *Hah.* Tell me, if the war's going so allfired good like the Republicans say it is, how come there's a *need* for the Indiana Legion? Answer me that, will you? Ah, I don't hear no one speaking up. Well, I didn't think I would. You can't answer, can you? You down there, Bill Hooper! How old are you? Sixty? What? How's that? Sixty*four?* And ain't that the uniform of the Indiana Legion you got hanging on you? Now then, Bill, don't misunderstand me. I expect you're as good as the next man when it comes to a fight, but you *are* sixtyfour for the God's sake! Bill, I say to you it's a damn shame a man of your age has to be pressed into service by a government of fools and jackals and brutes who can't even provide you protection! Ah, surely, I know what you want to say, Bill! You want to say that Charley

Wells is a peace sneak! You want to say that two years ago Charley
Wells spoke words and held opinions you thought were treasonous! Perhaps you still think I speak treason! But just hear me out a little bit longer!
This here is the month of June in the year 1862, and the Republican war
is fourteen months old, and just what's it got us? It's got us *nothing—that's*
what it's got us! Nothing except a lot of bloodshed! And what about this
black Republican government that's supposed to be conducting the war?
Two months ago that stupid ninny of a Secretary of War ordered all the
recruiting stations closed, now didn't he? You *know* he did! He said the
war was just about won, didn't he? Then how come last week he ordered
all them recruiting stations opened again? What the hell is the matter with
such a man? Is he fit to be Secretary of War? Well, if he's fit to be Secretary of War, then my name is Abraham Lincoln! Ah hah! Some joke
ain't it? Ah, but I got a message for you—Abraham Lincoln is an even
bigger joke! He's the biggest and most goddamn horrible joke this country's
ever had perpetrated on it! Him and his stories! Him and his funny stories!
All he does is tell his goddamn funny stories, and every day boys is dying
down in them battlefields in Tennessee and Virginia and wherever, and
what the hell sort of *President of the United States* is it who all he can
think of at a time like this is to tell funny stories? I got a friend over by
Clapham Junction! Some of you know him too! His name is Silas Pomeroy!
He was at that fight in April down by Shiloh Church in Tennessee when
the rebels ran all over us for a day and a night until we just in the nick of
time managed to hit back and drive them from the field! You want to
know something about my friend Silas Pomeroy? He's got only one leg
these days! Before Shiloh Church, he had two! His other leg it's buried
in mud somewheres along the bank of the Tennessee River! And so he's
invalided out, and he comes home, and he picks up the black Republican
Evansville *Courier* and he reads of how Lincoln and Stanton and all them
other boobies in Washington are talking about a victory before the end of
the summer, and you know what my friend Silas Pomeroy does? I'll *tell*
you what he does! He laughs! He's heard a funny story! Oh that Lincoln,
such an amusing sort of feller! *Victory before the end of the summer!* Ah,
how my friend Silas Pomeroy does laugh! He just laughs and laughs until
he ain't got no breath left in him! Only it ain't in no ways a decent *kind* of
laugh! It's like milk that's gone off! It's like vinegar! It's like alum! So you
listen, my friends! If any goddamn black Republican tries to tell you how
good the war is going, *you* just tell *him* he's full of you know what! Or,
maybe better, have him go pay a call on Silas Pomeroy! Two years ago
there was some of you called me a peace sneak! Now then, there's something I want to tell you about Charley Wells! Sure, two years ago he *was*
against the war! But how can you say he was a sneak? He stood right here

and hollered out his convictions! He was no sneak, and you know it! All
right, the past is past; done is done! What about Charley Wells *now?* How
does he feel *now?* Well, my friends, *now* there *is* a war, and we all got to
accept it! I am a loyal American! I support the war! The South has made
a grievous mistake! It has violated the Constitution! It must be brought
back into the Union! But that is the *only* reason we're fighting this war!
The only reason we *should* fight it! As long as it is conducted with that
end in mind, I'll give it my support! But, at the same time, I want to tell
you we should be on the lookout for that hideous monster called *abolition!*
If the goddamn radical war Republicans attempt to impose it, if they
violate the spirit of this conflict by introducing that sort of goddamn ir-
relevancy, then we'll have opened up a brandnew can of worms, and I
for one will have to take another look at the situation! I *got* to! I don't
want to see Titusville and Titus County ruined! I love it here, and I
don't want the niggers to take over! Yes, you heard me right! *I don't
want the niggers to take over!* We got a state law says free niggers can't
come here and put good white men out of work, but them abolitionists
they don't care about our state law! They want to interpose the power of
the federal government over our state law! And that means giving white
men's jobs to free niggers! I don't hold with it! And neither do I hold
with them New England Yankees thinking that they can call all the
tunes and we'll dance to them like we was dumb beasts! Who's this war
benefiting anyhow? Who's making the money from it? You take a look
at the map of this here nation of ours! Now that the Mississippi River is
closed to us, how do we send our goods to market? On the *railroads* by God,
and most of them are owned by them New Englanders, and ah Lord I
wish I was sharing in the profits! Them New Englanders got us where
it hurts most, my friends! *They got us by the pocketbook!* Three years ago
the tracks of the St Louis & Northeastern's Ohio River Division was laid
through here, and now we're connected with Evansville to the west and
Indianapolis to the north, and I recollect how loud the bands played and
how mighty the people cheered the day the first train came through—
but how about now? How many of you would cheer the St Louis
& Northeastern *today?* You, Henry Ventry, you and old Sherman Gentry
you got yourselves a nice little sawmill ain't you? The Ventry and the
Gentry folks call it, and it's as fine a sawmill as there is in this
part of the state! The good old Ventry and Gentry! But, now you tell
me, how much have the St Louis & Northeastern shipping rates
gone up in the past year or so? Thirty percent? Eh? How's that? You
say thirty*five* percent? Ah, wellnow, how about that? And you know who
the president of the StL&NE is? His name is Grimm! And you know where
he lives? I'll *tell* you where he lives! He lives in *Boston,* and that's a fact!

And Boston is in Massachusetts! And Massachusetts is in New England! And the people who live in New England are called Yankees! And Yankees is the biggest abolitionists there is! So, here we are, my friends, right back on our little vicious circle! It's got no beginning and it's got no end! The Yankees are making money hand over fist, and the Yankees want the niggers to be free, and just who the hell is this war being fought *for*? If it preserves the Union, fine, but let's make damn sure it doesn't ruin us, and let's make damn sure it doesn't bring a hundred thousand niggers splashing across the river! And, ah God, the hypocrisy of them Yankees! Here in Indiana, we're supplying tens of thousands of troops to the Union cause, but *up there*, do you think *those people* are supplying troops in those numbers? Don't be dense! They're too busy draining the nation of its wealth! Up there in New England, they got to *import people* from Ireland and Germany and God knows where else so the states can meet their quotas! *Ireland,* for the God's sake! *Germany!* Next thing you know, they'll be bringing in boatloads of the Heathen Chinee! And I'm not exaggerating! They'll bring men from wherever they can, provided those men got strong backs and weak minds! So, my friends, next time some black Republican comes strutting up to you and tells you how hunkydory everything is, what with all the dying and all the greed and all, you just tell him to go to hell! But, and I got to warn you, don't say the words too loud! You just might get yourself arrested! Seems a man can't speak his mind no more! Seems old Stanton calls it sedition! My friend Silas Pomeroy, him who's got only one leg, the man who laughed so sour when he read in the Evansville *Courier* all about how the war maybe would end soon, if old Stanton had of heard Silas Pomeroy laugh, he'd of had Silas Pomeroy throwed in jail, one leg or no! Oh, you got to watch yourself with these here Republicans! The country is tiptoeing on a narrow edge! *And there's only one thing you can do about it! Vote the Democracy, my friends! Bring reason back into government! Elect men who will bring this war to a speedy and successful conclusion without violating the Constitution! Vote the straight Democracy all the way down the line!* I thank you kindly for hearing me out! Now then, there's still plenty of beer! We don't want it to get warm! Ain't nothing sets a stomach to going sour faster than warm beer! So help yourselves! Hot day like this, it tastes mighty fine! Then, grinning, patting his vest and the unfastened button, Charley jumped down from the keg, and the volume of the applause just about brought tears to his eyes. Men shook his hand, clapped him on the back, toasted him with their beer. Times had surely changed, and hallelujah. One of those who congratulated Charley was a man named Jim Ordway, a great bearded fellow with crossed eyes and hands like sides of beef. He was the father of young Ezra Ordway, Charley's tormentor the day Charley had made the ill-advised speech from the recruiters' table. You sure do get wound up, said Jim Ordway, smiling. Well, said Charley, I feel kind of strong about the things I say. And Jim Ordway said: I just expect you do. And Charley said: How's your boy? And Jim Ordway said: Well, Ezry was at Malvern Hill with the rest of them, but he ain't yet fired a shot in anger. Charley nodded. He had heard about the Malvern Hill adventure. The Dick Harris regiment now was called the 198th Indiana, and only one man was hurt in that battle, which was the first battle it had seen. It was in reserve, however, and did not fight. The injured man's name was Crofutt. He was from over by Evansville. His rear end was cut when something fell on him. Charley grinned, started to tell Jim Ordway about Crofutt, but Jim Ordway interrupted: Yes. I know. Ezry told me about him in a letter. Seems Crofutt now goes around bragging about what a big hero he is. Charley nodded. Well, he said, that's war. A smile from Jim Ordway, and then Jim Ordway said: Charley, I got to give you credit. Said Charley: For what? Said Jim Ordway: For asking about Ezry—after what he done to you last year. Said Charley: Aw, the hell with it. Said Jim Ordway: No. Don't push it away so quick. It shows you're a pretty good feller. I aim to study on the things you said today. Said Charley, smiling: That's all I can ask. And, uh, next time you write to your boy, tell him Charley Wells says hello. Jim Ordway stared at Charley for two or three very long seconds. They also were very warm seconds, and they just about made Charley itch. But his eyes did not waver, and finally Jim Ordway nodded and said: Fine, Charley. Fine. I'll do her. That night Charley just about sang himself to sleep. The Professor would have been proud of him. Ah, what a splendid canvass this showed every sign of being. And it was. In every way except the final result. It was a nervous Frank Sturdevant who stood for reelection. The man's apprehensiveness became abundantly clear on the Fourth of July, when he did not put in an appearance for the traditional debate at the picnic in Garmaker's Grove. His excuse, conveyed by his wife, was illness—a stomach ailment of some sort. Charley grinned. He told Mrs Sturdevant he surely did hope and pray nothing *serious* was wrong with old Frank. Charley was sober as a Baptist preacher that day, and he complimented Mrs Sturdevant on her bonnet. He perambulated through the holiday crowd, spoke in sorrowful tones of poor *old* Frank Sturdevant's *unfortunate* indisposition, shook his head, stroked his chin. His heart was full of mockingbirds and laughter and the shy music of harps, and he had caused God to flee. *God.* For the first time since the beginning of the canvass, Charley had a sure and certain knowledge that he was making headway. Had the election been held that day, he no doubt would have won. He grinned, wondered if old Frank knew or even suspected what a good turn he had done him. He still was afraid

of debating old Frank, and that was a fact. Had there been a debate that
day, old Frank probably would have addressed Charley as Son, and the
tactic would have cost Charley a minimum of (he estimated) fifty votes.
But old Frank was more ascared of a debate than Charley was! Ah,
Lord, Lord, could it be that Charley was going to win? Charley now
thought so, and so did Morton C. Hightower, who told him: Keep working at it, my boy. You're getting there. I mean that. I can feel it. A great
disaffection is at work, and the Republicans will be hurt by it. So don't
stop. Keep your momentum. And Charley stepped up his canvassing, de-
voting sixteen and sometimes twenty hours a day to it. He made numerous beer keg speeches, and they were all well attended. He produced his
newspaper cuttings, waved them to his audiences, recited the casualty statistics for Shiloh Church, Malvern Hill, Second Bull Run, Savage Station,
Gaines Mill, Antietam, spoke of blood and death and pain and horror
and niggers and abolition. And the cheers for him became louder. And
from time to time men shouted back to him: God damn this war! You tell
the truth, Charley Wells! Swear God you do! And, one night in early
September, Jim Ordway brought his son Ezra to hear one of Charley's
beer keg speeches. Ezra Ordway was just home from the war. He was
blind. An exploding caisson had burned out his eyes at Cedar Mountain
the month before. Jim Ordway guided his blind son by an elbow. After
taking a quick look at Ezra, Charley told himself: You handle this right,
it'll be worth a hundred votes. Charley kept his face solemn, but he could
have embraced Ezra. In his speech he made no reference to Ezra, but then
he didn't really have to. Everyone knew Ezra was a large vertical example of all the things Charley had been saying. At the end of Charley's
speech, Ezra applauded very loudly. He beat his palms together in great
deliberate rhythm, ponderous and profound: womp . . . womp . . . womp
. . . womp . . . and each heavy echoing blow meant more votes for good
old oafish Charley Wells, and it was all good old oafish Charley Wells
could do to restrain himself from shrieking for joy. Later, Charley and
Ezra solemnly shook hands. Ezra's eyes were bandaged. The bandage was
dirty. I . . . I sure am sorry, he said. If I'd of knowed then what I know
now . . . ah, well, I expect you know what I'm trying to say. Charley
squeezed one of Ezra's arms. Of course I do, he said, and kindly please don't
bother yourself about it. Ezra Ordway smiled. I won't bother myself about
it, he said. I don't hardly bother myself about nothing no more. Ezra's
father made a clucking noise. Now, Son, he said, that's no way to talk.
And Ezra Ordway said: I expect I've earned the right to talk like I want.
Jim Ordway grunted. Ezra was breathing with his mouth open. Charley?
he said. You still there? Charley patted Ezra on a shoulder. I'm right here,
he said. Said Ezra Ordway: George Peters, our major, he's a friend of

yours ain't he? Said Charley: Yes. Or, anyhow, he *was*. I ain't seen him in oh I expect it's about six years. Said Ezra: He likes to give speeches. Said Charley: I wouldn't be surprised. After all, he *was* an actor in a traveling show. Said Ezra: He's a good officer though. Goes where the men go. At Cedar Mountain he waved his sword. Waved it and hollered: *For Indiana!* Real loud like that. But old General Banks he fucked us. He let the rebels come in on us from the left. We got enfiladed. Only six men was killed, though. Six killed and thirtysix wounded, and I'm one of the thirtysix, and I won't never see nothing no more. I can't hardly believe it even now. And, the thing is—we would of done good if it hadn't of been for General Banks. When it comes to fighting a battle, he don't know shit from chocolate cake, and that's the truth. Hadn't of been for him, we'd of sent them skedaddling in no time at all. But they hit us from the left, and so *we* was the ones who skedaddled. All of us. Even the major, your friend George Peters. I was just running past that there caisson when it blowed up. Last thing I seen in this life was a man named Monks running alongside me. He's from Boonville, and he's the homeliest feller in the whole 198th Indiana, and I mean that, and ain't *that* a hell of a last thing to be seeing? The colonel, Mr Harris, I hear he got sick the night after the fight. It was our first *real* fight, you know. At Malvern Hill, all we done was set on a hill and *watch*. Well, anyhow, I hear he got good and sick, and I expect maybe he ain't much of a colonel as colonels go; I expect maybe he should of stayed here and run his tannery and left the fighting to younger men. Shoes, belts, harness—the country needs shoes and belts and harness; the country needs somebody to see to it that the hides is tanned good. He got *real* sick, I hear. Took to his tent, I hear. Well, I expect that's enough of *that*. I expect I talk too much. I expect Papa and me ought to be getting on toward home. I'm sleepy. I sleep a lot nowadays. Here Ezra Ordway paused, rubbed at his nose. He smiled. Charley, he said, you keep on talking. I wouldn't be surprised there'll be more and more who'll listen to you. Charley nodded. He watched Jim Ordway lead the blind boy away. A week or so later, the Antietam battle was fought. The date was September 17, a Wednesday. Colonel Dick Harris was hurt that day. He fell from his horse and broke an ankle. A week and a day after the battle, Colonel Dick Harris was home on convalescent leave. His visit cost Charley the election. When Colonel Dick Harris returned to Titusville, people said they'd never seen anything like it; his appearance had been changed *that* much. In the first place, he was a great deal thinner. Secondly, his hair was a great deal whiter. Third, he was angry about something. Or perhaps he was frustrated. No one could quite tell. All his life he had been that fine fellow Dick Harris, a rich man who had inherited a prosperous tannery from his father and grandfather, an amiable and slightly lazy beneficiary of a prosperity he'd had no hand in creating. Childless, married to a woman whose chief characteristic was an insistence that sunlight be permitted to enter all the rooms of her home, he had never been known to exchange angry words with a single other human being, and his kindness had been grand and legendary. People said he understood serenity; people said he understood the wisdom of making peace with his good fortune. But now the serenity had apparently been done away with, and his gentle good will had been replaced by a sort of rancorous frenzy. His wife met him at the depot the day he came home. He had to be reminded to kiss her. He was heard to complain about what he called the filthiness of the StL&NE steam cars. My nose, he told his wife, feels as though it has been pounded full of cinders. Ruth Harris clucked, kissed her husband, helped him to a waiting buggy. They drove off. Within a day or two, the town and the county learned why the colonel was behaving in such a peculiar manner. Letters arrived from the men of the 198th Indiana. It seemed the colonel had skedaddled at Antietam. It seemed he had skedaddled real good. It seemed he was a coward. George Peters now held temporary command of the regiment. He had at first, out of loyalty to the colonel, the letters said, turned it down. But then he'd been *ordered* to take it. He had obeyed, but with the understanding that he would be in command only for as long as the colonel was incapacitated. When Charley learned about the affair, he could have kissed the colonel. First Ezra Ordway's blindness, now *this*. Ah, the Almighty was kind. Shaking his head mournfully, Charley told his cronies it surely was a shame, a fine man being so damaged by this foolish war. He never was cut out to be a soldier, said Charley. He is a good man, but it don't follow that a good man has to be a good soldier. He got nothing to be ashamed of, though. It could of happened to anybody. There's worse things in this life than running away from a fight. I hope folks got enough good sense to understand that. I hope they see how damn foolish it is to be thinking all the time about heroism and that sort of pig shit. This here war. Some war. I ask you—where's it getting us?

Then one morning the colonel paid a visit to Charley's store. The colonel was wearing his uniform. His buttons glistened. He walked on crutches, and the broken ankle was in an immense cast, and he seemed so *old*, so sort of *frail*. He came stumping into the store and he would not shake hands with Charley. Wesley and Verda Thornton and several customers were in the store, and their ears just about fell off from the twitching.

I understand you've been talking about me, said the colonel.

Sir?

About my running. At the Antietam fight.

Wellsir, all I said was—

I don't give a damn what you said. Perhaps you mean well. I won't be so presumptuous as to question your motives. They probably are political, but I won't make any accusations. But I will make a demand. I demand that you stop speculating on my behavior.

Mr Harris, I didn't mean no—

Of course. You meant no offense. I grant you that. But, you see, you don't have to speculate. The truth of the matter is: I ran. I saw what was happening and I could not bring myself to participate in it. I ran. I ran. *I ran.* I left the field to your friend George Peters, and he conducted himself with gallantry, and that is all there is to it. Later that day I fell from my horse, and that is how I broke this ankle. But I shall recover. And I shall return to the regiment. I want you to understand that. *I am going back, Wells.*

Yessir. Good for you, sir.

You never mean offense, do you?

Well . . .

You try to undermine the government, but you mean no offense.

Sir, I simply say what I think.

You say what you *say* in order to win an election.

No sir. Winning the election would be fine, but I say the things I say because I *mean* them. Win or lose.

The Republic means that little to you? You would destroy it?

I don't want to destroy nothing. All I want is for the Democrats to win the election.

Boys die. Every day boys die. They die for the Republic. You would undermine them.

No sir, that's not—

They are very brave. Some of them run, but most of them stay and fight. And, even the ones who run, most of them eventually come back. And then, the next time there is a fight, they stay. Do you understand manhood?

Charley smiled. Now, sir, he said, don't get all—

Duty. Trust. Willingness to adhere to principles and obligations.

The war is about those things?

Yes.

I don't believe it.

You pig.

How's that?

I shall do everything I can to see to it that you are defeated. I am a coward. I ran. But I'll go back. Perhaps the next time I'll not run. In the meantime, however, I'll remain in Titusville a month or so. I promise you I'll work with the utmost diligence to make certain my friend Frank Sturdevant is reelected.

Sir, I didn't say nothing *bad* about you. There's no sense calling me a pig.

It doesn't matter what you say about me. It does matter what you say about the war. It does matter that you are undermining it. By undermining the war, you are undermining the Republic. Such behavior can be expected only from pigs.

Now, I don't care who you are. You stop calling me a pig.

What do you propose to do? Wrest my crutches away from me and strike me on the head with them? I probably would whimper. I whimpered that day when I ran. I whimpered when I broke my ankle. Would you care to see an old coward whimper?

That's not a fair thing to say. You don't understand.

I understand very well.

The final tally was Sturdevant 712, Wells 699. It was almost literally true that the election was purchased by Colonel Dick Harris. He made no speeches, waved no banners, but the eloquence of his electioneering was profound and telling and went a large sight beyond rhetoric and slogans. He hired several dozen men to help Frank Sturdevant with the Republican canvass. He bought and paid for six mass rallies, all held in the Titusville Opera House. All Charley had to offer was oratory and beer. The Sturdevant rallies also provided oratory and beer, but the oratory and the beer were augmented by whisky, *and* bouquets for the ladies, *and* sweets for the children, *and* gigantic suppers, *and* music. The gigantic suppers were held in the Opera House basement. The building, which had been built just before the war, happened to be owned by Colonel Dick Harris. The suppers were stupendous. Entire beeves were consumed, plus pork, ham, sausage, chicken, lamb, veal, fish, potatoes, peas, beans, carrots, squash, yams, cakes, pies, cookies and even French pastry (imported from Evansville). Several of the rallies were highlighted by the appearance of the renowned Rockport Musics, perhaps the most skilled brass band in southern Indiana. All thirtytwo members of the group made the trip by the steam cars, with all expenses paid by Colonel Dick Harris, that admitted coward and shirker, no longer amiable, no longer plump, yet still and all a patriot, a lover of war, of heroes, of Deeds. The band played martial medleys, and it played sweet romantic airs, and the crowds joined in singing the rugged anthems and hymns of the war, the sentimental ballads of doomed lovers and defunct heroes, and yes, by God, it all was bought and paid for, and so were whores bought and paid for, and the banners shouted THE UNION FOREVER! and the orators shouted *Do not embrace those who would defile the flag!* and Charley felt it all sliding away, and he didn't see where there was a blessed thing he could do about the situation. The Sturdevant rallies even included speeches from wounded veterans. These men spoke slowly, and sometimes their voices barely could be heard, but these fellows were heroes, and the people loved heroes, and it mattered little that the heroes' voices were weak. Frank Sturdevant, godly and placid and apparently no longer ascared, introduced the heroes, spoke glowingly of their exploits, their golden valor. And always, somewhere or other at the periphery of the audience, standing on one leg, leaning on his crutches, unsmiling and skinny, Colonel Dick Harris took in the proceedings, and people admired Colonel Dick Harris; they truly did, and this was a thing Charley could in no way understand. The fellow had skedaddled! He was a coward! How could the people still admire him? One night Charley discussed this with his friend Lew Bixby, and Lew Bixby said there was nothing at all puzzling about it. Just because Dick Harris skedaddled that day, said Lew Bixby, that don't mean he ain't a *man*. Said Charley: Yes. I *know*. I've said so myself. I've said *exactly* that. Said Lew Bixby: Then what's so peculiar about the way people are behaving? They see what you see. Said Charley: You mean for once I got the right idea about something? Said Lew Bixby: Sure appears that way. Said Charley: I'm going to lose this here election. Said Lew Bixby: Appears that way. Sure does. Said Charley: He surely does hate me. Said Lew Bixby: No. I don't think so. I think he's just doing what he believes he's got to do. And it sure is a bad piece of luck for you. A month or so ago you probably would of won. But now the bad luck has got to you. He's come home. And how are people supposed to put him off? He's been honest about his skedaddling. And he loves this country. His skedaddling had nothing to do with *that*. And, in some peculiar way, the skedaddling makes the things he has to say stronger than if he *hadn't* of skedaddled. It don't cost a brave man a thing to be a patriot. A coward, though . . . it costs a coward a whole lot. And, you got to remember—Dick Harris is going back to the fighting. People respect him for that. Sighing, Charley nodded, told Lew Bixby yes, you sure God probably got the right slant on it all. The last month of the canvass, attendance at Charley's beer keg speeches declined, and a number of men went so far as to call him to his face a Copperhead skunk. Charley denied this, swore that he simply sought to have the conduct of the war brought more under the auspices of his beloved Democracy, disavowed any affiliation with the Knights of the Golden Circle or any of the other covert peace organizations that had sprung up in Indiana and Illinois and Ohio in the previous year or so, but no one really believed him, even though he really was telling the truth. Oh, from time to time he had been visited by representatives of the Knights of the Golden Circle (narrow hawkfaced men, most of them; dissidents, haters of niggers, men of shady and surreptitious reputation, many of them with roots in the South), and these men had sought to bring him into their organization, but he had told them all to go to hell. In the first place, their ideas bordered on treason. Secondly, those ideas had not the remotest chance of success. The KGC wanted to blow up ammunition stores. It wanted to organize a Midwestern Confederacy. It wanted to assassinate Union army recruiters. It wanted to foment an army mutiny. As far as Charley was concerned, none of these proposed cabals came anywhere near being *possible*. So he would have nothing to do with the KGC and its ridiculous ambitions. But nonetheless he became involved with the KGC, and he was tarred with the KGC brush, and it happened just before the election. It did in the last of his hopes. It all began on the Sunday morning before election day. Charley had a visitor in his home. It was about 8 o'clock, and Charley was getting dressed for church. Since the beginning of the canvass he'd not missed a single Sunday morning in church. He knew better. A candidate for public office could be many things, but he could *never* under *any* circumstances be thought of as ungodly. Charley was lacing his shoes when someone began pounding on the front door. His visitor was a tall grayfaced man, mottled and skeletal, with an enormous rumbling voice and an adamsapple that bounced and twitched. His coat and vest were frayed, and a long white thread depended limply from his left sleeve. His shirt was gray, and harsh little hairs squiggled from his nose and ears. His beard was lush and silvered and not particularly clean. He wore a cap that had a narrow bill. He whipped off the cap when Charley opened the door. Mr . . . Mr Wells? he said. Charley nodded. That's my name, he said. I'm . . . I'm Jesse Hubbell, said the man. From, uh, Evansville. Charley again nodded. Well, he said, good for you. And Jesse Hubbell said: Could I, uh, have a word with you? Said Charley: You're having it. Said Jesse Hubbell: Inside perhaps? What I have to say is of a rather, uh, delicate nature. Charley looked closely at this Jesse Hubbell and then said: You from the KGC? Jesse Hubbell jumped a little. *Please,* he said, please permit me to come inside. Charley shrugged. He opened wide the door. Come on in, he said, only how many times do you people have to hear me tell you no? Jesse Hubbell smiled meekly. His teeth were brown and green. He rubbed his hands together. They were like old leaves. He followed Charley into the parlor. He seated himself on the edge of a straightbacked chair and then he said: Is anyone else in the house? After Charley shook his head no, Hubbell continued: You're absolutely certain? Said Charley: *Yes.* God's *sake.* You people and your goddamn secrecy. Hubbell quickly nodded. Sorry, he said, I meant no offense. It's simply that there is a need for discretion.

What I have to say is extremely important, sir. It would not do for us to have eavesdroppers. Said Charley: Well, rest assured we have none. Please get to the point. Said Hubbell: Mr Wells, a group of us met in Indianapolis Thursday night. We are always, as you perhaps know, seeking to expand our activities. A number of names were brought up. Names of young men of vigor. Names of young men whose services are needed by the movement. Said Charley: The movement? Said Hubbell: The movement for justice. Said Charley: The KGC is interested in justice? Said Hubbell: Oh yes sir. Justice for Indiana. Justice for the United States of America. Defense of the Constitution. Said Charley: Let's cut this short. You want me to organize the KGC in Titus County, isn't that it? Said Hubbell: Yes sir. That is so. Precisely. Said Charley: God *damn* you people. You know how many men the KGC has sent to me? Well, Mr Hubbell, you are the seventh. The *seventh*. And I've told the other six what I now officially tell you—that is, and to wit, go to the Devil. Said Jesse Hubbell, smiling: Noted. Said Charley: So kindly get out. Said Hubbell, making no move to leave: You know of course of the desertions and the paroles. Said Charley: How's that? Said Hubbell: The desertion rate from the federal army is the highest it's ever been. And then there is the matter of paroles. Seems more and more men are volunteering to surrender to the Confederate forces without as much as firing a shot. They seek to be paroled, to be sent home and thus be relieved of any further obligations toward this preposterous war. Entire companies have capitulated without getting off even a single volley. We have documented proof of this. Said Charley: So? Said Hubbell, clearing his throat: Tell me, do you believe in this war? Said Charley: Not particularly. Said Hubbell: Do you believe in freedom for niggers? Said Charley: I don't care one way or the other. Said Hubbell: Do you believe that niggers should take away the work of white men? Said Charley: No. Said Hubbell: Do you believe we have any right enforcing our will on the South? Said Charley: Only insofar as the Union is preserved. Said Hubbell: Does the Union mean that much? Or is that just talk for the benefit of the voters? Said Charley: Are you calling me a hypocrite? Said Hubbell: I am calling you nothing, sir. I am simply trying to set your thinking in order. Said Charley: Thank you kindly, but I'll attend to my own thinking. Said Hubbell: When our government is formed, you could have a very high position. Said Charley: Your *what?* Said Hubbell: Our government, sir. We intend to force the secession of Indiana from the Union. Said Charley: Oh my God. Said Hubbell: Our friends will find themselves in fortunate circumstances. Said Charley: Mr Hubbell? Said Hubbell: Yes? Said Charley: Get out of here. Said Hubbell: Sir? Said Charley: I don't care for violence. Never have. But now and then there comes a time for it, and— At this point,

Jesse Hubbell stood up. He gnawed on his lower lip. Then he spoke: Mr
Wells, the trouble with you is you don't know what you believe. Charley
stood up. Good day, Mr Hubbell, he said. Hubbell exhaled. His lips
flapped. He shrugged. He turned and walked from the room. Charley
followed him. At the front door, Hubbell hesitated. He wheeled around.
Charley drew back a step. Hubbell rubbed his hands together. Then:
Mr Wells, *think*. Said Charley, his voice trembling: Good . . . good *day*.
Hubbell grunted. He went out the door. It slammed behind him. Charley
watched him walk across the front yard toward the road. He walked in a
sort of shamble, and his coattails flapped. Charley tried to smile. He could
not. He went into the kitchen and brewed himself a pot of coffee. He
did not attend church that day. Late in the afternoon he was visited by the
Titus County sheriff, a man named Ben Stork. The fellow's first words
were: Charley, I expect you owe me five hundred dollars.

Charley looked at Ben Stork. They were standing at the front door.
Ben Stork was grinning. Ben Stork had a harelip. Ain't you going to let
me in? he said.

Charley shrugged. He escorted Ben Stork into the parlor. Ben Stork
seated himself in the straightbacked chair that had been occupied by
Jesse Hubbell that morning.

Charley did not sit down. Now, he said, explain yourself.

Ben Stork still was grinning. He was a large man. Like most harelips,
he talked through his nose. He had been a Whig, and now he was a
black Republican, and he had three sons in the army, and he had about
as much use for Charley as a cat did for soapsuds. He had been sheriff
a dozen years. He had killed a man for each of those years. He was known
as Bloody Ben, and his reputation in that part of the state was considerable. It was a wise criminal who stayed clear of Titus County. Rubbing
his mouth, Ben Stork nodded. Then he said: It's about a man named
Hubbell.

Who? said Charley. His ears suddenly were very warm, and he felt
sweat pop from his forehead.

Hubbell, said Ben Stork. According to the papers we found in his billfold, his name was Hubbell, Jesse A., of Evansville, a dealer in feed
and grain.

Was?

Yessir. He's sort of dead now. I had to shoot him.

Oh.

He came at me with a gun, the stupid sonofabitch.

Mm, said Charley.

Right on Titus Avenue it was. Hour or so ago. He seen me, and he tried
to shoot me. Damn if he didn't.

He . . . he had a gun?

Yessir. One of them little singleshot pistols. Had it in his vest.

His vest?

Yep. Sort of a tackylooking vest it was. But he got the gun caught in the lining. Good thing for me he did.

Yes. I expect so. But what's all this got to do with me?

Don't fuck at me, Charley.

What?

Don't fuck at me, you Copperhead bastard.

Ben, are you crazy?

The piece of paper was in his billfold.

What piece of paper?

The piece of paper with your name written on it: Charles P. Wells, Titusville, Indiana.

My name?

Yes. I expect you're going to fuck at me and tell me you don't know nothing about it. And I expect you're going to tell me you don't know nothing about the murder neither.

Murder?

Ben Stork grunted. Well, he said, maybe your friend Hubbell *didn't* tell you about *that*.

God damn it, Ben, I don't know what you're talking about.

Over by French Lick it was. Your friend Hubbell and another man ambushed a recruiting officer on the road south of town. Kilt him deader than hell. Well, seems the other man was caught in Indianapolis last night. Must of been sort of a soft feller. Wasn't no time a tall but what he was telling the Marion County sheriff about how he and Hubbell done it. Went on to say he thought Hubbell was heading down thisaway. So the Marion County sheriff sent me a little old telegram and I went out looking for this here Hubbell. And in maybe an hour or so I see him, big as you please, walking along Titus Avenue like he ain't got nothing on his mind but his goddamn hair. I holler at him to halt, and that's when he starts fumbling for that little pistol. So what can I do? I shoot the sonofabitch. I got to aim in a hurry, and it ain't too good, but the bullet it does pass through the top part of his head, and that's the end of him.

And you say my name was on a piece of paper in his billfold?

Charley, I told you. Don't fuck at me. Old Jesse A. Hubbell was out here to see you this morning.

No.

Sherman and Idarose Gentry *seen* him. They was on their way to church. They seen him walk across the yard here in front of your place.

And they seen you standing at the door. They was driving past in their buggy. They seen him real clear, and they seen you real clear.

They were mistaken.

Ben Stork grinned. Don't matter none, he said.

What?

Your friend Mr Hubbell the bushwhacker, nobody in the world except Sherman and Idarose Gentry and *me* know he came calling on you this morning. And you don't have to fret none about Sherman and Idarose. I can take care of them. They ain't nohow brave, if you get what I mean eh Charley?

Ben, you don't understand any of—

Charley, don't *fuck* at me. It all was in the wire from Indianapolis. Hubbell was a big man in the Knights of the Golden Circle. He came here to see you about something. Maybe it all was as innocent as Sister Susie's doll, but it's going to cost you five hundred dollars for me to keep this here mouth of mine shut. Cash. No cheques.

You're wrong.

Ben Stork jumped to his feet. He pulled back his crippled lips. *Wrong, my ass!* he hollered. Don't tell *me* I'm *wrong*, you sonofabitch! I got three boys fighting in this here war. By rights I ought to shoot you! You get me that five hundred—and no sass!

I've never had a thing to do with the Knights of the Golden Circle!

There you go! Fucking at me again! hollered Ben Stork. He took a step toward Charley.

Charley held up his hands. All right! he shouted. He spread his palms, moved his hands in short chops. All right! All right! Hubbell *was* here! But I wouldn't have a thing to do with him!

Ben Stork's hands shook. He closed them in fists. He took several deep swallows of air, then said: I got three boys just came through Antietam. They send me letters, and in them letters they say: Papa, you make sure none of them peace sneaks gets away with a goddamn thing in Titus County. They say: Papa, there is nothing we hate worse than peace sneaks. We don't even hate the rebels that much. At least the rebels is *men*. At least the rebels meet us *out in the open* for a *fair fight*.

Ben . . . Jesus, Ben . . . what do I got to say to make you believe I—

You say nothing. You give me the five hundred dollars, you fucking hog turd you. I don't like you, and I ain't never liked you, and I'd just as soon kill you as look at your goddamn skunk of a face. If it wasn't for old Dick Harris, I'd of run you out of the county two years ago like I wanted to.

What? said Charley. He blinked, shook his head. He backed toward the sofa and sat down.

Surprise you? Wellsir, back in '60, first time you stood for the legislature, I wanted to run you out. And I *could* of, too. I got ways. But old Dick said no. He said you had a right to speak your goddamn traitorous piece.

I don't believe it. *Not* the beloved colonel. Not *him*.

You keep a decent tongue in your mouth. I ain't lying. If it wasn't for Dick Harris, I'd of scattered your ass from here to Muncie. And this time too. After he came home from Antietam, I went to him and told him I'd have you out of the county in two hours. But he said no. He told me to leave you be. He said you was *sincere*. That's the word he used. *Sincere*.

Lord have mercy, said Charley.

At noon the following day, Charley met with Ben Stork in Bagwell's Saloon and gave him the five hundred dollars. In cash. Then Ben Stork gave Charley a scrap of paper. Charley's name was written on it, and of course the handwriting could have been anyone's, even Ben Stork's, but Charley said nothing. Ben Stork was not a stupid man. For all Charley knew, Ben Stork may have hatched the entire thing in his mind after talking with Sherman and Idarose Gentry. But this didn't matter. Ben Stork had a firm grip on Charley's balls, and there wasn't a thing Charley could do about the situation. All he sought was to get shut of it. And to think that he had *ejected* the shambling Jesse Hubbell from his home. Without the slightest by God by your leave. Jesse Hubbell, the murderer of a recruiting officer and only the Lord knew how many other people. Jesse Hubbell, who had been carrying a pistol in his tattered clothing. Jesse Hubbell, such a sicklylooking fellow, such a sort of nibbler. Jesse Hubbell: God. The next day was election day, and Charley really did better than he had expected. To lose by just 13 votes out of 1,411 was, he thought, a remarkable achievement. Election night, after the tally was certified, he shook hands with Frank Sturdevant on the steps of the courthouse. I gave you a better run this time, said Charley. I don't think I got a thing to be ashamed of. Frank Sturdevant nodded. His grip was slippery, and his forehead gleamed with perspiration. Sweating in November. Great Jesus. Later that night, Charley repaired to Bagwell's Saloon and drank until he fell down. In early December he received a note from his old mentor, Morton C. Hightower. It said: *May I see you at your earliest convenience?* The next morning Charley paid a call at the old lawyer's office. Charley, said Morton C. Hightower, trembling, dropping his hands behind the desk so Charley could not see them shake; Charley, I have been hearing a rumor. Said Charley: Oh? Said Morton C. Hightower: This man Hubbell, the chap who was shot dead by our old comrade Ben Stork, did you know him? Said Charley: No. Of course not. Said Morton C. Hightower: Please. I am putting the question to you for your own good—*did you know him?* Said Charley: Well, I *met* him. Said Morton C. Hightower: On the morning of the day Ben Stork killed him? Said Charley: Yes. Said Morton C. Hightower: I expect it is Ben who is behind the rumor. He hates you. I don't imagine that's any surprise to you. Said Charley: What rumor, sir? Said Morton C. Hightower: That you are a member of the Knights of the Golden Circle. That Hubbell came to see you in his capacity as an officer of that organization. Said Charley: It's not true. Hubbell approached me, but I wouldn't have anything to do with him. Said Morton C. Hightower: I like you. I truly do. All things being equal, you by rights should have been elected this time. You must know I like you. Said Charley: Yes. But what's that got to do with Hubbell and Ben Stork? Said Morton C. Hightower: I am leading up to something. I am leading up to advising you to get out of town. Said Charley: Sir? Said Morton C. Hightower: Matters may become extremely dangerous for you. Said Charley: You mean you think people are believing the things Ben Stork says? Said Morton C. Hightower: Yes. Precisely. Said Charley: You think they're going to come after me with a rope? Said Morton C. Hightower: They might. Or at least some of them might. You know as well as I do that the KGC is not popular in this county. Not popular at all. It is one thing to be known as a Democrat. It is quite another to be known as a member of the KGC. Too many people here have sons fighting in this war. They have no use for the KGC, for obvious reasons. Said Charley: But I'm not a KGC man! Said Morton C. Hightower: I believe you. But I fear there are many who don't. Said Charley: But I love this town! Where would I go? Said Morton C. Hightower: Kindly hear me out. In the first place, I am not suggesting you leave Titusville forever. Sooner or later this war will end. The Union will win. Don't for a moment believe otherwise. The Union is too large, too strong. The Confederacy may be winning most of the battles, but it will lose the war. When this happens, matters will go badly for the KGC people. They also will go badly for those who even are *suspected* of being KGC people. I want to spare you that. You have a large future. If you leave town now, the rumor will die. Nothing Ben Stork can do will keep it alive. When the object of an argument vanishes, so does the argument. People move on to other rumors, scandals, disturbances. So the thing to do is remove yourself . . . temporarily. You are an attractive political person. We do not want to jeopardize your large future. Said Charley: All right. Suppose I grant you that what you say makes sense. That still doesn't answer my question—where would I *go?* Said Morton C. Hightower: How does Our Nation's Capital strike your fancy?

It turned out that Morton C. Hightower had been in contact with an old colleague, an Illinois Congressman named Lansing H. Ingraham.

This Ingraham needed a secretary. He owed Morton C. Hightower several favors from the old days, and so he agreed to take on Charley as his new secretary—on a trial basis. And so Charley went to Washington, and Lansing H. Ingraham was delighted with his work and quickly made Charley a permanent member of his staff. Ah, Washington. Charley learned in that city all there was to know about whores. He encountered whores the likes of which he'd not imagined in even the most frenzied of his lonely bachelor grapplings with his carnality. And it was in Washington that Charley learned to play poker really well. It was a splendid place for the development of all sorts of surreptitious skills, and he was not so stupid that he did not take advantage of his opportunities. His employer, Congressman Lansing H. Ingraham, was elderly, gray, rather fishfaced, a lifelong Democrat whose southern Illinois district contained more overt Copperheads than any comparable area in the nation. He was a close personal friend of the fabled C. L. Vallandigham, and Charley got to know Vallandigham quite well. He surely was a talker, was this Vallandigham, but he clearly believed the things he said. There was, however, one serious reservation Charley had about the fellow: C. L. Vallandigham was most madly and wholeheartedly in love with himself. It was a wonder to Charley that Vallandigham didn't hug himself in public, or perhaps kiss the back of one of his own hands. Ah well, Vallandigham was a good enough sort, and after all, no one was perfect.

Charley arrived in Washington in early January of 1863. He took a room in a hostelry called the Hotel Nonpareil, then went straight to the offices of Congressman Lansing H. Ingraham. The man's handshake was damp, but he did manage a sort of smile, and then he said: Mort Hightower thinks a great deal of you. That is a large recommendation. I do hope you work out. Said Charley: Thank you, sir. I'll surely try to do the best I can. Lansing H. Ingraham frowned. He removed his spectacles, leaned forward, lowered his voice and said: Did Mort tell you about John Stapleton? Said Charley: John Stapleton? No sir. Never heard of him. Said Lansing H. Ingraham: John Stapleton was my previous secretary. Shot himself in the mouth with a horse pistol. It was over a woman. Wife of a black Republican Senator from a state we shall leave nameless. John loved her, but then she showed a rather distressing lack of breeding. She gave him the clap, she did. Said Charley: The *clap*, sir? The wife of a *Senator*? Said Lansing H. Ingraham: You heard me correctly. And don't be so in awe of the fact that the woman's husband occupies a chair in that august body. I know for a fact that it cost him fifty thousand dollars at the very least. Legislatures come dear these days. And, besides all that, it is my belief that he was the one who *gave* the unfortunate woman the clap. You'd be astonished if I were to tell you their name. Said Charley: Yes

sir. I expect so. Said Lansing H. Ingraham: Are you discreet? Said
Charley: Yes sir. When the situation calls for it. Said Lansing H. Ingraham: It will be necessary, if you want to fill this position on a permanent basis, for you to be very discreet indeed. John Stapleton was very
discreet. He was truly quite a fine fellow. Said Charley: I'll do the best
I can, sir. Said Lansing H. Ingraham: Now then, as to our political views.
I trust they coincide. You're not interested in the colored, are you? Said
Charley: No sir. Not at all. Said Lansing H. Ingraham: Do you believe
in the rights of the several states to determine their own peculiar institutions? Said Charley: Yes sir. That I do. Said Lansing H. Ingraham:
Would you assassinate that contemptible Lincoln if you had the opportunity? Charley hesitated. Then, smiling, he said: No sir. I have no desire
to be a martyr. Said Lansing H. Ingraham: Good. That was the proper
reply. Hate Lincoln all you want to. But please do not conduct yourself
in the manner of a zealot. I have a yardstick that I apply to my own
conduct. I ask that you apply it to yours. Here Lansing H. Ingraham
settled back, replaced his spectacles on his rather long and thin nose. He
made a church with his fingers, and then he continued: I want to be
a member of the United States Senate someday. I shall do nothing to
jeopardize that goal. I ask you to remember that. I ask you to do nothing
to endanger my chances. Hate this damnable war all you want. But never
—and I mean under absolutely *no* circumstances—involve yourself in
cabals that could lead to violence. I want my name linked with no plots,
no treason. Remember that, my friend. Use it as your yardstick. Said
Charley: Yes sir. I surely will. Said Lansing H. Ingraham: You just might
make a good secretary. At least you know the proper things to say. Now,
tell me, where are you staying? Said Charley: At the Hotel Nonpareil,
sir. Said Lansing H. Ingraham: That place is little more than a common
whorehouse. Said Charley: Yes sir. I know. I asked Mr Hightower to recommend a hotel that had such a reputation. I gather that back in his
congressional days he visited the place several times. Or perhaps more
than several times. Chuckling, Lansing H. Ingraham said: Why, the old
fart. But that doesn't explain why you want to *live* in such a place. Said
Charley: Wellsir, to be honest about it, I haven't been fucked much lately.
Back home I had a steady woman for a number of years, but then we
mutually agreed to terminate the relationship, and since then there
have been just a few casual whores whose services I obtained when I went
to Evansville on various business errands. You see, I ran for office twice
in my home county, and it was not expedient for me to lay about as a
seducer. It is not the best way to gain votes. Again Lansing H. Ingraham
chuckled. Quite so, he said. Well, I'm not going to make an issue of your
place of residence. Perhaps you *could* find a more respectable place to live,

but then again perhaps you could not. Just about every building in this city, large or small, imposing or humble, is a whorehouse these days. My God, sometimes I wonder why the earth does not tremble. Ah, but you will no doubt find out all these things for yourself. All I ask is that you remember to be discreet. Said Charley: Yes sir. Discretion.

Within a month Charley had the job on a permanent basis. The life agrees with you, said Lansing H. Ingraham. It is good to see a young man take hold so well. Bodes well for the future of the race. One is encouraged when one sees a young fellow understand his world. Charley grinned, told Lansing H. Ingraham he surely was grateful he had been found adequate. His duties covered two fields. First, he protected Lansing H. Ingraham. Now that Washington had become such a place of insanity, it abounded with scamps, cranks, swindlers, profiteers, officeseekers, deserters, bullies, drunkards, poseurs and fools. And apparently all of them had the most pressing business with the Congressman. Charley was charged with turning them away. His second function was to serve as intermediary between Lansing H. Ingraham and representatives of various rail, manufacturing, munitions and mining interests that sought certain specific favors involving pecuniary considerations. Lansing H. Ingraham was serving his tenth term in the House, and he was a ranking minority member of the Committee on Appropriations—a fact that was not lost on those who sought to do business with the government. And thus it fell to Charley to keep furtive appointments in hotel rooms with men who had need of the assistance of Lansing H. Ingraham. Sometimes these men gave Charley packets, and sometimes they gave him plump envelopes. He delivered the packets and the plump envelopes directly into the Congressman's hands. He never opened them. He never asked questions. Not that he had to. He would have been the premier chowderhead of the universe if he'd had to. His official salary was one hundred dollars a month, but it was augmented by certain surreptitious increments tendered by Lansing H. Ingraham. This money, plus funds that came by cheque from Titusville (Morton C. Hightower was handling his affairs there, and the Thorntons had agreed to stay on and operate the store), enabled Charley to live quite comfortably in the Hotel Nonpareil. The place housed seventeen whores. Their activities were supervised by a man named Wendell Archer Doggett. He was quite fat, and he insisted on the use of all three of his names. Charley liked the man. He reminded Charley a little of the vanished Prof Tobias G. Frye, PhD (Harvard), even though his command of rhetoric in no way approached that of the Professor. He surely was no hypocrite. I am a whoremaster plain and simple, he told Charley, and I am not a bit ashamed of it. I provide a necessary service at fair rates, and my girls know I tolerate no thievery or other shenanigans. In my own way, I am an honest man, and I take serious offense when I am accused of being anything less. Of the seventeen whores, Charley's favorite was a thin little girl named Irene Weaver. There was nothing she would not do. On Sunday mornings she attended the Congregational church around the corner, and she admitted to having something of a case on the minister. She was very good at quoting Scripture. She never told Charley a thing about her background, and he figured it was not his business to ask. From time to time he sampled the fleshly delights offered by the other girls, but Irene Weaver remained his favorite. It was the best sort of relationship with a woman. Value was given for money received. There was no mention of love. Thus was the *mortality* admitted, and Charley was grateful. All in all, his time in Washington (it continued until April of 1865) was pleasurable beyond anything he reasonably could have anticipated. He was surviving this war. He was learning from it. He was tilling the good earth that would bear some day his greatness. And of course the fact of the death of his old *friend* George Peters helped matters a good deal. Good old George, the seeker of a Deed, had been killed in the battle of Fredericksburg back in December of '62, and glory, glory, hallelujah, such a blessing. Good old George had led a charge up a hill at the banks of the Rappahannock River. A rebel bullet had hit him smackdab in the face. It had taken away his face; it had rendered him most heroically dead, and glory, glory, hallelujah indeed. Word of his death reached Titusville shortly before Christmas. Charley paid an epic visit to Bagwell's Saloon. He spent more than fifty dollars on drinks for one & all. That Fredericksburg battle had been a true wonder. It had been without question the worst defeat the Union had suffered in all the war. Poor old Muttonchop Burnside had made a perfect botch of it. He had insisted on sending division after division in a series of foredoomed attacks against Lee's army, which was aligned across a ridge. Naturally the attacks had failed, and naturally Burnside's losses had been huge, and ah the poor heroes, the poor dead and maimed fools. Now they were either wormy jelly in their graves or broken puling invalids, and Charley Wells still was taking nourishment, thank you kindly, and just exactly what had the heroes proved? Ah, if it weren't so foolish, it almost would be tragic. Oh well, better the dead and maimed heroes than a dead or maimed Charley Wells. Better anyone. Better the world. Among the maimed, perhaps the most notable was Colonel Dick Harris. The Fredericksburg fight surely had done a good job of work on *him*. Colonel Dick Harris, a damned imbecile if there ever was one, had rejoined the 198th Indiana shortly before the Fredericksburg fight. He had promised to do this, and so he did do it, even though his broken ankle still was in a cast. The day after

George Peters was killed, Colonel Dick Harris rode at the head of the 198th Indiana as it advanced toward the rebels on that damn ridge. He had been a coward at Antietam, and he did not want to be a coward again, and so he rode at the head of his troops. And the inevitable came to pass. His horse was shot out from under him. He was thrown to the ground, and the dead horse fell on his legs, crushing them, snapping them like sticks. The fall also opened a great lateral gash across his face. He was more dead than alive when he was dragged from the field, and no wonder. He was removed to a hospital near Baltimore, and a few weeks later he was invalided out of the army. Now he was back home in Titusville, and, according to a letter Charley received from Morton C. Hightower, he was being treated with *respect if not downright adulation by the people of this town. They do not choose to remember his cowardice at Antietam. He is never absent from patriotic rallies, & apparently his scarred face & twisted legs serve him as a kind of shield of Honor. I am at a loss to give a reasonable explanation of their curious conduct. But then I make no claim to understand the emotions engendered by a war. All I can do is note & report.* And, after reading this letter from Morton C. Hightower, all *Charley* could do was shake his head. He never would understand. Never. Why was it so important that a man be measured in terms of how badly or how well he behaved in a contest that proved nothing beyond the unalterable fact that a human being was no match whatever for miniéballs and canister and chain shot and grape? Flesh was terribly vulnerable, and *torn* flesh *hurt*, and these were truths to which even *children* were privy, and what was it about a hero, a seeker of a Deed, that made him so hideously stupid? And why the respect, if not downright adulation, that invariably greeted him from a bemused civilian populace? For the God's sake anyway. Hell with it. Hell with all heroes. Hell with all lovers of heroes. There was no understanding their lunacy, and anyway, Charley had better things to occupy his attention. *Washington:* this great rude flatulent city was more than enough to take his mind off the imponderables of heroism. *Washington:* the Stars & Stripes flapped and curled at every streetcorner, and every streetcorner was Babylon, and every streetcorner was a place where convened mud and whores and cigar butts and parasols and the hobbling wounded. *Washington:* Charley Wells was a country boy and hadn't been particularly anxious to leave his home town, but now all that was changed. He had his work, and it was marvelously devious and corrupt, and he had whores enough to astound an Arabian prince, and he had poker games, and he had an embarrassment of saloons and tap rooms in which to share stories and rumors with the tophatted scoundrels who had, with the outbreak of the war, invaded the city like vermin invading a heap of fresh warm garbage, men who dealt in goods and services that promised quick and usurious profit, men whose salivary glands reacted promptly to the slightest clink of gold dollars, the most surreptitiously dry rub and slap of greenbacks. Ah, such a splendid life it was, and Charley didn't care if it never ended. It was no life for heroes, but it surely was a life for Charley Wells, and the odor of all the fresh warm garbage offended him not a stitch. There were worse odors. As, for example, the odor of dead heroes. *Washington:* Horse mess. Official capital wifedom, all puffy and pink in the swish and whisper of its new gowns. Elegant ladies, girdled and glittering, riding in trim little gigs. Clerks carrying their lunches in paper sacks. Drunkards. Checkered vests. Narrow hats. Bartenders, vast and dewlapped. Sniggers. Spittoons. The clank and grunt and pound of dusty regiments marching down Pennsylvania Avenue. Joe Hooker riding a white horse. Poor Joe Hooker, a good Democrat and not a bad general, even though his nerve did fail in front of Lee in May of '63 at the Chancellorsville crossroads down in Virginia not far from Fredericksburg (it was said Hooker had been dazed from a blow to the head rendered by a falling pillar that had given way on his headquarters verandah at the height of the battle; this may have had something to do with his failure of nerve); Joe Hooker, who was fired from his job after the Chancellorsville debacle, whose place at the command of the Army of the Potomac was taken by a sourfaced individual named George Gordon Meade just before a great battle was fought near a little Pennsylvania town called Gettysburg. *Lee had invaded the North!* Great God almighty, what a calamity this black Republican war had become. Could anyone deny this? Charley discussed the situation with Lansing H. Ingraham, and the Congressman speculated on the possibility of a coup. He spoke of a little general whose name was George B. McClellan. This fellow had twice commanded the Army of the Potomac, but his excessive caution had caused President Lincoln to remove him both times. But McClellan was extremely popular with the troops, as was Joe Hooker. Really, said Lansing H. Ingraham, there is an excellent chance for a coup. Needless to say, the prospect delights me. Both McClellan and Hooker are Democrats, and they surely have reason to hate that hapless booby in the White House. I am told there are any number of divisions that would follow McClellan and Hooker anywhere, even in an attack on the government. Lincoln never should have fired McClellan the second time. But, once having done *that,* he *surely* never should have fired *Hooker,* especially on the eve of such a large battle as this Gettysburg affair evidently is. Oh, I know, there are those who say Hooker has welcomed his dismissal. They say he has no stomach for meeting Lee again. But I find that hard to believe. I *know* Joe Hooker. He is a braggart and

a bully, and I can't say as I approve of his practice of importing prostitutes for his officers, but he *does* fight, and I cannot feature him shrinking
back from a second confrontation with Lee—especially after the first one,
that Chancellorsville business, went so badly. He is not the sort of man
to eschew the opportunity for revenge. Ah well, perhaps from *our* stand-
point Lincoln's troubles with his generals are the best possible news. A
presidential year is coming, and I feel we have an excellent chance of
defeating him if our candidate is strong and our canvass vigorous. A
coup, on the other hand, would be messy and might just make Lincoln
a martyr. In any case, he has made a severe error in firing McClellan
and then Hooker. Both are Democrats, and thus the firings smack of
politics, and next year we surely should be able to make capital of the
situation. Provided, of course, the war continues to go badly for our dear
friends in the other party. Here Lansing H. Ingraham chuckled. Ah
yes, he said, the poor fellows. My compassion for them is profound.
Charley laughed. I just expect *so*, he said. He and Lansing H. Ingraham
repaired to the nearest saloon. Grinning, they drank a discreet toast to
the impending federal defeat at that place called Gettysburg. But there
was no defeat. The fight didn't turn out at all the way Lansing H. Ingraham had expected. Meade, the sourface, pushed back Lee's army after
three days of the most severe fighting of the war. And, almost simultaneously, the Mississippi town of Vicksburg capitulated to Union forces commanded by a notorious inebriate named U. S. Grant. It had been a long
and dismal campaign for this Grant, but he had prevailed, and now the
Mississippi River was totally under federal control, and the Confederacy
had been effectively split in half. For all intents and purposes, Arkansas,
Louisiana and Texas had been amputated from the rest of the rebel nation. A week or so after these two rather surprising developments, Lansing
H. Ingraham delivered a mournful prediction. Gone now was his optimism, his talk of a Democratic election victory in '64. If the war continues
in this distressing manner, he told Charley, we can forget all about '64.
We won't be able to dislodge Lincoln from the White House unless we
employ explosives. The South may have only six months more, perhaps
a year. She has been sundered, and her manpower has been drained
bloodless, and she does not have the industrial capacity to conduct an
indefinite war. I very much fear the Republicans have done well by this
conflict of theirs. If I am correct, the Democratic party must prepare itself
to endure a substantial ordeal. These are grim words, I know, especially
in view of my optimistic pronouncements of only a few days ago, but
facts are facts, and nothing is to be gained by hiding from them.

Except for the fact that the South survived longer than he had anticipated, Lansing H. Ingraham was quite accurate as a prognosticator.

In '64, after a rancorous convention that was badly divided over the issue
of whether the war should be supported, the Democrats nominated the
little general, George B. McClellan, the twice unfrocked commander of
the Army of the Potomac, as their Presidential candidate. The McClellan canvass harped on one major contention—namely, George B. McClellan could oversee the conduct of the war more successfully than Lincoln.
A year or two earlier, this contention might have had some merit. But
'64 was too late for George B. McClellan. The man has no chance whatever, Lansing H. Ingraham told Charley, and so we'll not fret ourselves
about him. I have my own canvass to attend to. It will be work enough.
Charley accompanied the Congressman to his southern Illinois district
and helped him with his canvass for reelection. The men in this district
were mostly coalminers and operators of small farms. The majority of
them were transplanted Southrons, and nearly every town had an active
chapter of the Knights of the Golden Circle. In Illinois, this part of the
state was known as Egypt, and only the mines prevented it from being
one of the most impoverished areas in the nation. The war, and the demand for coal, had brought a sort of prosperity to Egypt, but this prosperity had in no way dimmed the place's enthusiasm for all things
Confederate. Charley never had seen coal mines. After visiting Egypt,
he decided he'd not missed a great deal. For one thing, they stank. For
another, they were so damp they made the bones ache. Accompanying
Lansing H. Ingraham, Charley went down into the mines. He always
came out filthy. So did Lansing H. Ingraham, but the Congressman apparently was enjoying himself hugely. Whether I *do* enjoy myself is not
germane, he told Charley. The point is: I must *appear* to. These miners
represent too many votes. I must not permit myself to appear too high and
mighty to enter the mines and go down where the filth is. If I allowed
that idea to run unchecked, these people would turn me out of office in less
time than it takes a grasshopper to spit. Lansing H. Ingraham was extremely enthusiastic about the future of coalmining. The steam locomotive
is converting to coal, he told Charley. The steel industry also needs coal.
And more and more coal will be required for the heating of homes. The
mining business offers excellent prospects for a man who seeks to become
rich. Excellent. When the war ends, new cities will spring up in no time.
They will demand coal by the millions of tons. And think of the West.
As soon as the Southrons surrender, our next order of business will be
the final defeat of the Indians, a consummation that should be achieved
within, oh, ten or fifteen years. Once this is done, the West will be
inundated with immigrants. And they will proliferate. And they will build.
And coal will be needed, coal to make the steel that will go into their
plows, coal to operate the steam trains that will carry their goods to mar-

ket, coal to heat their stoves, coal, coal, coal, world without end. Ah, I
tell you: if anyone asks you to invest in a coal mine, don't hesitate. Find
the money somehow. Charley supposed there was some merit to Lansing
H. Ingraham's enthusiastic talk about coal, but he was damned if he
cared an awful lot. As far as he was concerned, the mining of coal was
a dreary affair, and the mining towns just about made him sick. His
mind catalogued Egypt, and it saw nothing good. Tipples, for the God's
sake. Slag heaps. Coalgas. Railroad tracks. Foulsmelling mules pulling
immense groaning wagons. Buildings that leaned with the prevailing
winds. The slap and clatter of loose boards. All the miners appeared to
have dust in their eyes and noses. They forever blinked. They forever
breathed through open mouths. They talked in accents of Tennessee and
Kentucky and Arkansas and Alabama, and Charley was barely able to
understand what they were saying. Their speech seemed to consist of
nothing but vowels. Charley walked the dank Egyptian streets with Lansing H. Ingraham, and everywhere they went the Congressman laid on
hands and addressed people by their Christian names, and the beer flowed
mightily when Lansing H. Ingraham visited the Egyptian saloons and
asked the patrons of said Egyptian saloons to do him the ineffable honor
of voting for him; Charley and the Congressman waded through sawdust
and gobs of spent chawtobacco; they breathed the yellow fumes of stale
beer and overripe eggs; they went clattering off into the gray backcountry;
they stumbled across cornfields and passed the time of day with lean and
tattered farmers who chewed and stared, chewed and nodded, chewed
and scratched themselves; they beat the bushes of the Congressman's district with dedication and zeal, and always Lansing H. Ingraham smiled,
always he was the compleat canvasser. Charley, who thought he knew
something about smiling *and* canvassing, was astounded. When it came
time to participate in the almighty hunt for votes, Lansing H. Ingraham
was absolutely without weariness. In Washington, Lansing H. Ingraham
was considered to be rather chilly. But back home in his district he was
the great handshaker and backslapper of the North American continent.
Ah yes, he told Charley one morning, on occasion I just about pull my
lips out of shape from all the grinning. But you must remember it all is
in a good cause. The name of that good cause is Lansing Horatio
Ingraham. This is a delicate canvass, my friend. If I seek to perpetuate
myself in office (and *that* of course is the ultimate goal of all elected
officials, or at least those that have their wits about them), I must move
carefully. You note, I trust, that I am discussing no issues. I am simply
addressing people by their Christian names and bestowing on them my
worldrenowned smile. This is a year I can ill afford to become involved
in controversy. Elsewhere in the state, Union sentiment is at a flood. *Here,*

however, the KGC rules the roost. And so I am betwixt and between, especially when one takes into account my ambition to be a member of the United States Senate. The Democratic party in this state includes many influential Unionists. Without their support, I cannot ever be a Senator. So perforce I am keeping my mouth shut about my sympathies. At the same time, however, I must get myself reelected to the Congress from a district that is as Copperhead as any in the nation. So I can say nothing. I smile. I shake hands. I buy beer. I visit. I trust you apprehend my dilemma. Upstate, I am suspect because allegations have been made that I am a Copperhead. Heh. Yes. Allegations. On the other hand, there are those down here who say I am not loud enough in my denunciation of the war. Hah, if I were to say *a single word* in favor of the war to these constituents of mine, it would be tantamount to pressing a pistol to my temple. In the past three years the KGC chapter *in my home county alone* has been responsible for at least sixteen murders. These killings have included seven members of one family. *Seven.* A man, his wife, their three sons, their two daughters. The man and the three boys had committed the heinous crime of enlisting in the army. The recruiters had been in the county seat for three weeks, and not a soul had stepped forward. Then one day Henry Quade and his sons got up their courage. The youngest of the sons was just sixteen. They went to the courthouse and saw the recruiters and signed the papers and were sworn in. They were to leave for St Louis the next day, but that night Henry Quade and all his family were shotgunned to death. And their home was burned to the ground. They were buried in sacks, all seven of them. They had no funeral. There was not a preacher man enough to step forward and say the words. Not a one. Three county commissioners rode with the raiders, and so did the sheriff. Needless to say, there were no more enlistments. And then, a year or so later, when the draft registrars came to my county, two of them were chased buck naked down to the river, where they had to run for their lives. It finally required the presence of a company of militia before order was restored in the county seat so that the registration could proceed. And this wasn't the *draft,* mind you; it simply was the *registration.* So, as you perhaps can deduce, I try to be as noncontroversial as possible. I do not delude myself. No one ever will mistake me for a statesman, and I have no ambitions to be a towering historical figure. I have always attempted to keep my purposes in line with my abilities. I admit I would by no means be an outstanding Senator. But, on the other hand, I would not be a poor one. I do have some decent impulses. Perhaps they have not as yet penetrated your awareness, but they do exist; take my word for it. Ah, but come, first things first. I must get myself reelected. Let us be about. There are hands to be shaken, grins to be exchanged. The sun hangs high and warm. The morn is clear. Onward.

Lincoln had no trouble defeating McClellan, but at the same time Lansing H. Ingraham won reelection by 4,902 votes to 1,128 for his black Republican opponent. Charley spent the election night with the Congressman in the Illinois town that had seen the beginnings of that distinguished legislator. Lansing H. Ingraham's plump wife, Undine, and three of their six homely daughters also were present on this gala occasion. A good deal of wine was consumed, and the Ingrahams' youngest daughter, Betty, was seized with a fit of giggling. This Betty was just twenty, and she was immensely infatuated with Charley. She was fond of batting her eyes. She had no chest. Her mother took her upstairs to bed. The Ingrahams' home—or home away from their Washington home, as the Congressman called it—was a huge drafty place that had been built in 1822. It had seen three additions, and it had at best count nine bedrooms. A clutch of Ingraham cousins now lived in the place, but every two years they made room for the Ingrahams when they came back for the canvass. Charley had an attic room that was across a narrow hallway from the one occupied by the smitten Betty. Sniggering and snuffling, she visited him that night. She wore a pink nightgown. When he lifted it, he discovered she had by God absolutely no tiddies whatever. She snuggled and threshed, and her breath was warm, and she fell asleep before anything of a carnal nature took place. Grinning, Charley carried her back to her room. He was grateful he had not been called upon to perform on poor skinny little Betty. There were already more than enough complications in his life. He grinned himself to sleep, and the next morning he received a telegram from Wendell Archer Doggett: *Do you know a man named Tobias G. Frye? He is dying and wants to speak with you. He says to tell you it has to do with a Rev and Mrs Weeks. He says you will understand.*

And Charley did understand—or at least partly. Here were, as he knew them, the details of the infamous Weeks-Frye affair, a wretched piece of business that was acknowledged by one & all to be quite the most succulent scandal ever to have been visited upon Titusville:

The first part had been supplied to Charley by Prof Tobias G. Frye, PhD (Harvard), himself. From 1853 through 1860 the Professor and Mrs Sara Weeks were lovers. Her husband, the Rev Abner D. Weeks, a thin little man with a tic, had not (according to what Mrs Weeks told the Professor) exercised his husbandly perquisites since their wedding night. He called her his Beloved Sister, and they spent most of their leisure hours engaged in the reading of Scripture. From time to time, using various feminine stratagems, she had attempted to make the Rev Mr Weeks

perform in a manly fashion, but he had sternly—and successfully—resisted her. He told her she did not know what she was doing; he told her
she was being betrayed by her flesh; he told her she was the Devil's agent.
On at least one occasion he beat her when she attempted to lure him
into her bed. All the foregoing information had been relayed to Charley
by the Professor. The remaining details, beginning with the suicide of
Mrs Weeks, were more or less public knowledge. One spring afternoon
in 1860 a man named Harvey Ewald was passing by the Presbyterian parsonage when he heard wild laughter coming from within the place. A
moment or so later, Mrs Weeks ran out onto the front stoop. She ran
back and forth, and she was flapping her arms, and her wrists were bleeding, and she was absolutely bone naked. Poor old Harvey Ewald, who
was something of a drinking man and neerdowell, just about fell over
dead on the spot. He hurried to the stoop and stared at Mrs Weeks. Hers
had been the wild laughter. It still came from her throat. She flapped,
twitched, leaned against the front of the house. She was a skinny blond
woman. Too skinny for Harvey Ewald's taste, he later told his cronies
when they filled him full of whisky in Bagwell's Saloon. You could see
the bones where her ribs was, said Harvey Ewald, and damn me for eternity
if you couldn't. Well, at any rate, Harvey Ewald stood there and stared
at Mrs Weeks for some time. Then she walked to him and said one word.
That word was: *Toby?* Then, without saying anything else, she fell in
a faint. During all this, there was no sign of the Rev Mr Weeks. Harvey
Ewald went running for a doctor. Ten minutes later, a Dr Findley was
ministering to Mrs Weeks there on the stoop. She blinked, looked up at
Dr Findley (and Harvey Ewald, who was staring at her over the doctor's
shoulder) and said, quite calmly: Go fuck yourselves. (Later, both Dr
Findley and Harvey Ewald took their solemn oath that they were neither
hard of hearing nor so insanely imaginative as to have concocted the
obscene quotation.) After Mrs Weeks' wounds were bandaged, she was
carried into the house by Dr Findley and Harvey Ewald. Then they
searched the house for the Rev Mr Weeks. For all they knew, Mrs Weeks
had murdered him. After all, what other explanation was there for her
attempted suicide? But the Rev Mr Weeks had not been murdered. Dr
Findley and Harvey Ewald found him upstairs in his bedroom. He was
unharmed. He was sitting on the edge of the bed. He said nothing. His
tic was not functioning. His razor lay in a filled washbasin on his dresser.
The razor was bloody. So was the washbasin. So was the dresser. So was
the wall behind the dresser. Apparently Mrs Weeks had slashed herself
right there in front of her husband. This was the only reasonable explanation. The Rev Mr Weeks never did relate the exact details, which
probably was just as well. The town applauded him for his discretion.

And the details never were learned. Nine months later, *he* also was dead, murdered most foully, and the details went with him. But, on that spring morning, he was not a bit dead, and Dr Findley and Harvey Ewald were grateful that they had been spared further horror. They shouted at the Rev Mr Weeks, asked him whether he heard them. He nodded. He said nothing, but he did nod. His eyes were large and dry. They were very dark eyes, and their dryness made them dull, and they did not remember to blink. Well, said Dr Findley to Harvey Ewald, there's nothing we can do for him right now. Let's get back downstairs. Mrs Weeks lay on the sofa in the parlor. Dr Findley and Harvey Ewald had stretched her out; her body was pale; she was dead. Shreds from the doctor's bandages were lodged between her teeth. She had bitten loose the bandages from her wrists, and she had bled to death, and the rug was covered with spots and smears and curls of blood. Over the mantel was a sampler that said: GOD IS GOOD. Charley was in the large crowd that attended the funeral and the graveside services. The Professor also was there, but he said nothing to Charley, and Charley said nothing to him. A visiting preacher, a Rev Mr Gassaway from Evansville, presided. The bereaved Rev Mr Weeks was silent throughout the funeral and the graveside services. His tic was not functioning. His adamsapple occasionally wobbled and danced, but otherwise he showed not a thing. The Professor, however, was not so successful at restraining himself. Just as the coffin was about to be lowered into the ground, the Professor rushed forward and seized the Rev Mr Weeks by the lapels. *Do you feel better now?* screamed the Professor. *Is everything all right? How can you stand there and not be ill?* Then the Professor began hitting and kicking the Rev Mr Weeks. The Professor was weeping. Three men jumped on him and pulled him away. The Rev Mr Weeks' face remained bland, calm. This incident took place near the middle of June, about a week after Charley had delivered the first of his beer keg orations for the Democracy. What with the canvass, he did not see the Professor as often as he would have liked. In point of fact, he did not learn of the Professor's disappearance (and the simultaneous end of the Southern Indiana Eclectic Institute) until a few days after it had taken place. The canvass also kept Charley from paying any particular attention to the activities of the widowed Rev Mr Weeks. But the rest of the town did, and the good parson's rather peculiar behavior was duly reported to Charley by various friends and acquaintances. Within a disgracefully short span of time after his wife's death, the Rev Mr Weeks had begun sparking various girls and women of the town. And he was often seen to laugh. He escorted the various girls and women to socials and suppers; he took them buggyriding; he picnicked with them down by the river. The talk was that the Rev Mr Weeks was a fast

man with a warm hand. It was talk that Charley had a great deal of
trouble believing. He remembered what the Professor had told him. It
didn't seem possible that a man who'd treated his wife as his Beloved
Sister could be so quickly transmogrified into something more nearly resembling a man. Still, the fellow *was* sparking the girls and women, and
Charley knew of only one reason why girls and women were sparked.
Ah well, the devil take it. Charley had his canvass to worry about. The
Rev Mr Weeks' business was his own. But then, in the fall of that year
of 1860, the Rev Mr Weeks turned his attentions to just one female, the
very young and wellformed Widow Grimes, *née* Charlotte Quimby,
younger sister of Nancy. This development revived Charley's interest in
the Rev Mr Weeks. At the very least, he admired the fellow's taste. Since
the death of her elderly husband, Charlotte Quimby Grimes had been
courted by a number of men, but she'd shown no permanent interest in
any of them. If it hadn't been for the damn canvass, Charley himself
probably would have come sucking around her dooryard that summer. It
was, after all, the summer her sister Nancy married that Evansville man,
Henry Ferris. But the canvass kept him too busy. Then, when the election
was over and he had all the time anyone would have wanted, Charlotte
Quimby Grimes was unavailable to him. She was seeing the Rev Mr
Weeks and the Rev Mr Weeks *only*. They made a strange couple, the
Widow Grimes and the Rev Mr Weeks. She was a head taller than he,
and she probably outweighed him by ten or fifteen pounds. No one ever
had accused Charlotte Quimby Grimes of being inconspicuous, and at
twenty her proportions were splendidly firm. But, on the other hand, they
were not rigid. A distinction had to be made. Rump and bosom, hip and
thigh: flesh and warmth. Ah, she truly was something, and Charley just
had to be envious of the Rev Mr Weeks. No young man in proper possession of his faculties *wouldn't* have been. Rump and bosom, hip and thigh:
flesh and warmth: a full mouth, pouty: wild thick hair dark and stormy:
the girl was a blessing and a vision, and the Rev Mr Weeks was acknowledged (by Charley, at least) to be a very lucky man indeed. But
then one night in January of 1861 the Rev Mr Weeks' good fortune took
abrupt flight. He was murdered. To be specific, he was strangled. The
body was found by none other than poor Harvey Ewald. The Rev Mr
Weeks' tongue was blue. It protruded. His eyeballs had rolled up out of
sight. He wore not a stitch. The body was found at the edge of the river,
a little downstream from the wharf and Bagwell's Saloon. The night
had been extremely cold, and when Harvey Ewald found the body early
the following morning, it was frozen to the earth. Sheriff Ben Stork had
to use a shovel to pry it loose. After seeing to the removal of the corpse,
the sheriff went to the parsonage. The Rev Mr Weeks' clothing was strewn

across the bedroom floor, but otherwise nothing in the house had been disturbed. The sampler that said GOD IS GOOD still hung over the mantel. The sheriff decided that perhaps the Widow Grimes could shed some light on what had happened. He and Dr Findley called at her home. They found her crouched behind the stove in her kitchen. She was weeping and moaning. She was unable to form words. Apparently something had driven her out of her mind. She never was able to reveal what it had been. Her parents moved into her home that afternoon. They put her to bed. She subsided. Never again did she weep or moan. She simply lay there. She could do nothing for herself. Her parents fed her and changed her as though she were an infant. The following spring, Nancy and her husband Henry Ferris came for Charlotte. They took her back with them to the Ferris farm near Evansville. And that was the end of the story, as far as anyone in Titusville knew it. Of course there was one person who probably knew a large sight more, and of course that one person was Prof Tobias G. Frye, PhD (Harvard). The consensus was that the Professor had sneaked back into town that night. The consensus was that he had strangled the Rev Mr Weeks in full view of the Widow Grimes, thus destroying her mind. The consensus was that he had carried the nude corpse to that place by the river, perhaps in an attempt to humiliate the Rev Mr Weeks as thoroughly as Mrs Weeks had been humiliated. In any case, Sheriff Ben Stork was convinced that the Professor had murdered the Rev Mr Weeks. A warrant was issued for the Professor's arrest. Circulars were mailed. But the Professor never was found, and the murder of the Rev Mr Weeks still was officially listed as unsolved. Those were the details of the Weeks-Frye affair as Charley knew them. He assumed that the Professor would be able to clear up the unanswered questions. The assumption was correct. The answers, however, were not those he had anticipated.

Lansing H. Ingraham, jubilant from his overwhelming victory at the polls, was sympathetic when Charley showed him the telegram from Wendell Archer Doggett. I once knew this man very well, said Charley. If it is all right with you, sir, I should like to return to Washington by the first train. Lansing H. Ingraham nodded. Of course, he said, go and be quick about it. Charley thanked the Congressman, then went upstairs and packed his grip. He bumped into Betty in the hall. She was pale. She said nothing to him. Her hair was uncombed. Smiling, Charley took his leave of the Ingrahams, caught the first train east. He telegraphed ahead to Wendell Archer Doggett, who was waiting for him at the B&O depot in Washington. Charley was very tired, and his mouth felt gritty, but he wanted to see the Professor immediately. He asked Wendell Archer the name of the hospital. He is in no hospital, said Wendell Archer Doggett.

He is at the Nonpareil. He refuses to go to a hospital. He says he wants
to die in a whorehouse. He says it is most appropriate that he die in a
whorehouse. Charley nodded, chuckled a little. That surely does sound
like him, he said. Wendell Archer Doggett helped him with his grip. They
left the depot and hailed a carriage. Inside the carriage, Wendell
Archer Doggett said: It is his heart. I have had physicians in to see him.
They say he could Go at any time. He must lie very still. He looks dreadful. Said Charley: Have you known him long? Said Wendell Archer
Doggett: Nearly twenty years. He came to the Nonpareil as a client shortly
after I opened the place. He stayed one night to play poker. The damned
rascal just about cleaned me out. Damned old rip. Said Charley: How did
he ever find out I was living there? Said Wendell Archer Doggett: Well, it
happened after his attack. He heard I think it was Gertrude mention
your name. He asked her if this particular Charley Wells was from a
little Indiana town called Titusville. When she told him yes, he asked her
for God's sake to have me get in touch with you. So I did. And here you
are. And he still is alive. But we don't know for how long. Said Charley:
How did he have the attack? Wendell Archer Doggett smiled. He cleared
his throat, studied his hands. Ah, he said, wellnow, he was, uh, well, to be
candid, he was in the act of mounting little Dorcas Pfaff. Said Charley:
What? Said Wendell Archer Doggett: You know little Dorcas? Said
Charley: Of course I know her. Redhaired girl. Very firm tiddies. Lost her
husband at Antietam. Said Wendell Archer Doggett: Well, I guess you
do know her. Heh. Well, at any rate, our friend the Professor had just,
uh, begun his labors, so to speak, when his heart acted up on him. The
poor girl. As you can imagine, she just about had a fit. We left him in her
bed. He has lain there ever since. I visit him three or four times a day.
We talk about the old times. He is quite cheerful. He knows the end is
near. I was the one who told him. I know him. I know he would not have
taken kindly to lies. I have no idea why he is so anxious to see you. He
refuses to discuss it with me. Does it have something to do with that home
town of yours? Charley nodded. Yes, he said, it does. Then Charley told
Wendell Archer Doggett the story of the Weeks-Frye affair. When the
recitation was done, Wendell Archer Doggett made a kissing sound. The
carriage clattered, and the great city roared, and Wendell Archer Doggett followed the kissing sound with a solemn shake of his head. I see,
he said. My God. I surely do.

Prof Frye's face was purplish in the light from the fancy whorehouse
lamp on the table beside his bed. The skin around his eyes was puffy, and
he appeared very old, a great deal older than Charley had remembered
him. He wore a green nightshirt, and he was reading a copy of Harper's
Weekly. Skin hung from his neck in immense folds and flaps. He was

wearing eyeglasses. He had pushed them to the end of his nose, which now abounded with broken bloodvessels. Charley did not remember the broken bloodvessels. He supposed they were new. The Professor grinned at him and laid aside the magazine. Welcome, young Mr Wells, he said. Welcome to the bedside of the dying Falstaff.

Charley laughed, went to the Professor and pumped his hand. Ah now, said Charley, the dying Falstaff my ass. All you want to do is laze about a whorehouse and be waited on hand and foot like some goddamn sultan.

Ah, said the Professor, you dissembler you.

Charley pulled a chair to the side of the bed and sat down. Now, he said, what's all this sheep dip about your heart?

I am dying.

Now, now, that's a lot of—

Please, there's no need to dissemble. I know you mean well, but there's no *need*. I know what is happening and I accept it. I await my Creator in perfect serenity. I am in a whorehouse. Which means I am amid familiar surroundings. Which means I am at peace. My seizure came to me as I was joyously fucking a marvelous young woman who has the miraculous name of Dorcas Pfaff. I have coined a small alliterative aphorism for the occasion. It goes like this: *A Frye dare not fuck a Pfaff. For, if a Frye fuck a Pfaff, a fatal failure follows.*

Oh Jesus, said Charley, rolling his eyes.

Now, now. Please. Let's not include *Him* in this conversation. I rather suspect He might blush. And anyway, I have no desire to antagonize Him at *this* point.

You old bastard.

Yes. Yes indeed. Excellently put. Now then, how have you been?

All right. Very busy, but I like my work, and I like this city.

Yes. I imagine you would. My friend with the trinity of names, Mr Wendell Archer Doggett, Esquire, whoremaster, rip, swindler, carnal degenerate, tells me you are still in politics and still espousing the Democracy.

That's right.

Do you want to hear about the murder now, or shall we delay matters further by manufacturing more of this witless small talk?

Charley grinned. If you want to talk about the murder, he said, talk away.

Good. I need to get it all out.

Do you feel up to it?

The Professor snorted. He removed his spectacles, cleaned them with the corner of a sheet. Then, after replacing the spectacles at the end of his nose, he said: *Yes.* I feel up to it. And please stop staring at me as though what is happening is some sort of great volcanic tragedy. It is not.

So get that stricken expression off your face. My death will be trivial. I
am no martyr; I am no great man; the only sacrifices I've ever made have
been to my own selfindulgence, and if that is a contradiction, make the
most of it. But for God's sake please do not endow my leavetaking with
any nobility. I have all the nobility of a burlap bag full of jackass vomit.

Yessir. Whatever you say. Jackass vomit. Yessir.

Ah. That's more like it. Now, as to the murder. Contrary to popular
belief, I did not kill the Rev Mr Weeks. However, I do know who did. It
was a young woman. Her maiden name was Charlotte Quimby. I do not
recall her married name.

Grimes, said Charley. He tried to keep his voice even. He leaned forward.

Yes. Grimes. That's the name.

Charley placed his hands on his knees. He was very warm. The lamp
spat. I don't believe you, he said.

I didn't think you would. But you will.

Oh?

Yes. Not that I didn't *want* to kill the Rev Mr Weeks. I most assuredly
did, and I had stolen back into Titusville that night to do precisely that.
But I was deprived of that great privilege. By this Quimby girl. What did
you say her married name is?

Grimes.

Grimes. Yes. Well. Let me explain. Let me outline for you my activities
since I left Titusville back in '60 after my Sara died.

Take your time, said Charley.

Don't worry. *Please.* Let me get it *out.*

All right.

I had about fifty dollars when I went away from Titusville. My first
stop was Columbus, Ohio, where I decided to go into the, uh, apothe-
cary business. I purchased some twenty dollars' worth of various ingredients, including cod liver oil, sugar, cinnamon and sassafras. I rented a
room in a disreputable hotel (a hostelry even more disreputable than this
one, I might add), and then I hired a nigger to fetch me several tubs of
hot water. I mixed the cod liver oil, the sugar, the cinnamon and the
sassafras into the hot water. Then, after straining the mixture and allowing it to cool, I funneled my noxious nostrum into several dozen pint
bottles I had just purchased. I subsequently visited a printer and had
labels made. I called my concoction Dr Boyle's Stomach Purgative &
Bowel Cleanser. After affixing the printed labels to the bottles, I took up
a position on a nearby street corner. I took with me a box of the bottles. I
began to speak. A crowd gathered. Within half an hour I had sold more

than three dozen of the bottles at one dollar each, thus recouping my original investment and leaving myself with a substantial profit, considering the expenditure. In all, before the Columbus police ran me out of town, I'd made nearly a thousand dollars in clear profit and I was embarked on a career as a, God forgive me, chemist and physician. I am quite proud of the name: Dr *Boyle's* Stomach Purgative & Bowel Cleanser. Rather a good pun, if I do say so myself.

Ah, whoa. Hold on. A pun?

You clot. When one's soul is subjected to the torments of hell, it can fairly be said to Frye, is that not so? Well, it also can fairly be said to Boyle. Hence, the transmogrification of Prof Frye into Dr Boyle.

Oh, said Charley.

The Professor smiled. An apt comment, your *oh,* he said. It bespeaks volumes, nay, *libraries.* But the devil with all that. Please permit me to return to my recitation. As I was saying, I earned nearly a thousand dollars before the Columbus police were so inhospitable as to run me out of town. I proceeded east. Everywhere I went, my odious preparation coined money for me. I'll make you privy to a substantial truth, my friend. If you seek to do well in this life, it might pay you to traffick in Fear of Death. No one wants to die, and anything that promises to postpone this inevitability will be welcomed with unquestioning enthusiasm. The successful purveyor of pills, salts, syrups, emetics, cathartics and the like will have medals struck in his honor, and women will leap into his bed with the alacrity of frightened gazelles. *I* know. *Believe* me I do. My spurious pharmacology made me the toast of the sickly and the fretful, and it all was a most rare experience. I can *guarantee* you *that.* I recall this one asthmatic old bitch in Scranton who clambered into my bed and just about chewed me to death and then the next morning, while ministering over my bloodied corpus, actually *proposed marriage,* one that carried with it a dowry of something near a quarter of a million dollars. Her late husband had been in the foundry business or some such thing. It seemed that after quaffing one draught of Dr Boyle's Stomach Purgative & Bowel Cleanser the old girl had the most damply passionate carnal urges she had experienced in something like twenty years. She called me her godhead, the savior of her womanhood. She called me all sorts of things. Oh Lord, what *didn't* she call me. Well, ah, as you can see, I did not suffer from lack of womanly companionship, although I was forced to quit Scranton in a most surreptitious fashion, sneaking down my inamorata's back stairs at four in the morning and scuttling like a thief in the night to the nearest railway depot. Ah, but I found it all most amusing and stimulating, and it nearly enabled me to push away the memory of the terrible thing that had happened to my beloved Mrs Weeks. You see, I'd honestly loved that woman. Which of course was a personal catastrophe—*and* a contradiction of a belief I had held sacred for more years than I care to admit. Tell me, do you recall my talking to you of what I called my Fucking Principle?

Yes.

Well, I violated my Principle. Instead of acknowledging the *mortality* of my feelings, I was seduced by love and—faugh!—romance. My darling pale little Sara Weeks had taken possession of my ratty and tattered soul, and her death—what I then believed to be a suicide—twisted my heart out of joint, plunged me into the most degrading spasms of an astonishing grief. You remember how I lost control of myself just before she was lowered into the ground? You remember how I tried to attack her husband? Well, that sort of thing was not typical of me.

Charley nodded. I know, he said. But then along came your bowel cleanser or whatever, and you were able to recover.

Yes—but only to a certain extent. Never wholly. You see, I was able to deduce what I was reasonably certain had happened that day in the Weeks' bedroom. This may come as a surprise to you, but several weeks before her death Sara had discontinued our assignations. For years they had bothered her conscience. She was originally, you see, from Vermont, and she was the sort of person who set great store by contracts. Even though her husband was a mad zealot with testicles like dried walnuts, even though he had beaten her because she had sought to lure him into performing in a husbandly manner, *even though* and *despite* these acknowledged truths of her existence, she nonetheless was his *wife,* and the final sum and total of her guilt and her Vermont upbringing eventually made her unable to abide any further betrayals. So, even though she still professed love for me (and, God knows, *I* loved *her*), she put an end to our meetings and once again set out to restore her lunatic spouse's manhood. It mattered not to her that he called her the Devil's agent when she was engaged in such activities. All that mattered was that she was bound to him by a contract, and she would honor the contract or die in the attempt. Well, naturally, I felt I was able to visualize what had happened in their bedroom that day. She'd probably made another attempt to take him to her bed. (After all, she *was* nude.) And of course the attempt had failed. I do not know how many such attempts she had made, but apparently *that particular attempt* was one too many. It snapped her; it literally did her in. And so she seized the razor and slashed her wrists and subsequently expired. That was my theory at the time, and I saw no reason to question it.

Well, said Charley, it sounds reasonable.

Of *course* it does. And my pain was exquisite. It represented truth that could not be borne. I kept telling myself: Perhaps there was more you could have done. You are mighty persuasive. No doubt you could have talked poor Sara into running off with you. Had you done so, she still would be alive. Ah. Well. Now then, young Mr Wells, you are not insensitive. Surely you can understand how I felt. And surely you can understand that all I could do was flee. I had to put it behind me. And to a certain extent I was successful. At least my picaresque adventures as Dr Horatio U. Boyle, quack and poseur, provided a *diversion*. They enabled me to survive . . . until that night in New Haven . . .

New Haven?

Yes. New Haven. It was a night in January of '61. I was in my hotel room. I had just completed the preparation of about ten dozen fresh bottles of Dr Boyle's Stomach Purgative & Bowel Cleanser. (Incidentally, before I continue, let me tell you what happened to me the only time I *drank* some of the hideous stuff. It was in the interests, mind you, of scientific curiosity. Well, I shat for forty minutes straight. Without respite. I shat with such dedication and force that I honestly feared I was in grave danger of expelling my small intestine. I shat so diligently that I damn near fainted. When finally I was able to shit no more, I was weaker than a dying cat, and, believe me, I never again permitted that foul mixture to touch my palate. Not even when I was constipated. There is such a thing as a laxative. There also is such a thing as gunpowder. It is the wise man who does not confuse the two. Especially where Dr Boyle's Stomach Purgative & Bowel Cleanser is concerned.) But enough of my gastrointestinal misadventures. Let us return to my tale. As I said, the place was New Haven, and it was a January night. It was quite a cold night, and snow had begun to fall. Just as I was corking the last of the bottles, I heard a succession of screams and shouts. They came from the street, just outside my window. I went to the window and looked out. A woman was lying in the street. She apparently was dead. She lay in a sort of smear. I put on my hat and coat and ran down the stairs and out into the street. The woman's breast had been ripped open. A man stood over her. He held a large bloody knife. A considerable crowd had gathered, but no one ventured near the man. Snow caught at his hair. His face was unremarkable, utterly without expression. Perhaps there was a trace of a smile at the corners of his mouth, but I was not absolutely certain. Well, after a bit a constable came along. He approached the man with the knife with some caution, but the fellow was quite docile. He did not resist when the constable took the knife from him. He was led away, and he said not a word. An hour or so later I learned the whys of the incident. An hour or so after *that* it was revealed to me how much this murder had to do with my own situation, the one involving the Rev Mr Weeks and my late beloved Sara. You see, the dead woman out there in the street had been the wife of the poor wretch who had killed her with the knife. It was her *left* breast that had been ripped open. He had made a literal attempt to cut out her heart. You see, he'd believed the Devil had taken possession of her heart. I learned all this from a constable whom I encountered in the hotel tap room. I bought the man several drinks, and he gave me the entire story. God as my witness, said the constable, poor old Luke Corwin he really and truly thought Maizie's heart had been captured by the Prince of Darkness. And so he done the only thing he could of done. He went after her with that knife and tried to cut out her offending heart. Well, young Mr Wells, I was properly horrified by the constable's grisly tale, but it wasn't until later that night that I realized how profoundly it applied to *me*. I was lying in bed. I was thinking of this stranger, this Luke Corwin, this pitiable madman who had seen the Devil grinning at him from within his wife's heart. And poor Maizie, who had been in fact the Devil's agent. It was at that moment, of course, that the truth was revealed to me.

The truth? said Charley. The truth of what?

The Professor held up a hand. Please, he said, allow me to move on. As I recall, I sat up in bed and uttered a loud groan. That woman had been the Devil's agent! Her husband had removed the Devil with a knife! Great God, could not *another* husband, a lunatic preacher residing in Titusville, Indiana, have cut out the Devil with a *razor*? I remembered Sara telling me that he had accused *her* of being the Devil's agent! Oh sweet Jesus, it made such magnificent *sense!* It all—

Sh. Now. Don't holler. Your heart.

The Professor nodded. He smiled. Yes, he said. My heart.

That's it. Just settle back.

Thank you. I shall try to be calm.

Good.

All right. Now. I am calm. I shall continue. The Devil's agent. You can see, I'm sure, the sense it all made. My Sara had put an end to the assignations. Her marriage had meant *that* much to her. She was prepared to suffer as many rebukes as were necessary in order to make her husband into a man. She had suffered a great many of these in the years of her marriage to that twisted twitching zealot. So did it make any sense for her to have killed herself simply because of another rebuff? No! It made no sense at all! She had *not* killed herself! He had murdered her! That was why—

Professor. Easy. Sh.

Oh. Oh yes. All right. I shall try to suppress my agitation. But it is understandable, is it not?

I suppose so.

Suppose so? That swine had *killed* her. He had done away with what his mind saw as a vessel of Satan's will. The way he reasoned, he had done the only proper thing. He had struck down evil. He was a rock of Jehovah. And so of course *I* tried to do what *I* had to do, the only proper thing.

You went back to Titusville so you could kill him?

Yes. But I was a few minutes late. The young lady had already killed him, depriving me of the pleasure that unquestionably would have been the greatest of my raffish and seedy life.

Yes, said Charley. I can see that.

God bless you, my friend, for being so perceptive.

Now. Don't be sassy, you old fart.

Heh. Pardon me. Ah, such a free one with a jest I am. Even *now*, under *these* circumstances. It probably bespeaks a great deal about me. Ah well, it is too late to change. I shall get on with my story. There is a final chapter, and it is an eloquent study in absurdity, and perhaps you can learn something from it. As you know, I returned to Titusville. I rode the steam cars to Indianapolis, where I purchased a horse for the remainder of the trip. I could have traveled from Indianapolis to Titusville by rail, but I did not want to be at the mercy of the St Louis & Northeastern Railroad. A horse would provide me egress from Titusville at any time I chose. So I rode south from Indianapolis. I rode all day. The countryside was gray. There had been a severe killing frost the previous night. I did not stop to eat, but I did have a bottle of Irish whisky with me. I nipped at it from time to time. It kept me remarkably warm. I rode and nipped, rode and nipped, stopping only to feed and water and rest the horse, and I rode and nipped on into the night, and a brandnew razor was folded in a pocket of my waistcoat. I had personally honed that razor. It glittered. You should have seen it. Such a splendid instrument for my vengeance. You see, *I* sought to kill *him* in precisely the manner *he* had killed *Sara*. I blush to say this, but I fear my thoughts were all bound up in a cocoon of melodrama and romance, florid justice, all that sort of thing. In point of fact, I saw my killing of the Rev Mr Weeks as a . . . as a . . . well, I hesitate to say.

Go ahead.

Ah, you see, I saw it as a totally selfless act.

Oh?

The first totally selfless act of my life.

Oh, said Charley.

I have always resisted selflessness. As I have resisted love. But my Sara had brought me to love. And by killing the Rev Mr Weeks I would be brought to selflessness. I was quite drunk on the Irish whisky by the time I arrived in Titusville. It was perhaps midnight. I could see my breath. It was clouded, dank, foul. I felt my greatcoat flap in the cold black midnight wind. My horse went galloping through the north end of town, and then I slowed it to a canter. I rode to Kentucky Street and proceeded eastward toward the Presbyterian parsonage. I saw not a soul. I curled a hand around the folded razor in my pocket. Oh I felt very vengeful indeed, very selfless, and I could not wait to fulfill my bloody Purpose. I sought to get it over with as quickly as possible, then leave town with despatch. I had no intention of surrendering to the law after performing the deed. I am not, even in my most floridly vengeful moments, a martyr. And anyway, why should I have been punished for doing away with *that* cockroach? Only one light was on in the parsonage. It was in an upstairs window. I reined up, dismounted, tethered my horse to a tree. My stomach felt a bit queasy, so I leaned against the tree for a moment. I fear I had become a victim of the Irish whisky. To be perfectly candid, I damn near threw up. But a few moments later I forgot about my uneasy belly. A scream came from the parsonage. *No! No!* someone shouted. It was a woman's scream, and for an instant I thought the voice was Sara's. But that was nonsense, and I knew it was nonsense, and I told myself I was an imbecile. Then came a second scream. I rushed for the front door. The screams had come from upstairs, where the light was. I hurled myself against the front door. It flew open. I went lurching across the threshold and apparently tripped over something. At any rate, I fell on my face. In so doing, I received a fine dry mouthful of carpet. Ah, such drama. Oh yes. Wager your life on *that*. I shook my head. A large lump blossomed on my forehead. I groaned. I spat out the carpet, licked my lips, stood up. I climbed the stairs to the room where the light had been shining. As I started up the stairs, I heard the Rev Mr Weeks' idiotic falsetto voice, then two loud thumps. I opened a door. I entered what apparently was the preacher's bedroom. He was dead. He lay next to the bed. He wore no clothes. A razor was in his right hand. A girl sat in a rocker next to the bed. She was a large girl, very pretty—the Widow, uh, Grimes you said? She was naked, and she was staring at her hands. I went to where the body lay. The preacher's tongue hung out. It was clear what had happened. He had come at her with his goddamn razor. In protecting herself, somehow she had strangled him. I picked up the razor. A fleck of blood lay on the blade. I wiped away the blood, placed the razor on the dresser. The Rev Mr Weeks' clothing was scattered on the floor. I did not bother with it. I looked at the girl. She still was staring at her hands. I asked her what had happened. She did not reply. One of her wrists had a shallow cut. It then occurred to me that perhaps she'd *married* the Rev Mr Weeks. But she wore no ring, and anyway, the thought was preposterous. I shouted at her. I even went so far as to wave my arms. She did not acknowledge me. It had to be *tonight?* I said to her. Why couldn't this have happened some *other* night? I railed at her for some time, but her eyes were vacant, and I might as well not have existed. Finally I decided I had to do something for her. And, indirectly, in a most romantic way, for myself. Her clothes also were on the floor, intermingled with those of the Rev Mr Weeks. I gathered them up and assisted her into them. She did not hinder me. She did not help me either. I had to do a great lot of grunting and twisting before I finished dressing her. I have never been, heh, particularly adept at or interested in *dressing* females. Still, amateurish fumbling and all, I finally managed to clothe her. I helped her down the stairs and out of the house. She leaned against me. She did not walk very well. I knew where her home was—or at least I *thought* I did. I have reference here to the home she shared with that old fellow she'd married. At any rate, that is where I escorted her. The walk is half a mile or so, wouldn't you say?

Yes. About that.

Well, I took her around to the back door and left her sitting in the kitchen. I was very cold, but of course I was no longer drunk. I had a Purpose. It was not as highminded as the one that had brought me back to Titusville, but it was all I had remaining to me, and I was determined to bring it to fulfillment. I returned to the parsonage, slung the preacher's naked corpse over a shoulder and went back outside. I carried the body to a spot down near the river. I left it lying in mud. This was the least I could do. I mean, I *had* wanted to humiliate him the way he had humiliated Sara. So at least I derived some satisfaction from *that.*

And then you left town?

Yes. I returned to the parsonage, remounted my horse and rode off. I made my way along the river road to Evansville, where I fear I became extremely intoxicated. I remained in an almost continuous state of inebriation for about four months. Can you understand why?

I think so.

Tell me.

Charlotte had taken away your chance to do something selfless.

Correct. For the first time in my life I had sought to indulge in a romantic gesture. She had frustrated me.

But he was dead, wasn't he?

Yes. But not by *my* hand.

And that made a difference?

Of *course* it made a difference. You see, I was caught up in romance, my friend. Caught up most thoroughly. Trussed. Helpless. Your old friend George Peters, I recall that several times he spoke to me of what he called a Deed. A declaration of existence, so to speak. I scoffed at him. I still do. But, for that one night, I too sought the accomplishment of a Deed. The romance had taken possession of my sense. And of course we both know romance is madness. Of all the persons I have encountered in my picaresque peregrinations, *you* perhaps understand the madness better than anyone.

Me? said Charley. Why me?

Because you never will put aside, even for a moment, your awareness of the *mortality* of romance. When I spoke to you of that mortality, I found a most receptive pupil. You were quick to grasp the uses of reality.

But you haven't seen me in more than four years.

Doesn't matter. Your political activities showed me what you are.

But how do you know I haven't changed?

You wouldn't change. You're too intelligent.

Professor, that's not fair. I ran for the legislature twice as a Democrat. If I were so goddamn . . . uh . . . *realistic,* how come I didn't go over to the Republicans?

You were taking an intelligent risk. Suppose the war had gone badly. You would have been in a very fine position for gain.

You're saying I don't really believe in much of anything?

Precisely. Which is why I had our friend Wendell Archer Doggett send you the telegram. I had to see you. I had to tell you my story.

Why?

So you could learn what happens when a realist is seduced by romance. I've said it before and I'll say it again: God *damn* romance. I don't want you to slide backward, young Mr Wells. You understand the truth of mortality. I don't want you to lose that understanding. I had to reiterate that truth to you before I died. You can be great, but you have to keep the reality uppermost in that devious mind of yours. Now then, do you understand how stupid and wasteful it is to give a damn?

Yes.

Will you ever give a damn?

Not if I can help it.

Be kindly. Even be generous, if you can. But never give a damn.

All right.

Do you promise never to give a damn?

I do. For whatever my promise is worth.

The Professor chuckled. Ah, he said, yes indeed.

Why is all this so important to you?

My boy, I must justify.

Justify?

Yes. The rules of conduct that—with just that one exception—I have always obeyed. The Fucking Principle, all that sort of thing. They are the only right and proper rules, my friend. The only right and proper rules. God as my Witness. I mean, look what happened to me when I ignored them. Because of my love for Sara Weeks, I sought a Deed. And it was denied me. Tell me, am I at least wanted for that murder?

Yes.

Splendid. At least I fulfilled my secondary Purpose. Having failed to accomplish the Deed, at least I was able to arrange things to *look* as though I had done it. I was in Evansville a total of nine months after the night of the crime. I did not particularly hide myself. You see, had I been apprehended, I would not have been too distressed. Now then, how is *that* for romantic conduct?

Pretty awful.

You must make me a promise.

What's that?

That you'll never reveal what I've told you. I want to die with Titusville still thinking of me as a murderer. It pleasures me to imagine my portly flapping shade haunting that town. So, will you promise?

I promise.

You mean it?

Yes.

Thank you. Now, tell me—what is new in Titusville? How is our friend George Peters? Has he achieved his heroism?

George is dead.

Dead?

Yes. At Fredericksburg in December of '62. His face was shot off.

And he achieved no Deed?

Not that I know of.

The Professor sighed. A pity, he said.

Ah, fuck him, said Charley.

What?

He was full of shit. Goddamn *hero*.

Ah, I am proud of you, said the Professor, chuckling. *That's* the spirit.

Well, what's wrong with the way I see things? *I'm* alive.

Exactly. And George Peters is dead. And it is better to be alive than dead.

That's right.

You will go far, Mr Wells.

I hope so.

It is inevitable. As the night follows the day. You will be a great man. Oh?

You understand *possibilities*. You understand *mortality*. I am gratified that you arrived here in time. My story has perhaps reminded you of the calamities that await those who even temporarily abandon such awareness.

Yes. I see what you mean.

Give only what you can afford to give.

Yessir.

Always leave open paths of retreat and escape.

Yessir.

Subscribe to no causes.

Yessir.

Trust no one.

Yessir.

Avoid heroes.

Yessir.

Rascality, my boy. The word is rascality. What does it profit a man? It profits a man the world, and the world is enough.

Yessir. Rascality. Profit.

Prof Frye died six days later. Dorcas Pfaff was mopping his forehead with a damp rag. He had a convulsion of some sort. He heaved, gasped. His face became quite red. He pissed the bed. Dorcas Pfaff screamed, but by that time Prof Frye was dead. About a hundred dollars was found among his personal effects. According to documents in his billfold, he was sixtyseven years of age and his real name was Thomas F. Byrne. The documents did not reveal where he originally was from. In his last six days, he had held several more conversations with Charley, but he had said nothing of either his youth or his antecedents. Charley had questioned him about them, but his only reply had been: Please, my boy. Please do not attempt to pry. Nothing is to be gained from it. I am a scamp and a fraud, and *there* lies the truth of me, and further information is not necessary. But the Professor did tell Charley what had happened to him in the years following the murder of the Rev Mr Weeks and the four drunken months in Evansville. You may not know this, he said, but telegraphy long has been an avocation of mine. Upon emerging from my drunken debauch, I obtained a position as telegrapher for the Evansville *Courier*. After five months with that newspaper, I repaired to Indianapolis, where I was hired by the Indianapolis *Crisis*. A little less than a year after *that*, I journeyed to New York. I found a job with the New York *Call*, a journal of dubious reputation and low pay.

But I was reasonably content. The work was easy, and I had a good deal of time for my, uh, private pursuits. Of course I *could* have returned to the peddling of Dr Boyle's Stomach Purgative & Bowel Cleanser, but I no longer had the spirit (forgive the hideous pun), nor did I have the energy, for such a strenuous undertaking. I fear the Weeks business had taken much of the starch and fraudulent oratory out of me. One must be nimble of lip and quick of foot if one is to purvey patent medicines successfully. I no longer possessed such agility. So I turned to telegraphy —and actually, as matters turned out, I had more than enough excitement for these old bones. The New York *Call* made me a battlefield telegrapher, and I was on the scene sending dispatches from Antietam, Fredericksburg, Chancellorsville, Gettysburg and The Wilderness. Ah, my boy, this war. That damn Grant. Men are not *men* to him; they are *instruments*. But please do not think I disapprove. I do not disapprove. Grant understands the nature of modern war. He does not concern himself with such obsolete and pluperfectly romantic considerations as honor and human life. He understands *mortality*. He understands the structure of the apparatus of attrition. This apparatus has no room for honor, bravery, Deeds. Grant will win this war for the Union. No question about it. As an engineer, he is a genius, and he guides the machine with a sure and certain hand. And it is grinding down those poor gallant foolish rebels. I fervently hope they hurry and surrender. Otherwise, the machine surely will destroy them all. Grant understands all there is to understand about the machine. Its components are men, but men as *instruments*, and they outnumber the rebels, and the outnumbering is all that matters. You and he are very much alike; you both embrace reality as truth. You both are great men. Ah, but enough of my mournful philosophy. Tell me—how are the whores in this place? I fear my own experience here has been, ah, limited. . . .

Charley and Wendell Archer Doggett donated the Professor's hundred dollars to a Baptist temperance and Bible study society. They shared equally in the costs of the Professor's funeral. They decided it would have to be a very elaborate funeral. They figured the Professor would have been very amused by it. They even hired a band, and Charley told the bandsmen to play the most heroically lugubrious music in their repertoire. They engaged a Methodist church, and the preacher recited several appropriately gloomy prayers. Charley had insisted on the gloomy prayers. The gloomier the better, he told the preacher, and the fellow did splendidly, including among them the fiery hyperbole of Revelation: *And I saw the dead, small and great, stand before God: and the books were opened: and another book was opened, which is the book of life: and the dead were judged out of those things which were written in the books, according to their works. And the sea gave up the dead which were in it; and death and hell delivered up the dead which were in them, and they were judged every man according to their works. And death and hell were cast into the lake of fire. And whosoever was not found written in the book of life was cast into the lake of fire.* And, as a coda, in a truly inspired choice of Scriptural quotation, the preacher (who was not a stupid man, whose church was directly across the street from the Nonpareil, who knew damn well what was going on there), recited these words: *He that is unjust, let him be unjust still; and he which is filthy, let him be filthy still; and he that is righteous, let him be righteous still; and he that is holy, let him be holy still. AND, BEHOLD, I COME QUICKLY; AND MY REWARD IS WITH ME, TO GIVE EVERY MAN ACCORDING AS HIS WORK SHALL BE. I AM ALPHA AND OMEGA, THE BEGINNING AND THE END, THE FIRST AND THE LAST. Blessed are they that do his commandments, that they may have right to the tree of life, and may enter in through the gates into the city. For without are dogs, and sorcerers, and whoremongers, and murderers, and idolaters, and whosoever loveth and maketh a lie.*

At the final amen, Charley nudged Wendell Archer Doggett and whispered: Dog. Doggett the Dog.

Sorcerer, whispered Wendell Archer Doggett, covering his mouth.

Whoremonger, whispered Charley.

Murderer, whispered Wendell Archer Doggett, sniggering.

Idolater, whispered Charley.

God damn you, *stop* it, whispered Wendell Archer Doggett.

All the whores, including a weeping Dorcas Pfaff, attended the funeral. Charley and Wendell Archer Doggett and the whores marched behind the band and the hearse all the way to the cemetery. Wendell Archer Doggett puffed and gasped. Ah Lordy, he said to Charley, the curse of fat. The Professor's grave was high on a green hill that faced across the Potomac. A week or so later, his tombstone was put in place. Charley and Wendell Archer Doggett had had these words inscribed:

BYRNE
FRYE
BOYLE
1797–1864
GONE TO JESUS
(PERHAPS)

Greatness: the Professor had predicted it, and Charley had fulfilled it. Now, here in this pretty little village of Paradise Falls, Charley figured the Professor would have been proud of him. The necessary betrayals had been accomplished. He had learned never to give a damn. His muzzle velocity continued to increase. His happy worm continued to feast. The birthing was done. The man had emerged. And now the worm demanded that he destroy a foolish old relic named Ike Underwood. And this he would do. By whatever means were necessary. And of course hate had nothing to do with it. Which was why Charles Palmer Wells was so relentlessly great. He told Millerspaugh to keep up the good work with the *Journal*. Let us roast Mayor Pillsbury, he said. Let us remove him. It will be the first large step. Said Millerspaugh: The first large step toward what? Said Charles Palmer Wells: Just you never mind. When the time comes to tell you, I shall. Said Millerspaugh: Yes sir. You're the boss. Said Charles Palmer Wells: Correct.

1871 . . .

The 1870 census statistics are released by the federal government. They reveal a total Paradise County population of 5,885. The Paradise Falls population is 3,202. That of Blood is 624. The rest is classified as rural.

The C. P. Wells Coal Co opens another mine, the Tuesday Creek. Ike Underwood admits to his wife that C. P. Wells is out to chop him down. And what are you going to do about it? Phoebe wants to know. I don't guess I know, says Ike. Then, smiling, he changes the subject. They discuss their son Philip, who has been graduated with honors from Harvard and now lives in New York City, where he is involved in the editing of a small but influential literary magazine. They are extremely proud of Philip. As well they should be. He visits them every Christmas, and his dark good looks and quiet good manners have caused many a maidenly heart to thump and flutter. Phoebe wishes he would get married soon and come back to Paradise Falls to live, but Ike tells her to give the boy time. A young man needs time, says Ike. Mm, says Phoebe. Well, says Ike, take my own case. If I'*d* of gotten married early, I never would have married *you*. Says Phoebe: That would have been, I expect, the tragedy of the age. Says Ike: Ah, Lord. A person would think that after all these years I'd of learned to keep my mouth shut. Says Phoebe: Yes. That's true.

Warrior:

VIRGIL, THE TROUBLE WITH YOU IS YOU HAVE SOFT BONES: his father, a good and honest man, had said those words. There had been no better or more honest man than Joseph William Light, carpenter and cabinetmaker, and Joseph William Light had assisted old Ike Underwood in the building of the village of Paradise Falls, and there never had been a way to live up to what he had demanded. The man never had been afraid to face into high winds. He never had been *afraid*. He saw existence in terms of standing up, of facing up. The rules were in the Book, and the rules were explicit, and soft bones were not tolerated. Virgil T. Light knew all the rules, and he understood them, but he had soft bones (his father, who had been infallible, like the Pope of Rome, had said so), and so sometimes he slunk away from the rules. Now, today, this day in early November—the leaves were gone, swept, raked, burned, suppressed— he sat rigidly and embraced himself, squeezed his inadequate bones, and Catherine Anne finally was dying, finally was *getting on* with it, and he closed his eyes and saw his friend's wife offering to lick his feet, and with God as his most holy Witness he had no idea why he had so monstrously offended heaven. So perhaps he did have soft bones. Perhaps his father had been most eminently correct in that awful bruising summation. But was it such a crime? Did soft bones somehow connote evil? He opened his eyes, looked upon his dying wife. He rubbed his hairless head. In the war, men had respected him. They had addressed him as *sir* and *captain*. They had looked to him for guidance. They had sought from him ways to survive. Motes. Sunlight now, thin and white. Catherine Anne could not last out the day. Dr Reeser had said so. Shaking his head, shooting his ruffled cuffs, the plump little doctor had said: It is pneumonia. She is too weak for pneumonia. You understand that, don't you? And Virgil T. Light, commander of the Paradise Falls Post, Grand Army of the Republic, had said: Yes. I understand. Poor old girl. The doctor had frowned. Mm, he'd said. He was gone now. He'd returned to his home for a few hours' sleep. Virgil T. Light sat beside Catherine Anne's bed. His son Bill was downstairs with Mrs Pett. They were eating their noon meal. Bill was twentyone now, a man. Bill worked in the store. Girls and ladies liked him. There wasn't too much Virgil T. Light knew about his son. The war had taken away too many of the large formative years. The war was more than six years dead, but Virgil T. Light still knew little about his son. But then of course Virgil T. Light had soft bones. Virgil T. Light also had a large voice. It stood him well as a candidate. He was going to win this election. Charley Wells and Dave Millerspaugh had told him so. He was county Republican chairman, and he had the support of the aggressive little *Journal,* and he would overwhelm George Pillsbury. No doubt about it. More motes. A swirl. The curtains were open, and sunlight streaked Catherine Anne's face, pink now from the pneumonia. Her breath had a sound to it of gravel. She wore a white nightdress, and her hair was in braids. Her eyes were closed. She knew. She had to know. And about more than the dying. About his friend's wife as well. His friend whom she hated. He and Nancy had perhaps kept their secret from the village, but *he* had not kept it from his wife. Catherine Anne knew. There was nothing about him she did not know. As a girl, when they were courting, she had said: I love you *so* much. Oh my darling Virgil, my sweet, my dearest, bless you. I love you so much I am going to spend the rest of my life finding out everything there is to know about you. Ah, smoke your pipe. I like to kiss you after you've smoked your pipe. You look so wise with a pipe. Wedding night: Catherine Anne pale, Catherine Anne smiling, Catherine Anne drenched in lace: Oh. Now. Ah. Yes. There will be no secrets. My hair. Kiss my hair. I have washed it, and it will taste good.

Virgil? she said. Her eyes were open.

He smiled down at her. Yes? he said.

I can see the trees from here.

Well. Ah. Good.

The covers were to her neck. I'm cold, she said.

He reached out, tucked the covers closer to her neck.

She nodded.

He kissed her forehead.

I wish I could memorize the trees, she said.

Sh.

Oh it's all right. I do not feel feverish or out of my head. Just a little cold.

Ah, said Virgil T. Light. Fine. You're a good strong woman.

Even though they have no leaves, I wish I could memorize them. Even bare trees are better than no trees at all.

Yes. That's the truth.

Where's the boy?

Downstairs. He and Mrs Pett are eating.

Oh. Well. That's good.

Virgil T. Light smiled at his dying wife. You look very pretty today, he said.

You and your flattery.

I *mean* the things I say.

Of course you do.

I *do*.

Catherine Anne closed her eyes. The trees, she said. Bless the trees.

Martha, Lester, even poor little Barbara . . . they'd all died. Perhaps, if they'd not died, his father would not have accused him of having soft bones. Without the grief, perhaps his father would have had patience with weakness. It was the consumption. Martha was eleven, Lester eight and little Barbara just three. They lay together in one bed, and it crackled and slapped from the force of their coughing and hawking. At thirteen, Virgil was the oldest, and he had his own bed. The consumption never even brushed against him. His father sat stolidly with the three dying ones. His father read Scripture. Little Barbara was the first to go. She died in the night, and no one realized she was dead until the following morning. When she was lifted from the bed, she was stiff and brittle as a stick. Next was Martha. She died sitting up. She died weeping. She died with her hands in fists, and after she was dead the room had an odor of damp hair. Then came Lester. He died threshing and spitting. They all died within a week. Virgil helped carry all three coffins to the graveyard. His father had made the coffins. Virgil had offered to help, but his father had said: Get out of my sight. Apples: God, how the boy Virgil had loved them. Apples and quiet. Fishing. The sound of the river. Dreams. Sky. Insects. He stole an apple from one of the trees in Mr Sidlo's orchard and ran down to the river and ate the apple and washed away his tears in the crisp white water. He even ate the seeds and core of the apple. He ate all of the apple except the stem. He liked to squash the seeds between his teeth. The bitter brown taste was to him a delight. Get out of my sight, his father had said. His father had been a great carpenter, a virtuoso. His father had needed no help. His father had had hard bones.

Bill came into the room.

Virgil T. Light held a finger to his lips.

Catherine Anne opened her eyes. They were white.

Bill bent over his mother and kissed her on both eyes. He looked across the bed at his father. His face was puffy. You can go eat now if you want to, he said. I'll sit with Mama.

Yes, said Catherine Anne. Yes, Virgil. You go eat.

I'm not hungry, said Virgil T. Light.

Then go lie down, said Catherine Anne.

You, Papa, said Bill. You must be tired.

Virgil T. Light nodded. He stood up. He cleared his throat. He left the room. On his way out he heard Catherine Anne say something to Bill about the trees. He crossed a hallway to his bedroom. He lay down. He looked at the ceiling. Then, straining his neck a bit, he looked at the silhouette of his father. A silhouette artist had come through Paradise Falls in 1847; he had been a very skillful artist; his rendering of the silhouette of Joseph William Light had been a very accurate one; it truly was remarkable what a person of talent could do with a pair of scissors and a simple sheet of black paper. The boy Virgil had paid for the silhouette. The artist, a large florid man, seated Joseph William Light on a folding chair on the boardwalk in front of the Harlowe Morris store. Joseph William Light grumbled and snorted, called it damn nonsense. Virgil was nineteen that year, and nothing he'd ever done had pleased his father. He stood and watched the artist work. A crowd gathered. People shook their heads. My, they said. Isn't it remarkable? The silhouette cost a dollar. The boy Virgil had it framed. He made the frame himself.

Mrs Pett came into his bedroom. Don't you want anything to eat? She asked him. There's some nice leftover ham.

Virgil T. Light shook his head no.

Mrs Pett shrugged. All right, she said. She went out.

He closed his eyes. He had worked hard on that frame. Fastidiously. He had been apprenticed to his father. He had wanted to please his father. When he gave his father the silhouette in its frame, his father said: Vanity, vanity. A waste of time and effort. It's a shame you don't put all that time and effort into your work. Those studs in the kitchen of the Garfield place. I'm going to have to rip them out tomorrow. You got them in wrong. I expect I still have to watch you every minute. A silhouette: it was only a silhouette, a trivial thing. He could have been decent about it. He could have said thank you, son, I appreciate the thought. He died in 1849, and Ike Underwood was among those who told the boy Virgil what a truly outstanding man Joseph William Light had been. Virgil and his mother, a gray little woman with a wen on her neck, were left with an estate in excess of ten thousand dollars. Virgil made the coffin. It was a large coffin. As far as he was concerned, it was just as good a coffin as the ones his father had made for Martha, Lester and little Barbara. After the funeral and the burial, Virgil walked down by the river with a girl whose name was Catherine Anne Crozier. She was tiny and dark, and it did not seem to concern her that Virgil already was beginning to lose his hair. They walked without touching, and after a time he said: I've never meant anyone any harm. Do you believe that? And Catherine Anne said: Of course I do. I love you. I know you.

He opened his eyes. No, he did not want to fall asleep. He looked away from the silhouette. The voices of his wife and son came from across the hall. He could not make out what they were saying.

Oh dear God, he said aloud. He rubbed his belly. It felt thick. The terror and the shame pushed at its walls. Perhaps someday it would rip open the skin and emerge in a great foul spurt.

Virgil and Catherine Anne were married a week after his father's funeral. The wedding had been planned before his father's death. There was no real reason to postpone the wedding. Death was death, and a wedding was a wedding. His mother wept. She scratched at her wen, and her tears were warm and comfortable. The boy William was born a year later, and that also was the year Virgil T. Light opened his furniture store. He was just twentytwo that year, and his hair was almost all gone. Ah well, said Catherine Anne, shaking her head, I have more than enough for the both of us. She spoke gently to him. She told him she detected a fine sweetness in him. A man should not be ashamed of sweetness, she said. She carried the baby high. Small women often did. The store did well almost from the start. Virgil discovered he liked to talk to people. He'd never realized this before. He hired a carpenter named Osterhaus, an energetic young fellow newly arrived from Prussia, to build him a home. He had no desire to build the home himself. He was not that good a carpenter, and he knew it. After all, his father had told him often enough. But he was not a bad cabinetmaker, and *that* he also knew. Soft bones or no soft bones, he was patient and careful with detail work, and this was one of the principal reasons he went into the furniture business. Although most of his merchandise was of necessity Shipped In, he nonetheless found the time to work on his own tables, chairs, dressers and the like. He loved the delicacy of the work. He loved the odors. After a few years, there were some who said he was an even better cabinetmaker than his father had been. He sometimes wished there were written testimonials. He would have opened his father's coffin and waved the testimonials in the dead face.

He rolled on his side and looked out the window. The sunlight came crisp and hard. I should be in the other room, he told himself. I should be there with her. They call me the Warrior. It is incumbent upon me to display courage.

He placed his fists against his eyes.

The lace. Lord, the lace. And the quiet love, so optimistic and moist. I have more than enough hair for the both of us, said Catherine Anne. Hair today, gone tomorrow, said Virgil. Quiet laughter. Oh you *scamp,* she said. The baby was thin and alert, and right from the start it was silent. I never knew a baby to bawl so little, said Catherine Anne. Poor little fellow. Sometimes I wish he would just let *go*. Oh well. I expect most mothers would envy me. I should not question a blessing.

He removed his fists from his eyes. He brought up his knees. He loosened his belt, and this helped a little to relieve the thickness in his belly. I have my shoes on, he told himself. I should have removed them. Now I'll get the spread dirty. Mrs Pett won't like me. Mrs Pett will be in a pet. Poor Mrs Pett.

The business prospered. His mother died in 1852. That also was the year both of Catherine Anne's parents died. Her father had been in the feed and grain business. His estate was more than twelve thousand dollars. Virgil T. Light closed down the feed and grain store, sold its assets for five thousand dollars. Well, he told Catherine Anne, you'll surely be well fixed if anything happens to me. Said Catherine Anne: Nothing is going to happen to you. I won't *allow* it. Said Virgil: You're awfully friendly, ma'm, to an old bald fellow. Said Catherine Anne: Ah, such a scamp the world has never known. The days moved briskly. The business gave him a knowledge of the uses of friendship, and perhaps it didn't matter that he had soft bones. He became active in the local militia, the Paradise Falls Blues. Big men surely do look fine in uniforms, said Catherine Anne, smiling, brushing lint from his tunic. She took excellent care of his uniform, and she attended all the parades, and she always made the little boy wave at his daddy.

Bill came into the room. He seated himself on a chair next to the door. Mrs Pett is with her, he said.

There any change? said Virgil T. Light.

No, Papa. No change.

Well, you know what the doctor said.

Yes. I know.

Your mother spoke to me of trees.

Yes. She also spoke of them to me.

I feel so helpless.

Yes, Papa.

The election and all. And *this*.

Bill nodded. He folded his hands in his lap.

Maybe I can catch a little sleep.

Yes, Papa. I'll just sit here for a bit.

All right, said Virgil T. Light. He closed his eyes and listened to the terror. It had a sound like broken glass. He rolled to one side, pulled the pillow over his ears. He could hear Bill's breathing. He listened to it very carefully. After a time Bill sighed. He stood up and went out. The door closed softly. Virgil T. Light removed the pillow from his ears.

She was sixteen when he married her. She was perhaps twentyfive when it occurred to her that in all probability she despised him. He saw the knowledge come to her, and he supposed it was because of his soft bones. There was no one specific incident. The atrophy simply grew, like a wart. She told him: Virgil, why is it so important to you what other people think? She told him: Can't you be your own man? The boy took to going off by himself to fish. The boy was towheaded and silent, and his face was a bit pinched, and loud noises made him wince. Perhaps he too had soft bones. You and your cronies, said Catherine Anne. You and your Paradise Falls Blues. Why don't you try to talk to the boy? My goodness, I'll wager that some fine day you two will pass on the street without even nodding.

Virgil T. Light sighed. He flopped over on his back. Across the hall, Catherine Anne began to cough. She coughed and coughed and coughed. He lay quite still. He stared at the silhouette of his father. He blinked. He thought of the election. He said to himself: I am going to be mayor. I will be addressed as the *Honorable* Virgil T. Light. The GAR boys will put me across. They are *my* boys, my *friends*. They call me the Warrior, and some of them laugh at me, but I can count on them. One can always count on one's friends. One needs friends. Who wants to be friendless?

The boy took to going off by himself to fish, and wasn't that hunky-dory. One would have thought he was the first boy in the world to go off by himself to fish. Ah, but did he savor apples? Did he dream? Did he understand that courage would have to be found? In the late 1850's, when the despair and the contempt invaded the marriage of Virgil T. Light, there was not a soul who knew a thing about it. The village saw Virgil T. Light as being something of a windbag, but it detected nothing anguished within him. Said Catherine Anne: Oh no. You are perfectly safe. You are Virgil Light the good fellow. You need not concern yourself about what is happening to us. Oh, Virgil! Virgil! All I ask is that you be whatever it is you *are!* It doesn't matter what people think of you! It doesn't! (Fine. A fine speech. But what did she know of soft bones? Suppose they became common knowledge? He, Virgil T. Light, was nothing. His father had said so. He had offended his father by surviving. His father had spoken of soft bones, and his father had possessed all wisdom, and a man who had soft bones clearly could never afford to be himself. That was only common sense.) A large bald man with a large bald voice—this was the Virgil T. Light the world would know, and to hell with apples, to hell with the river and dreams. He involved himself with the Masons. He involved himself with the Odd Fellows. He taught himself always to speak in the large bald voice. He had many friends. He was ah such a fine fellow. Catherine Anne had been ill more than two years when the war came. He went away gratefully. He left her in the care of Mrs Pett, and he hired an old man named Sam Reddy to look after the store. It did not even matter that the men of the Paradise Falls Blues had elected Fred Magill captain over him. He did have a lieutenant's commission, and the war no doubt would provide many splendid opportunities for advancement. Chancellorsville. Gettysburg. The Wilderness. Petersburg. Fred Magill was raised to major, and Virgil Light to captain, and those were the great days, and not a word was said about soft bones.

Bill came into the room. Papa? he said.

Virgil T. Light sat up.

She wants to see you, said Bill.

Thank you, son, said Virgil T. Light. He quickly came out of the bed. He wiped his eyes, hurried across the hall.

Catherine Anne's head was propped up with pillows. I can breathe better this way, she said. I have water in my lungs. I don't *feel* the water in my lungs. But that's what the doctor says. Remarkable, isn't it?

Virgil T. Light went to the bed and sat down next to it.

Bill stood at the door. Mrs Pett stood next to him.

Catherine Anne inclined her head toward Bill and Mrs Pett. Would you please go downstairs for a little bit? she said.

Yes, Mama, said Bill. Of course. He took Mrs Pett by an elbow and they went out of the room, closing the door softly behind them.

Catherine Anne smiled at her husband. Her face was more pink. Her teeth appeared to be too white. Just sit here with me, she said. You don't have to say anything. Just sit here. I feel so peculiar. I always thought I would be out of my head when the time came. But no such thing. I see everything so very clearly. Lungs full of water. Can you imagine?

Virgil T. Light said nothing.

It's been too bad, said Catherine Anne. I'm so sorry.

You're sorry? You . . . you have nothing to . . .

Yes?

No. Never mind.

Virgil. Ah, my poor Virgil.

Virgil T. Light looked at the floor. He listened to his wife's breathing. She said nothing. He thought of the whore Pauline. He'd had her at Falmouth. She had been supplied to him by an aide to General Fighting Joe Hooker. His tent was high on a bluff overlooking the Rappahannock. He told Pauline about Catherine Anne. Pauline had been very kind. Make believe I am your Catherine Anne, she told him. And he did. Or at least he tried. All night long he tried, and the next morning Pauline was not angry. You should not be ashamed, she told him. This happens to many men. She was a large girl, and her busts were too vast. In no way did she resemble Catherine Anne. He pressed his face against Pauline's pale whore belly and he said: She has never permitted me my weakness. She sought to investigate me, but there was nothing much to be found. And so now she despises me. What did she expect? Who does she think I am? My papa told me: Son, he said, the trouble with you is you have soft bones. And Pauline stroked Virgil T. Light's bald head. There, there, she said, you sweet man, don't take on so. In the long run, nothing matters anyway. Always keep that in mind. *I* always have, Lord knows.

Virgil?

Yes?

I feel it . . . I feel it all leaving me. It is a . . . peculiar . . . ah . . . it's all been so difficult, hasn't it?

I'll call Bill.

No. Please. Please . . . let's just sit here quietly.

He looked at her. Now she breathed with her jaw hanging loosely. Spittle trailed from a corner of her mouth. He wiped it with his handkerchief.

Thank you, said Catherine Anne. Thank you. Ah. I love the trees. Even in November. The sleeping trees. So thin. See how they scratch the sky.

He leaned forward and took her hand. He squeezed it. She smiled. Her eyes still were wide open. And they were dry. He blinked. The whore Pauline: he had thought of a *whore* at a time like this. He cleared his throat, snuffled. Again he squeezed Catherine Anne's hand. He remembered how it had been in the army. Perhaps the war would enable him to be whatever it was she wanted him to be. He walked through that war large and bald and proclamative. Oh, he still talked too much, but he was no coward, and everyone in the Paradise Falls Blues knew it. At Gettysburg, that day General Dan Sickles had overextended the III Corps into that infernal peach orchard, Virgil T. Light, the brave captain, had stood right alongside his men when the rebels came at them from two directions, rolling up their salient, and he and an elongated corporal named Ferris had by their example kept the men from breaking and skedaddling (when they finally did withdraw, they did so in reasonably good order), and by the Lord Harry he could still *hear* that day, even now, here on this scratchy Paradise Falls autumn afternoon with its sleeping trees and vanished leaves and crisp sky. There had been that Gettysburg day sounds beyond sounds, sounds that fell and bounced like boulders: it was the second day of July in the year 1863, and the fear came thick and boiling into his mouth; it burned his throat; it clouded his vision; it laid a layer of fur across his tongue; he told himself: If you get through this, you can get through anything. They came, those rebels. They came yipping. They came waving their hats. The men of the 33rd Ohio Volunteer Infantry met them at the point of the peach orchard salient. Fred Magill stood in full view of the rebels. So did Virgil T. Light. And Virgil T. Light was weeping, but of course no one could hear the sound of it. The weeping was like knives in his skull. The enemy came bouncing and whooping through the high grass, all those damnable rebels in their ragged uniforms (those who *had* uniforms), and Virgil T. Light withdrew his sword from its scabbard and waved the sword high above his head in great whirling circles. And he ran it through two rebels. And he shot four others. And he lost his hat. And both legs of his britches were torn. And he wet himself. Whatever Fred Magill could do, so could Virgil T. Light. No *man* had soft bones, and everyone said Fred Magill was a *fine* man, and so it was incumbent upon Virgil T. Light to be just as fine, just as brave; that way, he could exorcise the soft bones.

Catherine Anne coughed. It was not a loud cough. Her body barely moved.

He smiled at her.

Now her breathing was more shallow. She said: It is . . . it is as though . . . I am lying next to a bonfire. I tried . . . to be the best . . . the best wife . . . I knew how.

Virgil T. Light nodded. Yes, he said. Yes. And you *are* a good wife.

I . . . forgive you.

What?

You want me to forgive you. You know you do. I do so. I do hereby forgive you. I expect it all was as much my fault as it was yours.

You forgive me for what?

She pulled her hand free of his. She shuddered. The woman, she said. The Wells woman.

Oh God . . . Catherine Anne . . .

Don't cry.

No . . . I won't . . .

Please. Yes. No tears. Good Virgil. Yes.

Virgil T. Light covered his face with his hands. He made no sounds. He was able to hear Catherine Anne's breathing quite clearly. He squeezed his cheeks. He wrenched his hands away from his face. The door opened. Bill and Mrs Pett came back into the room. Catherine Anne coughed. Mrs Pett leaned over her and made shushing sounds. Catherine Anne's eyes still were dry. She knew about Nancy. She knew about Nancy. She knew about Nancy. There it all was—out. Virgil T. Light stood up. Bill stared steadily at him. Did Bill also know? Virgil T. Light shook his head. He made a moaning noise. He went out of the room. He crossed the hall, reentered his own room. This time, however, he did not lie down. He went to the window and seated himself in a straightbacked chair. Motes. Sun. The air was thin today, thin and uncompromising and very clean. He looked out over rooftops toward the low blue hills. He embraced himself. He said to himself: After the election, I will be addressed as the *Honorable*. He thought of The Wilderness. He thought of Petersburg. He remembered the Petersburg trenches with special clarity. Mud. Inescapable. He was away for four years. Not once did he come home on leave. The other men of the Paradise Falls Blues came home on leave, but not Virgil T. Light. He had excellent reasons—there was always so much to be done. He was not expendable; after all, he was the Warrior, a large bald Warrior with a large bald voice. It occurred to him that perhaps he didn't want to leave the war because he hoped it would kill him. He told himself: That is madness. What I am is what I proclaim myself to be, and she will have to make her peace with it. I enjoy the company of my fellows, the pleasures of jests, of debate, of the small pomps and intrigues of human intercourse. Petersburg: the trenches gave him plenty of time to think. The mud was the sky, and the sky was the mud, and the men of the two armies yelled foully goodnatured insults at each other, and Virgil T. Light had an embarrassment of dank hours to crouch in his dugout and dissect his wife's contempt. And no one knew a thing. He was all smiles and good fellowship, and not even Fred Magill knew. A war required its large bald windbags. Virgil T. Light was fulfilling a necessary function. The candle wavered and curled in the dugout, and its shadows were bleak and dreary, and oh how he did have the time to think. It finally came to him that she had no *right* to her contempt. It finally came to him that he did not at all want to die. He would live the only way he knew how, and the Devil take its fraudulence. The devil take her cold eye.

A sparrow, anonymous and threadbare, flew to the windowledge. It perched there. Virgil T. Light pressed his nose against the pane. The sparrow stared at him. The sparrow was steadfast. When it blinked, it jerked its head. Virgil T. Light bared his teeth. The sparrow did not move. He tapped the pane. The sparrow flew away.

Mr Sparrow, said Virgil T. Light aloud, the trouble with you is you have soft bones.

The scroll had been Virgil T. Light's idea. He saw it as giving him a leg up on Fred Magill. He figured Fred Magill would be running for office. He didn't want Fred Magill to run for office. Fred Magill had been the commanding officer. Fred Magill had had enough glory. Throughout the four years of the war, Fred Magill never said a critical word to Virgil T. Light, but of course he didn't have to. Fred Magill was a *fine* man. Didn't everyone say so? Oh yes. Fred Magill: prince of the elect. It was *Fred Magill* the men cheered the loudest. It was *Fred Magill* who marched at the front of all the parades. It was *Fred Magill* who had received the compliments of General Armbruster the day the 33rd Ohio had helped cover the retreat of General Ledlie's division after the Crater disaster. No sir, by God, when the war ended the world would no longer revolve around Fred Magill. It would be Virgil T. Light's turn. (Apples: where was the boy who had delighted in the bitter brown taste of the squashed seeds? Ah, the poor little fellow, the world and the contempt had assassinated him.) And anyway, there was nothing immoral in the idea of the scroll. The man's name had been Ferris, and he had hailed from Indiana, and he had transferred into the 33rd Ohio after an incident in his Indiana regiment in which he'd almost killed a man who'd insulted his wife. He was only a corporal, but he'd seen action at Cedar Mountain and Antietam, and he was very helpful in preparing the Paradise Falls Blues for their first big fight, at the Chancellorsville crossroads in May of '63. He was an angry and profane sort of fellow, but nothing frightened him, and he showed the officers of the Paradise Falls Blues what it meant to *lead*. He told the men: I don't give a damn about Ohio, and that's the truth. I'm an Indiana man and proud of it. But, as long as I'm stuck with you fellers, I'm going to see to it that you do some soldiering. So, all of you, stand up straight there, God damn it. Look smart. Be men. I'm going to make it so you drink blood for breakfast, and you might as well believe it, because I God damn give you my oath it's going to happen. Even the officers were in awe of the stupendous Ferris. Even the *fine* Fred Magill. They gathered with him often, and he told them: Ain't nothing to it. All you got to do is make sure they face in the right direction. Wave your swords for them now and again. You do them things, they'll be all right. They're just men like other men. Ferris was killed the third day at Gettysburg while in command of a squad that had been sent out on flank picket down below Little Round Top. One other man in the squad was killed, and the others were taken prisoner. It was several months before the Paradise Falls Blues learned what had happened to that squad. One of the prisoners was paroled, and he sent Fred Magill a letter as soon as he arrived home. There was a feeling of loss, no question about it, and it was magnified with the passage of the long months that stretched to the end of the war. Virgil T. Light was aware of it, and he had no trouble whatever obtaining the signatures for the scroll. Old Ferris was a good man, he said. Old Ferris taught us a lot. This here scroll seems like the least we can do. His wife'll appreciate it, you just mark my words. Virgil T. Light personally visited every veteran of the Paradise Falls Blues in the first six weeks after the men came home from the war. The wording of the scroll was his. He had it done up fancy in the job printing shop of the Paradise Falls *Democrat*. J. K. Bankson, the paper's hunchbacked little editor, congratulated

him on his choice of words. Well, said Virgil T. Light, you got to understand it all comes from the heart. That late spring and early summer of
'65 was a good time for Virgil T. Light, and never mind his wife, never
mind his silent son. The *great,* the *fine* Fred Magill was dying of dysentery. He would be no threat. As for Catherine Anne, well, nothing had
changed. She was thinner, and she coughed more often, and her words
had a quality of sour grease, but he was neither shocked nor surprised. If
she didn't like the way he was, bad cess. As for the boy, his life was his
own; he could make of it what he would; Virgil T. Light had no objections.
A young former lieutenant named Tom Messer accompanied him when he
traveled to Indiana to present the scroll to the Widow Ferris. She was not
what they had expected. In the first place, she was quite young. Secondly,
she was almost beautiful. Her breasts were huge, and she carried herself
very well. If it hadn't been for her somewhat weak chin, she would have
been a genuine beauty. As it was, both Virgil T. Light and Tom Messer
were very impressed. The Ferris farm was just outside Evansville, and it
wasn't much of a farm at all. The Widow Ferris lived alone in a small
house that really was little more than a shack. But the place was clean
enough, and she was very hospitable. She wept when Virgil T. Light gave
her the scroll. She said it was quite the finest thing that had happened to
her in years. Her weeping caused her breasts to tremble. Virgil T. Light's
belly felt tight. He began to talk. He told her she always would be welcome in Paradise Falls. Tom Messer looked at him. Virgil T. Light told
the Widow Ferris her late husband had been almost revered by the men of
the Paradise Falls Blues. He told her their community always would have
room for the widow of such a fine and brave man. The Widow Ferris
smiled at him through her tears. She nodded. She told him she was most
humbly grateful. Returning to Evansville in their rented gig, Virgil T.
Light slapped the reins and said to Tom Messer: My God, what a woman.
Said Tom Messer: Yessir. Yes *sir.* (Thoughts. Dreams. The apples were
forgotten, but flesh was not. Perhaps someday she *would* come to Paradise
Falls. The world abounded with miracles, and what harm could come
from a little innocent carnal wishing?) Virgil T. Light dreamed often
and well of the Widow Ferris, and then later that summer there came
that fine day he encountered the Widow Ferris in front of the Paradise
County Court House. She was with a grinning fellow named Wells, and it
turned out this Wells was her new husband. Virgil T. Light's face immediately became quite red.

He pushed back his chair from the window. He stood up, rested his
forehead against the pane. Catherine Anne, he said aloud. Catherine
Anne. Catherine Anne. Ah, thank you for the . . . for the, ah, forgiveness . . . I . . . well, I don't know why it . . . happened . . .

Bill came into the room. Papa? he said. Did you say something?

Virgil T. Light turned from the window. No, he said.

Bill nodded. She wants to see you again, he said.

All right, said Virgil T. Light.

They crossed the hall to her room.

Virgil T. Light sat down next to the bed.

Her eyes still were open, still were dry. She reached for his hand. She squeezed it. Her own hand felt like twigs. Lean forward, she said.

Virgil T. Light leaned forward.

She whispered into his ear: I didn't *know*. I only *guessed*. But that doesn't matter. What . . . what does matter is that . . . you can have what . . . you want: I . . . forgive . . . you . . .

He drew back.

Catherine Anne smiled.

Bill and Mrs Pett stood at the foot of the bed.

Just . . . stay here with . . . me, said Catherine Anne.

Virgil T. Light nodded. So did Bill and Mrs Pett.

Motes again. He almost wanted to lick at them like a cat. He rubbed the skin on his head. It was stretched tight. He thought of Nancy, the way her hands scrabbled at his belly and his balls. He moistened his lips, sucked spit. Catherine Anne squeezed his hand. Her chin wobbled. He said to himself: Charley Wells is my friend. A man needs friends. Charley Wells did *not* burn down my store. I don't care *what* Nancy says. And anyway, she's admitted she doesn't know it for a *fact*. She says she thinks Fritz Voss does. Well, I wouldn't trust *him* any farther than I could throw a mountain. Virgil T. Light shuddered, shook his head. Bill frowned at him. Catherine Anne's eyes still were open. Water in the lungs. She was drowning. God. She had sought to learn everything there was to know about him. Ho. Such a joke. The village believed Charley Wells had cheated him out of his share of the land up there at Blood, the land that now *just happened* to be worth what? Millions? Yes, all of it in coal, and the coal would last forever, and the village said: Ah, pity the poor Warrior. He surely was snookered. But what did the village really know? It knew *nothing*. Charley Wells had come to Virgil T. Light's assistance after the fire. If Charley Wells hadn't bought Virgil T. Light's share of the land, the poor Warrior would have been ruined. Charley Wells was a *friend*. Yes, a *good* and *true* friend, and he'd never said a word about soft bones. And look now at the situation. Virgil T. Light's furniture business was more vigorous than ever. His fire losses had forced him to sell his house (to Dr Reeser, incidentally), but last year he'd bought a new place (also built by the carpenter Osterhaus), and it was larger and more elaborate than the first one had been (with even an indoor upstairs lavatory for Catherine Anne's use), and the new house had complete plumbing and gas facilities, and it was four rooms larger than the old one had been, and it sat tall and sturdy in a grove of oak trees halfway up the Cumberland Street hill, a redbrick structure, filigreed with fancy ironwork and surrounded by a high castiron picket fence, a splendid domicile with a granite birdbath out in the back yard among the shrubs and the rhododendron and the box hedges, a pride and a glory of a house, a place of *substance,* a right and proper residence for a man of influence, a man who had many *friends.* Including Charley Wells. No matter what Catherine Anne said. No matter what *Nancy* said. How had the betrayal begun? That time he'd accompanied Charley to the Hollingshead woman's whorehouse in Columbus . . . Charley had looked upon it as being right and natural. He'd even joked about it. But was that enough of an excuse for the betrayal? Catherine Anne and Charley—Catherine Anne who had loved him, Charley who was his friend: how could a man live with such treachery? It began back in the days when Charley and Nancy were living in the Acterhof House. Virgil T. Light stopped in one afternoon to say hello. Charley was in Columbus, and Virgil T. Light told her he had not been aware of this. She wore a white dress that day. She looked like a virgin bride. He is in Columbus today, she said, and of course Virgil T. Light apologized for the intrusion. She smiled and said: Don't be foolish. I'm always glad to see you. Please come in. He thanked her, told her he would only stay a minute. They talked briefly of the weather, the furniture business, the GAR. And then Nancy said: It really was very kind of you to stop by. Said Virgil T. Light: Well, ah, I'm only sorry Charley's not here. Said Nancy: No you're not. Said Virgil T. Light: I beg your pardon? Said Nancy: You knew he wasn't here. He told you day before yesterday he was going to Columbus. I was with him, remember? Virgil T. Light cleared his throat, said nothing. He looked past her shoulder, and his cheeks were warm. Said Nancy: I saw it back in Indiana. Said Virgil T. Light: You saw what? Said Nancy: The wanting. Most men can't hide it. Even though I cried a whole lot that day, I could see it. Very clear. It's all right. It wasn't like you were the first man to look at me that way. Said Virgil T. Light: I don't know what— Nancy shook her head from side to side. Please, she said, no polite lies. You're here because you knew I'd be alone. It's all right. Really. He's not at me as much as you might think. Said Virgil T. Light: What? Said Nancy: He's . . . well, I expect he's used to me. Those things happen. Especially when a man visits so many whores. He gets sort of tired. Can I call you Virgil? Said Virgil T. Light: Yes . . . ah, go ahead. Said Nancy: Thank you. I want to call you by your Christian name. Then Nancy stood up. Virgil T. Light also stood up. She opened her mouth. She shook her head, closed it. She rubbed her chin. She moved toward him. The white dress rustled and snapped. He looked at the swell of her breasts. He was almost ready to believe he could see her nipples. He held his breath. She smiled. He expelled his breath in a tight burst. Come halfway, she said. She stood in the middle of the neat little Acterhof House sitting room. He moved toward her. *Why?* he said, almost bleating. It is the least I can do, said Nancy.

Catherine Anne squeezed his hand. He flinched.

Mrs Pett made a noise deep in her throat.

Virgil T. Light smiled at his wife.

Please . . . please believe me about him, said Catherine Anne.

About who?

Wells. Your friend . . . Charles P. Wells . . .

What about him?

Ah, never . . . never mind . . .

Virgil T. Light patted his wife's hand.

Lean forward, she said.

He leaned forward. The odor of flesh and sheets was milky.

She whispered into his ear: There is . . . nothing . . . you can do, is there? The Wells woman has made it . . . safe . . . for her husband . . .

He embraced her. He murmured: Catherine Anne, please don't say these—

She whispered: Don't you see? You can't hate him, can you? You . . . don't . . . *dare.* I mean, how can you hate a man you've . . . betrayed?

Virgil T. Light pulled away from his wife.

Catherine Anne smiled. Lean forward, she said.

He leaned forward.

She whispered: The Wells woman did it for her . . . husband . . .

No, said Virgil T. Light. Again he pulled away from his wife.

Catherine Anne smiled.

Another growling noise from Mrs Pett.

No. No. Wrong. Not true. Catherine Anne's feverish dying insight was a delusion. Virgil T. Light rubbed the backs of his hands. He breathed shallowly. He and Nancy had come together because of passion; there had been no secret design to it. He could *not* believe such a thing. It was too monstrous. He thought of her as *his* Nancy. When they were together, they seldom mentioned Charley. He saw her whenever the opportunity presented itself, and sometimes they ran grave risks. She murmured to him words of love. When she became pregnant with the little girl Nell, he told her it was best that they discontinue the meetings. Nancy smiled. The meetings were not discontinued. (Flesh. Sweat. Groans. Occasionally he took her on the floor. Charley had built a fine new house on Grainger Street, and it was quite the finest house in town, a place of cupolas and *two* marble fireplaces and six bedrooms and two lavatories and a nursery and even a conservatory complete with grand piano which neither Charley nor Nancy could play, and Virgil T. Light visited her there on nights when Charley was out of town, and sometimes they fell upon one another without even waiting to climb the stairs to her room, and she did anything he asked her to do: she even licked his feet. She told him: Charley did a terrible thing to you. Poor Charley. It's important to him that he do terrible things. He wouldn't be Charley if he didn't. Ah, Virgil, Virgil, it surely is a life we lead. All of us. Good *or* bad.) He asked her if the baby was his. She smiled. She did not reply. He repeated the question. Still she did not reply. When he asked the question the third time, she said: No. I don't *think* so. Beyond that, what can I say? Come here. You have a large physical presence, do you know that? Hah. The way I talk. You should have heard me a few years back. Little Susie Blockhead from the farm. But now I have many books to read. If Phoebe Underwood ever invited me into her Atheneum, I expect I could show those ladies a thing or two. Take a look some day at the titles in Charley's library downstairs. Remarkable. Ah, you have no idea how much I read. Why, back in Indiana the people I knew would be shocked out of their wits. Little Susie Blockhead has become the lady of the manor. Ah. My goodness. The way of the world.

Bill seated himself across the bed from his father.

Catherine Anne was gasping now.

Bill embraced his mother. He wept against her neck.

At the foot of the bed, Mrs Pett began to keen.

Sh, said Catherine Anne to her son. She gasped, coughed, patted the back of Bill's neck.

Mrs Pett covered her face.

Sh, said Catherine Anne to her son. Be . . . brave . . .

It occurred to Virgil T. Light that someday he'd just *have* to take the time to make something with his hands again. He'd not put together a piece of furniture since before the war. He squinted, tried to recollect the odors of wood and varnish. Thin. Tight. New. Yes, and perhaps soon he would find himself an apple. Charley grinned broadly at him: Now then, old friend, I know you could do the job a damn sight better than that old fool of a George Pillsbury. He's been nothing but Ike Underwood's toy on a string since time out of mind. It's about time a change

was made. We need to cut old Ike down a peg or two. He's never liked
me, and he's never liked you either. If he had liked us, he'd have seen us
through that furniture factory thing. And at least he would have lent you
the money to build back the store. So how about it? You'd be a good
mayor, and you could get elected on the GAR vote alone. And, God
knows, I'll have Millerspaugh and that little *Journal* work like Trojans
for you. Dave is putting together a pretty fair paper these days. Influential. There should be little trouble. Said Virgil T. Light: But what about
George Pillsbury? Said Charley: What *about* him? There's something
you got to learn about power, old son. It's no damn use to anybody if it's
not exercised. George Pillsbury is an old man. If he loses his mayor's job,
it's not as though he hasn't *held* it for a few years. And he's not about to
starve to death. He still has that fraudulent *position* of his with the Paradise Falls Clay Products. Said Virgil T. Light: But what'll the county
committee say? Said Charley: God damn it, didn't I pay that fool of an
Ed Maxwell five thousand dollars to step down from the county chair-
manship because of his socalled high bloodpressure? *You're* the county
chairman now, Virge. If the committee doesn't like it, tell the committee to
go to hell. You'll be a good mayor. You got nothing to be ashamed of.
Said Virgil T. Light: All right. Seeing as how you put it that way, I'll do
it. (And of course he'd had no intention of not doing it. *Mayor* Virgil T.
Light! Ah, a splendid prospect.) The canvass was a fine one. The *Journal*
performed energetically, again dragging out that business of George
Pillsbury's buying a buggy at city discount and using Paradise Falls Clay
Products brick in the construction of the new village hall. And Virgil T.
Light worked on his GAR cronies. Signs were posted everywhere. They
said: LET THERE BE LIGHT. The idea for the slogan came from Dave
Millerspaugh. At first both Virgil T. Light and his friend Charley vetoed
the idea as being too impious. Dave Millerspaugh asked them to think it
over. It's catchy, he said, and it's short and to the point. Who's going to
say it's sacrilegious? A couple of old women? Well, gents, let me remind
you that women, old *or* young, do not have the vote. And so Virgil T.
Light and Charley finally were persuaded that the slogan was a good one.
The signs were printed, and Dave Millerspaugh hired a crew of small
boys to post them everyplace in the village where there was a blank wall
or fence or side of a building. Virgil T. Light's candidacy came as a
complete surprise to old George Pillsbury. He and Virgil T. Light still
were cordial when they met on the street (they even managed to joke a
bit), but the old mayor's eyes had a pale shattered look to them. My Lord,
said Virgil T. Light to himself, a person would think I'd poisoned his
dog. Ike Underwood and the *Democrat* got behind the mayor, and in one

particularly angry editorial J. K. Bankson wrote: *The jackals of expediency and unfair play are roaming the streets of our village. This is no ordinary electoral contest. Rather, it is a struggle between Reason and untrammeled Radicalism. The future of Paradise Falls as we know it is surely at stake in this election. Do we seek to deliver our village into the hands of a stranger who has displayed only greed as the touchstone of his philosophy? Make no mistake, Virgil T. Light is not the true opponent of Mayor Pillsbury. The name of that true opponent is Charles P. Wells. We do not oppose reasoned progress. We do, however, view with horror and distress the spectre of greed that could take possession of our village should Mr Wells' handpicked candidate defeat Mayor Pillsbury. It is our heartfelt belief that Mr Wells will not be satisfied until he controls the lives and destinies of every man, woman and child in Paradise County. This cannot be permitted to happen.* The first time Virgil T. Light saw Nancy after the editorial had been published, she asked him what he thought of it. He shrugged, told her it was no secret that Ike Underwood never had had a bit of use for Charley. It goes back to the time Charley and I bought that land from him, said Virgil T. Light. I don't expect you can blame him. And Nancy said: But *you* don't hate Charley do you? Said Virgil T. Light: I don't hate him. I got no reason to hate him. You're wrong in what you say. He didn't burn my store. He didn't. He didn't. Nancy laughed. It was short and dry. She shook her head.

A cough.

Virgil T. Light blinked at Catherine Anne.

She still was embracing Bill. Lean close, she said to her husband. He leaned to her.

She whispered: Virgil? Are you there?

Yes.

William?

Yes, Mama, said Bill, sniffling. I'm right here.

She whispered: Trees and sky. Stop from time to time. Look.

Father and son looked at each other over Catherine Anne's chin and nose.

She whispered: Sweet. My tongue. My tongue tastes so sweet.

Mrs Pett gave a great wail. She went around the bed and threw herself on Catherine Anne's legs. The covers rustled.

Catherine Anne whispered: There never is enough time. Smell the air. Always. Do. That. The trees are lovely even when they have no leaves. I forgive everybody everything. Sweet Jesus. Lovely. Oh. I am so warm. Nice. Oh.

Bill wept.

Catherine Anne whispered: Sh.

A high sound came from the roof of Virgil T. Light's mouth.

Catherine Anne coughed, seized one of her husband's wrists, coughed again, drooled, died.

The election was held the day after her funeral. Virgil T. Light won easily with 528 votes to Mayor Pillsbury's 307.

1872 . . .

Mrs Dwight T. Templeton, wife of a telegrapher for the CPV&M, grows a tomato that measures seven inches in diameter. C. P. Wells is elected to the Vestry of Grace Episcopal Church. Claude Dill, saloonkeeper, has his fourteen remaining teeth removed. On thirtynine separate occasions, Mrs Isaac (Ike) Underwood asks her husband what he intends to do about the Wells person. St Mark's Presbyterian Church is the setting for the ceremony that unites Mr Arthur Carmichael and Miss Priscilla Caroline Purvis in holy mortal wedlock. Mrs Templeton cannot bear to let her family eat her epic tomato, and so she permits it to spoil. Death claims Queenie, the elderly Spitz bitch owned by the Rev and Mrs Edwin P. Rathbun. Mrs Henry I. Plowright, wife of a laborer for the Paradise Falls Clay Products, bakes eleven mince pies in one day. Mrs Wilhelm Soeder gives birth to her fourth child, a girl. The infant is named Katherine. The other three also are girls. They are: Ida (born 1862), Margaret (born 1863), and Martha (born 1868). No day passes but what Wilhelm Soeder does not pray for a son. The little girls are very pretty, and he loves them dearly, but what sort of man is it who has nothing within his loins but the seed of females? The political situation is rather interesting. There is more Greeley sentiment than one would imagine.

Arthur Carmichael:

THEY WERE SERENADED by dogs the night she told him yes, she allowed as how marriage to him did not exactly strike her senseless with fear and loathing. They were sitting on the back porch of the Purvis place, and Priscilla wore a pale blue dress, and the sounds of the dogs came in waves of lonely twilight yowls. Peculiar how they get going like that, said Priscilla. First just one, and he starts howling like that because he hasn't anything better to do. Then he's answered. Then some other dog joins in. Then, first thing you know, it's like a mess of old women at a wedding or a funeral.

Yes, said Arthur Carmichael. He held her hand.

I always was partial to blond fellows, said Priscilla.

Good, said Arthur Carmichael.

They always have made me stand up and take notice.

Arthur Carmichael nodded. He listened to the dogs. He could hear no other sounds, not even his breath. He had been courting her for three years now, and three years was enough. He had saved nearly a thousand dollars. He was a good worker. His employer, Bill Osterhaus, was the first to admit this. He had done a good job helping Bill Osterhaus put up the C. P. Wells home, which was the county's acknowledged showplace, and not once in those three years had he had carnal knowledge of a woman, and enough was enough. He said: Priss?

She said: I know what you want to say.

And?

It'a been two weeks since the last time you said it. Two weeks tonight. And?

You'll have to support Editha too. She's just sixteen.

I know that.

And you don't mind?

No. I don't mind. How many times do I have to tell you that?

I just want to be sure you understand your responsibilities.

I understand them.

I'll quit my job with Mr Morris. I expect he's going to close down his store soon anyhow. Last year or so, he's sort of lost interest. Age. He just sort of potters around the place, you know what I mean?

Yes.

Priscilla shook her head. The dogs' sad debate continued. *My,* she said, just *listen* to that.

I am.

She worked her fingers between his. I could be younger, she said.

You're young enough.

The twilight was heavy and green. There was an odor of earth, perhaps from some neighbor's garden freshly turned. The people in this village were very fond of gardens. Arthur Carmichael had heard that day of a woman named Templeton who purportedly had raised a tomato measuring seven inches in diameter. He breathed slowly, listened to the dogs.

Two weeks tonight since you last said it, said Priscilla.

Arthur Carmichael nodded.

I been waiting for you to say it again.

All right. I'm saying it again.

Say it *nice.*

Yes. Ah. Hm. Priss . . . ah, *Miss Purvis* . . . will you marry me?

That I will.

What?

I'm saying yes.

Oh my Lord, said Arthur Carmichael. He stood up.

She smiled up at him. My stars, she said.

He dropped to his knees. He kissed her. He pressed his face against her belly. She rubbed his head. He swallowed. The dogs scolded and grieved.

Said Priscilla Purvis: You are really a good man.

He closed his eyes.

Her hand was warm on his head. My flesh feels good, she said.

I know, said Arthur Carmichael.

I love you, she said.

He opened his eyes. She'd never said it before. He kissed her.

I do love you, she said. Her hair glistened.

He ran his hands over her breasts and belly. Yes, she said. Do that. I am twentyseven years old. It is about time.

You are so pretty . . .

Thank you.

So strong . . .

Ah, you and that Ulster rhetoric of yours, said Priscilla. She smiled. Her teeth were quite good. She was a large girl, but she was pretty for a large girl, pretty in a way that had to do with her dark hair and heavy lips and firm bosoms. It was a sturdy prettiness, dependable.

He pulled away from her. He stood up. He turned his back on her. You don't have to be ashamed, said Priscilla.

He wiped at his eyes with his thumbs.

Yes indeed, she said, I always have been partial to blond fellows.

He turned to face her.

She smiled. Do something for me? she said.

Anything.

From time to time bring me surprises?

Surprises?

My papa used to bring home surprises. Bonbons. Licorice. Things like that. One time it was a ribbon for my hair. A blue ribbon. Just about the color of this dress.

I'll bring you surprises.

We don't want it to wear out.

It won't, said Arthur Carmichael.

A lot of people, it wears out for them.

We're different.

Ferd liked you very much, she said.

Well, *I* liked *him.*

Poor Ferd. I still think about him a great deal.

So do I.

We'll live here in this house. With Editha and Pinky.

Yes.

My, those *dogs.*

They were married in July, and in September she told him she did indeed believe she was in the family way. You have brought me, she said, my first surprise. And then she laughed, and so did Arthur Carmichael, and he limped across the parlor and just about squeezed the breath out of her, family way or no family way.

1872 . . .

Ike Underwood quietly slips away to Columbus on four occasions during the first three months of this year. His bank, the Paradise County State, has been purchasing shares in the Columbus, Paradise Valley & Marietta Railroad. By the end of March, it owns more than twenty percent of the road. While in Columbus on his secret visits, old Ike always calls on the CPV&M president, a man named Timothy R. Reavis. He and Reavis are involved in some sort of dispute. Ike Underwood threatens to vote his bank's twenty percent of the stock with a man named Smeed, a minority stockholder who is lusting after control of the CPV&M. I don't see what the hell you're so reluctant about, says old Ike to Timothy R. Reavis. All I'm trying to do is make you rich and at the same time get rid of that damnable Wells. This is a true opportunity for you and your goddamn railroad. Don't force me to give it to Smeed. (Besides Timothy R. Reavis, the only person who knows what old Ike is up to is Mrs Underwood. She is delighted. I find it all very offensive, says Phoebe Underwood, but at the same time I have to admire you for thinking of it. Says old Ike: Well, thank the Lord for small favors. Says Phoebe: I must be getting old. All of an instant I'm telling you what a fine fellow you are. Bah. Senility.)

There is a heavy clattering agony in the skull of the former mayor, George McC. Pillsbury. Daily he spends hours washing and polishing his buggy. He is often absent from his job at the Paradise Falls Clay Products. Not that he is needed. What he does not know about the brick and tile business would fill a book the size of Scripture.

O God of coal mines, praise Thee. We, Thy most unworthy servants, do give hearty thanks for the riches that have accrued to us since the opening of the C. P. Wells Coal Co mines. In Paradise Falls the miners spend their money most enthusiastically, and our retail merchants do most humbly prosper. O God of coal mines, there are those of us who have come to understand that it matters not the most remote damn whether the apple withstands the worm. We are the future, and we shall prevail. In the name of the Father, and of the Son, and of the Holy Ghost. Amen.

To those who say C. P. Wells is crass and greedy, he makes a most eloquent reply. He purchases thirty acres of land south of the river not far from the old Ike Underwood grist mill near the falls. He donates this land to the village for use as a park. The land is gratefully accepted by

Mayor Virgil T. Light. It will be called Elysian Park, and money already
has been appropriated for benches, swings and a picnic shelter. The *Journal* quotes Mayor Light as saying: Each and every resident of Paradise
Falls is, I am certain, grateful that Paradise Falls has the benefit of the attentions of such a man as Mr Wells. The park will be a perpetual monument to his remarkable largeness of spirit.

In Blood, six children die of tuberculosis. Another is killed by a rat
said to have been as large as a suckling pig.

The morning of Tuesday, July 22, former Mayor Pillsbury awakens with
a pain in his chest. He says nothing to his wife about it. He has a fine
breakfast of sausage, fried eggs, potatoes and coffee. He belches several
times as he hitches up the buggy. It is, of course, gleaming. He sits high
and straight in the buggy. He is going to his job at the Paradise Falls
Clay Products. Not that he has any work to do, but he *does* have an office
there. And anyway, where else is there for him to go? There has been a
dry spell, and the horse's hoofs clack against the hard earth streets. The
pain worsens. He nods at passersby. He even manages to smile. The effort
brings pain to his lips. He tells himself: I worked hard for them. All of
them. No fear. No favor. Only hard work. He glances up and down the
treacherous streets. He listens to trees. He is warm. He unbuttons his
frock coat. Perhaps this afternoon he will pay a call on his friend Ike
Underwood. Perhaps there is something Ike can give him to do. He says
to himself: I never took a penny from anyone. Ike knows that. He smiles
at the passersby, and what he wants to do is leap down from the buggy
and seize them by the scruffs of their treacherous necks and tell them:
I am no criminal! I did nothing wrong! He tells himself: I have a good
wife. I have good sons. Why should they have to bear all this? One seeks
love. One works diligently in the pursuit of it. Former Mayor Pillsbury
fiddles with his pince nez. He slaps the reins. He tells himself: I was man
enough to sire seven fine sons. This betrayal never should have been permitted to happen. I never harmed anyone. I have been an honorable man.
Ah yes, look at them. See them smile. They still can smile. They elected
that Virgil Light over me and ah, if only I had a penny for every tooth
that has been exposed in my presence. Ah, if only. Clucking, former Mayor
Pillsbury decides it is not so important that he drive directly to his place
of alleged employment. He decides he will drive over by the old mill. He
squeezes the bridge of his nose, adjusts his pince nez. The drive is a pleasant one, despite the heat of the day. There is an odor of honeysuckle in
the air. Honeysuckle and somewhere meat frying. He tells himself: I
like the people here. I always have. He takes a handkerchief from a pocket
and wipes a spot of anonymous moisture off the empty seat next to him.
He is aware that there are those who ridicule him because he takes such
good care of his buggy. He is sorry that he is ridiculed, but he knows he
cannot help being whatever it is he is. The pain in his chest is so intense
that he has to bend forward. He grimaces. He focuses his mind on his

doughy wife, his seven sons. The pain relents. There is still the agony within his skull, however. He straightens up and again uses the handkerchief, this time to wipe away the sweat that has gathered in bright little drops on his forehead. He reins up the horse at a tree close by the river and Ike Underwood's old mill. The sun is sweet God so hot. He climbs down from the buggy and tethers the horse to the tree. He walks to the edge of the river. He places his hands on his hips and smiles at the white water that comes crisp and riotous over the falls. He removes his hat, frock coat, vest. Carefully he folds the frock coat and vest. He seeks out a grassy place. He finds one in the shade of a willow, gray and graceful, murmurous. He places the folded frock coat on the grass. He places the folded vest on the folded frock coat. He places his hat on the folded vest that is on the folded frock coat. Then he removes his pince nez. He places his pince nez squarely atop the hat that is on the folded vest that is on the folded frock coat. He seats himself next to this fastidious little pile of his possessions. He hugs his knees. He breathes deeply of the grass and the earth and the river and the falls and the willow. The pain returns to his chest. He tells himself: I am warm. I am very warm. I do not want to be warm. He removes his watch and billfold from a pocket of his trousers. The watch is quite large. He received it from his wife on the occasion of his fiftieth birthday. He places the billfold on the pince nez which are atop the hat which is on the folded vest which is on the folded frock coat. He places the watch on the billfold which is on the pince nez which are atop the hat which is on the folded vest which is on the folded frock coat. He tells himself: If God strikes down the last tree, it will be no outrage. But what if the dead hand of man is there before Him? God save me, I am too warm, and I am too tired, and the pain is too much. Sighing, former Mayor Pillsbury stands up. He clears his throat. For some reason he remembers bells. Cowbells. The farm where he had lived the days of his slender dreaming boyhood. His father's herd. Ashtabula County, fifty years ago. Cowbells. A sound like no other sound. Hollow. Calm. A sound of the rightness of God's order. Over yonder, not too far away, just beyond those ancient unremembered Ashtabula County hills. Ah, but all hills are ancient, and these Paradise County hills are just as good as any (and they are remembered; they are visible; they bend in from the east, and they are warm), and former Mayor Pillsbury blinks at the hills, and the absence of his pince nez makes the hills to him hazy and hallucinatory, and he scrambles down a shallow bank to the river, and at the edge of the river he pauses to remove his shoes. He places the shoes neatly next to one another. He wiggles his toes. Ah. Relief. The air now is cool against his feet. He steps into the water. The pain beats on him with a hammer. He was a farmer's boy from Ashtabula County, and he came to this place and made a name for himself, and the village records always will include that name as a onetime MAYOR, and he is able to smile, and the water is not as cool as he hoped for, but one presses on, and he cannot swim, and the sound of the bells increases with the depth of the water, and his eyes smart, and he wishes he knew an appropriate hymn. Inscribed upon the great bell at the Grace Episcopal Church are the words: LET EVERY THING THAT HATH BREATH PRAISE THE LORD. This bell, the largest and loudest in the village, was given to the church by Ike and Phoebe Underwood. It has a reluctant castiron sound to it, and its reverberations shake the building's foundation. It tolls for former Mayor Pillsbury, whose remains are found three miles downstream four days after he does away with himself. The face is severely chewed by fish and perhaps musk-rats, and the body is not placed on public display. The story is that he had a coronary attack and somehow fell into the river. The story is perhaps not even accepted by babes in arms. The bell tolls. The bell tolls. The bell tolls. *Laudate Dominum.*

The widowed Heinz Burkhart sets places at the kitchen table for his dead wife and daughter. He does this every day—morning, noon and night. He works his farm alone, and it is as neat and prosperous as ever. He sells off his hogs to Wilhelm Soeder. They are too dirty, he tells Wilhelm Soeder. I cannot abide dirt any more. I do not know why. I wish I did. I have always been a neat man, but never to this extent. Perhaps, Wilhelm, I am mad. Could that be? I keep seeing that dead Purvis fellow on the kitchen floor. Him and his tongue. Says Wilhelm Soeder: Perhaps you need a new wife. Says Heinz Burkhart: Ach. Do not be foolish. Evenings, when the sun goes down and there are no more chores than can be done, Heinz Burkhart sits in his parlor and stares at the photograph of himself that hangs over the mantel. Such a fine little fellow. Such a splendid uniform. Ach.

Ike Underwood is seventy this year.

Mrs Templeton's tomato is the subject of half a column of type in the *Journal* one rainy day. She purchases twenty copies.

Another of old Harlowe Morris' peach trees dies.

Little Nell Wells is talking now. Her father has inundated her with dolls. She is tall for her age and rather plain. She brings little girls into her big house to play with her. The little girls are frightened by the high ceilings. Their voices echo. They visit her once or twice, then do not care to return. Nell begins thinking of herself as a princess locked in a tower. She loves her mama, and she even loves the man who visits her mama when her papa is away. The man is very important, and he has no hair. He is what is known as a mayor, and it is a large and scary thing to be a mayor. He has a loud voice, and he and Nell's mama apparently like each other a whole lot.

Ike Underwood finally prevails upon Timothy R. Reavis to go through with the plan as outlined. It fails. The failure represents the first of two defeats inflicted on old Ike this year by the damnable Wells. The second defeat is political. Ike Underwood is a delegate to the Liberal Republican convention that meets in Cincinnati in May and nominates Horace

Greeley for the presidency. Old Ike—and apparently millions of other Republicans—cannot tolerate the prospect of four more years of U. S. Grant in the White House. There are those who have taken to calling the man U. S. Graft. They cite the Crédit Mobilier railroad construction scandal (*even the Vice President of the United States,* that wretched booby of a Schuyler Colfax, was involved in *that* one). They cite the land giveaways, the whisky tax fraud, the bribery of Secretary of War Belknap, the rigged Navy Department contracts. This is intolerable, says old Ike to his wife. I have supported the Republican party since its inception, but now I must leave it—or at least leave *what now passes* for the Republican party. Says Phoebe: But can this man Greeley win? Says old Ike: Perhaps—if the Democrats go along with us. The Democrats, who are in such a poor condition that they have little choice, do go along, and thus Greeley becomes the nominee of a coalition that has as its sole objective the ouster of Grant. Old Ike sets J. K. Bankson to writing daily Greeley editorials in the *Democrat.* At the same time, C. P. Wells' *Journal* comes out strongly in support of Grant. This is the second public confrontation between Ike Underwood and C. P. Wells within a year. Phoebe Underwood questions its wisdom. This Greeley person doesn't seem to have much of a chance, she says. Not with the GAR and the colored people lined up for Grant. Says Ike: I know that, but I have to do what I believe is right. Says Phoebe: Well, you old fool, you always *were* stubborn. Then Phoebe nudges her husband with an elbow, which coming from *her* is the same as a kiss and a hug around the neck from any *normal* woman. This is Ike Underwood's second major change of politics. He was originally a Democrat, which is why his newspaper bears that name. But he became weary of the doughfaces, the Polks and the Pierces, whom the Democrats were putting up for the Presidency. And so, in '52, his paper came out in support of the Whig, General Winfield Scott, and in '56 it went Republican, backing John Charles Frémont. Until this year, it has not swerved in its espousal of all things Republican, but this Grant person is too much. So J. K. Bankson furiously grinds out the editorials, as does Dave Millerspaugh of the rival *Journal.* The Democratic county chairman, an impecunious lawyer named F. B. Crabb, offers his congratulations to old Ike Underwood. Be damned to you, sir, says Ike. This is a Greeley canvass, not a Democratic canvass. Kindly stay out of my way. I shall have nothing to do with you and your people. (Crabb, under whose guidance the Paradise County Democracy has not won a single office since 1858, immediately repairs to Claude Dill's saloon and drinks himself out of the ordeal he has just undergone. F. B. Crabb has been for many years more than eager to heal his wounds with the heavy waters. He and his skinny little wife are childless, and it is said he beats her two or three times a week. He wears stovepipe hats, and he is bearded and very tall, and there are those who say he bears an extraordinary resemblance to the late President Lincoln. There are others, however, who say that if F. B. Crabb bears a resemblance to the late President, then so does the man in the moon.) The *Democrat*'s editorials are vigorous, but the zeal of their language is put to shame by the invective loosed by the *Journal*. If I do say so myself, Dave Millerspaugh tells C. P. Wells, I can pile more abuse per square inch than a shovel can pile pig shit. The *Journal* editorials remind one and all that Horace Greeley was one of those who went bail for Jeff Davis shortly after the end of the war. They point out that the Greeley forces have aligned themselves with the party of treason, Tammany and the infamous Ku Klux Klan. They ridicule Greeley's messy and eccentric physical appearance. Mayor Virgil T. Light and his GAR men hold a number of gala torchlight parades in support of their beloved commanding general. C. P. Wells laughs. This has to be his finest year. C. P. Wells laughs like the devil. He reminds himself that he already has defeated old Ike in the squabble earlier this year with the CPV&M. Old Ike *had* to be behind that fuss, sure as the sun rises in the east. And now the old fart is hanging himself again, this time by supporting Horace Greeley. The election is closer than '68, but Grant still has little trouble carrying the county, 1,004 to 611, and Paradise Falls, 551 to 354.

A Great Man:

OH THAT LOVELY PLUMP WORM: how it gorged itself. Erich Kahler's fine fiduciary brow was a sight to behold. The C. P. Wells Coal Co was becoming one of the largest corporate enterprises in southeastern Ohio, and Charley's name had penetrated quite a sight beyond the tight boundaries of Paradise County. His magnificent new Grainger Street home, built with care and devotion by a carpenter named Osterhaus, had to be one of the glories of the age. Its turrets, its filigree, its great high ceilings, its plethora of lavatories, its hedges, its trim and geometric lawn —all contributed to the undoubted splendor, and surely there was no one who could in all candor question the greatness of Charles Palmer Wells. And he was just thirtyfour years of age. Ah, boys, the grandeur of genius. Such a muzzle velocity. (He put on a bit of weight, and all of it was in his face and belly. He told himself he was an ass. He took off the weight. He would not permit himself to become fat and sluggish. There still was too much to be done. He'd not yet defeated old Ike Underwood. And, once the defeat of the old bastard was accomplished, there no doubt would be other projects. No, a great man could not afford fat.) Nancy seemed delighted with the house. My, she told him, we surely have come a distance. Ah, good old Nancy. A fine wife. A heroically constructed creature whose physical enthusiasms still were able to give him delight. Not as often as in days past, but then that was to be expected. A great man required more than one woman; a great man's appetites required that he sup at more than one table. He supposed Nancy knew he visited the girls at Irene Hollingshead's fastidious whorehouse when he went to Columbus on his business trips. He figured she maybe even understood. Certain rules were not for certain men. She was not so stupid that she could not acknowledge this. And besides, now she had little Nell, and clearly she loved the child devotedly. It was necessary that a woman have a child to love. Kept her mind from considering boredom and mischief. Four years ago, when she'd screamed out the words having to do with the betrayal of the betrayer, he had wondered if perhaps they'd had something to do with his associate Fritz Voss. He knew her attitude toward Fritz had changed from distaste to a sort of admiration. And so he'd asked her if there was anything she wanted to tell him. And she'd told him no, not a thing. Which was good enough for him. And anyway, he was rather pleased that she had her admirers. Fritz was one. And so was that windbag of a Virgil T. Light, who now was Charley's private mayor. And so, for that matter, was Virgil T. Light's son, young Bill. But Charley could not feature these men, any of them, as the seducers of his wife. Not *Nancy*. She had better sense. Perhaps from time to time she felt sorry for herself, and perhaps she even resented Charley his whores, but she was wise enough to keep her feelings to herself, and this was all that mattered. Charley Wells was a man who trafficked in *possibilities* and *mortality*, the real and the tangible, and those things that were unsaid did not exist. (And, beyond that, there was the matter of courage, or its lack. He did not *want* to know what she really thought; he did not want to know what *anyone* thought. It was enough for him to grapple with the clear and present intrigues of each day; he had no desire to be burdened with concepts. He had learned well from the revered Professor. Dying and retribution would come soon enough; in the meantime, he would nourish the worm, and the Devil take eternity.) In that year of 1872, he saw himself as playing at the top of his game. The election of Virgil T. Light as mayor had been accomplished, and it was the first large step in the demolition of Ike Underwood. And, as soon as the opportunity presented itself, there would be another step. And then there was the matter of the Elysian Park. He purchased the land and donated it to the city because he figured it was about time he did something to silence those stupid carpers who were forever complaining about his alleged despoliation of the Blood country. His mines had brought unparalleled prosperity to the entire county, and what difference did it make that holes had to be dug and trees chopped down? What in the name of God did those people expect? Ah, but the Elysian Park affair had done a great deal to muffle their weeping and wailing. Charley had become a bloody goddamn *benefactor,* a fine fellow, a true Christian gentleman more than willing to share the fruits of his labor, and now how would it be possible to call him a monster? Yes indeed: the top of his game. And, in the meantime, his two principal associates—Fritz Voss, his general superintendent, and Erich Kahler, his banker and bookkeeper—were playing at the top of their game as well. In the spring of 1872, Fritz was married to a plump and tawny farm girl named Elke Brandt, and she almost immediately became most heavily gravid. As for Erich Kahler, well, the man had a quality that made him lovable—no doubt about it. He was a great one for giving candy to children. Old ladies adored him. He liked to tell innocuous little stories. His laugh was shy, and he daily brought bread for the birds that gathered outside his window at the Paradise Valley Farmers' & Merchants' Bank. The birds learn quick, he said, who their friend is. Two days after I started bringing the bread, they were sitting there on the sill waiting for me. I enjoy feeding them. It how you say sets up my entire day. Erich Kahler still was unmarried, but he'd not given up *looking,* oh Lord no. Charley had heard young women remark that Erich was the most fervent one for *looking* they'd ever encountered. Erich still sang bass in the Lutheran choir, and every other week or so he was called on for a solo. His voice was quite loud, and he smiled as he sang, and it was as though squadrons of cherubim were romping across the vast pale virgin expanses of his immortal soul. (Or at least Charley *figured* Erich to be a virgin. He'd never quite gotten up the gall, however, to ask.) At any rate, Erich Kahler appeared to be a happy man, and Charley surely could find no fault with the fellow's handling of the fiscal affairs of the C. P. Wells Coal Co and the Paradise Valley Farmers' & Merchants' Bank. Nor could he reasonably criticize Fritz Voss' performance as general superintendent of the mines. Both men clearly knew their jobs; both carried them out splendidly. Both surely were playing at the top of their game. The notice from the CPV&M came in the mail one morning in early July. The damn cowards. Didn't even have the courage to notify Charley personally. Had to send the notice in the mail. Effective immediately, coal shipping rates were being raised fifteen percent. As soon as Charley read the notice, he summoned Erich Kahler to his office. The news made Erich Kahler flop in a chair. My *Gott,* he said, this could ruin us. Said Charley: It won't. Said Erich Kahler: But we cannot pay. Said Charley: We won't. Said Erich Kahler: But how will the coal be shipped? Said Charley: By the CPV&M, same as always. Those sonsofbitches won't get away with this. They want the mines for themselves. It doesn't take much of a brain to figure *that* out. Well, they've got themselves another fine think coming. Said Erich Kahler: How do you propose to fight them? Said Charley: I don't have the slightest idea. But I'll come up with something. Just have faith. Said Erich Kahler, grinning a little: Do I have any choice? Said Charley: Those people don't know it, but they have just become involved in a pissing contest with one of the world's truly outstanding skunks. Said Erich Kahler: I do not doubt that for a minute. Then he laughed, and so did Charley.

The next afternoon Charley was sitting in the Columbus office of Timothy R. Reavis, president and chief executive officer of the Columbus, Paradise Valley & Marietta Railroad. This Timothy R. Reavis had excellent manners, and his voice was smoother than a baboon's ass. He was about forty, and there was no fat to him. He had brown eyes, thin sandy hair, a square jaw. He reminded Charley a little of his old dear departed *friend* George Peters, and he surely did look like a Leader of Men, and he surely did look like he was full of shit. Smiling, he offered Charley a cigar. It was accepted. Then he offered Charley a shot of sour mash whisky. It also was accepted. Reavis had taken care to make sure Charley was seated in the most comfortable chair in the room. It was leather, and it made comfortable flatulent noises when Charley seated himself in it. After giving Charley his drink, Reavis lifted his own glass and said: Health.

By all means, said Charley. He lifted his glass and drank.

Reavis also drank. Then he seated himself behind his desk and said: I expect you are here because of our rate adjustment.

Adjustment? said Charley, smiling.

A euphemism, of course, said Reavis.

Mm.

You are here to remonstrate, of course.

Yes.

I'm sorry, Mr Wells, but with all respect to you, sir, we cannot reconsider.

You're trying to put me out of business. You won't put me out of business.

Of course not, sir. That was not our intention.

You're not going to raise your goddamn rates.

I beg to differ with you, Mr Wells.

Said Charley: You put me in a nice soft chair. You give me a cigar. You give me a drink. And then you as much as tell me I'm finished. All right. Come out with it. You and your goddamn railroad want my mines, don't you?

Reavis smiled. You waste no time getting to the point do you? he said. I'd be obliged if you did the same.

Fair enough. The board has met on this matter. We are prepared to offer you half a million dollars for your holdings.

Oh? That so?

And we shall assume your bank obligation. And, if you agree to our terms, you will be voted a seat on the board. Or, if you do not care to serve on the board, we would be amenable to appointing you chief executive officer of the mining operation—at a substantial salary, of course.

No.

Does that mean you agree to the increased rates?

It means no.

Please try to understand our position.

Oh?

Yes. Hear me out, Mr Wells. These are not good days for the CPV&M. The rate adjustment is perfectly legitimate, sir. In order to keep our heads above water, we must raise our coal shipment charges. If you like, I can give you a copy of our most recent financial statement. It shows how—

How many companies ship coal on your railroad?

Oh. Several dozen.

Shit.

I beg your pardon?

For all it *matters,* you got *one* coal shipper—*me.* A good ninety percent of your coal business comes from me. You know it and I know it. Who else you got? A couple of tacky little flybynight operations over in Athens and Washington counties? They aren't worth a fiddler's fart, and that's the fact of the matter, and kindly don't tell me any different. And how come, if your road's so goddamn poor, it's offering me half a million dollars? Not that half a million dollars is even a twentieth of what my holdings are worth, but by God it's a whole lot coming from a road that's supposed to be on the edge of bankruptcy. No, Mr Reavis, you are full of shit up to your eyeballs. You can take your half a million dollars and stuff it up your ass. And, if there's any room left, you can maybe squeeze in that seat on the board. Hah, some seat on the board *that'd* be. I'd sit there about five minutes and then you and your cronies would vote me out. No sir, I was *not* born the day before yesterday. I am going to whip you, Mr Reavis, and I am going to whip you good and proper. You and your cigar and your drink and your soft chair. I am going to make you curse the day you ever tried to get the best of *me.*

Reavis drummed his fingers on his desk. I regret you feel that way, he said.

You're going to regret it more.

You're an unpleasant sonofabitch aren't you?

Yes.

Well, it'll give me pleasure to destroy you. I tried to be polite. I tried to be a gentleman. But apparently you have no use for gentlemanly conduct. Very well then. So be it. Effective midnight tonight, our service to your mines is suspended. If and when you choose to honor the adjusted rates, it will be restored.

This is going to cost you a whole lot, said Charley.

Cost *me?* said Reavis, chuckling. How?

Your railroad has got just one main line.

So?

A chain is only as strong as its weakest link.

Reavis stood up. I don't know what you're talking about, he said. Perhaps you are out of your mind.

Charley struggled out of the flatulent chair. He was shaking. His eyes were hot. I never did a thing to you, he said. I came here willing to talk over the situation. But all you do is tell me to go to hell. I am going to chew you up real good, you piece of shit.

Get out of here!

Kiss my ass, you sonofabitch.

Reavis came around his desk and advanced on Charley.

Charley retreated toward the door. My, he said, look at the polite *gentleman.* Then Charley opened he door and went out. He slammed the door in Reavis' face. That night, on his return to Paradise Falls, he held a council of war with Fritz Voss, Erich Kahler, ElRoy Mauk and Winfield Wainscott. He had a plan, and it was a very florid plan, and his associates clucked and grunted when he outlined it for them. They told him it did not have the slightest chance of succeeding. He told them shit, they were of weak spirit and little faith. They argued with him. They said he was as much as taking the law into his own hands. They were unanimous in their condemnation of his plan. He grinned, told them to buck up, old Charley Wells was on the job, and old Charley Wells would get the job done. Finally his associates surrendered. Said ElRoy Mauk: All right. We're in. We wouldn't want you to face the firing squad alone. Said Charley: Thank you kindly. And don't fret yourself about any firing squad. Before this is over, Reavis'll be wishing *he* was in front of a firing squad. He'll welcome it. Said Fritz Voss: You're sure you'll be able to get Virgil Light to go along with all this? said Charley: Virgil Light is an honorable man. I put him where he is. He'll pay his debt. And besides, everybody knows I'm his friend. And that's a fact. I've been a good friend. Go on. Laugh. All of you. Enjoy yourselves. You fellows just don't understand friendship. Later, after the laughter had subsided, Charley said: It'll all work. I promise you that. We got a sight of things to stuff up that Reavis' hightoned Columbus ass. Now let's all get some sleep. Beginning tomorrow morning, we go to work . . . or war . . . or whatever you choose to call it. Then, grinning, Charley shook hands with his associates and sent them on their way. He got to bed at about midnight. He had trouble sleeping. Nancy reached out for him and hugged him. She moaned in her sleep. Her body was hot, sticky. When he finally fell asleep, he dreamed he was being pursued by a large cow that had moist and luminous eyes. The next morning he called on his good friend Mayor Virgil T. Light. He told old Virge what he wanted, and old Virge promptly gave him a large bald frown. *Well*now, said old Virge, we couldn't pass such an ordinance. It wouldn't hold up in a court of law. Said Charley: It doesn't have to. If matters progress the way I want them to, a day or two is all we need. The CPV&M won't be able to get to court that quickly, so what difference does the legality make? Said old Virge: Ah, but I took an oath to conduct myself in a proper manner. Said Charley: Please. Let's not cloud the issue with *that* sort of sheep dip. Virge, do you realize how much wealth the C. P. Wells Coal Co has brought to Paradise Falls? *And* the county? At midnight last night the CPV&M did a thing that not only could ruin me and the company, but what about all the people who have come to depend on the mines? And I don't mean those miners up in Blood. They were brought in, and I expect they can be taken out. The things I'm talking about are: Number One, the county tax duplicate has been increased by about thirty percent since the first mine was opened, and you know as well as I do that a lot of that money has gone to this village; Number Two, the prosperity of one Charles Palmer Wells has given this village one new bank and one new newspaper *and* the reputation of being a community where large things are beginning to happen; Number Three, the retail merchants and the saloonkeepers are thriving to a degree they never could have hoped for before the mines were opened; and Number Four, God damn it, Virge, you owe me a favor. Friendship is a reciprocal thing. All I'm asking is that you bend the law for a day or two. You're no lawyer. Neither is anybody on the village Council. You can't be expected to know whether every piddling little ordinance is proper. Nobody's going to blame you a damn bit. So please. Do this thing for me. Finally, with a good deal of reluctance, after shaking his head and drawing several score wet fretful breaths, old Virge agreed to do Charley this favor. Charley thanked him most heartily, then took a jaunty little stroll over to

the courthouse, where he conferred with Sheriff Lester W. Bowles, the
gimpy Gettysburg veteran. The sheriff told Charley yes, he had heard
about the dispute with the CPV&M. I understand, he said, the CPV&M
pulled all its engines and rolling stock off the Blood branch last night.
Ran six engines up there and took out every one of its gondolas, closed
the depot, laid off four train crews. Said Charley, smiling: Four train
crews? Good enough. How many men to a train crew? Five? Four times
five is twenty. Looks like I got twenty allies. Well, fine. The more the
merrier, yes *sir*. Now then, Lester, let's not beat around the bush. We got
a little serious talking to do. Charley and the sheriff conferred for about
fifteen minutes. At the close of those fifteen minutes, they shook hands.
Charley gave the sheriff a large sealed envelope. Again he and the sheriff
shook hands. The sheriff told him he surely was a sketch. Charley
grinned, took his leave of the sheriff. He walked home. He told Nancy and
little Nell he had to go to Blood on business. Nancy told him she'd heard
about the fight with the CPV&M. Said Charley: Don't concern yourself. I'm taking care of it. Said Nancy: I'm not concerned. I'm sure
you'll take care of it just fine. Charley smiled, told her that was the spirit.
He went outside, climbed into his buggy and drove the eleven miles to the
village of Blood. The first thing he did was visit all five of the C. P. Wells
Coal Co mines—the Nancy #1 (1868), the Orland (1869), the Nell
(1869), the Nancy #2 (1870) and the Tuesday Creek (1871). He
chatted briefly with the foremen. They showed him the large hand
printed notices that had been posted at all the mines by Fritz Voss early
that morning. The notices read:

DUE TO THE GREED AND PERFIDY OF THE COLUMBUS,
PARADISE VALLEY & MARIETTA RY CO, THESE PREMISES
WILL BE CLOSED UNTIL FURTHER NOTICE.

THE OWNERS AND MANAGEMENT OF THE C. P. WELLS
COAL CO WISH TO ASSURE THEIR WORKERS, HOWEVER, THAT
THEY ARE BENDING EVERY EFFORT TOWARD A QUICK AND
HONORABLE SETTLEMENT OF THE MATTER.

IN THE MEANTIME, THE OWNERS AND MANAGEMENT
DEEPLY REGRET ANY HARDSHIPS THAT MAY BE SUFFERED
BY THEIR WORKERS BECAUSE OF THE UNJUST ACTION TAKEN
THIS PAST EVENING BY THE CPV&MRR.

AT 3 P.M. TODAY, MR C. P. WELLS, PRESIDENT OF THE
C. P. WELLS COAL CO, WILL DELIVER AN ADDRESS FROM
THE STEPS OF THE BETHEL ME CHURCH, BLOOD, O. HE
WILL EXPLAIN THE SITUATION AS IT PRESENTLY IS FOUND.

ALL EMPLOYEES OF THE C. P. WELLS COAL CO ARE IN-
VITED TO ATTEND WITH THEIR FAMILIES. REFRESHMENTS
WILL BE SERVED.

F. F. VOSS
GEN'L SUPT

JULY 10, 1872

Back in the days when Blood had been a farming settlement, the Bethel
ME Church had been a crisp white little building, narrow and frail, high
on a hill, with a graveyard behind it. James Perry Blood's energetic progenitors had built the church, and the figure *1829* had been carved in its cor-
nerstone. But now the Bethel ME Church was neither crisp nor white. It
lay in the path of the winds that came from the west, and these winds first
passed the C. P. Wells Coal Co's Tuesday Creek mine. As a result, the little church now was caked and smeared with coaldust. According to talk
Charley had heard, the place probably would be abandoned soon. The
coming of the mines had driven away most of the congregation. Member-
ship was barely twenty, and the little church was open only one Sunday a month. The preacher, a young fellow named Pratt, had resigned the
previous year to accept a more promising post in the town of Brockton,
Maine. Now the monthly services were conducted by the Rev Clovis T.
Reader, pastor of the First ME Church of Paradise Falls. His monthly
visits to Blood were something of a chore for him, seeing as how he had to
rush there after conducting a full Sunday morning of services in his Paradise Falls church. Surely, on the face of it, there appeared to be little doubt
that the Bethel ME Church would soon be abandoned. The miners had
increased the population of Blood several times over, but most of those
people were Papists. They also were visited once a month—by the Rev Fr
Paul K. Messer, pastor of St Thomas Aquinas Church of Paradise Falls.
The Rev Fr Messer, a portly and jovial chap with a fondness for wine
and steaks and blueberry tarts, was much beloved by his parishioners in
Paradise Falls, but he was a German, and so were most of them. The Papists
of Blood, however, were Irish and Welsh, and they barely could understand Fr Messer's words, his Teutonic accent was that impenetrable. As a
result, they didn't much care for him. He tried to make friends among
them, but they gave him little encouragement. I much fear, he told his
intimates, they hold me to be an enemy. It is a pity, and I do indeed wish
I could do something about the situation. But, I ask you, what *can* I do?
The Rev Fr Messer's monthly Masses were celebrated in a tent provided
through the largesse of the C. P. Wells Coal Co, but these facilities were

far from adequate, especially when there was rain, and most especially in
the winter, when the cold whipped down from the hills. Charley understood all this, and for the past year or so he had made a great show of
trying to find these people a decent place where they could fall down and
grovel and kiss the priest's ring, or kiss his ass, or whatever it was they did
in their exotic Papist rituals. There had been some agitation among them
for a church of their own, but they had barely enough money to nourish
their bodies. The feeding of their immortal souls would have to wait for
better times. With this in mind (and figuring it wouldn't cost him much
and at the same time would gain him a great deal of popularity), Charley
had gone so far as to call on the Rev Mr Reader and suggest to him that
perhaps the miners could use the Bethel ME Church for their Masses.
The Rev Mr Reader, a small young man with dark jolly eyes, was very
sympathetic, but there was nothing he could do. You see, he said, I rather
suspect that some of the, uh, more *zealous* adherents of the Methodist faith
hereabouts would take an exceedingly dim view of such an arrangement.
They would call it desecration. *Miners* and a *priest* in *their* church . . .
oh my, they would just about all of them enter into severe convulsions.
Said Charley: Suppose I bought the church. Said the Rev Mr Reader:
Yes, that would be a fine solution, but I'm afraid it's out of the question.
Said Charley: Why do you say that? Said the Rev Mr Reader: You have
to remember that there *are* a few people who still attend Bethel. And, to a
man, they consider you to be the most frightful villain ever to have entered their lives. They hold you responsible for what they consider the
destruction of their village and farmlands. I think they would sooner burn
their church to the ground than sell it to you. And then of course there is
the matter of your old friend John Ellsworth, who is a deacon. As you
know, he still lives in Blood, and he's not forgiven you for sending him
off to jail. I am very sorry, Mr Wells, but your chances of purchasing
Bethel are less than remote. Said Charley: Well, I thank you anyway. For
your time and your candor. It is good to hear the unvarnished truth of a
thing. I expect I'll have to figure out something else. Said the Rev Mr
Reader: I imagine you will. You surely do appear to be a person of deter-
mination. Charley smiled, shook hands with the Rev Mr Reader. Later,
he told his associates to spread the word to the miners and their families
as to how diligently he was working to find them a church. The word
duly was spread, and it gave Charley something of a leg up as far as popularity was concerned. This pleased him considerably. He was not unap-
preciative of the uses of popularity and good fellowship. The way he saw
it, a popular employer had an easier time keeping his workers' wages low.
As long as the miners thought of him as being such a considerate fellow,
they would give him little trouble, and he could continue paying them

twenty cents per man per ton of coal brought out of the mines. He had all this in mind on July 10, 1872, the day he went to war with the CPV&M. The miners didn't know it yet, but they were about to become footsoldiers in the army of the godly and the righteous. He was about to play on them the way that Italian fellow Paganini had been said to play on the fiddle. The war officially began that afternoon when he stood on the front steps of the gray little Bethel ME Church and spoke to the miners and their families. It was a brilliant afternoon, an afternoon without shadows, an afternoon free of wind and thus also free of swirling coaldust; there was heat, but the heat was not muggy; it was the sort of heat that rubbed the skin and reddened it but at the same time did not inflict pain; it was the sort of heat treasured by small boys and liverspotted old women; it was picnic heat, wildflower heat, polecat and chipmunk and sniggering girl heat; it was heat to exalt the optimist and confound the cynic; it was heat that complemented beer and lemonade and melons and cold tea; it was loud britchesbusting take your darling into the bushes heat, and Charley knew he couldn't have *had* a better day for a declaration of war, and they came, these miners; they came with their wives and they came with their children; their faces were gray; they blinked in the brilliant sunshine; they wiped their mouths with their forearms; they squinted with pale querulous puzzlement at Charley and the other men who stood on the steps of the Bethel ME Church; they squinted and shrugged and spoke in dry whispers, and all around them was evidence that this was not an ordinary day; planks had been set on sawhorses in an adjoining grove, and displayed on those planks were all the fixings for a massive picnic, and the fixings included kegs of beer, pitchers of cold tea, sides of beef, sides of pork, mounds of chickenlegs, chickenbreasts, chickenthighs, platters of watermelon, plates piled with onions and potato salad and sausage and ham and cookies and candy and taffy and cakes and pies and relishes, pails of milk, buckets of coffee—all of it immense and splendid and unutterably terrific, a majestic symphony of food and drink, a sight to make the senses fall down, the heart whistle, the belly gurgle. At 7 o'clock that morning Fritz Voss had hired a dozen local women and girls to prepare this epic feast. The ingredients had been brought by wagon from Paradise Falls. The assignment had been accomplished with efficiency and dispatch, and that was Fritz Voss for you. Charley stood on the top step at the entrance to the little church. He was in his shirtsleeves, and his hands were on his hips. He grinned at the miners and their families. He grinned until his teeth hurt. The people gathered below him. They gathered in an arc. He motioned to them to sit down. They spread themselves crosslegged on the grass. Charley took a large breath. He recalled his beer keg orations for the Democracy. He was able to smell the grass. He also was able to smell his audience. One of his shirt buttons was unfastened. Fritz Voss and Winfield Wainscott stood at the bottom of the steps. They also were grinning. Charley had told them it was very important that they grin. We can't show them fear or lack of confidence, he'd said. If we do, then we're whipped before we start. What we got to do is get them *mad*. If we do, then—what with the whisky and all—it won't take much for them to get the idea to do what we want them to do. Oh that Reavis. He's going to curse the day, and that's a fact. Now, grinning down at his audience, Charley felt as good as he had felt in years. This was even better than Virgil Light's victory over George Pillsbury; it was even better than being with a whore. A happy tightness came to Charley's belly, and finally, still grinning, he held up his arms for silence. The noise of the crowd fell away. Charley opened his mouth to speak. A bluejay squawked from a tree. *Quiet, you!* hollered Charley, pointing an accusing finger at the bird. Everyone laughed. The bluejay flew off. Charley leaned forward a little. It's a fine thing, being a boss, he said. You can't even get a bluejay to keep still when you want to talk. More laughter. The hell with the bluejay, Mr Wells! hollered a man in the rear. *We'll* listen to you! Talk away! Charley nodded. Thank you, friend, he said. I appreciate that. Truly I do. Now then, over there in that grove are a whole lot of things to eat and drink—for *you* to eat and drink. So I'll try to keep this little talk of mine short. After I'm done, you're all of you to go over there and help yourselves, have yourselves a nice picnic, courtesy of C. P. Wells. That all right with you? The answer came in cheers and applause. You got beer over there? a man hollered. Yes sir, said Charley. Hot damn! hollered the man. Then another man spoke up: If you don't feel up to making a speech, it won't hurt our feelings none! Charley laughed, and so did just about everyone else. Ah, he said, I fear nothing in this world is free. You'll have to hear me out first. So let me be about it. I'm as hungry as you are, and that's a fact. Here Charley paused for a moment. He smiled. Then, looking out at his audience in a narrow squint, he said: It surely does look like we got us a fight on our hands. Another pause. Men and women were fanning themselves with their hats. The odor of these people was yellow, with a trace of the odor of coalgas. Said Charley: It surely does look like the CPV&M wants to ruin me. Or, I should say, *us*. That's why the mines are closed. I expect most of you heard all the commotion last night, the commotion at the CPV&M yards I mean. You been down to those yards today? You been over to the depot? Well, for those of you who haven't, I'll tell you something—the CPV&M has pulled every piece of its rolling stock out of here. You won't find so much as a little old *handcar*. And the depot's closed down tighter than an oldmaid's . . . ah, *lips*. Again came laughter, punctuated by hoots from a number of the men. Charley held up a hand. He continued: The fact of the matter is the CPV&M is just plain and simple trying to run me out of business. Ah, how about that, eh? I can just see what some of you are thinking. You're telling yourselves: Well, what *about* it? Since when are C. P. Wells' troubles *our* troubles? Ah, my friends, there's only one thing I can say, and it's this: *C. P. Wells has been a good friend to you*. Now, now, don't laugh. It's the truth. I am *not* the champion liar of the universe. Let me remind you of a few *facts*. First, I pay the prevailing wage. Second, I pay in *money*, not *scrip*. Which means you can do your buying anywhere you please, not just in my commissary. Third, last year I arranged with the CPV&M to take care of the train fare for anyone who wanted to go down to Paradise Falls of a Saturday. Far as I know, I'm the only mineowner in the country who provides such a service for his people. And it doesn't come cheap. Fourth, I got honest scales. I don't cheat. A man digs a ton of coal, he gets *paid* for a ton of coal. Not for half a ton. Not for threequarters of a ton. For a *ton*. I opened my first mine four years ago next month, and in all that time there's not been a single man come to me to complain about my scales. Not a single man. Not a married man either, for that matter. Heh. Ah. I beg your pardon. Now. The things I've said to you are all *facts*, and you know they are. All right, I'm the first to admit that a miner's life maybe isn't the easiest life a man could choose for himself, but at the same time—*and maybe, my friends, you'd better let this sink in*—you all came here of your own free will. Nobody pressed guns to your heads. And, let's not delude ourselves, you *know* you're getting a better shake out of the apple tree than you ever got anywhere else. Now then, the whole purpose of the CPV&M closing down its Blood operation can be summed up in one sentence: *The CPV&M wants to take over the mines*. The name of the thing, my friends, is Greed. I got a letter two mornings ago. The postmark was Columbus, and the letter was from the CPV&M, and it told me the coal shipping rates were being raised fifteen percent. Well, for those among you who understand arithmetic, I don't need to tell you that's fifteen cents on every dollar's worth of coal that comes out of the mines. Now, with God as my most holy and revered Witness, I say to you I cannot afford such an increase. Why, damn it all, it's the sort of thing that'd make even a Jew blush. And so yesterday afternoon I went to Columbus where the highest and most colossal poobahs of the CPV&M sit in fat and sassy comfort on their soft city rear ends. I had a personal interview with the road's president, a highandmighty fellow named Timothy R. Reavis, and oh was he ever the polite one. He gave me a cigar, and he gave me a drink of whisky, and he insisted I sit down in the softest chair in the office. I thanked him for his hospitality, sat me down in that chair and told him I surely was sorry, but I could not afford the new rates. Well, you got no idea the change that took place in the highandmighty Mr Timothy R. Reavis when I told him that. All of a sudden his good manners went off somewhere and hid. And Mr Timothy R. Reavis proceeded to tell me to go to the Devil, either I took the new rates or his railroad would suspend service and starve me out. Well, my friends, I'm not about to go to the Devil. And I'm not about to be starved out. The CPV&M is never going to get those mines. Do you hear me in the back? I said *never!* Here Charley spread his arms. And it's not just because of Charley Wells that I'm going to fight that railroad! he shouted. It's because of *you people* too! If the CPV&M comes in here and runs the mines, you can rest assured you'll be paid in scrip! And you can rest assured you'll have to put up with crooked scales and company police! How about *that,* eh? Has Charley Wells ever hired company police? The answer is *no,* and by God I'll shout it like thunder! There's never been a single company policeman here! There's never been *reason* for one! Charley Wells has got good people working for him! He has respect for them, and they have lived up to his respect! So I'm not going to betray myself, and I'm not going to betray you! We're going to fight the damned CPV&M! And we're going to win! *Am I right or am I right?*

You're *wrong,* you sonofabitch! someone hollered.

Necks were craned. The crowd had begun to applaud, but the voice had done away with the applause.

The voice was John Ellsworth's. He stood next to a tree out by the road. His legs were spread wide apart. He cupped his hands to his mouth: The railroad is going to whip you, Charley Wells, you swindling bastard! God bless the railroad!

Charley moistened his lips.

Heads swiveled. The crowd looked up at Charley and waited for him to say something.

Well? hollered John Ellsworth. Ain't you got nothing to say?

Charley sighed. He cleared his throat. He smiled. He scratched his belly. He leaned forward and down. He was taking the crowd into his confidence. He made a clucking noise. It came from somewhere behind his nose. It was a shy little cluck, and it contained a good deal more sorrow than anger. He said: Friends, that man doing the hollering back there, I expect most of you know him. I feel sorry for him, and that's a fact.

What's that? hollered John Ellsworth. Can't hear you! Speak up!

Charley straightened. He beckoned. Come on forward, John! he yelled. We won't hurt you! Come on forward and you'll be able to hear just fine! We won't hurt you! We washed our hands this morning! Wouldn't want all that hard work to go to waste!

The crowd laughed.

Roaring, John Ellsworth lunged forward.

Gasps.

A number of miners got to their feet and seized John Ellsworth. He threshed and kicked. I'll kill him! he shouted. Let me go! He spat and twisted, but the miners would not release him.

Charley smiled. John, he said, I just don't know why you got to fuss at me all the time. I just don't. I'm sorry about the time you did in jail, but you did attack me on a public street, and there's a law against that sort of thing.

More laughter from the crowd.

You swindled me! hollered John Ellsworth, still squirming, still kicking at his captors.

Oh? said Charley. That so?

John Ellsworth spat. Some of the spittle dribbled into his beard.

Friends, said Charley, I gave this man more money than he ever saw in his life.

You swindled me!

You already have said that, John. Think of something else to say.

You're taking millions out of my land, and all I got to show for it is five thousand dollars!

You mean to tell me you still *got* the five thousand?

What?

I *said*: You still *got* the five thousand?

That's got nothing to—

John, you're just trying to hold me up. You think you can scare me into giving you more money for the lease. You've spent that five thousand on the whisky and I don't know what all. Maybe you've spent some of it on a big club. I've heard tell you like to beat on your wife. How about it, John? That true?

I never beat on my wife!

Oh now, *John* . . .

You bastard! You stinking—

Sh. *John*. The ladies and the little ones.

Fuck the ladies and the—

A miner's red Irish fist cracked against the side of John Ellsworth's jaw. John Ellsworth fell. Then came applause. Charley smiled. Grunting, several of the miners kicked John Ellsworth in the ribs. Charley, benign and mildly reproachful, held up a hand. Now, *now*, he said. Please. None of that. Why don't you fellows just sort of drag him over into the shade of that sycamore tree yonder? He's got him a little nap coming. Let's make him as comfortable as we can. Laughter from the crowd. Grinning, the miners dragged the unconscious John Ellsworth to the tree. They laid him out flat on his back. He groaned. Wish we had a couple of candles for old John, said Charley. One for his head. Other for his feet. More laughter, and presently Charley resumed: All right. Our little diversion's done with. Let's get back to the serious business of the day. I was, I believe, talking about the CPV&M. Well, you can take my word for this: *I, Charles Palmer Wells, do solemnly affirm that, with your help and forbearance, I shall never surrender.* Here Charley paused. He pulled a handkerchief from a pocket of his trousers. He wiped his face and his forehead. The crowd was silent. He wadded the handkerchief, stuffed it in the pocket, then said: I'm sorry. I don't mean to get so worked up. But, by glory, I can't help it. This entire matter is such a damnable outrage. Well, now then, let's get down to what's going to happen. I hate to say this, but it's clear I can't keep the mines open. No sense digging coal if there's no way to ship it out. Now then, this is going to cost me a lot of customers, but believe me, that's just about the least of my worries. The biggest worry I got right now, and I swear I'm speaking the truth, is this—*what about you people?* With the mines shut down, I expect some of you'll want to pull out. I expect some of you are thinking this thing'll last a long time. Well, I got a proposition for you. I'd like to know what you think of it. First of all, you got to eat. I know that. All right, I tell you what I'll do. For the duration of this shutdown, or at least as long as my money holds out, I'm taking it upon myself to feed each and every one of you. As of tomorrow, you all will have unlimited credit at the commissary—within reason, of course. Heh. I wouldn't want any of you men running over there and making off with a case of Kentucky whisky. Unlimited credit, yes, but I can't allow it to be abused. I think that's only fair. But enough of that. Let me get to the good part. As of tomorrow, all commissary prices will be cut in half. And, as long as the mines are closed, those prices will *stay* cut in half. *And,* if the mines are closed more than sixty days (which means that your bills will by that time be considerable), you will be free to leave without paying. Won't matter anyway. If we stay closed more than sixty days, I'll be a whipped man. Now, I expect you're asking yourselves how come Charley Wells is being so generous. That's a good question, and it's got a simple answer. When the mines *do* open, I'll have a lot of catching up to do, and I'll be needing experienced help. I won't be able to send Fritz Voss here traipsing all over Creation on a hunt for experienced help. I'll be needing to get started *right then,* and a man in the mining business can't just snap his fingers and expect good people to come flapping down out of a clear sky. Which is why I want all of you to stay here and stand fast. It won't be easy for you. I'm not saying it will be. But then it won't be easy for *me* either. Friends, I'm in debt to a Columbus bank clear up to my bellybutton, and that's a fact. Four years ago the debt was clear up to my eyebrows, but I've worked hard, and so have you, and now the debt's only as high as my bellybutton. Still, it's a long way down from my bellybutton, and I got a sight of work yet ahead of me. When this thing's ended, I'll drive you like you've never been driven before. We'll work around the clock. We'll dig coal like it's never been dug before. There'll be plenty of money to be made by those with the energy and the gumption. And so I ask you to stand by. I ask you to give me your support. I've tried to be fair to you, swear by Almighty God I have. So please, if you can, bear with this thing. And, if you do, there's something I hereby give you my oath I'll do for you when this is all over and done with. As of today, according to the figures Fritz Voss keeps for me, there are one hundred and seventyseven men on the payroll. If, when this thing is settled, there still are one hundred and *fifty* men on the payroll and ready and willing to go back to work the first day the mines reopen, I'll build you a church. I repeat: *I'll build you a church.*

Silence from the crowd.

A church, said Charley. A church of your own. A thing of brick and stone. It'll mean you can have a priest of your own.

A Catholic church? someone hollered.

Yes. So how about it?

One of the miners stood up.

Charley looked at him.

Necks were twisted. A sound of leaves. Flapping hats.

The miner was grinning. Cupping his hands to his mouth, he shouted: Mr Wells, my name is Jack McBurney, and Jack McBurney says fair enough!

Another miner stood up. And so does Tom Flynn! he hollered.

The applause began, and it was followed by cheering. Here and there were weeping women. Charley grinned. He held up his arms. Thank you! he shouted. Thank you very much! God bless you all!

Cheering. On the steps below Charley, Fritz Voss and Winfield Wainscott were grinning. More cheering.

Charley's arms still were outstretched. We're going to win! he yelled. No railroad is going to take over these mines and pay you in scrip and cut your wages and cheat you on the scales and send company police to beat on your wives and your little ones!

We're with you, Mr Wells! hollered Jack McBurney, clapping.

Good! yelled Charley. Now then, I've said enough! Let's us have at that food and drink over there in the grove! Then, slowly, Charley lowered his arms. He had forced several tears from his eyes. One of the tears, round and golden in the reflected sun, squiggled down a cheek. God bless that tear. God bless the sunshine that was making it visible to the miners and their families. Now they were roaring and whooping. They clapped. They whistled. Women wept. Children jumped up and down, and their faces were contorted, pink, and some of them even screamed. Charley leaned down and spoke to Fritz Voss: Got the whisky spotted around?

Fritz Voss nodded.

Good, said Charley, straightening, waving at the crowd.

It all happened precisely as Charley had promised his associates it would happen. The picnic became a feast, and the feast became a rite of the heavy waters, and the rite of the heavy waters became a debauch, and the debauch led to a sort of jolly mischievous violence, and the results of the violence brought *genuine* tears—tears of joy—to Charley's large mendacious eyes. Fritz Voss had spotted the whisky intelligently. More than five dozen bottles were found by the feasting miners and their wives and children. No one questioned where they'd come from. A miner was not the sort of man to throw salt into the mouth of a gift horse. All that mattered about the bottles was that they were there. The miners were good drinkers. The miners were dedicated drinkers. The miners saw drinking as no idle halfhearted pursuit. They saw drinking as being just as profound as fear of God, just as pleasurable as love of woman. The bottles materialized at the base of trees. They materialized at the bottom of baskets of bread. They materialized inside great mounded bowls of potato salad. They materialized down among the rocks that sat slick and dark in a creek that coursed through a corner of the grove where the picnic was held. They materialized in low scraggly patches of brush and fern. Within an hour, the picnic had formed itself into a loud staggering Easter egg hunt, but of course the participants were not children, and of course the game in no way resembled the innocent gambols of the little ones. Charley watched the proceedings from the front steps of the church. Winfield Wainscott had fetched him a chickenleg and a bottle of beer. Winfield Wainscott and Fritz Voss sat with Charley. From time to time they sniggered discreetly at the whoops and flailings of the picnickers. After an hour or so, several men staggered up to Charley and told him this surely was some picnic, all right, all right. He smiled, thanked them, told them to have a good time. Fritz Voss and Winfield Wainscott covered their mouths and made trapped sounds. Charley gnawed on his chickenleg, sipped at his bottle of beer. The miners and their families tore into the food. Some of the women made off with bread and meat and vegetables. And then the time of food became a time of garbage, and the little grove yielded to bones and rind and broken glass. The miners and their families ate with their hands, and their hands ran with grease, and they wiped their mouths with their sleeves. They picked their teeth with their fingernails, and of course their fingernails were thick and gummy with coalmine filth. They grinned at

each other, and their teeth were ragged, and they belched and farted with
deepthroated urgency, moist and echoing. And they didn't give a whoop
where they scratched. And they didn't give a whoop who saw where they
scratched. They gabbled and honked, and the men among them drank
from the miraculous bottles of whisky, and so did some of the women,
wrenching the bottles away from the men, lifting their skirts, curtsying,
swallowing deeply, gasping, shaking their heads, remarking happily on
the warmth of the good stuff as it coursed down into their rumbling bellies.
And then some of the women began to shriek and giggle, and some of the
men began to pinch and prod and tickle some of the women, and surreptitious hands sought out valiant wellused breasts. Now some of the
food lay in smears across the grass. But a good deal more of it lay in the
bellies of the miners and their wives and children. And a good deal more
had been pilfered. For a day or two at least, the children would receive
more than raw potatoes and fried dough for their supper, and all the mothers, all the Irish mothers and all the Welsh mothers, all the Moiras and
Bridgets and Brendas and Mildreds, congratulated each other on their
Christian foresight in seeing to it that tomorrow would not be quite as
bleak as yesterday had been, and some of the younger men wandered off
with some of the younger women, walking very casually and altogether *too*
casually, and Charley rather envied some of those younger men. There
were several most enchanting and juicy girls here at this picnic that had
become a rite of the heavy waters and was fast becoming a debauch, and
Charley clicked his teeth and told himself: God damn. He smiled at everyone, and everyone smiled at him, and one elderly woman—fragrant and
blurred from the heavy waters—even kissed his hand. The church, said the
elderly woman. A church for us. Ahhh. God love you, Mr Wells, and
make His countenance to shine down upon you. Charley thanked the
elderly woman, patted her shoulder, told her: Yes. A church. As long as
your men stand fast. So do what you can to see that they do, all right?
The elderly woman nodded, said she surely would. She lurched off. Fritz
Voss and Winfield Wainscott permitted themselves a few pinched mewling
noises. Charley continued to smile. Ah, such an inspiration, this idea of
the church. A good four of every five of these mining families were Catholic, and this ratio even included the Welsh. About threefourths of the
families were Irish, and of course solidly Catholic, but there were a great
many more Catholics among the Welsh than one would have imagined.
The idea of the church probably had no appeal to those of the Welsh
who were Protestant, but their numbers were small, and Charley figured
they had the good sense to keep silent about the matter. And anyway, a
Protestant could become just as intoxicated as a Papist, and right now
intoxication was the order of the day. The thing that now was required

was the jolly mischief, which was the purpose of this debauch, and at nightfall—ah, hallelujah, praise God—it began, and of course it drew no religious lines. The men had been singing songs of Ireland and of Wales, songs of love, of sentiment, of death, of dear mother, of famine, of injustice, of revolt. One man had run home and had fetched a flute. Another had run home and had fetched a fiddle. A third had run home and had fetched a wrinkled old cornet. These men began to play, and they played with vigor, and they played very badly, but by that time the sound of the singing had just about done away with any other sounds, and so their incompetent tootling and scraping went largely unheard. The singers sat around trees. Arms were draped on shoulders. The singers regarded the twilight sky, and their silvery songs rose to that sky, touched it with gentle foolish sooty fingers, then slipped back down into the hills and ridges of the alien land called Ohio, this place of rocks and tipples and an intransigent and most noxiously foul railroad. It never was determined whose mind was responsible for the idea that led to the fulfillment of the jolly mischief, but its source was really of no consequence. Suffice to say that the jolly mischief came from the heat of the day, from the whisky, from the songs, from the promise of the church, even from the prideful manhood of the young boys who had taken their darlings into the bushes: it came from the sum and total of *all* these things, from the mass and spirit and essence of a most remarkable day. And so it all began, a mischief born in anger and weaned on the heavy waters, and it came with a sweet sweating spontaneity: the flutist laid aside his flute; the fiddler handed his fiddle to his wife and told her to take it home; the cornetist dropped his battered instrument to the ground (he never recovered it); dozens of men surged to their drunken splayfooted full height and rolled up their sleeves and kneaded their hands and fingers: and then came shouts, and the shouts were nipped at by laughter and oaths, and the children clapped their hands and danced impromptu little jigs, all the while flailing and screeching, and the women shook their heads and predicted that it would be a long night indeed, and off they all moved, in ragged revolutionary procession, toward the yards and the depot of the Columbus, Paradise Valley & Marietta Railroad. Charley did not witness the events of that night. He'd had to return to Paradise Falls. He had important affairs to transact there, affairs that also had to do with his war against the CPV&M. But Fritz Voss was a witness to the things that happened that night in Blood, and so was Winfield Wainscott, and they laughed until they just about fell down. They stood atop the Tuesday Creek tipple and they saw the entire spectacular demonstration, and they hollered and bleated, and then they pummeled one another, and then finally all they could do was gasp. The miners all were singing, but they were singing no one particular song. Each man had his own song, and each man *hollered* his own precious song, and each precious hollered song jostled all the other precious hollered songs, and the resultant sound was all sounds, sounds beyond sounds, a single creation of high beauty and terror, dark and heavy, jagged, moist with emanations of coalgas and whisky and meat and belly and crotch and foot and belch: sounds of holy righteousness. And someone broke into a shed, and upon the door of that shed were posted the words KEEP OUT PROP M OF W DEPT CPV&MRR, and several men laughed, and crowbars were removed from the shed, and shovels were removed from the shed, and picks were removed from the shed, and the men brandished their new weapons, and one man (he had arrived after the supply had been exhausted) could find only a screwdriver, but he went ahead like a good fellow and brandished *it*. And then, laughing and staggering, still hollering their precious songs, the men moved through the yards of the CPV&M, and gangs of them went to work with their new tools, and up came spikes, popping reluctantly from the ties, and the rails parted, and the rails were pulled loose from the ties, and the ties were flung about like twigs, and switches were smashed, and somewhere someone found some kerosene, and ties were set afire, and the heat from the burning ties bent the rails, and Fritz Voss and Winfield Wainscott laughed fit to fall down and expire from burst bloodvessels, and the miners advanced on the CPV&M depot, and crowbars were hurled through windows, and doors were smashed, and desks were split with mighty blows from the picks and crowbars of the hollering righteous, and telegraph instruments were pulverized (seeing as how the CPV&M had closed the depot, it really should have had better sense than to have left its telegraph instruments sitting there so vulnerable: ah, the poor CPV&M; truly it did not have the intelligence the Almighty gave a sack of salt), and then someone climbed onto the depot roof and doused it with kerosene, and then everyone withdrew to a safe distance, and then a can of flaming kerosene was tossed through a window, and a wind came up at just that precise instant, a wind of God, and the wind lashed and twisted the flames, causing the roof to fall in almost immediately, with a hollow sound that was like *whum*, and a great brave cheer rose over the sound of the flames (atop the Tuesday Creek tipple, Fritz Voss and Winfield Wainscott were hugging one another so they would not fall down), and then someone ran across the yards and set a CPV&M privy afire, and children ran dancing, dodging the sparks that came from the burning ties and the burning depot not to mention the very briskly burning (and hotly stinking) privy, and some of the more outgoing of the women lifted their skirts and gleefully pissed on the tracks of the detested CPV&M, and by morning very little remained of what the CPV&M had called its property there in that dark and violent village of Blood. With dawn, with the first shrill urgings of birds, with the pale silver hillcountry dew, the extent of the damage was revealed in all its magnificence. It was as though a retreating army had passed through the CPV&M yards, a retreating army charged with the destruction of all it left behind. It was like, in a sense, what the *advancing* Cump Sherman had done to the fair Commonwealth of Georgia back in '64. It was all smoke and dust and hissing embers, and it was sublime, clear evidence of the existence of a most loving and warmly vengeful Creator. Women prowled the ruined yards. They were searching out their husbands, victims of the grog by heaven, holy warriors whose eyes had been a mite larger than their capacities. The fallen heroes lay quietly. A few jerked their legs in weak spasms, and a few moaned, but most of them had the good sense to lie quietly. Their wives bent over them. Their wives clucked. Grunting, they were helped to their feet by their wives. They lurched. They shuddered. They hugged their bellies. The field was theirs, but the air stank, and some of them had to bend forward and gag, and somewhere nearby the last rooster in the world proclaimed its lonely grief, and the warriors squinted, spat, leaned on their wives, shaded their eyes from the cruel and excessive new day's sun. The battle was done. The foe had been demolished. The sparks flew upward. Victory.

Word of all this was brought to Charley that morning by Fritz Voss and Winfield Wainscott. They drove their buggy straight to Charley's home, arriving there at about 8, just as Charley was sitting down to breakfast with his wife and daughter. Little Nell, dark and silent, flat of face and voice, would soon be four years old, and Charley did wish there were more little girls willing to play with her. But, ah well, that was Nancy's concern. He loved his daughter, and surely little Nell knew that: there were, after all, the regiments of toys. His love was large and profound, but what on earth was he expected to do about finding her playmates? No, that was Nancy's job. Nancy would see to it. Nancy was a good wife. And anyway, little Nell still was very young. She would be all right. He had to be patient. Time, assisted by wise guidance from little Nell's mother, would do its work. No indeed, there was not a thing to worry about. When Voss and Wainscott walked into the diningroom, Charley smiled and motioned to them to sit down at the table. Then he said: Well?

Mr Wells, said Wainscott, you are a genuine wonder.

That so?

Nodding to Nancy and the little girl, Voss and Wainscott seated themselves. It did indeed work, said Voss. They performed just as you had anticipated.

They rip and tear?

Yes *sir,* said Wainscott. Burned the depot to the ground. Ripped up ties and track. Even burned a privy to the ground. Then, blushing a bit, Wainscott smiled at Nancy and said: Ah, I beg your pardon, ma'm.

For nothing, said Nancy. Now then, would you gentlemen care for some coffee and maybe some ham and eggs?

I'd be obliged, said Wainscott.

I too, said Voss, smiling primly. We've had no breakfast, having, ah, come here straight from the, ah, field of battle.

Nancy stood up. I'll see to it, she said. She smiled at the little girl and said: Come along, Nell. Your daddy and these gentlemen have a lot to talk about.

Nell's mouth had a faint moustache of milk. I want to *stay*, she said.

No, dear. Come along with me.

I want to stay with Daddy.

Charley smiled at his daughter. Please go with your mama, he said.

Yes, Daddy, said Nell. She rose and went out of the room ahead of her mother. She did not look back.

Nancy followed. Her shoulders were hunched forward a little.

Wainscott smiled. A pretty little girl, he said. She'll really be something when she grows up. Your daughter, I mean. Ah. Heh.

Thank you, said Charley. Then, to Voss: No one was hurt?

Not a soul.

Good. I wouldn't have wanted that.

And the damage truly was extensive.

How much?

Twenty thousand dollars' worth. Easily.

Good, said Charley, nodding. He impaled a slice of ham on his fork. He chewed slowly, wiped his mouth with his napkin, then said: My news is good too.

Oh? said Voss. The ordinance was passed?

Unanimously. And Virge Light signed it. Right there on the spot.

Oh *ho!* said Wainscott. *Now* we've got them!

Yes, said Charley, I expect we do.

Voss sniggered.

Charley threw back his head. He laughed loudly. His throat worked. He shook. His eyes were moist. Yes! he hollered. Yes! Yes! *Yes!*

Nancy brought ham and eggs and toast and jam and coffee for Voss and Wainscott. The little girl did not return. She had gone out back to play silently in the dirt at the edge of her mother's rosebushes. Charley told Nancy to bring whisky. Voss and Wainscott looked at him. Now, now, said Charley, don't go telling me it's too early in the day. This is an *occasion*. Nancy poured the drinks for the three men. She also poured a drink for herself. Charley glanced at her but said nothing. Glasses were lifted. To the destruction of the enemy, said Charley. Everyone drank. Nancy's face flushed. She smiled. I expect it'll be another hot one to-day, she said. Voss and Wainscott nodded. Charley fussed with his napkin. At noon that day, the CPV&M tracks were barricaded at both ends of the village. Sections of rail were torn out, severing the CPV&M main line. Several hundred copies of the new ordinance had been run off that morning in the *Journal* job shop. One was delivered to the CPV&M stationmaster. You could have knocked him over with a baby's breath. He immediately sent a wire to his superiors in Columbus: *The village Council here has passed an ordinance assessing us $100 per train passing within corporate limits. Kindly advise the course of action to be taken.* While Ed Clapp awaited his instructions, a number of armed men, sworn in as deputies by Village Marshal Adolf W. Kolb, manned the barricades. They grinned and joked, and some of them even fired their pistols in the air. Most of these men were GAR cronies of Mayor Virgil T. Light. Marshal Kolb remonstrated with them about firing their pistols in the air. They laughed, assured him they weren't about to hurt anyone. Each barricade detachment was commanded by a chief deputy who carried a copy of the ordinance. There never had been any particular love between the village and the CPV&M. Ten years earlier, there had been talk that the CPV&M planned to build car shops in Paradise Falls, but nothing came of the talk. The shops were built in Lancaster. Then it was rumored that the CPV&M would split its main line into two divisions. Since Paradise Falls was the only place of any size anywhere near the halfway point on the main line, there were those who figured the CPV&M surely would construct a substantial locomotive servicing facility there. But the CPV&M did nothing. The officials of the road learned of the rumor, and forthwith they issued a statement. It pointed out that the CPV&M was too short to accommodate two divisions. It claimed its locomotive servicing facilities —at Marietta, the road's southeastern terminus—were more than adequate. But the statement did the CPV&M little good. The rumor had been permitted to circulate too long. As far as Paradise Falls was concerned, the CPV&M had plainly and simply reneged. And then there was the matter of the CPV&M's relations with its employees. The road had a strict policy relating to injured workers. If they were injured while on the job . . . well, the world sometimes was a cruel place indeed. The workers could expect no aid from the CPV&M. Payment of medical bills was the responsibility of the injured. This rule also applied to funeral costs. In Paradise Falls alone, there lived two former brakemen who had only one hand apiece, two former engineers and one former fireman who had only one leg apiece, and one former conductor who had no legs at all and only one arm. Every one of these men had been maimed while carrying out their duties for the CPV&M. And this total did not of course include the dead. Since the road's opening, a total of twentysix CPV&M employees had been killed in wrecks, and nine of these twentysix had been from Paradise Falls. Now then, all these men, the dead and the maimed, had large families, and the members of these families never exactly went out of their way to stand up and applaud whenever the CPV&M was mentioned. So, what with all this accumulated hate, there was no lack of men to stand at the barricades and assist Marshal Kolb in the carrying out of his duty. At 1 o'clock that afternoon, the first train was stopped. It was Number 6, an accommodation passenger train from Columbus and Lancaster. The conductor was handed a copy of the ordinance. God damn, he said, and he scratched his head. His name was Earl McBride, and he was a Paradise Falls man. Despite his name, he was a thirtysecond degree Mason, and he'd once served on the Council that had passed this ordinance. God damn, he said again. He squinted forward, and his eyes took in the tornup track. He was leaning against the cowcatcher of the locomotive, a trim little 4-4-0 called the Martha. The armed deputies stood around him in a semicircle. Behind him, the locomotive made hollow clanking sounds. He fumbled in his pockets and came up with a handkerchief. He wiped his forehead, blew his nose. He said: You know, boys, I kind of think Charley Wells has got this here railroad by the balls. Everyone laughed. Earl McBride went around to the side of the locomotive and hollered up to the engineer to get ready to back the train to Egypt and await instructions. What about the passengers? yelled down the engineer. Well, if they're going to Paradise Falls, they can walk the rest of the way! yelled Earl McBride. If they're going any farther, good luck to them! More laughter from the deputies. Earl McBride walked back to the coaches. He announced to the passengers what had happened and the option they had. There was a sight of grumbling, and a number of children decided that then was as good a time as any to whimper and bawl. In the rear coach, a fat man stood up and made a speech about what a damnable outrage it was. Oh yes sir, said Earl McBride. Ain't it the truth. The passengers disembarked. Some of them hollered at the deputies, and of course the deputies again had to laugh. Several of the passengers were Paradise Falls people. Included among them were former Mayor George McC. Pillsbury and Mrs Pillsbury, returning from a visit to Mrs Pillsbury's sister in Columbus. Earl McBride always had liked George Pillsbury, but damn if he'd not voted for Virgil Light in last year's election. George Pillsbury had become a mite long in the tooth, and it was Earl McBride's studied opinion that younger and fresher blood was needed to conduct the village's affairs. He helped George and Irene Pillsbury down from their coach. Is this Light's doing? said George Pillsbury. Ah, well, I wouldn't be surprised if Charley Wells had something to do with it too, said Earl McBride. George Pillsbury snorted. Oh yes, he said, the master orders, and the dog obeys. The distance into the village was about a mile. Several of the deputies set up a shuttle buggy service to take the stranded passengers to their homes and hotels. Awful goddamn decent of you fellers, said Earl McBride to one of the deputies. Well, said the deputy, we don't want to put people out no more than we have to. Earl McBride grinned. What's so funny? said the deputy. I'm just thinking of the look that's probably on Mr Timothy R. Reavis' face along about now, said Earl McBride. Who's Mr Timothy R. Reavis? said the deputy. President of the CPV&M, said Earl McBride, and I expect his face it's got a look on it like he's swallowed a wart hog sideways. The deputy laughed. Earl McBride punched him on a shoulder, supervised the unloading of the rest of the passengers. Then he gave the engineer a wave. You and the boys can take this here train back to Egypt now! he hollered. I'm going on in to the Paradise Falls depot! The engineer nodded. The fireman and the head brakeman were standing on the steps behind the cab. They grinned at Earl McBride. The rear brakeman waved at him from a coach. The whistle blew. The drivewheels spun, caught. The train backed down the track toward Egypt. Earl McBride sighed, shook his head. He watched the train until it was out of sight. Then he trudged past the barricade and the tornout track and on toward the depot. His wife was waiting for him at the depot. Word of the ordinance and the barricades was all over the village, and she had come to the depot to see what she could see. Oh, Earl! she cried. I was so worried about you! Earl McBride had a favorite name for his wife, whose actual Christian given name was Hortense. She was a small chirpy woman, and so he called her Little Bird. He went to her and hugged her and told her there, there, everything was just fine; the deputies had been very decent about the whole thing. She clapped her hands. Tears were in her eyes. Chirping, she said: Oh, Earl! Isn't this the most exciting thing you've ever *heard* of! Earl McBride moistened his lips. They were dusty from his walk. Then he laughed. He made fists, and the fists chopped the warm air. My Lord, he finally said, a person just never knows. You start a day, and it sure seems just like any other day, and then everything blows up in your face. Yes, Little Bird. *Yes,* by God. I'm enjoying this. I truly am. Then Earl McBride again hugged his wife. He told her she was a grand and beautiful princess. Tush, said Hortense (Little Bird) McBride. Tush and pish. Chuckling, Earl McBride escorted his wife into the depot. There he conferred with Ed Clapp, the stationmaster. No word yet from Columbus. A man named Dwight Templeton sat at the telegrapher's desk. Earl McBride went out into the waiting room and fetched his wife. They sat in the office—the four of them, Earl and Little

Bird McBride, Ed Clapp and Dwight Templeton—and waited for the word
from Columbus. Dwight Templeton got to talking about a tomato his wife
had raised in her garden. A diameter of seven inches it had, said Dwight
Templeton, so help me Hannah. At 3:30 the official word came. Dwight
Templeton took it down quickly: *Effective immediately, all freight and
passenger operations between Athens and Lancaster are suspended until
further notice.* The wire, which carried the signature of Harry E. Smallsreed, general superintendent, was sent to all mainline stations. It was
accompanied by a wire for Ed Clapp personally. Mr Smallsreed and the
road's president, Mr T. R. Reavis, would arrive in Paradise Falls by special
train at 5 P.M. Would Mr Clapp be so kind as to meet them? This wire
also was signed by Mr Smallsreed. Ed Clapp looked at Earl McBride.
Well, he said, I expect the fur it's going to fly tonight. Earl McBride
agreed. So did Little Bird McBride. So did Dwight Templeton. Earl
McBride announced he was calling it a day. Can't say as I blame you,
said Ed Clapp. I only wish I could too. Said Earl McBride: Well, good
luck. Said Ed Clapp: Thank you kindly. The McBrides went on home.
By 5 o'clock, when Ed Clapp drove his buggy out to the northwest barricade to meet the special train, he had received more bad news—if it could
be believed. A rumor had reached him that the miners up in Blood had
run amok, as the saying went. According to the rumor, the miners had
ripped out track *and* had burned down the Blood depot. Apparently they
had been most thoroughly lubricated, and it didn't take the mind of a
genius to figure out who had provided the lubrication. Despite himself, Ed
Clapp had to smile. That C. P. Wells surely was a caution: no getting
around it. Lord God, this surely did figure to be a long day for Mr
Reavis and Mr Smallsreed, and Ed Clapp didn't envy them a bit. When
he drove up to the barricade, the deputies all grinned and waved at him.
He told them why he was there, and they were delighted. *Hey* now, said a
man named Graves, we're to be *honored.* Hugh Graves was employed by
the C. P. Wells Coal Co as a bookkeeper. He did not, however, look like a
bookkeeper. He looked more like a circus strong man. His head was
shaped like a cannonball, and his voice came rumbling from somewhere in
the vicinity of his navel. He was wearing overalls and an old shirt, and the
sleeves of the shirt had been cut away in order to give his arms freer
play. Ed Clapp grinned at Hugh Graves. It was wise to grin at Hugh
Graves. It was not wise, for obvious reasons, to have Hugh Graves as an
enemy. Ed Clapp came down from the buggy and walked to the barricade.
He looked at the stretch of track that had been torn up. Mm, he said,
now I got to call that a real neat job. He looked at the deputies. Any of
you boys over in Blood last night? he wanted to know. Sniggers from the
deputies. Hugh Graves spoke up. Oh, he said, you heard about it too eh

Ed? Said Ed Clapp: Yessir. That I did. Said Hugh Graves: Wish I'd of knowed about it. I would of liked to of helped out. Mr Wells is a good man. He pays me good. You and your damn railroad got no right trying to run him out of business. Said Ed Clapp, smiling: It's not *my* railroad, Hugh. I got enough things to fret at. I don't need no *railroad*. Said Hugh Graves: Ah. Well. Sure now, Ed. I know that. You're a good fellow. I didn't mean it that way. All I'm trying to say is I like Mr Wells a whole lot. You remember how it was when I came back from the war? Remember how people laughed when big old clumsy Hugh Graves said he liked arithmetic and wanted to be a bookkeeper? Remember all that, Ed? Said Ed Clapp: Yes, Hugh. That I do. Said Hugh Graves: But nobody gave me no job keeping books, did they? And so I had to go back to doing what I'd been doing before the war—carrying bricks for the Paradise Falls Clay Products. But then three years ago I paid a call on Mr Wells and told him what I wanted to do, and you know what that man said? He said: All right, Hugh. This is a new company and a new day. I'll give you the chance. If you're so good like you say you are, you'll have a job with me as long as you want it. And so I went to work for him, and he ain't had no reason to regret it. I'm a good bookkeeper, God damn it, that I guarantee you. Said Ed Clapp: Yessir, Hugh. That you are. No doubt about it.

The special train consisted of a locomotive and just one coach. When Reavis and Smallsreed came off the train, they were accompanied by three burly men. All three of these burly men were wearing derbies. Reavis' face was red. He squinted at the deputies and said: Which one of you is Clapp?

Ed Clapp stepped forward. Me, sir, he said.

You have a buggy for us?

Yessir, said Ed Clapp, pointing toward a nearby grove where his horse and buggy stood in the shade.

Good, said Reavis. Now, tell me, do you know where I can find Wells?

Ed Clapp shrugged. Wellsir, he said, it's late in the day. I expect maybe he's gone home. Then Ed Clapp scraped a toe of a shoe across the earth. Sir, he said, you know about what happened over at Blood?

Blood?

Yessir. There was—

Hugh Graves interrupted. He shoved himself forward until his belly was just about touching Reavis' chest. He grinned and said: Mr Reavis, my name is Hugh F. Graves.

Reavis made a scratching noise in his throat. Ah, he said, kindly stand aside. I am talking to Mr Clapp.

I'll stand aside when I'm good and fucking ready, said Hugh Graves. I got a few things to say first.

Reavis gasped.

Mr Reavis, when you open your mouth to say Mr Wells' name, it's *Mr* Wells, not *Wells*. And, if you're wondering about Blood, it's only a beginning.

Beginning? Beginning of *what?*

Hugh Graves grinned. Mr Reavis, he said, you lost yourself a depot up there. Burned to the ground. Sure must of been a sight. And I hear tell you lost a lot of track too. Appears to me them miners up there don't like you an awful lot.

Reavis backed away a step. He said: Are you trying to tell me railroad property was vandalized?

If that means tore up and burned down, I got to say yes.

Where is he? Where is that damn Wells?

His name is *Mr* Wells.

Oh go to the devil, you damn oaf!

What?

Reavis was trembling. He tried to push past Hugh Graves. He might as well have tried to push past the Great Wall of the Heathen Chinee. Hugh Graves clucked, gave Reavis a mighty shove. Reavis staggered back. He flailed. One of his hands smacked across the adamsapple of Smallsreed, the CPV&M general superintendent. Smallsreed bleated, gagged. One of the three derbied men lunged toward Hugh Graves. He was quite a large fellow, and his derby was perhaps half a size too small. Hugh Graves smote the derbied man in the belly. Rach, said the derbied man, and his derby went flying. Several deputies laughed. A second derbied man came toward Hugh Graves. Grinning, Hugh Graves seized this second derbied man by the scruff of the neck and the seat of the pants, turned him upsidedown, pumped him like the handle of a churn, then dropped him on his head. The first derbied man came gasping to his feet. Someone tripped him. Yelling, he flopped back down on the ground. Now dust was rising. Ed Clapp decided to withdraw to his horse and buggy and await the resolution of this matter. Four more derbied men came out of the coach. Ed Clapp recognized them. They were railroad detectives. They rushed Hugh Graves. The deputies joined in, and the fighting became general. The engineer smiled down from his cab. T. R. Reavis, president and chief executive officer of the Columbus, Paradise Valley & Marietta Railroad, was knocked down several times. His clothing was torn. So was the clothing of H. E. Smallsreed, the general superintendent. Derbies rolled and skipped in the dust. Ed Clapp never had owned a derby. He crept to the periphery of the melee and picked up one of the derbies. It had picked up dust. He brushed away the dust. Carefully he placed the derby on his head. It felt fine. He wished he had a mirror. The fighting was vigorous and quite gay. From time to time Hugh Graves was heard to guffaw. The engineer and fireman came down from the cab. They hurled themselves into the dusty fray, but it was difficult to determine which side they were fighting on. Perhaps they simply were fighting for the sake of fighting. At one point, the engineer delivered a titanic blow that struck the side of Smallsreed's head. He apologized. Smallsreed nodded, staggered off. The engineer grinned. Ed Clapp seated himself in the shade of a beech tree and watched the proceedings. He removed the derby from his head. He brushed it again, then tossed it back toward the melee. He was hungry. He hoped this damn affair wouldn't last all night. The emergency had caused him to miss his noon meal, and he wasn't the sort of fellow to miss a meal with much good grace. He listened to grunts. He sighed, examined his fingernails, used a toothpick to dig out some dirt. The fight continued for about a quarter of an hour, and Hugh Graves and his numerically superior forces were the clear victors. Four of the derbied railroad detectives were knocked senseless. Two others were tossed into a ditch, where they simply lay and rubbed their bruises. The seventh derbied railroad detective retreated back into the coach and locked all the doors. The engineer and fireman, after getting in their licks for whichever side it was they favored, scrambled back up into the locomotive. T. R. Reavis lay gasping at the lip of the ditch. His fly had been ripped open, and his modest and quite understandably dispirited private parts were exposed. Apparently he was not aware of his condition. Or, if he was, he did not care. H. E. Smallsreed, the general superintendent, sat crosslegged like a tailor. He was bent forward, and his arms were folded over his head. Ed Clapp, whose salary as Paradise Falls stationmaster was a not precisely princely fifty dollars a month, worked very industriously on his fingernails. When Mr Reavis and Mr Smallsreed wanted him, they could call. In the meantime, there was the matter of his fingernails. Hugh Graves and the rest of the victors stood grinning down on the fallen enemy. Hugh Graves walked around with his chest out, and his grin stretched to the moon. He nudged one of the deputies and said: God damn but what I don't feel like I got five girls in the family way all in one night. Said the deputy: Sure must be some feeling. Then along came a buggy. It pulled up next to the place where sat the industrious Ed Clapp.

Ed? said Charley Wells.

Ed Clapp looked up.

Fritz Voss and Winfield Wainscott sat next to Charley. What in the name of God is going on here? said Charley.

Ed Clapp blew on his fingernails. He flipped away the toothpick. Fight, he said.

Charley grinned. That so? he said.

Yessir. And your side it won.

My side?

Yessir. That Hugh Graves, he's a wonder. Some bookkeeper.

Charley squinted toward the track and said: Isn't that Mr T. R. Reavis sitting by the ditch? He looks like something's chewed on him.

Yessir. And I expect if you was to look real close you'd see his pecker hanging out.

All three of them—Charley, Voss and Wainscott—leaned forward. Wainscott shaded his eyes.

Well, goodness gracious, said Charley.

Wainscott began to snigger.

Voss cleared his throat.

Charley frowned at Wainscott and said: Why, *Winfield,* is this a time to be laughing?

Said Wainscott: Now, Mr Wells, you . . . you *stop* that . . .

Charley grinned. Good old Wainscott. Wainscott and all his children. Wainscott who gathered his family together every evening to read Scripture. Wainscott the sniggerer. Wainscott the farmer with the soul of a clerk. Wainscott the discoverer of coal. Ah, God love him, this Wainscott. And God love this day. It was turning out even better than yesterday, and that was a fact. An hour or so ago, he'd been told of the impending arrival of Reavis and Smallsreed. The information had been supplied by Earl McBride, who had stopped at Charley's office on his way home with his chirpy little wife. Charley had thanked Earl McBride most heartily, and Earl McBride had said: No need to thank me. On the money they pay me, they can rot. You know what I mean? Said Charley: I expect so. Then Earl McBride and Charley shook hands, and Charley complimented Mrs McBride on how well she was looking these days. Grinning, the McBrides departed. Charley's chest was large with jubilation. So far, the CPV&M had reacted exactly as he had anticipated. Now, if Hugh Graves performed as planned and successfully picked a fight and did a job of humiliating Reavis and Smallsreed, there was an excellent chance the entire matter could be settled within a few hours. Charley sent word to Sheriff Bowles, Mayor Light and Marshal Kolb to be in his office by 6 o'clock. Voss, Wainscott, Erich Kahler and ElRoy Mauk had already been so informed. The windows of Charley's office were open. He heard the special train's whistle quite clearly. Voss and Wainscott had already arrived for the 6 o'clock meeting. Charley fetched them. Come on, men, he said. Let's take us a little buggyride. Our friends are coming in on a train, and Ed Clapp's gone to meet them, but something tells me . . . some small voice . . . there just may be some trouble.

Voss and Wainscott looked blank.

Charley chuckled. Come on, he said.

Voss and Wainscott followed Charley to the buggy. Charley cracked the reins, and the buggy moved down Main Street toward the western edge of town. Wainscott was the first to speak. I'm sorry, he said to Charley, but what you said up in your office about trouble—what did that mean?

There's a hundred dollars in it for Hugh Graves, said Charley.

For doing what? said Voss.

Picking a fight with Reavis and his people.

How's that? said Wainscott.

Ah, please don't misunderstand. I don't want Reavis *hurt*. All I'm thinking about is his dignity.

Dignity? said Voss.

Charley nodded. Now the buggy was headed west on Grainger Street, which would veer northwest in a moment and become the Lancaster road. They were just about at the town limits. A quarter of a mile or so beyond the town limits, the buggy made a left turn onto a narrow rutted track and bounced across a field and through a grove toward the place where the northwest barricade had been erected. Said Charley: This has been a bad day for our friend Mr Reavis. About all he has left to him is his dignity. I want to take it away from him. The word here is humiliation. I want Hugh Graves to humiliate him. Not *hurt* him, you understand. Only humiliate.

Oh, said Wainscott.

Voss said nothing. Voss cast bland eyes in the direction of the horizon.

If he is sufficiently humiliated, said Charley, it all will be over.

Some men are more dangerous after they have been humiliated, said Voss.

True, Fritz. A good observation. But Reavis isn't that sort of man. He has a very large opinion of himself. If we can damage that opinion, he will become amenable to anything.

How do you know that? said Voss.

Oh, it has to do with a number of things. First, only a truly great man is able to reassemble himself after a humiliation.

Oh? said Voss.

Yes. And then of course there's the matter of anticipation.

Anticipation? said Voss. What sort of anticipation?

Said Charley: It is never enough simply to do a thing. One must take into account all possible reactions to an action. If one has an opponent, one must get to know that opponent so well that one is able to anticipate his reactions. Once that is done, the opponent is whipped. That is the philosophy of Charley Wells, my friends. Charley Wells never makes a move unless he knows damn well what the other fellow's response to it will be. Take those miners. They aren't my enemies, of course. Still, I had to anticipate what they would do. My speech, the promise of the church, the strategic deployment of the whisky bottles—I envisioned a certain specific response to those factors. And it came to pass. And where was I when those people burned down that depot and ripped up that track? I was *home*. My wife and I were sitting in the parlor, and I was God as my Witness eating gingersnaps and drinking oolong tea and reminiscing on an octaroon woman I once knew in Evansville, Indiana. Her name was Rachel Something, and I never did fuck her, and I have long considered that failure to have been one of the most profound tragedies of my life. But, ah, never mind that. The point here is: *in the literal sense* I had nothing to do with what happened in Blood last night. Yet at the same time it would not have happened had I not provided the ingredients. Do you follow me?

Yes, said Voss. I follow you very well. But what is all this about Hugh Graves?

I spoke with him this morning. I did not know *for a fact* that Reavis and Smallsreed were coming here, but I *did* figure they would *have* to. I was, you see, anticipating. I'd split their railroad for them. I'd promised Reavis I would do that. I told him a chain was only as strong as its weakest link. I *told* him. But he chose not to pay me any mind. Well, now perhaps he knows differently. Cha. Horse. Yes. Good boy. That's a fine fellow. Good. Cha. Do you gentlemen ever think about manhood? *I* do. I think about it a great deal. I have reached some conclusions. They perhaps are not the conventional conclusions, but I do believe they contain a great deal of wisdom. For instance, I never have held with violence as a thing that bred manliness. Or at least not the sort of manliness I have in mind. Your average fellow can withstand violence. He has to. It is expected of him. By violence I mean pain. Physical pain. A knife across the belly, things of that nature. Now then, in the ordinary view, a fellow who subdues that sort of violence has performed in a manly way. We are all brought up to accept that view, and it is delivered as some sort of large shining truth. Well, I personally never have held with this violent view of manliness. As a matter of fact, I've never held with violence itself, violence involving my own person I mean. I consider violence to be superficial, and therefore anyone who has withstood it has *not* proved himself a man to *me*. A little while ago I spoke of humiliation. Now *there*, my friends, is a *true* test of manliness. Catch a fellow pulling his pudding in the privy. Catch him fucking his dear old mama's cat. Catch him eating snot. If you catch him doing any of those things, or any of the rest of those activities the world chooses to call shameful, if you catch him *that* way, he is humiliated. And *then*, if he manages to *throw it off*, if he picks himself up and seeks out the fragments of his soul and puts them together again, *then* you have found yourself a *man*. And, if later he becomes your enemy, he could very well defeat you. He has been tested by sterner means than a knife across the belly. If you want to find a real man, don't bother to send him off to war. He may very well stand up to bullets and yet not be much of a man. After all, *and this I must emphasize,* it is *expected* that he stand up to bullets. No, if you seek a man, smear him with tar. Stick feathers up his nose. Run him out of town. Turn him into a damn *animal*. Then wait and see what happens. One man in a thousand will recover from such an indignity. He'll wash away the tar and remove the feathers, and then you'd just better look out. Which is why I talked with Hugh Graves this morning and promised him the hundred dollars.

How's that? said Wainscott.

Said Charley: I don't believe Reavis is man enough to withstand a humiliation. If Hugh Graves does a job on him, he shouldn't be any trouble.

My God, said Voss.

I beg your pardon? said Charley.

You think of everything.

Well, I *try*.

Charley's estimate of Reavis was eminently correct. By 8 o'clock that evening a settlement had been reached—although Reavis did make something of a valiant effort to restore some of his dignity. But, in the final judgment of the matter, poor Reavis failed. And so the settlement was reached. It was a splendid settlement. It was in effect an unconditional surrender—a hasty white flag run up by the CPV&M. And Reavis did everything short of handing his sword to Charley. Ah, poor Reavis. Poor Reavis and his sword. Erich Kahler had given him some pins to hold together his fly, but from time to time poor Reavis' fly popped its pins, and ah, his poor sword.

Charley and Voss and Wainscott were very apologetic when they drove up to the barricade and saw what had been done to Reavis and Smallsreed by those *oafs* and *ruffians* led by Hugh Graves. Charley made a special point of speaking sharply to Hugh Graves. You ought to be ashamed of yourself, said Charley. These gentlemen have come here peacefully. All they seek is to get this unfortunate affair straightened out. They are very important men. Hugh, I just don't know what I'm going to do about you. You and your damnable fists.

Hugh Graves performed well. He lowered his head, scruffed at the dust. He mumbled several words no one could hear.

Said Charley: If it weren't for your wife and eleven little ones, I'd see to it that you were rolled out of town in a barrel.

Hugh Graves nodded. Yessir, he said. Won't happen again. (Hugh Graves was as belligerently stubborn a bachelor as the village ever had known.)

Said Charley: I really should discharge you, but I hate to think what would happen to your family.

Sir, said Hugh Graves, whining a bit, it won't happen again. Swear God it won't. I'd be obliged to you if you let me keep my job. So would Myrtle.

Myrtle?

Yessir. My wife. Little Myrtle. The mother of my, uh, eleven children. Ah, yes sir. Eleven. Sometimes I sort of lose track. Sure is a lot of responsibility, I tell *you*.

Well, you think of, ah, Myrtle and the little ones the next time you try this sort of thing.

Yessir. Thank you, sir. Thank you kindly.

Now you can just help Mr Reavis to the buggy.

Yessir, said Hugh Graves. His shoulders were rounded, humble. He bent over Reavis, who still sat at the edge of the ditch. He mumbled something solicitous to Reavis. He helped Reavis to his feet. Then he guided Reavis to the buggy. In the meantime, Voss and Wainscott were giving assistance to Smallsreed, who was sniffling a little. One of the recumbent railroad detectives got to his feet and moved loosely, staggering, toward the buggy. The contrite Hugh Graves interposed himself between the detective and the buggy. The detective hesitated, frowned. Ah, he said. Yes. Ah. Well. Mm. He rubbed his jaw. He looked toward Reavis and Smallsreed. They paid him no mind. The detective shrugged. Grunting, he sat down beside the track. He made a loose movement with a hand. A number of the deputies had scuttled off to the other side of the train. Hugh Graves' story of Myrtle had been too much for them. They gasped soundlessly. Their breath came falsetto and pinched. Ed Clapp drove up. Charley smiled at him. You can go home, Ed, said Charley. These two gentlemen are my guests. Ed Clapp quickly nodded. He glanced at Reavis and Smallsreed, then made a pinched sound that was not unlike the pinched sounds that were being made by the deputies. He flapped the reins. He drove off. Hugh Graves assisted Reavis and Smallsreed up into Charley's buggy. The ride into town was slow. When the buggy pulled up in front of the building where Charley's offices were, a small crowd stood waiting. Included in this crowd were a little boy and his mother. The little boy's name was Valentine Schmidt. He had a square face, and he was about seven years old, and Charley never would forget him. As soon as Reavis and Smallsreed were helped down from the buggy, little Valentine Schmidt began to jump up and down. Everyone looked at him. Squealing,

he pointed toward Reavis' fly. Look, Mama! he hollered. The man's got his
dingle hanging out! Valentine Schmidt's mother gasped, slapped his face.
Reavis gasped, reddened, covered himself with cupped hands. Charley examined the sky. Wainscott coughed, cleared his throat. Charley was aware
of shooting pains in his chest. Voss rubbed his mouth. As quickly as possible, Reavis and Smallsreed were escorted upstairs to Charley's offices.
Charley was wheezing a bit, and tears nudged his eyes, and he would
love Valentine Schmidt forever and ever, world without end. Mayor Light,
Sheriff Bowles, Marshal Kolb, Erich Kahler and ElRoy Mauk were waiting
in Charley's private office. They all rose when Charley and Voss and
Wainscott entered dragging the wounded. They all made solicitous noises.
Reavis and Smallsreed were gently deposited in two large comfortable
leather chairs. Reavis' fly still was covered by his cupped hands.

Erich Kahler smiled, fumbled in a vest pocket, came up with a small
steel box. He opened the box, withdrew a small pincushion. He removed
a number of pins. I, sir, am a bachelor, he said to Reavis. As a result, I
must make do for myself as far as minor repairs to my clothing are concerned.

Reavis looked at him.

Erich Kahler went to Reavis and held out the pins. Here, sir, he said,
perhaps these can be of some use to you.

Reavis grunted, took the pins, bent them, fastened his fly.

Everyone watched him very closely.

He worked hastily. When he was done, he said to Erich Kahler: Ah,
I thank you.

You are most welcome, sir, said Erich Kahler.

Charley made the introductions. Hands were grasped. Grunts. Then
Charley began to speak. He allowed as how nothing was to be gained by
beating around the bush. He spoke quietly. He told Reavis he surely did
regret all the trouble that had befallen the CPV&M in the past twentyfour hours. He said he surely did wish it could have been avoided. He nodded
toward the sheriff. The sheriff had visited the village of Blood that day.
Lamentably, damage to CPV&M property there had been considerable.
Charley listed the extent of the damage. Shaking his head, he told Reavis
the sheriff had been unable to apprehend those responsible. Apparently
scores of men had participated in the hideous mischief, and the task of
sorting the guilty from the innocent was patently impossible. The sheriff
nodded confirmation. Reavis glared at the sheriff. Smallsreed made a hapless gesture with his hands. Charley reminded his two guests that the
CPV&M had, by closing its depot, deprived Blood of telegraphic communication with the outside. Had the line been open, the sheriff no doubt
would have been on the scene hours earlier, and perhaps arrests would

have been made. Ah, well. No matter. Done was done, eh? Yes. No
sense bewailing what might have been. After a pause, Charley addressed
himself to the ordinance that had been passed the previous evening by the
Paradise Falls village Council. It was called, for want of a better term, the
Train Ordinance. It authorized the levying of a fee of one hundred dollars for every train that passed within the village's corporate limits. Charley explained to Reavis and Smallsreed that the Council had felt the
ordinance to be necessary because of the smoke and soot.

Smoke and soot? said Smallsreed.

Yes sir, said Charley, that is what I said.

You mean the smoke and soot from our engines?

Precisely. You see, there have been numerous complaints from owners
of homes. These people say the smoke and soot have forced them to paint
their dwellings more often. They say this condition has been in effect since
the day the CPV&M inaugurated its service here. The expense to these
people has been considerable. They have sought equity. The Council, being responsive to the needs of the citizens, thus came up with the idea of
the Train Ordinance. You see, it is not the—

Said Smallsreed: I still don't see what housepainting has to do with the
ordinance.

Said Charley: Ah, I was just getting to that. The citizens simply seek
equity. They certainly have no desire to run the CPV&M out of business.

Not *much*, said Reavis.

Charley smiled. Ah, he said, *please*.

You swine, said Reavis.

Charley still smiled. He said: Ah, now, now. No names. Please. Permit me to continue. As I was saying, the word to focus on in this situation is *equity*. It is felt that the levying of a train fee will enable the
county commissioners to lower property taxes, since less money from
property tax revenue will be needed by the village. Thus, if the taxes
are reduced, the owners of homes will have achieved the financial equity
that will enable them to afford to be able to paint their dwellings more
often. We treasure cleanliness here, gentlemen. Many of our residents
are of German origin, and no one is cleaner than a German, no one in the
world. Do you follow me so far? I hope you do. Your railroad runs twenty
trains or so into Paradise Falls every day. From now on, it will cost you a
hundred dollars a train for that privilege. Or approximately two thousand
dollars a day, a figure that comes to about three quarters of a million
dollars a year. Ah, gentlemen, *cleanliness*. You cannot begin to understand how deeply we of Paradise Falls treasure it. I don't suppose I have
to remind you that next to godliness there is no more profound and en-
nobling—

Both Reavis and Smallsreed began to shout. Charley's smile did not go away. Mayor Light fidgeted. Marshal Kolb glanced out a window. Sheriff Bowles tugged at an ear. Fritz Voss stared at his lap. Winfield Wainscott cleaned his spectacles. Erich Kahler linked fingers across his belly. ElRoy Mauk's eyes were moist, and two words were written there in all the dampness, and the two words were: RASCALITY TRIUMPHANT. Reavis and Smallsreed shouted for some time. Charley nodded, clucked, pursed his lips, scratched his chin. His eyes were jolly. Reavis and Smallsreed threatened legal retaliation unparalleled in the annals of American jurisprudence. They called Charley a scamp, criminal, skunk, jackass, cockroach, cur and bastard. It surely was fine talk coming from such a couple of important Columbus gentlemen, and it made Charley's belly shake for joy. Reavis and Smallsreed told him they would *blockade* Paradise Falls if necessary. They accused Charley of bribery, arson and inciting to riot. They told him they would rebuild their railroad if necessary clear *around* Paradise Falls. They asked him just precisely how he thought Paradise Falls would survive without the railroad. They asked him whether he had consulted with Ike Underwood. They told him Ike Underwood was going to be mighty angry with him. After all, if the railroad abandoned Paradise Falls, how would the brick and tile manufactured by the Paradise Falls Clay Products be shipped to the outside world? They told Charley he was ruining the village. They took turns shouting, did Reavis and Smallsreed, and their promises of doom made the windows rattle. They swore eternal hostility. They flapped their arms. Their words came laced in spit. It was only gradually that they became aware of the giggling. It began with Winfield Wainscott. Next was ElRoy Mauk. Then Erich Kahler. Then, in a burst, the others. Charley was the last to succumb. Even Mayor Virgil T. Light, who was clearly frightened out of his large bald wits, began giggling before Charley did. Charley was rather proud of this. His selfcontrol was, as far as he was concerned, another proclamation of his greatness. But finally he could restrain himself no longer. His giggling became outright laughter, and so did the giggling of the others. Reavis slammed his fists against the arms of his chair. *Stop that laughing!* he yelled.

Charley cut short a guffaw. He dabbed at his eyes. Can't help it, he said.

Said Reavis: Oh you think you're so goddamn wise, don't you? Well, this thing is nowhere near being—

Reavis, said Charley, your cock is hanging out.

Quickly Reavis looked down at his fly.

Said Charley: Poor little thing. I expect the pins worked themselves loose.

ElRoy Mauk spoke up: If I were you, Mr Reavis, I wouldn't make
any abrupt movements. For all you know, one of the pins has worked its
way inside your fly. I'd be greatly distressed to think of you as a boy
soprano. Honestly I would.

Laughter. Winfield Wainscott actually laughed so hard he was seized
with a coughing spell. Mayor Virgil T. Light gave him a large bald clap on
the back.

Reavis blushed. His fingers groped hesitantly inside his fly. He stuffed
his penis back inside his fly.

Winfield Wainscott's coughing spell subsided. He looked solemnly at
Reavis and said: Sir, how come your cock is yellow?

Reavis made a sound like a croak. He said nothing. His fingers sought
out the pins.

A yellow cock, said Sheriff Bowles. I swear before God, I never knew
there was such a thing.

I'd call it more of an amber, said Charley.

Look how he plays with himself, said Sheriff Bowles.

Sign of a diseased brain, said Charley. Back in Indiana, our little town
had a fellow who waved his old whang in front of little girls no more
than six or seven years of age. Can you imagine such a thing? Well, old
Alf Tubbs he got taken away, and good riddance. Anything makes my
flesh run cold, it's the sight of a degenerate.

No dignity, said Fritz Voss.

Charley looked at him. Exactly, said Charley.

Reavis stood up. Tears ran down his cheeks. Pins fell from his fly.
Charley guffawed, and so did the other men—all but Smallsreed. Now
Smallsreed was trembling. He came out of his chair. He moved toward
Charley. His hands were in fists. The sheriff intercepted him. Smallsreed
knocked off the sheriff's spectacles. Reavis moved to help Smallsreed.
Mayor Virgil T. Light seized Reavis, pulled him back. The sheriff groped
for his spectacles. Smallsreed tried to step on the sheriff's spectacles, but
Fritz Voss pushed him back. Winfield Wainscott sat in a corner and
whinnied. Mayor Virgil T. Light and Fritz Voss pushed Reavis and
Smallsreed back into their chairs. The sheriff groped. Charley's eyes were
hot. He closed them, shuddered, covered his mouth with a hand. He
chided himself for not having had the foresight to hire an orchestra. I
could have played some nicely appropriate music for the solemn buck and
quadrille that had just been performed in front of him by Sheriff Bowles,
Mayor Light and the Messrs Reavis and Smallsreed. It had been like one
of those French sissy ballets, and that was a fact.

Finally, after Reavis and Smallsreed were safely returned to their chairs,
Charley spoke. He looked directly at Reavis and said: You stay in that

chair until I tell you to get up. If you do *not* stay in that chair, I'll have Marshal Kolb here arrest you for indecent exposure.

Reavis opened his mouth.

No sass, said Charley.

Reavis breathed deeply. He swallowed, said nothing.

An amber cock, said Charley. Maybe you ought to forget the railroad business and get in touch with that man Barnum.

Laughter. Winfield Wainscott beat his fists against his knees.

Charley still was looking directly at Reavis. After the laughter had faded out, he said: We have you, Reavis. We have you good.

No, said Reavis.

Oh now—

We'll take you to court. We'll turn you upsidedown and shake you until by God . . . by God even the fillings will fall out of your teeth.

You can't. You'd like to, but you know you can't.

What?

A chain is only as strong as its weakest link. Now you keep still. Let me finish. I won't bother any more with talk about the Train Ordinance and all that shit. It was just a means to an end. You aren't about to pay two thousand dollars a day so your trains can pass through here, and I can't say as I blame you. I wouldn't pay either. But I've got you. The CPV&M has just the one main line, and I've cut it, and you can't starve me out. Your damn railroad isn't in condition to starve out a chipmunk, and that's a fact. You're all bluff, Mr Reavis. And I got more brains than to be taken in by you.

You swine.

Ah, you've said that. You running out of words?

I'll destroy you.

Horse *shit*. You're not *man* enough. I expect you could if you wanted to, but you'd have to destroy yourself right along with me. You'd go down with me. You'd have to spend all your railroad's money, and all your own money: I'd hold out that long. *That* I give you my oath on.

He means it, Mr Reavis, said Winfield Wainscott, winking.

Thank you, Winfield, said Charley. Then, to Reavis: If there are going to be fillings on the floor, yours'll be down there too. Sure, if you want to fight me you probably can reroute your trains through Nelsonville and Logan on the Hocking Valley, but the Hocking Valley'll make it mighty dear for you. And you can go to court. Go ahead. Maybe in a year the matter will be resolved. But a year is too long to wait, isn't it? Cut in half the way it is now, your railroad can't last but about six months. And don't tell me anything different. So go ahead. Just do that. Walk out the door and go back to Columbus and starve me out. Chances are you can make me go under—*but so would you*. One way or the other, it'd happen sure as hell. Suppose somehow I went under before you did, and suppose you and your railroad still had money, you know what I'd do then? Well, I'll make you a promise. If, as and when I'm run out of business, I'll personally see to it that each and every one of my mines is doused with kerosene and set on fire. You got any idea how long a coal mine can burn? A hundred years? Two hundred years? In other words, the mines'll either be mine or they'll be no one's. So let's settle this thing. Cut your rates back to what they were. The minute you do is the minute we get rid of the Train Ordinance. ElRoy Mauk here is legal counsel for the village. All he has to do is tell the Council the ordinance is discriminatory and therefore illegal. So let's end this stupid business.

Never, said Reavis. His voice was harsh and torn.

Tim, said Smallsreed.

Reavis looked at Smallsreed.

We can't fight this, said Smallsreed. We really can't.

Reavis glared at Smallsreed and said: You're suggesting we give up?

Yes. It's not that we've lost anything. All that will happen is that the situation will revert to what it was.

You . . . you realize what you're saying?

All I'm doing is talking sense.

You're . . . you're betraying me . . .

Tim, that's sheep dip.

I am president of this road! I don't have to—

Don't shout at me, Tim.

You—

I don't deserve being shouted at. All I'm trying to say is that we have made a mistake. You know that. Admit it. This, too, shall pass.

But you've seen what they've done! You've seen how they've been . . . ah, *ridiculing* us!

Smallsreed shrugged. Perhaps we gave them no choice, he said.

What? How's that?

Tim, I'm tired. I want to go home. I want to change my clothes and take a hot bath. If we leave now, we can be back in Columbus by ten-thirty or eleven.

Bath? Did you say bath?

Yes. I said bath. A hot bath. Ella was going to fix lamb chops for my supper tonight. I have a large fondness for lamb chops. Maybe she'll still fix them for me—if I get home early enough. She really can fix them. Crisp. And yet a great deal of juice.

Lamb . . . lamb chops, said Reavis, sagging back in his chair.

Tim, I want to go home. We're not about to wrest Wells' mines away from him. He's licked us, and we've made asses of ourselves. Yelling. Fighting. I even tried to step on a man's spectacles. Godalmighty. I am sixtyone years of age. A man's spectacles. Lord.

What . . . what if I refuse to give up?

Smallsreed sighed, spread his hands. He said: In that case, you'd have to go on without me.

You'd . . . you'd resign?

Yes. I'm too old to behave like an ass. Too old to be thrashing about and trying to step on a man's spectacles. I am not a petulant child.

Neither am I!

Well, Tim, you could have fooled me.

Reavis gasped.

Charley smiled. This was all very enjoyable. Charley's associates were leaning forward, and their eyes were large. It had been years since Charley had felt such a terrific surge of his greatness. He supposed he was grateful to Reavis. The man had caused the muzzle velocity to reaffirm itself. Ah, good old Reavis. Him and his amber whang, his humiliation.

Smallsreed stood up.

Reavis stared at him.

Come on, Tim, said Smallsreed, holding out a hand.

Reavis' breath made a dry abrupt noise. He reached for Smallsreed's hand.

Smallsreed pulled Reavis to his feet.

Reavis still held a hand cupped over his fly.

Charley opened his mouth to say something.

Smallsreed interrupted: No, Mr Wells, no words are necessary. We . . . ah, what I should say is . . . the rates are, ah, restored. Yes.

Charley nodded.

Smallsreed placed an arm around Reavis' shoulders and escorted him out of the office.

Charley and Wainscott drove the two railroad officials back to the barricade and the waiting train. Charley told Smallsreed the track at the barricades would be restored first thing in the morning.

Ah, thank you very much, said Smallsreed.

Of course, said Charley. But you understand the CPV&M will have to stand the expense of repairing its facilities in Blood.

Smallsreed nodded. Yes, he said. We understand that.

Reavis said nothing. He sat hunched forward, and his hand remained cupped over his fly.

Charley flapped the reins. He was quite grateful to this fellow Smallsreed. If it hadn't been for Smallsreed's intelligence, the thing could have dragged out, and perhaps it wouldn't even have been settled at all. Smallsreed had given Reavis an opening. He had had the intelligence to understand that Reavis was not the sort to surrender voluntarily. Reavis was of course a very weak man, and he had been humiliated quite ferociously, and very weak men always were reluctant to surrender voluntarily. No weakling was happy with his weakness, and thus he invariably fought to the death to hide it. Charley knew this, and clearly so did Smallsreed, which meant Smallsreed had done him a large good turn. By surrendering first, he had given Reavis an excuse for his own surrender. Ah, good old Smallsreed: a fine fellow, one Charley probably could have been quite fond of. Under other circumstances of course.

Smallsreed assisted Reavis up the steps into the coach. Then Smallsreed came back down the steps and spoke with Charley. A thin string of weariness lay across his voice. Mr Wells, he said, it's a shame there is no decency in you.

Oh? said Charley. He stood with his hands on his hips. He cuffed at the dirt roadbed with a shoe. The buggy was a few yards away. Wainscott sat holding the reins. He was grinning, and Charley could see the grin, darkness or no darkness.

Smallsreed nodded. Yes, he said, if there were decency in you, you could be a figure in history.

Well, thank you kindly for your generous words.

I am not joshing. I do not make it a practice to josh. You are a remarkable man, but I cannot say that I admire you.

Mr Smallsreed, with all due respect, I must say that I do not give a shit what you think of me.

Yes. That goes without saying.

Hasn't it occurred to you that all I've done has been in the simple defense of my property from the machinations of a goddamn railroad that was trying to bludgeon me out of it? Who was the wronged party in this matter? *I* was, and you know damn well I was.

I am not talking about the justice of your fight. I am talking about the *deviousness*. Great God, I thought *I* was devious. Hah. Compared with *you*, I am about as devious as an elephant's fart.

I'm taking that as a compliment.

I figured you would.

Charley kept his word—the church was built in Blood for the miners and their families. It was constructed entirely of brick purchased from the John K. Farr Brick & Tile Co of Zanesville. The Paradise Falls Clay Products was not even asked to submit an estimate. Since the death of former Mayor Pillsbury (a death anyone in his right mind knew was a suicide) and the beginning of the presidential canvass, the final traces of cordiality between Charley and old Ike Underwood had been scraped away. Charley was convinced old Ike had had something to do with the railroad's plot to take control of the mines. Which meant this was a very bad year for old Ike. First he had to throw in with the Liberal Republicans, whose Greeley was bound to lose, and then he went so far as to make his feelings public when the *Democrat's* Greeley editorials began to appear. Charley told Dave Millerspaugh to roast Greeley a thousand ways come next Thursday in the *Journal.* Have no fear, said Dave Millerspaugh, it will be done. And it was. Dave Millerspaugh perhaps never would be a candidate for the community of the saints, but he surely did understand billingsgate, and the day Charley had hired this fellow had been a very fine day indeed. Ah yes, such a splendid year it was for the discomfort of old Ike. The greatness of Charles Palmer Wells inflated itself like a bladder; the worm feasted; the year was all sunshine and sweet chirping birds. And it reached its zenith late in November, when the new church was dedicated. Charley and Nancy and little Nell were the honored guests at the consecration ceremonies. They were met at the new Blood depot by a delegation of miners and their families. The new parish's priest also was there. He was a florid middleaged fellow named McQueen. There was a warm smell of whisky to him. It was a good deal stronger than the smell of wine that invariably hung about the Rev Fr Messer. Nancy and little Nell were given flowers. The priest grinned and scraped. When he said the word fine, it came out foine. A monsignor was there from Columbus to preside at the consecration. The monsignor's name was Schwabacher, and he was quite thin and pale. He was perhaps seventy years old. He did not smell of whisky. Nor did he smell of wine. He smelled of nothing other than some sort of harsh ammoniacal soap. The delegation escorted Charley and Nancy and little Nell to the church. The building lay in a gully just east of the Nancy #2 mine. It was at the end of a street lined by small frame houses built by the C. P. Wells Coal Co and rented to the miners. The new brick of the church was a brilliant red. Leaves slapped along the earth, and the crisp air had almost done away with the stink of the mines. Alas, only almost, but ah well, such was the price demanded by progress. Nell got a stone in her shoe. Nell was four now, and she gave no sign whatever of growing up into a beauty. She began to whimper. Sh, said Nancy. My *foot* hurts, said Nell. Nancy squatted next to Nell and removed the shoe. She shook the stone out of the shoe. Fr McQueen smiled down on Nell. Nancy replaced the shoe on Nell's foot. Thank you, Mama, said Nell. Nancy smiled, patted Nell on a shoulder. Oh *you,* she said. Everyone was standing at the front entrance of the church, which was to be called St Malachi's. Men scruffed their feet against the leaves. Charley smiled and bowed at everyone. Some of the men applauded. Nancy also smiled. She had developed a fine skill at smiling. The past few years had done wonders for her. She tucked a hand inside the crook of Charley's arm and smiled and smiled. She was really quite a good wife, no getting around it. And even now, at thirtyfour, she turned more than her share of heads. Her undergarments were firm, and her opulent tiddies still possessed a great deal of their girlish thrust. Charley grinned. Nancy's hand was warm against his arm. After the monsignor conducted the ceremony of consecration, Fr McQueen delivered a lengthy sermon. He made numerous references to the goodness and loving kindness of the one & only Charles Palmer Wells. He complimented the miners on their loyalty to their sainted employer. Smiling, he raised an arm and let it swing in an arc. Ah, he said, here for the glory of God and the consolation of Man are the fruits of that loyalty. It was a foine thing you did. There are few virtues that exist on a higher plane than loyalty. May you call thanks to God that you possess it in such righteous abundance. May this church, consecrated today in the name of our beloved St Malachi, be a constant reminder of your resoluteness in the face of adversity.

That night, after Nell had been put to bed with her dolls and stuffed animals and whatnot, Charley and Nancy sat in the parlor and discussed the priest.

Where on earth did they get him? Nancy wanted to know.

They're assigned by the Papist church. The diocese I believe it's called.

You think he *believed* the things he said?

I have no way of knowing.

Did *you* believe them?

Don't be foolish.

He was frightened to death of you, said Nancy.

I don't know why.

You know people. You know the soft places. And you got the stomach for working at the soft places.

Nancy, what are you talking about?

I don't hate you. Please don't think I do. But, my stars, there's no one you wouldn't corrupt is there?

I don't understand this.

You have corrupted him.

Corrupted who? The priest?

Yes.

That's stupid. How could I have corrupted him? I only just met him today.

You know what I mean. That man is just a man, and he knows which side his bread is buttered on.

That's foolish. You don't know what you're talking about.

Charley! Charley!

Nancy, calm down. There's no sense Nell hearing all this.

The priest was corrupted the moment he opened his mouth. All he wants is to please you. He is afraid.

So? All right, suppose what you say is true. What difference does it make?

Charley . . . my Lord, Charley . . .

Why are you getting so worked up? What's the sense in it? You know the way I feel. It just so happens I got little use for *rhetoric* and *concepts* and the sort of thinking that holds Man to be the finest thing ever to have stood in the sunlight of Creation. Man is *mortal*, which means he is *imperfect*, which means there is no real health in him, as the Papists themselves say in their prayers. Look, did I make the world? Of course not. Sin is Sin, and Weakness is Weakness. Which was here first, Sin or Jesus? I almost feel sorry for poor old Jesus. The other side had such a big head start.

Charley, please don't talk this way . . .

Then don't get so worked up. I don't kick crippled dogs.

Oh . . . Charley . . . Charley . . .

You listen to me. You look around the world. The people who matter are the people who pursue their own interests. I'm nothing special, not when you get down *to* it. There are millions who feel just the way I do. They pursue their own interests. Maybe I've worked harder and been luckier than most of them, but there's no *real* difference. And what's so terrible about it? And, even if there is something terrible about it, just exactly what can be done about it? Oh that priest, oh how you groan and carry on about him, but there's one point you miss. You say I've corrupted him already. Well, maybe so. But, don't you see, he *wanted* to be corrupted. Otherwise, he wouldn't have said the things he said. I'm a stranger to him, but he understands where the power is, and so he sells himself to it. He has to. That's his nature. He has given in to his mortality, his Sin, his Weakness. So tell me—what difference does it all make? If he's mortal and Sinful and Weak to begin with, how can it matter that he's been corrupted? Anyway, how can I corrupt a man beyond what he's already been corrupted by God on the day he is born? Man is born to die. All that matters is how interesting he makes the days in between. Concepts are hogwash. So is eternity. I learned that. Remember back in Titusville when I stood up for what I believed in? What did it eventually get me? Tar. Feathers. My ideas and my good intentions were kicked out of me. Ah yes, your beloved *human beings* did me that kindness. So why should I care about them? A priest comes along, and he needs to attach himself to someone strong, so he gets down on his hands and knees and licks the feet of Charles Palmer Wells. What am I supposed to do about it? Kick him in the face?

Charley?

Yes?

Your face is very red. *You* really shouldn't get *your*self so worked up.

1873 . . .

Mayor Virgil T. Light is reelected without opposition. The Carmichael baby is a boy, dark and frail. It is named Arthur Junior. Harlowe Morris, who is ninety this year, decides to close his grocery store. A goodly crowd is on hand the day the store's stock, furnishings and equipment are auctioned off. After the auctioneer's fee is deducted, old Harlowe realizes $1,004.12 from the sale. Dr Jerome K. Reeser, he of the fastidious manner and the fancy ruffled shirts, drops dead of a coronary thrombosis. Little Miss Nell Wells has names for all her dolls and stuffed animals. Legions of them occupy her bed at night. She tells them: We all of us love the world, don't we? The Wall Street panic is felt by Ike Underwood to a mild degree. He had invested five thousand dollars in Jay Cooke & Co stock. I should have known better, he tells his wife. Serves me right. Says Phoebe: What do you mean? Says old Ike: Well, I wanted something for nothing. Cooke is a speculator, and his methods always have been shady. Speculators promise a great deal for very little. But they usually give very little for a great deal. The collapse of Jay Cooke & Co is no great loss to the nation, believe me. I feel sorry, though, for the people who can't afford what's happening. And the people who'll lose their jobs. There's going to be a sight of bankruptcy, take my word for it. And unemployment. Says Phoebe: It seems a shame. Says Ike: It *is* a shame, but business is a very complicated thing, and these calamities are bound to come along now and then. Says Phoebe: Yes. I suppose so. Says Ike: Like Wells. Says Phoebe: I beg your pardon? Says Ike: Wells is a calamity. Says Phoebe: Yes. I would say *so*. Do you, ah, have any further plans regarding him? Says Ike: I only wish I did. Ike shakes his head. He is seventyone years old, and plans no longer come easily to his mind. Twenty years ago a C. P. Wells never would have been allowed even to make a start. But now is not twenty years ago, and old Ike is weary. At seventyone, he figures he has a right. He is fortunate in one respect, however. After the failure of the CPV&M to take over the C. P. Wells Coal Co mines, he unloads his stock in the railroad—and at a profit of nearly ten percent. The transaction is consummated just sixteen days before the start of the panic.

CPV&M stock promptly plummets. Great God, he tells his wife, if I'd
have waited sixteen days more, I'd have lost something like seventy thousand dollars. Says Phoebe: Praise the Lord. You are a genius, Isaac. No
question of it. Mayor Light's son, young Bill, meets secretly with Mrs
Nancy Wells and says to her: Why? Why did you do it? It was obscene.
Says Mrs Wells: I don't know. It just seemed like the right thing at the
time. Says Bill Light: God damn you, I hate you. Says Mrs Wells: No.
That's not so. Bill Light drops to his knees and presses his face against Mrs
Wells' thighs. She strokes his hair. Find a wife, she says. Hurry. Please
hurry.

Philip Isaac Underwood:

THERE HAD BEEN NO DARKNESS at the beginning, but of course now was no
longer the beginning, and the darkness sucked and slapped: Phil Underwood's head shrieked from it, and yet (Phil Underwood being Phil Underwood) the world knew not a thing of his terror. He seldom remembered
butterflies. There were larger things to be remembered. The largest of
them all was his joy in blood and broken bones. It came the night he had
the erection in Paul Starling's apartment after giving Lipscomb the sissy
such a beating. The fellow had attempted to seize Phil's genitals, and
surely he had been made to pay. Phil was an excellent student, and in
the summer of 1869 he was graduated from Harvard *summa cum laude*,
but for him there was no larger truth learned than the one he encountered that night in Paul Starling's little flat in Cambridge. Lipscomb of
course left Harvard. The last anyone heard of him, he was teaching rhetoric in a small college in Michigan. Phil often thought of Lipscomb. He
wished he would meet the man someday. There were certain things that
needed explaining. Such as, for example, the theft of a necessary war by
parents whose love could not be resisted. Phil loved his mother and father;
he did; he *did*. But they had betrayed him. Perhaps the world would not
understand how he felt. Perhaps the world would not be capable of seeing
love as the agency of a betrayal. But Phil was not concerned with what the
world thought. All he knew was that the betrayal had been made. All he
knew was that he had to find his own war. All he knew was that the beating of Lipscomb had produced an erection the sweet pain of which had

almost made him faint, gasping, like a girl with the vapors. After his graduation from Harvard, Phil did not return to Paradise Falls to live. The thought was intolerable. He needed room to fulfill the darkness, and he did not want it revealed to his mother and father. And so, after paying them a brief visit, he went to New York, where a position was waiting for him on a literary magazine called *American Crisis*. Its publisher was Paul Starling's father, a man named Lloyd L. Starling. Phil rented an elaborate suite of rooms in a new brownstone on Christopher Street, and two or three times a week he went out in search of vagrants to punish. He usually dragged them into alleyways, and he was not satisfied until he felt something break. The vagrants invariably whimpered and puled.

Phil did very well as an editor of *American Crisis*—so well, in fact, that within three years he was named editorinchief. Lloyd L. Starling became quite fond of him. A large man with great gray brows, moist lips and a full Burnside beard, Lloyd L. Starling was a widower, the only heir of a family whose previous generation had amassed a fortune in lumber and wood pulp. He had two children, Paul and a daughter Christine. Paul became a Harvard teaching assistant after his graduation. His field was Roman history, and he firmly believed Gibbon to be the most gifted writer the English language ever had produced. Christine was three years younger than her brother. She was slender and gentle and blond, and she blushed whenever she was in the same room with Phil. He supposed she thought she was in love with him. Lloyd L. Starling made no particular bones over the fact that he would not exactly flop over dead if Phil were to marry Christine. Phil liked the girl, even though her blushing was a bit tiresome, and he supposed someday he might marry her at that. But not right away. There was too much else to do. His work on the magazine put him in contact with scholars, poets, writers of fiction. He was a good editor. He despised excessive rhetoric. He demanded precision of thought. He would not publish Whitman. He met Whitman one night at a party, and the man struck him as being something of a shaggy poseur. Phil found Whitman's work embarrassing. The nakedness of it was not Art; it was simply public display. Art demanded discipline, structure, knowledge of effects. Whitman understood none of those things, and his alleged poetry made Phil uncomfortable.

Phil's apartment, large and elaborate as it was, nonetheless was furnished simply. He found delight in bare floors, unpapered walls. He knew he was an anachronism, but he didn't particularly care. The ornate, things of glass and velvet and ormolu, things filigreed and doilied and antimacassared—all were rejected. Only in his apparel did he indulge himself. His vests were stupendously elaborate, and he owned sixteen tailormade suits, and he always carried a stick. His library was handsome.

He favored the works of Pope and Tennyson. He detested Wordsworth and Byron. He tolerated much of Shakespeare, but the excessive melodrama really did infuriate him. If only the man had had a feeling for form! Phil was comforted by things, persons and attitudes that did not yield. Sentiment, on the other hand, made him uneasy. He had been deprived of his war, but he would not permit this betrayal to destroy him. He never used his stick on the vagrants. That would have been dishonorable, unmanly. He used only his fists, and of course they were sufficient, and he supposed that the darkness would forever spit and snigger about him.

For a year or so he kept an actress named Stella Charles. She laughed a great lot, and she was tall, and she made a splendid appearance on his arm when they dined in public. His *American Crisis* salary came nowhere near paying for his apartment, his mistress and his wardrobe, but his parents were more than generous. He visited Paradise Falls every Christmas without fail, and Ike and Phoebe were hugely impressed with whatever it was their elegant son had become. Especially Phoebe. You have done awfully well, she told him, for a boy from the country. Phil invariably smiled in response to this observation. And he invariably thanked his mother for her kind words. Phoebe Underwood had lived in Paradise Falls for decades, but she still was a Connecticut person in her heart of hearts. And a wellborn Connecticut person. She was, after all, the former *Phoebe Bowers* of *New Haven,* and her father had been *Cyrus O. Bowers,* and the Bowers name still meant something in that stern and implacably traditional part of the nation. And Phil was pleased by this. In a way, he was unhappy that his parents had packed him off to Harvard instead of Yale. Still, he could understand their reasoning. There were squadrons of his mother's relatives still in New Haven. Had he attended Yale, his social obligations would have left him no time for his studies, and he probably would have been expelled. As it was, he spent many of his Harvard weekends in New Haven. He was forever being invited to visit his mother's innumerable cousins and aunts and uncles. It was in New Haven, in point of fact, that he met Stella Charles. It was the spring of his senior year, 1869. One night he and several male cousins and friends attended a performance of *Faust.* The performance, given by a secondrate traveling company, was execrable, but the Helen of Troy was altogether magnificent, and Phil was taken by her immediately. Stella Charles, as Helen of Troy, was clad in a flowing white robe, and its decolletage was colossal, sublime, a miracle of God. How, after being in the presence of such a majestic wonder, could one doubt the existence of a Supreme Being? After the performance, Phil went backstage. He was escorted by his cousins and friends. He stopped an old man who was wearing what appeared to be an extremely uncomfortable pair of velvet tights. He asked directions to the dressingroom of Helen of Troy. The old man hitched at his crotch, shook his head no. Phil frowned. The old man smiled. Phil's frown was gentle, almost kindly, but for some reason the old man began to tremble a bit. Quickly he pointed an uncertain finger down a long dark corridor. Phil politely thanked the old man, who scuttled away. The cousins and friends laughed. Phil looked at them. He gave them the same frown he had given the old man. The laughter stopped. He told the cousins and friends he had some private business to transact. He left them standing there. He walked down the corridor. He opened the dressingroom door without knocking. Helen of Troy was in the room with four other women. He told the four other women to get out. He smiled at them, and his words were soft. The four other women protested, and for a moment the room was full of squeals and tintinnabulations. Then Phil decided to go ahead and frown and see if it had its effect. It did. The women drew back. Helen of Troy smiled. She smiled at the women. Go ahead, girls, she said. It'll be all right. The women did not argue with her. Quickly they went out of the room. Phil was succinct. He told Helen of Troy he was a senior at Harvard. He told her he had enjoyed her performance immeasurably. He told her it didn't matter that she'd had no words to say. Helen of Troy smiled and said: In this company, the less a person has to say, the better off he is. Said Phil: Yes, ma'm. You would seem, judging from tonight's performances by the other actors, to have a point. Helen of Troy laughed, and then Phil told her he had a fine position awaiting him in New York. He told her he wanted her to resign from this ridiculous company. If she did, he would set her up in New York. She looked at him, and her eyes were like slabs of noon, and her laughter pounded and rocked, and finally she summoned the breath to tell him he was out of his mind. Phil stood rigidly. He was carrying his stick. He tapped it on the floor once, twice, three times. Helen of Troy looked at it. The laughter went out of her and she said: Now, *now*. Said Phil: All right, Miss Charles. I shan't make a fool of myself. My name is Philip I. Underwood. I shall withdraw myself from your presence, but I shall not withdraw the offer. After June, I can be reached care of the editorial offices of *American Crisis*, 277 Broadway. Please feel free to get in touch with me at any time. Then Phil turned and went out. He closed the door quietly behind him. When the cousins and friends asked him what had happened, he simply turned down the corners of his mouth. They left the theater, crossed the street to a saloon. They drank a great deal of whisky, but Phil answered no questions. He toyed with his stick, tapped it on the floor in triplets, once, twice, three times, in unhurried rhythm.

A year later he again encountered Stella Charles. It was in New York, at a party given by a theatrical impresario named Kelly. It was quite a grand party, and even Jim Fisk and Josie Mansfield were there. Josie Mansfield was supposed to be a great beauty, but she was too fat and loud for Phil's taste. So was Jim Fisk too fat and loud, for that matter. The man and his plump inamorata were vaguely disgusting, and Phil stayed away from them. Stella Charles was escorted to the party by an actor named Sergius Laughlin, a large proclamative sort who that season was scoring a considerable success in *Macbeth*. One of the performances had been attended by no less a couple than Vice President and Mrs Colfax, and after the final curtain they had gone backstage to give Sergius Laughlin their personal congratulations. Accounts of the visit had been in all the newspapers. Phil recognized Stella Charles as soon as she entered the room on the arm of the impressive Sergius Laughlin. And Stella Charles recognized Phil. Her eyes became large, and then she smiled, and the smile had something in it of fear. Phil returned the smile. He bowed. She looked away. She wore a dress of crimson velvet, and nothing save a narrow beaded necklace covered her vast creamy decolletage. Phil decided he would have to maneuver Sergius Laughlin into a fistfight. He would have to thrash the fellow good and proper. Phil sipped champagne, drifted across the room. Then, when he was within earshot of Sergius Laughlin, he engaged a man named Easterly in a conversation about the Irish. Easterly, who was rather drunk, did not notice how near Laughlin was standing.

Yes, said Phil to Easterly, I doubt whether those people ever will be able to fit in. Once an Irishman, always an Irishman. Once an Irishman, never an American. The way the Irish live, for example. Disgusting, I call it. No decent selfrespecting *black Negro* would consent to exist the way the Irish do. I am told that the only way one can tell an Irishman from his pig is by the fact that the pig keeps its person cleaner.

Easterly laughed.

Phil shook his head. Drunkenness, he said. License. I do not mean to sound like a prig, but there *are* standards of civilized conduct.

No, no, said Easterly, you're not being priggish, old fellow. I understand what you mean. Perfectly.

Apparently our Irish friends are as ignorant of civilized conduct as they are ignorant of just about everything else save whisky and their loveless prolific fornications.

Ah, said Easterly. Well put, sir.

Sergius Laughlin came up to Phil and placed a hand on his shoulder. Easterly swallowed, backed away.

Phil smiled at Sergius Laughlin.

Sergius Laughlin also smiled. Wellsir, he said, you're not a very pleasant person, are you now?

Please take your hand off my shoulder.

You have a loud voice, said Sergius Laughlin. Perhaps it is *too* loud a voice.

Please take your hand off my shoulder, you Irish pig.

A whisky glass was in Sergius Laughlin's free hand. He flicked the whisky into Phil's face.

Phil pulled back from Sergius Laughlin's hand. He removed a handkerchief from his vest pocket. Carefully he wiped his face. He set his champagne glass on a table, cleared his throat and said: The first pig I see, I must apologize to it. I used its name to insult an Irishman. I should be ashamed. The poor pig. The day an Irishman is the equal of a pig is the day the sun comes up green.

A woman gasped. Stella Charles stood against a far wall. Her arms were folded across her bosoms, and her eyes were white.

Kelly, the host, stepped between Sergius Laughlin and Phil. Kelly was smiling. He also was perspiring. Jim Fisk and Josie Mansfield stood behind him. Jim Fisk was smiling. He whispered something to Josie Mansfield. She nodded, blinked, grinned. Kelly was a small man with pink hands and ears. He was quite a successful theatrical impresario, but no one really knew why. His friends had coined a soubriquet for him. They called him, in acknowledgment of his pink hands and ears, Bunny. Now, now, everyone, said Bunny Kelly, this is a *party*. There is no need for—

Phil reached out and pushed Bunny Kelly aside. Perhaps, he said to Sergius Laughlin, this matter can be settled outside.

Sergius Laughlin bowed. Splendid, he said.

Smiling and chatting, Sergius Laughlin and Phil went outside to an alley. The other guests followed. Even Bunny Kelly came along. The fight was brief. Phil broke Sergius Laughlin's nose and four of his ribs. Someone hailed a passing hansom. Sergius Laughlin, who was whimpering, was carried to the hansom by three of the guests. They clambered in after him and took him to a hospital. Phil offered Stella Charles his arm. They returned to the party. The following week he established her in a flat on Houston Street. The *Macbeth* closed nine days after Phil had put its principal player in the hospital. Sergius Laughlin's understudy had been most inadequate. Phil's demands on Stella Charles were not inordinate. His lusts for female flesh had never been overwhelming. Once a week or so and he was perfectly content. He did insist, however, that she see no one else. And he did insist that she be fastidious in caring for her physical appearance. He gave her a generous allowance for clothes, perfumes, jewelry, soaps and the like.

In a way, you know, I am insulted, she told him one night in bed.

Oh? said Phil.

Yes. A person would think I hadn't *taken care of* myself before meeting *you*.

I didn't intend it that way. It's just that you make such a miraculous appearance. I want you to be able to enhance it as much as possible.

Well, said Stella Charles. Thank you very much, kind sir. Then she laughed (she was fond of laughter), and she pressed his dark little face against her bosoms.

The arrangement remained in effect about a year, which was just about what Phil had expected. He had no illusions. Stella Charles had jettisoned Sergius Laughlin with great alacrity; sooner or later she would jettison Phil with equal dispatch. Also, there was the fact of his perfunctory lusts. He was not so stupid that he did not realize that such an epic creature required more frequent carnal adventures. Still, she did look splendid on his arm, and it was with some regret that one evening he called on her unexpectedly and found her fornicating with none other than Bunny Kelly.

He had known that some night he would find her fornicating with *someone*, but certainly not *Bunny Kelly*. Great heavens!

The confrontation was brief and quiet and really quite reasonable. If it hadn't been for the few frightened tears that meekly issued from Bunny Kelly's tiny blinking brownish eyes, it would have been concluded in even less time than the five minutes or so it did take. But Bunny Kelly insisted on weeping a little, and it was necessary then that a few rancorous and really extremely distasteful words be uttered. Still and all, nothing got out of hand, and later, thinking back on it, Phil decided he had suffered through a great many far worse experiences.

They both sat up when Phil entered the apartment. They had been sprawled on the couch. They both were nude. They were illuminated by moonlight. A comforter was at the foot of the couch. Stella grabbed it, covered herself and Bunny Kelly.

Sighing, Phil struck a match to the gaslight on the wall by the door. He turned up the light.

Stella and Bunny blinked at him.

Phil was carrying his stick. He tapped it on the floor once, twice, three times.

Caught, said Stella. She smiled.

Yes, said Phil. He smiled.

Bunny looked at Stella and then he looked at Phil. Are you going to beat me? he asked Phil. His voice squeaked.

No, said Phil.

And why not?

I beg your pardon? said Phil. He tapped his stick.

I have betrayed you, said Bunny, squeaking.

Nonsense, said Phil.

The color deepened in Stella's cheeks. She no longer smiled. She hugged the comforter. It means that little? she said.

Bunny Kelly was trembling. I'm willing to take my beating, he said.

No, said Phil, there will be no beating.

Now the few frightened tears were meekly issuing from Bunny Kelly's eyes. He threw back the comforter and stood up. His body was pink and gray and altogether without hair save at the pubis.

Phil smiled at him.

Grunting, Bunny Kelly assumed the stance of a boxer.

Phil chuckled.

I . . . I am Irish too, said Bunny Kelly, trembling still. You never thought of that, did you? I love her, and I am Irish, and do you want me to throw whisky in your face?

No, said Phil. Please sit down and cover yourself. You look ridiculous.

Bunny wheezed.

There is no need for melodrama, said Phil. And, beyond that, there is a chill in here.

Stella looked up at Bunny. Yes, darling, she said. It would be better if you sat down. I know you love me. I know you want to stand up for me. That's all that's necessary. There's no sense your getting hurt.

But maybe, said Bunny, maybe for you I *want* to get hurt.

No, said Stella. I *know* you love me. Please sit down. Please.

Bunny Kelly glared at Phil. Then, sniffling, shrugging a little, he sat down and gathered his share of the comforter around his chest and mid-section.

You say you love her? Phil asked him.

Yes. And I mean it.

Good, said Phil. Then, to Stella: I enjoyed it all. Truly I did. But please don't ask me to destroy the flavor with a lot of sentimental lies.

Wouldn't think of it, said Stella.

Thank you.

Would you like to know something?

I always seek knowledge.

He is better than you. Bunny here, I mean.

Ah, is that so?

Stella smiled. You've been good to me, she said. I'll never say otherwise. But I don't like you. I never have. You frighten me. And you know too much about how to hurt people. You wouldn't even consider beating

Bunny, would you? That would be too simple, wouldn't it? This way, by not *deigning* to as much as *touch* him, you're *really* expressing your contempt, aren't you? Ah, Phil, such a clever fellow you are. Now perhaps it would be best if you got out.

Phil nodded. He pointed his stick toward her midsection. Farewell, holy temple, he said.

Stella looked down at herself. She shuddered.

Bunny Kelly squeaked, tried to rise from the couch again.

Stella pulled him back. No, she said. No. Don't rise to it. Don't give him the satisfaction. I know how that mind of his works. Please. Let's not do what he wants us to do.

Bunny Kelly nodded, settled back.

Phil bowed. He smiled. He withdrew, closing the door gently behind him. Briskly he walked the midnight streets. His eyes were alert for vagrants. He found an elderly man huddled in a doorway. He dragged the elderly man into an alley and gave him a severe thrashing. He did not of course use his stick. He went home to a dreamless sleep. Bunny Kelly and Stella Charles were married several months later. She gave him three children in three years, and their marriage was acknowledged to be one of the great love matches of the age. People smiled about it, but their smiles were not without admiration. Even Phil had to smile. He did not believe himself to be a malicious person, and certainly such an emotion as common jealousy was unbecoming and petty, and he would have nothing to do with it. He despised instincts, lusts; he kept himself tight and pinched; he listened to the sounds the darkness made. For him, the large word was Control. Most people kept their distance from him, and this was excellent. Philip I. Underwood, an aloof dandy with bare unfiligreed tastes, had the darkness for a companion, and the darkness was enough. All right, his mother and father *had* betrayed him, *had* deprived him of his war. He was by no means lost. He had taste, and he understood beauty and Control, and there always were plenty of vagrants to supply the blood and the broken bones. Life moved on. His days were like clean white birds. Then, because he was the last of his line, and because he had an obligation to his parents (and never mind their betrayal), he decided to marry the worshipful Christine Starling, and in so doing he happily destroyed himself, banishing the darkness.

1874 . . .

Pianos and lettuce and a drunken miner hollering for more beer. Fish and nails and evergreen boughs. The wart that depends from the tip of the chin of Mrs Lucille Sidlo, whose husband sells shoes. Hands that stroke, stuff, pick, scrape, pat, strike, slap. Sniggerings. Down with the pants, my darling. Ah. That's a good girl. *I believe in one God the Father Almighty, maker of heaven and earth, and of all things visible and invisible: And in one Lord Jesus Christ, the only begotten Son of God; begotten of his Father before all worlds, God of God, Light of Light, very God of very God; begotten, not made; being of one substance with the Father; by whom all things were made: Who for us men and for our salvation came down from heaven, and was incarnate by the Holy Ghost of the Virgin Mary, and was made man: And was crucified also for us under Pontius Pilate; he suffered and was buried: And the third day he rose again according to the Scriptures: And ascended into heaven, and sitteth on the right hand of the Father: And he shall come again, with glory, to judge both the quick and the dead; whose kingdom shall have no end. And I believe in the Holy Ghost, the Lord, and Giver of Life, Who proceedeth from the Father and the Son; Who with the Father and the Son together is worshipped and glorified; Who spake by the Prophets: And I believe in one Catholic and Apostolic Church: I acknowledge one Baptism for the remission of sins: And I look for the resurrection of the dead: And the Life of the world to come. Amen.* Voices. Words. God's crushing mystery. Sausage. Dandelions. Hairribbons. Teeth. Gossip. Love. Noses. Rooftops. Mud. Sun. The wide beseeching arms of a stone Beauty. Potatoes. Breath. Sumac. Frogs. Coal mines. Cats, pregnant, dragging their bellies. Peach trees. The old man sits among his peach trees, and the peach trees are dead and dying, and the old man remembers he knows not what. His memories are sweet and vague and much blessed. Soup. Tatting. Eyes. Poems. Tombstones. Swine. Corn. Barns. Earth. Fiddles. Girls. Combs. Frost and leaves and a white sky. The midnight sounds of doomed locomotives. Salt and horses and a picket fence. God bless God.

A Lady:

SHE WAS NO SIMPLEMINDED CLOT from the country, no braying *arriviste*. She was the former *Phoebe Bowers* of *New Haven,* and at fiftyfive her dress size was the same as it had been at nineteen, and her posture still was most abundantly erect, militant, indomitable. She still was without loose flesh. She would not tolerate it. She and her husband were Lloyd L. Starling's house guests for the week of the wedding, and the first thing she did when she arrived in New York was purchase more than five hundred dollars' worth of dresses. She bustled and crackled, and from time to time, when no one was observing her, she even smiled.

She forbade Isaac to chew his hideous tobacco—except late at night, when they were alone in the guest room of the Starling home on East 23rd Street. She made him go sit in a far corner when he chewed the frightful stuff. When he was done with it, he dropped it out a window— after first leaning out to make sure no one was standing below. Fortunately, the window looked down on a cluster of rosebushes in the Starling garden. Now be careful where you pitch it, she told Isaac. For heaven's sake don't drop it too far *out.* I wouldn't want it to land in the *birdbath,* for heaven's sake.

The month was June, and it was a warm June, and she awakened every morning to the glorious sounds of the city. She'd always adored New York. As a girl, she'd often visited New York to attend dances and parties. Her beaux had all been handsome and gallant, and they'd always presented her with flowers. She had been snippy little Phoebe Bowers in those days, and the young men hadn't ever been able to anticipate what she would say. There had been those who had called her Forward, and there even had been those who had called her something of a Hussy, but she'd not cared a fig about those people. They could say whatever pleased them. She would lead her own life, say what she wanted to say. Those had been frail and peppery girlhood days, and she looked back on them with a fine proud nostalgia. She had no regrets. Truly she did not. Isaac was an old man now, but there still would be good times. He was seventytwo now, and if he could live to seventytwo, he surely could live to a hundred. In the past few years he'd undergone a number of defeats, most of them at the hands of that Wells person, but the struggle was not yet ended, and someday perhaps Isaac would find the means to deal with the fellow. In the meantime, as a good wife, Phoebe would continue to prod, jab and exacerbate her husband in the accepted manner. Their skirmishing was as natural to them as breath, and without it they both probably would have withered away like old leaves. Surely it had enabled them to survive a great deal, and especially the death of little Sarah. (To focus the eye of the mind on the days of little Sarah, the halfremembered suckling times, the poor thin little creature so foully taken at the age of nine months, the diphtheria wrenching the life out of her feeble bones . . . for Phoebe, the recollecting no longer had pain, only a vague sadness. Poor little Sarah. If she'd remained alive, she would have been thirtyone years old now, and Phoebe probably already would have been a grandmother. This thought was impossible to accept. Sarah had been an infant, nothing more. How could an infant be capable of giving birth? Ah, stupidity. Praise God for His gift of days and unremembering. Praise God for His gift of the love of a good man, a love that had made the days and the unremembering bearable. A girl child it had been, a first child, a sweet creature of blue eyes and wispy hair and a splintered voice. Phoebe had dressed Sarah for the coffin. She had dressed Sarah all in pink. The child's face had been tight, like a dried berry. And now Phoebe prayed: Ah, dear God, smile upon that innocent child. And smile upon Philip and this marriage of his. Phoebe's prayers were fervent. They could not have been anything else. She knew of no other way to pray. When she and Isaac gave the great bell to the Grace Episcopal church, she had been the one to choose the inscription: LET EVERY THING THAT HATH BREATH PRAISE THE LORD. It splendidly mirrored her feelings on such matters.) She was delighted with Philip's choice of a wife. The girl was really quite pretty, and the Starling lineage was as much as any mother could ask for her handsome and dapper son. Ike and Phoebe had been anxious for him to get married. Perhaps then he would come back to Paradise Falls. They'd discussed this possibility with him, but he'd avoided giving them a direct answer. To his mother he'd said: Mama, one thing at a time. Give us a chance first to get up a head of steam in this marriage of ours. Later will be time enough to discuss Paradise Falls. I realize Papa's at the age where he wants somebody to help him with the bank and the Clay Products and all, but you'll just have to give me a bit more time. If I came back too early, I might resent him—and you. I wouldn't want that to happen. Please. Try to understand. And Phoebe did try to understand. And she supposed she could. People were young only once. They had to make up their own minds as to when they would lay aside the childish things. Not that Philip was *childish*. It was just that he'd never had much responsibility. Well, marriage would change that. Marriage and, hopefully, a prompt fatherhood. Then he would come home, and Isaac would have help in his struggle against Wells and that clutch of vulgarians that had attached itself to Wells. Yes, this month of June in the year 1874 was providing Phoebe and Isaac and their son with a large change, and hurrah for the change. The rigid peppery spirit of Phoebe Bowers Underwood rejoiced.

The night before the wedding, Isaac sat in the corner and chewed his vile tobacco and said: All the money I got, and here I sit like a dunce.

Phoebe, who was sitting in bed, said: Then dispose of your tobacco and come to bed.

I'm just getting to the flavor.

Oh. Well. In *that* case.

I wish I could have gone to that bachelor party Phil's friends are giving tonight.

It pleases me that you were not invited.

Thank you, Phoebe. I can always count on you to say the right thing.

I only meant you probably would have found it all very taxing. After all, we must consider your age.

Isaac nodded. My age, he said.

Well, you certainly cannot hold *me* responsible for *that*.

Isaac grunted. He chewed, rolled the tobacco from cheek to cheek.

Isaac?

Yes? You got more meanness to speak?

No. For heaven's *sake*. It's just that today I had an idea. I want to see what you think of it.

All right. Go on.

It's about Paradise Falls, and our friend Mr Charles Palmer Wells. It's occurred to me that perhaps we'll never defeat him through outright opposition.

What?

We have to outdo him in something. Something constructive.

Oh?

It's not enough to oppose. Too much opposition is, uh, sour grapes.

Phoebe, will you please get to the point before I die of old age?

Phoebe clucked. She arranged the covers, patted them, then said: This afternoon when I went to the tea at Mrs Astor's home I had an idea. I saw all the grand buildings and all the magnificence, and they caused a notion to cross my mind.

And what was that notion? God's sake. Get on with it.

In order to outdo him, we must *create* something. Something that will outlive us—and him. When he's gone, nothing will remain except that park. Admit it, he stole a march on us by giving that land to the city. Well, I propose that we steal a march right back on him.

Godalmighty, woman, get on with it I said.

I propose we build a great hall.

A . . . a *hall?*

Yes. For Paradise Falls. A hall for theatrical and musical entertainments, oratory. Perhaps we can start a Lyceum, bring in important persons from all over the land. The buildings in this city—have you really examined them? They are beautiful. Their turrets, their minarets, the delicacy of their masonry, ah, it all inspires one.

Now wait a minute. It doesn't inspire *me.* The buildings in this city got too much fuss and commotion to them. How come you can't understand the good of a thing that's plain? Ever since you got the commissioners to put that damn statue on top of the courthouse you've been all—

Please, Isaac. Please don't curse. I do find it so terribly offensive.

Yes, Your Majesty. Now. Getting back to what I was saying, you and your love of all things that are fancy. If any hall's to be built by me, it's going to be plain. And that's no threat, my girl. That's the fact of the matter.

Phoebe smiled. Ah, she said, the idea has merit?

Yes.

And I don't have to argue with you about it?

No. That disappoint you?

In a way, yes. What I mean is, I've always found our arguments great fun. Haven't you?

Ahh, said Isaac. He walked to the window, removed the tobacco from his mouth, peered out the window, carefully dropped the tobacco into Lloyd L. Starling's rosebushes. Then he went to the bed. He embraced his wife. An old fool, he told her, is the worst sort there is.

Yes, Isaac, said Phoebe.

The next day Lloyd L. Starling took them to the church in a magnificent brougham drawn by a pair of matched grays. The brougham was freshly painted, black with gold trim. Lloyd L. Starling personally drove the brougham. Forgive the vanity, he said, but I always have been inordinately fond of this contraption. I've owned it since the day it came from the carriage works, and that was seventeen years ago the eleventh of September. The G. L. Stamper Co of Trenton, New Jersey. Finest carriagemakers in the East. No question about it. Said Isaac: Yes sir. It's a fine vehicle. I had a friend back home who was very keen on carriages. He would have appreciated this one. He was a fine fellow. Died before his time. Lloyd L. Starling nodded, said: Ah. A shame. The day was Saturday, and sun and sky stood white and remote. The brougham moved with stately grace through the crowded Manhattan streets. It clicked, and from

ime to time the matched grays nickered discreetly. Phoebe was wearing
one of her brandnew New York dresses, a blue and white creation, ruffled
nd crisp. Her hat was wide, with a light veil. She had an odor of toilet
water, and the flesh of her arms felt sleek. The church also was fragrant.
Several of the windows had been opened to admit a soft cooling breeze.
Seated in the front pew on the groom's side, Phoebe blinked at the windows and the altar. She twisted around and looked at the guests. She saw
hats, teeth, cutaways, moustaches. Oh, such a splendid wedding, such a
day, such a time: it all was made in heaven. Then, abruptly, Phoebe
frowned. She faced forward again. Now *you*, she told herself, you just
stop your gushing. The ceremony went off without a mishap of any sort.
Christine was white and misty; her voice was timid. Phil stood erectly; *his*
voice was clear. At the conclusion of the ceremony, when bride and groom
marched back down the aisle, Christine did most valiant battle with her
tears and the wobbling that had taken possession of her chin. Phoebe
smiled, dug at an eye with the back of a finger. The reception was held
in a hall on Broadway. More than three hundred persons attended, and
Lloyd L. Starling had hired a string orchestra. The champagne punch was
delicious, and poor Isaac became a trifle tipsy. At one point, Phoebe found
her husband standing in a corner and quietly giggling. When she asked
him what was so amusing, he said: Ah, the poor rosebushes.

Three nights later Phoebe and Isaac were on their way back to Paradise
Falls. In their Pullman suite, Isaac said: We'll do it.

Do what?

That hall.

Oh? Well, fine.

Isaac glanced out the window. We ought to be around Harrisburg by
now, he said.

Well, that's very nice, dear.

Fighting him is no good.

Fighting whom?

Wells.

Yes, dear.

Since he came to Paradise Falls in '65, not much good has happened to
us.

Well, we still have our health.

Isaac examined his knuckles. I don't know, he said. I suppose it's age.
But just think of the things that have happened since then. First I closed
the chair factory. Then I closed the shoe factory. Then I backed George
Pillsbury, and you know what happened to *him*. Then I got involved in
that business with the CPV&M, and you know what happened to *that*.

And poor Greeley, you know what happened to *him*. It all comes out to a good deal of losing. I'm not used to losing. I don't like it.

Well, for heaven's sake don't whine, said Phoebe. She clicked her teeth. Then: You have to remember who you are.

Isaac nodded.

It will help us with Philip, too.

What?

Well, if there's a hall in Paradise Falls, a place for theatricals and the like, he'll have more of an interest in coming home, bringing his wife and settling down. He enjoys such things. At the wedding, remember all those theatrical people who were present at his invitation?

Yes. That I do. There was one, a woman named Stella Kelly . .

Well, never mind *that*. I know the woman you mean. The one with the breasts, correct?

Yes ma'm, said Ike, smiling.

Really, Isaac, you are *impossible.*

Mm, said Isaac. Again he glanced out the window. Yes ma'm, he said, this surely has got to just about be Harrisburg.

1875 . . .

There are those who are born to do and there are those who are born to think about it. Charles Palmer Wells is a doer, and so (in her way) is his wife. She decides to discontinue her meetings with Mayor Virgil T. Light. She remembers his son's face against her thighs. She must defeat her itch for once and for all. It is no longer enough of an excuse that her husband visits whores. It never really was that much of an excuse. Betrayal is betrayal. She is now thirtyseven years old, and the rituals of carnal love are no longer that important. And, beyond that, there is the matter of her daughter. She tells the Honorable Mayor: Find yourself a wife. Everyone should find himself a wife. Marriage is a holy estate. Find yourself a wife and leave me be. And don't speak to me of love. I know nothing of love. I am an authority on nothing other than shame. I sought to degrade Charley, and what did I do? I degraded myself. So please *please* leave me be. I don't mean to hurt you, but it's final, and I'll thank you not to argue.

The children roll their hoops, and the women cinch their corsets, and the bland and prosperous sky spreads smugly over the tarnished Arcadia. The time now pursues a zeal, and the zeal picks and hacks at the village

nd the county. The name of the zeal is progress, and only the empty-
neaded would deny it. The trees. The tall trees. The tall trees fall. The
ate Mayor George McC. Pillsbury would have left the felling of the trees
o the Almighty, but then perhaps this is one of the reasons he is dead.
Horses fart, and coalgas rises, and the prosperous belch from eating too
much, and the way of the world is the way of Paradise Falls is the way of
Paradise County is the way of the world.

Trash:

HE WAS ROPY AND BLOND, and even at fourteen his muscles stood in knots,
which made him fortunate. A Masonbrink needed muscles. He told his
little sister Ada: At least I can beat back things. And Ada said: Me too.
I'm strong too. I can lift rocks. And young Sam Masonbrink said: I expect
that's all to the good. And Ada said: Me too. All to the good.

They lived in a cabin—Sam and Ada and their mama and papa—and
the cabin had cracks between the logs, and the cracks were stuffed with
muslin, and when the muslin became damp it rotted, and when it rotted
it stank. Sam's mama made wine from dandelions, and she made wine
from berries, and the thing he always would remember about her was the
dark fragrance of her fingers. He came to boyhood very aware of odors,
odors of wine, rotten muslin, mud, flesh. The days were all bones. They
were like nails in the throat. His papa's name was Earl William Masonbrink, and his mama's name was Martha Anne Masonbrink, and they had
been first cousins. They both drank a good deal of the wine. The cabin
leaned at a slant, and small hairy things scrabbled beneath the floor. His
papa and mama did not have much to say. He wanted to go to school, but
they would not permit it. You work, said his papa. Never mind about getting grand ideas. You're a Masonbrink, and that's that. Go away from me
with your grand ideas.

The best days, the days that were without bones, were the days Sam and
his little sister Ada escaped into the hills. She was four years younger than
he, and she was happiest when she held his hand. Her hand was feathery.
He liked holding it. They walked barefoot, and he lifted her over large
rocks and fallen trees, and the feel of his muscles in his chest and shoulders
made him proud. His little sister Ada also was blond, but she really had

no muscles at all, even though she did brag on how she was able to lift rocks. She picked wildflowers for her hair. She pranced. She giggled. She told him: Sam, flowers is the best thing there is. The wildflowers were her crown, and she knew where all the berries were, and they always had plenty to eat on those days when they escaped into the hills. There were streams in those hills, and the water was white, and Sam and his little sister Ada liked to watch the minnies slither and skim. One day Ada put an arm in the water, and a minnie ran straight up the arm, and Ada shrieked, and the minnie flopped back into the water, and then Ada ran to Sam and hugged him and said: Sam, minnies is the best thing there is.

But most of his days were the days that had bones. He worked the fields with his papa, and sometimes—when his papa had slopped down too much wine—he worked the fields alone. The fields were good for nothing other than corn, and it came up at a slant, and more times than not it was washed away by the first good rain. He told his little sister Ada: You know, seems like there ought to be something better. And Ada said: Yes. For me too. Something better. I want something better too. He hugged her, told her she was like the echo down by Uncle Frank's ravine where all the frogs croaked so loud of a summer.

He knew all about what it meant to be a Masonbrink. His father had told him. He understood how it didn't matter that the Masonbrinks had come here first. He understood how the rest of the county was his natural enemy. Never have nothing to do with no highandmighties, boy, said Earl Masonbrink. Never have nothing to do with nobody except your own kind. People who got the same blood as you won't kick you in the head. Maybe we'll all of us starve, but least we won't get kicked in the head.

Papa?

Yes?

No disrespect, sir, but I sure would admire to read.

Won't do no good. A Masonbrink's a Masonbrink.

But I sure would like to try it.

Don't sass me, boy.

Yessir.

Fetch me another glass of this here wine.

Yessir.

The days had bones, and the days had splinters, and the days forever ran in mud down the sides of the hills. From time to time, when he had had too much wine, Sam's papa crucified dogs and cats. The crucifixions made Ada shriek and run and hide. The dogs and cats were crucified alive, and Sam's papa stood and watched the blood run. They were crucified on trees. They screamed. There's got to be something, said Earl William Masonbrink to his son, that I can do bad to. And anyway, it ain't so bad. They most of them die sort of quick. I only do it to them when they're old, when they can't catch no more mice or run after the game. I ain't never nailed up a young cat or dog, and I never will. People look at me funny, you know that?

The boy Sam Masonbrink studied on his father's words. He said to himself: Their paws got pads on them, and them pads is soft and smooth, and the nails go in quick and easy, and how come that's the way they got to die? A good cat works hard all its life, looking under everything, picking and scraping for mice or whatever. How come when it's old it's got to have pain? How come he ain't never found nothing else he could get the best of? I mean, someday I'm going to go to him and I'm going to say: Papa, here I am. Nail *me* up instead. It means so much to you, do it right.

Beyond the barn and the creek and the hills was the road that wandered north to Paradise Falls. About three miles up that road was a little country school. A person could learn to read there. It was beyond the Masonbrink crossroads and the Masonbrink store. There was, atop one of the hills, a place where Sam could lie flat on his belly and look down past the store and see the school, and the elms that surrounded the school, and the haze that pressed against the elms. He could lie flat on his belly and scrabble at the earth and *taste* that school. Sometimes he had to hug the muscles in his arms. Sometimes he had to hold his breath. He told himself: There got to be something better. Got to be. I don't aim to end nailing up cats and dogs. Lord God, the way he stares at them. Mouth hanging open the way it does. Hammer tight in a fist. All the twisting and all the howling and all the blood. Nothing nobody says does no good. He got to do it, he says, because there got to be *something* he can get the best of, and poor Ada, her so white and thin, laying on the ground and wailing like something's pulling her apart with its fingernails. No. There got to be something different. There got to be something *more*.

One day, when he was eleven, Sam ran off with an old black tabbycat his father had been about to crucify. The tabbycat fell asleep in Sam's arms. He ran with it all the way to the home of a man named John Fry, a second cousin. John Fry lived alone. He had outlived three wives and six children. A man who lived alone needed a tabbycat to keep him company. The tabbycat was black and gray, and most of its teeth were gone. The old girl had given birth to something like a dozen litters. Her belly sagged and flapped. John Fry was grateful for the tabbycat. You're a good boy to be thinking of me, he told Sam. He gave Sam a piece of bread and some honey. He gave the old tabbycat some honey too. The tabbycat licked up the honey, sighed, retired to a corner of John Fry's front room and promptly fell asleep. She's a fine mouser, said Sam. You'll get a lot of good use out of her. John Fry nodded. Yes, boy, he said. Yes. Thank you kindly. When

Sam returned home, his father beat him with a length of plank. Sam made no sounds. His father ordered him to sleep in the barn for a week. That night, lying in the barn, Sam stroked his bruises. He smiled. His father had for once brought his strength to bear against something deserving. Sam smiled, stroked. It had been a good day. From then on, he abducted all elderly cats and dogs whenever he sensed his father was about to go after them with hammer and nails. He carried them for miles, then let them run loose. He embraced them before he released them. He became very large in Ada's eyes. She told him she truly wished the whole world was like him. Occasionally his father beat him to the cats and dogs, but most of the time he was able to save them, and after a year or so his father didn't bother any more with the length of plank. Apparently the occasional crucifixions now were enough for Earl William Masonbrink. Apparently he was more interested in the wine.

It was one of the days of the wine when Sam ran off for good. It was in the fall of the year 1875, and he was fourteen, and he told his father: Papa, I expect it don't matter none no more what you think. I'm real sorry, but I got to go to that there school and see about studying on reading and writing and sums.

Earl William Masonbrink sat crosslegged with a jug. His back rested against the trunk of a pinoak, a scratchy little old thing that stood in the side yard near the barn. It was an afternoon in late September, and Sam had come in from husking corn out behind the barn. He wiped his hands on his britches. He waited for his father to say something. But Earl William Masonbrink apparently wasn't about to say a word, and so finally Sam said: Well, Papa?

I'll kill you first, said Earl William Masonbrink.

No, Papa.

It'll be easier on you that way. Me killing you will be better than *them* doing the job.

Papa, nobody's going to kill me.

Earl William Masonbrink drank from the jug. He wiped his mouth. He said: You don't know. You got no way of knowing.

Knowing what, Papa?

You think I *like* this?

Like what, Papa?

Being here like this. Setting here like this. Me and all the time the wine.

Well, I don't know, Papa. I figure it's your life and you got your own way of living it.

My life. Shit boy shit shit you don't know a damn thing. Shit. God damn you.

Papa . . .

You think this is the way I had it figured out? Well, it ain't! The way I had it figured out was I was going to get me a nice farm up by Lake Township where the land is flat and good and the crops is like miracles from heaven! But the world, boy, the *world* wasn't about to let no *Masonbrink* have it that good! It's been more years ago than I can reckon, and me and my brothers and my old dad went to Paradise Falls and seen that banking man, that Ike Underwood, and you know what he done? He told us to go to hell! He told us we wasn't never going to amount to a hill of cow flop! He told us to get out and not come back! That's your *world* for you, boy! I'm telling you—stay away from it! We got enough here!

No, Papa. I got to do this thing.

Earl William Masonbrink flung the jug at his son. It struck Sam's forehead, fell to the earth and shattered itself. Wine ran. Dandelion wine. Sweet. Warm.

Sam staggered back. He rubbed his forehead.

Earl William Masonbrink got to his feet. You're my son! he hollered. You do like I say!

Sam shook his head no.

Earl William Masonbrink went to his son and slapped him across the face.

Weeping, Sam still shook his head no. He reached to embrace his father.

Shit! said Earl William Masonbrink, drawing back.

Sam's mother and little sister Ada came running. Ada took one look at Sam and began to cry. Get him away from me! hollered Earl William Masonbrink. He lurched off toward the house. Sam shook his head. It'll never work, he said. His mother asked him what he was talking about. I got to go, said Sam. Go where? said his mother. Away, said Sam. *No!* said Ada. She pounded his chest and waist. I got to find out, said Sam. *No!* said Ada. Sam looked around. Now his mother also was crying. This is the time, said Sam. He looked at the house, and suddenly he was aware of the stink of rotten muslin. He pulled away from Ada. He pulled away from his mother. I surely am sorry, he said. His father came out of the house. Earl William Masonbrink was carrying a shotgun. No, Papa, said Sam. He walked to his father. Earl William Masonbrink trembled. His teeth clicked. Sam took the shotgun away from his father. He dropped it to the ground. Goodbye, Papa, he said. His mother wailed. He turned, smiled at her. Goodbye, Mama, he said. Ada made a sound that put him in mind of one of the crucified cats. Now Earl William Masonbrink also was weeping. No, Sam, he said. No. No. I didn't mean to throw that thing at you. No. Please, boy. Sam drew a deep breath. Another no nod, this one brief and quick. He walked out to the road. Ada followed him. His father and mother did not. Now they understood. It only remained for Ada to understand. At the road, she fell down and rolled and kicked. He looked down at her. He told her she was too big a girl to be acting up that way. He said: I got to go. He bent over her, patted her head. She kissed his hand. She rubbed her cheeks against it, and the dampness from them was cool. Her face was dirty. Sam rubbed his forehead. He went off down the road, and Ada curled in the dust behind him, and he did not look back. There was no sense in that sort of thing. He slept that night at the side of the road, and the next afternoon he rode out of Paradise County in a gondola car.

1875 . . .

Mayor Virgil T. Light is reelected without opposition.

Prof Karl J. Baer still gathers wildflowers for his wife, the former Madeleine Magill. Her sons have come to accept him as their father. John, who is twentyone now, is a senior at Ohio Wesleyan, and he is considering entering the Methodist ministry. Frederick Junior, sixteen, has a decided bent for the natural sciences, and he is beginning to hint that perhaps he would like to study medicine. Prof Baer still wears his villainous moustache and still smokes his cheroots, but appearances are not always everything, and the village no longer sees him as a scoundrel. He insists that a photograph of the boys' late father remain in a prominent place on a table in the parlor. He tells his wife: Madeleine my darlingk, do you understandt the how you say *depth* of my love? I have never been vhat I seemedt to be. Ah, my darlingk, praise *Gott*. John's tuition fees have all been paid out of the pocket of Prof Baer. The professor has been giving music lessons in Paradise Falls for nearly twenty years; his bank balance is in excess of ten thousand dollars; not once since their marriage in '69 has he asked her for a penny. Her first husband's estate, which didn't amount to an awful lot in any case, has not been touched. Says Prof Baer: Mr Magill vas a fine man, ant a goodt soldier. I only vish I had known him better.

A baseball team is organized, the Paradise Falls Superbs. Its captain is the massive Hugh Graves, who plays first base. In their first game, the Paradise Falls Superbs defeat a team from Nelsonville by a score of 89 to 20. The team plays eight games in all and loses not a one.

Of the original twentytwo trees in old Harlowe Morris' peach orchard, only nine still live. The dead ones, however, have not been cut down. Old Harlowe Morris will not hear of it. Mrs Priscilla Carmichael visits him every other day or so. She brings him food, straightens up his house. She is more fond of him than she likes to let on. Back in '65, after her father died on the floor of Heinz Burkhart's kitchen, old Harlowe Morris gave her work. It is difficult for unmarried young women to find employment in Paradise Falls. She has always been grateful to him. She supposes he is too irascible and eccentric for most people, but Priscilla Carmichael is not most people. She sits and actually *talks* with him. He speaks at some length of the old days, and his words are not always very well organized. He speaks in a sort of whine, and his memory is not particularly good except when it addresses itself to funerals.

Ike Underwood secures the services of a Columbus architect, a man named Howard K. Ives. At Phoebe's suggestion, the hall will be called the Aeolian Temple.

Mayor Light has no choice but to accept Mrs Wells' insistence that their assignations be terminated. He remonstrates with her, but to no avail. He speaks to her of love, and his words make her smile.

Earl McBride, a conductor for the CPV&M, succumbs to a stomach ailment.

Remember, says Ike Underwood to Ives the architect, I want this to be a plain structure. No fuss. No goddamn busywork. Do you understand that?

From time to time Priscilla Carmichael calls out a name in her sleep. Her husband recognizes the name. It is the name of Christian Soeder. One night, during a particularly vivid dream about Christian Soeder, Priscilla Carmichael literally *shouts* his name. In so doing, she wakes herself up. Her husband is already awake. She embraces him, tells him she is mortified. Arthur Carmichael smiles, strokes her hair. No need to be, he says. A life is a whole thing. I don't expect you to cut away what you felt before we were married. Sh. Now, now. It's all right. Good girl. Sh.

Ike Underwood rejects six Ives sketches as being too fancy.

Little Arthur Carmichael Junior, age two, becomes infuriated when his mother refuses him a piece of chocolate. He bites her thumb, drawing blood.

Peter O. Rothermel, shoe merchant, succumbs to a bladder ailment.

Ike Underwood approves the seventh Ives sketch. The Aeolian Temple will be three stories high and constructed entirely of brick supplied by the Paradise Falls Clay Products. It will be free of all representations of lions, gargoyles, birds, horses, &c. A local man, Bill Osterhaus, receives the contract to put up the building. His carpentry business has been so successful that he now is a fullfledged building contractor. The Aeolian Temple will cover twothirds of a square on the north side of Main Street between Market and Mulberry streets. To make room for it, two smaller buildings are razed. Both of these smaller buildings are empty. One had housed old Harlowe Morris' store, the other Rothermel's Shoe & Boot Emporium. The estimated cost of the Aeolian Temple is one hundred thousand dollars.

Bill Osterhaus hopes to finish the job by the end of 1876. A crew of twenty men is put to work on it. Foreman is Arthur Carmichael.

Mrs Dwight F. Templeton, grower of a legendary tomato, succumbs to a brain hemorrhage.

Young Bill Light begins courting Editha Purvis, who at nineteen is one of the village's most astonishing beauties. She likes him a good deal. He is the first young man she has permitted to kiss her with mouth open.

J. K. Bankson, editor of the *Democrat,* reads a novel entitled *Sevenoaks,* by a man named J. G. Holland. It has to do with a New England factory-owner who makes a great deal of money over the prostrate bodies of his workers. After reading the novel, J. K. Bankson mails it anonymously to C. P. Wells.

There is little enthusiasm hereabouts for a third term for President Grant.

Philip Isaac Underwood:

SHE TORE AWAY HIS DARKNESS, but he murdered her with his seed, and so it was with a full and loving heart that he entered into his destruction. He had never understood what a mighty juggernaut was simple goodness. It could even do away with the need for blood and broken bones. It seduced; it laid open the heart; there was no way to resist it. And so he permitted it entrance, and its frail light pushed away all of his darkness, and he almost was willing to believe he could see the outlines of her sweet forbearing God. But then he assassinated her, his darling Christine, and back came the darkness, and he reached gratefully for his damnation.

But first had come the light. Their honeymoon was in London and Paris, and he became aware of the light late one Paris night, a July night ochre with stars and reflections, a warm thing abounding in faint threads of music, of laughter, of damp sighs. He lay next to his wife, and she was asleep, and she was golden. He did not know what to think of her. Christine, Christine, Christine . . . when would she reveal what she sought from him? Where was her darkness? Ah, but perhaps she sought *nothing* from him. Perhaps she possessed *no* darkness. The idea made Phil's belly twitch. She spoke to him constantly of love, and her pale romantic words were fervent, relentless, fearless. He could not understand any of them.

Love was an instinct, and instincts offended him. She was a narrow girl with a soft belly and large gray eyes, and her fine blond hair had a consistency of breath and feathers. She spoke softly, and the sound of her words had a shy murmuring grace that tore at him with hooks. He had not expected any of this. He had married her because he had felt it was necessary that he marry *someone* in order to fulfill his responsibilities as a perpetuator of his line. He had sought no light; he had contemplated no reformation; he had wished for no love. But there it was, and its goodness was pushing away the foul bloody darkness. He found himself thinking less and less of betrayals, of the war that had been stolen from him. He found himself wondering whether the war really ever had been that important. He often felt tears nudge his eyes. Her words were open: Phil, I would crawl naked over shredded glass for you. I mean that. I pray we have babies. I pray we have many babies. That would please you, wouldn't it? You don't have to answer. I know it would. I know you better than you think. I love you. Little Christine Starling has loved you since that first evening Daddy brought you home and told her you were going to work for the *Crisis.* I don't know any of the whys or hows or whats of it; all I know is that I love you so much, dear Phil, that I even would sacrifice goodness for you if that was what you wanted. I have always wanted to be good, but if *you* want something else from me, just tell me. Whatever it is, I'll try to give it. My daddy and my brother call me Pious, and sometimes they call me Miss Priss. I suppose that's because I like to pray. I mean, doesn't the thought of God just *thrill* you? Sometimes I feel as though my heart wants to fly out of the top of my head. God is so many things. Have you ever smelled the breath of a baby rabbit? There are rabbits up at our summer place near Peekskill, and I've smelled the breath of the baby rabbits. Ah, there is so much, my darling Phil. We must go to Peekskill when we get back. The river, the hills, everything blue and white and clean. I want you to see the summer place. We can have picnics, and I'll collect leaves, and we can press them in a book along with a lock of my hair. I would enjoy that. Wouldn't you? Say yes. I would be obliged.

Lying wideawake in that ochre Paris night, thinking back on the words of his bride, Phil had to grimace. The hour was secret and lonely, and there was no way to escape the truth of himself. He was without his vest, and he was without his stick, and he did not gleam, and there were no vagrants to punish: he was simply a papery little man who did not really want his darkness. She had made him understand that. He wanted to weep. But he could not weep. It was not within him to weep. So he lay silent and coiled, and he thought of blood and broken bones. Could she remove him from the blood and the broken bones? Was her goodness truly that irresistible? Phil blinked. From outside the open window came a sound of a woman's laughter. It was a shriek, abrupt and carnal. He winced. He stared at the ceiling. This was a fine hotel, and the ceiling was decorated with a design of plump pink angels. Next to him, Christine breathed in a reedy whistle. She lay flat on her back, and she was covered by just a sheet. He sniffed. He smelled what seemed to him to be warm leaves and roasting meats. Christine sighed in her sleep. She plucked at the sheet. It slipped away from her shoulders and breasts. He kissed her shoulders. Her tiny golden breasts were exquisite. He lay the tip of a finger gently on a nipple. He did not stroke the nipple. He simply let the finger rest there. He had not anticipated this, and the word for it was Love, and it was an *instinct,* and reasonable men were wise if they kept their distance from such an afflic-tion. He closed his eyes. He said to himself: I have no *right.* He tried to think long and hard on the beatings, the pale unshaven faces of all the poor vagrants. He tried to picture the faces of Henry Oliver, the tormen-tor of the horse apple episode; Lipscomb, the degenerate; Sergius Laugh-lin, the proclamative actor. Henry Oliver was dead, and Lipscomb had withdrawn into lonely Michigan exile, and Sergius Laughlin was no longer a principal player (his broken nose never had been reset properly), and only God knew what had happened to the vagrants, and again Phil wanted to weep, and again he could not weep. And anyway, what pur-pose would there have been to it? Face it, he told himself. Face the vio-lence. For once look at it squarely. You are nothing more or less than a gleaming fastidious brute. You must strike chop lacerate smash hack cut break. Phil opened his eyes. He shuddered. No, he said aloud, it doesn't have to be that way. No. No.

Christine came awake. She rolled on her side, and his finger came away from her nipple. Is there something I can do? she said. Her eyes were clouded.

Phil trembled.

She hugged him. She kissed his cheeks, his eyes, his mouth. What is it? she wanted to know. What *is* it?

He moved his head from side to side. He studied the pink angels. It's . . . it's nothing, he said.

All right, my darling. All right. Yes.

The night simmered and ululated. Phil's chest roared with terror.

Christine placed her hands on his chest. They were warm and boneless. Phil made fists.

She stroked his chest. Yes, she said. Yes. Yes.

I want to . . . want to . . . God I really do want to . . .

Want to what?

Phil groaned. He embraced her. He kissed her nipples. Murmuring into her neck, he said: How do I get clean again?

What? I didn't hear you.

He pulled his face away from her neck. Now his tears were in front of his eyes. I . . . ah, I . . . you take away my sins, he said. You . . . ah, there is much *talk* of angels, but . . . ah, how many of us are privileged to *see* one? Oh, you sweet . . . ah, love. Yes. *Love*. And then Phil wept, and Christine made puzzled clucking sounds, and he fell asleep with his head between her breasts.

The next day she did not mention the incident, but Phil did. He told her she had done a large thing for him. He told her he did believe there was hope for him. And of course she thought he was joking, deprecating himself. Hope for *you*? she said. Why, you talk like the world's biggest sinner! Shame on you! And then she plopped down on his lap and asked him to kiss her ears.

Thus came, wavering and flickering at first, but finally blazing up clean and undefeated, the light. The wedding trip was a wedding trip beyond which there were no wedding trips. Christine gasped and giggled most of her waking hours. She acquired more color, and her teeth glistened. First was Paris, where everywhere people sat in spindly uncomfortable chairs and happily drank up the days. The days were hortatory, and they laughed for being hortatory; the nights hummed and clapped. Phil and Christine rode in elegant carriages, and everywhere abounded grand leafy boulevards. He took her to the most fashionable boutiques, and small owlish Frenchwomen fussed and scrabbled over her. They told her in quick peremptory voices that ah, her coloring was sublime, a gift of God. He bought her elaborate dresses, and she smiled and pirouetted for him, showing him an ankle, a leg, an occasional unabashed knee. They visited bistros, and they saw sissies and prostitutes and toughs. They visited exquisite restaurants that had high ceilings and frail china and obsequiously busy waiters, elegant of lip and moustache. They climbed the steeples of immense musty old churches. They stood in warm belfry winds and looked out over the great city and its spangled midsummer roofs and chimneypots. She squeezed his arm and she pressed a cheek against his shoulder, and it all was instinct; it all was Love. She loved him gently, and naked she was shy. Her hands made tentative movements at her throat. Then was London, and there they met Mr Charles Dickens. It was at a dinner party given by a publisher named Geoffrey Eggleston, and it was a very fine dinner party indeed (candelabra, silver salvers, lint, odors of venerable velvet cushions, an immense roast of beef, hearty redfaced Englishmen speaking in grunts and ejaculations of victory and empire and dreams, angular Englishwomen, nasal and majestic, chatting of tea and whist and cuckolds), and Mr Charles Dickens made a special point of speaking with Phil and Christine. He apparently was

delighted when Phil expressed a loathing for Whitman. Splendid, said Mr
Charles Dickens. Yes indeed. One must always be zealous in defending
the holy relics against the barbarians, eh boy? While in London, Phil
and Christine of course visited Westminster Abbey. Christine knelt and
prayed, and she pulled him down to pray with her. He mumbled, and his
belly was heavy and fearful. They visited the House of Commons; they
visited St Paul's; they took a boatride on the Thames; they bought greasy
foods from sidewalk vendors who reminded Phil of his vagrants (the sidewalk vendors all had wobbly teeth, and their tongues were black, apparently covered with fur); they walked and chatted, and always Christine
gasped, always she giggled; her goodness beat at his darkness with sticks
of laughter; her eyes were cups of innocence. At night she always smiled
for him, and her fists always beat a happy loving tattoo on his shoulders
and his back. He functioned with warmth. It was the first time he'd ever
functioned with warmth. In the Stella Charles nights he'd functioned with
a certain coiled fastidious expertise, but never could it have been called
warmth. The wedding trip lasted three months. They returned to New
York in late October of 1874. Their last night on the boat he told her: I
love you, and I am going to try.

Try what? she asked him.

To be a man in the proper way. Knowing goodness.

Now, *Phil*. You know goodness. Don't belittle yourself.

And I shall attempt to practice it.

Sh. Don't talk that way. You're already a good man.

You mean so much. You are so large.

Large?

Now, now, you know what I mean.

I don't think I'm large.

All right, Christine, I understand your little joke.

But I want to *be* large!

Oh?

With a . . . well, you know, with a . . .

Baby?

Yes. Yes, Phil. Darling Phil.

The breath of baby rabbits. I must love you.

What?

Phil smiled. If anyone else in the world had spoken to me of the breath
of baby rabbits, he said, I probably would have laughed myself into a
premature grave. You have changed me, Christine. You have no idea
how greatly. I love you. I swear that is the truth. You can talk about the
breath of baby rabbits all you want. You can talk about anything all you
want. No matter what you say, it is profound.

Now, *Phil* . . .

It will be a good life. Ah. My love. Your dear breasts.

I . . . I want them to nurse.

They will.

They moved into his Christopher Street flat, and she was sorry, but there were a few things she had to do to the place. She bought doilies. She bought china. She bought horsehide chairs, a horsehide sofa. She bought thick drapes. Phil did not protest. His bare tastes had been a condition of his brutish past. He did not want to be reminded of it. He told her all her acquisitions were in excellent taste. He came to her almost every night, and the idea of course was to get her pregnant. Their life chirped and chattered, and from time to time he was aware of a witless and very happy ringing in his ears. He still was a dandy, and he still carried a stick, but he no longer withheld his smiles, and people began to talk of what a wonderful job Christine had done in bringing him *out* of himself. And for once people were right. Usually people were wrong, but not this time. Christine became pregnant in December of 1874. She told him at supper one snowy night. The city made muffled sounds outside. She told him by candlelight, and the colors in her eyes were all stuttering flashes of red, white, green. He went around the table and knelt in front of her and embraced her legs. She giggled, stroked his ears. He immediately wrote his parents. He told them he and Christine would come to live in Paradise Falls once the baby was born. *I am resigning my position with the* Crisis, *wrote Phil.* It is about time I faced up to my responsibilities. Christine is very happy with my decision. And I am a very fortunate man.

(It was all so clear now. Phil Underwood, the distinguished editor, *bon vivant*, lover, devotee of elegance and style, had been pulled away from his hell by nothing more than simple goodness. In acknowledgment, it was necessary that he address himself to a life of goodness. And the largest opportunity for that life lay back in Paradise Falls. His father was an old man, and his father needed help, and no *good* man turned his back on his father. It was all so clear. She had saved him. He would devote himself to being worthy of the effort.)

The baby was a splendid boy, robust, with a great deal of blond hair. He was born less than an hour after he signaled his arrival, and there barely was time to rush Christine to the Gramercy Lying-In Hospital. She hardly knew what happened, and she was quite proud of herself. Nothing to it, she told Phil the next day. She smiled, and the sturdy little boy rocked in her arms, and she said: I expect he favors my side of the family. The blond hair and all, I mean. Ah, I'll tell you the truth, toward the end I was a little bit frightened, but I expect that just goes to show you what a foolish ninny I am. Ah, Phil, please kiss me. Your foolish ninny loves you. She hopes you are pleased with her. Bending over the bed, Phil kissed his wife. Her mouth was wet and warm. It had a flavor of milk and sugar.

(She had saved him. He would devote himself to being worthy of the effort. He had understood nothing of her goodness. To him she had been a pretty little thing who had blushed ferociously whenever she had been in his presence, a shy and inarticulate girl with pale hair and a skin that could not abide too much sun. But she had been convenient, and his responsibility to his bloodline had decreed that he marry her, and he'd not understood even a hint of her goodness. She had saved him. She had saved him. She had washed away his sins.)

At 6 o'clock the next morning, someone pounded on the apartment door. Rubbing his eyes, Phil answered it. A bearded man stood in the doorway. He identified himself as an orderly from the hospital. Yer wanted over there right away, he said. I got a hansom waiting right downstairs. Phil nodded. Quickly he pulled on a shirt and a pair of trousers. He kicked his feet into a pair of slippers. He hurried outside with the bearded man. It was a chilly morning for early August. Phil and the bearded man jumped into the hansom. The bearded man ordered the driver to take them to the hospital. The hansom lurched away from the curb, and Phil was thrown across the bearded man's lap. I beg your pardon, he said, straightening up. Then he asked the bearded man what had happened. Damn if I know, said the bearded man. All I know is that Dr Ewbanks sent me to fetch you. Don't ask me why. I got no idea. Doctors. Huh. I been working at that there hospital eight years, and the things doctors do . . . well, let's just say that sometimes they put me in mind of blind men hunting a black cat in a coal mine. Yessir, the stories I could tell. Phil nodded. Please, he said, please be quiet. The bearded man shrugged. Yessir, he said. Phil jumped from the hansom as soon as it came clattering into the hospital courtyard. Running across the courtyard, he lost one of his slippers. He did not bother with it. (She had saved him. She had saved him. She had washed away his sins.) He ran limping, staggering. He burst through the front doors. Her room was on the second floor. He took the stairs two at a time. He heard a sound of squalling. Babies. Many babies. The place was full of babies. He said to himself: Feeding time. Dear God it is feeding time. Son of mine, you seek a breast, isn't that so? Dr Ewbanks was waiting for him at Christine's bedside. She was golden and rigid and dead. Dr Ewbanks cleared his throat. He mumbled words that had to do with something called the cervix. An infection, he said. We didn't know. It affected her blood, and apparently some time during the night it became critical. I am sorry. We didn't know. We thought she was coming along fine. We had planned to discharge her tomorrow. I am so very sorry. We just didn't know. There are so many things we don't know. Ah, but your son is in fine health. Have no fear about that. Phil stood quietly. He very carefully listened to the doctor's words. He stared down at his dead wife. He did not touch her. He felt dry. He was quite aware of his skin. It was like tissuepaper. Had there been a draft in the room, he probably would have swirled witlessly through the air, slapping against the walls and the ceiling. The doctor's breath sounded like mucus and saliva. Phil looked at the doctor and said: I am going to kill you. He charged the doctor, smote him across the adamsapple. The doctor gagged. Again Phil smote him across the adamsapple. The doctor tried to shout, but all he could manage was a sort of cough. He staggered back, knocking over a table. Several vases of flowers had been on the table. The vases crashed to the floor. Water ran. Phil's bare foot stepped on shards. He yelped. The doctor backed against a wall. He was a middleaged man, and a great deal of him was belly. He bent double, put his hands over his face. Phil bent down, seized the doctor by the chin, pulled him to an upright position. He plunged a fist into the doctor's belly. The doctor bleated. Phil's foot spurted blood. A nurse came into the room. She shrieked, turned and ran out. Phil used both fists on the doctor's belly. The doctor slobbered, choked. Two orderlies rushed into the room. They pulled Phil off the doctor. *Guilty!* screamed Phil. His foot stung. The doctor collapsed on the floor with the flowers and the water and the broken glass. The orderlies dragged Phil down a corridor to a room that had no windows. They tied him to a cot, and then another doctor came and bandaged his foot. This doctor smiled at Phil and said: I understand. Believe me, I sympathize with you completely. Then this doctor pressed a rag against Phil's face, and the rag had chloroform, and Phil went to sleep. When he came out of it, he felt calm and remote. An orderly sat outside the door. He called for the orderly, and the orderly fetched Dr Ewbanks, and Dr Ewbanks was remarkably decent about what had happened. I understand, he said. Had I been in your position, I no doubt would have felt the same way. There was a bandage on Dr Ewbanks' left hand, but otherwise he appeared none the worse for the experience. The body was taken to Paradise Falls in a leased Pullman. Phil and his fatherinlaw and his brotherinlaw and his baby son and a nurse rode with it. The men wore cutaways, silk hats, black armbands. Lloyd L. Starling had been quite decent about burying her in Paradise Falls, a village she'd never seen. Phil, said Lloyd L. Starling, she was your wife, and she was happy with you, and it is only right that she be buried in your family's plot. From time to time Lloyd L. Starling wept. So did his son Paul. Phil, however, did not weep. Phil's flesh still was papery. He said very little; he simply sat and listened to the clatter of his thoughts; the darkness had returned. (She had saved him. She had saved him. She had washed away his sins.) The coffin was splendid, with brass handles. They glistened. The coffin lay in the lounge section of the Pullman. The trip to Paradise Falls was made via Albany, Syracuse, Rochester, Buffalo, Erie, Ashtabula, Cleveland, Galion, Columbus and Lancaster. The trip took more than twentyfour hours, but Phil did not even lie down, let alone sleep. Neither did the other two men. The baby was quiet most of the time. The nurse, a tall woman whose thin gray hair was done up in rats, said she was very proud of the little fellow. Phil nodded, told her to go away. He blinked, sighed, thought of Christine. (She had saved him. She had saved him. She had washed away his sins. She had *not* saved him. She had *not* saved him. She had *not* washed away his sins. No one could escape the consequences of his acts, no matter *how* much goodness came to his aid.) From time to time he glanced out a window and saw anonymous railway yards and silent gray fields. He said to himself: It was my idea that we stay in New York until the child was born. That way, I told her, you will have the best of medical attention. Ah, God. Perhaps, had we returned to Paradise Falls, the doctor *there* would have detected the infection. Ah, God. Madness. The train pitched and rolled, and occasionally the coffin slid a bit, making squealing sounds against the Pullman's varnished floor. Christine was buried in Oak Hill Cemetery. She was buried next to little Sarah. The grave was on a hill, and the hill faced the morning sun. Next to the grave was a plot reserved for Phil. The day of Christine's burial was a gift, a glory of a day, sunny and full of birds. More than two hundred persons were present for the graveside prayers. The Rev Edwin P. Rathbun, rector of Grace Episcopal Church, presided. Phil stood between his parents. They held him by the elbows. Not since the time of the chloroform had he slept more than an hour or so. His fatherinlaw and brotherinlaw stood at the far side of the grave. They both were sobbing. Birds swooped down. Phil wished he had a gun. The birds were bright and nervous; they hopped and chirped and preened. Phil surely did wish he had a gun. The Rev Mr Rathbun spoke: *Man, that is born of woman, hath but a short time to live, and is full of misery. He cometh up, and is cut down, like a flower; he fleeth as it were a shadow, and never continueth in one stay.* (A bird tugged at a worm that lay in the earth where Phil's grave would be. Phil studied the bird. He thought: Pull, Sir Bird. Pull so you can eat. Eat so you can live. Very important. Yes.) *In the midst of life we are in death; of whom may we seek for succor, but of thee, O Lord, who for our sins art justly displeased?* (The bird extracted the worm. Down went the worm. Nodding, the bird flew away. It was a robin, and its chest was magnificent, and it put

Phil in mind of bishops and Senators.) *Yet, O Lord most holy, O Lord most mighty, O holy and most merciful Saviour, deliver us not into the bitter pains of eternal death.* (Phil shook. His mother squeezed his elbow. He closed his eyes and saw great and terrible beasts. They flapped. They spat. They hooted. They came at him with green teeth. He opened his eyes.) *Thou knowest, Lord, the secrets of our hearts; shut not thy merciful eyes to our prayer; but spare us, Lord most holy, O God most mighty, O holy and merciful Saviour, thou most worthy Judge eternal, suffer us not, at our last hour, for any pains of death, to fall from thee.* The wind was murmurous and timid. Somewhere someone wept. Someone else, a man, busily cleared his throat. Phil was nudged by his mother. He stepped forward. So did his fatherinlaw and his brotherinlaw. They all bent and picked up handfuls of earth. It was damp. Phil stared at his handful. All he could think of was dog whoop. The Rev Mr Rathbun resumed: *Unto Almighty God we commend the soul of our sister departed, and we commit her body to the ground* (the gravediggers began lowering the coffin, and Phil and his fatherinlaw and brotherinlaw sprinkled earth on it); *earth to earth, ashes to ashes, dust to dust, in sure and certain hope of the Resurrection unto eternal life, through our Lord Jesus Christ; at whose coming in glorious majesty to judge the world, the earth and the sea shall give up their dead; and the corruptible bodies of those who sleep in him shall be changed, and made like unto his own glorious body; according to the mighty working whereby he is able to subdue all things unto himself.* (Phil smiled. The earth was gone from his hand. The coffin lay at the bottom of the grave. He stepped back. So did his fatherinlaw and his brotherinlaw.) *I heard a voice from heaven, saying unto me, Write, From henceforth blessed are the dead who die in the Lord: even so saith the Spirit; for they rest from their labours.* (Phil still smiled. He remembered how as a boy he had collected leaves and pebbles. He had kept himself very busy gathering up the leaves and the pebbles and placing them in the little box he had kept in his room. He had been a frail and gentle child, and yes, the sight of dead animals had made him weep. Oh yes, and his tears had been genuine.) The Rev Mr Rathbun said: *The Lord be with you.* And, mumbling, those in attendance said: *And with thy spirit.* And the Rev Mr Rathbun said: *Lord, have mercy upon us.* And those in attendance said: *Christ, have mercy upon us.* And the Rev Mr Rathbun said: *Lord, have mercy upon us.* (Phil still smiled. He was recalling warm belfry winds and a spangled Parisian horizon of roofs and chimneypots.) The Lord's Prayer was recited, and then the Rev Mr Rathbun said: *O merciful God, the Father of our Lord Jesus Christ, who is the Resurrection and the Life; in whom whosoever believeth, shall live, though he die; and whosoever liveth, and believeth in him, shall not*

*die eternally; who also hath taught us, by his holy Apostle Saint Paul, not
to be sorry, as men without hope, for those who sleep in him; We humbly
beseech thee, O Father, to raise us from the death of sin unto the life of
righteousness; that, when we shall depart this life, we may rest in him;
and that, at the general Resurrection in the last day, we may be found
acceptable in thy sight; and receive that blessing, which thy well-beloved
Son shall then pronounce to all who love and fear thee, saying, Come, ye
blessed children of my Father, receive the kingdom prepared for you from
the beginning of the world. Grant this, we beseech thee, O merciful
Father, through Jesus Christ, our Mediator and Redeemer. Amen.* Then
came coughs, a sound of scuffling feet. Phil glanced at his mother. She
was smiling in the direction of the Rev Mr Rathbun. It was a polite smile,
distant and a bit chilly, the sort of smile one certainly would expect from
the former Phoebe Bowers of New Haven. Phil glanced at his father. Ike
Underwood was shifting his weight from one foot to the other. Phil
glanced across the grave. His fatherinlaw and brotherinlaw were bent
forward, as though perhaps their intestines had contracted. Phil began
to whinny and screech. He pulled himself free of his mother and
father. He was wearing an expensive and very tasteful and dandified
black suit. He tore at it with his fingernails. He ripped loose several of his
fingernails, all the way to the quick. Blood came from his fingertips in
dollops and sprays. He leaped into the grave. He embraced the coffin. He
ate dirt. The coffin was cold. He whinnied. He screeched. *Guilty!* he
shouted. *Guilty! No man can avoid the responsibility for his own acts!*
GUILTY! GUILTY! He ate more dirt. He drooled on the coffin. He
shook. His darkness kissed him, laughed. *Guilty!* shouted Phil. *Guilty!
There was no goodness large enough! I should have known!* Several men
jumped into the grave. He grasped the coffin's brass handles. He pressed
a cheek against the mahogany surface of the lid of the coffin. A mahogany coffin. Ah, the extravagance of the rich. (She had not saved him.
She had not saved him. Nothing could wash away his sins.) The men
tugged and grunted. Finally they pried his hands loose and pulled him
from the grave. His darkness clapped and sniggered, prodded him with
spears. He kicked and wept. His suit was shredded. His fingers bled. His
foot hurt. Dirt lay like mud on his tongue. He heard clucks, gasps. He
heard a woman say something about the awful power of grief. He grinned,
licked his lips, swallowed mud. GRIEF? he shouted. *Grief? Not Grief!
Guilt! I say guilt!* His mother went to him and seized him by the shoulders
and shook him. She shouted directly into his face: *Philip! Be quiet!*
He'd never before heard his mother shout. Never. Her teeth all were
exposed, and she shook him and shook him. He was dragged to the family
carriage. He chuckled. He drooled. His poor fingers. His poor foot.

1876 . . .

Little Arthur Carmichael Junior, age three, becomes infuriated when his Aunt Editha tells him he cannot climb the tulip tree in the Carmichael back yard. He smites her across the legs with a board. The spring floods are especially violent this year in and around Egypt. Property damage is estimated at more than one hundred fifty thousand dollars, and three members of the Frank Neumark family perish in the high waters. They are Frank Neumark himself, and his two sons, Henry, nineteen, and Peter, seventeen. They drown when their barn collapses and traps them. They had gone inside the barn to get out a wagon and plow. Frank Neumark leaves a wife, Gertrude, and two small daughters, Margaret, six, and Lotte, four. In December Gertrude Neumark is married to the widower Heinz Burkhart. She weighs two hundred pounds to his one hundred forty. He tells her: You mind me good, and everything will be fine. He moves into the Neumark place, rents his own home to a family named Schwab. The combined Burkhart-Neumark acreage is 1,007. Mayor Virgil T. Light heads the committee that is in charge of the observance of the one hundredth anniversary of the birth of the Republic. He pledges himself to make the celebration a memorable one. The C. P. Wells Coal Co pays the final installment of its loan from the Columbus bank. Charley Wells gives a party for his cronies. Twenty cases of champagne are shipped in from Columbus. A great many of the guests, with Mayor Virgil T. Light in the vanguard, become intoxicated. Mrs Wells, the former Nancy Quimby Ferris of Titusville and Evansville, Indiana, is spectacular in a purple velvet dress. For a woman of thirtyeight, she still is a glory and an inspiration, and the gentlemen drink numerous toasts to her beauty and good health. Philip Isaac Underwood lives with his parents now. He is seldom seen on the streets—at least in the daylight hours. There are many, however, who have seen him prowling the village at night. He speaks to no one, and of course no one is so foolish as to speak to him. He apparently sees himself as wearing the mark of the beast. No one knows why, but whatever the reason is, it is no doubt delicious beyond belief. Says Editha Purvis to young Bill Light: I . . . ah, isn't it . . . ah, please don't think me forward, but isn't it time we talked about our . . . ah, *plans?* I mean, it's been a whole *year* now, and a year is a long time. Wilhelm Soeder has heard nothing from his brother Christian since 1871. The zenith of the centennial observance will of course be reached on the Fourth of July, says Mayor Light to the members of his committee. Construction of the Aeolian

Temple proceeds apace. The Rev Clovis T. Reader, pastor of the First ME
Church, confers with Mrs Underwood on the feasibility of forming a
Lyceum. Mrs Underwood is enthusiastic about the idea. She says: Yes
indeed, Mr Reader, it is an excellent proposal. As you probably know, my
son Philip was very interested in the theater when he lived in New York
City. I feel certain he can give us a great deal of help. And perhaps this
sort of activity will do something toward reviving his spirits. Poor Philip.
He really did love his wife very dearly. Yes, the theater. And musical entertainments. And lectures. A fine idea. I am sure Philip will be extremely
interested. Naturally, Prof Karl J. Baer is tapped by Mayor Light to lead
the band for the Fourth of July celebration. Normally, he leads only the
Masonic band. On this occasion, however, he augments it with the GAR,
Grange and Knights of Pythias bands. Mass rehearsals are held in a vacant
lot at the edge of the village. A grand total of ninetyseven musicians are
under Prof Baer's baton. The sound of them carries for more than a mile.
It is a miraculous sound. It makes people pause and smile. The GAR,
Grange and Knights of Pythias memberships are very cooperative in
giving Prof Baer the extra musicians. He personally visits the meetings of
each of these groups and gives a brief speech of thanks. He has kind words
for the leaders of these bands. In the interests of good will, he confers
upon each of those three men the title of associate conductor. Phil Underwood smiles, tells his mother he has no interest whatever in the formation of a Lyceum. She tells him he cannot spend the rest of his life brooding. He says he is not brooding. It is far beyond that, he says. You have no
idea how far. God willing, you never will. Young Bill Light groans, removes a hand from Editha Purvis' bosom, tells her he is not being a bit
fair. She kisses him with her mouth open. She says: I love you. I love you.
I love you. I am forward and I am cheap, but I cannot help saying what I
have to say. Again young Bill Light groans. He clutches at Editha. They
are sprawled on the sofa in her front room. Both her feet are off the floor.
Her sister Priscilla has told her never to allow herself to be worked into a
position where both her feet are off the floor. It is a good year for oats,
barley, corn. The CPV&M now operates six trains daily to and from Columbus, three trains daily to and from Blood. Miss Amelia Metcalf, a
teacher, is charged with the training of a children's choir that will sing at
the gala Fourth of July celebration. Miss Metcalf, who weighs barely
ninety pounds, drills the children with the zeal of a Prussian infantry
sergeant. She is fortysix years old, and twentyseven years ago she was left
at the altar by a man named Floyd Royalton, and her wedding dress still
hangs, clean and crisp, in her closet. Within the past decade or so, a
reddish down has sprouted on her chin and cheeks. C. P. Wells decides
that it might not be a bad idea to destroy the Aeolian Temple once it is
built. The more he thinks about it, the more the idea appeals to him.
Swings are installed at the Elysian Park, along with benches, tables and
a picnic shelter. Contract for the work goes to a Columbus firm. Mayor

Virgil T. Light receives an honorarium of two hundred fifty dollars. Elmer Strapp, a farmer whose place is out in Lake Township, tells his wife their daughter Ethel can bake a cherry pie better than anyone in the world. Strapp's wife, Abigail, is a bit put out. She has been baking cherry pies for him for thirty years, and now along comes Ethel at age twelve, and Elmer has to say a thing like that. Along comes Ethel at age twelve and everything Ethel knows has been learned from her mother, and what is it about men that makes them so thick in the head? The matter of Ethel and the cherry pies becomes something of a bone of contention between Elmer and Abigail Strapp. The Honorable Ross T. Plowman, who since 1869 has represented the congressional district that includes Paradise County, regretfully declines an invitation to deliver the principal address at the gala Fourth of July celebration. A previous speaking engagement in his home town of Lancaster is given as the reason.

(Mrs Nancy Quimby Ferris Wells cannot of course tell a soul her reasons for betraying the betrayer. But, at the same time, she *is* able to address herself. She says: Well, was it so terrible what I did? I mean, didn't he have it coming to him? Her voice, when addressing herself, is loud and firm and false, drenched in shame.)

Mayor Virgil T. Light decides to give the Fourth of July oration himself. It will be delivered from a platform to be erected in front of the Elysian Park picnic shelter. Mabel, a collie bitch owned by Kenneth I. Vance, a druggist, drops a litter of six. All the puppies are sleek and well formed. The identity of their father is known but to God. Abigail Strapp tells her husband: I'll never bake you a cherry pie again. A delegation of ladies, representing all churches, even the Catholic, goes to work sewing flags and banners for the gala celebration. Claude Dill, the saloonkeeper, holds a confidential conversation with C. P. Wells. I don't mean to be blunt, says Claude Dill, but we got to do something about them miners who come to town of a Saturday night. Says C. P. Wells: Oh? How so? Says Claude Dill: Well, not to make too fine a point of it, but what this town needs is a whorehouse. C. P. Wells laughs uproariously. I'm *serious,* says Claude Dill. Damn if I ain't. Some of them been taking their business to Nelsonville and even clear up to Lancaster. They say there ain't no women for them here, and you know well as I do they're right. Says C. P. Wells: My God, you're going to make Ed Maxwell happy. Says Claude Dill, frowning: What's Ed Maxwell got to do with it? Says C. P. Wells: Everything. Just hold your horses and I'll explain. Arthur N. Sturgeon, a young attorney, is accepted into partnership by ElRoy Mauk. The Republican presidential nomination of good old R. B. Hayes is welcome news indeed. After all, the man was three times governor of Ohio. There is little doubt hereabouts but what he will deliver a severe thrashing to the sourfaced Democratic nominee, Sam Tilden. The GAR boys drill twice a week in preparation for the gala Fourth of July celebration. Young Bill Light (at twentysix not really so young any longer) tells Editha Purvis he cannot marry her. She weeps. She beats at him with her fists. It is late June, and they have gone picnicking downriver not far from the hamlet of Earlham. She wears a white dress. She rubs her hands together. The sun sends its light in a slant, thin and full of motes. She and young Bill Light are seated on the ground in the shade of a great white birch. The hills are all around them, and the hills are blue, and young Bill Light's saliva tastes oily. Says young Bill Light: I'm sorry. I'm just not ready for it yet. It's got nothing to do with *you*. Believe me, if I was to marry *anyone*, it'd be you. Says Editha: Can't you . . . can't you give me a *reason*, I mean something I can get my *teeth* into? Says young Bill: A terrible thing happened to me a few years back. I can't get it out of my head. Says Editha: What was it? Says young Bill: I can't tell you. He glares into the thin trembling sunlight. Editha leans back against the trunk of the tree. It's me, she says. Something I've done. Young Bill shakes his head. The time's just not right, he says. I'd like to ask you to wait, but I can't do that. Wouldn't be fair. That night, Editha Purvis weeps into her older sister's lap. Priscilla Carmichael's face is hard. Well, she says, there are other fish in the sea. And besides, I never *did* think much of him, him or his father the almighty *mayor* either. Phil Underwood keeps himself busy writing poetry. His son, who has been named William Henry, is a solemn and silent little fellow, with square bones. Phoebe is delighted with him. Ah, she tells old Ike, from the look of him I wouldn't be surprised if he never has a sick day in his life. We are fortunate in our choice of a grandson. God bless him. Says Ike: Yes. Very good. But what about Phil? Says Phoebe: I don't know. I wish I did. Ike and Phoebe discuss their son almost every day. What do you imagine it is he thinks he's *done?* Phoebe wants to know. Says Ike, shrugging: Damn if *I* know. Says Phoebe: Please. Must you punctuate everything you say with profanity? Says Ike: Who ever heard of teaching an old jackass new tricks? Says Phoebe: You are the most insufferable man I've ever met. Says Ike: Well, if a man's going to be a thing, he might as well be the best. It is a good year for blackberries and pumpkins, and the two little Neumark girls, Margaret and Lotte, lie together in bed and decide they hate their stepfather, Heinz Burkhart, very much. He is forever patting them on their buttocks. They wonder if there is a safe way to murder him. They giggle and snigger, and their talk has to do with knives and revolvers and fresh blood. Sometimes the prospect is so delicious that the girls clap their hands and hug and thresh. The Ed Maxwell situation, as outlined by C. P. Wells to Claude Dill, is very amusing. Ed Maxwell is a former county commissioner and former county Republican chairman. A few years back, C. P. Wells gave him five thousand dollars to resign as Republican chairman. His place was taken by Virgil T. Light, and the next year—after receiving two thousand dollars more from C. P. Wells—he chose not to stand for reelection as county commissioner. His place was taken by Winfield Wainscott. Now all three of the county commissioners are solid Wells men. At the outset of the rise of C. P. Wells, Ed Maxwell was one of those who viewed him as an untrustworthy outsider who gave not a damn about either Paradise Falls or Paradise County and only sought to seize power. Ed Maxwell was in those days a loyal Ike Underwood man. Ike Underwood's bank had loaned him the money to set himself up in the bakery business back in '52, and Ed Maxwell was the type of man (and still is, for that matter) who liked to think of himself as being fiercely loyal to his friends. His bakery prospered, and for years he told one & all he owed his success to the faith in him that had been exhibited by Ike Underwood. But then a quite natural and human thing happened to Ed Maxwell. His wife, a thin little woman who had borne him six children, died in 1863, and his bereavement was a thing of many facets. Not the least of them was the ache her loss created in his groin. He was (and still is, for that matter) a large and hearty fellow. For the past two decades his weight has exceeded two hundred fifty pounds, and he thinks nothing of devouring six, eight and even ten pork chops at one sitting. And his carnal appetite is just as large. But for years it was inhibited by his political position. But then, one day in the summer of 1868, he visited Irene Hollingshead's fastidious Columbus whorehouse with C. P. Wells, and a strange and miraculous thing happened to him—at the age of fiftytwo, fat and wheezing, too red in the face for his own damn good and the good of his bloodpressure, Edward B. Maxwell fell desperately in love. Now, eight years later, he still is in love, and he wants to do the honorable thing by it, but the object of his affections (none other than Irene Hollingshead herself) absolutely refuses to marry him. Ed Maxwell has discussed the deplorable situation with C. P. Wells many times, and the word he uses most often when describing his beloved is Stubborn. He is now sixty years of age, and he moons about like a lovestruck pup, and sometimes C. P. Wells just laughs and laughs until his sides hurt. Mayor Virgil T. Light's plans for the gala Fourth of July celebration are acknowledged to be splendid beyond belief. The church ladies sew more than two hundred flags and banners. Under the inspired direction of Prof Karl J. Baer, the massed bands rehearse diligently, and after just three weeks they are playing in unison most of the time. The GAR fellows apply themselves energetically to their drills. The mayor's large bald voice is excellent for the calling of cadence. Bill Osterhaus builds the speakers' platform free of charge. Miss Metcalf's singers respond to her commands with terrified enthusiasm, and their voices are made pure and sweet and harmonious beyond even her most desperate hopes. Her sharp brown eyes rattle and snap, and her young choristers sing away like squadrons of angels.

(Mrs Nancy Quimby Ferris Wells, her oratory silent except within her skull, where it hoots and whimpers and snickers and whines, says: It wasn't as though I ran out into the street and grabbed Virgil with a hook. It wasn't just *anybody* I took. It was Virgil because Charley had cheated him. It was Virgil because of the way he looked at me back on Henry's

farm when he and the Messer boy came to see me with their scroll and
their words. Poor Virgil and his invalid wife. Poor man. Charley was off
visiting his whores, and so why not? The boy, though. I surely am sorry
about the boy. I hope he gets married real soon. Ah, so stern and righteous
he was: You and my father have done a terrible thing. Ah, such a young
fellow, and his face was tight and full of pain, and I said to him: You
should not have spied on your father. It is not honorable to spy. And he
said: Who are *you* to talk about *honor*? And I said: You don't know all
the facts. And I stood up, and I was smiling, and I said: You sweet boy.
Come here. Let Nancy hug you. Nancy doesn't know much about much
of anything, but this she does know. Come here. Yes. Nice boy. I have
seen the way you look at me. You want to tell Charley, don't you? You
want it all so very nice and *honorable*, don't you? You want your father
punished for his betrayal, don't you? Sh. Nice boy. Nice young fellow.
Kiss me. Ah. I get damp so easily. You would be surprised. Sneak
ing around after your papa like this. Shame on you. And the boy said:
Nancy! Nancy! And I said: Sh. This is only a hotel. The walls are thin.
Sweet darling. Yes. Ah. And I lay down for him, and of course I was his
first woman, and his warmth came into me so quick and deep I was just
about ready to believe I could feel it tickling my throat. But only the one
time did I let it happen. It was all that was necessary. After that one time
how could he cast stones at his father?)

Mayor Virgil T. Light begins composing his Fourth of July speech in
early May. Little Nell Wells has become very fond of scrabbling in the
dirt and building cities and palaces of mud. It is a poor year for cabbages,
potatoes, geraniums. The Aeolian Temple foundation is completed by the
end of April, despite cold weather and heavy rains. Says Claude Dill to
C. P. Wells: You think you got a way of getting Ed to bring the Hollings
head woman *here?* Says C. P. Wells: Yessir. That I do. If it's really neces
sary, I expect it can be arranged. I have all sorts of friends. You would be
surprised. Says Claude Dill: Well. Good. And, uh, the whores too? Says
C. P. Wells: Yes. Of course. The whores too. Quilts. Cookies. Logs. The
cold clink of the stonecutter's hammer and chisel: GONE TO JESUS. REST
IN PEACE. SACRED TO THE MEMORY OF. HERE, SERENELY AWAITING THE
FINAL JUDGMENT, LIES. Pianos in the parlor. Gentle maiden fingers
Czerny. Papa strokes his moustache, reclines on a hassock, listens to the
frail hesitant music. Skirts crackle. God damn those Indian savages. Custer
and two hundred sixtyfour men are killed up in Montana by a band of
Sioux under a chief named Sitting Bull. Both the *Democrat* and the
Journal devote dozens of columns to the massacre, and hereabouts the old
timers recall the banished Mingoes and say: You just can't expect nothing
else from them people. Phil Underwood begins submitting anonymous
poems to the *Democrat*. Only his parents and J. K. Bankson know that he
is their author. He signs the poems Piper Hell. C. P. Wells discusses
Claude Dill's whorehouse idea with a number of the village's business and

political leaders. They all express proper shock, but they do admit that the establishment of a whorehouse would no doubt bring more money into Paradise Falls. A dollar spent here, says George Acterhof, the hotel man, is a dollar that helps us all in the long run. And a whorehouse dollar is no different than any other. Says Erich Kahler, the bachelor banker: A house of prostitution, you say? Ah. Well. Dear me. Heh. In the fall, the parents of Ada Louise Masonbrink, age eleven, permit her to enter school. They have received no word from their son Samuel. The Paradise Falls Superbs, again captained by the massive Hugh Graves, win eleven games and lose just two. Both the defeats are inflicted by a traveling professional team from Toledo. O God of coal mines and whorehouses, preserve Thou our unquenchable spirit, the beauty of our Arcadia. In the name of the Father, and of the Son, and of the Holy Ghost. Amen.

(Again, Mrs Nancy Quimby Ferris Wells: Far as I know, Charley is her father. Far as I know. He asked me about it. So did Virgil. I told them both it was my beloved husband. And that's the truth. Far as I know. A village like this is the sort of place where everybody is supposed to know everything about everybody else. The women here, they look at me and my bosoms, and my bosoms make them go all tight and lemony in the mouth, and I expect there's all sorts of bad things they want to believe about me. Most of them don't even get damp when they go pee, and, like Charley says, that's a fact. But they never suspect a thing about Virgil and me. It was beyond their imagining. Anyone else maybe, but not *him,* and sometimes I swear I almost laugh. Only the boy ever found out, but I took the boy that one time, and that one time was enough to keep him from casting the stones. I don't guess I'm altogether stupid, no matter what Charley thinks, him and his whores and all the time the betraying and like he's got it coming to him as his right. Sweet Nancy: that's how he sees me. Sweet Nancy sit by the fire. Charley, I was willing to try. When we came here to this place Paradise Falls my Lord it's been eleven years ago now, when we came here all I wanted was to be a good wife to you and we'd go on picnics and listen to band music and raise babies and I'd give you all you wanted under the covers. That was what I wanted, and that was what you would not let me have, and so now I have punished you, and you don't even know it, and I'm still sweet Nancy sit by the fire, and that's all right too. At least, because I picked Virgil, I made it so he can't hate you for cheating him out of that land. He thinks you're his friend, all (like ElRoy Mauk says) contrary evidence notwithstanding. He felt terrible because he was betraying you. Oh ho. Some life. Henry, you should have lived. You were a hero, and I have a scroll to prove it, and I wish you'd have been a coward, so you could have lived and come home to me, and then there would have been no Charley Wells and no betrayals and no poor boy with his head against my thighs and his words coming out like slivers of raw meat. I told him: Get married. I said: Leave it all behind you. It doesn't matter. And so he went out and sparked the Purvis girl, and she would have made him a good wife, but he won't marry her. He tells me: I am no better than my father. How can I smear that girl with my filth? And I tell him: You are no better than a human being. And he shudders, and why did he follow his father to the hotel that night? Why can't people tend to their own business?)

The rain begins the evening of Saturday, July 1. It comes gray and soft and warm, more of a mist than a true rain. Children lick at it, and green odors abound. Horses blink, nicker. Thunder soughs down from the hills, but it is distant thunder, and neither it nor the rain causes any alarm. There are certain ladies of the village who hide themselves, all quaking and squealing, inside closets whenever there is a storm. But this is no storm, and the ladies neither quake, squeal nor hide. The rain slaps and spatters all night, and it is a good night for sleeping. Cats crawl under porches. The next morning, out in Egypt, the river has risen ten inches. This comes as something of a surprise to the people out there. They had no idea the rain was that heavy. The wind begins late in the morning of Sunday, July 2. It comes from the west, swirls the mist high into the hills. The falls shout. Shortly after noon, Mrs Horace N. Bloomer, wife of a deputy sheriff, receives a cut forehead from a falling branch. Almost simultaneously, the umbrella carried by Erich Kahler, bachelor banker, is turned inside out. Now the rain comes in sheets, and Mayor Virgil T. Light begins to worry about the gala Fourth of July celebration. The Republic will be one hundred years of age only once, and the text of the mayor's oration contains nothing but hard bones, and it surely would be a pity if an act of the Almighty interfered with the festivities. At 4 in the afternoon, the river overflows at Egypt. This is the latest a flood ever has plagued that luckless community, and the residents of Egypt ask each other whether perhaps the end of the world is at hand. Grimly they evacuate their homes and flee to higher ground. At 10 o'clock the CPV&M's Egypt depot is inundated, and mainline service between Paradise Falls and Lancaster is suspended. Early in the morning of Monday, July 3, the waters rush into Ike Underwood's old grist mill. Old Ike can scarcely believe it. My God, he tells his wife, that means the whole southwest end of town will go. First time it's ever happened. Grimacing, he stands at the front parlor window and looks out across his front yard. It is littered with leaves and branches, and the rain swirls and flaps like sides of canvas. Five of Harlowe Morris' dead peach trees are bent and splintered. The roof of the new Elysian Park picnic shelter collapses. Three of the swings are blown away. Bill Osterhaus' speakers' platform still stands, however. Now the closet ladies are all hidden. Phil Underwood stands in the yard behind his parents' home. He waits for lightning to strike him, or perhaps a tree to fall on him. Drops cling to his nose and chin. He regards the sky. He waits. Finally his mother comes scuttling out and prods and jostles him back inside the house. His son, little William Henry, sleeps warm and pink. Water enters the CPV&M's Paradise Falls depot. It also enters the

Depot Hotel. All guests are transferred to the Acterhof House. By nightfall, all of Mineral Avenue, Front Street, River Street, Railroad Street and Clay Street are flooded. The Paradise Falls Clay Products kilns are soaked. A total of twentysix homes are evacuated. Most of the Fourth of July flags and banners are gone from Main Street, torn off buildings and poles by the wind and the rain. Not a street in the village is passable. The mud is like pudding. The old Ike Underwood grist mill is sucked away by the water. Along with it goes some six thousand dollars' worth of brick that had been stored inside. Lightning crackles. The closet ladies quake. Among them are Mrs Madeleine Magill Baer, wife of Prof Karl J. Baer; Mrs W. W. Phipps, wife of the owner of the W. W. Phipps Hardware, Saddle & Harness Store; Miss Amelia Metcalf, the downyfaced teacher (she wraps herself in her wedding dress), and Mrs Edwin P. Rathbun, wife of the rector of Grace Episcopal Church. F. B. Crabb, the impecunious lawyer who heads the Democratic party in Paradise County, is prevented by the flood waters from paying his daily visits to Claude Dill's saloon. In lieu of his drinking, he beats on his skinny little wife. His voice is shrill, and his face is the face of the gentle martyred Lincoln, and he smacks his wife with the flat end of a spatula, and his movements are choppy, skittish, almost girlish. Early in the morning of Tuesday, July 4, it is apparent that there will be no gala celebration of any sort. The rain still falls. The flood waters proceed as far north as Meridian Avenue, and now parts of High, Market and Mulberry streets are inundated. Trees scream, splinter, fall. A large elm falls through the kitchen roof of a family named Sturgeon, on Meridian Avenue. These people are the parents of Arthur N. Sturgeon, the young attorney. Fortunately, no one is in the kitchen at the time. Treetrunks sink in the mud. Everywhere are leaves. Mayor Virgil T. Light is rowed around the southwest end of the village in a skiff. Hugh Graves is the oarsman. The mayor's large bald voice shouts instructions to the men who are aiding the families that are evacuating their homes. Fallen trees block Grainger Street at eleven different locations. The rain whips like pins. The closet ladies squeal. The rain continues until late in the evening of Wednesday, July 5. The gala celebration never is held. Fortunately, there is no loss of life, but property damage is estimated at three hundred thousand dollars, and a grand total of one hundred six trees are uprooted. Seventeen homes are a total loss. Mayor Light saves the text of his speech. With a few revisions, it will be perfectly adequate next year.

(Again, Mrs Nancy Quimby Ferris Wells: I am ashamed. I admit it. But what was I to do? I gave him no reason to betray me. He thinks he is above obligations. Well, no one is above obligations. He has been punished right and proper. It doesn't matter that he doesn't know. All that matters is that I know. The betrayer betrayed. O dear God, why hast Thou forsaken me? Forgive me my lies. I promise Thee I'll be good. My little Nell, I'll see to it that bad things don't happen to her. I can be good. I was born good. I loved George Peters and I loved Henry and maybe I could have loved Charley, but do You know that on our wedding night he left me alone and went off and tried to stick himself inside a *nigger* woman? He thought I was asleep. He thought I'd had too much champagne. But I'd only dozed off for a bit, and then I went roaming the floors of that Evansville hotel, and the door to the nigger woman's room was open, and there they were, the nigger woman and Charley, and she was calling him names, and I ran back to our room and fell on the bed, and I cried until my eyes ached, and how is *that,* dear Lord, for a betrayal? I am sorry, and I know I am bad, but I did what I did because I had to. So please do not forsake me. I didn't want anything any way but the good way. Someday maybe he'll tell me he's sorry. Someday when we're both old. Then maybe we'll be all right. With the dying close. Please, don't You see? I didn't do any of it *on purpose.* I swear that. On Your most precious Blood.)

Total deaths for the year is 86. Total births for the year is 149. The July flood and subsequent bad weather cause a delay in the construction timetable for the Aeolian Temple. Bill Osterhaus apologizes to Ike Underwood. No need for that, says old Ike. I can't hold you responsible for this damn weather. Just do the best you can. That's all anyone has a right to ask. By Christmas, the outside work is finished, as is perhaps half of the interior trim. Bill Osterhaus estimates that the job will be done by April, weather permitting. Two days after Christmas, a man named Percy T. Disney comes to Paradise Falls. He registers at the Depot Hotel as Philip T. Dilworth, a hardware salesman from Meadville, Pennsylvania. He meets secretly with C. P. Wells, who gives him five thousand dollars in cash, small bills. In the meantime, C. P. Wells has held a number of conversations with Ed Maxwell, the baker and former county commissioner and Republican chairman. I take it, says C. P. Wells, that you would marry her if you could. Says Ed Maxwell: You mean Irene? Says C. P. Wells: I don't mean Jenny Lind. Ed Maxwell laughs, tells C. P. Wells he envies him his sense of humor. Says C. P. Wells: Never mind that. If you really want to marry Irene, I believe I can arrange it. Then, placing his fingers together in a steeple, C. P. Wells leans back and says: This town needs a whorehouse. No doubt about it. He explains to Ed Maxwell what he has in mind. Ed Maxwell becomes even more red in the face than he normally is. He says: But what'll my children think? Lillian's husband—you know him, Wayne Bradley, sells shoes for Sidlo—he just got himself elected a deacon of the Presbyterian church. He'll just about fall down and have a fit. And my girl Martha and my boy Paul, I know *them.* They won't speak to me long as I live. Says C. P. Wells: Do you care that much? Says Ed Maxwell: Well, ah, maybe I don't. Says C. P. Wells: You got how many children? Says Ed Maxwell: Six. Says C. P. Wells: Let's see now, three from six leaves three. Suppose Lillian and Martha and Paul don't speak to you, you still got three, correct? Says Ed Maxwell: Yes. Andrew, Ed Junior and Tom. Says C. P. Wells: And will they speak to you? Says Ed

Maxwell: Yes. Matter of fact, Andrew and Ed Junior have already met Irene. She treated them real good. Served them *tea,* by God. Says C. P. Wells: Then why make such a fuss because the other three maybe'll get all worked up? At your age, what do you care? I'll fix it so Irene'll be glad to marry you. Leave it all to old Charley. Now, tell me, you old bastard, what were Andrew and Ed Junior doing calling on her? Says Ed Maxwell: Ah, traveling door to door. Selling Bibles. Ah, bound in leather. C. P. Wells laughs. He rises, claps Ed Maxwell on a shoulder. My congratulations, he says. The two men shake hands. C. P. Wells journeys to Columbus two days later. He points out the alternatives to Irene Hollingshead. She is angry at first, and he tells her he can't blame her. But finally she laughs, calls him a devil, agrees to marry Ed Maxwell and bring her whores to Paradise Falls as soon after the first of the year as practicable. The Hayes-Tilden election is close nationally, but Hayes has no trouble carrying Paradise County, 1,319 to 595, and Paradise Falls, 608 to 361. Tilden, however, wins the election. Or at least that is what most of the newspapers, including both the *Democrat* and the *Journal,* report.

A Great Man:

THE WORLD, THAT PAINTED OLD WHORE, was now performing every service for him short of licking the balls of his feet, and the clap and wheeze of his days had assumed a sort of perpetual triumph; the days grinned and chirped; the days existed for the Having; all winds were sweet. And hats were removed in his presence. Yes, by God, *hats.*

He still visited Irene Hollingshead's prim little Columbus whorehouse as often as he could, and he had himself an absolutely splendid girl. She was a tiny redhead named Rose Mast. She had a sweet singing voice, and she played the mandolin for him. Her skill on the instrument was more than perfunctory. And horizontally she was one of the wonders of the century. She attended a Unitarian church, and of course Charley did not understand the Unitarian church. He knew no one who did, not even those few Unitarians he had encountered. One time, when he questioned the vagueness of Rose Mast's religion, she smiled a pale delicate smile and said: Ah, Mr Wells, that's precisely the point.

How's that? What's the point?

The vagueness, said Rose Mast, tittering.

Charley laughed with great vigor. He kissed his dear little whore squarely on her dear little whore mouth. Grunting, he worked at the buttons of her dress. She helped him. She lay down. She was all mouth and thighs.

Yes, by God, *hats*. His greatness was beyond dispute, and the world was his very own painted old whore. And he respected his world. He'd always respected whores. They never permitted concepts to get in the way of what they did. Charley appreciated this sort of attitude. He had learned well from the revered Prof Frye—or Byrne, or Boyle, or whatever the fat old fraud's name had been. Thanks to the mad Mrs Weatherly, he had severed himself from bravery. Thanks to his dear late unlamented *friend* George Peters, he had seen honor and heroism as delusions. Thanks to the tar and the feathers inflicted by the town of Titusville, he had come to understand the idiocy of belief. And the revered Professor had crystallized his jaded philosophy for him, speaking to him of *mortality* and *possibility*, and now he had his own catalogue of regulations, and he adhered to it without question. The only reasonable goals a great man could pursue had to do with power and wealth, things of the world, and all talk of eternity and retribution was a lunatic gabble. He often reminded himself of the Professor's dictum: *What does it profit a man? It profits a man the world, and the world is enough.* But of course his greatness was not the sort of greatness that could survive inactivity, and so he filled his clapping and wheezing days with things to do. In this year of 1876, the largest of them still was the destruction of Isaac (Ike) Underwood. He knew he did not hate Ike Underwood, and because he did not hate Ike Underwood he figured he would succeed. Hatred served no useful purpose; therefore, the one & only Charles Palmer Wells would have no part of it. Hatred had no place in the activities of a great man. There were two reasons why Ike Underwood had to be destroyed. One, he was there and he was large. Two, the village never truly would belong to the one & only Charles Palmer Wells until Ike Underwood was made ridiculous. Now that the C. P. Wells Coal Co was free of debt and being operated smoothly by such underlings as Fritz Voss and Winfield Wainscott, Charley was able to devote most of his attention to the job of grinding up old Ike. He had stolen march after march on the old bastard, and there remained only one final crushing humiliation. He had snookered old Ike out of land that was worth millions; his candidate, Virgil T. (Let There Be) Light, had wrested the mayor's chair from old Ike's flunky, the late George McP. Pillsbury; he had turned back Ike's attempt to take over the mines through the CPV&M (and oh yes, Charley knew now for a fact that old Ike had bought CPV&M stock and had threatened poor Reavis with loss of control of the railroad unless Reavis went ahead and raised the coal shipping rates; word of Ike's stock purchase had come to Charley about a year after the great CPV&M war of 1872; it came from a man named Smeed, head of the syndicate that had tried to wrest the road from Reavis; Charley and Smeed had become close friends; they visited Irene Hollingshead's whorehouse together, and Smeed had given Charley a number of invaluable pieces of stock market information); no, there was little doubt that one final humiliation would take care of old Ike for once and for all. There was the word: *humiliation*. Ike Underwood had founded this village; he had created it in an antique Arcadian image. Not until this aspect was changed would the village—and the county—truly belong to the one & only Charles Palmer Wells. And the only way it would change permanently would be with the destruction of Ike Underwood. And for the word *destruction* substitute *humiliation*. A man could be destroyed but not defeated. Humiliation was much more profound. Only a great man recovered from humiliation, and Charley did not see old Ike as being a great man. Old Ike showed too many signs of love and other debilities. Yes, the word here was *humiliation,* and for four years Charley waited for his chance. Then, when plans for construction of the Aeolian Temple were announced, Charley saw his chance, and it dazzled, and his nights became warm with happy anticipation. In the meantime, though, there was the matter of the whorehouse. Charley's conversation with Claude Dill gave him a splendid idea. Why not a whorehouse indeed? Why should he be forced to travel to Columbus each time he sought honest female companionship? And, beyond that, the establishment of a whorehouse would be one more crack in the antique Arcadian aspect of this village. The world was a painted old whore, and Paradise Falls was a thing of the world, so why not bring some painted *young* whores there? And, beyond that, it would be one more slap in the face of old Ike, a small slap that would be a prelude to the large blow to be delivered later, the *coup de grace* so to speak, the final humiliation. Ah, the worm that resided within Charles Palmer Wells gave a great happy shout: Yes, yes, old fellow! You are a genius!

Humiliation: the word indeed.

It could be endured only by uncommon men.

Charles Palmer Wells knew this.

He had been taught it.

He had been taught it expertly.

It had been the final lesson for him.

It had been the largest lesson for him.

O God, Charles Palmer Wells said aloud after it was done, I thank Thee for permitting me entrance to it.

He said the words in a woods, and the tar was black in his mouth, and the feathers made him sneeze, and he dropped to his knees and rocked from side to side and his gratitude was immense, unconquerable, loud as doom. He spat tar. He grimaced. Yes, Lord, he said aloud, yes, Lord, yes, now I know all that needs to be known . . .

The lesson came to him in the spring of 1865, and a funeral train was hooting across the damp April fields of the state of Indiana, and he should have known, and that was a fact . . .

He had gone home to Titusville. The war was done. He had resigned his position with Congressman Lansing H. Ingraham, and he had gone home, and it didn't take the town of Titusville long to break out the tar and the feathers. All because of that damn simpleton of a Wilkes Booth . . .

His decision to go home had not been a difficult one. He made it in Washington shortly after New Year's Day, 1865. He had been doing some strenuous thinking on certain aspects of his final conversations with the late Professor, and a great many of the old fart's words had made sense. Especially the words that had had to do with not giving a damn. About anything and anyone, that is, beyond himself, the one & only Charles Palmer Wells. And so, with his own ambition and welfare in mind, Charley decided to quit Washington as soon as practicable. Once the Confederates finally gave up, the money no longer would be there for the grabbing. A buyer's market, and a cheap one at that, would be created for the favors of intelligent young men who were secretaries to influential Congressmen. The rag and belch and scamper of the city would be wiped away by the peace. Yes, all things considered, it was time for Charley to consider shifting his headquarters. His mind dwelt with a special devotion on the Professor's prediction of greatness. Of course the Professor had been a hideous bag of gas, but this did not mean he had been stupid. There was a great deal of merit in his prediction; now it was up to Charley to fulfill it. And fulfill it he would, by Jesus. The one & only Charles Palmer Wells understood *mortality*. The one & only Charles Palmer Wells understood *possibility*. The one & only Charles Palmer Wells understood the obsolescence of honor and heroism and belief. The one & only Charles Palmer Wells understood the rightness of the methods employed by the U. S. Grants of this life. He had all the skills, and by Jesus there was no reason on earth why he couldn't be a great man if greatness truly was what he desired. He followed the Grant campaigns with interest. Grant was a great man, and there was much to be learned from his generalship. The damn fellow was literally grinding the rebels into a pulp. Richmond was in danger. The siege of Petersburg was bound to succeed. It was simply a matter of time, and Grant viewed time in the same light as human beings—both were expendable. If it took forever to grind the rebels into a pulp, Grant would *take* forever. If it took five hundred thousand lives, Grant would *take* five hundred thousand lives. He was a wholly admirable man, and he did not waste his mind and energy on concepts and belief. A fine person. A man of this world. A despiser of Romance. In Washington that winter of 1864–65, most of the talk had to do with when the war would end. Charley figured the Confederates surely would collapse by the end of May. Once warmer weather set in, Grant's forces would gain mobility, and the rebels' contracting defenses would be smashed. It was some winter. Inch by filthy frozen inch, Grant's enormous army was chewing up the tattered enemy in Virginia. At the same time, old Cump Sherman's forces had torn across Georgia, capturing and burning Atlanta, blazing an immense scar clear across that anguished Commonwealth from northwest to southeast, finally occupying the seaport of Savannah and thus cracking apart the Confederacy at still another place. The rebels barely were able to turn occasionally for rearguard actions, let alone mount any sort of effective offensive. In Washington, the Republicans and the Unionist Democrats and the abolitionists were utterly beside themselves with delight, and every night there were galas, and the saloons were aswarm with jubilant Union officers (as were the whorehouses, including the Hotel Nonpareil, which that winter entertained—by actual count, kept by Wendell Archer Doggett himself—no less than *sixteen* big as life and twice as sassy *generals*), and the churches were crowded to their very highest most pious rafters with multitudes of the grateful and the exultant, and gamblers were making heavy wagers on exactly when R. E. Lee would surrender the Army of Northern Virginia to the Grant juggernaut, and ah, no question about it; the war had become a fine free delight of a war; yes indeed, such a happy city it was. (Yes indeed. And so had been Sodom. And Babylon. Yes indeed. Once one accepted the fact that elsewhere a great lot of men were being slaughtered, one could participate in all the joy with a singing heart. Yes indeed. Bless Mr Lincoln's war. Bless Mr Lincoln's butchery. Yes indeed.) But of course the joy would quickly go out of the city with the final echo of this immensely stirring and profitable war, and for Charley Wells it would be time to go away. And of course there was only one place he could go, and that was home. In the early months of 1865, Charley decided that the largest opportunity for greatness lay back in Titusville. To begin with, he had a large affection for the place. His *friend* George Peters, the late seeker of a Deed, had sneered at Titusville, had said Titusville was not the world. Well, George Peters had been full of cow flop. Titusville *was* the world. It was as much the world as Washington was the world, as the United States Military Academy was the world, as life on the stage was the world. And, beyond that, Charley still had ties in Titusville. He owned a home there, and he owned a store, and Titusville was where people *knew* him, and in time they would forget the war and his late espousal of what so many of them liked to call Peace Sneakism. He would charm them, by Jesus. He knew how to smile. He was conversant with the more oleaginous uses of rhetoric and hyperbole. He would work hard. And, sooner or later, they (those people of Titusville, cinched and grim and patriotic, reciters of psalms, red and sinewy from sun and grain and earth, awkward of tongue, large and virtuous and really, most of them, not too goddamn bright) again would clasp him to their collective bosom with the proverbial hoops of steel. Yes, within Titusville lay goals that were *possible*. He would find a design, and it would be an optimistic design, and he would carry it through. And from it he would achieve power and wealth, and the power and wealth would be the ultimate proclamation of his greatness. One thing was for certain. Nothing really had defeated him. Not even Nancy. Oh, he had had *setbacks,* but—thanks to the Hand of God—she still was *possible*. The Hand of God had given Charley another opportunity to take her for himself. Her husband, Henry Ferris, the farmer from over by Evansville, was dead. He had been killed at Gettysburg. The story of his death had come to Charley in a letter from Morton C. Hightower, the palsied old lawyer and Titus County Democratic chairman: *I have my account from none other than our old friend, Rufus Quimby, and so perhaps some of the details are questionable. But, in toto, I suspect the essentials are accurate enough. As Quimby tells it, Ferris had not been a member of the 198th Indiana Volunteer Infantry since early in 1863. It appears he had a severe physical encounter with a man named Underhill, a reputedly shiftless fellow whose farm adjoins the Ferris place over near Evansville. It seems this Underhill had some obscure grudge against Ferris. At any rate, Underhill had been badgering Ferris for some time in re: the former relationship of Mrs Ferris and the late Geo Peters. As Quimby tells the story (and perhaps, since he still drinks heavily and talks far too much, he has colored it a trifle too vividly), Ferris one day picked up Underhill and flung him against a tree, quite effectively breaking his back. (I find this difficult to believe. Perhaps Ferris injured the fellow, but the breaking of his back seems a bit farfetched to me. Rufus Quimby insists, however, that this is true. When I expressed skepticism, he said: It's all in a letter we got from Nancy. I'll show you the letter if you don't believe me. I'm not lying. I'm proud of my soninlaw. He's a good man, and I don't have to make up stories about him.) So, I leave it up to you, Mr Wells. Believe the story or not, as you choose. For myself, I believe most of it. My credulity is stretched a bit, however, by the thought that one man can break another's back simply by throwing him*

*against a tree. If this is true, then Ferris must have been a man of epic
strength. But enough. Back now to the narrative, as recounted by Quimby.
The incident occurred, said Quimby, in a bivouac near Falmouth, Virginia, less than a month after the lamentable Fredericksburg battle. The
upshot of the affair, according to Quimby, was that Underhill was placed
in a hospital and Ferris was given what is known as a Dishonorable
Discharge. His superiors did not take the incident very seriously, however, and the Dishonorable Discharge was simply a formality, a slap on
the wrist. For, you see, after receiving this apparently meaningless document, Ferris promptly signed enlistment papers with an Ohio regiment.
The commanding officer of one of the companies in this regiment is a
cousin of the wife of Major (now Colonel) Ezra Dreyer, of Evansville,
who has succeeded our friend Richard T. Harris at the command of the
198th Indiana. Ferris' new company was made up of men from a southeastern Ohio community that bears the exotic name of Paradise Falls.
(I have consulted an atlas, and yes, there is such a place.) At any rate,
the veteran Ferris quickly became a sort of hero to the greenhorns of
this Ohio company, which had not then yet seen serious action. To hear
Quimby tell it, even the officers took their orders from Ferris. This is
probably an exaggeration. Suffice to say that the officers did find Ferris'
experience valuable. And evidently it was transmitted to the men. In any
case, they conducted themselves well at both Chancellorsville and Gettysburg, and Quimby tells me Ferris was conspicuous in his gallantry. Then,
on the third day at Gettysburg, while participating in a minor skirmish
at the extreme left flank of the federal position, Ferris was killed by a bullet from a sniper's rifle. The men who were with him (Quimby says they
numbered fewer than ten; they apparently had been sent on a scouting
expedition, or whatever it is called in the army) all were either killed or
captured, and it was several months before the specifics of the affair came
to light. This occurred when one of the captured men was exchanged.
And so Ferris is dead. And you and I survive. I seriously question whether
either of us ever will die. We are probably, as the saying goes, too ornery.
Please pardon the incompetence of my handwriting, but my palsy has
become a great deal worse in the past year or so. Still, I otherwise feel
fine, and I see no reason to believe I will not live for centuries.* This letter was dated January 30, 1864. It went on to report that Nancy and her
lunatic sister, the Widow Grimes, the girl the Professor said he had found
sitting naked with the corpse of the Rev Mr Weeks, still were living on
the Ferris farm just outside Evansville. Charley promptly wrote Nancy a
letter of condolence. It was quite flowery and hortatory. She did not
answer it. Later he sent her a letter about Washington and its intrigues.
It was a splendidly chatty missive, absolutely awash with exclamation

points and parentheses and flamboyant little ampersands. She did not answer that letter either. Ah well, no matter. The point was: Nancy Quimby Ferris had returned to that domain where *possibility* governed. And once again, when the time was right, Charley would—to paraphrase that fine fellow, U. S. Grant—move upon her works. And this time, by Jesus, he would invest her. He would extract unconditional and immediate surrender. She was a large reason he decided to go home. Along with the opportunities he figured Titusville afforded his nascent greatness, she probably was the largest. But there was one other large reason, and it puzzled him. He did not quite know how he was supposed to accept it. On one hand, it reinforced his belief that people weren't worth an awful lot. On the other, however, it was a painful thing. After all, he *had* gone out of his way to perform an act of Christian charity for Wesley and Verda Thornton. He had saved them from ruin. He had given them back their dignity, a dignity that had been torn away from them when their sons had died and Wesley's hardware business in Evansville had gone bankrupt. The Professor had warned him that sooner or later the Thorntons would come to hate him, but this belief represented a cynicism that even Charley was unwilling to believe. When he hired the Thorntons to work in his grocery store, they performed splendidly, and their gratitude gave him a good deal of pleasure. But now the plain fact of the matter was they were swindling him. When he went to Washington, he left them in charge of the place. He increased their pay to one hundred twentyfive dollars a month (plus groceries, of course), and specified that they were to render a monthly accounting to Morton C. Hightower, who had power of attorney for all Charley's affairs in Titusville during his absence. Well, almost immediately Morton C. Hightower began to have his suspicions. Wartime inflation had increased prices, but the store's books —as kept by the Thorntons—showed profits at or near the 1860 levels. In a letter sent to Charley in late 1864, Morton C. Hightower wrote: *I cannot understand your appalling forbearance. Those two are spooning off money by the buckets. Why not permit me to discharge them? I surely shall be able to find someone to operate the store and keep the thievery within reasonable and civilized bounds. As you may already have suspected, I am not opposed to thievery per se. However, I do draw the line at vulgar display. Perhaps if our friends the Thorntons had not bought the old Peters place from Jim Otis for cash money, I would not be so distressed. But when they flaunt their larcenous activities, I am deeply offended. Stringent measures are in order, Mr Wells. Kindly permit me to take them.* Charley's reply: *As soon as this war ends, I am coming home. I feel the Thorntons have a right to explain themselves. Please do not misunderstand. It is not that I am being sentimental. It is simply that I am reluctant to believe that I was such a stupid judge of character. I fear my high regard for myself has been damaged. Thus, I cling to the desperate hope that there is some sort of honest and truthful explanation for their apparent rascality.* On April 9, 1865, at a place in Virginia called Appomattox Court House, R. E. Lee called on U. S. Grant, and the rebel surrender was arranged. The following night, while participating in an exquisitely Babylonian celebration that occupied the top two of the four floors of the Hotel Nonpareil, Charley made up his mind that then was as good a time as any to return to Titusville. He lay naked in an immense bed, and to his left lay a naked Irene Weaver, and to his right lay a naked Dorcas Pfaff (the thin little thing whose carnal energy had caused the Professor to suffer the attack that eventually did him in), and Wendell Archer Doggett reclined naked on a chaise longue with a naked whore named Dorothy sprawled on the floor next to him, and everyone was drinking champagne, and from time to time Dorothy licked and nibbled at Wendell Archer Doggett's massive feet and legs and thighs, and outside the window there was a fine and splendid sound of fireworks and bands and cheering and cannon, and the windowpanes rattled, and there was rain (but no one minded), and all day long crowds had stood in front of the White House, and all day long those crowds had hollered *Speech! Speech! Speech!*, but President Lincoln, just back from a trip to the captured Rebel capital of Richmond, had given no speech (he had appeared twice at a window, however, and the cheering had been stupendous), and Charley grinned at Wendell Archer Doggett and said: Well, old fellow, you old sorcerer, you old dog, you old whoremonger you, what are you going to do now that the war's over? Said Wendell Archer Doggett: This may come as a surprise to you, but I'm going to run a whorehouse. Charley laughed. Said Wendell Archer Doggett: Whorehouses are a bulwark, one might say, of civilization. Along with the barber and the undertaker, the lowly prostitute will always be necessary within what we think of as society. Perhaps from now on my profits will be a little less, but I shall endure. Who ever heard of a whoremaster starving to death? The next day Charley delivered his official resignation to his employer, Lansing H. Ingraham. The Congressman was quite decent about it. I understand, he said. After all, you have your own destiny to pursue. It would be unintelligent of you to attach it to mine. I only hope you have learned some things. I only hope your experience has been broadened. I rather think you are a remarkable young man. Ah, by the way, I know about Betty. I know she visited your room last year when I took you home with me for the canvass. She confessed it all to me a week or so later. I thank you for being a gentleman. The poor skinny little creature. Said Charley: Well, ah, sir, I don't know what— Said Lansing H. Ingraham:

Yes. That's it. Deny it. Be a gentleman. I appreciate your kindness. Poor little Betty. Said Charley: Really, sir, I don't— Said Lansing H. Ingraham: Six daughters. Can you imagine that? *Six.* And none of them beauties. And only two of them married, and both as yet childless. Ah, Undine and I have loved them all. Someone must love the homely ones too. Undine and I have worked hard for them, and they are good girls, even Betty, but we have always deeply regretted never having produced a son, though Lord knows we tried. *Six.* Dear me. When I think of my poor ears. Wendell Archer Doggett and an even dozen of the Nonpareil whores escorted Charley to the B&O depot. It was the morning of Friday, April 14, Good Friday, and all over the city was a sound of church bells. In observance of the day, Wendell Archer Doggett had purchased Episcopal hymnals for the girls. Carrying their hymnals, the girls lined up in a column of twos and followed the two men into the depot. The girls wore no paint. Their eyes were clear. They were clad in muted grays and blacks. Their hair was done up in buns, and their dresses were without decolletage, and several of the dresses had lace at the neck. They walked in a solemn and most impressively pious lockstep, and their hymnals were open, and their voices rang clean and clear, echoing across the waiting room, as they sang:

> *O come and mourn with me awhile;*
> *And tarry here the cross beside;*
> *O come, together let us mourn;*
> *Jesus, our Lord, is crucified.*
>
> *Have we no tears to shed for him,*
> *While soldiers scoff and foes deride?*
> *Ah! look how patiently he hangs;*
> *Jesus, our Lord, is crucified.*

Wendell Archer Doggett and Charley walked with heads bowed. From time to time Wendell Archer Doggett made mumbling sounds and said: Amen. Yes. Yes. That's right, sisters fair. Amen. The whores sang on:

> *Seven times he spake, seven words of love;*
> *And all three hours his silence cried*
> *For mercy on the souls of men;*
> *Jesus, our Lord, is crucified.*
>
> *O love of God! O sin of man!*
> *In this dread act your strength is tried;*
> *And victory remains with love;*
> *For thou, our Lord, art crucified!*

The voices rang demure and silvered. Ah, said Wendell Archer Doggett under his breath, look how patiently he hangs. Then, after glancing around, Wendell Archer Doggett said to Charley: It would appear that we are attracting a crowd. Charley looked up. Sure enough, several dozen persons—men, women, children, even a few hobbling wounded soldiers— now trailed along behind Charley and Wendell Archer Doggett and their tarnished choristers. When they came to the track where stood the train that Charley would be boarding, Wendell Archer Doggett turned and raised his arms for quiet. The whores shuffled, coughed. The spectators smiled. Let us pray, said Wendell Archer Doggett. Heads were lowered, including Charley's. His belly trembled. Wendell Archer Doggett wore a heavy great- coat. He groped inside its folds and removed a book. He opened the book and read: *O merciful God, who hast made all men, and hatest nothing that thou hast made, nor desirest the death of a sinner, but rather that he should be converted and live; Have mercy upon all who know thee not as thou art revealed in the Gospel of thy Son. Take from them all ignorance, hardness of heart, and contempt of thy Word; and so fetch them home, blessed Lord, to thy fold, that they may be made one flock under one shepherd, Jesus Christ our Lord, who liveth and reigneth with thee and the Holy Spirit, one God, world without end. Amen.* Then, looking up, Wendell Archer Doggett addressed the crowd. My friends, he said, I thank you for joining with us in prayer. I hold here in my hand *The Book of Common Prayer*, which is of course an Episcopal document, but I am humbly grateful to those of you who are not of the Episcopal faith who have nonetheless shown the largeness of spirit to assist us in our loving petition this holy day. Then, pointing to Charley, Wendell Archer Doggett said: Dear friends, we are gathered here today in an endeavor that tran- scends narrow differences in theology, and thus it is meet and right that, no matter our faith, we join together to wish Godspeed to the Rev Dr Lucius Abernathy Marchbanks here as he leaves on the first leg of his trip to the faroff isles of Pussyhoha in the South Indian Ocean. Is there a more noble calling than that of the missionary? I know of none, and so it is an inspiration indeed that so many of you are participating in this fond adieu to the Rev Dr . . . uh, Marchbanks. His soul, my friends, is as un- soiled as the breath of lilies. The natives of Pussyhoha are fortunate in- deed. They do not know it, but God this day is causing His countenance to smile upon them. We wish the Rev Dr Marchbanks every success in this, his greatest challenge. God love you, sir! May angels protect you and keep you and shine their loving light upon you through the final echo of the last eternity! These young ladies, these innocent maidens, students of mine from the W. A. Doggett Select School of Bible Study and Christian Morality, join me—as you know—in the fervent wish that your days in

Pussyhoha be blessed with the love of Jesus Christ, our Mediator and Redeemer. Wendell Archer Doggett turned to the whores. All right, young ladies, he said. Now then, let us hear your voices in enthusiastic concert. Then Wendell Archer Doggett shook hands with Charley and pushed him and his luggage aboard the train. As Charley made his way to his seat, he heard the shaky whore voices again raised in sweet song:

> *For he's a jolly good fellow,*
> *For he's a jolly good fellow,*
> *For he's a jolly good*
> *feh*
> *heh*
> *low,*
> *Which nobody can deny!*
>
> *Which nobody can deny,*
> *Which nobody can deny.*
> *For he's a jolly good*
> *feh*
> *heh*
> *low,*
> *Which nobody can deny!*

Charley yanked open a window and grinned down at his assembled wellwishers. God grant you safe passage! yelled Wendell Archer Doggett, waving his hat. The whores all jumped and squealed. They blew kisses to Charley. Several of the spectators cheered. A number of women waved their handkerchiefs. Charley cupped his hands to his mouth and yelled to the whores: Young ladies! I shall pray for each and every one of you! Thank you for your kind attentions! Several of the whores blushed. Irene Weaver winked. He had fucked seven of those girls, and there was a catch in his throat, and that was a fact. He learned of the assassination the next morning when he changed trains in Marietta. Newsboys scrambled up and down the platform. There was a deal of shouting and shoving. Charley's eyes were hot. He had sat up all night. He'd never been able to sleep in the steam cars. He purchased a copy of a newspaper that called itself the Marietta *Standard*. The assassination account ran down the first three lefthand columns of the front page. The story was headed:

IMPORTANT!
President Is Shot!
J. W. Booth, Actor, Sought
Little Hope Held for Recovery
of Lincoln

SEWARD STABBED!
But Will Live
ASSASSINS!
REBEL PLOT!

Charley seated himself on his suitcase and read the details. He dug at his eyes with a fist. Jesus God. Jesus God Almighty. Grit was in his eyes. He wet a finger with his tongue, bathed his eyes. He blinked away the grime. After reading the newspaper, he pushed his way inside the depot and bought a cup of coffee. The morning was gray and close. He was aware of the smell of his body. It was a sour smell. Everyone was talking about the shooting of the President, about Booth the actor, about the stabbing of the Secretary of State. Voices were shrill. My God, said a man, it's chaos! Charley blew on his coffee, shook his head. A man ran out of the telegraph office. The man was skinny; he wore spectacles from which depended a black string; he waved a scrap of paper. It is over! he hollered. He is dead! The President is gone! The skinny man ran out a door. A bald man was sitting next to Charley. The bald man began to sob. All around Charley, women and children were wailing. Charley sighed. God damn. Children plucked at their mothers' skirts. Charley drew several deep breaths. He finished his coffee, returned to the platform. His train would be along in a few minutes. The platform was nearly deserted. Inside the station everyone was milling and hollering. Shaking his head, Charley again seated himself on his suitcase. He lighted a cheroot. Puffing, he looked out across the tracks and down a shallow slope that ended at the Ohio River. He had known Booth. It would have been difficult, if one was something of a rake and drinker and gambler, not to have known Booth. Charley and Booth had discussed the President not too many weeks before. Booth had talked for several hours, and spittle had formed at the corners of his mouth. The conversation had taken place in Derry's Saloon, at E Street and Pennsylvania Avenue. Booth was accompanied by a large sneering fellow he introduced as the Rev Lewis Wood. Charley later learned the man's true name was Lewis Paine. The talk was that this Paine had once served in the rebel army. That night in Derry's Saloon, Booth made no bones about his hatred for Lincoln, and Charley finally had to smile. He reminded Booth that the war was as good as over. Said Booth: No, my friend. Not so. Suppose, ah, suppose something happened to Lincoln. Suppose he was, ah, abducted. Said Charley: Abducted? Said Booth: Yes. Fear for his safety would no doubt force the government to deal honorably with the Confederacy. Said Charley: That's ridiculous. Are you so foolish as to believe that the government will *negotiate* at *this* stage of the war? The rebs can kidnap Lincoln *and* the Vice President *and* all the members of the cabinet and it won't make a particle of difference. Said Booth: Then perhaps he should die. Said Charley: You mean Lincoln? Said Booth: I do. You're damn right I do. Said Charley: You're out of your mind. Said Booth: This has been an *immoral* and an *unjust* war, and its foremost perpetrator should be made to pay the most profound penalty. Then, glancing at his huge companion, Booth said: Isn't that right, Reverend Wood? And the big fellow said: Sure, Johnny. Whatever you say. The conversation continued for some time, but the Rev Mr Wood made no further contribution. Instead, he drank. He apparently had an unlimited capacity. From time to time the right corner of his mouth curled upward in a rather sinister sneer, but otherwise he simply stood there and poured down whisky. *The Rev Mr Wood!* Hah, if this fellow was a minister of the Gospel, then so was Joe Hooker, the general who was said to take prostitutes with him to the field. Ah, poor Booth. Apparently he and this Rev Wood were attempting to hatch some sort of mad conspiracy. Charley grinned, shook his head. He had known Booth for the past couple of years. He had attended several plays featuring Booth, and he'd not been too impressed with the man's acting style. Oh, Booth surely was handsome enough for the stage (he was dark and slight, with a drooping moustache, good teeth and large, almost girlish, eyes), but his style was excessively flamboyant; he was more of an acrobat than an actor, and he was notorious for delivering his lines far, far too loudly. Still, for all that, and despite his bizarre political beliefs, Wilkes Booth was not a bad sort. He was a generous drinking companion, and he certainly always knew where to find women. In a way, however, he reminded Charley of his late *friend* George Peters, the defunct seeker of a Deed. One night, while drinking with Charley in a saloon called Tartavul's (which, by the way, was smack nextdoor to Ford's Theater), Booth said: The world does not understand how it is with me. You see, ordinary affairs will not do. I have a sure and certain Purpose on this earth. Its precise nature has so far eluded me, but I am confident that sooner or later, when the times are right, it will be revealed to me. Once this happens, I shall not be stayed. You always will remember me, my friend. Some day you will tell your grandchildren you were a drinking companion of Wilkes Booth. Ah, now, don't look at me that way. I am perfectly serious. There is an immensity within me. I can feel it. It churns, and it provides heat rather than warmth, and it affords me great intimations. You just wait. You'll see. Some day a name will be writ huge and bold across the bright blue sky of this Republic, and that name will be: BOOTH. Well, now, sitting there on the platform of the Marietta depot, Charley couldn't say he hadn't been warned. He puffed on the cheroot, tucked the newspaper under an arm. He would save the newspaper for his grandchildren. He smiled. He supposed he probably *would* tell his grandchildren he had been a drinking companion of Wilkes Booth. Ah, poor Johnny. The poor madman. Charley shook his head, threw away the cheroot. His train came alongside the platform. A trainman jumped down from one of the cars. Is he dead? the fellow shouted. Charley nodded. The trainman gave a great wail, ran inside the depot. Charley boarded the train. The coach was empty. The train was made up here in Marietta, and so he had his choice of seats. He took one halfway between the forward and rear wheels. There was less pitch and sway in the middle of a coach. He sighed, settled back. The train began to fill. Women wept. Everyone spoke loudly. He closed his eyes (they again were hot). He changed trains again in Cincinnati and Indianapolis (there was no direct connection between Cincinnati and Titusville), and his ears clapped and stung from the groan and keen of all the grief he heard. He bought a newspaper in Cincinnati. He bought another newspaper in Indianapolis. After reading them thoroughly, he packed them away—along with the Marietta paper—in his suitcase. Yes, his grandchildren no doubt would be greatly interested. He was willing to wager a thousand dollars it had been Paine, alias the Rev Mr Wood, who had stabbed Secretary Seward. He felt sorry for Seward. To be attacked in one's bed by *that* great sneering oaf—ah, Lord, the thought was enough to make one's blood turn to sand. In the Cincinnati depot, black crepe already had been hung from the rafters. Outside the building, the flag was at half-mast. Charley saw a number of men wearing black armbands. Women stood and wept. The sound of their weeping was small and frail. Charley did not give two whoops and a pile of dead skunks about Abraham Lincoln, but he did have to acknowledge (to himself, at least) that nothing was more certain to earn a man a sentimental immortality than a bullet from an assassin's pistol. Ah, poor Wilkes Booth. He would be captured, and he would die, and his only accomplishment would be the guaranteeing of an immortality for the one man he had hated above all others. In the Indianapolis depot, Charley almost became involved in a riot when he attempted to buy his newspaper. As it was, he lost two buttons from his waistcoat. He was clawed at, kicked and even punched. One man, very drunk and fat and malodorous, even made so bold as to attempt to knee Charley in the testicles. But his aim was poor, and Charley managed to push him away. The man lost his balance, fell against a wall, slid to the floor, made no effort to get up. Charley paid him no mind. Grunting, Charley used his elbows to push aside a small woman who had a brown wen on her forehead. She whooped, spat. He paid her no mind. Finally he managed to buy his paper. The train to Titusville was not crowded. Charley finally was able to get some sleep. It was Easter morning, and he really would have had himself quite a good nap if it hadn't been for the damn church bells. The train was an accommodation local, and it stopped in every village and hamlet, and in every village and hamlet the bells were tolling. The bells. The damn church bells. Ah, a splendid day indeed to be coming home. Finally he gave up trying to get any more sleep. He sat up. Bleary, grimy, his mouth and belly dry, he licked his lips, rubbed his eyes. He sat rigidly. He made a face, lighted a cheroot. The conductor came along. The conductor had a full white beard. He was portly, and his breath had an odor of eggs, an odor that was so strong that not even the smell of Charley's cheroot suppressed it. He sat with Charley for a time. Ah, he said, old feller like me, sometimes my feet hurt real bad. I expect I maybe carry too much weight for them.

Charley nodded, puffed on his cheroot.

What do you think of the shooting? You think they're going to catch that Booth feller?

I wouldn't be surprised.

A man I seen this morning in the Indianapolis depot, he said it wouldn't surprise *him* but what it's all a Democrat plot to put Andy Johnson in the White House.

Mm, said Charley. That's a thought.

After all, old Johnson *is* from Tennessee.

Correct.

Wouldn't that be something if it was to turn out to be true? I mean, maybe the rebs didn't have nothing to do with it a tall.

Charley nodded. These are peculiar times, he said.

That's the truth, brother.

Charley rubbed his eyes. The cheroot had begun to taste foul.

The conductor stood up. Well, he said, nice talking to you. He moved off down the aisle.

Paugh! said Charley. He exhaled. His lips flapped. He opened the window and threw away the cheroot. He bathed his mouth with saliva, spat out the window. Yach! he said. Again he spat. The air was misty and cold, but he left the window open anyway, even after a woman across the aisle frowned at him.

The bells: a sound of tolling grief, measured and helpless. It was this sound that greeted Charley when that wretched accommodation local finally pulled into Titusville just as the muggy Easter twilight was settling over the town and the river. When Charley came down out of the coach, the sound of the bells rapped at his skull. No doubt about it—that contemptible baboon of a Lincoln was now a genuine martyr, and Easter was supposed to be a day of joy (*Hallelujah! The Lord has risen!*), but the death of the baboon had done away with the joy, and did these people propose to ring their damn bells forever? Charley walked slowly.

From time to time he set down his suitcase and dug soot from his ears and his eyes and his nostrils. He walked along Titus Avenue. He saw no one. He walked to his store. It was closed. A handwritten notice was in the front window. It said:

> DUE TO THE DEATH OF PRESIDENT LINCOLN,
> THIS STORE WILL BE CLOSED APRIL 17.
> —Wesley G. Thornton, Proprietor

Wesley G. Thornton, *Proprietor,* eh! *Well*now, imagine that! Charley chuckled. He shifted the suitcase from one hand to the other. He decided he would walk home along the river road. He crossed the street, headed south along an alley. The river road: Prof Frye had found him sitting by the river road the morning his parents had died. A good deal had happened since then. Ah, yes. Charley grinned. He moved along at a lope. *Home,* by God! Yes *sir!* And about *time* too. He'd not permitted Morton C. Hightower to rent out the old place. It had been kept locked up for more than two years. He supposed the first thing he would have to do would be to give it a good airing. He would open all the windows, then sit on the front porch for a time and look down toward the river and the blue Kentucky hills. The key to the place was in a pocket of his britches. Ah, bells or no bells, it was good to be—

Sheriff Ben Stork emerged from behind a shed. He was grinning through his harelip.

Charley stopped.

Wellnow, said Ben Stork, how are you, Charley?

Charley looked at him.

Ben Stork walked to Charley. Howdy, he said. Howdy do, Charley. He stuck out a hand.

Charley looked at the hand. The bells were loud.

Shake it, said Ben Stork.

Charley looked at the hand.

Shake it, you Copperhead skunk.

Charley's right hand came out.

The sheriff seized it and squeezed.

Charley yelped, bent forward. Tears filled his eyes. He dropped his suitcase.

Welcome home, said Ben Stork, squeezing.

Ah, said Charley. Ah. Oh.

Yessir, said Ben Stork, grunting and squeezing. Sure is good to be seeing you at a time like this.

Oh, said Charley. Ah. *Ben.*

Ben Stork released Charley's hand. The bells were loud. Ben Stork made a fist, rammed it into Charley's belly. The impact knocked Charley down. He gagged. Bile surged into his throat. He remembered the time Ezra Ordway had attacked him.

Peace sneak, said Ben Stork. Copperhead. You sure did pick a good time to be coming home, didn't you?

Charley coughed, tried to clear the bile from his throat.

You have anything to do with it? said Ben Stork. He was leaning forward. His face was close to Charley's.

Wh . . . what? said Charley.

You have anything to do with it? You know where Booth is?

Charley shook his head no.

Ben Stork kicked Charley in the ribs.

Charley bleated.

Get up, said Ben Stork. You're under arrest.

Charley looked up. He rubbed the place where Ben Stork had kicked him.

Get up, said Ben Stork.

Gasping, Charley stood up. His mouth was sour. The bells were loud. He shook his head like a wet dog.

Pick up your suitcase, said Ben Stork.

Charley nodded. He bent, picked up the suitcase. When he straightened, he said: Ben, what's this all about?

Never mind, you traitor shit. As if you didn't know anyhow.

You think I know something about Booth?

Think, hell.

I don't know anything about it.

Get moving.

Ben, you got no right—

Get moving, said Ben Stork. He seized Charley by the scruff of the neck and pushed him back up the alley toward Titus Avenue. He pushed Charley all the way to the county jail, which was in the courthouse cellar. The bells were loud. It occurred to Charley why this all was happening. It was the reward. According to the newspapers, Secretary of War Stanton had approved the posting of a $100,000 reward to be given to anyone supplying information leading to the capture of Wilkes Booth. The reward had not yet officially been acknowledged by Stanton, but there seemed little doubt that it would be. The goddamn reward—*that* was why Ben Stork was shoving Charley off to jail. Charley remained in jail for three days. It was just as he had figured. Ben Stork was holding him for questioning in connection with what good old Ben called Suspicion of Complicity in the Assassination of President Lincoln. He beat Charley

with the butt of a pistol. He beat Charley until Charley wept. He beat
Charley until a number of Charley's teeth were torn loose. He beat Charley until Charley's mouth was flooded with a taste of brass, and of course
the taste of brass actually was a taste of blood. He beat Charley until all
Charley could do was crawl. He beat Charley, and everywhere was a
sound of bells. Charley recalled all the men Ben had killed (including
Jesse Hubbell, the KGC organizer), and Charley supposed he was lucky
not to be dead. Charley screamed at Ben Stork, and blood flew from Charley's mouth, and Charley's words were thick and moist with blood: No,
no, Ben! I don't know a thing about it! I don't! I don't! Please! For God's
sake, Ben, *stop* it! And, grinning, Ben Stork hollered: Look who's bawling
about God! Damn fucking assassin! Ben Stork beat Charley in the morning, and he beat Charley in the afternoon, and he beat Charley at night,
and all Charley could do was snivel and crawl and spit teeth, and then
one night none other than ridiculous old Dick Harris, the crippled and
scarred former *hero,* the tannery man, the fellow who had been com-
missioned colonel and had raised a regiment, had skedaddled at Antietam,
had returned to the war despite the skedaddling, had performed bravely at
Fredericksburg in atonement for his Antietam cowardice, and had—as his
logical reward—been crippled and disfigured when his horse had fallen
on him, who walked now only with the assistance of crutches, who had
been the foster father of the late and despised George Peters; this Dick
Harris, whom the town apparently (according to letters Charley had received) revered despite his cowardice and his incompetence and his
scarred face and smashed legs; this fine saint of a Dick Harris, whose
purse had stolen an election from Charley back in '62; ah, this marvelous
Dick Harris, who was a kindly man and a gentleman and a black Republican and therefore an ass; then one night this selfsame Dick Harris
came to the huddled and whimpering Charley and stood over him and
said: Good God, Charley, what has he done to you? Charley, who was
drooling blood, tried to answer, but he did not have the strength to spit
out the blood. His tongue hurt. Patoo went his poor tongue, but nothing
much happened except that he swallowed blood and began to cough and
hawk and gag. A man bent over Charley. The man was not old Dick
Harris. The man was no less a personage than Wesley Thornton, the
proprietor of Charley's grocery store, the fellow Morton C. Hightower had
accused of excessive and tasteless thievery. Good evening, Mr Wells, he
said. He seized Charley by the shoulders and pulled him upright. Dick
Harris went limping off down a corridor. Wesley Thornton assisted Charley to his feet. Charley groaned, coughed. Then he heard two voices
shouting. He recognized the voices. One belonged to old Dick Harris.
The other belonged to Sheriff Ben Stork. Charley could not make out

their words. He shook his head. Steady now, said Wesley Thornton, steer
ing Charley out of his cell and down the corridor. The shouting contin
ued. Fear came hot and plump in Charley's belly. The shouting was loude
now, and it was clear that Wesley Thornton was taking him to Ben Stor
for another beating. Charley cringed, tried to pull away from Wesley
Thornton. No, said Charley. No. No. I don't . . . no . . . please . . .
don't want him to hit me any more. A cluck from Wesley Thornton. Ah
now, now, Mr Wells, he said, please don't concern yourself. There wil
be no more beatings. Mr Harris is arranging for your release. Mr Har
ris is a very influential man. You are very fortunate that he has come
forward in your behalf. Then Charley was outside, and Wesley Thorn
ton's arms firmly held him upright. He helped Charley inside a carriage
Charley heard the soft whicker of a horse. He sagged back. He saw the
light from a lantern. Dick Harris came limping to the carriage. Wesley
Thornton helped him inside. He settled back next to Charley. He sighed
Charley looked at him. Dick Harris smiled. Charley slumped forward
chin against chest. He closed his eyes. A series of convulsions jerked a
his belly. He opened his eyes, twisted his neck, looked back at Dick Har
ris. Yes? said Dick Harris. I . . . *uhhhhh* . . . said Charley, and a thir
spray of bile came from his mouth, and a great stink arose, and then he
simultaneously vomited and fouled himself, and he choked and shud
dered, and Dick Harris clapped him on the back, and the next thing he
knew he was naked, and Mrs Dick Harris was bathing him in warm
fragrant water, and she told him not to fret about his nakedness; she tol
him she had seen a naked man before. And then there were sheets, and
the sheets were clean and cool, and Mrs Dick Harris was humming
Lorena. She sat next to the bed, and she wore a black dress, and she wa
fussing with what appeared to be a piece of embroidery. Charley moaned
raised an arm. There, there, said Mrs Dick Harris, you just rest easy now
She smiled, and she really wasn't much of a woman to look at, and so why
was it he wanted to press his face against her belly? Then Charley's vision
became dark and warm, and Mrs Dick Harris vanished, and he slept, and
then he was aware of sunlight and a smell of toast, and he heard Mr and
Mrs Dick Harris discussing something or other, and Mrs Dick Harri
said: I wouldn't normally argue with you, Richard, and you know that
but it's stuck in my mind that it was only about six months or so.

No, said the voice of Dick Harris. It was oh perhaps three years.

Dear, I'm sorry, but you're wrong.

Well, said Dick Harris, when Charley here comes out of it, we'll as
him. He'll know.

All right, dear. That'll be just fine.

Anyhow, be that as it may, I expect it *is* a blessing she's dead.

Yes, dear.

It was a terrible business.

Yes, dear. And best forgotten.

Believe I'll go sit on the porch. It's turned out to be a fine day.

Yes, dear.

Call me if he comes out of it.

Yes.

Yes, said Dick Harris. A fine day.

Do you want me to help you?

No. I have to learn to make do for myself.

Yes, dear.

Then came a succession of thumping noises, apparently from Dick Harris' crutches. A door closed. Then came a sigh. The humming of *Lorena,* small and despondent, resumed. Charley lay in that bed without speaking for a day and a night and another day, and then he came back from wherever it was he had gone. It was a Friday morning, and it was the twentyfirst day of April in the year 1865, and there was no place he did not ache. But he did manage to sit up in bed. He smiled at Mr and Mrs Dick Harris, thanked them most heartily for their kindness. After determining from them what day it was, he said: Lord, there's not much I remember since Sunday.

Well, said Dick Harris, no wonder.

Charley probed with his tongue. How many teeth did I lose?

Dick Harris raised his eyebrows. I don't know, he said. Dr Findley was here to look at you, but I don't believe he took a census of your teeth.

Charley grinned. His mouth hurt. Back and forth went his tongue. As closely as he could tell, he had lost six teeth. He rubbed his jaw. Well, he said, at least Ben Stork didn't break my jaw. You say this is *Friday?*

All day, said Mrs Dick Harris, tittering.

I didn't have anything to do with it, said Charley.

With what? said Dick Harris.

The assassination.

Oh, we know *that,* said Mrs Dick Harris.

You do?

Yes. We know *you.*

Charley frowned.

Dick Harris smiled at Charley and said: You're not nearly the bad fellow you'd sometimes like people to believe.

Oh? said Charley.

I think you're a very sincere sort of fellow. We've had our differences politically, but I've never questioned your sincerity.

Ah, said Charley. Well. That's fine. I thank you.

Dick Harris nodded.

Now, said Charley, can you answer a question for me?

We'll surely try, said Dick Harris.

The other day—I can't recollect exactly what day it was; my head was sort of out of joint, if you know what I mean—uh, the other day you and Mrs Harris were talking about some dead woman.

Dead woman?

Yes. Something about her being better off dead. You were arguing about whether something had been six months or three years.

Mrs Dick Harris spoke up. Yes, she said, we were talking about Charlotte Grimes.

Nancy's sister? Nancy Quimby, I mean?

Nancy Quimby *Ferris,* said Mrs Dick Harris. Yes. Her sister. Poor Charlotte died about a week or so ago. Richard and I were trying to recollect how long she was married to old Oliver Grimes. I say it was six months or so. Richard says it was more like three years. Do *you* remember?

Charley frowned. Finally he said: Mrs Harris, I hate to contradict a lady, but it was more like three years.

It *was?*

Yes. Best as I can recall, they were married in '57. And he died in '60. I remember it was '60 because it happened during my first canvass for the legislature. I recall saying to myself at the time that I wished I had some spare time so I could sort of, uh, *call on* Charlotte. She was a handsome girl. But then, by the time the canvass was over, she was going everywhere with Rev Weeks, and I never did get the chance to call on her.

Dick Harris smiled at his wife. Aha, he said, I'm not *altogether* stupid.

Mrs Dick Harris frowned. Isn't that the strangest thing? she said. Where does the *time* go?

Who knows? said her husband, shrugging.

And I know they were married in '57, said Charley. My folks died in '56, and I know it wasn't too long after that. I date things from when my folks died, you know? It was just about nine years ago. Doesn't seem that long.

No, said Dick Harris. It surely doesn't.

Mrs Dick Harris, who appeared a bit put out, said she would fix Charley a nice hot bowl of soup. She excused herself. Her husband smiled at Charley. Dick Harris was seated in a straightbacked chair. His crutches were propped against his legs. The lateral scar across his face was white edged in pink. He said: Ruth is a gentle person, but she does *not* care to lose an argument.

Hardly anyone does, said Charley.

True . . .

Charlotte die over at Nancy's place by Evansville?

Yes. Or at least that's what her father tells me. Says Charlotte, who was a lunatic as I suppose you know, says Charlotte went to sleep one night and never woke up. She'd become very fat, he tells me, and apparently all the fat was too much for her heart. She never did tell anyone what took place that night with Weeks. And Prof Frye never has been apprehended. Ben Stork thinks Frye killed Weeks. I mean, still thinks.

Mm. And the Professor's never been found?

Not a trace.

Well. Imagine that.

Ah, do you know about Nancy's husband?

I know he's dead.

I owe my life to him.

Oh?

Yes, said Dick Harris. He rubbed his scarred face.

How so?

Ferris was the one who pulled me back to our lines at Fredericksburg after I was hurt. I don't know how many hundred yards he dragged me. Better part of a mile, that's for sure. Paid no attention to his personal safety. A fine fellow. It is a genuine loss. I'm sorry for his widow. Poor Nancy. Perhaps you didn't know it, but George was very fond of her.

Yes. I knew that.

We loved George, Ruth and I. He was a good boy. Quiet. Never caused trouble for us. Obedient. After his parents and his sister were killed in that *Molly B. Edwards* explosion, he was a son to us. A son we never had. Ah, I am being sentimental, womanish. Forgive me.

Charley said nothing. Ah, the poor fool. The things Charley could tell him. Charley rubbed his mouth. His gums hurt.

Dick Harris cleared his throat.

Charley smiled. What's the latest news on the assassination? he said.

Booth is still at large. Seward will recover. The President's body lay in state in Washington the better part of the week. It's being brought back to Springfield now. By very slow train. I understand it won't arrive there until May 1 or so. The funeral is to be held May 3. I must say, Stanton and Ben Wade and those people are milking it for all it's worth.

Yes, said Charley. I expect it's difficult to resist martyrdom.

Dick Harris nodded and said: Those people propose to deal harshly with the South. They no doubt figure they will have an easier time of it if they keep the populace all worked up. Hatred apparently can be useful in expediting political ideas. I would not presume to argue the point.

Well, said Charley, it sounds logical.

Yes, said Dick Harris, it does, doesn't it?

Hatred will always be with us.

Dick Harris shrugged. Yes, he said, I expect you're right.

I mean, *I* should know.

Ben Stork, you mean?

Yes.

Well, Ben gets carried away.

I hope to tell you.

What he did to you was shameful.

My feelings exactly, said Charley, smiling.

Dick Harris sighed. I suppose you'll try to get back at him, he said.

I don't know.

What?

If it's *possible,* I will. I won't endanger myself, though. That would be stupid.

Mm.

Tell me, do you think Wesley and Verda Thornton are cheating me?

Cheating you?

Yes. I understand they bought the old Peters place from Jim Otis. Where did they get the money?

Dick Harris spread his hands. Maybe you have a point, he said.

How come Mort Hightower didn't try to get me out of jail?

He did.

Oh?

Yes, said Dick Harris. Soon as he found out that you were in jail, he tried to get a *habeas corpus.* But he couldn't. The *habeas corpus* has been suspended.

Oh, said Charley.

A wartime measure.

Yes. I *know.*

Mort is in a most difficult position. He is trying to keep himself as inconspicuous as possible. He is a Democrat. The assassination has made the Democrats, ah, unpopular.

Charley grinned. Yes, he said, I know *that* too.

Well, he *did* come to *me.*

Oh?

Yes. I didn't even know you were back. He came to me and he told me Ben Stork was in the process of beating you to death. He told me he was unable to talk Ben into letting you out. He asked me to help him. So I paid a call on Ben Stork. I'm afraid we had . . . well, an argument.

Yes. I sort of vaguely remember the two of you having a shouting match. Well, don't think I'm not grateful.

Forget that. All I'm trying to say is that you shouldn't hold Mort Hightower to blame for anything.

All right, said Charley. I won't.

Good.

Could you send somebody to fetch him up here?

Yes.

I have some business to discuss with him.

All right.

I appreciate it.

No trouble.

Could I ask you a couple of sort of *close* questions?

Close questions? said Dick Harris, frowning.

It's the best word I can think of. I suppose what I mean is *important* questions.

Well, I'll try to answer them. I cannot guarantee how competent my answers will be.

Said Charley: I kind of think they'll be competent as hell. I kind of think you're a good sight more of a man than I ever gave you credit. Now then. Close question number one—do you think I have much of a future around here?

Dick Harris hesitated before answering. He ran his tongue over his lower teeth, then said: Yes.

Really?

But not right now.

Ah, said Charley.

For now, I would have to say no. Passions are quite a bit too high. I am certain too many people remember your, uh, *zealous* espousal of the Democratic party.

Yes. I expect so.

There is a violence in this town. I feel it.

Charley grinned. So do I, he said. I feel it all over.

Dick Harris chuckled. Well, he said, at least you have a sense of humor about it all.

A man has to. Now then. Close question number two—should I get rid of the Thorntons?

Of course. If they've cheated you.

Close question number three—have they made many friends here in the time I've been away?

Yes. They appear to be very efficient. And they work hard. And I have a feeling they have been undermining you every chance they've had.

Oh? That so?

Yes. In their quiet way, they are good talkers. They've let it be known that they've saved the business.

Saved the business?

Yes. They've told people you were an extremely poor businessman. They insist they've saved the store from bankruptcy.

That's not so. I did all right. There always was a profit. God damn them.

I do not doubt you. But remember, most of the people in this town, even the ones who supported you back when you canvassed for the legislature, most of them *now* want to believe the worst of you. And, in the final measure of things, people believe only what they *want* to believe. Which means only bad things about those they consider bad.

Yes, said Charley. That's the world for you.

You take a bleak view.

I take a *true* view. Didn't you just finish saying that people are perfectly willing to embrace lies if the lies suit their purposes? Now that's what I call a bleak view, don't you?

Yes.

But it's true, isn't it?

Yes.

All *right* then.

Dick Harris shook his head. He said: But man is capable of attaining great moments of nobility. His goodness prevails; he fulfills his obligations to God.

Mr Harris, you've been very good to me. And I thank you kindly for getting me out of jail, but I got to tell you your philosophy is shit.

Oh?

Nobility made it so you got to walk with crutches. Nobility killed George. Nobility is the worst shit there is. I was in Washington more than two years, Mr Harris. I've seen the divisions come marching back from the war, and there's no nobility to them, and *you* know *that*. Those men don't think about God. They are *dirty,* and they are *tired,* and all they want to do is find whisky and whores. Maybe there was nobility at the beginning. Maybe there even was some in '62 at Fredericksburg when George was killed and you got your face and legs hurt so badly, but '62 was a long time ago. Believe me, all the nobility is gone now. People don't even know the meaning of the word. Look at the way they talk about Grant. They call him a hero. Huh. Some hero. U. S. Grant is no more a hero than I'm a hero. He knows better. When he took over the running of the war, nobility was the first thing that went by the boards. This war was a new kind of war, a grinding war, and Grant understood it. He didn't fight the enemy; he chewed the enemy. Bravery gave way to simple endurance. From now on, all wars will be decided by one consideration

—which side can endure the longest. Nobility will be, uh, superfluous. Go on. Believe in nobility until the day you die. A lot of other people will do the same thing. But all you and the rest of them will be believing in is *words*. Read the papers. *Really* read them. You'll *see* how U. S. Grant won this war. It was all squeeze, squeeze, crush, strangle. It was all about as noble as mud. I mean that.

Dick Harris shrugged. All right, Charley, he said, whatever you say. You don't believe me?

No. I don't.

Charley sighed, spread his hands. He rubbed his mouth.

Dick Harris stared at Charley with an expression Charley supposed was meant to indicate a sweet loving forbearance. It was concentrated in Dick Harris' eyes and the corners of his mouth. It was wise, warm, almost amused.

Charley looked away.

Dick Harris settled back in his chair and was silent.

Charley closed his eyes. Had he been a violent sort of person, he might have tried to smack old Dick Harris right across the poor old fool's ruined face. Whenever Charley spoke of the stupidity of noble postures, why was it the Dick Harrises of this world regarded him with such sweet tolerance? Why did they treat him as though he were an adored child of imperfect mentality? Why did they refuse to accept the direction the world was heading? Why couldn't they recognize the hard truth of their obsolescence? Oh, they thought they were so goddamn wise; they thought they had access to some golden secret. Well, their secret was a lie. God damn them and their lie of a secret. God damn them and their blindness. They buried their mortality in flatulent concepts of nobility and Deeds, and they were as stupid as the ocean was deep. Why was he forever encountering such people? And why, for the God's sake, *why did they inflict on him such pain?*

That afternoon Morton C. Hightower came to see Charley. Morton C. Hightower's palsy was more severe, but otherwise he appeared not to have changed at all. Charley told him to put up the house and the store for sale.

What about the Thorntons? said Morton C. Hightower. He seated himself next to the bed. He pressed his hands against his thighs. This eased the trembling. He said: Are you taking legal action against them?

No. Never mind them. I'm leaving this town. You know what would happen if I brought the sainted Wesley and Verda into court—*me*, the filthy Copperhead. I'd probably be lynched.

Morton C. Hightower nodded. Yes, he said. Considering the temper of the times, you're probably being very wise. I have lived here all my life, and I have always tried to conduct myself as a patriotic citizen, and yet I know there must be those here who believe I was involved in the monstrous cabal that took the President's life.

Well, you are a Democrat. All Democrats are suspect these days.

Yes. Exactly.

And that's why I want to leave town as soon as I can.

Morton C. Hightower made a dry smacking sound with his tongue and palate and lips. Fine, he said. I'll get after the matter right away. Here, grunting a little, Morton C. Hightower stood up. His hands danced. He cleared his throat.

Thank you for coming, said Charley. And thank you for getting in touch with Dick Harris.

I know what you're thinking.

How's that?

Morton C. Hightower adjusted his spectacles. Then he said: You're wondering if I'll ever die. Well, ah, so am I. I must say, death has been on my mind a great deal lately.

Mine too, the past few days.

Morton C. Hightower did not appear to have heard what Charley had said. He looked at the floor. He pressed his hands against his thighs. He said: I am eightytwo years of age, did you know that?

Well, I knew it was around that.

I have served in the Congress of the United States. Henry Clay was a friend of mine. Can you imagine? *Henry Clay.*

Ah. Henry Clay. It must have been an enriching experience.

May I say some things?

Go ahead.

I feel as though at least some of them need saying.

Go ahead.

Morton C. Hightower drew a deep breath. He squeezed his thighs. He said: I . . . uh, this may astonish you, but for a number of years I have thought of you as a son.

Oh?

Yes. You interest me. There is something very strong within you.

Charley smiled. Well, he said, don't stop.

I had a son once.

Oh? I didn't know you'd ever married.

I never did.

Mm, said Charley. Well, you old rascal you.

He was a fine boy. He died almost twenty years ago. Malaria. In Mexico it was. He was a lieutenant of artillery. Personal friend of T. J. Jackson. His mother was the wife of a passport clerk in the Department of State.

The name was an ugly one—Burpee. The boy never knew I was his father. His name was Kenneth William Burpee, and he was twentyone years old when he was taken out of this life, and he didn't even particularly *like* me. I was a friend of the family, you understand.

Yes, said Charley. A friend of the family.

Morton C. Hightower sat down. He still was squeezing his thighs. He said: Kenneth leaned toward the Whigs. He wrote verse. He was, everyone acknowledged, something of a talented boy. Had my nose, my facial bone structure. It's a wonder to me Ted Burpee never suspected anything. Why am I telling you all this?

Charley shrugged. I don't have the slightest idea, he said.

I have never told a soul, said Morton C. Hightower, frowning.

Well, you don't have to tell *me* if you don't want to.

But I *want* to.

All right then.

There truly is something about you. I do not believe I approve of whatever it is, but it surely is very strong, and I expect there's more than a good chance that you'll abuse it. If I had to define it, I suppose I would call it an ability to *induce the exposure of unpleasant truths.* Not that you *do* anything or *say* anything to bring about the exposure. On the contrary. I have a feeling that unpleasant truths are *thrust* upon you. Could I be correct?

Charley thought for a moment. He summoned to his mind the Professor's dying confession of a reluctant innocence in the matter of the death of the Rev Mr Weeks. He recalled the time his employer, Congressman Lansing H. Ingraham, had spoken so feelingly of the inadequacies of his six homely daughters. Finally he said: Perhaps you have a point.

You have a low opinion of the human race don't you?

Well . . .

And so the human race, being ever obliging, confesses its sins to you.

That sounds mighty cynical to me.

Morton C. Hightower cackled. Cynicism? he said. Are *you* accusing *me* of *cynicism?* Hah!

Yes, said Charley, grinning. I am.

Young man, I am a fraud. My cynicism is simply an exercise in rhetoric. *Yours,* however, is something far more profound. It comes from the heart. I admire you. Truly I do. Your life has definition. I see within you what I would have liked to be. Which is why I think of you as a son. All that strength. You are to be envied.

Well, thank you.

Lansing Ingraham has written to me about you.

That so?

He has never failed to deliver admiring comments on your corruption.

Corruption?

Now, now, no insult was intended. In your case, the corruption is your strength.

Oh? said Charley. He adjusted the covers.

Yes. In his letters, my friend wrote that you took to the filth of Washington as easily as a dog takes to a stump. According to him, you were discreet; you made no comments on the tasks that came your way (I do not believe I have to enumerate the nature of the tasks to which I refer); you cheerfully associated with criminals and prostitutes; you flourished in the greed and hypocrisy. In other words, you were a man of your time and place, and your conscience was as unvexed as an infant's brow. You will go far. Others have told you that, I am sure.

Charley nodded.

But, ah, have you ever thought of death?

Yes. Everybody thinks of death.

I have a theory about my own death.

Oh?

I don't believe I'll ever die.

That so?

Morton C. Hightower held out his hands. They danced. I shall never die, he said. I shall live on and on and on, always trembling, always feeble and foolish, nearsighted and impotent, hollow of bone and cheek, clerkish and despised, and never shall I even be permitted to *aspire* to death.

That's a lot of shit, said Charley. He fussed with the covers.

Shit? said Morton C. Hightower. Do you not believe in punishment? What about God? What about retribution?

That's all a lot of shit. Like I said. Shit.

Would you like never to die?

Yes.

Even if living is a far worse punishment?

Living is no punishment. Not if a man is strong enough. There is nothing a strong man cannot endure.

Morton C. Hightower pressed his hands against his thighs.

Charley sighed. Just put up the house and the store for sale for me, he said. Don't bother me with your goddamn concepts of life and death.

Morton C. Hightower nodded.

Charley's hands were cold. He rubbed them together. Soon as I'm able, he said, I'm leaving this town. I'll write and let you know where to send the money.

All right.

You can go now.

Again Morton C. Hightower nodded. He stood up. He did not offer to shake hands. He smiled. Good luck to you, he said.

Thank you, said Charley. You can go now.

A dry sound came from Morton C. Hightower's nose. He lurched out of the room.

Charley sighed. He gathered the covers more closely around his chest and neck. His tongue sought out the hollow places where the butt of Ben Stork's pistol had knocked out teeth. He closed his eyes and thought of naked whores. They danced for him. They fondled him. They sang hymns for him. He grunted. He grimaced. He ached.

The Lincoln funeral train crossed Indiana the following Thursday evening. All the depots along the way were draped in black. The train did not pass through Titusville, but the night was observed there nonetheless. It was a grand celebration, and hundreds of persons turned out to participate, and they tarred and feathered Charley Wells with joy and zeal, and he was not surprised, and he was not even particularly angry. The tarring and the feathering had been a most distinct *possibility* all along, and Charley understood *possibility* better than he understood anything, so how *could* he really have been angry? Anger would have been illogical.

Morton C. Hightower had no trouble disposing of Charley's home and store. Both, together with their contents, were sold to the Titus County National Bank for twelve thousand dollars. The deal was closed on Monday, the twentyfourth. Charley had Morton C. Hightower bring him five hundred dollars in cash. The rest would be held for him at the bank.

Where will you be going? Morton C. Hightower asked.

Charley lay on a sofa in the Harris front parlor. He smiled. To Evansville first, he said. There's a woman there.

The Quimby girl?

Correct. Now that her husband is dead, perhaps she would . . . ah, wellnow, I'm sure you understand.

Oh yes.

And I'm going to look around. I want to get into some sort of business. *What* sort?

I don't know. Whatever appeals to me. Whatever promises a good return on the money I have to invest. Evansville seems as good a place as any for a beginning.

A beginning?

Yes. Of whatever it is that awaits me.

Mm.

Tell me, do you think the Thorntons will try to buy the store from the bank?

It wouldn't surprise me.

I like that, said Charley. It will mean that everything has worked out logically for them. They're very logical, those two. First they undermine me; then, after stealing from me, they buy my store. Very clean and neat. People after my own heart.

Ah . . .

Now, now, don't look at me like that, Mr Hightower. Remember, I am a genuine cynic. You said so yourself.

Yes. I did.

Wellnow, let *me* tell *you* something. You're absolutely correct. A few years ago, though, back when I was canvassing for the legislature, you wouldn't of been. You see, I never meant anyone in this town any harm. I was a peace sneak, people said, but by God I was an *honest* peace sneak. The things I said, I *meant* them. Well, fuck all that. From now on, Charley Wells doesn't worry himself about beliefs. From now on, all that matters is the good his words will do *him,* Charley Wells. God as my Witness, Mr Hightower, I tried to do what I thought was right. But now fuck it. I am tired of the damn abuse. I am leaving this town. They call me a traitor here. They beat on me. They knock out my teeth. Well, fuck them all. Do you follow what I am saying?

Yes.

Thank you kindly.

The tarring and the feathering were in no way spontaneous. The large mouth of Mrs Dick Harris gave Charley's enemies plenty of time to make their plans. She was a nice kindly woman, this Mrs Dick Harris, but her mental apparatus was about as substantial and inspiring as a leaky nose. The morning of Wednesday, April 26, Charley told the Harrises he would be leaving for Evansville the next day. My aches and pains are coming along right pert, he said. Give me one more day and I'll be out of your hair. The Harrises both protested. You're not *well* yet, said Mrs Dick Harris. You should stay here at least another *week.* Charley shook his head no. Smiling, he told the Harrises he was perfectly able to travel. He thanked them for their kind attentions, but pointed out to them that it was best he leave Titusville as soon as possible. There's no future for me here, he said, not for *now* at least. Maybe later I'll come back. In the meantime, though, it's best I get started as soon as I can on whatever line of work I find. The Harrises finally gave up trying to argue with him. That afternoon Mrs Dick Harris went to Hooper's Dry Goods Store to buy some material for a nightcap she wanted to make for her husband. Neither Dick Harris nor Charley had the presence of mind to tell her to keep her mouth shut. In order to avoid any possibility of trouble, Charley wanted to slip out of town as inconspicuously as possible. He would take the 7 o'clock evening train for Evansville. It arrived there at 11. It was a slow train, and not many people rode it. As far as Charley was concerned, it was thus a very safe train. There was little chance that Ben Stork would see him. He had no desire to encounter the sheriff again. For all he knew, the sheriff might get it in his head to jail Charley once more and go to work dislodging the rest of Charley's teeth. Charley's surviving teeth had become very precious to Charley. As had Charley's skin. But, unfortunately for him, Mrs Dick Harris did not keep her mouth shut—and, even more unfortunately for him, the fact of her loose mouth did not reveal itself in time for him to save himself from the tar and the feathers. Half an hour before train time, he was bundled into the Harrises' carriage. Next came Dick Harris, crutches and all, assisted by his wife. Finally Mrs Dick Harris clambered aboard, and she was gasping. Twilight was spread loosely, hanging in streaks and tatters, and there was a threat of rain. Dick Harris clucked at the horse, and the carriage started down Titus Avenue toward the StL&NE depot. At the corner of Titus Avenue and Kentucky Street, people began materializing. Strange, said Dick Harris. Street's kind of full for a week night. Charley nodded. He dug his teeth into his upper lip. Turning to Mrs Dick Harris, he said: You, ah, did you say anything about my leaving to anyone? Mrs Dick Harris stared at him. She opened her mouth, closed it, opened it again, then said: *Say* anything? Again Charley nodded. Answer him, Dick Harris told his wife. Quickly Mrs Dick Harris said: Ah, well, I did happen to mention it to Mr Hooper. Said Dick Harris: Was anyone else there? Said Mrs Dick Harris: No. Not a soul. Dick Harris smiled at Charley and said: Well, I don't guess we have much to worry about. Ted Hooper wouldn't tell you the time of day if you offered him a hundred dollars for the information. Last time he put ten words together all at once I understand his wife fainted dead away. Mrs Harris spoke up. Richard? she said. Yes? said Dick Harris. Uh, I did stop at this young man's store, his *old* store I mean, said Mrs Dick Harris. Her words came quick and timid, and they made Charley sit up straight and blink. You talk to the *Thorntons* about it? said Dick Harris. Yes, said Mrs Dick Harris, nodding. Charley drew a deep breath. Dick Harris pulled back on the reins. He looked at Charley and said: Maybe they're planning to jump you at the depot. We'd better drive over to Clapham Junction. Charley nodded. Yes, he said, that's a good idea. Dick Harris flapped the reins. The horse moved forward. Charley's chest hurt, and his cheeks were warm. He looked around. People were walking alongside the carriage. They were looking up at him. He looked back. People were walking behind the carriage. For some reason, he looked down at his feet. He looked at his suitcase. He hoped its contents would not be destroyed. He'd not been able to visit his old home, the house on the hill, the house with the grand view that extended twenty miles clear across the Ohio River and beyond, but he *had* sent the Harrises' handyman, old Harvey Ewald (the drunken neerdowell who four years earlier had found the strangled body of the Rev Mr Weeks), he had sent old Harvey over there with a key and instructions to fetch certain private papers and photographs. The private papers and photographs were packed away in the suitcase. Memorabilia. God damn. Here, at a time like this, he was worrying about *memorabilia.* Charley shook his head. The furniture, the silver, everything else in the house, now was the property of the Titus County National Bank, and he did not give a damn. *Memorabilia.* No sir, no memorabilia for Charles Palmer Wells. He who traveled light traveled fastest. Memorabilia equaled clutter, and clutter equaled sentiment, and sentiment equaled foolishness. Hell with it. The thing to do was make the amputation clean. Yes. Clean and therefore pure. That way, perhaps nothing would fester. He nudged Dick Harris. Those people who were standing back at Kentucky Street, he said, they're following us. Dick Harris nodded. Now the carriage was passing in front of Charley's old store. His attackers came running. Mrs Dick Harris gave a little shriek. Her husband laid the reins to the horse's back. The horse whinnied, lurched. A hand came up and wrested the reins from Dick Harris. *Give me those reins!* shouted Dick Harris. Someone laughed. Charley squeezed his eyes tightly shut. The horse made a sound that was like a bleat. *Come down out of there, you sonofabitch!* someone hollered. Charley recognized the voice, but he could not place the name. Hunching his shoulders, he bent forward. A hand seized one of his legs. He kicked. *God damn you!* shouted the same voice. Then another hand began to pull Charley's britches. Mrs Dick Harris screamed. Charley heard a sort of whirring noise, and he supposed it meant Dick Harris was wielding a crutch. Hands seized the carriage, began to rock it from side to side. The horse shrieked. Jesus Jesus Jesus, said Charley, not loudly. He opened his eyes. Blind Ezra Ordway was the first person he saw. Blind Ezra Ordway was one of those who was rocking the carriage. Blind Ezra Ordway was grinning, and his eyes were white and pink. He didn't have as many teeth as Charley had remembered. Now perhaps fifty persons were rocking the carriage and trying to pull Charley down from it. Blind Ezra's father, Jim Ordway, held the reins. Charley shuddered. Hands grabbed at him. A sound came from the crowd, but it was not a shout; rather, it was a sort of jubilant moan. It put Charley sort of half in mind of whores in heat. Dick Harris smote someone's head with a crutch. Mrs Dick Harris wept. Her lips were drawn back, and her chin was tucked against her chest. Charley's britches ripped. Someone laughed. Verda Thornton stood at the entrance to the store. She rocked from side to side in rhythm with the rocking carriage. From time to time she beat her palms together like a child about to receive a piece of chocolate. Charley fought. He thrashed. He kicked. But the hands that were tugging at him were too strong. He came out of the carriage. He came flying. In his descent, he bounced off several bodies. Someone kicked him across the neck. Someone else kicked his rump. A leg of his britches was torn off. He rolled over. He lay in mud. There had been rain that morning. It had been a good rain, a fine fragrant springtime rain. He saw nothing. A pointed toe slammed into his testicles. He screamed. A woman laughed. Then a man began hollering: *Hey, Charley! Your friend Booth is dead! We got the good news this afternoon on the wire! He got himself shot all to hell last night in a barn down there in your beloved Dixie! Too bad ain't it?* Charley got to his hands and knees. His mouth was bleeding. The pain from his bruised testicles had spread across his belly in an immense crimson smear. He opened his eyes. He saw feet. Someone kicked mud into his eyes. He blinked. The mud ran down his face. Someone kicked him across the side of the head. Moaning, he fell back. Then came laughter. Then a sound of feet. Then a shrill voice, and it pierced the laughter and the sound of feet. It was the voice of Dick Harris, and Charley couldn't quite make out the words. Someone seized Charley by his coatcollar and pulled him to his feet. He groaned. He cupped his hands over his testicles. A fist smacked into his belly. He coughed. A small bony hand tried to pry his hands away from his testicles. It was Verda Thornton's small bony hand. She laughed. She wept. Wesley Thornton stood behind her. His hands were on his hips. He'd always had watery eyes, but now for some reason they were dry. His kick was swift, but it struck Charley in the thigh instead of the genitals. Nonetheless, Charley screamed. He fell down, writhed. It had been very wise of him to scream. That way, perhaps Wesley Thornton would be satisfied. That way, perhaps he would not try again. A second attempt probably would have been a great deal more accurate. So Charley screamed and writhed. Charley was a very smart fellow. Dick Harris came staggering. Behind him, the carriage stood ignored. Mrs Dick Harris was bent forward, and she was weeping. She sat black and plump and quavering, and her eyes were lost behind her fists. Dick Harris' crutches slipped in the mud. He flailed, managed to keep his balance. Waving one of the crutches, he shoved aside several of those who were trying to get at Charley to kick him. *No! No!* shouted Dick Harris. A hand and arm came out of the crowd. It struck Dick Harris across the chest. He lurched backward. He would have fallen, but someone grabbed him by an elbow and held him upright. Jim Ordway came running. He bent over Charley and pulled him to his feet. Dick Harris was dragged away. Jim Ordway's breath was all whisky. He thrust his face close to Charley's and for a moment

Charley thought Jim Ordway was about to kiss him. As it was, Jim Ordway's breath made Charley flinch. *Sonofabitch!* hollered Jim Ordway.
Copperhead bastard! (The train, the funeral train . . . tonight the
train was beating slow and mournful across Indiana, past the depots
and their grieving crepe, past the silent witnesses to what had now become
an officially certified and acknowledged martyrdom, past throatclearing
men and weeping women and children who chewed on their knuckles,
and all eyes damply proclaimed the outrage. Charley could see the train.
It was tens and scores of miles away, but he could see it as clearly as he
could see the hatred of Jim Ordway and blind Ezra Ordway and the
Thorntons and all the rest of his tormentors; he could see it and he could
hear it, and nothing that was happening to him was really too much of a
surprise. After all, what sort of tragedy was it that had no villain?) Jim
Ordway bumped his belly against Charley's, and Charley staggered back.
Oh you surely did have me going! shouted Jim Ordway. *You surely had
me doing your Copperhead dirty work didn't you? I was a genuine convert wasn't I? Well, God forgive me!* Then, turning, Jim Ordway seized
his blind son Ezra by the neck. He pushed Ezra's face directly in front of
Charley's. Ezra's eyes actually were scarred. *This here boy is blind!*
shouted Jim Ordway. *He is blind and you and your goddamn Copperhead friends are just as much to blame as any reb ever fired a gun! God
forgive me for being such a nincompoop as to of voted for you, you dirty
shit you!* Charley blinked into the white and pink eyes of Ezra Ordway.
A deep sound came from Ezra Ordway's throat. Then he spat. The spittle
came in a gob; it struck Charley's nose. It ran, dripping down onto Charley's lips. Grimacing, Charley wiped it away. I hope you die, said blind
Ezra Ordway. I hope you die real slow. I hope, before you die, someone
rips out your goddamn eyeballs. I hope you puke and shit from the hurt
of it. Out came one of blind Ezra Ordway's hands. It collided with Charley's chest. Charley shuddered. Ezra Ordway's breath was foul. Charley
backed up until he was pressed against the front of his old store. Men and
women and even children crowded around him in a semicircle. The
President's being took across this here state tonight, said a voice, and you
killed him, you Copperhead filth, you killed him sure as if you'd pulled
the trigger. Charley's head moved from side to side. He recognized the
voice but could not place its owner. He looked down at his tattered
britches. He brought his hands together, lacing the fingers. No, he said, I
had nothing to do with it. Don't kill me. I ask you that. You shouldn't kill
me. Wouldn't be right. Please don't kill me. Charley held his laced hands
in front of himself. He squeezed them until they were beyond pink. His
legs were cold. No, he said. Please. No. Godalmighty. Someone tittered.
Hands reached out, tugged at his coat and shirt. He wriggled from side to

side. His coat was torn off his back. His shirt was torn off his back. More tittering. He squeezed his latticed fingers. A burly man came to him and spat in his face. Charley recognized this burly man. It was Fred Carson, the fellow who had married the Widow Bumpus. Charley supposed Fred Carson had waited a long time for this. Then Charley saw Nehemiah Ford and John Griswold, the two farmers who had helped him and Rufus Quimby drink all that cider back nearly five years ago when Charley had first canvassed for the legislature. It had been the Fourth of July, and Charley was to have debated Frank Sturdevant, otherwise known as God. But he never did. It had been a fine day, and the four of them had been assisted in their cider debauch by a couple of riverboat men named Carleton and Stringfellow, and it had been the sort of day a man looked back on with a grin. And now Nehemiah Ford and John Griswold were standing here with his tormentors. As was Fred Carson. And Fred Carson was grinning. And Fred Carson's spittle ran cool and slick down one of Charley's cheeks. And Fred Carson's mouth hung open. And Fred Carson's tongue played with his teeth. Charley's coat and shirt were tossed high in the air. They sailed out into the street, plopped down in a great lake of mud. The store's front door was opened. Wesley Thornton emerged. He carried a large bucket. It steamed. Verda Thornton followed her husband. She carried what appeared to be brushes. She said something to Nehemiah Ford and John Griswold. Sniggering, they scuttled inside the store. They returned a moment or so later. They carried large gunnysacks. Shouts came up. People yelled at Verda Thornton to give them brushes. She giggled. Excuse me please, she said to blind Ezra Ordway, pushing him back from Charley. She stared straight into Charley's eyes. My, she said, aren't you something. Aren't you just *it*. She turned, motioned to her husband. Toting the steaming bucket, Wesley Thornton moved to her side. Charley recognized the bucket's hot odor. He cringed. He licked his lips. No, he said, my God please no, please. His chest and arms were cold. His torn britches flapped. Fred Carson seized one of his arms. Nehemiah Ford seized the other. Charley squealed, wept. Verda Thornton dipped a brush into the bucket. Then, almost moaning, she spread warm tar across Charley's cheeks, his chin, his forehead, his lips. The crowd made a soughing sound. Tar got into Charley's eyes. He blinked. His tears made the pain worse. *Hah!* shouted Verda Thornton. *Look at the nigger!* She pressed her face close to Charley's. Her breath came laced in snot and phlegm. She turned, tossed brushes to the crowd. Laughing, John Griswold opened one of the gunnysacks and came up with a handful of feathers. He pelted Charley with them. It occurred to Charley that perhaps these people did not want to kill him. Perhaps they only sought to humiliate him. He smiled. *Look at him!*

a man shouted. *He's smiling!* Fingers grabbed Charley's lips. He squealed, tried to bite. He shouldn't have smiled. He was stupid. He had no business smiling. His world was being torn up and carried away, and there he was *smiling.* Fred Carson and Nehemiah Ford twisted Charley's arms. Charley bleated, opening wide his mouth. He tasted knuckles. Then he tasted warm wet brushes. His mouth was held open by the lips. He gagged, swallowed tar. He coughed, sputtered, vomited. Several persons were splattered. They punched him in the belly. Brushes were slapped against his chest and arms and back and belly. They tickled his armpits. Spitting bile, he giggled. Feathers were stuffed into his mouth. *Hey, Charley!* hollered Nehemiah Ford. *You remember when you hung them election signs over the door to this place? You remember how someone came along and turned them upsidedown? Well, it was me and old John Griswold here done it! What do you think of that huh you goddamn traitor! The only thing was—we was dumb! We ought to of hung YOU upsidedown!* Charley drooled, shuddered. His tormentors held up his head, smeared it with more hot tar. He saw nothing. He groaned, gagged. Then he heard the voice of Dick Harris: *No! No! You must not do this! He was sincere!* Then the voice of Jim Ordway: *You stay out of this! Go away!* Then a scuffling sound. Charley blinked, and his tears washed away some of the tar from his eyes. He saw two men move toward Dick Harris. He wanted to speak. He wanted to tell Dick Harris to give up. Talk wasn't about to do any good. Dick Harris swung at the two men with a crutch. It struck one man across the side of the head. The man bellowed, fell down. The crowd turned to watch. Dick Harris lost his balance. He crumpled. He lay in the middle of the street, and he lay in mud. His wife screamed from the carriage. Children yipped and danced. A woman laughed. Someone hit Charley across the adamsapple. Mrs Dick Harris came down out of the carriage. She went to her husband and sat down in the mud next to him and cradled his head in her lap. Someone slapped at Charley's ears with a hot brush. Feathers were inserted in his ears, his nostrils. He sneezed. Jim Ordway and a man named Hippler tied his hands behind his back. Now his vision again was gone. He tried to move his eyelids against it. He felt his eyelashes tear. The tar was gummy now. His mouth hung open. He spat tar. But each time he spat tar someone inserted another brushful in his mouth. He wailed. Someone tripped him. When he fell, he skinned his elbows. *Hit the sonofabitch!* someone hollered. *Hit him good! KILL HIM, BY GOD! KILL THE TRAITOR!* Charley recognized the voice. It belonged to Wesley Thornton. It was all tin and sticks and lunacy. Charley was kicked. He was pulled to his feet. He was knocked down again. He was kicked some more. He twitched and gurgled. He was pulled to his feet again. A voice spoke into his ear. It was Jim

Ordway's voice, and it was like Verda Thornton's voice had been—full of snot and phlegm. But it was calm, and it said: *Don't fret none, Charley. We ain't studying on killing you. We ain't going to dirty ourselves. We just aim to run you out. That ought to do her. I don't expect we'll ever be bothered with you no more. That's all we want . . . to get shut of you for once and for all. Huh. You ought to see yourself. You ain't even something a hog'd brag on. I mean, I seen things come out of a hog's asshole look better than you do. Like, for one of them things, hog SHIT. I mean, you are the sorriestlooking traitor bastard I ever seen or hope to see, and by God I expect maybe along about now you're thinking Booth was the one got off lucky. Right, Charley? Ah, good old Charley. Charley the hog turd.* Charley could feel Jim Ordway's beard against the side of his neck. Charley had to piss. He went ahead and wet himself. He didn't see where it made much difference. The stink of the tar was more than thick enough to cover the stink of his piss. He blinked. His sight was returning. Jim Ordway resumed: *I expect it's about time we seen how fast you can run.* Now Jim Ordway's words were louder, and the crowd was reacting to them with laughter and hoots. *Charley,* said Jim Ordway, *I got a broom here in my hands. Can you see it?* Charley shook his head no. He blinked, worked his cheeks; more tar drained from his eyes. Finally he was able to see the broom. He shook his head yes. *Ah,* said Jim Ordway, *good. You see, Charley old friend, I'm going to stick the handle of this here broom right up your ass. When I do that, I want you to skedaddle.* Laughter from the crowd, and then Jim Ordway moved around behind Charley and jabbed him with the handle of the broom. Charley gurgled, jumped straight up. More and louder laughter. Again Jim Ordway jabbed. Again Charley jumped. *Run, Charley!* hollered Jim Ordway. *Run sheepy run!* Charley began to run. Tears washed more tar from his eyes. He staggered. He fell. His hands still were tied behind his back. He saw Dick Harris, who still lay in the mud, head cradled in the lap of Mrs Harris. He crawled toward Dick Harris. A woman stepped in front of Charley. She lifted her skirts, danced a jig. She spat at him. Then she kicked him. A little boy pushed Charley flat on his face. He ate mud. Then he felt a jab, probably from Jim Ordway's broom handle. He got to his feet. Mud and tar dripped from his chin. He ran. He ran straight past the Harrises. He ran gurgling. He spat feathers. The crowd chased him. He was hit with switches and rocks. He spat more feathers. He blew feathers out his nose. *Run! Run! Run!* someone hollered. *Get out and don't never come back!* His chest was bleeding. So were his hands. So were his elbows and knees. He ran down the middle of Titus Avenue. He skidded in the mud. His pursuers laughed and whooped. A rock struck the back of his head. He wriggled his wrists. The rope that bound his hands was coming loose. Sheriff Ben Stork stood leaning against a storefront at the corner of Titus Avenue and Kentucky Street. He had out a large knife. He was cutting himself a chew of tobacco. He grinned at Charley, tipped his hat. Morton C. Hightower stood next to the sheriff. Morton C. Hightower's hands danced. He called out something. Charley could not make out the words. Charley ran. Charley ran and ran. He was jabbed, punched, prodded, kicked. He ran straight out of town. He ran until his breath was heavier than the end of the world. He spat. He sneezed. He tugged at the rope that bound his hands. Feathers swirled. Skin hung away from one of his elbows in a sort of flap, like old wallpaper. Finally he managed to work his hands free. Then he ran flailing. He ran beyond fright. He fell. He scraped his chin. Birds squawked at him. There was moonlight now, but it was reluctant, perfunctory. The tar cooled; it tightened his skin, split it. Charley ran. He ran and ran. He outran his tormentors. Finally, far beyond the town limits, they turned back. They laughed, yelled, shook their fists. Charley kept running. The road was thin and cold; his feet slapped; his arms churned; he ran and he ran and he ran; he ran until he was beyond breath, and then he was in a woods, and the sounds of the woods had nothing to do with human beings, and so he dropped to his knees, and the tar still was black in his mouth, and the feathers still made him sneeze, and it was then that he thanked God for permitting him entrance to his largest lesson. Beyond this lesson there was no lesson. The name of the lesson was humiliation. And beyond this humiliation there was no humiliation. He rolled on his back. Twigs cut and scraped his skin. He felt himself. Apparently he still was all of a piece. He grinned. He coughed; his legs shot out in weak spasms. He had been defeated, but by no means had he been destroyed. This was something they all were too stupid to understand. Charley grinned, giggled. Wild things scurried. They made dry sounds. Charley pulled feathers from his ears. He pulled feathers off his chest and arms. Each feather took skin with it. He winced, grimaced. The raw places were hot. When the footsteps finally came, he did not care. What else could be done to him? The footsteps were heavy. Voices called softly. Two voices. Female. Charley frowned. He thought he recognized the voices. He could not believe he was hearing right. He hugged his chest. He waited for the two women to find him. And they did. Miss Marie Killpack was just as plump and blond as he had remembered her. The Widow Bumpus (now Mrs Fred Carson) was a good deal heavier.

It was Miss Marie who found him. She nearly tripped over him. *Well,* she said, my *stars.*

Charley groaned.

Miss Marie squatted next to him. *Harriet!* she called. I *found* him! Over here!

Be right there! shouted a voice. A moment later, the Widow Bumpus came crashing through the brush. She knelt next to Charley and said: Oh dear God, Charley, are you all right?

Just fine, said Charley. Hunkydory.

Miss Marie looked at the Widow Bumpus and said: He's just as sassy as ever, I expect.

Mm, said the Widow Bumpus.

Again Charley groaned.

You feel anything broken? Miss Marie asked him.

No . . .

Good, said Miss Marie. I'm going to go fetch the coal oil. I'll be right back. The can's in the wagon.

Coal . . . oil?

Yes. We have to get the tar off of you, don't we?

With . . . coal oil?

Can you think of something better?

No . . .

All *right* then, said Miss Marie. She stood up. She moved off back toward the road. Her footsteps were brisk.

Ah, said the Widow Bumpus, my poor Charley . . .

Charley shuddered, twitched.

The Widow Bumpus stroked his face. Close as Charley could remember, she was a good fortyfive now. The reluctant moonlight showed her skin as being gray, doughy. She wore a housedress and a shawl. Her belly protruded, and her bosoms drooped. Great God: age. She had been such a wondrous carnal marvel, and now look at her. Marriage to Fred Carson had evidently drained the last of the starch out of her.

Again Charley shuddered. He closed his eyes.

Miss Marie returned. She carried some rags and a lantern as well as the can of coal oil. She lighted the lantern.

Charley opened his eyes. He blinked.

Well, said Miss Marie to the Widow Bumpus, we might as well be about our business.

The Widow Bumpus nodded, took a rag from Miss Marie.

The women soaked their rags, went to work. The coal oil stung. Charley gasped. The women rubbed briskly.

Sooner we get it off, said Miss Marie, the better you'll feel.

Charley nodded.

The lantern spat. Tar came off Charley in cakes.

We surely are sorry about all this, said Miss Marie, rubbing.

Sure, said Charley.

It was Harriet's idea, said Miss Marie.

Charley smiled at the Widow Bumpus, and damn if the Widow Bumpus didn't just about blush.

Harriet came to my house, said Miss Marie. I was lying on the settee. I was bawling. I was *that* ashamed. She came up in Fred Carson's wagon and she said she thought we'd be able to find you. She told me she maybe would need help in case you had to be carried. She is a good woman, Charley.

You . . . you both are.

Thank you kindly.

I argued with Fred, said the Widow Bumpus—Mrs Carson, rather. She rubbed the folds of Charley's neck. Her rag stank. Then she said: But Fred had to go and help out with it. Maybe you know why.

Charley nodded.

He's just a man, said Mrs Carson. I'm sorry he did it. I'm sorry he helped out. But I can understand why.

Yes . . . said Charley.

Miss Marie grunted. She was wearing a dark dress, a very proper dress for a teacher of piano, harp, organ and violin. I'm sorry about Verda, she said. She and that brotherinlaw of mine . . . I don't know what's happened to them. Ever since you left town, they've done nothing but undermine you.

Charley nodded.

I didn't have a thing to do with it, said Miss Marie. Didn't even know about it until it was too late. I swear that's the truth.

I . . . ah, I believe you . . .

They don't live with me any more. They bought the old Peters place.

Yes . . .

I don't understand them any more.

Harriet Carson spoke up. I think *I* do, she said.

Oh? said Miss Marie.

He helped them. He was generous. That made him a bigger person than they are. So they had to hate him.

Miss Marie rubbed Charley's ears. Well, she said, maybe you do have a point.

Harriet Carson leaned over Charley and rubbed his forehead. It all was planned, she told him. Wesley and Verda. Ben Stork. My husband. Jim Ordway. They got together in town last night. My husband told me he was going in for some harness. I didn't believe him. He told me to tend to my own knitting.

They all got together in the back room of the store, said Miss Marie.

Mrs Harris spoke when she shouldn't have. She told Wesley and Verda when you were leaving.

Yes, said Charley. I know.

She even told them the train.

Charley nodded.

I expect she's got brains like sand.

Charley smiled.

Ben Stork stayed out of it, but he was the one did the planning.

Mm, said Charley.

He had to stay out of it. As sheriff, I mean, he couldn't—

Yes, said Charley.

Miss Marie grunted. She rubbed. Harriet Carson plucked feathers from Charley's head. Hair came with the feathers. Charley winced. A little later, the women led him to a creek. The water's going to be cold, said Miss Marie. No matter, said Charley. He waded into the creek and bathed himself. The women helped him back to the road and the wagon. Harriet Carson had brought him fresh clothes. They were her husband's, and they were too large. She apologized. Charley told her to hush. He withdrew behind a clump of bushes, removed his torn britches and put on the fresh clothes. He transferred his billfold to his new trousers. His tormentors had not taken his billfold. He grinned. Some people surely were as stupid as death was long. He returned to the wagon. He asked the women if they would take him over to Clapham Junction so he could catch the early train for Evansville. They told him they would be happy to. The ride was silent. Charley sat in a sort of crouch. It was a good nine miles to Clapham Junction, and the trip—what with the darkness and all— took more than two hours. It was a trip punctuated by owls and the wind, a wind that pushed clouds in the path of the moonlight. Charley hugged his midsection. Harriet Carson drove the wagon. The horse was quite old. Its haunches were bony. Flies prowled.

Clapham Junction was nothing more than a depot and perhaps a dozen houses. It lay in a ravine about a mile or so back from the river. The wagon creaked, slid. All of the houses were dark. The wagon descended into the ravine. A few minutes later it had pulled up next to the depot. Harriet Carson sighed. The depot was dark. She and Miss Marie helped Charley down from the wagon. It can't be much past midnight, said Miss Marie. When does the first train come through? About six in the morning?

Far as I know, said Charley.

We can wait with you.

No. I thank you kindly, but I wouldn't want the sheriff out looking for you. I'll find a tree and curl up. I could use some sleep. Train'll wake me up, I expect.

Miss Marie nodded.

Charley turned to Harriet Carson and said: I thank you, Harriet.

Harriet Carson sighed. It's all right, she said. You're not such a bad sort of person.

Don't be too sure about that.

Harriet Carson made a sound that was perhaps a laugh. She and Miss Marie escorted Charley to a large old elm that stood perhaps a dozen yards from the darkened depot. Sighing, Charley sat down. Ahhh, he said, my *bones*. He smiled up at the women. I thank you both, he said. He fumbled for his billfold. He opened it, extracted two fifties. Here, he said, these are for you.

They drew back.

Charley! said Miss Marie.

No, said Harriet Carson.

Now look . . .

Put them away, said Harriet Carson.

Don't talk that way, said Charley. You got a right to them.

Put them away.

Charley blinked at the money. He shook his head.

Yes, Charley, said Miss Marie. You just put them away.

Charley shrugged. He slid the money back inside his billfold.

Harriet Carson spoke. Her voice was flat. Charley, she said, there is such a thing as affection.

Oh? Well, *I* know *that*.

Then act like you do.

All right.

I got affection for you. You were good to me.

Now, Harriet, you—

It's all right. Miss Marie here knows about it. Everybody in town knows about you and me. What you and me *were*, I mean. But that's not the point. The point is *affection*. I got affection for you. You helped me when I needed it. We sort of, ah, helped *each other*, correct?

Correct, said Charley.

You helped me over a bad time. And I helped you, well, *find out* some things. It was good, Charley. I'd be a hypocrite if I was to say it was anything else. I'll always remember it.

Well. Ah. Thank you.

And I get along pretty good with Fred Carson. And my girls got a good roof over their heads.

Fine. Glad to hear it.

You were decent about him, Charley. You could have made trouble.

Well, things end.

Yes, said Harriet Carson. Yes, Charley. They do. Like being young. I'm fat now. I thank you for letting me have my last chance.

Ahhh . . .

Which means I got affection for you. And I'm sorry Titusville treated you the way it did tonight. Wasn't fair.

Miss Marie spoke: Charley, we've been happy to help you. If you can, make allowances for those people tonight. It's politics, Charley. Politics and the war. Please try to make the allowances.

Surely, said Charley. Allowances.

By noon the following day, Charley was in Evansville. He had slept in the train. He did not take a room in a hotel. Instead, he bought a horse and saddle for twenty dollars, then asked for directions to the Ferris farm. All traces of the tar and the feathers were gone, but of course he ached considerably. Before setting out for the Ferris farm, he visited a doctor who treated his scraped elbow. What on earth happened to *you?* the doctor wanted to know. Charley grinned. A fight, he said. There was maybe a hundred of them and only one of me. The doctor clucked. After treating the elbow, the doctor spread a cool salve on the raw places on Charley's skin. I detect an odor of tar, said the doctor. You fall in some? Again Charley grinned. Never mind, he said. How much do I owe you?

Charley rode slowly. His belly and throat were hot, and from time to time the pain in his belly made him bend double. And, despite his sleep, first in the shade of the oak tree and then aboard the train, he was tired. To his bones. Nancy couldn't have been more surprised if the Great Lord Jehovah had knocked on her door. She had been scrubbing floors. Her hands were soapy. Her hair was up in a knot. She stood at the door, and she gasped, and her first words were: My Lord, you been in a fight?

Charley grinned. All the fighting was on one side, he said. Uh, you going to let me in?

Nancy shrugged, stood aside.

He entered the house.

Don't walk where the wet places are, said Nancy.

Yes ma'm.

She led him into the kitchen. She asked him would he care for some coffee. He said he surely would be obliged. She was older. No doubt about it. But then who in Creation wasn't? She worked silently. Charley wondered what he should say. Finally he said something about the damp spring weather. Nancy nodded. Yes, she said, surely is damp all right. Lines were at the corners of her eyes, but her majestic tiddies were just as much of a miracle as they ever had been. She was twentyseven, same age as Charley, but damn if she didn't look better than any woman of twentyseven *he'd* ever known. She had lost weight, and her buttocks no longer were so heavy. Maturity had even taken away some of the weakness in her chin. Her hair still was dark, and she still wore it very long. If she were to undo it, he supposed it would trail down below her hips. The thought of her hair trailing to her hips brought a tightening to his groin. He told himself: Godalmighty, you are without hope. The kitchen smelled of soap and lard. It was quite a clean kitchen. In point of fact, the entire house appeared almost to *gleam*. Charley cleared his throat. He told Nancy he had been sorry to hear of the death of her lunatic sister Charlotte.

Well, said Nancy, fussing with the coffeepot, she's better off dead.

I suppose you're right.

You know she was a lunatic?

Yes.

You know how it happened?

Yes. I was living in Titusville at the time, remember?

Oh. Yes. So you were. Well. Anyway. I'd surely like to get my hands on that Professor friend of yours.

Said Charley: Mm. I expect so. (He wondered if he should tell her the late Professor's version of what had happened that night in the home of the Rev Mr Weeks. He decided not to. He didn't see where it would serve any useful purpose. And what if Nancy didn't believe him? No, there was no point accusing her sister of an ancient murder. He would keep his mouth shut. And anyway, hadn't the Professor expressed an enthusiasm for the idea that he would forever be remembered as a fugitive assassin? A ghostly terror, flapping into dark legend—yes, this was the proper role for the poor proclamative Professor. Charley would do nothing to disturb it.)

Nancy brought the coffee to the table. The mugs were heavy. The coffee was very hot and strong. Charley sipped at it. It hurt his raw throat.

Nancy seated herself, sipped at her own mug. She blew on it. She brushed a strand of hair back from her forehead, then said: You been back to Titusville? That where you got into the fight?

Charley nodded. *I* didn't fight, he said. It was *the other people* did the fighting.

She asked him what he meant. He told her of his return to Titusville, of the beatings by Sheriff Ben Stork, of his recuperation in the Harris home, of the tarring, the feathering, his flight, his discovery by Miss Marie and Harriet Carson; he told Nancy all of it, and from time to time she pursed her lips and nodded, but she made no comment. She blew on her coffee. When his story was finished, she smiled a little, started to say something, then thought better of it. She shook her head.

You want to say something? Charley asked her.

No.

I mean, don't you want to kiss my wounds or something?

No.

You didn't answer my letters.

Letters?

Yes. When your husband was killed, I sent you a letter. And I sent you a second letter later. A later letter. Latter litter. Ladder liter.

What?

Oh. Excuse me. I'm tired.

Well, maybe you ought to be starting back for Evansville.

Oh, I expect I'll just sit here a little longer.

My husband was a fine man, said Nancy.

I'm sure he was.

A man in every way there is.

Yes. Of course.

I'm sorry you got beat on, but maybe you'd better go now.

Not right just yet.

His body still hasn't been found.

Oh? Well, that's too bad.

I used to think that maybe some sort of mistake had been made.

Charley nodded. I can understand that, he said.

Yes, said Nancy. I used to hope that he was still up and around. But he's not up and around. Just because his body hasn't been found, that don't mean a thing. There was witnesses to his dying. *That's* what matters.

Yes. I expect so.

He's dead. Dead and dead and dead. *Dead.* Maybe some day his body'll be found. Don't matter though. A body is a body, and a body don't matter. He loved me. He truly did.

Well, he should of. You're the sort of girl it doesn't take much to love.

Girl?

Woman.

Nancy nodded. I'm a woman now, she said. And don't talk to me of love, Charley, please don't do that.

All right.

He didn't care none about my busts one way or the other. I mean, he *liked* them all right, but he'd of loved me even if I'd of had a chest like a chicken.

Well, you'll never be guilty of *that.*

I know why you're here. You don't have to look at me so innocent, Charley Wells. I know *you.* You're here like maybe it's ten years ago.

What?

Nancy stood up. She went to the stove, poured herself another mug of coffee. You care for some more? she asked him.

No thank you.

She returned to the table. She sat down, blew on her coffee.

Now, what's all this about ten years ago? Charley asked her.

Nancy sighed. She sipped at her coffee, and then she said: Ten years ago, all you done was try to take me off somewheres and grab me.

Oh, said Charley. He grinned.

Nancy's tongue moistened her upper lip. She said: There's been two men for me in my whole entire life—George Peters and Henry Ferris. The war killed both of them. You want to know something? What those people in Titusville done, with the tar and the feathers I mean, I expect it wasn't right—but that don't mean I can't understand why it was done. I can. I honest can.

Would you of helped them?

Maybe.

Charley twisted in his chair. He coughed. Ah, yes *ma'm,* he said, you are the *honest* little woman aren't you?

I'm trying to be.

You're doing fine at it.

No offense to you in particular, Charley.

No. Of course not.

You remember my little brother Bill?

Yes.

He got killed too. And it was at Fredericksburg, same as George, only Bill was fighting on the rebel side. God. Bill is dead. George is dead. Henry is dead. Charlotte is dead. Tell me, Charley, how come you and me are still alive?

Charley shrugged.

Bill ran off to Virginia. Couldn't abide Titusville. He ran off to Virginia and he worked on a farm there and when the war came he enlisted, and he's dead too. Sometimes I get to thinking the whole world's dead. He couldn't abide Titusville because of the way people treated us Quimbys. Like we was slop to be tossed to the hogs.

Well, Nancy, your father never has—

I *know.* You don't have to *tell* me. He's not worth a whoop. I *know.* I *know.* But that don't mean people had to take it out on Bill.

No. You're right.

Other boys picked on him on account of he was skinny.

Mm.

Nancy banged her mug down on the table. Coffee slopped. She paid it no mind. Her eyes were crisp. You want to take me into the room where the bed is don't you? she said.

Nancy, I just want to talk to you.

You want to grab me. I know what you want to do.

Please. Let's don't fuss.

You want to grab me, said Nancy. You want to grab me. You want to *grab* me. You know when was the last time I was with a man? I want to *scream*, Charley! The last time I was with a man was pritnear *four years ago!* She hesitated, swallowed, then: It was the night before Henry went off to the war. He never did come home on leave. It's been four years, and sometimes at night I get myself in such a state I got to go outside and run in the fields. You ought to see me. A sketch. In my nightgown, sort of running into the wind. Smell of earth. Sky, stars, all that there kind of thing. Some sketch it is. Two men, and both dead. I remember how you used to grab at me. I laughed, didn't I? You were good old Charley, and you were sort of thick with your breathing and all, and so I went and I laughed. I was young, and I didn't have to go running into the wind, and so I went and I laughed real good. Now I don't want to laugh. I want you to go away.

You don't.

You going to tell me you love me?

You want me to?

Tell you what. You go back into town. Buy a wagon. Fill that wagon with Bibles. Drive the wagon back out here. Then swear on those Bibles. Swear you love me. Do that. Swear up and down.

Charley grinned.

You stop that grinning!

Charley stood up. He came around the table. Nancy stood up so quickly she knocked over her chair. She backed toward the stove. She groped behind her back. She came up with a long wooden spoon. She held it above her head.

Charley, she said, if you try to grab me I'll hit you on the head with this here spoon.

I doubt that very much, said Charley, advancing.

Charley!

Four years is too long a time for a big healthy girl like you . . .

Charley!

He seized her. She blinked. She dropped the spoon. It clattered. He kissed her. Promptly her mouth came open. He pressed against her, and he was hard. She tasted like soap and coffee. He pulled her out of the kitchen. They went into the room where the bed was. It smelled white. He was on her quickly, and he tore her dress. She bit her lower lip until it bled. Charley kissed the blood, licked it. Her head went from side to side. He heard birds. Small birds. Field birds. He grinned. He ached, and his raw skin was hot, and he grinned and grinned. She was luxuriant.

She was deep. She was damp beyond dampness. He entered large and pink, and she clawed at his ears. He pounded her. The fragrant white bed creaked and bucked. She breathed through her nose. She seized his buttocks, pressed him more deeply inside her. His bandaged elbow sang. He grimaced. On and on. Over and over. Grunts. Pale odors of juices. She scratched him. She licked him. She pressed his mouth against her tiddies. The precious pussy was sleek and damp, and he shoved and jostled and grinned. He undid her hair, and sure enough it trailed down below her hips. It smelled like corn and sun. She stroked his wounds and bruises. She kissed them. Her nipples swelled until it appeared they would burst. They were dark nipples, darker than her hair. He licked them, nibbled on them. She squealed. She embraced him. She crooned. On and on went the birds, chatting. Later . . . a good deal later . . . Nancy and Charley did some chatting of their own. They lay naked, side by side, and the room was humid with their odors.

Said Nancy: I ought to get back to my floors.

Charley chuckled.

Well, I got pride in the way I keep up this place.

Tomorrow.

What?

Get at your floors tomorrow.

Oh. All right.

They'll still be there.

Yes.

Godalmighty . . .

What?

Oh, nothing. I was just thinking of all the years I've wanted this.

And you call it nothing?

Charley smiled. I call it a lot, he said.

I'm bad.

No you're not.

Henry was good to me. This here bed was his and mine.

Well, he's dead now. The living go on living.

Yes, Charley.

He moved in with her. He told her he wanted to marry her. He supposed perhaps he was telling her the truth. Marriage would represent the final surrender of the precious pussy long withheld. Ah, God bless fate. She had been so easy, so *ready*. Four years without a man had truly ripened her. She made him feel large, and that was a fact. He told her he believed that someday he would be a great man. She did not laugh. She did not even smile. She said: I expect maybe you're right. I know I wouldn't want to wager against it. She told him they were committing a terrible sin.

He told her yes, maybe so, but then how come they were compounding the terrible sin every night and sometimes even in the afternoon? She told him he was nasty. He grinned at her, and within a week all his pain was gone, and his elbow had scabbed over quite nicely. She changed the dressing every other day. She did not speak to him of his cowardice the day of the storm and the mad Mrs Weatherly. Perhaps she had forgotten all about it. He hoped so. He spoke to her of Washington, of Wendell Archer Doggett, of Congressman Lansing H. Ingraham. He said not a word, however, about the late Professor. It was a warm damp spring. The Ferris farm did not amount to much. The river flooded, and water came to the doorstep. When the water finally receded, it carried away great slabs and chunks of earth. Had he spoken to her of the late Professor, she would have asked too many questions, and perhaps he would have been forced to tell her that her late sister Charlotte had been the real murderer of the Rev Mr Weeks. He did not want to do this. In the first place, such a reve-lation would have given Nancy great pain. Secondly, she probably would not have believed it. In any case, she probably would have ordered him from her house, thus depriving him of the precious pussy. This thought he could not abide—not *now*, not after finally having *attained* it. He journeyed into Evansville twice a week or so. He took a box at the post office. He had Morton C. Hightower mail him a cheque for the balance of the twelve thousand he had realized from the sale of the store and house. He deposited the cheque in an Evansville bank. In another letter, sent to Dick Harris, he made inquiries about his suitcase. Dick Harris' reply was prompt: Yes, he had managed to save the suitcase that night of the tarring and the feathering. Where would Charley care for it to be sent? A week later, Charley's suitcase came by express. Ah, now he had his precious memorabilia once again. Now he was a whole man again. He grinned, chided himself for being a sentimental ass. Perhaps he had caught the affliction from Nancy. When it came to sentiment, Nancy was its most ardent practitioner. She was particularly fond of reminiscing on her late husband: Henry always had a terrible time with this farm. It was his father's place, and he lived here alone for a long time after his father and his mother and his sister died, and he could of sold it off, but he never did. He had a stubbornness. He wasn't about to give up. He'd lived alone I don't know how many years before I met him at the Fourth of July picnic back in '60, the day you was supposed to of debated Tom Sturdevant, re-member? Ah *hah*, I can see by the look on your face that you surely *do*. Ah well, getting back to Henry—he was the gentlest man in the world. You wouldn't of knowed it to look at him, him being so sort of *big* and *grim* and all, but he *was*. Charley, it could of been a real fine thing. I mean, I never would of complained. I *had* him. And *he* had *me*. And *I* don't

mean Having like owning niggers or a horse or a pretty hat. I mean Having like Loving. With *you* now, the Having is like the niggers or the horse
or the pretty hat. We didn't even have a year together, Henry and me, but
I pray to God I'll always remember every day of it. You know what him
and me used to do? We used to watch the clouds, that's what. We'd look
for faces in the clouds. Old men mostly. Old men with beards. I'd pack us
a little lunch and we'd go set by the river. I made my own dresses, and
they were pretty dresses, and I'd set there by the river and spread my skirt
pretty as I could, and likely as not he'd say something soft and kind about
how I looked. He liked bacon. I'd make him bacon sandwiches. With fresh
bread. Bread I'd baked that morning. Bread still crumbly and warm. Hah,
you and your Having. I know *you,* Charley. All your life you've wanted to
Have me, and so now you Got me, and I hope it means something to you.
But I'll tell you the truth, Charley: I don't see how it can. In order to
Have, a person has got to Give. And I don't see you doing that, Charley.
I don't see you doing that *ever,* for *anybody.* But then maybe for you that
don't matter. All you care about is taking a human being like a human
being was a nigger or a horse or whatever. All right. Fine. That's the way
you want it; that's the way I got it to give. I mean, what choice do I have?
Look, the day you came calling on me, what was I doing? I was scrubbing
floors. You scrub floors and then they get dirty again and so you scrub
them again. A person can use up a lot of days that way. A sight to look forward to, oh surely. You scrub floors and you scrub floors and you scrub
floors, and always you're alone, and then along comes your old friend
Charley Wells, and so what do you do? You do a terrible thing. You claw
and flop and groan and shout. It's been four years, and how else are you
going to keep track on whether you're alive? I mean, at least Charley
Wells is somebody you *know.* Around here, I been the Widow Ferris,
and the men they sort of click their teeth together whenever they see me,
me and my big busts I expect it is, and it surely does make me sick. Only,
God forgive me, it don't make me *too* sick. And so then *you* come along,
and you're somebody I *know,* and right away, soon as you walk in the
door, it comes over me that I'm going to be bad. That's the word, Charley:
bad. (She spoke quietly while telling him all this. Her hands were folded
in her lap, and her voice was glassy, the voice of a little girl delivering a
school recitation.) So, Charley, let's keep it clear in our minds what this
all is. It's like skunks in a hole. Animals, Charley. The beasts of the field.
(The voice of a little girl delivering a school recitation. Tiny. Splintered.
No love. Only tiredness. It was clear to Charley that she thought she
didn't care any more about much of anything. The way she saw the world,
one day was no different from the next. The sky was vague, and the faces
in the clouds had fled, and both her men were dead, and there were only

so many men a woman could expect. Well, she was wrong. She, this precious pussy, had herself a third man, whether she admitted it or not. And she would accompany him to his greatness. He would, in short, Have her.)

He bought fancy dresses for her in the best Evansville stores. But she seldom wore them. He had to holler at her to remind her to comb her hair. She remained clean enough, and she spent a great deal of time scrubbing the floors, but seldom did she come to him except in old dresses and with her hair mussed. He began making more frequent trips into Evansville. He drank a good deal, played poker, became known as something of a rakehell. He told himself he was looking for some sort of business venture in which to invest his money. For some reason, however, he kept postponing the project. Perhaps—and he tried to be candid enough with himself to admit this—Nancy's hard words had in some measure wounded him. At any rate, he devoted most of his Evansville visits to the pursuit of whisky and cards. The poker games turned out to be disastrous. Within six weeks, he lost more than four thousand dollars. The games were held in a suite in the New Evansville House. The heavy winner was an old friend—Nig Stringfellow, one of the boatmen who had become drunk with Charley at that infamous Fourth of July picnic back in 1860. Nig Stringfellow was a rich man now. He never told Charley precisely what had made him rich, but it evidently had something to do with the running of whisky up from Kentucky. Now he wore suits that cost fifty dollars each if they cost a penny, and he openly cohabited with an octaroon woman, a former slave named Rachel Timmins. This Rachel Timmins was rumored to have been the onetime mistress of a rebel major general, and Charley could believe it. Her skin was yellow and smooth, and her eyes were green, and there was nothing about her Charley was unwilling to believe. She served coffee and whisky and sandwiches to the poker players. She almost always hummed. Her voice was contralto. It made Charley's belly feel as though it were full of pins. Perhaps, for all he knew, the presence of Rachel Timmins was the reason he did so badly in the games. He often caught himself concentrating on her bosoms instead of the cards. Oh well, all men had Weaknesses—even great men. He supposed his Weakness was a hell of a lot less unpleasant than most. There were ways of being ruined and ways of being ruined, and some of those ways just weren't hardly painful at all. But Nig Stringfellow apparently didn't want to see Charley ruin himself. He said to Charley one night (the game had just ended, and Charley had dropped almost a thousand dollars): Charley my friend, you ought to stay out of this game. It's too much for you. A man's got to understand his limitations. Ain't it enough you got tarred and feathered? Why don't you find a nice business and settle

down while you still got some of your money in your pocket? If you want
that girl to marry you, I expect she will. From what you tell me about her,
it ain't likely that she's going to be too fussy. So, Godalmighty, get aholt of
yourself. You look like a fish flopping out of the water. (And Nig Stringfellow was right. Charley admitted it. There was no sense in all this drinking and gambling. There was no future in it; it contained no *possibilities.*
He *was* flopping. He was being a fool. He was behaving as though it was
some sort of tragedy that she'd never spoken to him of Love. Jesus Lord &
Saviour, he'd abandoned concepts of Love long ago. The hell with her.
The thing he had to do was get started in pursuit of his greatness. Nothing else really mattered, and certainly not Love. Ah, of all the frauds
foisted upon a gullible humanity . . .)

Nancy?

Yes?

Dress up for me.

What?

I bought you a lot of dresses. Please wear one.

Why?

Because you're pretty. Because it'd please me.

No.

The pink. I like the pink the best.

No. I'm *bad.*

What?

Charley, I'm terrible. I wish you'd go away.

I can't do that.

Well, I won't dress up for you.

But why not?

There's no sense lying.

Lying?

Yes, Charley. *Lying.* That's what this here whole thing is.

He was puzzled, and that was a fact. What difference did it make
whether she wore the dresses he bought her? He was *Charley Wells,* and
he understood the *possible* and the *mortal,* and Love was the biggest lie
there was, a base and stupid dream fit only for posturers, heroes, seekers
of Deeds. It was a waste of time; it exhausted the spirit; it provided no return; it was the most cruel and foul of myths, food for fools in the sad cold
hours of their vacant days. So what was it he felt? Why was the wearing
of the pink dress so important? Ah, it was a debilitating *sentimentality—*
that was what it was, and nothing else. The dream of the pussy long withheld had finally been fulfilled, and so now—like a romantic idiot—he
sought the fulfilling of another dream, a dream of Love. Hah. *Dreams.*
(Ever weigh a dream? Ever sell one? Ever float one on the river? Ever

use one to drive a nail or fry an egg?) So why then, since he understood the lie so well, was he drinking so much? Why was he playing so much bad poker? Why was he losing so much money? What in the name of God was going *on*?

Greatness?

Greatness is a vertical and sober thing.

Yes. All right. But tomorrow is time enough for greatness.

For now, let us have our nip. Let us wet our whistle.

Tomorrow is time enough to get right down *to* it. Today is too warm. Today requires libation. Tomorrow perhaps the weather will be cooler. Then one will be able to roll up one's sleeves, spit on one's hands and set about capturing one's mighty destiny.

(Charley Wells sits grinning, and she clucks at him, tells him he is a perfect jackass, and he says: All right then. Tell me to leave. And she says: Go. Good riddance. And he says: You don't mean that. And she weeps, and quickly he renders her horizontal, and she tells him: God, God, I am so *bad*. Of course he does not volunteer to leave. The pussy long withheld is the pussy precious, and someday she will understand that she has no future with anyone else. For now, however, it is enough that she cannot bring herself to make him go away. One counts one's blessings. One embraces the *possible*.)

The farm. It was really such a small and inconsequential farm, and the house was gray, and the eternal floods had made rustcolored lines, antic wavy scribbles, on its outside walls. Most of the land had been leased to a neighbor named Elwell, a onelegged veteran who had served with the late Henry Ferris in the 198th Indiana. Elwell had a plump wife and nine plump children, and he was a good farmer. He talked a great deal, but he had admired Henry Ferris, and Nancy preferred him to most of her neighbors. At least, she told Charley, Perry Elwell don't look at my bosoms like maybe he wanted to eat them with a spoon. And he minds his own business. Which is more than a body can say for most people, here or anywheres else.

Most of the neighbors knew Charley was staying in Nancy's home. She let the word get out that he was a cousin. She didn't suppose many people believed her, but she didn't particularly care either. I don't expect I got much of a *right* to care, she told Charley. I'm doing terrible things with you, and if they want to punish me with their blabber and gossip . . . well, it's not much of a punishment at that. I mean, I kind of expect I'm beyond blabber and gossip. It can't do no more to me than it done when Charlotte was alive. Neighbor women used to walk for miles to visit me because they figured maybe I'd let them take a look at Charlotte. It was like she was something in Mr Barnum's freak show. You see, it wasn't

only that she was so fat and didn't have no mind no more. She had a moustache too. I had to shave her twice a week. And she'd been such a pretty
girl. A real beauty. More of a beauty than *me,* by a whole lot. This
chin of mine, I got it from Papa, and it sort of does away with beauty. If
you was to ask *me,* I'd say I look kind of *dumb.* But I don't know, though.
At least the Lord gave me these here big busts, and men surely do like
them. But Poor Charlotte, though. Whatever it was happened that night
with Preacher Weeks, it surely must of been awful. I mean, Charlotte
always was a sort of strong person. I mean, marrying Old Man Grimes
and all, with him all the time tweaking her. Oh well. Makes no difference
no more. She's dead, and I expect it's the best thing could of happened,
what with how fat and brainless she got, not to mention her moustache.
Lord. Poor Charlotte.

Nancy?

Yes?

It won't last forever.

What's that?

One of these days I'll get going again. It's just that maybe the tarring
and the feathering took more out of me than I thought.

Surely. You'll be all right.

Yes.

Something'll happen.

Yes.

Something'll happen, and you'll take advantage of it. I got faith in you,
Charley.

Oh?

Yes *sir.* Faith. Right now you're just sort of resting. But you'll be all
right. Right now it's enough that you and me got this itch for one another.
We're neither of us worth a nickel, but at least we understand it. So we do
what we do. Makes no difference.

Nancy, you talk like the world's passed you by.

Well, it *has.*

No. Not unless you want it to.

Don't talk to me like a preacher. Don't talk to me like I was that dumb.

Nancy, would you marry me if I asked you?

Marry you! Goodness, *no!*

Why not?

Because I know what married can be.

But what's going to happen to you?

Nothing much, I expect.

I could take you away from here.

You'd get tired of me. You'd find some *other* whore.

Don't talk about yourself that way.

Ahhh . . . Charley, Charley . . . just take it for what it is. You want to go lay down with me?

Nancy, for God's sake.

Who?

Then the thing came that showed Charley the way to his greatness. Nancy had been correct. He *had* been only resting. And she changed her mind about marrying him. She told him: All right. I expect we both need to get away from here. I'll marry you. But I might as well warn you about something. I'm going to try to make it *good*. One more time for me, Charley. One more time to try to build something out of my days. All right? Will you let me try? And Charley said: Of course. You'll be a good wife. I know you will. And I'll love you and cherish you. And Nancy said: Oh ho. Love me and cherish me. My goodness.

It—this thing that showed Charley the way to his greatness—arrived in June of that year 1865. The two strangers made a deal of racket when they approached the Ferris farmhouse in their rented wagon. It was about 4 o'clock in the afternoon, and Charley had been drinking all day. He lay on the bed in the back room. A bottle of Kentucky whisky was on the floor next to the bed. His tongue tasted yellow. When he heard the racket, he debated going to the window and taking a look to see what was happening. But his head hurt, and he decided the hell with it. Nancy would take care of whatever it was the visitors wanted. She was good at taking care of things. She took care of this house real good. And she took care of him, the one & only Charles Palmer Wells, just fine thank you kindly. Ah, said Charley to himself, belching gently and patting his belly, yes indeed. The men were named Light and Messer. The door was thin, and Charley was able to hear their conversation with Nancy quite clearly. They were from that Ohio town called Paradise Falls, and they had served with Henry Ferris in that Ohio regiment. They had been officers of an infantry company called the Paradise Falls Blues. Charley grinned, belched, covered his mouth. He listened closely, and after a time it was clear to him that a miracle had come to pass . . .

One of the men, the one who called himself Messer, had a very young voice. He said very little. The second man, the one named Light, had a very large voice. It rumbled. It was the voice of a man who perhaps had ambitions to stand for public office. It was this Light who did most of the talking. He said: Ah, we're here, ma'm, because of your late husband. We have been delegated by our comrades back in Paradise Falls to come here and . . . well, to put it bluntly, we simply seek to assure ourselves that you are all right.

All right? said Nancy.

Yes. Ah, we feel we have a duty to make certain you are encountering no hard times. We owe your husband more than you can be expected to understand. He was very . . . ah, very *helpful* to us. When we first saw fighting, that is.

We were very green, said Messer. Fresh fish, we were called. Your husband, ma'm, saw to it that many of us survived. Men who would not otherwise have survived.

(In the back room, Charley rubbed his eyes.)

We came here in the steam cars, said Light. All the way from Paradise Falls.

A day's trip, said Messer.

A day and a night actually, said Light.

Yes, said Messer. A day and a night.

Well, said Nancy. You must be tired. Please sit down.

Thank you, said Light. There were scraping sounds, and then he resumed: Mrs Ferris, I don't mean to be indelicate, but are your finances adequate?

What?

Ah, do you have enough money?

Yes. I'm all right. The farm is free and clear.

Said Light: You are, ah, a lovely young woman. Are there any children?

No.

No one to operate the farm?

I lease most of the land to a neighbor. Would you please tell me what this is all about?

Messer spoke up. We want to help you, he said. Any way we can.

Oh?

Yes, said Light. You see, your husband helped so many of *us*. He made us into real soldiers. His death was a profound shock to every man in the company. But, thanks to his example, we conducted ourselves with honor.

Oh, said Nancy.

(In the back room, Charley grinned.)

We remember the Mud March with special vividness, said Light.

That so? said Nancy.

(In the back room, Charley covered his mouth and sniggered.)

Yes, said Light. It was in January of '63. Your husband had just joined our company. General Burnside sent the army on a long march that was supposed to flank the rebels by coming across the Rappahannock upstream from Falmouth. Well, Mrs Ferris, it was a failure. The weather was wretched—snow, rain, sleet, and all of it continuous. Ah, I met General Burnside on two occasions. Social occasions they were, and he seemed to be a fine fellow. But I fear he was not much of a general. Well, at any rate, the Mud March was our first . . . uh, *engagement*. If you can call it that. We became hopelessly mired down in the snow and the rain and the sleet. And, I am frank to admit, we also became quite badly disorganized. It was a serious situation, no doubt about it. But, ma'm, your husband, our Corporal Ferris, was not a bit disorganized. Every man in the company was the beneficiary of his assistance. He pulled men out of the mud, helped them make fires; he shouted at us, laughed, told us the worst was yet to come, jollied us along with splendid energy and forbearance, saw to it that none of us froze to death, helped us with our tents. Ah, it was a magnificent performance. I do not know what we would have done without him. And then, at Chancellorsville, he exposed himself to enemy fire I don't know how many times. Why? Because he sought to provide an example. And he did. Our conduct was exemplary, and after the battle we were personally commended by Colonel Drabble, who at that time commanded the regiment. Suffice to say, madam, your husband was a man of valor and honor and dignity.

And you came all the way here to tell me that?

Yes ma'm.

Well. Goodness. I thank you.

We are the ones who are thanking *you*. Or, to be more specific, your late husband.

I appreciate it.

Tell her about the offer, said Messer to Light.

Offer? said Nancy.

Light cleared his throat. Yes, he said, you see, we thought perhaps you would care to come to Paradise Falls.

What?

Ma'm, you see, we got together, we of the Paradise Falls Blues, and we decided it was only right and proper that we offer you our hospitality.

I don't follow you.

Mrs Ferris, if you come to Paradise Falls, ah, if you should ever *need* to come there, if, ah, perhaps your situation would necessitate such a move, we would be delighted to assist you in any way we can.

Sounds like public charity. I don't need public charity.

No. No. There was, in point of fact, talk of getting up a purse for you, but the idea was rejected. You see, Ferris had spoken of you to many of our men. It did not seem, from what he had said of you, that you would be the sort to accept a purse.

Well. Good.

But we wanted to do something. So it was decided to delegate Mr

Messer and myself to come here and explain to you how we feel about your late husband. We have no base motives, believe me.

I believe you.

So, Mrs Ferris, it all comes down to this—we are here to put ourselves on record in acknowledgment of your husband's courage and devotion.

(In the back room, Charley rolled his eyes.)

Light continued: We simply want to tell you that, should the need ever arise for you to leave Indiana, Paradise Falls always will welcome you. We do not expect you to take charity.

Well, said Nancy, that's a nice thought. I appreciate it.

And there is also the matter of the scroll, said Light.

Scroll? said Nancy.

Yes, said Light. There was a rustling noise. Apparently Light was unrolling the scroll. (In the back room, Charley listened closely.) Then Light began to read: *To Henry Edwin Ferris, whose unquestioned valor and brilliant powers of leadership will live in our memory until the final judgment, we the undersigned, members of Company G, 33rd Ohio Volunteer Infantry, 2nd Division, III Corps, Army of the Potomac, do hereby certify and acknowledge a vast and profound gratitude. To his grieving widow, whose—*

Please! said Nancy. She was crying. The sound of it was like an animal in a hole.

Light coughed. Ah, he said, it has been signed by every man in the company.

Nancy snuffled. Thank . . . thank you, she said.

We shall leave it with you.

I . . . I appreciate it . . .

(In the back room, Charley was grinning. The idea had already occurred to him.)

Nancy mewled and gasped.

Ah, said Light. Wellnow . . .

I'm . . . I'm real sorry . . .

No, said Light. Please. We understand.

A scraping noise. Messer spoke: We don't want to bother you, Mrs Ferris. We'll go now.

More scraping noises. Footsteps. I'll just leave it right here on the table, said Light.

Yes . . . thank you . . .

The footsteps moved toward the front door. Light spoke again: Mrs Ferris, we seek nothing from you. It is up to you to decide when and if you should want to seek anything from us. That is the only reason we are here—to make the offer. And of course to make the acknowledgment that is written out for you there in the scroll.

Yes . . .

We have been honored to have met you, said Light.

A high sound came from Nancy's throat. Then, after a cough, she said: He *was* a good man wasn't he?

Oh yes, said Light.

Yes *ma'm*, said Messer.

The front door opened. Farewells were exchanged. Charley crept to the window and watched the men climb aboard their wagon. They waved in the general direction of the front door. They tipped their hats. Then, creaking, the wagon moved away. Sunlight caught at the mane of the roan gelding that was pulling the wagon. The men sat erectly. They did not look back. Charley grimaced into the sunlight. This was the first sunny day in weeks. Or at least it was the first one he could remember. He drew a deep breath. He returned to the bed and lay down. In the front room, Nancy still wept. Charley stared at the ceiling. He worked the idea in his mind. He could find no fault with it. Absolutely none. He reached for his bottle, took a deep swallow. *Ah*, he said aloud, *well*. The whisky stung the openings between his teeth. The new openings. The openings provided courtesy of Sheriff Ben Stork. Charley grunted, took another swallow, waited for Nancy. Finally he heard her clear her throat. Then he heard her blow her nose. She came into the back room. He grinned at her, then carefully set the bottle on the floor. He made sure the cork was tight. Nancy was pale. She was wiping at her eyes. Strands of hair trailed across her forehead and down the nape of her neck. She seated herself on the edge of the bed. Did you hear it? she asked him.

Yes.

All of it?

Yes.

And?

Well, said Charley, I expect that's sort of up to you.

What do you mean?

Well, I just mean it all depends on what you think you got the strength for.

I don't follow you.

The way you talk, it's like you're dead. Well, Nancy my girl, I don't believe that. I, ah, got reason not to. I mean, believe me, there's *life* in you. Yes *ma'm*. If you marry me, we can go to this place, this Paradise Falls, and we can start so to speak right from scratch.

Start what?

Finding whatever it is the rest of the years got waiting for us. You're
not dead, and neither am I. It's just that we need a new place.

But I'm so *bad* . . .

Be quiet.

Henry was a good man, and I've dishonored his home, and—

And he's dead. That's what he is. Dead. But *you're* not dead. What do
you want to do? Sit around this place for the next fifty years or whatever?

No . . .

All *right* then. Marry me.

You think maybe we could make things so they came out good?

Yes.

Please come into the front room with me.

Why?

I want to show you that there scroll.

Give me your answer first.

All right.

All right what? You'll marry me?

Yes.

That night she wore the pink dress. Laughing, he had her on the front
room floor. She wept. She spoke of bereavement. He told her to be quiet.
He told her it was better to be alive than dead. He told her it was better to
be anything than dead. He ripped the dress so severely she had to throw
it away. He bought her another one. He still had about eight thousand
dollars. She sold the farm to Elwell for three thousand. She sent fifteen
hundred to her parents back in Titusville, gave the rest to Charley. He
told her it was a good beginning, but he vowed that it was *only* a beginning. She sold the house's furnishings for three hundred dollars. He permitted her to keep that money. They were married by a magistrate in
Evansville. Their wedding night, Nig Stringfellow gave them a big
party in the New Evansville House. He rented the entire second floor. His
woman, the octaroon Rachel Timmins, wore a scarlet dress. Early in the
evening Nancy became quite tipsy on wine. Charley carried her into one
of the bedrooms, dropped her on the bed. She fell asleep immediately. He
did not go to bed. He knew he would not have been able to sleep. The
party still was too loud. He returned to the party. He fell into conversation with a little ravenhaired whore named Joanna Ochiltree. She had
quite a remarkable stutter. She had become very drunk on champagne. She
gave him a wet kiss. It was a warm night, and she was perspiring, and
her kiss had been as much tongue as it had been lips, and he promptly
achieved a substantial erection. She saw it. She giggled. He slapped her
on the rump, told her she was a little devil. Yyyyyes innnnndeed, said
Joanna Ochiltree, so I've been tttttold. Then, still giggling, she staggered

off in search of more champagne. The guests at this party included many
whores, thieves, pimps, politicians and other various & sundry rascals. It
reminded Charley of several of the excellent social gatherings he'd
attended in the Hotel Nonpareil. He wished Wendell Archer Doggett
were here. He would have liked to share a bowl with the old rip. Two
fiddlers and a cornet player held forth in one of the suites. Nig Stringfellow had even provided a cake. It was immense, white, warm. The musicians stood behind it and sawed and tootled. Nancy had managed to cut
it before succumbing to the wine. She had laughed, and her face had been
pink. Charley liked her best when her face was pink. It meant her blood
was warm. She was a fine person when her blood was warm. There was no
finer. He found Rachel Timmins in the suite where the fiddlers and the
cornet player and the cake were. She was eating a piece of cake. A crumb
had attached itself to a corner of her mouth. He smiled at her. She did
not return the smile. She was talking with a peglegged little gambler
named Webb Ralston. He was telling her about a poker game. He was
very drunk. He leaned against her in order to keep from collapsing. Charley still smiled. He looked straight toward Rachel Timmins and smiled and
smiled. She paid him no mind. She frowned at Webb Ralston, nodded,
ate cake. Charley could not quite understand how she was able to breathe
in that scarlet dress. He surely did envy Nig Stringfellow, and that was
a fact. Her great green eyes glistened. Her tongue came out, licked away
the crumb. Charley shook his head. She was a large woman, and there
was a possibility her breasts were even larger than Nancy's. Again he
shook his head. He told himself he was a hell of a bridegroom, thinking
a thing like *that*. Out in the hallway, Nig Stringfellow was making loud
drunken sounds. A moment later he came into the suite. He lurched to
the cornet player, threw an arm around the fellow's shoulders. The cornet
player was a middleaged man with no hair. He winced. Nig Stringfellow gathered the musicians into a huddle. He whispered to them.
They nodded. Across the room, Joanna Ochiltree was laughing and thrust-
ing her bosoms against the chest of the chairman of the county board of
tax assessors. The musicians broke into *The Battle Hymn of the Republic*.
Nig Stringfellow sang with them. His voice was high, tenorish. He sang
in the same octave as the cornet was playing. Charley brought him a
drink. Nig Stringfellow clapped Charley on the back, downed the drink
in three swallows. Charley brought him another drink. Nig Stringfellow's
voice took on the consistency of warm mush. Clinging to an arm of the
chairman of the county board of tax assessors, Joanna Ochiltree whispered
something in the man's ear that made him blush. She led him from the
room. Charley saw them cross the hallway to a smaller room. Joanna
Ochiltree slammed the door behind them. Charley grinned. Other people

were withdrawing into various rooms. Nig Stringfellow's knees began to give way. Rachel Timmins still talked with Webb Ralston. Charley went to Nig Stringfellow and led him across the hallway to one of the empty bedrooms. It adjoined the one occupied by Joanna Ochiltree and the chairman of the county board of tax assessors. Charley was able to hear her voice: Oh Hhhhhorace! You bbbbbig *mmmmman* you! Mmmmmm! Mmmmmm! Ahhhhh! Ohhhhh! I lllllove yyyyyou! Charley grinned. Nig Stringfellow was humming and mumbling. Yes, said Charley, you just sing. He helped Nig Stringfellow stretch out on the bed. The wallpaper had a design of the Parthenon, endless Parthenons, dozens of them, on the walls and the ceiling, a clamor of Parthenons. Nig Stringfellow drooled. Charley loosened Nig Stringfellow's cravat and shoelaces. I'll sing . . . her . . . I'll sing her . . . *good,* mumbled Nig Stringfellow. Then his eyeballs vanished and he passed out. Charley nodded, chuckled, went in search of Rachel Timmins. The sounds in the next room had caused a return of his Joanna Ochiltree erection. He crossed the hallway to the room where the cake and the musicians were. Rachel Timmins stood by herself. Apparently Webb Ralston had gone off somewhere to collapse. Charley walked to Rachel Timmins. He smiled. Her face was moist. A harness came into the line of her jaw. She said: Has he passed out?

Yes, said Charley. He placed a hand on one of her arms. It was cool.

My God, she said, this is your *wedding night.*

I'm afraid my bride had too much to drink.

Did you see to it?

No. It just happened. I expect the excitement was too much for her.

Would you really go through with it?

With what?

Please don't fence, said Rachel Timmins. You know what I mean.

Charley grinned. He stroked her arm. He said: All right. I won't fence. The answer is yes, I surely would go through with it if you gave me the chance. You are a *woman,* my dear. My Lord, I'll tell the world.

Rachel Timmins nodded. There was a film of sweat at her hairline. Her hair was pulled back in a tight bun. Is there an empty room? she asked him.

We'll find one.

No. We'll use Mr Stringfellow's room. The one he shares with me. Would that suit your fancy?

Anything you say.

The bed is enormous. You have never seen the bed, have you?

No.

I suppose it would be an experience.

Well, I'll do all *I* can.

I expect.

Rachel Timmins went out of the room. Charley followed her. They went upstairs to the thirdfloor suite she shared with Nig Stringfellow. Charley's breath hurt. He wiped sweat from his neck and cheeks. She took him into the bedroom, and the bed *was* enormous. The coverlets were white. She walked to the bed, turned, backed against a table and said: Well? Her contralto voice was shaky.

Charley grinned. He came toward her.

Her hands were behind her back. She seemed to be fussing with something in the drawer of the table. A small scraping sound came from the drawer. She smiled.

He stood in front of her. He could smell her breath. It was warm. Her body gave off a decided fragrance. He'd heard it said there was a fragrance common only to nigger women in heat. Maybe this was that fragrance.

She blinked, parted her lips. Her hands still scrabbled in the drawer.

What you got there? said Charley.

Sh, said Rachel Timmins.

He bent forward to kiss her.

One of her hands seized his britches at the waist.

Ah, said Charley, closing his eyes, leaning closer to her.

Kindly open your eyes, said Rachel Timmins.

Charley opened his eyes. He looked down.

Rachel Timmins held a knife. Its point was aimed straight for his crotch. I come, she said, from a long line of savages.

Charley shrieked.

Rachel Timmins laughed.

He wrenched his britches free of her grasp. He backed away.

She laughed more loudly. She closed her eyes and she laughed and laughed. A golden dollop of sweat dropped from her forehead onto a cheek.

Charley opened his mouth, closed it, opened it again.

She blinked open her eyes. She did away with her laughter. She tested the point of the knife with a thumb. Mm, she said. Excellent.

Charley shook his head no.

You pig, said Rachel Timmins. You son of a bitch.

Charley's groin ached.

She gave a great screech, leaped toward him.

He turned and ran for the door.

Behind him, Rachel Timmins again screeched. Her footsteps clattered. He felt something brush the back of his neck.

She caught him at the door. He wrestled her into the sitting room. She dropped the knife. Bastard! she yelled. Filthy! Filthy!

The door to the hallway was open. He heard a gasp. He glanced toward the doorway. No one was there. He pushed at Rachel Timmins. Whooping, she went spinning across the room. Her skirts swirled. She slammed against a wall, slid to the floor. He ran out. He went downstairs to the room where he had left Nancy. She lay flat on her back with her mouth open. He closed and locked the door. He went to her and stripped her naked. Outside the room, the sounds of the party still were loud. He bent and kissed Nancy's right breast, licking it until the nipple became hard. She groaned. He took off his clothes and lay down beside her. A long time ago, as a boy, he had lain by the river and she had taken possession of his dreams: Nancy, the precious pussy long withheld. And now he *had* her. Yes. By God. Any time he wanted her. He grinned. Ah, such a life. If it wasn't one thing, it was another. He chuckled, decided the hell with Rachel Timmins. His Joanna Ochiltree erection had transmogrified itself into a Rachel Timmins erection, and now by Jesus it was a Nancy erection. He climbed atop his bride. She gasped, spread her legs. Ah, he said, my darling girl. Forthwith the marriage officially was consummated. He sniggered himself to sleep. He tried not to shake the bed. It had been a long day for Nancy. She needed her sleep. Tomorrow they would be leaving for this place Paradise Falls, this village that surely would be the arena of his greatness. Ah, the ways of the world truly were wondrous to behold. Many were dead. George Peters was dead. This Henry Ferris was dead. But Charley Wells, oaf of oafs, was alive, and *he* had Nancy, and he would never be defeated. The years would be good. He had survived everything, even the final degradation of the tar and the feathers, and he would continue to survive everything. The final lesson—and the largest lesson—had been learned. Charley grinned in the dark. He supposed Rachel Timmins was feeling very pleased with herself along about now. He supposed she thought she really had humiliated him. Hah. How stupid she was, the poor nigger bitch. Humiliation? *She* humiliate *him*? Ah, the day never would dawn . . .

And so to sleep. And no particular dreams.

And the days abided.

Eleven years of days.

And the greatness came.

And the muzzle velocity was in no way lessened.

And hats were removed in his presence. Yes, by God, *hats*.

Those two men, Light and Messer, had come to visit Nancy on a mission of Christian mercy and goodness. Oh, such splendid fellows. Them and their words and their scroll. Heroism. Devotion. Duty. The scroll was aswarm with such words, and the scroll had brought Charley to Paradise

Falls, and God bless scrolls and words and mercy and goodness. Ho. The ways of the world.

And now, here in this year of 1876, the days hung bright and victorious, and the one & only Charles Palmer Wells, devious oaf of devious oafs, flourished, grinned, plotted, played at the utmost top of his game. And continued his campaign for the ruin of his enemy, his beloved and most desperately necessary adversary, Isaac (Ike) Underwood. (Necessary? Of course. How else to feed the worm? Without an adversary, greatness would starve.) The whorehouse idea was especially delightful. He'd already humiliated old Ike several times, but this time he would humiliate the village old Ike had built. And, in so doing, he would remove old Ike's image. As God had made Man in His image, so had Ike Underwood made Paradise Falls in *his*. This image had included no whorehouse. It had been a most decent and loving image, a quiet Arcadian thing epitomized by that ridiculous statue of Beauty that stood atop the Paradise County Court House. Well, perhaps that had been a useeful image forty years earlier, but times changed, and decency and love had to make way for more important considerations, and so by God there *would* be a whorehouse, and it would be a fine whorehouse, and one more humiliation would be spat up in old Ike's face. And so Charley conferred with Claude Dill the saloonkeeper. And he conferred with George Acterhof, owner of the Acterhof House. And he conferred with various retail merchants. And he conferred with Ed Maxwell, the former county commissioner and county Republican chairman. (Ed's removal as county Republican chairman had been quite amusing—and in more ways than one. Perhaps the most amusing aspect had been old Ike's wholehearted endorsement of Ed's successor, Virgil T. Light. Ike's view of the situation had been that the change would unite the Republican party and the GAR, since Virgil T. Light would be heading both. What he did not then know was that Virgil T. Light was Charley's man to his very back teeth. He found out, though, when Virgil T. Light ran against George Pillsbury and whipped him. Ah, such a world. A person just could not trust a soul, and that was a fact.) But, anyhow, the whorehouse. Mayor Virgil T. Light was brought into the conferences, and he warned Charley that there would probably be a great hooraw about it. He said: The ministers. The women. Schoolteachers. They'll all of them raise almighty hell. This village has never had a whorehouse, and to tell you the truth I don't see why it has to have one now. It could be a very dangerous situation. Next year there's another election coming up. I don't like it a bit.

Charley smiled. Virge, he said, I expect it doesn't much matter what you like.

Virgil T. Light was seated in a large leather armchair in Charley's office. He shifted his weight. The chair squeaked. He said: Ah, now there's no sense our becoming angry over this. Let's discuss it reasonably.

Said Charley: Of course. I always discuss things reasonably.

Then believe me when I tell you it could mean trouble.

From whom? A few ministers? A few women?

They have influence.

Virge, how many women voted in the last election?

That's not the point.

It is the point if I choose it to be the point.

Virgil T. Light sighed, stared at his hands.

We have to bring this village into touch with reality, said Charley. What?

The reality of Here and Now.

And that means opening up a whorehouse?

Yes.

A whorehouse is the Here and Now?

Yes.

I don't understand.

Charley still was smiling. At thirtyeight, he still had a fine boyish oafish smile. His dentures were splendid. He had bought them in the late summer of '71. He had visited a painless dentist in Columbus, and the painless dentist had removed those teeth that had not been removed by dear old Ben Stork, substituting the dentures, and the dentures had been expensive, remarkably comfortable. Charley smiled at his fine stupid friend Virgil T. Light, smiled and said: It's not really necessary that you understand, but I expect it won't cost me anything to make the attempt. You see, Virge, a whorehouse here has become a matter of economic necessity. Without one, Paradise Falls could lose business to other communities. The business provided by men, most of them miners, looking for a good time. And, as you perhaps know, a good time includes fucking.

What? said Virgil T. Light, and the color went out of his large bald face.

I said fucking.

Oh. Ah. Yes.

And so there will be a whorehouse. Our friend Irene Hollingshead will provide it. You remember Irene Hollingshead don't you?

Yes.

You look terrible. Do you feel all right? Would you like a glass of water?

No. No thank you. I'm fine.

Is there something about fucking that goes against your nature?

No. You know me better than that, Charley.

All right. Now then, as to your function in this matter . . .

My function?

Charley grinned. Don't lose control, he said. It isn't much of a function. All I want is for you and Dolph Kolb to stay clear.

But what about the ministers? And the *Democrat* will raise almighty hell.

The ministers will be taken care of. As for the *Democrat,* since when have you had to worry about the *Democrat?*

What about the women?

I expect they'll whoop and holler for awhile. But that'll pass. Everything passes.

Virgil T. Light rubbed his cheeks. He made a clucking noise, sighed, then, said: I just hope you know what you're doing.

Said Charley: Don't fret, my friend.

Charley journeyed to Columbus a few days later. He spent the night with Rose Mast. She serenaded him on the mandolin, and they discussed the Unitarian church, and he gave her a china elephant for her collection, her china zoo, as she called it. The china elephant was tiny and blue. She had begun the collection only six months before, but Charley already had given her seventeen china animals, one for each visit. The following morning Charley had breakfast with the whoremistress Irene Hollingshead, *née* Irene Weaver. They discussed the political situation, and he told her he suspected the people were tiring of the Republicans. It wouldn't surprise me very much, he said, if Tilden did in our friend Mr Hayes. Well, it would serve him right. After all, a man who drinks nothing stronger than grape juice probably is a menace to the body politic. I may not even vote for him myself, dedicated Republican that I am.

Irene Hollingshead smiled. Yes, she said. A dedicated Republican. Like back in the Washington days when you were working for that fellow, that Ingalls.

Ingraham.

Oh. All right. Ingraham.

I have reformed. I have come to the holy light of the Republican Party. I have been saved.

Yes. Surely. Have some more ham.

I am much obliged.

We aim to please.

When are you going to marry Ed Maxwell?

What?

He loves you dearly.

I have no intention of marrying Ed Maxwell.

I wouldn't be too sure of that, my dear.

Oh? I suppose you think you can force me.

Yes. In point of fact, I do.

Irene Hollingshead leaned back from her plate. She blinked. Well, she said, go on. You have something in that devious mind of yours. You might as well spit it out.

Charley nodded. He chewed thoughtfully on a slice of ham, swallowed, patted his lips with his napkin. He said: If you don't marry Ed Maxwell, I'll ruin you.

She moistened her lips. She fought her fear, but it could not be resisted. It showed in her eyes. They enlarged. The whites glistened. She said: Ruin me?

Yes. And I can do it. And you know I can.

You are a bastard.

Perhaps.

I always thought you liked me, Charley.

I do.

Then why do you want to ruin me?

I don't *want* to ruin you. And I won't have to, not if you do what I want you to do.

Please explain.

All right. I want you to marry Ed Maxwell and transfer your activities to Paradise Falls.

Activities? You mean the girls? You mean open a house there?

Yes.

But why?

Paradise Falls needs a house. I am interested in, ah, creating an adjusted aspect. An adjusted aspect of Paradise Falls.

Aspect?

Yes. It is about time Paradise Falls became a part of the world as it is.

That sounds like nonsense.

No, said Charley. No, Irene, it is not nonsense.

But why me? Why pick on me? I don't want to leave Columbus. I like it here.

I want you, my dear, because you are the best. And it will be pleasant to have my Rose so near. The trips up here in the steam cars can be tiring.

But what about money? I'll never earn in Paradise Falls what I earn here.

Yes you will. There is no house in the county.

No. I won't do it.

Yes you will.

Oh. Yes. I forgot. You said you'd ruin me. Well, just you try. I have friends here. They are very fond of me. They will protect me.

Not so. I will buy them.

What?

And I *can* buy them. And you *know* it. A public official. The chief of police. A councilman or two to rise in civic indignation and demand the closing of your *perfectly horrible* brothel. Politicians enjoy delivering orations on the evils of whoredom. You say you have friends. Well, perhaps you do. But you have to pay them. And I can pay them more. No matter *what* you pay them, I can pay them more.

Ah . . . Charley . . . Charley . . . damn you . . .

I know. I am a bastard.

Cor . . . Correct . . .

Charley smiled. Well, he said, I apologize.

Irene Hollingshead was chewing on her lips. She blinked. But why must I marry Ed Maxwell? she wanted to know. He's so *fat*. And he's *sixty* if he's a *day*.

Still grinning, Charley made a pious kissing noise. It was full of saliva. He said: Because Ed *loves* you.

Now be serious!

Charley chuckled. Again he patted his lips with his napkin. Then he said: Ed Maxwell used to be county Republican chairman. And he used to be a county commissioner. He owns and operates a respected bake shop. He is considered to be a leader in the county and the community. Well, I bought him out—from his honor, that is, not the bake shop. I paid him to resign as county Republican chairman, and I paid him to quit as county commissioner. He doesn't realize it, but it is important to me that he be degraded as thoroughly as possible.

Ed *Maxwell*?

Yes. Because, by degrading him, I degrade my own beloved enemy.

And who might that be?

A man named Isaac Underwood. You've heard of him.

Yes.

Ed Maxwell represents what Paradise Falls was before I came there. He is a creation of Isaac Underwood. To establish him as the husband of a woman who runs a . . . ah, *crib* . . . is a splendid humiliation of Isaac Underwood. And only an extraordinary man has the capacity to endure humiliation.

You really must hate this Underwood.

No. Please. I insist. I do not hate him.

Then why humiliate him?

Because it is necessary. Because Paradise Falls never will be mine until I have finished him off.

Sounds mighty devious.

It's not. Not if you think about it.

But why do *I* have to get involved in your private—

Charley held up a hand. It was a plump hand, a very successful and confident hand, the hand of a priest delivering a blessing. He said: Irene, I mean you no harm. If, as perhaps worries you, you feel you won't make as much money operating a house in Paradise Falls as you have made here in Columbus, then I promise you I shall make up the difference out of my own pocket.

Oh? said Irene Hollingshead.

Yes. And I shall take your word for whatever accounting you choose to make. You see, I firmly believe you to be an honest woman. In, eh, the larger meaning of the word.

Yes. I believe maybe I am.

All the arrangements have been made. I have spoken with the mayor of our village. And day before yesterday I conferred with your Ed Maxwell. I told him what I propose to do. He was delighted.

You are a pluperfect shit, Charley Wells.

Ah, I don't expect I can blame you for feeling that way.

No. I don't expect you can.

I think you will be surprised.

Over what?

The volume of your business.

That so?

Yes. There will be of course many miners.

Miners? They're so *dirty*.

I am certain you will draw up a set of rules. And, if I know you, and judging from the spotless and decorous condition of this place, they will be enforced. And, remember, a miner's money is as good as anyone's. Perhaps even better, considering all the hard work that has gone into the earning of it.

Miners . . .

Now, now. Don't fret. I'm sure you'll cope.

Can't I get along without them?

No. Definitely not. Remember, I own the mines. And, within reason, I want to keep the men happy. There is a great need for a house in Paradise Falls. If the need is not met, the miners will go elsewhere for their pleasures, and the economy of Paradise Falls will be damaged. I have spoken with a number of leaders in the business community. They all agree. In point of fact, it was one of them—a publican by trade—who first suggested the establishment of one. He told me his business was suffering. After all, men who drink also enjoy . . . ah, well, *you* know what they enjoy. And of course this also applies to men who do not drink. Paradise Falls must meet this need. Otherwise, business will suffer. And, as you know, the health of a community is the health of its business. I would hate to think of all those miners gallivanting off to Nelsonville or Athens or some such place simply because they were unable to enjoy themselves in my adopted village. Not to mention, of course, the harm such gallivanting would inflict on the dollars and cents health of the place. So, you see, what must be done must be done, and *you,* my sweet Irene, have been chosen.

My God, Charley, what if I don't *want* to be chosen?

You have no option.

God . . .

Charley chuckled. But it won't be all miners, he said. Your clientele, I mean. There will be many other customers. Men of substance.

Like you?

Like me. Yes. Indeed.

Irene Hollingshead sighed. She said: You probably know what I'd like to do.

Yes. You'd like to refuse. You'd like to fight me. But you know better, don't you?

Irene Hollingshead nodded.

Do I take it then that you agree?

Yes.

And to the marriage?

Yes.

You are very wise.

Irene Hollingshead closed her eyes. When she opened them, they were dry. She began to laugh. Her laughter had no sound. You . . . you devil, she said.

The one & only Charles Palmer Wells pursed his lips.

The specifics were quickly arranged. Irene Hollingshead told Charley she would require a few months to close her affairs in Columbus. He said he understood. He told her it would not be necessary for her to observe her marriage vows to Ed Maxwell with any particular zeal. Smiling sourly, she thanked him for his kindness. He told her he never sought to be unreasonable. If you find a man who suits you, he said, don't hesitate to take up with him, even if it means making Ed sleep in the broom closet. As I say, one of the principal purposes of all this is humiliation, and the more the better, as far as I'm concerned. Said Irene: It may surprise you, Charley, but if I marry Ed I'll be faithful to him. I was faithful to Mr Hollingshead. Said Charley: I'm sure you were. And there is only one comment I would care to make. Said Irene: And what might that be? Said Charley: It isn't *if* you marry Ed Maxwell; it's *when.* Said Irene: Oh you bastard. Said Charley: Yes. Indubitably. Say, by the way, I

understand you have met two of Ed's sons. Said Irene: Yes. Andrew and
Ed Junior. Said Charley: And I was told you served them tea. Said Irene:
Yes. Said Charley: Well. Good. Then it's not as though you are a stranger.
Irene Hollingshead shook her head. She muttered something that Charley
did not catch.

The sun sang and clapped that day, and Charley grinned all the way
back to Paradise Falls, dirty CPV&M steam cars and bumpy ride notwithstanding.

So much for the whorehouse. The new year would see its establishment. Next on Charley's schedule was the assassination of a dream. The
name of the dream was the Aeolian Temple, and it was a dream fervently held by his beloved adversary Ike Underwood, and the anticipation of its destruction made Charley's heart swell and thump. How would
old Ike be able to withstand such a tragedy? Ah, a splendid prospect, and
Charley watched with interest as Bill Osterhaus' construction crew worked
through the year on the great hall. Autumn came, and it was a particularly
rich and golden autumn, an autumn moist and fragrant with the residue
of the great spring and summer rains, and the falling leaves slapped rather
than snapped, slapped damply, adhering to the earth like postage stamps
freckled with yellow and crimson droplets, and the odors of autumn
came up like steam, thick and sturdy. There was an election canvass that
autumn, and Virgil T. Light and his GAR cronies waved the bloody shirt
of the late War of the Rebellion in espousal of the candidacy of R. B.
Hayes the Stalwart and virtuous and nondrinking Ohio Republican, but
the signs were not good (apparently too many voters were fed up with
both the bloody shirt *and* the clear and present imperfections of the Grant
Administration), and it was generally conceded that Hayes would have
trouble defeating the Democratic nominee, Sam Tilden, the sour and
austere governor of New York. As was indeed the case. Although Hayes
carried Ohio easily, he lost the election by more than a quarter of a million
votes. Godalmighty, said Mayor Virgil T. Light to Charley, this is a calamity. Those damn traitors and Copperhead skunks will destroy the government. It could be that we'll have to fight the war all over again. Said
Charley: Aren't you taking something of a melodramatic view of the situation? Said Virgil T. Light: No *sir*. Not a bit. I'm simply stating facts. Said
Charley: Well, let's just wait and see. Said Virgil T. Light: Don't say I
didn't warn you. Said Charley: I won't. (He smiled. He told Dave Millerspaugh to have the *Journal* follow whatever posture the Republican party
was taking nationally. It appeared that there was some question as to the
electoral college totals. Louisiana, South Carolina and Florida were in
dispute. Both sides were charging fraud and ballot tampering. If those
states could be certified to Hayes, he would win by one vote in the elec-

toral college. As the year dragged to its end, there was a great deal of excitement about this possibility. Charley did not share in the excitement. After all, Tilden had won by more than a quarter of a million popular votes. He would be inaugurated. No question about it. The Republicans had to face up to the situation.) But the hell with the election. Charley had a more important consideration on his mind—the Aeolian Temple. Bill Osterhaus was doing a remarkable job, considering the difficulties the rainy weather had presented earlier in the year. By December, the hall was close to completion, and Charley decided it was time to assassinate the dream. He mailed a brief note to his friend Wendell Archer Doggett in Washington. The reply came eight days later: *Our mutual acquaintance will be more than happy to oblige you. He will be in Paradise Falls on the 27th instant. He wishes to spend Christmas with his mother in Pittsburgh. I had no idea he was such a sentimentalist. At any rate, he will call himself Philip T. Dilworth, a hardware salesman from Meadville, Pennsylvania. He begs to tell you his fee for a task of such magnitude will be $5,000. He says he will register in the Depot Hotel and will be more than pleased to meet with you at any time that day it suits your convenience.* So Christmas came, a time of pine boughs and mincemeat pies and Handel (*Wonderful! Counselor! The mighty God! The everlasting Father! The Prince of Peace!*), of a gritty and reluctant snowfall, of hands and rum and the slap and click of harness as heigh ho, across the fields clattered the carriages and wagons and broughams and buggies and gigs, across the fields and along the hard winter village streets they went, a day of cheeks and breath and mittens: fruitcakes and cocoa and candles and scarves: hats and laughter: pussy asleep in front of the fire: the choristers sang and the children yipped and the huddled surly poor spat: Christmas, and the children gathered at old granny's skirt and tugged on it and begged for more cookies, and the yule logs burned sweet and pungent, and pussy stretched, yawned, looked around, settled back down, head in paws, hind legs twitching: Christmas, and bravely marched the lead soldiers, and small pale hands fussed at the crinkly skirts of blandfaced virginal dolls: Christmas, and the one & only Charles Palmer Wells gave his beloved wife a pearl necklace valued at more than two thousand dollars: Christmas, and that selfsame one & only Charles Palmer Wells gave his little daughter Nell a perambulator for her battalions of dolls and animals, and he also gave her a fur hat, a fur muff and fur mittens, and he also gave her a cameo pin, and he also gave her a tall and spindly wagon in which she could pull her battalions of dolls and animals when she tired of pushing them in the perambulator, and he also gave her a tiny blue umbrella, and he also gave her a great and elaborate box of crayons, and she was eight years old, and she thanked him, and she even curtseyed (her mother had taught her this frail art, and only the good Lord knew where *she* had learned it), and Charley held little Nell on his lap, and she was dark and silent and plain, and he bounced her, told her he would see to it that the world would be hers, and she told him Thank you Papa, and he laughed, and Nancy sat stiff and pale across the parlor from him, and Nancy's new pearls hung cunningly down over her miraculous bosoms: Christmas, and someone tied a red ribbon around pussy's neck, and pussy flopped and bit and nearly strangled: Christmas, and for the one & only Charles Palmer Wells it seemed unlikely that anything could vex the progress of his now undoubted greatness (hats were removed in his presence; yes, by God, *hats*): he sat high and proud, at the top of his game, muzzle velocity unimpaired, and his world was the best *possible*, and that was a fact. When he met with Disney, alias Dilworth, in the Depot Hotel two days later, he told the fellow: You have no idea how much this means to me. It will be my real Christmas. Said Disney: Well, it won't be easy. I don't want you to get the idea that it will be. A brick building never is easy. Said Charley: For five thousand dollars it hadn't better be easy. Disney chuckled. He had not noticeably aged. He still bore a remarkable resemblance to U. S. Grant. He still chewed on an unlit cigar. Charley hadn't seen the man in a decade, but he could detect no changes in either Disney's appearance or his manner. He was every bit as taciturn as he had been back in '66 when Charley had hired him to burn down Virgil T. Light's furniture establishment. And he still apparently was fond of conducting his business while flopped on a bed. He lay flat, and he chewed on the cigar, and he stared at the ceiling, and he said: If she's going to go, it'll have to be done from the inside. Where the wood is. The inside walls, the floors, they're wood ain't they? Said Charley: Yes. Said Disney: The doors in yet? Said Charley: Yes. Said Disney: Windows too? Said Charley: Some of them. As near as I've been able to find out, the builder expects to have the job done by oh the first of April at the latest. Said Disney: Good. That means there'll be a good deal of truck inside the place. Said Charley: Truck? Said Disney: Yes. Lumber. Shavings. Truck like that. It on the same side of the street the other place was? Said Charley: Yes. Just three or four doors east, as a matter of fact. Said Disney: And, as I recollect, the wind comes from the west, correct? Said Charley: Correct. Said Disney: Then some rags and some kerosene should do her. Said Charley: If you say so. I don't know anything about such matters. Said Disney: All right. Give me the money. Charley nodded. He gave Disney the money. Thank you kindly, said Disney. He threw the butt of his cigar on the floor. He rolled over on his stomach. You can go now, he said. I got to get me a little sleep. I never could sleep on the steam cars. Said Charley: You won't be needing me for anything else, will you? Said Disney: No. Good day to you. Said Charley: Well, good luck. Said Disney: Sure. The firebell began ringing shortly after midnight of the twentyeighth. Eyes wide open, Charley lay flat on his back and listened to it. He tried not to smile. Next to him, Nancy stirred in her sleep. She groaned. Her breath became stringy. He patted her belly, told her sh. She subsided. Charley was unable not to smile. He finally decided he could not resist going to take a look. He slipped out of bed, quietly got dressed. He went outside, hitched up the buggy, drove over to Main Street. The noise became louder, and the sky was pink. The odor of smoke was delicious. He grimaced. Disney had done a magnificent piece of work. Charley pulled up two squares from the Aeolian Temple. He hitched the horse to a post, walked the rest of the distance. The Aeolian Temple was yellow and crimson. He could feel the heat half a square away. Men milled in the street. They waved and hollered, and it didn't appear that they were accomplishing much. A floor collapsed. The sound of it was loud, made the earth tremble. Sparks flew out into Main Street. Men with buckets ran to the sparks and doused them. It was one thing for the Aeolian Temple to burn. It would have been quite another thing for the entire village to burn. The men with the buckets were very diligent. Something exploded inside the Aeolian Temple. Shouts. Screams. Men scrambled away from the building. The front wall collapsed. Hot bricks flew. There was so much noise that it was safe for Charley to giggle. The fire burned all night. It burned until well past noon the following day. The Aeolian Temple was a total loss. Old Ike Underwood's pocketbook had taken a one hundred thousand dollar thrashing. At 8 o'clock in the morning of Saturday, December 30, less than twentyfour hours after the last of the fire had been extinguished, Bill Osterhaus' men, supervised by their foreman, a gimpy blond fellow named Carmichael, began clearing away the wreckage. Charley stopped to chat with Carmichael. Certainly is a shame, said Charley. It would have been a fine building. Said Carmichael: It will be. Said Charley: How's that? Said Carmichael: Mr Underwood has told us to build it all over again. Then Carmichael moved away and hollered at a laborer named Ruhlmann to get cracking on those burnt timbers.

1877 ...

Hayes is inaugurated President. Grant leaves the country on a world tour. He is scheduled to be away for two years. The Democrats scream that the election was stolen from their man, Sam Tilden. Perhaps so, but the Democrats themselves were participants in the thievery. An official certifying board gives the disputed electoral votes of Louisiana, South Carolina and Florida to Hayes, thus making him the winner by 185 electoral votes to 184. Publicly, the Democrats shriek that the situation could mean a new civil war. Privately, however, their leaders are more than satisfied. The Democrats horsetraded Sam Tilden for what they hold to be a far larger consideration—removal of the last of the federal occupation forces from the South. With the departure of the troops, the final surviving carpetbagger-scallywag-nigger Republican state governments collapse, and old Dixie is returned to the loving embrace of the Democracy.

A whorehouse did you say?

That I did.

Where?

On Mineral Avenue. Ed Maxwell's place.

What?

Yessir. That there widow he married last week, she's bringing in whores.

I don't believe it.

Well, that don't make no nevermind to me. It just so happens I'm telling you the truth. If you don't want to believe the truth, I expect that's your right.

Chickens. Mice. Dogs. Woodpeckers. C. P. Wells visits every church in Paradise Falls and confers privately with the clergymen. The gist of his remarks: I am in total accord with you. I too deplore prostitution. But, on the other hand, there are certain, ah, *realities* that must be accepted. The larger good, you know. The larger good. Allow me to explain. In and of itself, a house of prostitution is evil. However, a considerable argument can be made for its necessity. There are, first of all, many unmarried young men in the community. Without a house of prostitution available to them, they of necessity turn to our daughters and our sisters; their energies become concentrated on seduction—and, in some extreme cases, rape. This of course endangers public morality, the very foundations of what we call decent Christian behavior. Not to mention the wretched dishonor that falls upon those poor girls who are made the victims of lust that has no place to turn for its fulfillment. Hence, the necessity for a wh . . . house of prostitution. Just between the two of us, sir, and I know you are a man of the world, I have it on good authority that the new Mrs Maxwell is a woman of some refinement—if you will permit me to use such a word to describe a woman in her, ah, profession. I also have been led to understand that she has given her oath that none of her young ladies is in any way, shape, manner or form infected with any of those loathesome ailments the nature of which I do not believe I have to elucidate for you. In short then, sir, we must consider here the greatest good for the greatest number. Is it not better to deal in a forthright manner with the facts of life than to endanger the honor of our decent daughters and sisters? I do hope you will take my views under close advisement. (The words come solemnly from the Godfearing mouth of C. P. Wells; he permits them to throb. He folds his hands in his lap, constructs a steeple with his fingers. And the clergymen listen closely, respectfully. He is, after all, a very rich man *and* a member of the vestry of Grace Episcopal Church. As such, he is not a person to be dismissed willynilly.) After hearing him out, the clergymen—all except one—agree with C. P. Wells that the greatest good for the greatest number *is* a point to be kept in mind. The gratitude of C. P. Wells is considerable. Each of the clergymen—with one exception—receives a cheque for one thousand dollars. Use the money for whatever purpose you wish, says C. P. Wells to the Catholic, Presbyterian, Lutheran and Episcopal recipients of his largesse. I am certain there are many good works that require looking after. He is thanked most heartily by the Rev Fr Paul K. Messer, pastor of St Thomas Aquinas RC Church; the Rev Durward E. Lillis, pastor of St Mark's Presbyterian Church; the Rev Horst G. Leppelmeier, pastor of St Luke's Lutheran Church, and the Rev Edwin P. Rathbun, rector of Grace Episcopal. The only dissenter is the Rev Clovis T. Reader, pastor of the First ME Church. He says: Mr Wells, why do you hate us? Have we offended you in some way?

C. P. Wells smiles. I am sorry, he says, but I don't see the point of the joke.

I am not joking, says the Rev Clovis T. Reader. He and C. P. Wells are seated in his study. Mrs Reader has just brought them tea. The Rev Mr Reader is what his name says he is. The room abounds with books. They have a thin yellow odor. Brown too. He is the youngest clergyman in Paradise Falls, and it has been rumored that he is fond of dancing the waltz.

If you're not joking, says C. P. Wells, then I expect I'll have to take offense.

You've destroyed Blood. Now you want to destroy Paradise Falls. Isn't that the truth of the matter, the *whole* truth?

No. Of course not. I resent your remarks very deeply.

You'll survive, Mr Wells. I rather suspect you're quite good at that.

What is it you want?

I don't want anything, Mr Wells. Except perhaps for you to go away.

I suppose you think I'm sinful.

Yes. In point of fact, I do.

All I'm trying to do is prepare this village for reality.

Your reality.

All reality.

No, Mr Wells, your reality has nothing to do with all reality. Your reality is not all reality. Not by a damn sight, if you'll pardon me for saying so. Your reality is filth, and so you say the world is filth, and that is a lie.

So what do you propose to do about it?

Speak out. I have remained silent far too long as it is.

I wonder . . . said C. P. Wells, rubbing his chin. He frowned.

You wonder what?

Would more money change your mind?

You swine.

C. P. Wells shook his head. He said: What's gotten into you, Reader? I always thought you were a fine fellow. I mean, a harmless sort of fellow. Pleasant. Pious. Full of love and all that sort of thing. What's changed you?

The Rev Clovis T. Reader sighed.

C. P. Wells smiled. You have yourself a woman somewhere? he wanted to know. Somebody else's wife maybe? She giving you backbone?

Please get out of here.

What do you propose to do? Deliver passionate sermons decrying a simple little whorehouse?

Yes.

It won't do any good.

Probably not. But someone has to speak out.

You are a fool.

No, Mr Wells. Not so.

But the Rev Mr Reader does not speak out. He cannot. A malignancy in his belly does not permit it. The morning after his talk with C. P. Wells he awakens with such a pain in his belly that all he can do is weep. His wife summons a doctor, a young fellow named Webb. That evening the Rev Mr Reader is taken to a hospital in Lancaster. He dies there six weeks later. In those six weeks, he loses seventy pounds, and at the end his flesh hangs in flaps. He dies holding his wife's hand. His eyes are clear. He dies with the Saviour's name on his lips. He dies smiling. His jaw is tight. The Irene Maxwell whorehouse is opened in April. Ed Maxwell serves as a sort of major domo. Business is excellent, far beyond Mrs Maxwell's expectations. Many miners visit the place, but they conduct themselves (most of them) decorously. The prim boarding school aspect of the place inhibits them (most of them) and they (most of them) behave in a more or less gentlemanly fashion. Ed Maxwell has never been happier. He turns over his bake shop to his son Andrew. Of Ed Maxwell's six children, only three (Andrew, Ed Junior and Tom) will have anything to do with him. The other three (Lillian, Martha and Paul) refuse even to speak to him on the street. Lillian is the wife of Wayne W. Bradley, a clerk in the Sidlo Shoe Store and a deacon of St Mark's Presbyterian Church. Martha is the wife of Walter M. Plover, county recorder of deeds. Paul, a bachelor, sells cravats, handkerchiefs, shirts and suspenders at Steinfelder's. The three of them visit their pastor, the Rev Mr Lillis. They ask him what can be done about the deplorable situation. The Rev Mr Lillis, a grim and unbending sort of individual, commiserates with them most profoundly, but then shrugs and speaks to them with heavy earnestness on the ways of the world. Licentiousness, says the Rev Mr Lillis, cannot be countenanced. *However*, if there must *be* licentiousness, better it be regulated. And we must remember, my friends, that the existence of this, ah, *establishment* should do a great deal to protect the virtue of our young women. The Rev Mr Lillis talks for more than an hour, and he even occasionally smiles. When Lillian Bradley and Martha Plover and Paul Maxwell leave him, their eyes are white and blank, and all they can do is spread their hands and make small choked sounds. In the meantime, their father is happier than a cat in warm cream. And so is C. P. Wells. And this despite the fact that the rebuilding of Isaac (Ike) Underwood's Aeolian Temple is progressing apace. Old Ike has large and dark suspicions about the fire that destroyed the place, but of course he cannot prove them. He says to his wife: Wells did it sure as hell. Says Phoebe: Yes. I wouldn't be surprised. Says Ike: Doesn't matter though. It's going to get built no matter what. Says Phoebe: Isaac, please don't faint or anything, but I do believe I love you. Says Ike: Oh my Lord! Get the smelling salts! (Their son Philip is losing weight, and he is not the sort that can afford to lose weight. He writes much poetry, and he knows it is wretched and undisciplined and trite, and it all is published in the *Democrat* over the signature Piper Hell, and sometimes he embraces his pillow and calls it dear Christine.) Sun. Manure. Skunks. Quilts. Teeth. Sheep. The Paradise Falls Superbs win twentyseven games, lose one. Editha Purvis says to her sister: I am going to be an old maid. He'll never marry me, and there's no one else I want. Oh, Bill! Bill! (Bricks. Voices. Locomotives. Tears. Milk. Sermons. Whores. Coal. Love. Dirt. Nutshells. Sofacushions.) Mayor Virgil T. Light edits his undelivered 1876 Fourth of July speech and delivers it this year. He is reelected without opposition.

Dear Edna:

GOOSEBERRIES, BLUEBERRIES, BLACKBERRY PIE: catch yourself a wollybog and stick him in your eye. Graveyards and tombstones give me a fright: I feel much better under Jesus' loving light. Too much turpentine makes me very ill: I have to go to Papa and get a big pink pill. The light from the forest is cool and fresh: little bumps jump up all over my flesh.

It was a time, clearly, for Words, and they galloped grinning across dear little Edna's mind (I know a little fish who is dark and sleek: he hides under rocks where I can't peek), and sometimes she wrote them down, and sometimes she was brave enough to tell herself: There are worse things to do with your time.

Her name was Edna Barbara Vance, and she was twelve years of age, and she really wasn't *little* at all. She stood five feet five inches tall, and sometimes there were those who laughed. And she had bosoms already, and she knew what it meant to carry the burdens of a woman (had known it since last year, the thirteenth day of November in the year 1876, to be exact), and her mama had told her: I expect you will bear many children. And Edna had said: I hope so, Mama. I like children. And her mama had said: Got any poems for me today? And Edna had said (thinking up the poem as she went along): God made voices; God made feet; God is loving, kind and sweet.

Her papa was Kenneth I. Vance the druggist, a thin and persnickety man with a voice like pages in a book. He was unquestionably the most successful druggist in the village, and ten years ago he'd built a fine home for his family on South High Street. It had turrets and it had a widow's walk and it also had a gazebo, and there even was a solarium, and Edna often went into the solarium to write her poetry. The solarium almost always was warm. It faced away from the hills, which meant that the sun had a chance to get *at* it. (I love the sun: the sun is fun: would you give me the sun for a nickel and a bun?) She had three brothers. They all were older than she; Carl by six years, Howard by three, Walter by one. (Carl is big and loud and fat: Howard is thin and dark and flat: Walter is neither this nor that.) She was in love with a boy named Harold Keller. His father owned a grocery store. He had blond hair and a massive torso, and all the girls in the sixth grade adored him. In all her whole entire life, she'd never been spoken to by Harold Keller. (I love you madly, Harold Keller: you are such a handsome feller.) She often dreamed of Harold Keller. He wore a velvet doublet in her dreams, and from his mouth issued fragrant and gentlemanly words of love. They were very extravagant words, and the more extravagant the better. She collected picturebooks of animals. She had both a puppy and a kittycat. The puppy's name was Omar; the kittycat's name was Beatrice. She combed Beatrice's fur every day. She liked to watch Beatrice walk with tail straight in the air like a flagstaff. (One day in May, one very pretty day, Omar and Beatrice went to play: they chased their tails, and they dined on snails, and they took a nice nap in Mama's milk pails.)

Perhaps at some time there had been someone who had led a better life, but Edna could not quite believe this. It did not even matter that perhaps she was too tall. She would simply have to find a tall boy; that was all there was to it. (Harold Keller was tall.)

One day in August of 1877, one bright Sunday of tall skies and plump riversmells, the Vance family went on a picnic. Some cousins named Belter had a small farm a few miles southeast of the village. It wasn't much of a farm (too hilly, too rocky, too altogether Masonbrinkish), but it did adjoin the river, and the swimming there was splendid. Mama prepared a great feast of fried chicken and potato salad and baked bean salad and pumpernickel bread and poppyseed bread and preserved beets and preserved tomatoes and green onions and radishes and apple pie and lemonade, and of course everyone ate far too much, and Edna had to go take a nap. She found herself in a place in the shade of a stand of willows down by the river. The river plashed, salivated, cleared its throat. The sounds were simultaneous, and they made Edna smile. (River, river, I've ate my fill: won't you kindly just be still?) Edna patted her belly. She was a good eater, always had been. She wished her good eating would hurry up and put more meat on her bones. Even if she *did* have breasts, she still was far too skinny. It just wasn't fair. And it wasn't as though she was homely. With a little meat on her bones, she would be more than acceptable: this she knew. (Mirror, mirror on the wall: am I so ugly? *Not at all!*) Sighing, she flopped on the ground. The sound of the willows was soft, like the wings of angels, the breath of kittens. She closed her eyes. Papa and Mama had gone over to the Belter house to visit with the cousins. She supposed her brothers would soon be going swimming. She fell asleep. She dreamed of Harold Keller. His words were extravagant. She blushed, squirmed. She hugged herself. She rolled over, and her skirt hiked itself up. A breeze moved up her legs. Vaguely she was aware of the breeze, and it was very pleasant, very cool. She spread her legs wide apart. Ah, such a breeze. She supposed she was coming awake. She did not *want* to come awake. Harold

Keller was gone. His words were gone. She pursed her lips. His words. Goodness, if only she could kiss them. She made a face.

Which stand of trees? someone hollered. It was her brother Walter's voice.

The one to your right! hollered her brother Carl.

I thought it was the one to the left!

No! The one to your right!

Howard joined in: *We wouldn't fool you, Walter boy! The one to your right it is!*

The voices came from the river. Edna opened her eyes. Her brothers: trust them to wake up everything within ten miles. She blinked at the tall sky. There was not a single cloud. She saw dancing gray spots. They were like insects. The breeze tickled the insides of her legs. She did not bother with her skirt. She closed her eyes. She did not hear Walter come splashing out of the water.

He gasped.

She opened her eyes, sat up.

He was naked. He dripped. From behind him came a sound of guffaws. He was hairy. His mouth was open. She could see his tongue. He was so terribly hairy. And pendulous. She tried not to look. She tried and tried.

Hey, little brother! shouted Carl from the river. *Something the matter?*

The trees . . . ah, the trees, said Walter. They . . . ah, they blocked my . . . view. Edna, I . . . I didn't *see* you . . . I thought my clothes were up here . . .

Edna did not want to look. She really did not.

He took a step toward her. He squealed.

She looked down. Her skirt was up around her thighs. Quickly she pulled it down.

Now Walter, her brother Walter, was no longer pendulous.

She opened her mouth.

Walter squealed.

There was something severe that she needed to say.

Walter touched himself. He was pink and brown. Edna, he said. Lord God.

Edna screamed.

Walter's eyes were moist. He turned and ran back into the water. Carl and Howard laughed for days about their little joke. Walter had gotten his bearings confused. His clothes had been lying near another stand of willows. Carl and Howard had always been great ones for playing their little jokes on Walter. He never spoke to her about the incident. That night, alone in the privy, she threw up the fried chicken and the potato salad and the baked bean salad and the pumpernickel bread and the

poppyseed bread and the preserved beets and the preserved tomatos and
the green onions and the radishes and the apple pie and the lemonade.
(My brother Walter's big stiff dingle caused my heart to leap and tingle.)
She told no one about the vomiting. She did not fall asleep until well past
midnight. She decided she was evil and diseased.